D1084389

RAWN

BOY
WONDER

Books by James Robert Baker

BOY WONDER

FUEL-INJECTED DREAMS

von Riesen Library
McCook Community College

BOY WONDER

James Robert Baker

NAL BOOKS

NEW AMERICAN LIBRARY

NEW YORK AND SCARBOROUGH, ONTARIO

PUBLISHER'S NOTE
This book is a work of fiction. Names, characters, places, and
incidents are either the product of the author's imagination
or are used fictitiously, and any resemblance to actual persons,
living or dead, events, or locales is entirely coincidental.

Copyright © 1988 by James Robert Baker

All rights reserved. For information address New American Library.

Published simultaneously in Canada by
The New American Library of Canada Limited

 NAL BOOKS TRADEMARK REG. U.S. PAT. OFF. AND FOREIGN COUNTRIES
REGISTERED TRADEMARK—MARCA REGISTRADA
HECHO EN HARRISONBURG, VA., U.S.A.

SIGNET, SIGNET CLASSIC, MENTOR, ONYX, PLUME,
MERIDIAN and NAL BOOKS are published *in the United States*
by NAL PENGUIN INC., 1633 Broadway, New York, New York 10019,
in Canada by The New American Library of Canada Limited,
81 Mack Avenue, Scarborough, Ontario M1L 1M8

Library of Congress Cataloging-in-Publication Data

Baker, James Robert.
  Boy Wonder / by James Robert Baker.
     p.   cm.
  ISBN 0-453-00597-7
  I. Title.
PS3552.A4278B68   1988
813'.54--dc19   87-33953
                                             CIP

Designed by Julian Hamer

First Printing, August, 1988

1 2 3 4 5 6 7 8 9

PRINTED IN THE UNITED STATES OF AMERICA

(18.95)

gift

4-2-88

For John

ACKNOWLEDGMENTS

This oral history of Shark Trager—a man whom Edmund R. Frye once described as "arguably *the* quintessential Hollywood wunderkind producer of the last quarter of the twentieth century, and therefore almost certainly the definitive narcissistic genius-as-monster of an atrophying art form's, if not an entire civilization's, final phase"— this *print documentary* would have been impossible without the candor of a great many people, most of whom speak in these pages with a bracing, forthright and often moving eloquence. A few who, for reasons of structure, "ended up on the cutting floor" nonetheless have earned my gratitude for their honesty, however redundant it at times proved to be. For the few who chose *not* to participate, and luckily none was crucial, I can only offer my regretful understanding, tempered in a few instances with a certain contempt where, it seems, reticence was grounded less in a desire for privacy than a wish to produce an independent "quickie" confessional, exploiting a sometimes ephemeral, not to say fleetingly sexual, involvement with Shark Trager—a predictable trend in the light of Trager's controversial life, immense popularity, equally immense vilification, and sudden spectacular death.

To be fair the list of those I should thank would have to include everyone I interviewed. But I owe considerable special debts to Greg Spivey, Neal Ridges, Woody Hazzard, Brian Straight, Drake Brewster, Simone Gatane, Kenny Roberts, Lorna Trager, Brad Jenkins and Narges Pahlavi-Bardahl. Elliot and Sue Bernstein, two of our most respected and prestigious film producers, were especially warm and generous; as a result of the time we spent together on this endeavor they have become two of my dearest friends. If anyone was justified in wishing *not* to relieve the pain of the past, surely it was another gifted producer, Carol Van Der Hof; she is a brave and charming woman. My hat is off to Mac Trager; I know how difficult it was for Mac to dwell at such length upon the son he had come to loathe so intensely. Yet key scenes of Shark's boyhood would have remained blank film without Mac's careful recollections.

Finally there is one person without whose candor this book would have been unthinkable. For if there was a "Rosebud" in Shark Trager's life—to use an obvious but wholly appropriate analogy—it was surely not a sled but a woman. There are no words to properly thank Kathy Petro. She is a warm, intelligent, tender and funny and indelibly beautiful survivor.

James Robert Baker
Los Angeles, 1988

Contents

1/ **Gun Crazy** (1950–1957)

Buzz Payne

You bet I remember the night Shark was born. I was sixteen and had just gone to work at the Flying Wing Drive-In in Costa Mesa. I helped at the snackbar during intermission and the rest of the time I rode a bicycle around through the cars, using a flashlight to discourage too much carrying on, since Mr. Krogfoss the manager liked a family atmosphere. I hadn't seen much yet except a lot of kissing, though I was both afraid and kind of hoping that sooner or later I was going to see a whole lot more. So when I heard this woman moaning in the back of a Chrysler I got pretty shook up. Just moaning and groaning, like some guy was really letting her have it. I went up and shined my light in the window like I was supposed to, and almost crashed my bike, 'cause it was this woman having a baby.

Myrtle Butts

It was a hard pregnancy for my sister, being so frail and all. I'd come out from Nebraska while she was in her seventh month, not long after my husband Jop got killed in a cropdusting accident. I'd called Winnie and sobbed on the phone, and she'd said, "Come on out to California and start over, Sis. That's what Mac and I did." So I slept on their sun porch while I grieved over Jop and looked for work.

Winnie was no spring chicken when she had Shark, you know. She was almost forty, though Mac thought she was thirty-five. Winnie had her heart set on a girl, but Mac wanted a boy—Lord, how they'd squabble over that! Winnie was a whiner, you know. And Mac was always on a low boil. Whining and boiling. After two months of that my nerves were a wreck.

The night Shark was born Mac and Winnie argued over what to watch on TV. Mac wanted to watch wrestling, Winnie liked that

1

Goldberg show, but Mac didn't go for Jews. He didn't go for anyone, you know. Negroes and Jews and what-all. He really went for that Joe McCarthy though. So Winnie finally said, "All right, Mac, you watch your wrestling, Myrtle and I are going to the show."

That drive-in was new then and I remember it was packed. Some shoot-'em-up movie, not my cup of tea. Winnie kept smoking—she really went for those Chesterfields. "Mac makes me so bad," she kept saying, till that old Chrysler was so filled up with smoke I had to roll down my window. People didn't know then that pregnant women shouldn't smoke.

The baby wasn't due for a few more weeks, but I was still worried that Winnie was in such a tizzy. "I'll go get us some Coca-Colas," I said, and got out to go to the snackbar.

On my way back I heard Winnie moaning and dropped those Coca-Colas and ran. There she was in the back seat, Shark sliding out into this young man's hands.

Buzz Payne

Suddenly this baby was just coming out of her and I had to catch it. "Get Mr. Krogfoss," I yelled. But people started laughing and tooting their horns. I don't know what they thought, the way that woman was moaning.

Finally the lights came up, making it hard for people to see the screen, so they started yelling, "What the hell is going on?" 'cause it was right at the good part where somebody was about to be killed.

"A woman's having a baby," I yelled. "Somebody get Mr. Krogfoss!"

Greg Spivey

Shark once told me they were showing the B-movie film noir *Gun Crazy* at the drive-in the night he was born. He claimed he remembered it, which is preposterous, of course. But that's what he said—that the first thing he saw in this world was not even real life but a motion picture.

One afternoon in 1979 we screened *Gun Crazy* as part of the preparation for *Red Surf*, and I asked him, half-jokingly, "So which scene was playing when you popped out the womb, Shark?"

He smiled, then a few minutes later said, "This is it here, the first thing I ever saw."

It was the climax of the film, where the guy shoots the girl and the cops shoot him.

Mac Trager

They called me from the hospital and said, "Mr. Trager, your wife's just given birth to a healthy baby boy." I'd been half-asleep, but I dashed right out and jumped in the pickup. On my way to the hospital I had a head-on collision on Pacific Coast Highway. It was the other guy's fault—he crossed the line. Luckily for me, he was in an MG, so all I got was some cuts from flying glass. He died though, and later I came to wonder if it hadn't been an omen.

Kenny Roberts

We lived across the street from the Tragers on Mackerel Drive. When you say Newport Beach, people think of yachts and sports cars and fine beach homes, which is all true—but not Mackerel Drive. It was within the city limits, but it might as well have been Pacoima. Well, maybe not that bad. But Mackerel Drive was definitely on the wrong side of PCH—no ocean view, just a crummy little suburban street with trees that dropped these berries that stained the sidewalks and ruined people's paint jobs and everything else. The Tragers had this tract house with a white rock roof, and they'd painted the stucco this bright, almost Day-Glo aqua blue that really pissed off all the neighbors. It was a deliberate eyesore that stood out from all the other timidly pastel houses. But then it was the 1950s, wasn't it? All you could do was paint your house a bright color in a pathetic little stab at defiance.

Myrtle Butts

That house was always a mess and it got even worse once Winnie came down with that lifting disease. I forget what they called it now, but she was so weak she had to rest all the time. And she couldn't lift anything if it weighed much more than a pound. She'd open a can of Campbell's soup and be so exhausted she'd have to go lay down. That ruled out the vacuum cleaner and the scrub pail.

Kenny Roberts

Yes, Winnie's lifting ailment. I don't remember what it was called either. I don't think anybody does. It was one of those ailments you could only have in the fifties. Of course, it was psychosomatic. Her silent, inarticulate protest against a dull, stifling life.

Mac Trager

It was bullshit. There was nothing wrong with her except in her mind. I see that now, though at the time I indulged her. "All right, Winnie," I'd say. "Go stretch out in the den and watch 'I Love Lucy.' I'll do the housework." Then I'd run that vacuum a minute before I said, "To hell with this! Does John Wayne do housework?" He used to come into the station, you know.

Kenny Roberts

Mac had the Shell station down on PCH. He always seemed to be there till all hours of the night, probably to get away from Winnie. She was a whiner, you know. That's my earliest memory of Shark's mother. A frightened, whiny semi-invalid coming out to get the paper in a ratty floral housecoat. Not the Sunday paper though, she couldn't lift that. "Hon-*eeyy*?" she'd whine pathetically. Voices carried in the summer with all the windows open. "Hon*eeeyyy*?" And Mac would bark: "What the *hell* is it now!" He was this gruff ex-navy guy with a steel-gray flattop, a mean, stocky man who looked a lot like Glenn Ford.

Myrtle Butts

I had my own place for a while, but I moved back to Mackerel Drive when Shark was six months old since it had reached the point where Winnie could no longer care for him. At first she could still lift him and bottle feed him, then one day she dropped Shark in the rumpus room. Shark hit his head on that linoleum floor, Mac rushed him to the hospital, but it turned out not to be serious.

So I slept on the sun porch and played nursemaid to Shark, though we were still calling him Gale then. I'm not sure where Winnie got that name, though I do know she really went for that Gale Gordon on "Our Miss Brooks." "What a fine gentleman he is!" she would say.

"You're going to turn my boy into a fruit," Mac would say. "Gale's a broad's name."

"So is Marion," Winnie would say, "and that's John Wayne's real name. You don't think he's that way, do you?"

That steamed Mac something awful. He looked up to John Wayne in a big way.

Mac Trager

I loved the man, I'm not ashamed to admit it. He stood rock-hard for Americanism at a time when our great country was under attack from enemies both within and without. I still get misty-eyed when I think about Duke Wayne. That's why I feel a terrible rage even to this day when I remember why he quit coming into the station. I hate to recall how close I came that afternoon to killing my wife and only son.

Myrtle Butts

It was a beautiful Sunday afternoon and I had taken Winnie and Shark out for a drive. Shark was in the little baby seat in that old Chrysler, and Winnie was all bundled up in a pink coat and scarf even though it was warm, with that cupid lipstick she tried to do like Lucille Ball's. We were passing the station when Mac saw us and waved, so I pulled in. Only then did we realize that the tall man standing by his new Cadillac convertible was none other than John Wayne! Well, I almost died, never having seen a real movie star before. Mac insisted we get out and met Mr. Wayne, who owned a house down by the beach. I was just as flustered as a mare. But Winnie turned cross and moody, which embarrassed Mac, though he tried not to show it. Mr. Wayne was gracious, though I could tell he was eager to move on. Then Mac saw my camera, this old Kodak kind you had to hold at your waist and look down into. So he said, "Let's take a picture."

Well, I didn't want to, I could feel the tension in the air between Mac and Winnie. But Mac hissed at her to get out of the car and bring the baby over, even though he knew she couldn't lift the child. "Honey, I can't," Winnie whined. So Mac finally picked up Shark, and then Mr. Wayne took him and said, "Cute little fella." And Mac got the camera and made Mr. Wayne and Winnie stand in the hot sun by the Cadillac forever while he tried to get the camera right. Mr. Wayne started to perspire in the sun and Shark began crying, and Winnie started getting a weak attack. Mac finally snapped the picture, but Shark went potty in his diapers, and Mr. Wayne could tell and tried to hand the baby back to Winnie. But Winnie dropped Shark and he fell into the convertible. He wasn't hurt because he landed on the seat, but his diaper came off and he got some B.M. on Mr. Wayne's nice new upholstery. Mac flew into a terrible rage, saying horrible things to Winnie, while John Wayne just wiped off his car seat with one of those blue paper towels, and got in and drove off without saying a word.

Elliot Bernstein

As Shark described it in high school, one of his earliest "directly experiential memories" involved his "mother, a hot car, a gila monster and a nuclear blast."

Myrtle Butts

We'd all gone to a hotel in the desert, where Winnie got an awful sunburn when she fell asleep by the pool. She was all bundled up, but her hands and her face around her sunglasses were just red as a beet.

She was still in pain the next morning as Mac drove out along a desert road to a place where we could watch the A-bomb test that was planned.

When we reached the spot Mac got out, while I stayed in the car with Winnie and Shark, who was almost three years old then.

"Now you make damn sure they don't look," Mac said to me and walked a ways away to set up his Polaroid Land Camera on its tripod.

The bomb was supposed to go off at twelve o'clock noon way off across the desert but we'd got there early. Mac put on his war surplus goggles and got his camera all set and then we all waited, but that car was hot. The sun was pounding down and I started to perspire, and Shark got cranky and Winnie started looking funny, licking her dry lips, so I got out and went to Mac.

"Mac, the car's too hot," I said.

"Goddamn it, Myrtle, it's almost time," he snapped, without taking his eyes off the viewfinder.

Before I could say another word Shark let out a scream.

Elliot Bernstein

Shark was in the front seat of the car, his mother in the back, where she suddenly began "keening breathlessly in terror." Shark looked over the seat and saw a large black and orange gila monster crawling over Winnie's leg. Apparently, the desert reptile had gotten into the car the night before and gone undetected until then. Shark had no idea what a gila monster was, that it was in fact highly poisonous. But instinctively, he said, "When that fat, ugly, foot-long thing flopped between my mother's rigid pedalpusher-clad thighs, I yelled, 'Daddy, Daddy, Daddy!'"

Myrtle Butts

"Shut that kid up, shut him up, shut him up," Mac barked at me as I hurried back to the car. When I saw that lizard between Winnie's legs I let out a scream they must've heard in Reno.

Just as Mac turned from the camera the whole sky behind him flashed white. "Oh God, woman, cover their eyes!" he yelled, and I threw myself on Shark, grabbing Winnie by the hair, pulling her head down.

The whole ground quaked. I thought we'd gone in too close and were going to die.

Elliot Bernstein

Shark remembered Myrtle's "humongous spongy bazooms crushing my face," then a glimpse of his father "frantically snapping pictures of the rising mushroom cloud."

Mac Trager

I got some pictures of it, some good pictures of it. Black and white though. It was before Polaroid made color.

Myrtle Butts

Mac finally came and used a rolled-up map to flick that lizard out of the car. He yelled at me for almost letting Winnie and Shark look at the blast, and slapped Winnie 'cause by then she'd gone all hysterical.

"And you shut your trap, mister!" he yelled at Shark who was scared and crying too. Then he ran back and took some more pictures.

Elliot Bernstein

Shark remembered his father telling him as they drove off, "You almost made your mother go blind."

Not understanding, Shark began to cry again, and Mac yelled, "Shut up, you little pansy. I'm telling you for the last time!"

Shark held in his tears, and they drove on in silence, "everybody holding everything in." In a while Mac had to squirt water on the windshield and run the wipers to clean away the ash.

Myrtle Butts

As we drove off all this soot started coming down. "Oh my Lord, Mac," I said. "You don't think it's radioactive?"

"No," he said crossly. "I've told you twelve times already, we're well outside the limit. It's dust, that's all. Those things kick up some dust."

But in a minute he said, "Goddamn it, Myrtle, will you close your windwing?"

Kenny Roberts

One day Shark and I were playing in my backyard—we must have been about three or four, and he was wearing a new Hopalong Cassidy cowboy outfit—when he put down his cap gun and innocently opened his trousers to pick at a white Band-Aid wrapped around his penis.

Myrtle Butts

Mac had this old wire recorder—like a tape recorder except it used spools of thin wire instead of tape—which he used to record Senator McCarthy off the TV set. He kept all the neatly labeled little spools in a metal fishing tackle box—"in case there's a fire," he said. And one day he came in and found Shark playing withthe spools on the rumpus room floor. They were all unraveled, the wires all snarled, and Mac saw red.

He yanked Shark up and started spanking him so fast he didn't notice that one of those snarls of wire had gotten into Shark's baggy shorts and snagged his little you-know-what. Do I have to say the word? His penis.

I was in the kitchen when I heard Shark screaming bloody murder and raced into the rumpus room.

"Oh my Lord, Mac," I cried when I saw what had happened. "Stop, you're about to tear off his—"

Praise the Lord, Mac stopped in time, and there was no real harm done. I think the worst part was taking off that Band-Aid. Did Shark ever squeal when Mac did that!

Kenny Roberts

My parents felt sorry for Shark. I think that's why they started letting him come over all the time. Plus I was an only child as well—spoiled rotten I might add. I had everything but a playmate. My parents came to regret their hospitality though, because they became virtual babysitters, especially after Gladys entered the picture.

Myrtle Butts

I moved out after Mac made the pass at me. He was a drinker, you know. He liked that wrestling and that Brew 102, a cheap beer he just drank by the gallon. One night after Winnie had gone to bed we were watching the Gleason show in the rumpus room when he said, "Myrtle, why don't you make us some hot-buttered popcorn?"

So I did, but when I came back with it he said, "How 'bout it?"

and tried to pull me down onto the recliner with him, and I spilled popcorn everywhere.

I said, "Mac, it's not right, you're married to my sister." And he started to cry. It was the only time I ever saw Mac Trager cry, and it was just too awful for words.

He sobbed and said there'd been no love for years, even before Winnie got weak, that the night they'd conceived Shark Winnie was sleeping, or pretending to be, and there'd been nothing since. Then he described what he did in the bathroom to satisfy himself till I covered my ears and said, "Please stop."

I packed my bags in the morning. Not long after that Gladys moved in. Lord, what a scandal that caused!

Kenny Roberts

Gladys was this trashy blonde. She looked like Gloria Grahame with that same cupid lipstick thing Winnie tried to do, only Winnie always botched it. Gladys wore these tight pedalpushers and tight blouses with Peter Pan collars and had these incredibly pointy tits that caused gasps of flustered shock when she pushed a shopping cart through the Alpha Beta. And the perfume! A scent that just screamed cheap. She was supposed to be a nurse or something, but everybody knew what she was. The word my parents used was *tramp*.

Gladys Frazer

I met Mac in '55 not long after I left my third husband. I had this stupid little Nash Metropolitan that broke down one night on the coast highway, so I footed it back to the last whistle stop, which was Newport Beach. Jerks kept pulling up beside me, offering me a lift—I had a good body in those days and knew it—but I told 'em what they could do.

Mac was just closing up as I reached his Shell station and there was something about him I liked right away. He was good-looking, a little like the movie star Glenn Ford. But more than that he just seemed, I dunno, solid. We drove back to my car in his pickup truck. He took one look at my engine and said it was done for. Then he offered to drive me into Long Beach back to this sailor I'd just left.

On the way we stopped for a six-pack of Brew 102, which we drank as he drove and told me about his wife and kid.

"What you need is a live-in nurse," I said. "Too bad I don't do that anymore."

Then he said, "Where'd you get that shiner?"

"From this sailor you're taking me to," I said.

So we laughed, then he turned up this road and said, "I haven't slept with a woman in over four years."

At the end of the road was an old gun emplacement from World War II, put there in case the Japanese ever attacked, but they'd removed the guns by then. We parked there. It was a warm night.

"Shark? That's a funny name for a kid," I said as we finished the beers. "How come you called him that?"

" 'Cause the first time I ever took my boy fishing that's what we caught," Mac said.

Then we made love standing up in one of the concrete slots where the big guns used to be.

Myrtle Butts

I'd heard that Gladys had moved in but I could barely believe such a thing. So one afternoon I went by to see for myself. As I pulled up to the house I heard loud, exotic music playing—you know, that Martin Denny. I rang the bell but I don't suppose they heard me. So I let myself in.

The first thing I saw was poor little Shark on the rumpus room floor before the TV. He was wearing a spaceman's helmet, a big plastic fishbowl sort of thing, just like the one worn by that Captain Jet on TV. Except for that helmet, which was smeared with peanut butter and jelly, the child was not wearing a stitch!

"Where is your father?" I said, absolutely livid.

"In the garage," Shark said.

Well! Mac was in the garage all right. And so was that woman— her toreador pants hanging from the fin of that new Buick Mac had just bought. More than that I do not wish to describe.

I marched back in the house straight to Winnie's room, and found her sitting up in bed, watching her own portable TV. "Do you know what is going on in your house?" I said.

She looked up at me and smiled this funny smile and said, "I love him." And I saw that she meant the handsome game show host on TV. Then she smiled again, a sweet, peaceful smile just like a saint, and I knew she'd finally gone round the bend.

Mac Trager

It was a grim time. I'd always known in my heart that Winnie's condition was but a symptom of a far more profound and progressive mental illness. And I had loved her once, I don't care what anyone says.

Naturally, she hated Gladys on sight, though Gladys tried to tend to her needs. Gladys had been a nurse at one time, the facts will bear me out on that. But Winnie said terrible things to both Gladys and me, and then she just seemed to shut down.

Kenny Roberts

People were so hard-up for excitement in the fifties that what was happening at the Tragers really seemed like a big deal. I remember, when Shark and I started kindergarten Gladys would sometimes drive us, though my parents were under considerable pressure to take a dim view of her. My parents had voted for Stevenson, you see, and prided themselves on being "open-minded." But the rest of the neighborhood was hardcore Ike and felt compelled to act scandalized by the "shameless adultery" taking place in our otherwise tediously wholesome community. "How can you let *that woman* drive your son to school?" other parents said to mine.

In retrospect it was like something out of a lurid James M. Cain novel. Overheated suburban sex, the make-up-for-lost-time syndrome—at least in Mac's case. After school Gladys would quickly deposit Shark at my house so she and Mac could go fuck hanging from the pole lamp while the neighbors watered their flowers far too frequently and gasped in titillated shock when they heard Gladys's orgasmic cries coming from the Trager house. God only knows what Shark overheard or saw when he was at home.

Gladys Frazer

One evening Mac and Shark and I were watching "Father Knows Best" when a pleasant neighbor lady came to Robert Young's door. "I'll bet she wants to give him a blow job," Shark said as Robert Young let the woman in.

Mac turned his head to Shark in slow-motion. "*What* did you say?"

Shark cringed. "Nothing."

But Mac grabbed him and just spanked the living daylights out of him. "Don't you *ever* use talk like that in this house," Mac yelled.

"Mac, stop, for God's sake," I said. "He's just a child. He didn't know what he was saying."

I felt awful because I had a pretty fair idea where Shark had heard that expression. Mac's favorite trick was to come up and hug me from behind in the kitchen and whisper: "What say you give me one of your prize-winning before-dinner blow jobs?" He was not the world's most romantic man.

Mac Trager

I know what you're going to hear, that I was having sex with Gladys hanging from the rafters till it finally drove poor Winnie off the deep end. Well, it wasn't like that. I had certain needs and Gladys tended to them, but we were always discreet. When I realized the Pillsburys next door might be able to see her giving me a b.j. on the service porch, I made it a point to draw the shades the next time.

Seriously though, I wish I'd done something about Winnie sooner, but for a long time I still thought she was faking. She'd stare at that TV all day long and refuse to acknowledge me when I entered the room. But unlike the true catatonic she continued to chainsmoke. And she ate like a horse, though never in my presence. But I'd leave a plate of food and when I came back later it would be licked clean, and she'd be sitting there staring blankly at "Ozzie and Harriet," smoking an after-dinner Chesterfield.

And then, just like that, she could snap right out of it. She wouldn't speak for weeks and then suddenly she'd say in a normal tone of voice, "Mac, honey, would you please bring me the *TV Guide?*"

Gladys Frazer

The doctor came to see Winnie—they still made house calls in those days—and said it might be the change of life. He prescribed some pills, which seemed to help a little—at least we tried to believe they did. We started bringing her out of her room, propping her up at the breakfast table. She still had that funny smile, like an idiot almost. By then she'd got over her fight with me. I brushed her hair and did her nails and bathed her just like you would a child or a retarded person.

It was my idea to take her along to Disneyland the day we went.

Elliot Bernstein

It was Shark's first visit to the Magic Kingdom, and I don't suppose I have to tell you what Disneyland was like for a kid in those days. It was really the ultimate thrill.

Mac took Shark on a lot of the rides. "It was undoubtedly the best day of my early childhood," Shark said. So strong was his capacity for fantasy that he was nearly able to block out his mother's painful presence—"a specter shuffling up Main Street on Gladys's arm, a vegetable in pedalpushers and harlequin sunglasses with a smeary red idiot grin."

Gladys Frazer

"Mac, we should go," I said in Tomorrowland. "Winnie's getting tired." By that point we'd been stomping around for three hours.

But Mac said no. "Not till my boy and I go to the moon."

Kenny Roberts

In the line for the Moon Trip attraction, Shark and Mac ran into the Weltys, a family who lived one block over on Bonito Drive. It was Mr. and Mrs. Welty and the twins, Christopher and Christine—or Chris and Christy as they were known—who were also six years old and in the first grade with Shark and me. They were these perfect blond, blue-eyed twins, and the Weltys were absolutely *the* most perfect family in the neighborhood. Ray Welty was this incredibly "nice guy" type of dad—smiley, genial, completely Robert Young. And Mrs. Welty—God, I think her name was actually June—was just perfect perfect perfect.

They had recently put in a swimming pool, and I remember Shark and I going over there once with a bunch of other neighborhood kids, and everything was so great, the Weltys were so loving and joyful, that it made Shark sad. "I wish I lived here," he said to me in the pool. "I wish Mr. and Mrs. Welty were my parents."

He also developed kind of a crush on Christy—that sort of airy, innocent first-grade kind of thing. She was extremely precocious and believed in UFOs.

"Someday the saucers are going to come and take me back to my real parents," she said on the playground one day. Which, when you stop and think about it, is really pretty weird, considering how perfect her parents were.

Elliot Bernstein

During the Disneyland moon trip Shark sat beside Christy Welty, a girl from his first grade he had a crush on. When the plastic seats began vibrating as part of the rocket trip simulation Shark experienced a "transcendent elation, a visceral excitement mixed with dreamy feelings towards Christy, which was really the peak moment of my life up to that point."

Stepping out of the moon trip attraction Shark and his father were abruptly brought back down to earth.

Gladys Frazer

"I can't find Winnie," I told Mac. "I left her sitting right here on the Coca-Cola Terrace. When I came back with the drinks she was gone."

Well, we looked all around but we couldn't see her anywhere. Mac started getting mad. "Why the *hell* didn't you watch her?"

We walked around Tomorrowland, Mac tugging Shark along, getting madder and madder. "Bringing her was your idea, Gladys. I hope you're happy now."

"She's got to be here somewhere," I said.

Then we heard a young boy say to someone, "Guess what? There's some crazy lady in the Monsanto house taking off all her clothes."

Mac Trager

I have no idea what she thought she was trying to prove. But there she was, naked as a jaybird in the House of the Future while everybody and their mother gawked.

Gladys Frazer

She was just standing there in the futuristic living room stark naked, holding out her hands like a madonna with the peaceful smile of a saint.

People were giggling and had funny looks in their eyes.

Mac was furious. He picked up her clothes and threw them at her, telling her to get dressed.

"Mac, she's not responsible," I said, and led her back into the streamlined kitchen where I helped her back into her clothes. By then she seemed confused.

Some park people came and threatened to have Winnie arrested. But they soon saw that she was crazy and let us call the hospital instead. Then we couldn't find Shark. We realized he'd disappeared as soon as we heard about Winnie.

Kenny Roberts

Shark couldn't handle what his mother was doing. While Mac and Gladys were rushing to the House of the Future, Shark took off in the opposite direction and caught up with the Weltys.

"My father says I'm supposed to go home with you," Shark told Mr. Welty.

Mr. Welty assumed Shark just meant a ride. And though he didn't understand entirely he took Shark along when they left.

But when they pulled up to the Trager house, which was still dark, Shark said, "No. My father wants me to live at your house."

Well, the Weltys realized something was wrong, so they took Shark to their house, and finally reached Mac later that night.

Mac Trager

I was furious and worried sick by the time Ray Welty called and said Shark was over there. Disneyland was closed by then and we knew Shark wasn't there. We were beginning to think he'd been kidnapped.

If that wasn't enough I'd also had to deal with having Winnie committed.

Gladys Frazer

The ambulance backed right up to Tomorrowland and took her straight to the mental ward in Santa Ana.

Mac Trager

She was in the hospital for about two weeks, and the doctors couldn't figure it out either. One of 'em said, "We could give her a lobotomy," and I said, "Why bother? The way she sits around like a bump on a log it's like she's already had one."

So they gave her electroshock and a hysterectomy instead.

Gladys Frazer

After the hospital she was actually worse. She sat in her room and stared at the TV like she didn't even see it, and I had to feed her like a baby.

Kenny Roberts

I think Shark tried hard to lose himself in a fantasy world so he could forget what was going on with his mother. You know how you can transform reality when you're a child? Shark did that, pretending he was Flash Gordon—that old Buster Crabbe serial was running on TV in those days. In his imagination he was Flash and Christy Welty was Dale. She wasn't playing though—it was strictly Shark's fantasy. She was completely stand-offish, constantly snubbing him, only playing with other girls. But he'd say things like, "Someday I'm going to rescue her, and then she'll be different."

Then one day the Welty twins didn't come to school and Mrs. Healy, our first-grade teacher, said, "I have a very sad announcement, class. Yesterday evening, both Chris and Christy stepped onto a rainbow."

"*What?*" I said to Shark. I wasn't familiar with the expression.

"She means they're dead," Shark said.

Gladys Frazer

It was a terrible tragedy. The Weltys had a swimming pool and somehow while Mrs. Welty was in the kitchen fixing dinner and Mr. Welty was on the phone, the twins drowned.

Kenny Roberts

There was always something kind of weird about it. Just the fact that both of them drowned. The theory at the time was that one had tried to save the other, and in panic they'd drowned each other—which happens, I guess. But it just seemed very strange to me.

At recess after we heard about it Shark was very disturbed. That was probably why he forget it was Friday, and when the air-raid siren went off at ten o'clock, which it always did in those days, he thought it was really a nuclear attack and peed in his pants.

Gladys Frazer

The school called and said Shark had had an accident and I'd have to come and get him and change his clothes. So I did and he was very embarrassed. "I thought it was real," he said. "I thought we were all going to die."

"I know. It's all right," I said, and got him changed and drove him back to school.

When Mac came home that evening and I told him what had happened he saw red. "Oh Christ, that's the limit," he said.

"He couldn't help it, Mac. He thought the bombs were falling," I said, and tried to explain about the Welty twins drowning, since I knew that was part of Shark's distress.

But Mac wouldn't listen. "Out to the garage," he said to Shark.

Mac kept a paddle out there, and Shark started bawling as Mac dragged him out through the sliding glass door. Then I heard Mac say, "Goddamn it!"

He'd tripped on Shark's toy truck on the patio, and Shark had got away.

Kenny Roberts

Shark ran up Mackerel Drive. He had a pretty good headstart on his father but as he rounded the corner he looked back and saw Mac coming. Shark ducked up the alley and hid there. In a minute his father reached the alley, but not seeing him, continued on to Bonito Drive.

Shark ran on up the alley, his heart pounding, and as he passed the Welty house he heard someone splashing in the pool. Though he wasn't sure why, he said, that splashing sound—the knowledge that someone was using the pool—made his blood run cold.

He looked through the fence and saw Mr. and Mrs. Welty swimming in the pool—the pool where the day before Chris and Christy had drowned. He said they weren't saying anything to each other, they were just silently swimming. Shark got a very funny feeling because they didn't seem particularly sad.

Then they climbed out, first Mrs. Welty and then Mr. Welty, and they were both naked. Shark had never seen a naked adult before—he knew he shouldn't be looking. They dried off and lit cigarettes, never taking their eyes off each other, but still not saying a word.

Suddenly Shark stepped on a twig and the Weltys heard it. As they looked at the fence with alarm he took off in terror.

He ran to the end of the block, and then ran up Eel Road. In those days there was nothing on the other side of Eel Road except a field. And in the night sky above the field Shark saw it.

Elliot Bernstein

A band of flashing lights. He knew instantly that it wasn't an airplane or a helicopter. It was hovering in the night sky, silently hovering. There was only one thing it *could* be. Shark would always describe that moment as "one of the most truly ecstatic of my life." After having been exposed to so many movie flying saucers, but always believing, you know, that it was essentially bullshit—now to actually *see one.* To see plainly and clearly what could be explained in no other way.

Shark was mesmerized. Then he heard running footsteps closing on him. But he wouldn't take his eyes off the craft in the sky. He knew why it had come. "Here I am," he said silently, knowing they could read his thoughts. "I'm ready, please take me. Please." He heard the footsteps getting closer. "Please save me. I don't care if you have scaly skin and huge exposed brains, it doesn't matter, as long as you take me away from here."

But the craft did not descend. And Mac grabbed him. "Now you're really going to get it, mister."

As his father began spanking him Shark at last identified the flying object. It was the Goodyear blimp—with a moving band of lights wrapped around it, the bulbs spelling out an advertising slogan for a popular product of the day. *No Bugs, M'Lady Shelf and Drawer Paper*, it said.

Kenny Roberts

All things considered, Shark and Gladys seemed to get along pretty well. But then she indulged him tremendously. He ate what he wanted, when he wanted. But no matter how many times he gorged himself on Bosco and Three Musketeers, no matter how intense his fantasy life, I believe his mother's continuing deterioration affected him deeply. I think he was profoundly enraged at his father, but at seven years of age there wasn't much he could do about it.

Only once do I recall Shark's submerged resentment toward Gladys surfacing in a truly lethal way—though his chief aim may well have been to simply get at his father by depriving him of his tawdry sex obsession. Gladys was up on a ladder in her skin-tight pedalpushers hanging Christmas tree lights along the eaves of the house, giggling and wriggling as Mac held her hips—when suddenly, there was little Shark, pedaling directly toward the ladder on his tricycle, head lowered for the kill. At the last second Mac saw him coming and kicked over the tricycle, causing Shark to crash face-first on the lawn. He cut his chin pretty bad on a sprinkler-head—that's where that scar came from. I can still see him lying there bleeding on the dichondra while his father gave him hell.

That was the year that Winnie stepped onto a rainbow.

Mac Trager

Winnie wasn't getting any better, and a few days before Christmas the doctor came to see her and agreed she should be permanently committed. Those arrangements were in the process of being made when the man upstairs called her number.

Greg Spivey

Shark told me the story of his mother's death the Christmas Eve we got drunk together in Beirut during the filming of *Blue Light* in 1983. That it was Christmas Eve brought it back, no doubt, and as the tale unfolded I could easily see why he'd repressed it for years, for it was surely the most heart-rending Christmas story I had ever heard.

He described how as a little boy he'd go into his mother's room, toward the end I guess, and talk to her, trying to get her to respond. But she wouldn't, or couldn't. And then finally on Christmas Eve she did.

Shark said his father and Gladys were in the rumpus room that night watching TV, and there was a Christmas tree in the living room but his mother had never come out of her room to see it. And so, remembering how in previous years she'd loved the holidays, how they'd been her only joy in a neurotic, psychosomatic life, he went to her bedside and said, "Mommy, come look at the Christmas tree."

At that his mother smiled at him, Shark said, seeing him really for the first time in months. She smiled like a saint and said, "My precious baby." And Shark, who was seven then, led his mother into the living room and she looked at the brightly lit tree and there were tears in her eyes.

Then she looked at the bare tip of the tree and said, "Why, there's no angel." Then she smiled at Shark and said, "*You* can be my angel."

She led Shark back into her bedroom and dressed him in a long flowing white nightgown of hers so that he might roughly resemble a Christmas tree angel. And then, with floating, dreamy motions, she placed one of her hats, a white hat, on Shark's head. "Now you are mother's angel," she said, and lightly hugged him to her.

At that precise moment Shark's father burst into the room, wordlessly grabbing Shark by the arm, tearing off the nightgown, tearing off the hat. Then Mac threw Winnie back across the bed, slapping her again and again, until Gladys came in and pulled him off.

Shark, who didn't understand what was going on at all, ran to his mother, crying, "Mommy, Mommy." And Mac, still without saying a word, yanked Shark away from his mother, shoved him into his own bedroom, and slammed the door.

Shark said he was terrified all night and didn't sleep at all. He had no idea what he'd done or what his mother had done. All night he lay awake listening for the arrival of the one person he knew he could count on to provide at least momentary solace. But Santa Claus passed by the Trager house that night.

Then shortly after dawn, when Shark should have been excitedly anticipating opening his gifts, Mac returned. He threw open the door, glared about the room, then walked out.

He was looking for Winnie. It appeared she'd run off. But a few minutes after Mac left the room Shark heard Gladys scream.

Gladys Frazer

It was a terrible thing to do to a child on Christmas Eve.

Of course, you know Mac was something of a bigot. I didn't dare tell him my second husband had been Jewish. Or that I'd once made love to a black jazz musician in New Orleans. He would have dropped me like a hot potato if he'd known about that.

More than anything he hated homosexuals though. That was the worst thing, along with being a Communist—since both could happen to anyone regardless of skin color or religion. And he'd heard somewhere that mothers made their sons go that way by dressing them as girls.

Mac Trager

I admit I lost my temper, but I'm glad I did. It may have been the thing that stopped my son from going queer. And in that case it was worth it.

Gladys Frazer

It was an awful night. When Mac and I finally went to bed he wanted to make love, but I didn't. After what had happened I just wasn't in the mood.

I got up once to check on Winnie. She was sleeping and did not appear to be injured, though when Mac was hitting her those slaps were loud. She was supposed to go into the hospital the day after Christmas. That had been my idea—to at least wait until after we'd opened the gifts, if only for Shark's sake.

When I went to her room in the morning she was gone.

We thought she might still be in the neighborhood, so we got in the car. There was this freezer in the garage, the flat kind with the door on top, and as we were backing out I noticed all this frozen food defrosting on the work bench, packages of peas and venison Mac had shot on a hunting trip, and I got a sick feeling in the pit of my stomach.

"Stop the car, Mac," I said and got out.

Then he saw the food and started to get angry. "What the hell. My venison! Has she completely lost her mind?"

Then I opened the freezer and there was Winnie inside. That was when I screamed.

Greg Spivey

Shark ran out to the garage and his father said, "Don't look in there," but he did.

He said his mother was naked and her skin was very pale. Her eyes were closed and she looked peaceful. Shark said it wasn't terrible or gross at all, there was no sense of indignity or indecency, that on the contrary she looked like an angel, as if her lifeless body were reflecting where her soul had gone. Shark said he felt very peaceful looking at her and was barely aware of Gladys screaming hysterically behind him.

Kenny Roberts

I was opening presents when we saw the ambulance pulled up across the street. Soon everyone on Mackerel Drive was out in the street to see what had happened, and I heard someone say, "Winnie crawled in the freezer and died."

I caught a few other comments to the effect that it was Mac's fault this had happened—what he and Gladys were doing was bound to lead to something like this. You know how people are.

I went up the Tragers' driveway as the ambulance attendants were removing Winnie's body on a stretcher. She was covered with a sheet

von Riesen Library
McCook Community College

but one foot was sticking out. I remember the chipped red polish on her toenails.

I saw Mac with his arm around Gladys on the patio swing. She looked numb. Then I saw Shark alone in the living room, his back to me as I approached the sliding glass door. He was opening his presents under the tree.

When he saw me he smiled with a strange cheerfulness as if nothing at all had happened, and said, "Look what I got."

It was a Viewfinder. I looked into it and saw an eerie tableau of the Cisco Kid and Pancho on their horses, both of which looked stuffed.

2 / *Vertigo*
(1957–1961)

Myrtle Butts

Gladys left not long after Winnie's death, which was the best thing she ever did.

Gladys Frazer

I just couldn't take it, the way people looked at me at the local supermarket, and the things they said. Even the checker: "If you had any shame, you'd clear out."

And Mac wouldn't talk to me. You know how men get. He wouldn't say a word except, "Pass the salt."

Then one day he said, "My boy and I are going hunting." And I said, "Fine, but don't expect me to be here when you get back."

The last time I saw Mac he was backing out in that pickup, his rifle in the back window, Shark there beside him in his coonskin cap. The next day I caught the bus to Long Beach.

Kenny Roberts

Once Gladys left, people started to forgive Mac. It was like he was paying for what he'd done by being lonely again. People were so small minded in the fifties, don't you think? Making everybody pay for every crummy little thrill.

Mac felt guilty too, I guess, 'cause it was about that time that he started going to the Skylark Methodist Church, dropping Shark off at Sunday School, which my parents forced me to attend as well.

Sometimes I almost wish I'd been raised a Catholic, terror at least being more interesting than tedium. If there is a purgatory it must resemble a Methodist Church basement with old ladies moving biblical figures around on a feltboard in overpowering waves of sweet perfume. Jesus Christ and the reek of gardenias. Shark and I always sat together, talking and giggling like evil schoolgirls. Don't misread that—it was entirely innocent, we were only seven years old. But I see now that adults were already beginning to look at us as if there might be something "unhealthy" going on.

Myrtle Butts

I was heartened when I heard that Mac had begun attending church, and pleased when I heard he'd taken a fancy to Evelyn Burns, since she was certainly cut from a different strip than that Gladys.

Mac Trager

I did seek the comfort of the Lord after Winnie's demise, not out of guilt but simply because it was something I'd neglected. I had always had a deep faith in God and country, but had somehow felt I was too rough-hewn for church. Then I reflected on the fact that John Wayne went, and he was a man, so I gave it a try. I can't say I didn't feel awkward at first, but there was a certain serenity to be derived from it, and I believe it helped Shark too. He was troubled by his mother's death and had begun to put on weight, though it was far from the problem it eventually became.

I just couldn't be both father and mother to Shark, and I believed at the time the Lord sensed that. Those thoughts were in my mind, I know, the sunny Sunday morning the pastor introduced me to Evelyn Burns.

Evelyn Burns

My husband, Fred, whom I had worshipped, had passed away the previous spring after a long, excruciating bout with cancer. Toward the end his testicles had swollen up like footballs. It was ghastly and terrible and in grief I had turned to God.

I was not that impressed with Mac on first meeting. He was good-looking in a way, a little like Glenn Ford only more rough-hewn. But I'd heard things about him. I knew he had that Shell station, and in fact saw grease under his fingernails, and frankly felt I was a cut above that. Fred had been an executive at Petro-Chem in Costa Mesa, and we'd lived in a lovely home on Lido Isle, which sadly I had been forced to sell. When the proper time came for me to consider the possibility of remarriage I planned to look for a man still on his way up, not one pumping gas at the bottom of the ladder. But God, it would seem, had other ideas.

Kenny Roberts

Evelyn Burns took over our Sunday school class when one of the old ladies died. She was maybe thirty-five, though she looked much younger, a radiant vision of wholesome purity with a face and smile like Loretta Young. She was one sick cunt though.

Mac Trager

The next time I spoke to Evelyn was after Shark's prank. I was walking to the car with Shark after church when Evelyn came up and said, "Mr. Trager, can I have a word with you?"

Then she held up a flat piece of rough brown plastic and said Shark had put it on her Bible. "What is it?" I said. "It's plastic vomit," she said.

"Why did you do that?" I said to Shark.

"Because she makes me sick," he said, and I whacked his head right there in the parking lot.

Then I dropped Shark off and met Evelyn for coffee.

Kenny Roberts

Shark just had this aversion to Evelyn right from the start, like he sensed she was a phony or something. Then when Mac started going out with her a lot, Shark just went nuts.

Mac Trager

Evelyn was a stunning woman, as beautiful as Loretta Young, radiating a similar kind of goodness and decency. I knew of her late husband Fred because of his work on behalf of Americanism and was a bit intimidated by that at first. I'd heard him speak a few times and he was a real dynamo. So was Evelyn.

One Sunday after church I stopped by the small apartment she had on Pacific Coast Highway, and I laughed out loud and said, "Yes!" when I found out that she knew the score on the Reds and the niggers and the Jews.

Kenny Roberts

She was a grassroots American fascist just like her husband. I don't mean conservative, I'm talking Zionist conspiracies and blacks are monkeys trying to mongrelize the white race and the whole sick bit. It wouldn't surprise me to learn that Mac and Evelyn never actually had sex, but just lay in bed listening to Mac's old wire recordings of Joseph McCarthy's speeches.

Shark had inherited his mother's portable TV, which he and I watched in his bedroom all the time. The local stations seemed to show a lot of old costume adventure movies on weekend afternoons in those days. Shark liked the Errol Flynn stuff especially, *The Sea Hawk, Captain Blood.* One Saturday we were watching some piece of dreck with Louis Hayward when Shark heard Evelyn talking with Mac in the living room and he just went crazy. He started pacing around in circles, groaning as Evelyn cackled in the living room. Then he buried his head under the pillow and pounded the bed. I guess he sensed what was coming.

Mac Trager

I proposed to Evelyn on the second anniversary of Joe McCarthy's death. I took her out to a fancy prime rib restaurant and we drank a champagne toast to a man I have always considered a true American martyr, and then I popped the question. She was such a fine, decent woman, not a cheap piece of trash like Gladys had been, that I suppose I wasn't sure I deserved her. But she smiled and said yes, though we had yet to sleep together, and did not until the honeymoon. She was that kind of gal.

Kenny Roberts

Mac took Evelyn back to the house and together they told Shark they were going to get married. But things quickly turned ugly with Shark hitting Evelyn, you know, pounding her with his fists at about cunt level, saying, "I hate you, I hate you," until Mac whacked him and sent him to his room.

That night Shark climbed out his bedroom window and ran away. He was gone for nearly a week, and since he was only eight years old the cops were out looking for him, and it was quite a big deal.

They finally found him in the Balboa Theater. He had slipped in during a Saturday kiddie matinee and hidden in the balcony, which was closed off in those days. At night after everyone had gone he would gorge himself at the concession counter—which was what had finally precipitated a thorough search of premises. *Vertigo* was playing there that week. He told me he watched it something like twenty-four times.

Mac Trager

I was hopping mad as I brought Shark home. "You are going to pay a price for the worry you've put us through," I told him.

"What are you going to do?" he said.

"I don't know yet," I told him. "I haven't decided. I'll think of something while Evelyn and I are on our honeymoon. You'd better be trembling, mister. 'Cause it is going to be bad."

Then I left him in the care of the Roberts. Why I ever did that I don't know.

Kenny Roberts

It was Easter break when Mac and Evelyn belatedly went on their honeymoon, driving up the coast somewhere—though Berchtesgaden would have been more appropriate. One evening my parents took us to the Flying Wing Drive-In to see a movie I hated at the time, but which I rather like now, Orson Welles's *Touch of Evil*. It's a dark film, aggressively grotesque and bizarre, and at that point I was addicted to the sunny escapist world of musical comedies, you see. Shark, however, was galvanized by the film, responding to it as if it were somehow an exact representation of his inner state at the time— or so it seems in retrospect. I remember him chuckling cynically throughout the movie—a cynical eight-year-old!—chuckling in a way that mirrored Orson Welles's exhausted chuckle in the film, chuckling like a fat and evil old man as he wolfed down Milk Duds. Shark had quite a weight problem by then.

A few days later my parents took us to see *Gigi* and I was in rapture. I gushed about it for hours afterwards, asking Shark if he didn't agree it was the best movie either one of us had ever seen. He shrugged. "It's okay for what it is," he said.

Regardless, he did indulge my favorite pastime, which was lip-syncing showtunes before the dining room mirror. I would play *South Pacific* and *Carousel* and *Gigi*, and Shark and I would perform these little playlets for our own amusement, just having a gay old time. Actually, it was innocent, at least on Shark's part. It's funny, but in retrospect I see he always played the guy. Without even thinking, he would just instinctively do the Rossano Brazzi part while I would instinctively go for Mary Martin or whoever. But we were completely naive. We had no idea we were playing a dangerous gender role game.

Then one warm afternoon we were listening to *Oklahoma!* in the rumpus room as my parents lay sunning out by the pool. Shark and I were in our bikini swimsuits, which probably made it look even worse. Gordon MacCrae and Shirley Jones were singing their duet of "People Will Say We're In Love," Shark lip-syncing MacCrae's deep masculine voice as he held me in his arms while I batted my eyelashes repulsively camping it up as Shirley, when suddenly Evelyn walked in. She and Mac had come back from their honeymoon a day early.

The look she gave us could have killed bugs. Suddenly I just knew we'd been doing something terrible, something evil, though I didn't really know what it was exactly. In a fury, Evelyn tore the needle from the record, scratching it. The way she glared at me made my skin crawl. It was the first time I'd ever felt real hatred from anyone. She stormed out to my parents. Shark and I couldn't hear what she said to them, but my parents looked puzzled and then frightened.

Evelyn stormed back through the house and across the street to get Mac. Then Mac stormed in and yanked Shark by the arm all the way across the street.

The upshot was that Shark and I were forbidden to play with each other ever again.

Evelyn Burns

I saw right away that Shark's friendship with the Roberts boy was abnormal, so Mac ended it. He was determined that Shark would grow up to be normal, but after the Roberts boy left the picture Shark sulked and put on weight and refused to make new friends.

I tried to get along with Shark. The day I moved in, Mac and I sat him down and I said, "Listen, I know I'll never replace your mother . . ."

And Shark said, "You're right, you won't, you whore."

Mac hit Shark and he ran to his room. Later that night he tried to kill himself. Or so he said.

Mac Trager

He took a bottle of Sleep-Eze but nothing really happened. We wouldn't even have known if he hadn't told us. In the morning he came out with the empty bottle and said, "I took all of these last night. If she doesn't leave the house, next time I'll use one of your guns."

Evelyn sighed and said, "I've heard everything now."

I figured it was bullshit. But I did lock up my guns.

Evelyn Burns

Those two years with Mac were a nightmare. I don't know why I stayed as long as I did. Shark would barely speak to me at all. If I asked him a question he'd say, "Yip," or "Nope," the minimum possible. I could feel his hatred every time I stepped into that house.

Mac and I had our own problems though. He was in the mood all the time and I wasn't. I tried explaining to Mac that I couldn't do the deed without seeing Fred in his last days with his testicles swollen up like footballs. But Mac wouldn't listen. I went along for a while till the migraines started. Then I took this medication that did something to my skin so that it was painful to be touched.

Mac Trager

I worshiped Evelyn but she was cold as a fish. Then the headaches started and I watched the marriage slowly die.

Greg Spivey

Shark told me that the single high point during the years his father was married to Evelyn was the afternoon Mac took him to *The Searchers* at the Balboa Theater. Evelyn was out of town visiting relatives at the time, the marriage was already shaky, and in retrospect Shark said he realized Mac had begun drinking early in the day in a fit of self-pity and was drunk as he and Shark arrived at the theater just as the John Ford classic was beginning. Shark told me he felt that his father's intoxication accounted for what then occurred, a simple action rendered extraordinary by its utter absence from Shark's young life. As the two of them watched John Wayne move across the sweeping vistas on the CinemaScope screen Mac put his arm around his son and Shark rested his head against his father's chest.

Well, at the very end of the movie—which to my mind is one of the truly poignant moments in American film—where John Wayne stands framed in the doorway, watching the reunited family enter the house which he can never enter, then turns to the bright western vista, the comfort of family and culture forever denied him as he rides away eternally alone—just at that point, Shark told me, his father said in a choked-up voice, "That's you and me, son. We're both gonna end up like that someday."

Shark didn't understand what his father meant at the time. "But I do now," he told me twenty years later.

Mac Trager

Shark told me once in the late seventies that the one time he really felt close to me as a kid was when I took him to see Duke Wayne in *The Searchers.* I told him I had fond recollections of it as well. But the truth was the whole thing was pretty much a blank. I'd been drunk as a skunk that afternoon.

Evelyn Burns

Despite its side effects, the migraine medication did allow me to function, and in 1959 I took a full-time job at the local Republican headquarters, so I could be in on the ground floor of Dick Nixon's campaign.

Jeannie Goodhew

I used to babysit Shark, and I'm not sure to this day which of us was more lonely or miserable. We both had weight problems, and that's all we ever did: sit there and watch TV and stuff our faces. He liked those old movies they showed at night when the kids were supposed to be in bed. *Double Indemnity*, I remember that one. "I'm not sure you should watch this," I said. "It may be too adult." In those days people thought those characters were amoral.

There was one with Farley Granger where a carousel flew apart at the end. Shark really liked that.

His parents weren't getting along. His dad was always working late at the gas station, and his stepmother was always off doing something in politics somewhere.

Herbert Banton

Shark was in my sixth-grade class at Pizarro Elementary School and you could see he was a boy in trouble. He was fat and had no friends and the other kids made fun of him. His nickname was "The Blob," and the more his peers ridiculed him, the more obese he became, in a viciously circular attempt to further insulate himself from their ever-escalating cruelty. His work was listless and barely adequate. Here was a boy who had already given up on life, a fact driven home by the paper he turned in on what he'd done over Easter vacation. "I thought of different ways to kill myself," he wrote, and then listed fifty separate ways. It was clearly a cry for help. I called his parents in for a conference.

Mac Trager

Shark had turned into a fat sack of lazy shit, it was as simple as that. We met some yo-yo teacher of his who spouted out a lot of psychological crap. But I knew what Shark needed.

Herbert Banton

The conference was a disaster. As Mac Trager listened to my expression of concern his face grew redder and redder. Then he began punching his fist in his palm, plainly a nervous, compulsive gesture which nonetheless made me uneasy.

I showed the stepmother the suicide essay. She skimmed it, quickly losing interest, and began asking me very pointed political questions. Did I teach Americanism, that sort of thing. I said, "Mr. and Mrs. Trager, your son needs psychiatric help."

Mac Trager said, "This is horseshit," and they left.

Jeannie Goodhew

It was so sad. I used to drop Shark off at the kiddie matinee at the Balboa Theater. When I came to pick him up, he would be waiting there on the bus bench in front of the theater all alone. He was huge by then and so depressed he would barely even talk to me.

Then one afternoon the Balboa manager caught me and said Shark had broken a seat and would not be allowed in the theater again unless he lost a great deal of weight. "We can't risk being sued if he hurts himself," the manager said.

Shark was glum and said very little, but inside he must have been humiliated. On the way home he did his Alfred Hitchcock impression. He could even make his face look like Hitchcock's, and of course with the weight . . . But it wasn't funny, there was something despairing about it.

I think the only thing that saved him was that his stepmother finally left.

Lorna Trager

Evelyn was gung-ho for Nixon in 1960, and during the campaign there was some kind of coffee klatsch that Nixon dropped in on to thank all these Republican women who were working on his behalf. Evelyn was pretty high up in the organization by then, the head of some committee, and the way I heard it, right in the middle of the coffee klatsch, with all these people standing around, Evelyn said to Nixon, "Off the record, Dick, once you're elected what are you going to do about the kikes?"

Well, everybody just dropped their load, because that kind of thing wasn't said anymore. Supposedly, Nixon just laughed as if Evelyn was joking, then said, "Say, who baked this cake?"

But later he sent down the word that he wanted that woman out of the campaign, and the next day Evelyn was fired.

Mac Trager

The day Evelyn got fired from the Nixon campaign she came home and went completely berserk. At first it was just the Reds and the Jews and Nixon's "spineless advisors" she was mad at. I said, "Honey, I know," and tried to put my arms around her and she turned into a banshee. She said things to me then I could never forgive, even though I knew she was distraught. "You bore me," she said. "You make me sick, you always have."

Well, I hit her and told her to get out of the house and she left. I heard the car start and ran out to the street and said, "Oh no, you don't. You can walk." So we fought for the car keys, then she got out

Checkout Receipt

Longmont Public Library
04/09/12 03:23PM
303-651-8476
24-hr. Automated Renewal
303-774-4693

Patron ID: 42283

BOY WONDER
33060009541819   Due: 05/04/12

Total: 1

and walked, screaming, "You're no good in bed," for all the neighbors to hear.

As I walked back to the house I saw Shark watching from his bedroom window. "Are you happy now?" I said. By then several neighbors had come out to watch.

Shark just looked at me and pulled down his window shade. I could hear some old movie on his TV.

Lorna Trager

Mac was worried for a long time that Evelyn was going to take him to the cleaners. All he had was the station and that house. But Mac was funny. Once she was gone he wanted her back. She'd gone to Texas and he began calling her when he got drunk. But she met some Texas oilman and said, "I don't want anything you have, Mac. Just don't call me anymore." Then she got a new number.

Mac was bitter. I was bitter then too, since my husband Phil had left me for a younger woman in Kansas City. I hadn't seen my brother in almost ten years when Mac invited me out to California in 1961. I arrived that winter and slept on a little cot on the sun porch.

Shark and I hit it off right away.

3/ The Thrill of It All (1962–1965)

Brad Jenkins

I was Shark's best friend in junior high. We moved into the house across the street on Mackerel Drive when the Roberts moved out. I know Shark and Kenny Roberts had been friends at one time. I only saw Kenny once, but he acted just like a sissy. You could tell he was going to grow up to be a fruit.

I was tall for my age and had a bad acne problem. I got the nickname "Pus," which I hated, but it stuck. I was into math and science, and then after I met Shark, movies. We went to the show all the time.

Lorna Trager

Shark became best friends with Pus Jenkins, who'd moved in across the street where the homo boy used to live. Mac had a thing about homos, you know. I heard once he'd had a bad experience in a hobo jungle when he was a boy during the Depression. He was worried about Shark's new friendship with Pus until he eavesdropped on them talking in the backyard one day. They were talking dirty but about girls, you know. So Mac turned to me and said, "I guess it's all right."

Brad Jenkins

Shark liked Lorna. I guess everybody did. She wasn't too bright but she had a sunny disposition. She was pretty but not in a cheap way. She would always be out watering the flowers, or hanging clothes on the line, singing some tra-la song. And sometimes when the sun was behind her you could see through her dress.

Greg Spivey

Shark liked to say that his early childhood had been a "dark, grim, black and white era, about as much fun as an FBI surveillance film." But when his aunt came to live in the house "a luminous new WarnerColor age began." He felt that she'd literally saved his life and "probably prevented me from hating all women for all time."

Brad Jenkins

I think Lorna gave him his first movie camera.

Lorna Trager

It was my idea. Mac wanted to give him a set of barbells. But I said, "Oh come on, Mac. Let's pop for this Bell and Howell. It's Christmas. Don't you want to have some movies of the tree?"

Brad Jenkins

It was an eight-millimeter camera, not even Super 8—I don't think Super 8 was even around yet. Right away, Shark really got into it. And he didn't just do home movie stuff. Right from the start he tried to make real movies with plots and so forth, using other kids in the neighborhood. He was still fat, but that camera brought him out of his shell.

Julie Ferguson

I was in one of Shark's silent movies. I played a girl who saw a flying saucer land. He used this old pie tin for the saucer. Twenty years later when my husband and I went to see *Blue Light* and they showed the scene with the girl who sees the flying saucers, I said, "My God, Burt, that's me."

Brad Jenkins

We both liked science fiction movies. *Forbidden Planet*, *Earth vs. the Flying Saucers*, *War of the Worlds*—the kind of movies they showed at the Balboa Theater Saturday matinee. Shark and I would leave the theater and he'd talk about the movies all the way home. Then he'd make films of kids screaming and pointing, then cut to a shot of a Martian made out of red clay climbing out between two pie tins. Those movies were pretty good when you think that he couldn't even do any editing, except what he did just by choosing what he shot.

Mac Trager

I took a dim view of the camera from the start. It was just a way for his sick imagination to run wild when he should have been doing something physical. He was in some special P.E. class for spastics and queers because of his weight. When I found out about the queers I lowered the boom.

Lorna Trager

Mac sent Shark to a doctor who put him on a diet that included taking pills. In those days people didn't know as much about speed as they do now.

Brad Jenkins

Shark started losing weight as if by magic. He was glad, but I think it scared him too. By then he was used to being the fat kid all the time. Plus he was starting to develop. You know, his voice changed and he got hair and a man's dick. As the weight came off, his dad had him switched back to regular P.E. and put him on a crash sports course.

Lorna Trager

I was glad to see Shark lose the weight. But I think Mac pushed him too hard. Mac would do things like throw a football at Shark when he wasn't looking, shouting, "Catch!" too late. When the football hit Shark in the head, Mac would shout, "Come on, you pantywaist. On your toes!"

It got so that Shark would flinch when Mac just walked in the room.

Brad Jenkins

Shark's dad pushed him real hard. Shark started getting muscles but he was nervous and jumpy all the time. He was still making these little science fiction movies, but if somebody screwed up he'd lose his temper real quick. So after a while the other kids didn't want to do it anymore.

Then one day he said, "Come on, let's go see *Psycho*, it's playing with *The Birds*. I wanna check out that shower scene again."

Well, I got kind of excited because *Psycho* was forbidden. My parents wouldn't let me go see it back when it first came out because they'd heard it was too extreme. So we went off and saw it, sneaking in through this exit door. We watched it a whole bunch of times so that Shark could look at the editing. We watched it until it really *did* something to me, and Shark lost all interest in science fiction. "I'm going to make a movie like that," he said. And one afternoon he tried to get Julie Ferguson to take off her clothes in the shower.

Julie Ferguson

Shark tricked me into coming over to his house. There was no one there but Pus and him, and Shark took out his camera. "Come on, Julie, take off your clothes," he said with a funny look in his eye. When I said no he said, "Come on. Janet Leigh did it."

When I said, "No, she didn't, that was a movie," Shark picked up this knife.

Brad Jenkins

I don't think Shark ever intended to stab her or anything. He just wanted his way. But I made him put down the knife and Julie ran out of the house. Nothing ever happened. If she told her parents, they decided to drop it.

I thought about it later though, the look on her face when she saw that knife, and it made me hot.

Greg Spivey

According to Shark, he was playing sick to get out of taking a test the Friday President Kennedy was shot. He was home in bed, "masturbating to a *Nugget* magazine," and just about to "pop," using his term for it, when his aunt, watching daytime TV elsewhere in the house, cried out: "Oh God, no, no!"

Shark was subsequently "awed by the sense of history taking place," and exasperated because his portable TV had been temporarily taken away from him as punishment for bad grades, and his father, who'd never liked the president, obstinately refused to watch the extensive television coverage of the assassination's aftermath. "All the networks were live that weekend," Shark recalled, "but my father stayed tuned to a cheesy local channel showing "Highway Patrol" reruns and 1930s B westerns. If I hadn't been over at the Jenkins' Sunday morning I would've missed seeing Oswald bite the dust."

Shark confessed to "an illicit ambivalence" about that weekend. "As terrible as it was that Kennedy had been killed, the national trauma did provide an exhilarating sense of heightened reality, a feeling that life had broken free of its humdrum everyday restraints, that something had really *happened*. In an innocent adolescent way I guess I just found it very good drama and was so jacked up I barely slept the entire weekend, taking more of my weight control pills than usual, since I'd discovered they increased my alertness, though I knew nothing at the time about speed."

Brad Jenkins

Shark spent most of that weekend watching TV at our house. When Oswald got it, Shark clapped his hands and said, "Man, this is *wild!* I wonder who's gonna get it *next!*" And my parents kind of looked at him.

Lorna Trager

I could see the diet pills were affecting Shark's mind. He was jumpy all the time and started mumbling to himself. I talked to Mac but he said, "Aw hell, there's nothing wrong with him that running a few more laps won't cure."

Brad Jenkins

Shark really changed in junior high. He kept getting more muscles and hair on his chest and got one of the biggest dicks around. He was sex obsessed too. He told me he beat off five times a day. We would talk about different girls at school and I began to feel jealous because sometimes the girls would look at him, but they never looked at me except to throw up because of my acne.

Shark started dressing like a hood too. At Cortez Junior High there were hoods and soshes. The hoods wore white T-shirts and unwashed blue Levis while the sosh guys wore white Levis and Madras shirts. The hoods came from our neighborhood and the even worse area up by Costa Mesa while the soshes lived down in the nice houses by the beach. Shark went around with a rubber in his wallet saying, "I'm gonna get me some socialite ass."

It was about that time that he first saw Kathy Petro.

Paige Petro

We bought the place in Newport Beach in '64 so Jack could be near the Costa Mesa plant, which was expanding then. It was a stunning house, a showplace really, which we needed since we entertained. How I adored it, I truly did. The view, the sunsets! The ocean breeze! Orange County was the future then, the ideal place to raise a family.

Neal Ridges

There was an obsessively repeated tracking shot in Shark's notorious "non-linear" student film which, he told me in the late seventies, came as close as anything he'd ever put on celluloid to capturing his first impression of Kathy Petro. Although I had known nothing of Kathy Petro per se when I'd served as his student "line-producer" on the film in 1968, it was obvious from Shark's driven perfectionism as we set up the shot that he was bent on recreating a key moment of his life.

It took us an entire day to get that shot. The silver Mercedes had to sweep into the gas station at just the right speed, so that it appeared to be floating. The father who was driving—the Jack Petro figure—had to remain in darkness despite the bright sunlight of the Newport Beach day. His blonde daughter however, occupying the passenger seat, had to appear to "glow from within." That was hard to achieve. But we finally did it with a carefully adjusted sun-gun.

It was an extraordinary, near-hallucinatory shot, and it did capture the quasi-religious tone Shark wanted to impart to that "first enraptured emanation of love."

The silver Mercedes floats up to the pumps, the camera tracking in on the luminous teen angel, so fresh, so white, so light and pretty So blindingly blonde. So sunny, so cheerful, so rich and privileged, yet so innocent and unconceited. Startling green eyes and a sunshine smile, a California smile. Sweetly delicate peachfrost mouth. She places a nearly empty cream soda bottle to her lusciously pearlescent peach lips, and you can almost *taste* the vanilla as she takes a final swallow. Now she smiles at the camera—at young Shark in his father's gas station—she smiles so cheerfully, so good-naturedly, not stuck-up at all. "Hi," she says, holding out the empty cream soda bottle. "Could you do something with this?" she laughs lightly, infectiously, as if to indicate she doesn't mean to impose.

"Hi. Could you do something with this?" Again and again that shot replayed, at least two dozen times, a compulsive leitmotif of Shark's first sound film, as it was, I believe, and would always remain, of his mental and emotional life.

Kathy Petro

I remembered that first encounter later, of course. But at the time Shark made no special impression on me. He was just some hoody boy at the gas station I asked to take my cream soda bottle. If I smiled at him I certainly didn't mean anything by it. I tried to be nice to everyone in those days. The golden rule and all that.

Brad Jenkins

Once Shark and I walked past this big house on the Balboa peninsula, a big Spanish-style place with a tile roof and a silver Mercedes-Benz in the court beyond the iron gate. "I'm in love with the girl who lives there," he said.

Later I found out the Petros had moved in there. Jack Petro owned Petro-Chem and knew John Wayne and all these big Republicans. He was a millionaire many times over.

Neal Ridges

Shark said he became "actively obsessed" with Kathy Petro right from that very first encounter. He began dreaming of her at night, fantasizing about her. "If I'd seen the future," he told me, "I would have kept that cream soda bottle she handed me with her peachfrost lipstick on the rim as the ultimate icon of my life."

In retrospect he admitted that the speed he was taking had probably contributed to his fixation. "Speed is very mental. It makes it easy to stay locked on one thing." At the time, of course, he didn't really understand what his "appetite pills" were doing to him. But even without the speed, Shark contended, "I would still have lost my heart forever on a sunny summer afternoon."

Sometimes he would ride his bicycle past the Petro house in the evening, looking up at the windows, imagining what Kathy might be doing at that moment. He would visualize her seated at her vanity, applying her peachfrost lipstick, and instead of perfume the air would be laced with the scent of vanilla, the cream soda flavor Shark would then and forever always associate with Kathy Petro. He had already switched from Coke to cream soda, in fact virtually subsisting on little more than the soft drink and his Obetrol tablets.

One evening at sunset, he said, as he peddled past the Petro house he saw Kathy in an upstairs window. She was naked behind the diaphanous curtain as she prepared to dress and Shark was so mesmerized he crashed his bicycle into a parked car, severely bruising his leg.

Brad Jenkins

Shark and I were walking along the strand by the yacht club one day when he saw Kathy Petro coming up the landing from her father's boat. The way we were walking we were going to cross her path in about half a minute, and Shark whispered to me, "This is it. Disappear."

By then I was already sick of hearing about her, 'cause Shark talked about her all the time, even though they'd only met once at his dad's station. But he said he thought about her when he jerked off at night, and he knew she was thinking about him too. I told him he was crazy and he got mad. "You wait and see," he said. "It's just a matter of time."

So I stood there on the strand, pretending to look out at the boats, and let Shark go on ahead alone. He crossed her path as she reached the strand and she almost kept going. Then she stopped and she and Shark talked but it looked like she was in a hurry to continue on.

Kathy Petro

He startled me that day, I guess. I was in this extra-good mood, when suddenly he stepped in my path like a dark cloud blocking out the sun. He wasn't bad-looking exactly, but into this hoody thing I found very unappetizing. He tried making this awful, tense small talk, like was I going to Cortez Junior High in the fall and so forth, and something about him really made me uncomfortable. Not scared exactly, just, I don't know, repelled. He had this starving dog look in his eyes.

Finally Daddy called to me from the boat, which gave me an excuse to get away.

"Who was that?" Daddy said.

"I don't know," I told him.

Brad Jenkins

When Shark came back I asked him what happened. "She wants me," he said.

"Yeah, I could tell."

"What do you know, Brad?"

"I know she's out of your league," I said.

Shark exploded. "You don't know shit, you ugly geek. But I know one thing. I'm never going to get to first base with a stomach-turning creep like you lurking in the background. So take a hike, Brad. Okay? Get lost."

He really hurt my feelings that day. He apologized a few days later and we were friends again, but it was never really the same.

Neal Ridges

According to Shark, the kiss in *Tropics*—that swirling preposterously delirious shot of the lovers' juicy, sweaty faces, all Gauguin colors and crypto-von Sternbergian South Seas pictorialism—came the closest of any kiss in any of his films to conveying the "nearly unbearable rapture" of his first experience with Kathy.

It happened at the Flying Wing Drive-In on a Friday night late in the summer of 1964. Shark had gone there with a carload of older guys to drink beer and watch Ann Margaret in *Kitten with a Whip*. But the co-feature was still playing, Doris Day's unctuous vehicle, *The Thrill of It All*, when a new car swept in and Shark saw Kathy Petro in the passenger seat.

His heart started pounding, but several minutes passed before he got up the nerve to get out and approach the car, which had parked several rows down. As he did he saw the driver, an older girl friend of Kathy's, going off with a boy to another car, leaving Kathy to watch the movie alone.

Shark stepped to Kathy's window and said, "Hi." He said she looked at him "dreamily," and sighed but didn't speak. And although he'd been prepared to strike up a conversation, he suddenly realized with a stunning, galvanizing clarity that she didn't want him to, that it wasn't even necessary, that she did in fact want him as much as he wanted her. That what she wanted right then in that moment was simply for him to kiss her. And so he did.

He kissed her through the window, long and deeply, and she moaned. More excited than he'd ever been, Shark broke the kiss long enough to go around to the driver's side and climb into the car, where the kiss resumed despite the window-speaker counterpoint of a "classic Doris Day fit of mock-indignation in response to some 'wolfish male's' advances"—a seemingly inconsequential detail of considerable significance, I think. Kathy moaned meltingly, and Shark soon had a rock-hard erection, and knew that the time had come. But as he reached under her skirt, Kathy abruptly snapped out of her trance. "Oh my God, what are you doing? What am *I* doing? Oh no, look, you shouldn't be here. Oh, Jeez, here comes my girl friend."

That last remark jolted Shark sufficiently that he climbed out of the car, quickly pulling out his shirt tail to hide his erection, only then realizing that Kathy's girl friend was nowhere to be seen. Confused, he tried to open the car door again, but Kathy pushed down the lock a second before he could. Then she rolled up her window, locking the passenger door too.

"Look, I'm sorry," Shark said, thinking it was simply that he'd gone too far.

But Kathy wouldn't look at him. "Please go away," she said, covering her face in embarrassment. "Please just go away."

Shark walked a ways away, then lingered, watching the car for a while, hurt and angry, but most of all confused. "Her refusal to look at me," Shark told me fifteen years later, "that was the thing that really killed me. One minute she's giving me everything I've ever wanted. And the next it's like she's saying I'm a total piece of shit."

Kathy Petro

That night was so strange. I had this sinus problem and had taken an antihistamine which really knocked me for a loop. I shouldn't have even gone out, but I was curious about *Kitten with a Whip*, which was supposed to be racy and everything. But I was so woozy from the antihistamine I couldn't even follow the plot of that Doris Day film.

I didn't really even know what was happening at first when Shark started kissing me, I swear. Suddenly it was just happening and it felt good and everything, and the next thing I knew he was in the car. But when he touched my you-know-what, it was just like a bucket of ice water in the face. 'Cause I was fourteen and still a virgin and everything and suddenly realized: Oh my God, I can't do this, not with him. My reputation would be ruined forever.

Brad Jenkins

"She fucked with my head," Shark said one day at Cortez Junior High as we watched Kathy Petro crossing the quad. "But I still want her."

Then a few weeks later he approached her at lunch. She was with her blonde girl friends and Shark was only there a minute. He came back pissed off, and the blonde girls were laughing at him behind his back.

Kathy Petro

I tried to just block the drive-in incident out of my mind. Fortunately, I didn't have any classes with Shark. When I did see him at a distance I felt this flush of embarrassment though. At times like that I'd wish he'd just go away to some other school.

Then one day he came up and asked if I'd like to go see the Beatles' movie *Help!* "No," I said, just like that. It was at lunch and my girl friends were there and I was afraid he would say something about the drive-in. He was so hoody and everything I didn't want anyone to even think for a minute I would even consider going out with him, let alone anything else.

"Why not?" he said.

"Isn't it obvious?" I said. "I don't go out with boys like you."

"Why are you making it so hard?" he said, which scared me a little for some reason.

"Look, I'm just trying to eat my lunch, okay? Do you mind?"

At that he walked away.

Later I thought: It's too bad in a way. He could be cute if he weren't so hoody. If we were on a desert island it might not be that bad. But we weren't. Besides, even if we were it might not be that great, 'cause he had a look in his eyes that made me think he might actually be a little crazy.

Lorna Trager

Two policemen woke me up with their pounding on the door one morning. I got Shark out of bed and as soon as he saw the policemen he started shaking. Mac got up and when the cops told him what Shark had done he saw red. The cops went into Shark's bedroom and took all his movie film, and then they took him down to the station.

Kathy Petro

I'll never forget it. We were watching "Bonanza" in the den when the phone rang and Daddy went into the other room to answer it. In a minute he came back as white as a sheet. "Jack, what on earth?" my mother said.

When he told us I kind of went into shock at first. Then I started screaming.

Brad Jenkins

Shark told me later that one night he'd been thinking about Kathy and without really knowing why he just got up from his bed and got his movie camera and walked on down to her house. When he got there he saw a light on in her window, and the gate was open so he went into the court and climbed up the trellis to the balcony of her bedroom.

He saw her through the curtains, trying to decide what to wear that night, a Rolling Stones record playing on her 45 player. She was just wearing panties and a bra, he said, holding up these different dresses, looking at herself in the mirror, pausing every once in a while to take a hit off a bottle of cream soda.

Shark said he just watched her for a long time like he was spellbound. He said he loved her so much he felt like he could almost be content just looking at her forever. Finally though he lifted his camera and started to film her as she bounced around the room, singing to the records, modeling different clothes.

Then suddenly a record ended and the whirring sound of the camera seemed loud. Right then she started toward the balcony and Shark was sure she'd heard the camera and was going to catch him.

But she turned at the last minute and went into her own private bathroom. So Shark stepped over to the bathroom window, which was high up, the bottom of it fogged but the top part clear, so he could look right in and see Kathy.

He said she finished off this bottle of cream soda and then took off her bra and panties like she was going to take a bath, but she sat down on this pink velvet chair instead. Then she started doing things. You know, dirty things. And she finally used that cream soda bottle to do something real dirty.

Shark said he didn't want to film her doing that, 'cause he knew it was real wrong, but it was like he couldn't stop himself. By then there was more music playing so she didn't hear the camera, and his finger pressed the trigger till all the film was shot.

He said that what he wanted to do was open the window and crawl on in. But he knew that would really freak her out. So he left instead. Climbing down from the balcony, he was shaking so much with both fear and excitement he almost dropped the camera.

Then he was scared to get the film developed, 'cause back in those days anything dirty was still a big deal. Finally a week later he shot some more film of boats and took it all into Doolittle Camera. "Got some good boat stuff," he told Mr. Doolittle. But he said his heart was pounding.

When Mr. Doolittle developed the film he recognized Kathy with the cream soda bottle and called Jack Petro. Jack Petro called the cops.

Kathy Petro

The worst part was not knowing who'd seen the film. I could never go into Doolittle Camera again, knowing that rabbity little man had seen me like that. I asked Daddy if the cops looked at the film, and he said, "No, they gave it to me and I destroyed it." I didn't have the courage to ask him if *he'd* looked at it. I guess I didn't want to know. Years later Mom told me he had, just so he could see how bad it was.

Paige Petro

It was a terrible ordeal for Kathy, who was just so unaware of the perverse, awful things people can do to one another in this world. It was definitely a dark cloud. But we did all we could to make sure it passed as quickly as possible.

Lorna Trager

Once the cops were sure Shark's other movies weren't dirty, they were ready to let him go. They called around dinner time to say Mac could come down and get him.

"I'll tell you what, Gus," Mac said on the phone to this one cop he kind of knew. "Why don't you keep him till morning? That boy's been headed for trouble for a long time now, and this goddamn movie thing's the limit. Maybe a night behind bars'll teach him a lesson."

It didn't seem like that bad a thing since Shark was alone in the juvenile section of the city hall jail. But then this cop suggested another idea that would *really* put the fear of God into Shark.

Elliot Bernstein

The way Shark described it, he was alone in the juvenile hall section of the Newport Beach jail, "with nothing to do, nothing to read except the graffiti," when he heard the doors opening and assumed they were finally coming to release him. He felt both relief and apprehension, anticipating a severe paddling from Mac once he got home. But his fear of that survivable ordeal was quickly overridden by an incalculably greater terror.

"Come on, buddy boy. Not that way, this way," the cop said, steering Shark back through the station to a waiting prisoner transport van.

"But you're letting me go, aren't you?" Shark said. "My dad must be waiting in the front—"

"I don't know about any dad," the cop said with a chuckle. "We're shipping your ass to the big house. Let's see how tough you are in County Jail."

Shark began to hyperventilate.

Lorna Trager

The idea was to take Shark to the Orange County Jail and put him through the admission procedure, all the while acting like they were going to put him in with the hardened adult prisoners, but not really do it. They told Mac they could lead Shark through the cellblock and let the adult prisoners verbally taunt him so he would know what lay in store for him if he didn't straighten out.

But somewhere along the line somebody got their signals crossed, because the cops called Mac in the morning and said, "Mr. Trager, we're having some trouble locating your son."

Woody Hazzard

Shark would never really talk about what had happened in County Jail except to say he'd seen "some very bad things."

Lorna Trager

Mac was upset to the point of being kind of numb. The cops called back in a little while and said, "It's all right, Mr. Trager. We've found him."

"Is he . . . still my boy?" Mac said into the phone. His face was ashen.

Mac Trager

I felt like hell. I only intended to scare him, that's all. I didn't want to hear what had happened, I didn't want to know.

"I've got to go down and open the station," I said to my sister. "You'll have to swing by the jail and pick him up."

Lorna Trager

I felt awful for Shark. They said he was all right, that he hadn't been hurt, but he seemed too quiet. As we walked to the car outside the jail some prisoners started hooting from the windows, yelling awful things at Shark, things I blocked out of my mind, they were so awful. They said things to me too. I think they thought I was his mother.

We were both silent for a long time in the car. He stared out the window.

"Look," I finally said. "Your father didn't mean for you to be thrown in with those men—"

"What are you talking about?" he said softly, but clearly surprised.

I saw I should've kept my mouth shut. But it was too late, so I went on and told him about Mac's plan to teach him a lesson.

He hardly said a word, and his expression was blank, but I could tell he was shaken.

Then I said something stupid, trying to cover up my own bad feelings, I guess. "Anyway, that doesn't excuse what you did. How could you make that awful dirty movie? To violate someone's privacy like that—"

We were stopped at a red light and suddenly he bolted from the car.

Elliot Bernstein

Shark hitchhiked down Pacific Coast Highway, "running blind," he said. He had no idea where he was going, but home and his father were out of the question.

He never really told me what happened in County Jail, except to say he'd seen things that made him wonder "if man's so-called higher ideals aren't just a thin veneer of self-serving lies."

His last ride let him off in Laguna Beach, where he saw that the Surf Theater was playing a revival of *Rebel Without a Cause*. Although he'd seen the film on TV—the inferior, smeary "scanned" version, chopped up with commercials, that played in the early sixties—Shark had never really connected with the movie. He'd been too young to appreciate or identify with James Dean at the time of the young actor's death and initial stardom in the fifties and had even scoffed at the older guys who went around trying to act like Dean. His attitude had been: "He was just some young hayseed actor who died, too bad, but what's the big fuckin' deal?"

He was about to find out. He bought a ticket and entered the Surf Theater, and would forever describe the next hundred minutes in religious terms. Watching the film on TV had been like "looking at newsprint photo of the Sistine Chapel ceiling." Experiencing *Rebel Without a Cause* in its "full luminous mythic wide-screen WarnerColor grandeur" was "transcendent," "redemptive," "resurrective." As he sat there in the darkened theater a scant few hours after the worst terror of his life, he accepted James Dean into his soul "much as, I suppose, a born-again Christian must accept Jesus Christ into his heart."

As the film reached its climax, and Sal Mineo died on the observatory steps, Shark wept. "I felt as I *were* Sal Mineo," he said, "but also Dean. In the end more Dean, the survivor, than Mineo, the martyr. But a *part* of me died on those observatory steps."

He also identified the character of Judy with Kathy Petro, though it irritated him that Natalie Wood wasn't blonde. "But I felt that perhaps Kathy had a girlish crush on her father, as Natalie did on hers in the film. Perhaps *that* explained why Kathy had rebuffed me. And of course I still believed, despite what had happened, that as Jim Stark introduced Judy to his father over Plato's body, the day would come when I would introduce Kathy to my dad over the part of me which had died."

Only as the film ended and the lights came up did Shark realize there was just a handful of people in the theater for this early show. Somewhere towards the back he heard a girl weeping, reflecting his own silent tears.

Shark left the theater in a transported state, "revived and refreshed and determined to go home."

"I was fourteen," he said. "Practically speaking, there was not much else I could do. But stepping into the brisk night air I felt I had the strength to go on, to face my father, to do what I needed to do for the next few years so that when I did leave it would be to go off and make movies as indelible as the one I'd just seen."

As Shark walked around the corner he ran into the girl he'd heard crying in the theater, still with tears on her cheeks, though she was angry as well now, since her Vespa motor scooter wouldn't start. She was a Japanese/American girl, and Shark was immediately struck by her "simple, delicate beauty, matched to the sense of keen but gentle intelligence in her eyes."

Shark smiled and offered to take a look at her Vespa, though he in fact knew nothing about mechanics at the time. He noticed a paperback book stuck under the elastic on the rear part of the seat—a dog-eared copy of *Zen Flesh, Zen Bones*—and began asking her about it as he wriggled her spark plugs. Judy Oshima was somewhat skeptical of Shark at first, but then he said something that amused her, and for the first he heard her infectious laugh.

Lorna Trager

I'd insisted we call the police to report that Shark had run off. I was afraid he might try and kill himself.

"He damn well better not," Mac said.

I was sick with worry. Finally, around midnight we heard a car outside, then Shark coming up to the door, singing that Beatles "Love Me Do" song.

Mac was furious. "Where the hell have you been?"

I went and hugged Shark, hoping that would stop Mac from flying off the handle. "Shark honey, are you all right?"

"I'm fine," he said, like nothing had happened. "I just went to a movie, that's all."

4 / Blonde on Blonde (1965–1967)

Elliot Bernstein

According to Shark, his first evening with Judy Oshima began on a heavily verbal note. "I'd eaten another Obetrol part way through *Rebel*," he recalled a few years later, "so I was in a real chatterbox, Dean Moriarty mode. We must have stood there outside the Surf Theater for a good half hour yakking away while I dicked around with her Vespa."

When it became clear the Vespa wasn't going to start, Shark offered to help her push it home, an offer she accepted since home was several miles away, and uphill, in Laguna Canyon. As they walked up the road, Shark pushing the scooter, their intense conversation continued. "I think Judy was probably contact high from my speed vibes," Shark said.

The Oshimas lived in a small house behind the Canyon Nursery where George Oshima worked. As Shark and Judy came up to the house they heard George inside muttering angrily to himself in Japanese, and Judy motioned Shark to stop.

"It's no good, he's drunk," she said. The idea had been for Mr. Oshima to give Shark a ride home in return for his helping Judy with the Vespa.

"But my mother's due home soon," Judy told Shark. "She can get me the keys to the car. Come on, we can wait in the tree house."

In the tree house, which served as Judy's bedroom, she and Shark drank tea and began to make out. Suddenly they were disturbed by the sounds of Judy's father reeling into the patio below.

George Oshima was a genuinely tragic figure. Although he and Miko had both been born in California, after Pearl Harbor they had been interned, like thousands of other Japanese/Americans, in a relocation camp for the duration of the war, George forced to sell the modest but profitable fruit farm he'd developed in Costa Mesa for far less than its worth. By the time the Oshimas gained their freedom their immaculately tended orange and lemon groves were gone, replaced by the Brutalist bunkers and stinking expulsions of the Petro-Chem plant. George never recovered, financially or emotionally. He became an alcoholic, and in retrospect that may not have been the only thing affecting his brain. He was the insecticide man at the Canyon Nursery. For twenty-five years, until a few months before his death from cancer, he inhaled those fumes on a daily basis as he sprayed the lawns and gardens of the wealthy with a variety of chemical solvents, including the nerve-damaging and virulently carcinogenic Herb-Ex D4 manufactured by Petro-Chem, a compound finally banned in 1981.

Shark and Judy peered down from the tree house, Shark startled to see that George was waving a ceremonial sword. He staggered drunkenly about the patio, cursing in Japanese as he lashed out at the air, until at last he stumbled and fell to the ground, where he lay jerking "as if the whiskey he'd drunk had been laced with Raid."

Shark and Judy climbed down from the tree house and helped George to his feet. "He was gone, in another world," Shark said. "It was incredibly sad."

As they helped George to bed, Judy's mother came in. Only then, when he saw Miko, did Shark realize the Oshimas were the same Japanese couple who'd had a run-in with his father in the late fifties.

And Miko recognized Shark as Mac Trager's son—she had probably seen him working at the gas station where the painful scene with Mac had occurred.

"I want this boy out of our house," Miko said.

Lorna Trager

Mac had a special hatred for the Japanese because of his wartime experience. When he was in the navy he was on one of those aircraft carriers that had got attacked by kamikazes. He'd watched his best friend, a fellow sailor named Gene, get killed by a crashing kamikaze plane.

Gil Shirley

One afternoon in '59 when I was pumping gas for Mac Trager we seen this Japanese gal get out of an old Ford and head for the ladies room. It was okay by me, but Mac saw red. "She's using the crapper and she didn't even buy gas," he said. But that was just an excuse. The main thing was he hated all Japanese.

"Hey," he said to her through the ladies room door. "No-buy-gas-o, no-can-use-o." He tried the knob but she had the door locked.

"I'll only be a minute," she said through the door in perfect English.

"No nip-o shit-o," Mac said and kicked the door. "I mean it, you slit-eyed yellow monkey, this ain't *Teahouse of the August Moon.* Vacate now or I'll clean your Jap butt out of there with a flame thrower."

Mac kicked the door again, and right then George Oshima just sprung out of nowhere and *jumped him.* They both hit the ground and it was real bad for a while, like a genuine fight to the death, but me and Bud finally pulled 'em apart. Mrs. Oshima came out of the john, looking real shook up.

"Get off my property, you fuckin' nip," Mac shouted at George, so mad he turned the words around when he said: "And take that cunt-eyed slit with you."

"You're *dead,*" George yelled at him. "I'm gonna come back and *kill* you!"

But that was it.

Elliot Bernstein

Shark's first evening with Judy, indeed the relationship itself, appeared to be ending abruptly as Mrs. Oshima sent him packing. But he had only walked a short ways along the canyon road when Judy pulled up beside him in the family car—she'd grabbed the keys while her mother wasn't looking.

"Aren't you going to catch hell from your mom?" Shark said as they parked at the beach.

"Yes, but I don't care," Judy replied and they began making out again. Eventually, Shark opened her blouse and wanted to go even further. Although Judy wanted to as well, with a typical clear-headedness she declined since neither she not Shark were prepared.

"God, I wish I weren't leaving for Stanford in the morning," Judy said.

It would be another year before their paths crossed again.

Brad Jenkins

Shark's dad took away his camera after what he did to Kathy Petro. And he took all Shark's movies too. When Shark discovered that his movies were gone he went to his dad and asked for them back.

"It's too late," his dad said. "I've already thrown them away."

Shark got so mad he thought about breaking into the locked closet where he knew his dad kept his guns. "I'd like to blow his goddamn head off," he said.

"If you decide to really do it," I told him, "let me know. That's something I'd like to see."

It was about that time that they sent him to a shrink.

Lorna Trager

The psychiatrist was my idea. Mac wanted to send Shark to a military school till he found out how much it was going to cost. The doctor was cheaper. He zeroed in on the speed right away.

Raymond Dahl, M.D.

Shark came to me in a borderline psychotic state resulting from the overuse of Obetrol, a powerful amphetamine. I withdrew him in increments with the help of Valium, and Dalmane for sleep.

In therapy he was alternately sullen and sarcastic, and categorically refused to discuss the incident of camera voyeurism which had precipitated his coming to me. He displayed a profound ambivalence towards his parents—especially his late mother Winifred whose suicide he subconsciously interpreted as a form of abandonment. His father was a cold and dominating authority figure with an obsessive need to assert a masculinity he secretly doubted. The women in Shark's life, on the other hand, had either been smotherers or pamperers, or anal-retentive obsessive-compulsives and castraters, or in one case a pathologically lewd nymphomaniac he'd been encouraged to think of as a "substitute mother." In short, here was a teenage boy whose psyche was already stretched to the snapping point, whose only release lay in a fantasy life of the most intensely onanistic sort.

Brad Jenkins

Shark told me the shrink kept trying to steer him back to the subject of beating off.

Raymond Dahl, M.D.

Shark was a compulsive masturbator, massaging his youthful penis to the point of orgasm as frequently as five times a day. This concerned me a great deal as a symptom of far more profound psychic aberrances. But when I tried to discuss the issue with Mac Trager, he terminated Shark's therapy.

Mac Trager

This yo-yo tried to tell me Shark jacked off too much. And I said, I'm paying this asshole fifty bucks a crack so he and Shark can sit around and talk about jerking off? Who's jerking off who? To hell with this!

Lorna Trager

Things were better for a while though, once Shark got off the speed. I think he saw himself how close he'd come to really going crazy and maybe doing something a lot worse than making a peeping-Tom movie, and it sobered him a lot.

That last spring at Cortez his grades picked up. And when he started at Balboa High he really started studying. He had quite a high IQ, you know. Not gifted, but close to it. For a long time there things ran pretty smooth. I took it as a good sign when he made friends with the Bernstein boy, since he was real bright too. Mac didn't feel that way though.

Elliot Bernstein

I became friends with Shark our sophomore year at Balboa High. We were in gym and social studies together, then we started eating lunch together and hanging out a lot. I thought of myself as the school intellectual in those days, though in retrospect it was that terribly pretentious, adolescent sort of thing. But I read—Beckett, Burroughs, the *Evergreen Review*, and philosophy: Sartre, Husserl, Kierkegaard—and got Shark reading "seriously" too. We began having passionate "meaning of life" discussions that would go on for hours as we walked along the suburban streets of Newport Beach at night. "But that is precisely the *point* of phenomenology!" one of us might cry as we passed a house, catching a glimpse of "The Beverly Hillbillies" on TV. "To perceive the *thing itself*, free of discursive ideation. Which is precisely the goal of Zen!"

We lived on Squid Drive, a few blocks over from Shark's. My parents were not well off. My father had a small tailor shop on PCH, my mother was a bitter failed novelist. But my parents were relatively permissive, so Shark and I spent a lot of time at my place. I had moved into the garage, where we could play the stereo almost as loud as we wanted. It was the time of the Beatles and the Rolling Stones and Dylan, and we listened to that stuff till the records wore out. *Highway 61 Revisited*, I remember, had a profound effect on Shark. The first time I played it he became enraged, saying it was sick, that I'd "raped" his mind. Later, he made a complete turnaround, saying it was the greatest record ever made by man, and listened to it obsessively, endlessly quoting the lyrics. That was after we'd begun smoking dope, of course.

I never went to Shark's house at all because of his father's anti-Semitism.

Brad Jenkins

Shark changed in high school. We were still kind of friendly at first. But once he started hanging out with Elliot Bernstein he became this big intellectual and tried to get me to become one too. He gave me books to read, like Camus' *The Stranger*. When I said that book was sick he said I was stupid, and we had this big argument and quit being friends. It hurt my feelings a lot at the time, since he'd been my only real friend. Without one single friend in the brutal world of Balboa High my grip on reality soon became quite relaxed.

Elliot Bernstein

Shark and I started going to foreign films at the Surf Theater in Laguna Beach. They showed the latest Fellini and Bergman, and there'd be special weekend screenings of films like *October* and Carl Dryer's *Passion of Joan of Arc*. Afterwards we'd have heated discussions at the local Norm's Coffee Shop about what these films meant and how they were made.

I recall a particularly volatile debate over the merits of Jean-Claude Citroen's *Angel Street*. I considered it an essentially third-rate New Wave genre hommage, far inferior to either *Breathless* or *Shoot the Piano Player*, but Shark disagreed violently, quoting extensively from Sonya Heinz' rapturous review. By then he was something of a Sonya Heinz fanatic, tearing through each new piece in the hard-to-get *French Quarterly Review* as if it were an urgent dispatch from the frontline of cinema.

"*Angel Street* transcends genre!" Shark cried, pounding the table at Norm's. "Citroen is the only pure genius working in film today. I would gladly sacrifice one of my eyes if the one that was left could see as he sees." *Angel Street*, of course, was the last Citroen film with what we normally think of as a plot.

Shark told me about the eight-millimeter films he'd made in junior high which his father had destroyed, and spoke of his determination to get a "real" sixteen-millimeter camera. By then he was working part-time at the Jack in the Box and saving his money toward that end.

He'd never really said much about the peeping-Tom movie of Kathy Petro, assuming correctly that I'd heard about the incident. "It was a mistake," he said once. "The speed made me do it, I was nuts then." Despite his attempt to dismiss the matter as a nearly forgotten aberration, I sensed from a few occasions when we happened to see Kathy Petro on campus that his feelings about her were not all in the past.

Greg Spivey

Shark liked to say that Elliot saved his life. "There was nothing to read at our house except right-wing hate tracts and back issues of *Guns and Ammo*. Nobody ever talked about *ideas*. Elliot introduced me to the world of the mind, and that set me free. If I hadn't met him I would probably have become just like my father."

Elliot Bernstein

One night Shark and I went to the Surf Theater for a midnight screening of *Last Year at Marienbad*. The film was several years old at that point but Shark had never seen it, and I was curious to see what he'd make of it.

The lights were just about to go down when Kathy Petro and her current boyfriend came in and, oblivious to Shark's presence, took the two seats directly in front of ours. Presently, they began cuddling and cooing in one another's ears. I looked at Shark. He was staring at the blank screen, trying not to look at Kathy and her beau, which was virtually impossible. And he had begun to perspire.

By the time the film started Shark was pouring sweat, just imploding, Kathy and this blond jock sharing little impulsive kisses now, still completely unaware of Shark's presence. I was tempted to whisper to Shark, "Do you want to move?" But he was wound up so tightly by then, I was afraid to do or say anything at all.

Predictably enough, Kathy and her boyfriend soon grew restless with the film. He was your typical suntanned moron, and to be honest in my opinion in those days Kathy wasn't much more. I could certainly appreciate why Shark found her attractive physically. But she struck me as real zero, a pretty face masking a numbing vacuity.

The couple began talking, "I don't get it." "This is weird." "I can't follow this." "This is irritating." Then they'd start making out. Then they'd stop kissing and complain some more. Kissing and complaining, it just went on and on. And Shark was still sweating, but he'd also begun to tremble and had a near-demented look in his eye. Finally, during one of their kissing interludes, with a really terrifying abruptness Shark kicked the back of Kathy's seat and said: "If you want to fuck go somewhere else. This is a movie theater."

Well, I'll never forget the look on Kathy Petro's face. It was fear initially, shock and fear. But that gave way to . . . How to describe it? It was almost as if she'd *expected* something like this to happen eventually. As if, though she and Shark had had no contact for nearly a year, she *knew* on some level that it wasn't over, that in some incomprehensible and probably terrible way their fates were irrevocably intertwined.

Her boyfriend jumped up and did the manly thing. "How dare you talk to my girlfriend like that," or some such shit. And people began yelling: "Sit down!" By then Shark was on his feet too, but the standoff was brief. Kathy said something like, "Come on, it's not worth it." And she and surfer boy went off like they were going to sit somewhere else. But I think they just left, because when the film was over I looked around and didn't see them.

Shark was still mad as we left the theater. "That bitch, that cunt," he said as we walked up the street, and he was still looking around for her. I didn't know what to say, it was so crazy. The way he was acting you'd have thought they'd been passionate lovers who'd just recently broken up.

Kathy Petro

The incident at the Surf Theater was exactly the kind of thing I'd always feared. I'd see Shark around campus from time to time and just completely ignore him, and sometimes walk out of my way to avoid him. But I couldn't help but notice the way he was still looking at me. Not like he was angry exactly, or was going to do anything to hurt me. But it was like I had really hurt *him*, and his glance seemed to say: How could you? I just wanted to forget what had happened completely. Thank God we ran with completely different crowds and everything.

It was awful though because word had got around about the movie and all that, except you know how people exaggerate. There were even people saying they'd actually seen the movie, which of course was impossible. Though in time I guess people did get tired of talking about it, and moved on to other gossip. But it was definitely a cross I had to bear.

Elliot Bernstein

The summer of '66 was really idyllic, a kind of ultimate California summer. Shark was pumping gas at his dad's station and I had a boxboy job at the Alpha Beta, but we still managed to spend a lot of time at the beach. Before I met Shark I'd had this phobia about exposing my body, some bit of craziness I'd picked up from my parents, but Shark convinced me my body was fine and before long I was as sun-baked as any surfer. We'd lay there and look at the girls, the conversation drifting inexorably from Sartre to snatch. We were both sixteen and hadn't been laid yet and it was starting to drive us insane.

We met Woody Hazzard, which was something of a turning point, the night Debbi Henderson got him fired from the Taco Bell.

Woody Hazzard

I was eighteen then and I lived with my mom in this place she'd got from the divorce, this bitchin beach house on the Balboa peninsula right up the street from the Petro place. I was working nights at the Taco Bell and one night while Shark and Elliot were there I got into this thing with the manager after Debbi Henderson told him I spit in her burrito. I didn't really spit in her burrito, I just said I did to make her crazy while she was taking a big bite. She was this real square little blonde goodie-two-shoes type I really wanted to ball, but since I couldn't I teased her instead. But the manager had the hots for her too and took her side and canned me.

Shark and Elliot took my side, saying, "Yeah, that guy's a dip," and "Debbi's a cunt," till we all started laughing. So I invited them back to the house to get high. By then I had the whole house to myself since my mom was up in L.A. having a hot affair with her lawyer.

Shark and Elliot started coming over all the time, to get loaded and stuff, because that summer was rapidly turning into this big non-stop party. I'd heard about Shark's movie thing with Kathy Petro, but I just thought it was funny—it was probably part of what made me think Shark was cool. I mean, at the time he looked real square with short hair and so forth. But anybody who'd do something like that had to be intense, right?

We'd sit around on this weird blue shag carpet in the living room with the stereo pumping the Rolling Stones and smoke Mexican dope till we were stupefied. And there would be girls around—I'd been getting laid since junior high. But it was only too obvious that Shark and Elliot had not yet found a way to cross that border.

Then one night Shark came by with Judy Oshima and it was clear with one look at the smile on his face that she'd stamped his passport.

Elliot Bernstein

One afternoon in late August Shark was working at his dad's station when Judy Oshima pulled in to gas up her Vespa. Although Shark admitted he "hadn't really thought about her much" in the year since their first encounter, he felt the rapport and excitement of that night return as they made small talk while he filled her tank, the heat of their eye contact giving Shark a "pounding erection."

"What the hell were you saying to that nip?" Mac asked him after Judy sped off.

Shark stared at his father, then turned and walked away, whispering "Moron" under his breath.

"What did you say? Did you say something?" Mac said, going after Shark, whacking his head.

After work Shark hitchhiked up to Judy's despite a sudden freak tropical rain storm. Her parents were visiting relatives up north, in one of Miko Oshima's ill-fated attempts to get George to stop drinking, and Judy had the canyon house to herself. Shark was soaked by the time he arrived. "You'd better get out of those damp clothes," Judy said, the last words either of them spoke before losing their virginity. It was the beginning of a poignantly resonant, if tragically brief, affair.

Haiku Poem by Shark Trager, August 1966

For Judy
   dogs bark at thunder
   a peach drops in your tree house
   rain on your Vespa

Woody Hazzard

Everybody loved Judy Oshima, it was impossible not to. She was beautiful, but more than that she had this spirit about her, this sense of joy. She was friendly to everybody, not in a sappy way like a flowerchild, but like in this totally present way. She was always *right here*, in the moment, instead of being off in her thoughts somewhere like most people are. I guess that came from her Zen thing.

Elliot Bernstein

Judy introduced Shark to Zen meditation, which she had been practicing for several years at this point. When Shark got his VW bug they began driving up to Los Angeles on the weekends, where they would go to the Zen Center and then sometimes take in a film at the Toho La Brea where all the Japanese films played at the time. Shark reported being "wiped out" by Kursosawa's *Throne of Blood*, and "blown away" by *Naked Youth* from the iconoclastic young director Nagisa Oshima, to whom Judy was related. She was extremely supportive of Shark's cinematic ambitions, and there was a good deal of talk of their someday going to Japan to practice Zen Buddhism in its most conducive setting and perhaps find work in the film industry there.

These jaunts were undertaken with considerable subterfuge at first, since Miko Oshima would not have stood for her daughter going out with Mac Trager's son. But in September, despite her mother's protests, Judy took a leave-of-absence from Stanford, ostensibly to reassess her life direction, and using the money she'd saved from a summer waitress job, rented a small apartment on the Balboa peninsula, which was quickly converted into a spare, white-walled minimalist love nest. Clearly, her real motive for postponing college was to continue the affair with Shark. It was obvious to everyone how deeply she'd fallen in love with him.

I suppose all told they were only together for three or four months, but in those days that was somehow a lot longer than it is now. Knowing his father's special hatred for the Japanese—and for the Oshimas in particular—Shark's way of dealing with the potential for disaster was interesting. On the one hand he was fairly circumspect, telling his father he was staying over at Woody's when in fact he was spending the night with Judy. On the other, he barely took his hands off Judy in public, and they were all over town. He had to know it was just a matter of time until word got back to Mac.

But towards the end I remember getting a strong impression that Shark was growing tired of Judy, as if the novelty, the exoticism, was wearing off. With a sense of the pain it was going to cause, I began to suspect that he was in fact still obsessed with Kathy Petro, and he confirmed this one day. "I'm very fond of Judy, but I don't love her," he admitted. "I like her as a friend, but sexually I think I may be using her. She's wild in bed, but most of the time we're together I imagine I'm with Kathy. And when the sex is especially good, it kills me because all I can do is think: Why can't I be having these sensations with Kathy?"

A few nights later Shark had stopped by Woody's on his way to Judy's when the telephone rang and we learned that she'd been killed.

Woody Hazzard

She was on her Vespa when a Petro-Chem tank truck hit her on PCH. They said she was killed instantly. It was never established who was to blame. The Petro-Chem truck driver said she ran a stop sign. But at least one witness said the Petro-Chem driver was deliberately riding her tail, like coming on to her—"Hey, baby. Where you going on your scooter, sweet thing?"—when she stopped for a red light but he didn't.

Elliot Bernstein

Shark and I tried to attend Judy's funeral but Miko Oshima blocked the way. It was obvious she'd learned of Shark and Judy's affair. "I don't want you here," she told Shark. "Somehow this is your fault. You're just like your father."

After that rebuff, Shark and I stopped at the Norm's Coffee Shop in Laguna. Shark hadn't wept, he seemed numb, stunned. I guess we all were. "I should have said yes," he said as we sat staring at our coffees in the orange vinyl booth.

I asked him what he meant.

He said Judy had stopped by the gas station the evening she'd died, knowing Shark was on duty alone there till closing time. They had laughed and kissed and made plans for later. "I love you," she'd said lightly by way of parting, adding, "Do you love me?"

"Before I could answer I heard a car pulling in," Shark recounted. "When I saw that it was my father in his Buick my blood ran cold and I couldn't speak. I couldn't even say one word: 'Yes.' I watched Judy's expression change as she saw the fear in my eyes. I felt my father's hatred like a hot wind on my back, and I hated myself for being afraid. But I cringed when my father called my name, and watched Judy get on her Vespa and squeal away . . ."

For the first time Shark seemed about to cry.

"Shark, it's not your fault. These things happen."

"Elliot, if I'd said 'Yes,' she wouldn't have squealed away. A difference of even a few seconds—"

"Shark, you're not God."

He was still anguished when we parted that night.

But the next time I saw him, a few days later at Woody's, his mood had completely changed. He was smoking a joint with another girl, joking and flirting with her, although Judy had been dead less than a week. I convinced myself his pain was so great he'd had to repress it.

Later that evening he drew me aside in the kitchen and said, "By the way, our discussion at Norm's the other night—that never happened, all right?"

Lorna Trager

I knew Shark was seeing the Oshima girl. I'd heard talk about it, and one afternoon I saw them holding hands on the pier. But I didn't say anything to Mac.

When she was killed in that crash, I saw what it did to Shark and tried to get him to open up about it one day when Mac was out. "You really loved her, didn't you?" I said. "Why don't you just cry? Men cry, you know."

"I don't want to talk about it," he said and walked out of the room.

Woody Hazzard

Judy's death definitely put a damper on the holidays. Shark totally stopped his Zen meditation and got kind of manic for a while, like he couldn't let himself think about what had happened. He was still like that a month or so later when he and Elliot and I drove down to Tijuana.

Elliot Bernstein

Shark and I didn't know it was a dope run until we reached Tijuana and Woody went off to score. It wasn't the first time he'd done it, either. He had hollowed-out places behind the panels of his deliberately innocuous Oldsmobile. I almost crapped when I realized what he was up to since I'd heard some real horror stories about Mexican jails. Shark was scared too but tried not to show it. He was determined not to be a pussy in Woody's eyes. But I'm sure our fear of what might happen in the morning inspired our extreme drunkenness that night at Tijuana's notorious Blue Fox.

Woody Hazzard

The Blue Fox was legendary for having these raunchy sex shows. These really horrendous Mexican women would come out dancing, and then strip and bump their snatches right up in your face, while this sleazy MC said, "It's chowtime! Come and eat Maria!"

And if there happened to be a guy in the first row wearing glasses . . .

Elliot Bernstein

I wore thick Coke-bottle glasses in those days before they perfected contacts. Well, by the time the "show" started Woody and Shark and I were just blitzed on our butts, literally falling off our chairs. So the girls came out to this grungy mariachi striptease music, and we'd never seen anything like it—at least Shark and I hadn't. Just cheap and vile, yet incredibly exhilarating!

One particularly obese "dancer" gyrated over to me, doing her bump and grind routine practically in my face. I was so naive I actually imagined that contact with the audience wasn't permitted. So I was stunned when she suddenly took off my glasses and before I could object actually placed them inside her vagina! Then she snapped her fingers, lewdly undulating her crotch before my awestruck face, and said: "No hands."

Well, of course, I was far too dumbfounded to take her depraved hint.

Woody Hazzard

Suddenly Elliot was going down on this big Mexican babe to retrieve his glasses, and even after he did, he just kept chowing down like a starving man. Everybody was hooting and yowling, going totally apeshit, when suddenly I looked up and saw that Shark was stealing the show.

He was up on the stage just fucking the shit out of this young Mexican woman, who seemed like she might be pretty even though she was made up to look like a real whore. You know, fierce eyes and she's doing this whole fierce number: "Oohh, baby. *Yeah*, give it to me." Like really acting out everybody's fantasy of rowdy sex to the max.

And Shark's just fixated, like fucking her real slow with long, deep thrusts, like totally getting off on everybody watching. So everybody starts cheering him on, and then right at the last minute he pulls out just as he comes about a quart.

Elliot Bernstein

It was quite a performance.

Woody Hazzard

We were all sick with hangovers in the morning. But I was almost glad in a way because I was too ill to worry much about the border. So we started back and we were kidding Shark about the night before when he said, "Yeah, I'm gonna fuck the living shit out of her, just fuck and fuck and fuck her until one of us drops dead." Which I just took as meaningless bravado, you know? Like he was saying, Yeah, I'm gonna come back here every weekend from now on.

So we crossed the border with absolutely no problem, since we were in this very square Oldsmobile, and we were all taking pains to look equally square. Then north of San Diego when we were sure there weren't any narcs tailing us or anything, Shark said, "Pull over."

"Why?" I said.

Shark looked over his shoulder and said, "Juanita?"

And from the trunk came this muffled voice: "*Si*."

Elliot Bernstein

Juanita got into the back seat with Shark and they fooled around all the way into Newport Beach, and in daylight this girl was really tough looking. But Shark was clearly obsessed, with a driven look in his eye, and he wanted Woody to put Juanita up at his house on the peninsula.

Woody Hazzard

I said, forget it, Jack. No way.

Elliot Bernstein

So we dropped them off at Shark's. It was about three in the afternoon and nobody was home, but it was just crazy. Shark was acting as if he really thought he could smuggle Juanita into his bedroom and hide her there and nobody would ever know.

He told me later that she'd spent the night. They'd stayed in his bedroom, and when Lorna came home and then Mac, Shark told them he was sick with the flu. Then he and Juanita had fucked all night till she was exhausted and fed up. Because Shark had lied to her to get her to come back with him, saying he was a lot richer than he was, promising to put her up in an oceanfront house and all that, and now she knew the score.

So in the morning while Shark was still sleeping Juanita got up and dressed and stalked out of the house right past Lorna and Mac who were completely blown out. But Mac was probably pleased, since he didn't know about Shark's affair with Judy, and had always had an irrational fear that Shark was going to become gay.

Lorna Trager

I was flabbergasted to see that cheap Mexican girl in the house.

Mac Trager

I was relieved to see that his urges were normal. But when he told me where he'd met her I lowered the boom.

Elliot Bernstein

Mac Trager was a very strange, sick man. Shark told me that after the night with Juanita, Mac made him lower his pants every day for a week so Mac could inspect Shark's dick to see if it was dripping.

Lorna Trager

Not long after Shark spent the night with that Mexican girl something happened between Mac and him out in the garage. I still don't know what it was. But Mac came in looking white as a sheet, and Shark ran off up the driveway and didn't come back for three days.

For a long time after that Mac just seemed broken, as if Shark had said something to him that cut him to the quick.

Elliot Bernstein

Mac wanted to look at Shark's dick again—that's what happened. It was several weeks after the Juanita incident, and Shark was working in the garage when Mac stepped in and said: "Drop 'em, mister. Drip check."

Well, Shark had had enough. He exploded and yelled something like: "Not this time. You've ogled my dick for the last time, you latent homo!"

Mac was too wiped out to even get mad, Shark said—which was worse than anything, because it made Shark see that a remark made purely for its inflammatory impact might actually contain a kernel of truth!

Shark went to stay at Woody's for several days after that.

Mac Trager

Shark and I had an argument in the garage one day. We both got pretty riled up. But he said some things to me no son should ever say to his father. I tried to forgive him, but I don't think I ever really did.

Lorna Trager

It wasn't long after that business with Shark that Mac made a pass at me and I had to move out. He was drinking more than usual and we were watching "Green Acres" one night when he said, "Why don't you make us some Jiffy Pop?"

So I went into the kitchen and was standing there at the stove when he slipped his arms around me from behind. I jumped and said, "My God, Mac. I'm your sister, have you lost your mind?"

And he said, "Nobody will know."

And I said, "You *have* lost your mind."

And he said, "It's all right as long as you don't have a baby. I'll wear a rubber, how 'bout it?"

And I covered my ears and said, "This is sick."

Then he broke down and started sobbing and said, "I haven't slept with a woman in over six years, not since Evelyn left."

And I said, "Well, Mac, that's not my problem."

I left that night.

Elliot Bernstein

After Mac and Lorna had a fight and she moved out, Shark described his father as having fallen into a deep depression, drinking heavily and barely talking to him at all. "It's too grim, I can't take it there anymore," Shark said, and virtually moved into Woody's.

There was still a lot of partying, but Shark was always meticulous about his homework. He refused to light a joint until he was satisfied that his assignments were completed at a "B + level or higher." There was a calculation to Shark I'd never seen before, a capacity for coldly analytical judgment that could be unnerving. In a time when the greatest virtue was to live in the *now*, Shark was definitely thinking ahead. "I'm going to get out of here," he said, meaning Orange County. "I'm not going to end up like my father."

It was during our junior year that the really heavy dope dealing started.

Woody Hazzard

At first it was just grass. We made more runs down to Mexico. Grass had really caught on by then, so we were dealing to everybody. I mean, we were the big connection in Newport Beach.

We had a close call once in Tijuana though, when Shark ran into Juanita on the street. She started cussing him out in Spanish and her boyfriend or pimp or whoever he was pulled a knife. Mexico was getting freaky, we were afraid somebody was going to set us up. So pretty soon we started leaning more toward acid, making runs up to San Francisco.

Elliot Bernstein

We started taking acid at Woody's place. By that time his mother had virtually abandoned the house to him. I think she sensed what was going on there but didn't know how to deal with it.

Shark had his own bedroom with a view of the sea. He had affairs with different girls, but it was all light, party-time action. He was technically friendly, even jokey, but increasingly there seemed to be a part of him nobody could reach. I believed at the time that on some level he was still mourning Judy. Several girls got crushes on him and couldn't understand why he so quickly lost interest. I recall a girl crying on the sofa, "What's wrong with me? Why doesn't he love me?"

One night a bunch of us dropped acid and listened to records, you know, the Byrds, *Blonde on Blonde*, the Beatles—a typical sixties scene. And eventually Shark retired to his room with a girl named Cindi or Candi or something like that. But at dawn I saw him standing out on his balcony, alone.

He was looking off up the beach, sipping a bottle of cream soda. Sound carried at that hour, and you could hear laughter, bright girlish laughter, coming from beyond the wall that hid the Petro house.

Woody Hazzard

Shark was really the businessman. I had the contacts but Shark made the deals and kept track of everything. He just had a knack for it. I was too laid back to be a really tough negotiator, especially in a time where everybody tried so hard to "mellow." But Shark didn't give a shit if people thought he was uptight or not. We split the profits fifty-fifty. We made a lot.

Elliot Bernstein

In early 1967 Shark bought a new Camaro Z/28, a special limited edition with horrendous horsepower. It was silver, a stunning car, and you could hear it for blocks. A real head turner in the golden age of muscle cars. It impressed the girls, and everybody.

Mac Trager

Let me put it this way. I knew he didn't pay for that car by doing "odd jobs." I tried not to think about it. But I told him, "When the cops finally arrest you, you can have that Hazzard fella or that Jew boy post your bail, cause I won't."

Elliot Bernstein

That winter Woody and I put together a group called Black Light. I sold my old Martin and bought a Stratocaster, and Woody got a primo set of drums. Fred and Stu Dilday, who were twin brothers, had graduated from Balboa High with Woody a couple of years before, and had already been in a couple of other groups. We rehearsed at Woody's and at first we sucked. We made Blue Cheer seem accomplished. I wrote and sang the songs, which were dark and twisted. We wanted to be a kind of West Coast Velvet Underground. Soon, even though we still pretty much sucked, we began to get gigs locally in Orange County. Light shows were in then, which was part of the reason that Shark bought a camera.

It was a sixteen-millimeter Arriflex, and he shot the works, buying sophisticated lens and accessories, spending thousands of dollars. At first he shot a lot of pseudo-surrealistic acid-trip stuff, which we incorporated into our light show. Some of it wasn't bad—Shark definitely had a knack—though I imagine it would look terribly dated now. He would use whoever was around, creating these dreamlike Felliniesque episodes, though as time went on—after we'd seen a few D.A. Pennebaker documentaries at the Surf Theater—he began going for a more gritily "realistic" cinema verité approach.

One night he was running some footage he'd just got back from the lab—projecting it on Woody's living room wall—when suddenly the verité stuff of the band gave way to a telephoto shot of Kathy Petro sunning nude on a patio of the Petro house. She was with Jeff Stuben, a Balboa High quarterback from a wealthy Newport family, and he was also nude. As I watched in astonishment Kathy and Jeff began to have sex. Then Shark, who had been on the phone in the other room, came back and looked very freaked-out when he saw what was being projected—he clearly hadn't intended to show it— and immediately snapped off the projector. As it happened, of the people who were there that night, Woody and I were the only ones from the immediate area who were able to recognize Kathy Petro and understand that Shark had "done it again."

I figured out later that the only way he could have got that telephoto shot was to climb up to the very highest and most precarious point of Woody's tile roof.

It was hard to avoid the drug analogy: that Shark was a psychic junkie who had briefly cleaned up and experienced the beginnings of true happiness with Judy Oshima. But that serene happiness had come too easily and bored him, his craving for the unattainable had never really left him, and with Judy's death he had returned with an abject inevitability to his mainline blonde obsession.

Woody Hazzard

Shark had decided he wanted to go to film school and his first choice was USC. His grades were good enough that he could have got a scholarship—he played things very clean and straight at school. But when he heard that Kathy Petro was going to go to USC, he didn't even apply. "It's pointless," he said. "Her dad would make sure I didn't get accepted." Which was not even paranoid, since about that same time they'd announced there was going to be a new building named after Jack Petro at USC.

So Shark applied to UCLA instead.

Then I guess it was during the Easter break in '67 that Kathy came to the house.

Elliot Bernstein

Shark and I were alone in the house, smoking dope and listening to *Between the Buttons* as we watched the sunset, when suddenly there was a knock. We weren't expecting anyone, and we'd been getting a little paranoid lately. There'd been so much traffic Shark and Woody were sure the cops were on to them and had quit keeping large quantities of dope in the house. So Shark collected the joints with an eye on the bathroom while I looked through the peephole in the front door. When I saw that it was Kathy I opened the door a crack.

"Hi. Is Woody here?" she said.

"No, he isn't," I replied. And before I could say anything else Shark opened the door all the way.

"What do you want?" he said very neutrally.

There was a long look between them which I still to this day am not sure how to read. She certainly didn't seem afraid of him, I'll say that.

Finally Kathy said in that wholesomely sun-drenched way she had—I mean she could talk about shit and make it sound like apple pie—she said, "Well, I just heard you guys might have some LSD."

"We might," Shark said, and indicated his bedroom. She hesitated, then followed him in. Shark left his bedroom door slightly ajar.

Kathy Petro

To be honest I didn't want to go to Woody's at all. But Jeff Stuben, this guy I was going with then, had never taken acid, and so finally I said, "Okay, I think I know where we can score."

Later I'd wonder if that had just been an excuse. I had heard Shark was living there, I knew I might see him.

I don't know. I'd changed for one thing. And so had Shark. I'd seen him a few times roaring around in that Camaro he had, which I thought was really cool. Anyway, it was the sixties, you know what I mean? All the artificial barriers were breaking down, drugs—especially acid—kind of uniting everybody.

Shark *was* good-looking. I think it had occurred to me: Gee, you know, it's too bad that thing with the movie happened. But was it really that big a deal? Or was I just buying into my parents' values if I thought so?

I hate to say this, because I'm not for judging people solely on their looks. Other values are important. But if Shark had been a creep I might've felt less forgiving.

This is going to sound kinky, I know, but sometimes I would think about him filming me with that camera, you know, in the years after it happened, and it would excite me. It was like a fantasy or something. Like this really handsome guy watching me with a camera while I you-know-what. And I'd think: Gee, what if he'd put the camera down and climbed in the window? Well, if he *really* had I would probably have come unglued. But later I'd think about what might have happened and kind of imagine certain things.

I think what he did affected me in more ways than I knew at the time.

Elliot Bernstein

Shark and Kathy were only in the bedroom a few minutes. Then he walked her out to the street. They stood there talking a while longer, and she appeared to admire his Camaro.

Kathy Petro

Shark seemed really nice that day, which was maybe what I'd secretly been curious about. He sold me two tabs of acid, this orange sunshine acid everybody was taking then, and we even joked a little, though I think both of us were very cautious.

He certainly didn't try and push anything, and I made a point not to lead him on in any way. I mean, I just said, "Good-bye," not "See you later," or anything that implied any future at all. But a part of me was thinking, you know: Gee.

So I was just killed by what happened.

Woody Hazzard

Shark and I were alone in the house when a little after midnight the cops smashed down the front door. We had some grass which I managed to flush in time. But I didn't know until after they booked us that Shark had been holding twenty tabs of acid, which he'd managed to swallow before the cops slapped on the cuffs.

Elliot Bernstein

I was home in bed with the flu when Woody woke me at one in the morning to say he and Shark had been busted. He was calling from the jail, frantic because he couldn't reach his drug attorney. "The house is clean, they can't hold us," he said. "But we gotta get out of here quick, man! Because Shark's coming on to ten thousand mics." Which was, you know, a lot.

Well, I finally reached the attorney, but he couldn't get Woody and Shark released till morning. They spent the night in the drunk tank where, Woody told me later, he literally held Shark down all night, gagging him with a blanket while the drunks watched in awe. "I thought he was going to fucking explode, man," Woody said.

The cops were extremely pissed off and really tore the house apart looking for evidence. They definitely held Woody and Shark responsible for what had happened to Jeff Stuben.

Kathy Petro

I guess it goes without saying that it was up to then the single worst night of my life. But I never really blamed Shark, though naturally all the parents did. If anything, I blamed myself since I was the one who'd given Jeff Stuben the acid. Not that he hadn't wanted it. He'd been badgering me about it for weeks. Something in me always sensed that Jeff might not be able to handle it. I only wish I'd listened to that little voice of doubt.

His parents were in Hawaii for Easter, so we dropped at his place, this really stunning house on Balboa Beach. The setting was perfect— it wasn't the setting. We were cuddling on the shag, listening to Donovan as the acid started coming on. Right away it began going badly for Jeff. He started holding his head, saying, "I feel like I'm losing my ego, I don't like this!"

I tried holding him, saying, "Don't fight it, Jeff. Just go with the flow." I put on the Beatles, you know, *Revolver*. But nothing helped.

Then he went to the bathroom and I heard this terrible crash. I ran in and saw that he'd smashed the mirror with his head. There was blood everywhere. Now *I* started to freak, and said, "Jeff, here, use this towel." But he ran outside and that's where it happened.

There was this eucalyptus tree in the yard that had fallen down during a rain storm, and they'd been cutting it up to take it away. There was this chainsaw lying there, and Jeff picked it up and pulled the cord and it started buzzing. He just looked possessed by this time, and I was totally freaked out because I'd never been around violence before. I think his hormones were wrong or something because of playing so much football. He was just filled with all this aggression. I said, "Jeff, put that down, it's all right." For some reason I wasn't afraid that he'd hurt *me* with the chainsaw. So I took a step towards him. That's when he lifted up the chainsaw and cut off his own head.

Well, you know, first I barfed. I mean, what else could I do? And then I started screaming till the neighbors came.

I guess he didn't really cut all the way through his neck, but you could have fooled me at the time. There was blood squirting everywhere like in one of those awful Japanese samurai movies. He was dead long before the ambulance arrived.

Then Daddy came and I was completely flipped out, just screaming hysterically till Daddy slapped me and I told him where we got the acid.

Elliot Bernstein

Shark's mind was completely gone by the time he and Woody were released on bail. We took him to a friend's apartment and gave him some Thorazine. We thought he might be permanently damaged. But he slept all day and then seemed to be all right.

When we told him what had happened to Jeff Stuben he was awed at first, then incredulous—and ultimately rather darkly and coldly amused. He certainly didn't feel responsible. His attitude seemed to be: *Of course*, Jeff was precisely the sort of penultimate square you could expect to have a bad acid trip. I recall the way Shark smiled. Years later I noted DeNiro doing a similarly thin, wry smile in, I think it was *The Godfather, Part Two*, as he heard of the death of one of his rivals.

Woody Hazzard

It was real bad for a while. The parents really wanted to throw the book at us, but the cops had fucked up by neglecting to plant any evidence. Shark had really saved us by swallowing that acid. So there was nothing they could do to us.

But it was definitely the end of an era. A weird vibe was sweeping over the Orange County beach cities because there'd already been a couple of murders of young blond couples, what eventually became known as the Surf Killer murders, though it would be another six months and twelve victims later before they finally caught Brad Jenkins. But even though it was only June there was already this sense that, at least in Orange County, the fabled endless summer was over.

My mom made plans to sell the house, and Shark's dad told him, "You can stay till you graduate. Then you are on your own." Which was fine with Shark since he'd been accepted at UCLA.

Elliot convinced me and Stu and Fred that Black Light had a better chance if we went up to Frisco, where all kinds of groups were getting attention then. The week after graduation we were all set to leave, planning to hit the Monterey Pop Festival on the way up north, when we had this farewell breakfast with Shark one morning at Huck Finn's.

Kathy Petro

I was just totally wrecked by what had happened to Jeff. I kept having these nightmares about it. I'd wake up screaming till Daddy came in and slapped me. Then finally this shrink put me on some

Thorazine-type drug. But I was still just fragmented. It was decided I should spend the summer at a friend's villa in Spain just recuperating and thinking positive thoughts. The morning I was going to leave we all went out for breakfast at Huckleberry Finn's.

Elliot Bernstein

Huckleberry Finn's Family Restaurant was a huge, dementedly quaint Americana-style place on PCH, very conservative, a popular spot for well-dressed families to go for brunch after church. My hair was pretty long then, which was a tense issue at the time, especially in Orange County. Well, they let Shark and Woody and me in, but not without a few dirty looks. It was a buffet, so we got in line with the staid, conservative family people. But it wasn't until we had got our food and were sitting down that we saw the Petros at a table across the room.

Woody Hazzard

I knew something was gonna happen. Shark wouldn't take his eyes off the Petros. Off Kathy. She looked out of it that morning, completely withdrawn like she was on Thorazine or something. She ate like a zombie. Mrs. Petro was trying to ignore us. But Lance,* their asshole son, and Kathy's dad were drilling us with total hate.

Elliot Bernstein

Finally Kathy got up to go to the buffet table. And Lance, who was maybe twenty then, a big man like his father, got up too and accompanied Kathy, as if to protect her. And Shark got up before either Woody or I could stop him.

Kathy Petro

I was just numb that day, I barely even knew where I was. But suddenly Shark was there, trying to say something to me, I don't even know what. Then the next thing I knew he and Lance were fighting.

---

* Lance Petro would be dead within a year, succumbing to a rare form of liver cancer linked a decade later to Sol-Vex PPD, a popular pesticide manufactured by Petro-Chem. As Kathy recalls, "Daddy believed Lance should learn the business from the ground up. I can still see my brother coming in all sweaty, his bare torso glistening with that sweet-smelling chemical frost, after a hard day's work hosing down the vats."

Woody Hazzard

It wasn't much of a fight really. But Shark fell back into the buffet table, and it made a lot of noise when all this silver shit fell. I pulled Shark away and Jack Petro restrained Lance. And Mrs. Petro was kind of shielding Kathy, who was cringing. And then the maître d' was there, telling us we had to leave. So Elliot and I steered Shark toward the door, but by then his nose was bleeding. So when we reached the entry area Shark ducked into the men's room to get some paper towels for his nose.

Elliot Bernstein

Woody and I were waiting for Shark by the door when suddenly we heard screams and crashing in the dining room, and Jack Petro yelling, "You goddamn punk!"

We rushed in and saw Jack Petro just beating the living shit out of Shark, who was stumbling through the tables—stumbling because his pants were down around his ankles! Apparently, Shark had been taking a leak in the men's room when Jack Petro came in and saw him and completely flipped out, grabbing Shark before he even had a chance to button up his fly. Shark had tried to escape back through the dining room, his Levis slipping down, as Jack beat him every step of the way. By the time we reached him Shark could barely see, his face was cut and bleeding so severely, and Jack Petro was just completely insane, kicking Shark in the ribs when he fell, as if he quite literally intended to stomp Shark to death. People were going crazy.

Woody and I jumped Jack, and then Lance came at us. And then, somehow, it was over, all of us spent and panting for breath. There was poor Shark on the floor with his pants down in front of everybody—he never wore underwear. Woody and I helped him to his feet, and pulled up his pants, and got him out of there.

Paige Petro

It is not my favorite memory. But I did sympathize with Jack's vehemence. This young man had tried twice to ruin our daughter's life. If I'd known what was coming I might have entered that fray myself.

Woody Hazzard

Shark really got creamed. It wasn't a fair fight, what with Shark with his pants down. And Jack Petro was a big man, you know, like John Wayne or Ronald Reagan, while Shark was five-ten and maybe 140 at the time. Petro was in his fifties but he kept himself in shape.

Shark was getting stitched up in the emergency room when he went into this revenge riff: "I'm not going to forget this. Someday he's going to pay for this. I'm going to destroy that rotten old pig."

I understood how he felt but figured it was just talk, because Jack Petro had so much money and power it was kind of like saying you were going to get even with God.

5 / *East of Eden*
(1967–1968)

Letter from Shark Trager to Elliot Bernstein, July 14, 1967

Hey, bro:

The gods of Hollywood are already smiling upon me. I'm writing this letter from my bitchin new pad, a cruddy little A-frame in Sherman Oaks. Do you detect a note of inconsistency there? Yeah, you do. This place is a dump. The faucets drip, there are cobwebs in the rafters—and there's a scurrying sound under the floorboards I don't even want to think about. Then why is it so bitchin? Sixty bucks a month for one thing. But that's not the main reason I snatched (ooohhh yeah!) this place up.

It's the knowledge of who once lived in these walls, once slept on a mattress in the loft where I now sleep, once cooked on the cruddy stove, took a leak in the toilet, jerked off in the shower, parked his '55 Porsche Speedster in the shaded driveway. (Did I just give it away?)

Neal Ridges

I met Shark in the summer of '67 right after he moved into the James Dean house in Sherman Oaks. It was a rundown A-frame on an overgrown lot and at first I thought he was bullshitting about Dean having lived there. But he wasn't. It was really the place Dean had leased and lived in right up to the day he died.

Shark became a bit obsessed about that. We'd be sitting there smoking dope and he'd point to the bathroom and say, "Just think, Dean shaved in that mirror the last morning of his life."

It actually became a bit spooky. It was a time when people were taking a lot of acid and believed in "vibes," that a house most definitely absorbed the psychic energy of its previous occupants. So when

74

Shark told me he sometimes heard disembodied sobbing in the night—
"Dean was in pain when he lived here; he was on the threshold of
becoming mythic and it was tearing him apart"—I did not dismiss it
out of hand.

I was working on my thesis film project at UCLA that summer,
and Shark pumped me at great length about how the film school
worked. It was clear he had no interest in a college degree. He just
wanted to take advantage of the film school's facilities to make a
movie that would propel him out of academia into the real world.

Frank Forte

I was teaching a Project Two sixteen-millimeter production class
when Shark approached me requesting admission. According to the
rules he should have begun like everyone else with the Project One
class, which was eight-millimeter. But when he showed me his films
I was more than impressed. Arty, some of it, pseudo-Felliniesque,
but extremely well done. And the verité material—at least I *thought*
it was verité. When he told me it was "acted" I was stunned! To be
blunt I thought he might well be our generation's Orson Welles. And
I believed in art then, we all did—it had something to do with the
times, I suppose. I waived the requirements, the departmental rules
be damned. If he was a genius, we needed him now. The walls of
academia were crumbling. Revolution was here.

Neal Ridges

It was a volatile time and the film school was heavily radicalized.
Plot was out, "story" was considered a bourgeois conceit. Nobody
talked about money, about Hollywood "deals" or ambition. Hollywood was seen as corrupt. The studios could only make films like *The
Green Berets,* or smarmy youth culture rip-offs concocted by middle-
aged producers who fantasized about fucking hippie girls. We were
in it for art and to change the world. The cinema of "escape" was
dead.

Our idols were Godard, Truffaut, Resnais, Chabrol, Rivette, and
above all, Jean-Claude Citroen.*

Shark caught the fever, primarily from Simone Gatane, I think.
Simone was a stunningly beautiful and high-breasted, chain-smoking,

* Whose great-uncle, incidentally, was French car king Andre Citroen. In a
brief 1939 *scandale,* Jean-Claude sought to have the family name removed from
all of the automobiles (both retroactively and in the future), on the grounds that
the vehicles were "violent embodiments of capitalism," and "aesthetically absurd." The case was dismissed as soon as the complainant's age was ascertained;
the future *enfant terrible* of the *nouvelle vague* was then nine.

nail-biting Critical Studies major from France. It was well known that she and Jean-Claude Citroen had once been lovers.

Simone Gatane

I met Shark one day in the Steenbeck room, where I was working on a shot-by-shot analysis of *The Nutty Professor*—laughing out loud, clapping my hands in joy at the multiplicity of meanings in this subversive masterpiece of Jerry Lewis—when Shark spilled hot chocolate on the front of my blouse.

Naturally, I initially hated him for this. But when he apologized and told me he lived in James Dean's house we went there and made love into the night.

I soon moved in, for I found him stimulating as a lover, though his intellect was quite crude. I would speak of Bazin, for example, and he would laugh and say, "I don't care about these concepts, Simone. I want to *make* movies, not *talk* about the nature of film."

This would anger me and I would say, "Oh, now you're posturing, you're trying to play the primitive." And he would get quite mad. Then we would make love.

One night we saw *Neon City*, Jean-Claude's 1966 hommage and blow of death to American film noir. It had only then finally reached America and Shark was profoundly astonished. He had long admired Jean-Claude's early "narrative" films, but as Shark himself said as we left the theater, "This is a cinema *beyond* cinema! If only I knew how he dared to take such a quantum leap!"

That very night I saw to it that Shark read Jean-Claude's seminal essay, "The Death of Film as 'Entertainment,' " and it changed him forever. "Yes, yes, of course, I see now!" he cried, as we spoke with great zeal of Jean-Claude's revolutionary cinema far into the night, until at last near dawn we made love. Shark then took the conventional script he was working on and completely revised it in accordance with Jean-Claude's radical dictums. "I am going to do with the bedroom farce what Jean-Claude did with film noir," he said. "It's time somebody went for Doris Day's throat."

Neal Ridges

Most Project Twos were shorts, running maybe twenty minutes at most. But it soon became apparent that Shark was planning to shoot what amounted to a feature. When I finally saw the script I was floored. It was completely insane, a viciously satiric, deconstructive anti-"sex comedy" set in Newport Beach. The title, an obvious play on one of the key films of the genre, was *Pillow Fuck*.

Frank Forte

I considered the script unfilmable, less for reasons of "taste," than economics. I don't think Shark had ever written a script before and it was filled with intricate camera directions, elaborate tracking shots and the like. "Jesus, Shark," I said. "This is going to cost you at least twenty thousand dollars." Which in 1968 was a lot.

Simone Gatane

When Shark realized how much the film was going to cost he almost gave up on it. Then he said, "I know that this film was meant to be. I am going to proceed with pre-production. The cash *will* materialize."

So he began lining up the student crew and auditioning actors from the Theater Arts department. But I became concerned, especially after the cameraman mentioned that Shark had said if all else failed he would rob a series of "imperialist banks." In those days that was not crime, but a political act.

Luckily, it never came to that.

Neal Ridges

Shortly before the actual shooting began, at a time when if anything he should have been scrounging for cash, Shark pulled up to Melnitz Hall in a primo restored 1955 Speedster. White, like you-know-who's. I asked him how much he'd paid for it and he said three thousand. "Jesus, where are you getting your money?" I asked him.

He just smiled and said, "You don't want to know."

Elliot Bernstein

I called Shark from San Francisco in February to say I was coming down for the weekend to visit my parents, and hoped we might get together. "You should stick around," he said. "I'm going to be shooting in Newport Beach next week." Then he explained that through a third party he'd taken a two-week lease on the house next door to the Petro's.

When I arrived in L.A. a few days later and saw the Porsche, I said, "Are you dealing again?"

He said, "Yeah, but not dope."

What then, I asked him.

"Plastic explosives," he said.

Warren Dray

Simone Gatane introduced me to Shark one night at the Nuart Theater. We were all standing in line for Jean-Claude Citroen's *Honeymoon in Algiers* when Simone recognized me despite my disguise, in retrospect a rather pathetic black dye job and horn-rimmed glasses. I was already a fugitive then as a result of a troop train bombing up north. I knew Simone from UCLA where I'd been a film major before coming to see how pointless all that was.

After the film the three of us went to a dimly lit Mexican restaurant where I spoke bitterly of the impotence of art.

"But this is precisely what Jean-Claude is saying," Simone asserted. "That is why *Honeymoon in Algiers* has no 'meaning' according to the bourgeois or 'literary' notion of art. Because it is *film*. And film *as* film is *only* film, *not* something other *than* film."

Shark was very quiet, something clearly on his mind. When Simone left us for a moment to use the restroom, Shark looked at me and said, "Would *you* do what they did in the film?"

I knew he meant the sequence where the Algerian freedom fighters had butchered the smugly complacent bourgeois newlyweds.

"Yes," I said. "If it would stop the war."

Shark considered this, then said, "What if it would only mean saving a few thousand lives? Perhaps even just a few hundred Vietnamese babies from napalm?"

"Why are you asking me this?" I said, sensing correctly that the question was far from rhetorical.

"Because I have some privileged information," Shark said. "And enough plastique to blow Mount Rushmore off the map."

I looked around and noticed a couple at the next table who appeared to be eavesdropping. "Let's talk about this later," I said.

Darrel Tyrone

One day Simone calls me and says, "Darrel, my boyfriend's casting a student movie at UCLA and he's looking for someone to play a black terrorist."

So I say, "Simone, I *am* a black terrorist. I don't act in no honky movies no more."

And she says, "I know. That's why I thought of you. 'Cause this film is cool."

So I go out to Shark's place in Sherman Oaks, and the whole thing sounds like bullshit to me 'cause he don't have the money. Then this white chick comes by I get to tie up and rape in the script. So I say okay, and get this white chick's number so maybe we can get together and rehearse.

Then two nights later the pigs bust down my mother's door in Watts and shoot the lady in the spleen. They lookin' for me and a few other brothers, 'cause they hear we got some plastic explosives and plan to blow up Parker Center in revenge for their offing two other brothers they said offed a pig.

When we hear about this we go right away to where we stashed the explosives, since my mother knows where that is too. We got most of it loaded when we see the flashing lights. A high-speed freeway chase ensues. We're in a GTO so the pigs can't catch us. But on the Ventura Freeway we start running out of gas. "Get off here!" I shout to Lamel when I see the Sherman Oaks exit sign.

We reach Shark's house but there's nobody home. So we pull up the driveway, parking out of sight behind the house, while meanwhile the pigs are screaming up and down the streets. "We leave the car here," I say to Lamel, "and come back later when the pigs clear out."

So we set out on foot. Somewhere near Encino they close in on us, about fifteen pigs with their shotguns leveled at our heads.

Simone Galane

I received a call from Darrel Tyrone's attorney, saying, "Look, there's a hot GTO filled with plastic explosives parked in your driveway. You'd better get rid of it."

I said, "Yes, I know. My boyfriend is out looking at it right now. Do you mean all of that stuff piled in the backseat could blow up any time?"

Warren Dray

It was a sizable cache, though not worth the twenty thousand in requisitioned pig money we paid Shark. But we were desperate to strike a blow against the American Empire, and there was enough destruction there for a number of operations. The first blow—which Shark suggested—was too good to pass up. Along with the explosives he provided two hand-drawn maps: one of the Petro-Chem complex in Costa Mesa showing the unit where the napalm was manufactured, and the other a diagram of the Petros' pig residence in Newport Beach.

The only thing Shark asked was that we hold off till after the 27th, when his filming at the house next door to the Petro winter palace would be done.

Simone Gatane

I swear, I knew nothing of Warren Dray's terrorist plan. Shark left in the GTO the night Darrel's attorney called, returning several hours later on foot. "I left that explosives-filled car on a side street in Pacoima," he said, assuring me he had wiped it clean of his prints.

When not long after Shark announced that his film financing was "in place," I asked him how it was possible.

"Oh, I'm using my dope-dealing savings," he said.

"But I've seen your bank book," I said. "You have less than four thousand."

"Oh, no, I remembered another account," he said. "I guess I opened it on acid and then forgot. Isn't that something?"

I agreed that it was.

Elliot Bernstein

I told Shark he was crazy to film next door to the Petros. But he said it had to be there, the script called for Newport Beach. When I visited him at the Dean house a few days before filming began, things were already in high gear, people coming and going, consulting Shark on the details—it was almost as elaborate as a regular film.

And then the amphetamine arrived. Well, Shark was never able to handle speed, not that that ever stopped him from taking it. Soon everybody was just possessed and I knew something bad was going to happen.

"Come on, stick around," Shark said, and even offered me a part in the film as a soldier returning from Vietnam to find his wife being kept as a sex slave by a black guy.

"My hair's too long to play a soldier," I said, and split for San Francisco.

Simone Gatane

We began filming on a Friday morning, all of us having sneaked into the leased house as inconspicuously as possible. How exciting it was to be making this subversive film clandestinely in the very heart of the rancid American dream!

Shark worked feverishly, brutalizing the cast and crew. But no one minded for here was clearly a genius at work! He shot virtually in sequence, the film beginning normally enough. The first reel might easily have been mistaken for an insipid hommage to the films of Ross Hunter. Then, inexorably, all expectations are undermined until "logic" and "sanity" no longer remain.

Janet Bundy

I played the lead. I have to tell you it's not something I would do again today. I became a feminist a few years later, but at the time . . . Well, you've got to understand, it was the sixties. The sexual revolution and all that. The body—and nudity—were *in*. To think I actually thought it was art!

Neal Ridges

Shark really put Janet through the ringer.

Janet Bundy

My name in the film was variously Brenda, Jan, Doris, Kit, Tammy, and tellingly, Kathy. It was part of the intentional confusion of the script that all the other characters called me by different names.

Neal Ridges

Ron, the black acting student Shark got to replace Darrel Tyrone, was gay. Between takes he amused us with letter-perfect impressions of Dionne Warwicke and Diana Ross. There was a sequence where he was supposed to tie Janet to a lawnchair and then subject her to an interminable racial/political/sexual diatribe. It was an Eldridge Cleaver sort of thing, but Ron was irredeemably effeminate. "Look, you white ruling class bitch," he'd whine prissily. "I've got half a mind to just fuck the living shit out of you, except I know that's what you secretly want. All you honky snatches do is sit under your hair-dryers all day dreaming of a big, mean nigger cock."

Well, I didn't think the scene was supposed to be funny. But when I mentioned it to Shark, he said, "It's better this way. It'll twist people's heads even more."

Simone Gatane

The shoot was going fine, we were even ahead of schedule, when one night Shark was ready for a take and we couldn't find Janet. Then we looked out to the street and saw her smoking a cigarette and talking to a blonde girl who had pulled up to the house next door.

Kathy Petro

I was living in a sorority house near USC then, but I still came home on weekends a lot, and as I pulled up that night I couldn't help but notice all the bright lights in the courtyard of the Kenneys' house next door. I knew they'd gone to the islands and leased it out, so naturally I was curious. I saw this girl smoking a cigarette, wrapped in a blanket against the chill, and just looking incredibly bedraggled. "Hi. What's going on?" I said.

And she said, "He's crazy."

"Who?" I said.

Then I saw Shark.

Warren Dray

We'd been watching the Petro-Chem plant for a week, and we'd checked out the Petro house on the Balboa peninsula too. As far as we could tell Shark's maps were accurate. Then while watching the plant we observed on two separate occasions massive shipments of napalm going out.

"This is fucked," I told the others. "Babies are going to have their skin burned off while we wait for Shark to finish his stupid fucking movie. Art never changed anything, and it's not going to now. Fuck waiting. Let's do it. Tonight."

Neal Ridges

We were ready for a take on the courtyard scene when Shark saw Kathy Petro at the gate. At the time I didn't understand how closely the courtyard scene was modeled on a real life event.

Kathy Petro

I saw Shark and the camera and the movie lights but I just couldn't believe he was there. It was just too crazy. And he looked at me, you know, the way he *always* looked at me, as if every meeting we ever had was somehow *inevitable*.

Then before I could even react or anything, somebody started up this chainsaw! Well, you can *imagine* what that sound did to me! I could never go to any of those chainsaw movies that came out in the seventies, never, never, never. Because *that sound* just *did* something to me.

Then I saw that they had this muscular male dummy made out of flesh-colored plastic. The head was on a hinge or something, which they were trying to cover with makeup. And there was a pump device for the blood, you know? But the pump wasn't working right, and the blood was just kind of trickling down the dummy's chest from the neck. And then something blew and the blood started squirting every which way, just like it had in real life with Jeff Stuben. And I just started screaming.

Warren Dray

The plan was to kidnap Jack Petro and force him to admit us to the plant. That was to be no problem since he owned the fucking place. Shark pointed out, and I completely agreed, that if Jack Petro went up with his napalm it would be a warning to the other pig industrialists that their money and influence would not protect them either.

We decided on our own not to leave any witnesses. As for any janitors or night watchmen we might run into, we believed that people were responsible for their actions. There were no "good Germans" only taking orders. The same went for Petro's pig wife, the society bitch Paige. If she happened to be home the night we came for her hubbie she was due to be gutted. That went double for Petro's decadent daughter. If she was wriggling around that fascist household I would personally off that pampered blonde piglet.

Paige Petro

Jack and I were watching a late movie in the den when we heard Kathy scream outside. We knew the Kenneys had leased their place next door, but the properties were really quite private. We certainly had no idea Shark was there. Jack wouldn't have stood for it, needless to say.

Warren Dray

We pulled around the corner and suddenly there were cop cars parked at the Petro house dead ahead. We almost shit but we couldn't make a U-turn without attracting attention. "Stay cool, just keep going," I said to Randy who was at the microbus wheel.

We drove at a normal pace past the house where Shark was filming and saw cops in the courtyard under the movie lights. Then as we passed the Petro place we caught a glimpse of Jack and Paige comforting their sobbing debutante in a touching pig family tableau.

"Let's grease 'em," Randy said, his hand going to his AK-47. "Let's grease 'em now."

"Fuck, are you crazy?" I said. "There must be thirty pigs."

"Randy's right," Gretchen said from the backseat, fingering her own weapon. "Let's off 'em all." And her lover Luanne said, *"Yeah!"*

But several cops were already checking us out, microbuses being inherently suspicious. I stuck the barrel of my AK-47 in Randy's ribs. "Keep going at a slow pace or I'll blow your Marxist/Leninist guts out," I said, then glared at Gretchen: "And I'll blow off your radical lesbian head."

We kept going.

Neal Ridges

The cops shut us down, and told us to clear out, since we didn't have a location permit. Shark argued that we didn't need one since it was private property, and the cops threatened to take us all in. I imagine that was what Jack Petro was pushing for. At one point Shark started over to the Petro house; if he'd encountered Jack Petro I'm sure there would have been a bad scene. But the Petro gate was closed by then. Her parents had taken Kathy inside.

Kathy Petro

Mom took me up to my bedroom, and I was just kind of whimpering by then, so she left me there, I guess thinking that the worst was over. But no sooner had she left than I just flipped out again and started whirling around the room, screaming like an insane dervish. That was when Daddy came in, and trying to restrain me so I wouldn't hurt myself, yanked my arm so hard he dislocated my shoulder. A bunch of ligaments were torn and everything, and even though it healed it acted up for years to come, causing me intense pain, which led to some very bad things.

For a long time whenever I felt that horrible pain in my shoulder I cursed Shark, even though technically it was Daddy who had caused the injury.

Neal Ridges

Shark was furious about losing the beach house since the film was nearly half shot at that point, and he didn't have the money to re-shoot everything at a new location. Everyone assumed the film was lost until Shark decided the apparent disaster was actually a blessing in disguise. He would complete the film at a new location, then cut everything together, even though in a number of instances that meant the location would change from shot to shot within the same sequence. "It's a major opportunity to gut some of the most oppressive 'rules' of cinema," he said.

He found a beach house in Venice, a sterile modern place absolutely unlike the tropical Spanish ambiance of the house in Newport Beach. The only thing the two locations had in common was an ocean view.

Simone Gatane

So much of filmmaking entails exploiting chance. But only a genius would have dared such a leap.

Warren Dray

I caught up with Shark the night after the Newport Beach fiasco, wanting to find out what the fuck happened. And when he found out we'd jumped the gun he flipped.

"You stupid fucking moron," he yelled at me. *"You would've killed Kathy!"* At that time I had no idea he was fixated on her.

"You blew it," he said. "It's off." Then he threatened to warn Jack Petro and even call the FBI. When he mentioned the feds I went through the roof.

"Listen, you capitalist ass-licker," I said, jamming my gun under his chin. "You're in this way over your head. This isn't a movie, you simpering shit. This is a real gun with real bullets . . ."

Simone interceded, pushing my gun away from Shark's face. "Don't you see? This is precisely what they want, for us to fight among ourselves."

As it turned out we soon lost all interest in the Petro plan in favor of a much, much juicier target. A few weeks after the Newport Beach fiasco, Randy and I came back from casing a certain rather well-known Orange County theme park only to discover that Gretchen and Luanne had split with all the plastic explosives, leaving a note that said they were severing all contact with men.

Neal Ridges

We wrapped in May and I smelled disaster. I'd seen the rough footage and, the mismatched locations aside, the acting was wretched. Of course "good acting" was a bourgeois concept. But still . . .

Shark wanted to have the film finished in time for the June screenings in Melnitz Hall. Because of the delay caused by the location change that gave him less than a month. He got a new supply of speed and a stock of cream soda—have you ever tasted that stuff warm?—and worked around the clock in his editing room until his nerves were shot. If somebody laughed in the hall he'd step out in a rage, his eyes like Hitler's. "Shut up, goddamn you! How dare you disturb my concentration when I'm creating great art!"

I mean, it would've been funny if he hadn't been dead serious.

Simone Gatane

Shark poured his heart and soul into *Pillow Fuck*. I know because I would come to see him and say, "Shark, you haven't slept for many days, please come home." And he would yell at me and slam the editing room door in my face.

Neal Ridges

I believe he was nearly finished when he learned that Jean-Claude Citroen was coming to UCLA in June to screen one of his own films. This sent Shark into a complete frenzy. "No, this isn't right, I've got to redo it." He began tearing off splices, frantically searching for lost trims. Have you ever seen someone short-circuiting on speed? He was in a state of total panic because of course you know Citroen was his idol.

Simone Gatane

When Jean-Claude arrived in Los Angeles, he let the studio put him in a bungalow at the Beverly Hills Hotel so that he could experience firsthand the decadence of Hollywood and thus knowingly attack the capitalist factory of "entertainment." Though we had been lovers once, that was many years before, when I was fourteen. But when I saw Jean-Claude in his bungalow we made love together for old times' sake. Afterwards, as we smoked in bed, I said, "Oh, by the way. My boyfriend is screening his film tonight."

Neal Ridges

I remember the screening only too well. It started late because of the mob scene caused by Jean-Claude Citroen's arrival. Students crowded around him in the Melnitz Hall foyer, asking urgent, pointed questions about the future of cinema, a subject about which Jean-Claude always had a great deal to say. He was with Simone, who'd picked him up at his hotel, and I kept trying to get her eye, because Shark was just inside the theater, coming completely unglued. He looked terrible. I think he'd literally been up for a week, only hours before completing the final sound mix. His eyes, God. Like a character the actor Brad Dourif might play.

Finally, Simone steered Jean-Claude into the theater and introduced him to Shark, who could barely speak he was so exhausted, his voice little more than a hoarse whisper. Shark tried to express how much Citroen's *Neon City* had affected him. While Jean-Claude acknowledged Shark's admiration, he remained polite and reserved to the point of skepticism, as if he meant to indicate to Shark that he did not intend to let their mutual friendship with Simone color his critical reaction to Shark's film in any way—he took the art form of cinema that seriously. Given Jean-Claude's body of brilliant, unforgivingly incisive film criticism, I don't think Shark expected anything less.

At last everyone was seated and the lights went down. As they did I noticed Jean-Claude's hand sliding over Simone's knee.

Contrary to my earlier fears, based in part on Shark's occasional empathic references to Erich von Stroheim, the final cut of *Pillow Fuck* ran a concise ninety minutes. It was really a masterpiece of romantic deconstruction, beginning with an episode of coy telephone banter à la *Pillow Talk*, which quickly degenerated into obscenity and dementia. Needless to say there was no "plot," but simply a series of grating and increasingly fragmented vignettes, some of which were unmotivatedly violent, others intentionally tedious and repetitious, still others purposefully stupid and stultifying. I found that the "bad acting" worked after all. What in a Hollywood film would have been a kind of virtuoso Oscar-fodder acting moment became instead merely nauseating. The editing was aggressively chaotic or "bad," a senseless, arrhythmic jumble of jump cuts, pointless zooms, deliberately mismatched continuity—including of course the everchanging location. "Oh really?" Janet would say, smoking a cigarette in Newport Beach. "Yes," Ron would reply as the film cut to a shot of him in the beach house in Venice. Then cut back to Janet, sans cigarette, sitting now, not standing as before, nodding, in a different dress.

A few people walked out, the squarer students. Everyone else was galvanized—or at least awed.

I glanced at Jean-Claude during one of Ron's political harangues to see how he was taking it. The harangue was intentionally illogical, of course, an insane blend of Marxist and fascist cliché, while Jean-Claude was himself a grimly "serious" Marxist, so I thought this might be a touchy moment. But he was smiling with pleasure. Then I noticed that his hand had disappeared under Simone's miniskirt.

When the film ended there was silence. Then a thunderous standing ovation. I have no doubt it was one of the great moments of Shark's life. Vindication. Shark smiled wanly despite his exhaustion. Inevitably, he turned to Jean-Claude. We all held our breath, waiting for Jean-Claude's reaction. Finally, after an excruciating pause, Jean-Claude said to Shark, "I understand you live in the house of James Dean."

Shark smiled a bit shakily and said, "Yes. I'm having some people over. Would you care to join us?"

Simone Gatane

"He hasn't told me what he thought of my film yet," Shark said to me at the party, indicating Jean-Claude across the room in deep discussion with Janet Bundy and another girl.

"Perhaps you shouldn't press it," I said to Shark, sensing correctly that Jean-Claude's opinion meant far too much to him.

By then it had become all too apparent that Jean-Claude was deliberately avoiding his host. So finally Shark tossed back yet another glass of wine—how he was still on his feet I have no idea—and stepped

up to Jean-Claude. I cringed as I saw the look of helpless longing and anger on Shark's drawn face.

Neal Ridges

"So what do you think of my movie?" Shark said to Jean-Claude, loud enough for most of the room to hear.

"I'm sorry, what?" Jean-Claude said, torn from his conversation with the girls.

Shark repeated his question. And Jean-Claude looked right past him to the large French *Giant* poster on the wall.

"Ah, *Géant*," Jean-Claude said. "Dean moved into this house as he finished that film. Only to die in a matter of what? Days?"

Shark responded, his voice cracking with rage: "I don't want to talk about James Dean, man! I want to know what you thought of my fucking movie!"

"It was shit," Jean-Claude said, and several people gasped. "You're a moron, a poseur, you have no talent. You're not even mediocre, you're an incompetent fraud. An excreter of fake art, which is the worst kind, a cancerous tumor of capitalism which must be excised. You're a phony, a thief, a debased cinematic plagiarist, you will never do anything worthwhile. Anyone who spews out such drivel would be better off putting a bullet through his head."

I don't know, perhaps it was the James Dean aura of the house, but Shark's reaction reminded me of nothing so much as Dean's response to Raymond Massey's rejection in *East of Eden*—you know, the scene where Cal tries to give his father the money? It was like that, just awful, Shark reeling around the room in total incoherent agony. Just excruciatingly painful—if it had been a film, unwatchable. And no one knew what to do or say. Simone looked helpless. Finally, still groaning in unrelievable emotional pain, Shark reeled out the door. A moment later we heard the Porsche roaring out of the driveway.

Simone Gatane

I ran out after Shark but it was too late. In that Porsche like James Dean's he was screaming up the street.

Neal Ridges

Naturally, it occurred to us that Shark might try to kill himself. Later that night—after Jean-Claude had attacked a few of us who'd belatedly come to Shark's defense, and then he and everyone else had left—Simone said, "Neal, where did James Dean die?"

"On the highway to Paso Robles, I think."

We got out a map and located the highway, and set out in my VW bug at something like three in the morning.

I soon had second thoughts. "But Dean's death was an accident," I told Simone as we approached the Grapevine. "He broadsided somebody. How could Shark possibly hope to copy that fluke event? If he's really hot to kill himself I'm not at all sure he'll bother to drive all this way."

"He won't mind the drive," Simone said. "I know how his mind works, Neal. He will find the exact place where it happened and broadside someone there. And what's more, I'll bet they'll be driving a car just like the one Dean hit back in 1955."

It struck me as unlikely. But she certainly knew Shark more intimately than I did.

We reached the place where Dean had died around ten that morning. A super-highway had replaced the original road, and there was no intersection anymore. But there were still chunks of the old road running parallel to the highway, weeds growing up through the broken asphalt. Affixed to a tree near the old road we found a commemorative plaque identifying the spot where the crash had occurred thirteen years before.

"Maybe Shark stopped for breakfast at a roadside cafe," Simone said. So we waited—even though we both knew by then it was logistically impossible for Shark to reenact the crash no matter how badly he might have wanted to.

Finally around two I said, "Simone, this is inane." And we drove back to L.A.

For three days we heard nothing. I stayed with Simone who was literally sick with worry. Finally, we learned from Elliot Bernstein that Shark had sought refuge with his father.

Mac Trager

I hadn't seen my boy in a good nine months when he showed up late one night. I was watching Duke Wayne on TV in *Big Jim McLain*, feeling lonesome as hell, when I heard the doorbell ring.

Shark looked beat and said, all choked up, "Dad—I want to come home."

For some reason it got to me—I guess I'd been drinking some. It was all I could do not to cry like a goddamn girl. "Come on in, son," I said. "Come on in and pop yourself a brew."

He fell asleep in that old green recliner with a can of beer in his hand.

Elliot Bernstein

Shark called me in San Francisco from his father's the day after the UCLA screening. We made small talk for a while before he finally told me what had happened with Jean-Claude Citroen. Although he tried to make light of it he was clearly in a state of deep psychic pain. When he began making quips about "pulling a Hemingway" with his dad's shotgun I tried to keep him talking. But he began giggling distractedly—a bit like James Dean I remember thinking at the time—and then abruptly hung up.

Mac Trager

He was in a bad way. I knew it had something to do with that student movie he'd made. I'd heard about the deal next door to the Petros'. I figured he'd done something sick again and had to pay the price. And I could tell just by looking at him that he'd been on that speed drug. I should've kicked him out, but he got to my soft spot the way a lost, starving dog would.

Elliot Bernstein

I tried calling Shark back at his father's, until it became obvious the phone was off the hook. I was quite concerned by then, imagining his brains decorating the rumpus room. I considered alerting the Newport Beach police, but thought better of that, and called Simone instead.

"Simone, he's at his dad's with a gun," I told her.

"No, he's here," Simone told me. Perhaps two hours had passed since I'd spoken to Shark. "He's sleeping like a baby in the James Dean loft."

Mac Trager

I was under the impression that we'd had a good talk that evening. We drank some beers, and Shark said he was going to quit college, which was horseshit anyway, and come back to work for me at the station.

"We're a lot alike," I said to my boy. "Like father, like son."

I went out for another six-pack, but when I got back he was gone. Just like that. No note, no nothing. So I drank that six-pack myself and said: All right then, *to hell with you!*

Neal Ridges

I was with Simone in the A-frame when we heard Shark's Porsche pulling into the driveway. Simone and I had just finished having sex—there'd always been an attraction—and we dressed hurriedly as Shark came in the door. We weren't fast enough though. We were still in the loft—and in those days before VCRs there was little else we could have been doing up there *besides* having sex.

Shark entered and saw us but didn't seem to care at all. He was almost scarily calm, as if he'd done some very serious soul searching in the last three days, as if he'd given up a terrible struggle and in so doing found peace. Precisely because of this aura of surrender neither Simone nor I were at all prepared for what happened next.

Shark picked up the film cans that held *Pillow Fuck*, the work print, the answer print and—I realized with horror and incredulity— the original negative. I sensed he was not going to take them to a vault for safekeeping.

Simone Gatane

"What are you doing? Oh my God, no!" I yelled at Shark, as I tried to find my blouse. By the time Neal and I followed Shark outside he was squirting lighter fluid on the open film cans.

Neal Ridges

He was giggling—a kind of tortured Dean giggle—as he drenched the film with lighter fluid, holding the can at crotch-level so that there was a kind of unmistakable piss symbolism.

Simone tried to stop him from striking the match.

"*Noooooo*," Shark whined, as he pushed Simone away, sounding less like Dean now than Montgomery Clift. "Jean-Claude was *right!* It *is* shit!"

Shark tossed the match and the film ignited in the driveway as he groaned like an animal in agony, tears rolling down his grimacing face.

Elliot Bernstein

I spoke to Shark on the phone a week or so after he destroyed his film, and the conversation disturbed me a great deal. He was no longer suicidal per se, but he was mentally fragmented, burned out, rambling endlessly.

He'd left his father's, he said, "because there's a part of me that really wants to kill him. He's a bigot, he drove my mother to suicide, and he totally fucked me up for life. Sometimes it's all I can do,"

Shark added with heavy sarcasm, "to remember that he's still my dear old dad."

He was nearly broke, he said, though he made it clear he wasn't asking for help. Simone had gone back to France, he was losing the James Dean house, and his primo Speedster had "blown up on the freeway," forcing him to sell it for a fraction of what he'd paid.

"Where are you going then?" I asked.

He didn't answer, rambling on instead about the last half hour of *Giant*, how they'd receded Dean's hairline when he played Jett Rink as an old man. The way Shark was muttering reminded me *of* Jett Rink in that terrible, lonely banquet room scene that marked Dean's last moment on film.

"Look, Shark, when you know where you're going to be, let me know," I said finally and got off the phone, since I was paying for the call.

6 / Planet of the Apes (1968)

Neal Ridges

Shark got a part-time job at the UCLA Film Archives that summer and moved into a dumpy apartment in Venice. The campus was relatively deserted during those months, but I was there several days a week, fine-tuning my thesis film project, and sometimes gave Shark a lift home since he no longer had a car.

He changed radically that summer and it was all for the worse. He got fat for one thing, putting on maybe thirty pounds from eating junk food, which I suppose was all he could afford. Still, it was disgusting to watch him stuff five Der Wienerschnitzel kraut dogs in his mouth one right after the other like a starving pig. He let his hair and beard grow long until he looked like a blond Jim Morrison. Remember Morrison after he went to seed? That was Shark in the summer of '68.

Frank Forte

I saw Shark occasionally that summer and he'd become a disgusting slob. His hair and clothes were dirty—it went far beyond the hippie look of the time. He'd just ceased to care about his body and begun living entirely in his mind. His eyes had a kind of burning, Rasputin intensity as he lumbered through the corridors of Melnitz Hall, always with a number of dog-eared Critical Studies texts under his arm—Kracauer's *Theory of Film: The Redemption of Physical Reality* and the like.

One night I saw him at the Ray-Mar Theater in Mar Vista, which had just gone revival, using a pen-light to furiously scribble notes throughout a Jean-Claude Citroen double bill—*Neon City* and *Renée's Breath*. He was mumbling angrily to himself as he wrote until several other patrons shushed him. Clearly, he was researching a critique of Citroen's oeuvre, and was bent on intellectual revenge.

Eric Sievers

I worked with Shark in the film archives that summer. We were cataloging a cache of silent nitrate footage, which was badly decomposed and therefore extremely dangerous to work with. We were on a razor's edge of anxiety about it, and one day Shark actually came in *smoking!* Smoking and mindlessly flicking ash! He should have been fired on the spot.

But I think we all felt sorry for him. I know I did. I hadn't seen *Pillow Fuck*, but I'd certainly heard about it, and about the horrific aftermath. Anyone who'd destroy his own art . . . I don't know. In a way it was romantic—inevitably, you thought of Rimbaud—and yet it spoke of such pain. You could see that Shark was hurting, which in itself frightened a lot of people away. And his criticism of others was as merciless as Jean-Claude Citroen's had been of him.

Once after work we went upstairs to one of the screening rooms to watch the rough cut of a girl student's film. Well, it wasn't very good, but I mean she'd been working on it for months. So everybody was polite except Shark who asked her, "Where are you from?"

"Nebraska," she said.

And Shark said, "You're a zero. You should go back."

Well, she started to cry. It was just shitty, gratuitous cruelty on Shark's part, and there were many other similar instances of that sort of thing.

Neal Ridges

I stopped by Shark's one afternoon on my way to the beach. I'd never been inside before, and the building was indeed forbidding. Venice was a slum in those days, well before the gentrification of the seventies, and that rundown brick apartment house at Brooks and Speedway was a cesspool of burnt-out bikers and junkies.

Shark's room had an ocean view, though you'd never have known it. He had a ratty blanket tacked permanently over the window since the bright sunlight "hurt his eyes," he said. He sat on his lumpy bed, his lumpy body surrounded by fast-food debris and a dozen notepads, as he told me he was going to "annihilate" Jean-Claude Citroen. When I asked him how he hoped to do that he showed me a rough draft of a critical essay he was confident *Jump Cut* would publish.

Well, some of it was brilliant. But most of it was a demented screed. Every coolly rational critical point was invariably mired in a swamp of the most obviously personal vindictive bitterness, deranged diatribes which ran on for pages, rendering the essay completely unpublishable. That Shark didn't see that truly made me fear for his mind.

Eric Sievers

It must have been about the middle of the summer that Tom Field stopped by the archives one afternoon. I remember, Shark was watching *Kiss Me Deadly* on the Steenbeck when Tom walked in, and the two of them immediately plunged into an animated discussion of film noir that went on for hours. Then they left together still talking up a storm. It was amazing, the first time I'd ever seen Shark really excited and enthusiastic in a positive way. Obviously the beginning of an important friendship. Sad in a way too, because more than anyone I'd ever known—and more that summer than ever before—Tom Field radiated an aura of premature doom.

Neal Ridges

Tom Field had graduated a few years before and was really one of the bright lights of the film school. He was brilliant, absolutely brilliant. His thesis film, *Icons*, a kind of pseudo-verité *Citizen Kane* story of a rock star who commits suicide at the peak of his fame, was astounding. He'd won a number of festival awards with it and gone straight from UCLA into a studio development deal. And it was at that crucial point, sadly, that his health had given out. He'd had a severe recurrence of a childhood ailment, which had forced him to stay in bed for a year.

At the time he and Shark became friends Tom was back on his feet again but remained frail. He was, besides being brilliant, incredibly handsome, though in a delicate, almost feminine way. Poetic is the word, I suppose. He had the aura of a doomed poet—too sensitive, too beautiful for this coarse world.

Shark and Tom were soon together constantly, so much so that there began to be talk. There had always been rumors that Tom might be bisexual—though I think those were bred largely of either wishful thinking or envy, the desire to denigrate his genius in some way.

I never seriously thought that Shark and Tom were actually having sex, though the relationship was clearly intense—intense and exclusionary. They had a way of speaking a kind of private, intimate code, the way lovers do really, which was part of what fanned the rumors. One day in August Shark told me, as if it were a closely guarded secret, that he and Tom were writing a screenplay together.

Eric Sievers

I never believed the gay rumors. It's possible Tom may have experimented at some time in his life, but there was something totally asexual about Shark that summer—his body was just something that carried around his mind.

I'm sure his rapport with Tom was strictly mental, which is not to say there weren't some rather bizarre subtextual elements. I didn't realize it at the time, because I had yet to see Kathy Petro. But when I did see her a few years later I have to tell you I experienced quite a jolt. My God, I thought, looking at her face on the cover of a magazine. She could be Tom Field in drag.

Neal Ridges

There was definitely a resemblance, though I would describe it as more generic than mirrorlike. Tom had Kathy Petro's blonde hair, the exact same shade of pale blonde. He had her skin coloring, her green eyes. They were of a similar *type*, in the sense that people will speak of being attracted to a certain type.

Look, anything's possible. I have no way of knowing what was really going on in Shark's mind, either consciously or subconsciously, anymore than I or anyone will ever really know what happened the day Tom Field died.

Janet Bundy

I hadn't seen Shark for a couple of months, not since the *Pillow Fuck* screening, when I picked him up hitchhiking in Venice one day. I almost didn't stop, not recognizing him at first because of his beard and weight. "Janet, you've got to take me to UCLA," he said. "It's a matter of life and death."

On the way he explained that Tom Field had got the news that afternoon that the studio he had a deal with had decided to dump him. Then his agent had done the same thing, saying he had decided that Tom, however talented, was "a loser." Tom was devastated and had called Shark to say he was going to kill himself, mentioning that someone shooting a film on campus was using a real gun as a prop.

Even at the time I sensed that wasn't the whole story though. For one thing Shark's face was scraped, his lower lip swollen as if he'd just been in a fight. I'd heard some funny stories about Shark and Tom, which I'd tried not to believe.

When we reached Melnitz Hall, Shark barged right into the sound stage, ignoring the red light, spoiling a take. He was still looking around for the prop gun when we heard a shot in the archives and Eric Sievers crying, "Oh God, no! No no no!"

Eric Sievers

Tom came in that afternoon and asked if he could look at *Touch of Evil*. I was busy and said sure, and he went and got the film. He knew where it was since he'd studied it endlessly. It was his favorite Orson Welles film, if not his favorite film period. Later, I would recall that he seemed a bit moody, and remember noticing was that his knuckles were skinned as if he'd been in a recent fight.

I didn't give him much thought at the time though. I was painstakingly cleaning a nitrate print of *Greed*, and nearly jumped out of my skin when the gun went off less than six feet away in the Steenbeck room.

Janet Bundy

Shark and I rushed into the archives and there was Tom Field slumped over the flatbed. The gun was on the floor at his feet. It had been loaded with live ammunition so they could film a realistic close-up of it firing. There was blood everywhere.

Eric Sievers

As we went to Tom I couldn't help but notice the ending of *Touch of Evil* playing on the flatbed screen: a grotesquely bloated Orson Welles, shot by his partner, collapsing into the garbage-strewn waters of a Venice canal. Then a shot of Marlene Dietrich delivering her famous deadpan eulogy: "He was some kind of a man." Which she qualifies, with heavy poignance: "What does it matter what you say about people?"

At just that point the film ground to a halt, Tom Field's blood spreading like a magnified light-show effect over the close-up of Dietrich on the screen.

I looked at Shark. His expression was blank—stunned, I like to think—as he simply turned and walked out the door.

Elliot Bernstein

As it happened I came to L.A. about a week after Tom Field killed himself. I stopped by the UCLA Film Archives hoping to catch Shark, and Eric Sievers told me about the suicide. Shark had left the day it happened and had not been back since.

I went to Shark's Venice address. The apartment was empty, recently cleaned out, the landlady still angry about the mess Shark had left behind. It appeared he had simply taken off the night of Tom's death without bothering to return for any of his possessions, which were mostly books and papers.

As I was leaving the building I saw a screenplay in the trash with Shark's and Tom Field's name on it. All I knew of Tom Field at that point was the little Shark had written: that Tom was a gifted film-maker and a great guy, that they were working on something "incredible" together.

Impulsively, I took the script, perhaps curious to see how incredible it in fact was.

Neal Ridges

When Shark disappeared after Tom Field's death a lot of people feared the worst. Though it was true that Tom had lost his studio deal and his agent on the same day, the rumors of a fight—or to be blunt, a lovers' quarrel—between Shark and Tom spread. And now Shark, it was thought, might have drowned himself or OD'ed somewhere so that he could join Tom in death.

Elliot Bernstein

I was jolted when I read the script—which was called *Canyons* then—shortly after I returned to San Francisco. It was obvious that the main characters were modeled on Kathy Petro and Jean-Claude Citroen. It was essentially the story of a young California woman, blonde and rich with an industrialist father, who has an affair with a famous French auteur in Los Angeles. They lease a house in the Hollywood Hills which they use as their love nest. Then, while the director is away on location, the young woman and several of her friends are brutally murdered by a gang of psychotic hippies who break into the house on a random killing spree.

The script I read was a heavily annotated first draft. You could see that someone, probably Tom, had been afraid the film director might too closely resemble Citroen. As a result his name (Jean-Paul Peugeot originally) and nationality had been tentatively changed here and there, in one case making him Italian, in another Polish.

The violence was extreme by 1968 standards, though "artful," I suppose—if you consider the climax of *The Wild Bunch* artful. At the time I read the script I believed it was simply a wishful fantasy, Shark's way of exorcising his anger towards both Kathy and Citroen, the two people who had hurt him most, by placing them together in an imagined scenario.

Then a week or so later I saw a photo in *Look* magazine of Kathy Petro on Jean-Claude's arm. Eventually I learned that Shark had seen similar photos before he and Tom wrote the script.

Kathy Petro

Paris in the springtime, I mean any springtime, what can you say? But Paris in the spring of 1968—well, talk about being where *la action* was! Barricades and Pouilly Fuisse, tear gas and *chocolat souf-flé [sic]*. What a time to be young and *now* and free!

I was in this little cafe one night where Hemingway used to go when Jean-Claude came in. I'd never been a big fan of his movies, mainly because I didn't understand them. I mean, I'd always liked stories, and still do, so shoot me, okay?

So I was there with *my* friends and he came in with *his* friends and right away he looked at me with, you know, *that look*. Well, he was almost forty then, so I mean, my God. Then he asked somebody who I was and they must have said: Oh, her father's Jack Petro of Petro-Chem, the people who make the napalm and everything. Because suddenly he got this severe look and marched right over and just totally dressed me down. "Your father's a war criminal. Your sports car is fueled with the blood of the Third World, your college tuition is paid with the scorched skin of babies." He just went on and on, saying all these horrible things to me, until finally I broke down and cried.

"Look, I can't help what Daddy does," I said and ran out into the street.

And he came out after me, saying, "Wait, wait, you're right. It's not your fault. Please forgive me, I didn't mean to make you cry."

He brushed back my hair and caught one of my tears with his finger. And then, very gently, he kissed me.

Drake Brewster

Although I'd done a few drugs at one time, I was no fucking hippie and couldn't stand that bunch. So when I saw this grungy long-hair hitchhiking on the highway in Santa Barbara I had no intention of stopping. But suddenly the asshole stepped right in front of my car.

I veered to avoid him and hit the brakes. "You goddamn stupid fuck," I yelled back at him. And he reeled around like a goddamn drunk, so I threw it in park and jumped out.

"You fuckheaded dork," I said, about to waste him when he started whimpering like a fucking girl. It was so pathetic I just shook my head and said, "Man, I'm not even gonna dirty my hands on you."

Then he said, "I just lost my brother."

I see now he meant it in that bullshit hippie sense, like: we're all brothers. But at the time I thought he meant his *brother* and got a premonition. "What do you mean, man? In 'Nam?"

"Yeah," he said. "That's right. In fuckin' 'Nam, man."

I see now he meant it in the sense that the war was everywhere, so that everywhere was 'Nam. More of that hippie shit. But at the time it fuckin' moved me, man, since I'd lost my own brother over there in '65.

"Where you goin'?" I asked him.

"I don't know," he said. He looked like a poor fuckin' dog.

"Come on," I said. It was two in the morning. "You can sleep on my floor tonight."

I was living in this guest house then behind a big mansion in Montecito owned by an old Nazi. I mean a real German Nazi from World War II. I told Shark about that as we pulled up and he said, "So are you a Nazi too?" He meant my brown uniform.

"No. I'm a security guard," I said.

The next day was a Sunday and he'd got some sleep but I could see he was still pretty fucked up with grief. "Come on, the sun's out," I said. And we drove around Montecito in this old Nova I had, looking at all the rich people's homes.

"Boy, this place makes Beverly Hills look sick," he said.

"Damn straight," I said. "And the criminals know it too."

"What do you mean?" he said.

"See that house?" I said. "Couple of Mexicans shot the owner two weeks ago. All they got was an old clock. Too bad that was my night off." I opened the glove compartment so he could see my piece.

"You ever killed anyone?" he said.

"Not yet," I told him. "But last year I shot off a black guy's thumb."

That night we went to Taco Bell. There were two girls there, both interested in me—until they saw this grungy animal I was with. That irritated me, but when we got back to my place and drank a few beers and talked a lot more I had to admit Shark was not a bad guy.

He said he'd had to get out of L.A. because that city was a jungle.

"Yeah, you can get eaten alive in a jungle," I told him. "Especially when you're a fat fuckin' slob panting for breath like you." I told it like it was, since I worked out with weights and took good care of my body and couldn't stand slobs, I had no sympathy at all.

"I guess I have let myself go to seed," he said.

"Man, that's an understatement. Lift your shirt."

I was gonna let him have it about this fat fuckin' gut he had. But we ended up just laughing and I let him off the hook.

He told me he was broke and I said, "You might be in luck, a fella just quit. Do you have a clean record?"

He said he did.

Ernie Post

I managed the Santa Barbara office of Island Security then, and I hired Shark Trager on Drake's recommendation. Shark seemed like a level-headed young man to me, with something of a weight problem, but basically clean-cut.

Drake Brewster

Before I took Shark in to meet the boss I gave him a haircut, short as short could be, right down to the scalp. I shaved that dirty beard off too, since I knew how to handle a straight edge. I liked the body builder look for myself, without all that dirty hair, so I was smooth all over except for my butt. It's hard to shave your own butt, so I slapped on some lather and handed Shark the razor.

"Are you crazy?" he said and started to laugh.

Well, I saw red and we had our first fight. I pinned him to the carpet the way you might pin a child. "I've seen some fat sacks of shit," I said, "but you take the cake."

Ernie Post

Shark said he'd been in the ROTC and knew guns. So I told Drake, "Okay, go down and get him his permit and you break him in."

Drake Brewster

We got Shark a uniform but it was a joke. "Man, you're a lard ass," I said. "We gotta do something about you."

So I switched him to a high protein diet and made him jog every morning with me. Then I took him to the gym. He was panting and begging for mercy but I was brutal. "Come on, you fuckin' pussy," I'd yell when he wanted to quit.

The weight started coming off and he got some definition but only cause I whipped him like a goddamn horse. On our days off I took him to the pistol range and showed him how to handle my .357. The first time he fired it he flinched and I said, "Christ, man, you fire that thing like a goddamn fruit." I kept riding his ass till he got pretty good.

I showed him the route, pointing out what to watch for, strange cars and what-not. It was a pretty boring job unless you caught an in-progress, so a lot of the time we just talked about snatch. He told me about some French bitch who sounded like a real cunt, and about some other girl he still had the hots for. "Someday I'm gonna get her," he said once in a strange kind of voice that was filled with both anger and heavy-duty longing.

So I said, "*Get* her? What do you mean? Fuck her or kill her?"

I laughed and he blew up, saying, "Shut your stupid fucking mouth, Drake."

Well, nobody calls me stupid, so I hit him and we almost drove up onto this doctor's lawn.

Another time while we were jogging he said he'd gone to UCLA. "No wonder you were going crazy," I said. "All that shit they teach at college."

Then he set me straight about the guy who'd died the night we met being just a friend instead of an actual brother. When he said it was suicide, I said, "Man, that's a pussy's way out."

Shark said, "No, you don't understand. He was an artist and they drove him to it."

I said, "Fuck that shit. He was a loser. Only losers kill themselves like fucking little babies. Winners don't pull shit like that. That's what makes this country great."

We got into it on politics at first, 'cause he liked to spout this rancid radical shit this French bitch had filled him up with. But one day we passed some flowerchild types in Goleta and I said, "Look at those pukes. When all this *love* shit's over with, they're gonna go home to mommy and daddy. But where are you gonna go?"

Then one afternoon while he was spotting me at the gym he said the guy that had killed himself was a queer.

"How do you know that?" I said, feeling real nervous all of a sudden.

"Because he said he loved me," Shark said. And several other guys heard and gave us both funny looks. And I thought: Uh-oh, am I living with a fag?

"But I told him to get lost," Shark added. And I went: Pshew!

A while later in the showers he said, "You know I've been thinking. I think you're right. Tom *was* a pussy. If you can't stand the heat—"

"Damn straight," I said. "It's fuck or be fucked."

Just then a black guy stepped into the shower just as Shark stepped back, and they accidentally brushed. When Shark saw the guy was black he almost flipped. "Watch it, Sambo," he said, and there was almost a fight.

But the black guy shook his head and said, "Man, forget you."

Shark had a real problem with black guys.

"Yeah, it's a brutal world," I said as we drove back through Montecito. "Look at all these houses. You think the people who live in these houses got rich by taking it up the ass?"

We both laughed at that. Then we passed a couple of young babes in hot pants. "You see that one on the left, she's dying for it," I said. "They look like sisters to me. One for each of us. I wish they'd cut up that alley."

"Why?" Shark said.

"Cause I'm kind of into rape," I told him.

Elliot Bernstein

I'd heard nothing from Shark for over a month when he wrote me a letter from Santa Barbara saying he was working for a security patrol company and did not intend to return to UCLA in the fall. He said he'd quit drugs and was getting himself into shape "for combat," which struck me as a curious figure of speech since he had always been so passionately opposed to the war. What followed was even more disturbing. Less political than philosophical it was a kind of crypto-Nietzschean rant. Life is a jungle, the survival of the fittest, that sort of thing. The primacy of the will, the mandate of the strong to subjugate the weak—a brutal, insane philosophy which I mistook at first for parody. It was only as I came to his commentary on Tom Field that I realized how serious he was.

"Tom could never have made it in Hollywood," Shark wrote. "And he saw that himself. That's the reason he took the quick way out. Seen in this light his suicide was not cowardly, but was in fact the bravest act of his life. Tom was an artist but he was also a weakling. He was like a delicate poetess, Emily Dickinson, thrown into the Roman Colosseum. He was still shrinking from the sword with which he might have defended himself when they cast their nets and came in for the kill. This may sound heartless and self-serving, but I like to think that the weak, feminine, timid side of my own nature died when Tom pulled that trigger. Whenever I feel like pussing out I hope I'll see his bleeding head on that flatbed and remember what happens to 'suffering artistes.' "

I was extremely put off by this radical shift in Shark's weltanschauung, and showed the letter to Sue, whom I'd been living with for several months at that point. "I don't know what's going on with him," I told her. "This is not the Shark I used to know. Or perhaps one I want to know."

"He's been through a lot," Sue said. I had told her a great deal about Shark by then, though she had yet to read his and Tom's screenplay.

She read it that night. When she was done she came into the living room of our place on Haight Street and said, "This is the most far-out script I've ever read." She laughed with the joy of a great discovery. "I'm going to send it to Dad."

Drake Brewster

One night after we went to see *Planet of the Apes*, I turned Shark on to my philosophy of Zen rape. "The bitches want it," I told him. "That's the bottom line. And if you're a man you'll let 'em have it. That's what makes the world run. Everything else—society, the law, good manners—is all horseshit. Real men can take whatever they want. And if you're *real*, if you stay locked into the present on that animal vibe, the bitches won't complain. That's what I've found."

Up to then I'd nailed maybe seven separate babes, but not even one had gone and told the cops.

"Take her for example," I said as we saw some nurse getting off a bus. "I could nail her right now and she wouldn't do shit."

"You're crazy," Shark said. "You could go to prison."

"You're a pussy," I told him. "Watch this."

I made a U and pulled up behind the nurse as she walked toward an apartment building. "Come on, we can take turns," I said, thinking it would be a gas for us to watch each other fuck.

"You're nuts," Shark said.

"Quit saying that," I told him, cause I was getting turned on.

Then this nurse looked back and saw us in the car and started walking fast. By then I had a hard-on.

I pulled up and was about to jump out when she reached her door and this big Mexican dude came out.

"Damn, I hate it when this happens," I said, pulling out. "She had a nice ass too."

So we drove home and I jacked off, but I still felt frustrated and half-blamed Shark. If he hadn't been there giving me static, sure as shit I would've nailed that nurse before she even knew what hit her.

Elliot Bernstein

Sue and I met backstage at the Avalon after a gig and it was love at first sight. She was extraordinary, lithe with incredible legs, a stunning face with a large sensuous mouth, coal-black hair down her back, just a beauty. And intelligent! Really, her mind blew me away as much as anything. Her wit, her infectious joie de vivre.

She was still enrolled at Berkeley then. But it was 1968, you know, so the idea of actually attending classes and worrying about grades and all that just seemed incredibly unimportant. We spent the weekend together, dropping acid, and in the idiom of the day, we just merged. We barely spoke. Verbal communication was unnecessary, for we had entered a realm of tactile language, composing Italian sonnets and Dostoyevskian novels in and about one another's bodies.

Finally though, I had to drive her back to Berkeley to pick up a check she was expecting from home. That was when I first learned who her father was.

Sue Schlockmann

I was really embarrassed in those days about the kind of films Dad made. Of course film itself was cool, so if the subject came up I tended to color the truth. "Yes, my father runs a film company. He imports foreign films." The foreign film thing always sounded good. Maybe they'd think he was Janus or somebody, bringing Bergman films to the States. I'd usually change the subject at that point, because once I said Regal Pictures there would be this sneer that just killed me.

"Regal Pictures? Don't they make all those sleazy biker movies? And import those cheesy Asian caged-women flicks?"

I'd just be mortified because Regal was synonymous with the bottom of the barrel. I mean, let's face it, Dad made Roger Corman and AIP look like class operations. At least some of those B-films were kind of cool in a way, with a young Jack Nicholson or at least a name has-been. But Regal made Z-movies with sub-SAG morons no one had ever seen before or would ever see again.

Not that Dad cared as long as his films made money, and they almost always did. But 1968 had been a bad year. That was why I knew he'd consider Shark's script. He'd had high hopes for a depressing turd of a film called *Stews on Wheels,* and when it died he became despondent. He'd spent more than usual on advertising—I can still see the poster illustration of the buxom stewardesses scattering in terror as the grungy bikers roar up the aisles of the 747 on their Harley-Davidsons, with the tag: "They quit smiling the night the Angels ripped off their wings"—but still nobody came.

"I don't know, maybe I've lost touch," he'd said to me. "I don't know what these kids today want."

"Do this script, Dad," I told him on the phone the night I read Shark's screenplay. "It's cool and it's now, and it makes a statement about America that people of my generation will relate to. Plus—since I know this is important to you—it will also make a bundle." And then I told him, "Dad, if you don't screw it up it could even be art."

I knew that would get to him because by then he'd made so much money that it was really only a symbol. He'd talked cautiously for some time about someday mounting a "really class production," one that would give him the one thing that no amount of crass profit could provide: respectability.

I called him a week after I mailed the script and he said, "I couldn't finish it, I found it repellent. I don't mind turn-on violence, but this is turn-*off* violence, which is a whole other thing. These boys are sick. They should be in a mental hospital."

"One of them's already dead," I told him. "But the other one's a genius. At least that's what I hear."

He changed the subject and I didn't press it since at the time I'd spent my allowance on grass and acid and, you know, needed a few more dollars for food.

Woody Hazzard

Black Light played all over the bay area but for a long time nobody would sign us, cause they said we were "too dark." All these candy-ass psychedelic groups were being signed right and left and I got depressed, and when we didn't have a gig I just stayed in bed with Rat, this girl I was living with in a Sausalito houseboat.

Then suddenly in December this hot producer signed us. He said we were gonna be the next Doors. The studio dates were set in L.A., and Elliot and Sue and I drove down together in my VW, stopping to visit Shark in Santa Barbara on the way.

I don't think any of us were prepared for his roommate. The second I laid eyes on him I knew he was nuts.

Elliot Bernstein

Shark was out when we arrived. But Drake was sitting there in the living room watching "McHale's Navy" in his jockstrap, one leg over the arm of the chair as he rubbed his gun against the pouch of his jock. I thought at first we'd come to the wrong guest house. Then Shark pulled up in Drake's Nova.

Sue Schlockmann

I had a bad feeling about Drake right from the start. The gun-in-the-crotch business . . . I don't know. This was a few years before the women's movement and all the talk about sexism and machismo, so my reaction was not intellectual. It was just a gut feeling this guy was the enemy.

When Shark arrived he led us into the house and introduced us to Drake, who was glum and surly and refused to put on any clothes even after Shark asked him to. Drake muttered something like, "It's my fuckin' house," and strutted around in nothing but his supporter for the rest of the evening. He did have a pretty spectacular body, but his whole narcissistic thing was really a bore.

Woody Hazzard

Shark invited us to stay over, so I put my sleeping bag on the floor. Shark took the sofa and let Elliot and Sue use his bed on the service porch since they were still into this heavy sex thing. They went to bed early, partially I think to get away from Drake.

Then Shark and Drake and I smoked some dope, which Drake said he hadn't done in a long time. He said he'd taken peyote years before and had been hip when the word still meant something. Then he talked about how great Vietnam was, and at first I thought he was joking. But he wasn't, and he went into this incredible riff about how it must be like taking peyote to be in a battle, that it must be an "incredible rush to kill a man," that he'd heard it was better than sex.

"So why haven't you joined up?" I said.

And he said he wished he had because now it was too late. All the "pussy peaceniks" had fucked it up, making it impossible to "get off good over there."

I kept looking at Shark, trying to catch his eye 'cause I was sure he had to know his roommate was crazy. But every time I looked at Shark he quickly looked away.

Sue Schlockmann

The next day was a Sunday, a beautiful warm day, and since the guys weren't due in L.A. until Tuesday there was no real rush to move on. Drake had already gone to the gym by the time we got up, and Elliot and Wood went off to find some guy who might have some speed for the sessions. "Come on, grab a towel," Shark said to me. "Let's hit the beach."

Soon Shark and I were walking out across the toasty white sands of a stunning little cove which we had all to ourselves. "No need for tan lines," Shark said, and I suppressed a gasp as he pulled off his shorts.

This is going to sound corny, I know, but in many ways Shark was like a god back then. At least that's how he struck me that shimmering afternoon. With his blond hair and blue eyes, his golden skin and Greek statue physique—he was like a surfer or a Marine or maybe even a Viking.

And his talk was brilliant—though he could have been speaking Sanskrit and I would have still hung on every word. Soon I was topless and then bottomless myself, and I felt as if I'd taken acid, though in fact it had been nearly a week since I had.

There was a coolness to Shark however. Though our intellectual rapport was instantaneous he showed absolutely no sign of romantic interest. Of course I was going with one of his best friends. But still, you know, you can tell if there is repressed desire if you're really looking for it. And I was.

At the time I knew little of Kathy Petro. Elliot had mentioned in passing that the character of Karen in *Canyons* was based on a girl Shark had once known. I didn't really understand what that meant, though it was clear from the script that she must have hurt him deeply for him to imagine her murder as intensely as he had.

Eventually I steered the conversation toward film. Shark winced when I mentioned UCLA. It was obvious that wound was still healing. Then I revealed who my father was and, thank God, he didn't sneer. Instead he became bleak. "I don't care about movies anymore," he said. "I'm finished with that."

At that point I told him I'd read his script and for a moment I saw a look of real fear in his eyes. He was astonished when I explained that Elliot has retrieved the script from the trash in Venice and it had now gone all the way to Dad. For a second I thought he was going to be angry. Instead he laughed. "My God, that's funny, that's really funny. Our supposed masterpiece ends up going to Sam Schlockmann! Tom would fucking shit!"

Well, that remark cut me. Shark saw that he'd been thoughtless and immediately apologized, then asked almost timidly, "So . . . what does he think of it?" I saw his naked longing for approval— even from someone he respected as little as Dad.

I was still hurt and angry though, and tempted to say, "He thinks it's shit, below even him. So there!" But I couldn't bare to hurt Shark when I sensed how badly, on so many different levels, he'd already been hurt.

"He's still reading it," I lied.

Shark said nothing.

"*I* like it," I said, "I think if it's done right it could be art."

Shark snorted. "Then you're blind. There's a reason that script ended up in the trash."

Then he rolled away from me and I studied his tan back. God, I did want him that first afternoon.

Drake Brewster

I'd just about had it with Shark even before his fucking hippie friends came by. There was this little bitch in the big house, this old Nazi's niece, who used to wriggle her ass up the driveway after tennis. One day I was watching her through the window and I rubbed my crotch and said to Shark, "Man, if I don't shoot soon I'm gonna go crazy. Come on, man. Let's nail that little snatch right now."

And Shark said, "Man, you're crazy."

And I said, "Shit. You won't even fuck a Nazi. Man, I'd sure hate to be fighting next to you in World War II."

Then he called me stupid again and I chased him into the bedroom and threw him on the floor. I pinned him down and said, "Man, I've got half a mind to cram my dick down your throat just on general principle."

At that he threw me and pinned *me* down and said, "Don't you ever fuck with me again or I'll kill you."

I nodded okay and tried to act scared, but inside I was secretly smiling. Thanks to me, this guy who'd started out as a fat sack of shit that could've turned into a homo or a loser was now a real no-bullshit man like me.

Then a few days later I found a newspaper ad section with a few rentals circled on it. Some friend, right? He's gonna move out and he doesn't even tell me. I was all set to call him on it the night his hippie friends came by.

Those pukes made my blood boil. When I came back from the gym that Sunday and saw that their shit was still there I wanted to kill. I was alone in the house fixing myself a protein drink when I saw that black-haired hippie bitch coming back from the beach.

Sue Schlockmann

As Shark and I reached the driveway he went over to check the mailbox and I continued on to the guest house, eager to take a shower. I guess Drake saw me coming and thought I was alone.

I came in through the kitchen and the second I saw him standing there in his gym shorts I sensed what was going to happen. I tried to pass him and he grabbed me and forced me back against the sink. I fought him, but he was stronger, and he was just about to do it when Shark came in.

Drake froze and looked at Shark. Shark appeared stunned. Then Drake said, "Get in line, bro. Sloppy seconds."

Drake laughed and for a second I thought: Oh my God, Shark isn't going to help me, it's some sort of male thing. And for what seemed an eternity Shark didn't move, even as Drake turned his attention back to me.

Drake was just about to do it when Shark finally grabbed him, saying "Drake, let her go."

The two of them went at it, a grunting red-faced struggle, until both of them hit the floor. Then Drake got on top of Shark, pinning him down on his stomach. Drake's thing was still out, you know, as he abruptly tore down Shark's cut-offs, exposing Shark's buttocks. "Okay then," Drake said, "in that case I'll give it to *you*."

I tried to pull Drake off of Shark but he knocked me away. Then—thank God—Elliot and Woody barreled into the room and stopped Drake before he actually managed to do it to Shark. They pulled Drake to his feet, pinning his arms behind his back. By then he was like an animal—I'll never forget that insane red face—and both he and Shark were pouring sweat.

Shark got up, and refastened his cut-offs as best he could. Breathing hard he said to Elliot and Woody, "Let him go."

They released Drake, assuming as I did that the violence was over. But with a sudden ferocity that caught us all off-guard Shark laid into Drake, slugging him in the stomach and face again and again in a total rage, until Elliot and Woody managed to restrain him. By the time they did Drake was a bloody-faced mess beaten back into the corner.

Woody Hazzard

It was a bad scene. Shark really wasted Drake. If we hadn't stopped him I'm sure he would've literally killed Drake.

Elliot Bernstein

Sue was emotionally devastated. I took her outside while Shark packed his things, and there on the patio I said something incredibly stupid.

"Didn't you realize this might provoke him?" I said, indicating the sheer and skimpy bikini she was wearing. I'd never say anything like that now. But in those days people didn't really know what rape was.

"You asshole," she said, and pulled away from me.

Woody Hazzard

I helped Shark take his stuff out to the car. No way was he gonna stay there after what had happened. Drake was in the bathroom, mopping the blood off his face as Shark picked up a few final things.

"Hey, Shark," Drake called in this weirdly casual voice as if nothing that serious had happened. "Hey, Shark, can you run down to the drugstore? Looks like we're all out of mercurochrome, bro."

Shark didn't answer, but I remember there was almost a look of sadness on his face. Then he said, almost gently—too gently, I think, for Drake to hear, "Hey Drake. Thanks for . . ." But his voice trailed off, and then he snorted and said to me, "Fuck it. Let's go." And we left.

7 / Sex Kill à Go-Go (1968–1969)

Elliot Bernstein

Sue spent the entire drive down to L.A. talking film with Shark. Her attitude was so unctuously idolatrous you might have thought Shark was some sort of teenage Ingmar Bergman. Clearly, she was trying to make me jealous, but I refused to play that stupid game.

When we reached L.A. we dropped Shark off at Neal Ridges's place in Santa Monica. Then Sue—now in a cunty mood—and Woody and I met up with the Dilday twins at the Tropicana Motel in Hollywood. The first day in the recording studio Sue and I blew up at each other, and she ran home to mommy and daddy in Beverly Hills.

Sue Schlockmann

I hated being at home again back in my stupid Princess Anderson bedroom. I hated that kitsch Greco-Roman house on a street behind the Beverly Hills Hotel where all the houses were kitsch something. I moped and sulked, angry at Elliot, my Dad mad at me since by then he knew I'd screwed up at Berkeley.

Then one day Shark called. "I want my script back," he said adamantly. "I want it back right now."

I called Dad right away at the studio. And after checking around he called back and said someone had given the script to Nigel Blore.

Sam Schlockmann

Nigel Blore had run into trouble after being a British boy wonder. He'd made *The Hard Life* in '60, which wasn't too bad. Black and white, British losers, you know the kind of picture. Good camera work but downbeat—I skipped the last reel. I don't like to be de-

111

pressed, I don't think audiences do either. Maybe that's why his other movies went down the toilet, including *Method to Her Modness*—lousy title—which he shot for a bundle in Spain in '67. After that he couldn't get arrested—till I gave him a break since he was willing to work for scale.

Neal Ridges

Shark had been staying at my place a few days when he announced as I came in one afternoon, "Guess what? Nigel Blore wants to direct my screenplay."

Shark's tone was so neutral I wasn't sure how to respond. Was this good news or bad? Nigel Blore had been something of an auteur in the early sixties. But after *Method to Her Modness* he was considered washed-up.

"So how do you feel about it?" I asked Shark.

He shrugged and laughed. "It's Writer Guild scale." Which in those days was something like six thousand dollars for a low-budget script.

Sue Schlockmann

Nigel Blore was totally wrong for the project. He'd been good in his own "kitchen sink" element. But *Method to Her Modness* was just nauseating drivel, a complete misinterpretation of what the sixties were all about. It was so wretched it made *Myra Breckinridge* look like a film by Satyajit Ray.

As soon as I realized Dad was actually going to buy the script for Nigel I called Shark and said, "You've got to meet me at the beach house at once," meaning Dad's house on the Gold Coast in Santa Monica, which was closed up then. Shark and I could meet there and talk without anyone knowing.

Elliot Bernstein

I felt bad about my fight with Sue and called her one afternoon at her parents'. "Oh, she just left," the Schlockmanns' black maid told me. "She's going to the beach house, Mister Bernstein. You know where that is?"

Sue Schlockmann

Shark and I entered the beach house living room and I opened the drapes, bathing the room in bright sunlight. The Gold Coast is to my mind *the* choice beach in L.A., a broad vista of pure white sand and blue sea without the fires and slides and distance of Malibu. And what a history. Selznick, Thalberg and all the other giants—they'd all had houses there. John Kennedy had conducted his trysts with Marilyn at the Lawford house a few doors down. It was funny, but even in those first few minutes with Shark in that house I had a premonition we were going to live together there.

"Look, I know you're a genius," I told him. "It's something I sense intuitively, as well as a rational judgment I make on the hard evidence of your screenplay, and what I've heard about *Pillow Fuck*, your legendary student film. You went to bat for me in Santa Barbara, Shark. If you want me to I'll go to bat for you now with Dad. This may be your only chance. *You* should direct *Canyons*. My gut instinct tells me that this could be your *Breathless*, if not your *Citizen Kane*."

Shark said nothing for a long time. His back was to the window and the glare was so bright his expression was hidden in shadow. When at last he spoke he sounded old, old and scarred, even though at the time he was just nineteen. "I'll never direct another film," he said.

"Don't be foolish," I said. "Just because you had one bad experience—"

"You don't understand," he interrupted.

"Oh, yes I do," I said. "You're chicken—"

"Shut up," he said.

"No, I won't shut up," I replied. "I'll never shut up. I'm going to go on believing in you even if you don't quite believe in yourself. I know what happened with Jean-Claude Citroen—"

At that he grabbed my face—that is, he squeezed my cheeks between his thumb and fingers so that my mouth resembled that of a fish.

"This is not a subject I care to discuss with you," he said.

Our eyes met. Then he kissed my fish mouth, and soon we were stuck together like two ravenous kissing fish. Inexorably, we drifted to the sofa. We were making love there when Elliot walked in.

Elliot Bernstein

I said nothing to either of them. What could I say? I simply turned and walked out.

A few hours later I felt a terrible burning rage, which I quickly suppressed. Jealousy was considered very uncool in those days. We should all love one another without being possessive, it was felt. People changed partners in the dance of life. I see now what damage I did to myself by swallowing the fury I felt toward both of them, but in those days I was beatific whatever the cost.

Once our album was finished we decided to relocate in L.A. And so I would visit Shark and Sue—once a lover, but now a "dear friend"—after Shark moved into the beach house with her.

Sue Schlockmann

For a long time my parents weren't aware that Shark was living in the beach house with me. They thought I was there by myself, trying to "get my head together." My mother was fairly conventional about morality—which is to say she just didn't want to know. And Dad wouldn't have thought much of my living with Shark, especially after their disastrous first meeting.

Shark went to see Dad and Nigel Blore at the studio right after Dad bought the script, since both he and Nigel felt it needed some minor revision. Sadly, the moment when I might have convinced Dad to let Shark direct the script seemed to have passed. Given Shark's pained reaction to that possibility, I hadn't mentioned it to him again. For as fine as *Canyons* was, I had no doubt his mind would soon be fired with an even greater directorial vision.

The meeting with Dad and Nigel was supposed to be a positive, celebratory, "let's make a movie" sort of thing. But the minute Shark stepped into Dad's office he took a breath of Dad's cigar smoke and felt sick to his stomach. Dad was still in that terrible place in Palms with the noisy window air-conditioners. Even though the room was frigid, Shark said, the cigar smoke was just hanging in the air.

As Dad began to talk Shark said he almost laughed, because here was this "living three-dimensional cliché of the ultimate sleazebag Hollywood producer." (That designation stung me, though sadly I knew in my heart it was true.) Then Nigel began gushing effusively, "You're a gifted writer, it's an astonishing story, a fantastic script," when Shark stood abruptly with a snide, denigrating, "This is a joke," and walked out.

Dad was furious. "Who does he think he is? That arrogant punk. He's a nobody, fuck him." He was ready to kill the project then and there.

But Nigel interceded, making excuses for Shark's behavior. "James Dean was like that, you know. The boy may be a genius. Rudeness goes with the territory."

So Dad, who was desperate for a hit and had no more confidence in his own instincts, said what the hell and went ahead with the film.

Elliot Bernstein

One day I stopped by the beach house and Shark and Sue were arguing. "You insulted my father," Sue said.

"That's impossible," Shark replied. "You can't insult an old hack like your dad."

"Then I guess you don't want this, do you?" Sue grabbed Shark's screenplay check from Regal Pictures and tore it up in front of him.

Shark saw red and smacked Sue across the face. I intervened on her behalf, and she screamed at me, "Elliot, stay out of it!"

So I said, "Okay, fuck you both," and left.

Shark called the next day and apologized, mentioning that Sue had got her father to authorize a new check.

It was about that time that an FBI agent came around to see Shark. He'd registered for the draft in Santa Barbara, but had neglected to inform the board of his change of address, and the G-man told him to report for a physical or else.

Woody Hazzard

Shark told me he didn't have sex with Sue, or jerk off or anything, for like two weeks before his physical, and when the day came he didn't wear any underwear, knowing full well that all the guys had to strip down to their underwear to go through the procedure. So there was Shark walking around with his folder totally naked. Then, he said, he used all his powers of concentration to imagine he was having excruciating sex with Kathy Petro so that he got this huge fuckin' hard-on, and the army doctors and everybody became totally disturbed. They put him in the line to see the shrink, and while he was standing there, without touching himself or anything, he like totally shot off all over the place, getting jiz on the guy in front of him in line.

Everybody went apeshit, and they figured Shark was gay, so they stamped him 4-F and sent him home.

Sue Schlockmann

At the time I believed Shark had avoided the draft because he had a "John Kennedy-like back problem," though I would have been for anything that kept him from being turned into cannon fodder for that obscene war.

Early 1969 proved to be a difficult period though. Shark was irritable and directionless with too much time on his hands. With the money from the screenplay he didn't have to work. So he read a lot—books on Zen Buddhism especially—and we made love a lot, with the exception of a two-week period when his back was bothering him, and went for long walks on the beach. But he was restless.

The sex was quite good, though he held back emotionally. In an odd way I think that only increased my love for him. There was still such a sense that he'd been hurt so badly—by this Kathy person. And yet Shark was so beautiful in those days, with such an untapped depth of tenderness, that I was certain in time he would surely see how much I loved him and let down his guard and love me.

Once I hinted at the real possibility that if *Canyons* did well Dad might let Shark direct his next script, and Shark flared. "Fuck Hollywood," he said. "I don't care about any of that. There are other things in life beside movies, you know."

But one day I noticed that along with *The Three Pillars of Zen* he was also reading a paperback copy of *Memo from David O. Selznick*.

I was getting restless myself. As good as the sex was it began to seem like that was all Shark ever wanted to do. So in March I went to work as Dad's story editor, though the job was something of a joke. By the time a script reached Regal it was falling out of its binder, was generally wretched, and often genuinely psychopathic. Stories by geeks in Texas about women eaten alive by armadillos and the like. Very depressing.

Which I suppose was why I had such high hopes for *Canyons*. If Nigel Blore could relocate his pure artistic flame, the film might be another *Bonnie and Clyde*. Violent to be sure, but esthetically so.

Canyons rolled in April of '69. At the end of the first week I attended the dailies and actually threw up in the screening room.

Woody Hazzard

I was visiting Shark at the beach house when Sue flew in and said, "My God, I'm sick. Nigel Blore is ruining your script."

Shark snorted cynically, as if to say: So what did you expect?

I asked Sue what she meant and she said she was sick to her stomach in the screening room. "Why?" I said. "Because of the violence?"

"No," she said. "Because it's *Method to Her Modness* all over again."

Then she described how Blore was turning it into a cheesy psychedelic "art" movie, adding a bunch of disconnected visual stuff that wasn't in the script. For example, in the scene where the murders were taking place, instead of showing the violence he'd cut to a shot of a go-go dancing dwarf with this zoom going in and out, in and out real fast—which was the part that had made Sue sick.

"Let me talk to Dad," she said to Shark. "It may not be too late." Meaning that Shark might still be able to replace Nigel as the director.

But Shark stared out at the ocean and said, "Somebody else wrote that script, I didn't. I don't know what it's about anymore, nor do I care." Then he turned and looked at Sue and said in a cold, scary voice, "Both the losers who wrote that script are dead."

Sue Schlockmann

I couldn't bare to attend the dailies again, but it wasn't really necessary because word soon spread that *Canyons*, even by Regal standards, was a dog. Dad could have stopped the production but he didn't. He'd come back from the dailies shaking his head and tell me, "It's not even shit." Which translated meant it was arty as opposed to trashy—perhaps *that* was why he didn't pull the plug. "I don't know, is this what the kids want now?" he'd say with a terrible lost expression.

And Nigel *was* staying on schedule. He was shooting what was in the script, it was just that he was shooting so much more. But he was working so fast, and in a sense so ingeniously, that the film was still holding to its budget. I suppose from Nigel's point of view it was his last chance to make what he considered great art and as a result he was remorselessly brutal with the cast and crew and by all accounts completely possessed.

Nigel had made a number of seemingly minor adjustments to the script, many of which would eventually prove to be uncannily resonant choices indeed—though the most horrifying, thank God, had been avoided. Just prior to principle photography, Nigel had come up with the brilliant idea of making Daisy Withers, who'd been cast as the young blonde wife, pregnant. "It'll jack up the jeopardy," Nigel had enthused. "Look at *Rosemary's Baby*."

Dad, I'm sorry to say, had been on the verge of agreeing, grateful I suppose that Nigel was still making concessions to such outmoded conventions as jeopardy and suspense, but I'd argued against it in the only terms Dad would understand. "If you make Daisy pregnant she'll lose her sex appeal. You don't want that, do you?" The idea was dropped.

The final week of shooting was on location at a house in Coldwater Canyon, and that was where the shit finally hit the fan.

Sam Schlockmann

It's bad when you can't trust your instincts. I'd look at Nigel's rushes and think, this shit makes me sick. But if it's what the kids want . . .

Then he's shooting the murders up in Coldwater Canyon and he says: I wanna do the pigs. What pigs, Nigel? I say. There are no pigs in the script. Well, by now I'm used to that. He's done second unit go-go dancing dwarves, hunchbacked ballerinas, pinheaded debutantes—what he likes to call "surrealism." Fine. But pigs? I get a bad feeling. What do you mean, Nigel? He wants these pigs to fly across the swimming pool. He wants real pigs with wings attached. What are you saying, Nigel? You want a matte shot? No, he says. Live. I say how, Nigel? He says we run a wire through the pigs' mouths and out their assholes, then slide 'em down the wire across the pool. I say how do you keep 'em upright? He says we weight down their feet. I say Nigel that sounds painful for the pigs, there's gonna be a lot of squealing. He says I know, that's what I want. I say Nigel it sounds cruel. He says it's art and besides we'll get it in one take, we've got no choice. Why's that? I say. Because I'm gonna put a charge on each pig, he says, and when they reach the far side of the pool I'm gonna blow 'em up.

You're a sick man, Nigel, I told him. Go home, you're off the picture.

Sue Schlockmann

An hour after Dad fired him over the phone we learned that Nigel was still shooting, claiming that contractually Dad *couldn't* fire him. So we drove up to the location on a remote cul-de-sac in Coldwater Canyon, Dad primed for a confrontation.

When Dad picked up a megaphone and told the crew it was over Nigel went berserk. He called Dad every name in the book and threatened him with a Directors' Guild suit as the cast and crew stood around smirking. By then they all hated Nigel and thought he was completely insane.

Finally Nigel stormed off and got into his Jaguar, and at first it wouldn't start. He sat there pounding the wheel, pouring sweat, and you couldn't help but feel sorry for him. At last the car started. "You haven't heard the last of me," he yelled at Dad and tore out.

Not more than a minute later we heard a terrible crash.

Elliot Bernstein

I was smoking dope with Shark at the beach house when Sue came in and said, "Nigel Blore is dead. He had a head-on collision in Coldwater Canyon."

Shark was stunned and silent as Sue explained that Sam had been forced to fire Nigel, and that Nigel's devastation over that event had doubtless been a factor in his death.

Finally Shark said, "What's going to happen to the film?"

"I suppose Dad's going to write if off," Sue said bleakly. "It's crap. Unsavable. Which is a pity." She looked at Shark. "In the right hands it might have really been something."

I think Shark waited a day or two before he went to see Sam Schlockmann.

Minnie Schlockmann

Sam felt so bad about Nigel Blore's death. "I should've canned him sooner," he said sadly. Then he got mad and said, "Why did I hire him in the first place? That goddamn limey jerk."

Then he fell into a deep depression. "I'm too old for this business, Minnie. It's a kids' business now. Maybe it's time to bail out."

He was still depressed when Shark came to the door that Sunday afternoon. Shark was wearing a neatly starched white shirt and tie and was very polite and pleasant. "Good afternoon, Mrs. Schlockmann. Do you suppose I could have a word with your husband?"

Well, I knew Sam's first meeting with Shark had not been good. But Shark was so charming I said, "Yes, why don't you come in. Sam's out on the patio."

I watched from the window as Shark went out to Sam, who did not look happy to see him at all. They began talking. I was too far away to hear what was said, but in a little while Sam's scowl gave way to a smile. Then he laughed at something Shark said and saw me in the window. "Minnie," he called. "Why don't you bring our guest some wine?"

Sue Schlockmann

It was nearly midnight when Shark came in drunk, and I was mad as blazes. I'd cooked a meal that I'd had to throw out, and to be honest at that point I was insanely possessive and suspicious. "How was she?" I said.

"I was with your father," Shark said, and I was incredulous.

It turned out they'd been together since one that afternoon, getting drunk, then driving down to the studio where they looked at all the rushes of the film.

"I'm going to save the picture," Shark said. Then he went into the bathroom and threw up because he and Dad had been drinking Manischevitz all day, and Shark could never take sweet wine.

Woody Hazzard

"I jacked him off shamelessly, man," Shark told me a few days after Sam put him in charge of cutting the picture. "I had to be careful not to go too far. If I'd said I thought *Stews on Wheels* was art he would've known I was stroking him. So I used the veiled sexual approach. Regal Pictures represents 'rugged, masculine filmmaking, hard, assertive action pictures with a tough no-bullshit forward thrust.' The stupid old fart ate it with a spoon."

"Do you really think you can save the picture?" I asked Shark. And suddenly he quit gloating, like he was afraid he'd revealed too much. He turned real sober and serious and said, "Yes, I think so, Woody. And I believe passionately that Black Lights' music is going to be a major factor in my attempt to shape this film into something resembling art."

By that time, you see, our album had stiffed and our label was talking of dropping us. So we were only too willing to let Regal have a bunch of our songs for use in the film.

Sue Schlockmann

I was thrilled at first. If anyone could restore the film to its original concept, surely it was Shark. Amid all the artsy dreck the performances were not at all bad. Daisy Withers was especially convincing. Her protracted running-through-the-house-from-the-killers routine could have degenerated into giddy camp histrionics so easily. But Daisy made you absolutely believe her terror, as she ducked through door after door, hiding in the vestibule, then doubling back around as the knife-wielding hippie girls inexorably closed in. Sadly, it was Daisy's last movie role. Though I'm sure she didn't know it yet, botched silicone implants had resulted in malignant tumors in both of her breasts. Rather than face the double mastectomy she felt would end her career she took a lethal overdose of pills in 1970, allegedly inspired by the example of the starlet-with-breast-cancer in Jacqueline Suzann's *Valley of the Dolls*, a paperback copy of which was found beside her body.

Playing opposite Daisy, Reggie Bingum was quite good as Clay, the fashionable young designer who, still in love with Daisy's character, pays her a visit that hot summer night when he knows her auteur husband is away, and ends up paying the ultimate price for his obsession. Linda Carlisle was perfect as Andrea Grey, the British tea heiress, who is stabbed again and again on the lawn. All of the performances were actually quite naturalistic and believable. I was convinced that once Shark cut away the fat we might yet have a spare and serious crime drama in the realistic vein of *In Cold Blood*.

But I began to worry when he wouldn't let me see what he was doing. He was practically living at the studio, working with the editors till all hours of the night, and he made it quite clear that the editing room was "off-limits." I tried to attribute this attitude to nerves, or his abhorrence of criticism. Then too I knew he had begun taking speed to stave off his fatigue, and that was certainly a factor in his irritability.

Then one afternoon I heard he was "shooting some inserts" on one of the soundstages. I was puzzled since he'd said nothing about it, so I went over to see what was going on. I arrived just in time to see an extremely realistic miniskirted dummy being gutted. A knife would go in and what I presume were cow's intestines would spill out on the floor. "No, no, no, *cut*," Shark yelled, without seeing me there. "I don't believe how *fake* that looked! Come on, people, this isn't a comedy! Let's try it again."

I ran from the soundstage in shock and disgust, with no more illusions about what sort of film it was going to be.

Sam Schlockmann

I asked Shark to pick up some gore because Nigel had been too squeamish. Gore's funny. I don't know what it is, but a lot of guys get carried away, and Shark definitely did. Even after the trims I knew we'd get an X. But in '69 an X wasn't the kiss of death it is today.

Sue Schlockmann

"It's done," Shark announced as he came in one night, as if he had committed some terrible but inevitable and necessary crime. He dropped on the bed, exhausted. "Your dad likes my new title too," he said.

"What new title?"

"*Sex Kill à Go-Go*," he said, and laughed a terrible, bitter laugh.

I went to the studio screening a few days later, but walked out ten minutes into the film.

Elliot Bernstein

We let Shark use our music in the film because he led us to believe it was going to be an artistic statement sort of film. Violent, but toward a lofty end, like an Arthur Penn film or something.

So we were angry when we saw what a piece of shit it was. By then it was too late to get our music back, and we didn't really even say that much to Shark because at the time we believed he didn't really know how bad the film was. But of course he knew. He had coldly and deliberately turned the film into the garish trash Sam wanted.

Sam Schlockmann

I knew we had a winner when the exhibitors went gaga, especially the boys from the South. "This is the sickest piece of shit I've ever seen," one of 'em said. Which translated meant: Big bucks.

We opened wide in the last week of August with no press screenings. What do you think, I'm stupid? By the time the critics organized a lynch mob we would have cleaned up and blown town. Not that your typical drive-in redneck pays much attention to Vincent Canby.

I smelled success. The timing was right for this kind of picture. I knew the first weekend would be a killer. I had no way of knowing how true that would be in more ways than one.

Sue Schlockmann

The print ads were revolting. A chic couple strung from the beams of a living room ceiling, the woman's breasts about to pop from her blouse as a crazed bearded hippie threatens to cut off her buttons with a Bowie knife. And the tag: "To their friends they were rich, young, and beautiful. To their killers they were just a bunch of pigs."

I told Shark I thought it was tasteless and sick.

"Gee, I'm sorry you feel that way," he said. "Since I'm the one who thought it up."

"I hope you know what you're doing to yourself," I said. But I knew I was on precarious ground. Who was I, after all, to accuse Shark of whoring himself when my entire life-style was funded from the proceeds of the biggest whore in town.

Secretly though I was beginning to wonder if his fabled UCLA student film had really been as great as people said. Perhaps he had less in common with Orson Welles than he did with Russ Meyer.

Still, I loved him—though I see now how much that had to do with sex. He'd been too tired to make love during the editing period. But with the film in the can we resumed with a vengeance. He was good. To be blunt he knew how to use his hands and his mouth. And in those days I tended to romanticize all that.

Sam Schlockmann

We opened on a Wednesday, and the film left the gate like somebody'd fired a blowtorch up its ass. Even the matinees were packed, and it just kept building. There were lines around the block at the walk-ins, and the drive-ins were packed. It was the biggest opening we'd ever had. Whether it was the ads, or the word-of-mouth or what, I don't know. You can drive yourself nuts trying to figure these things. I know, 'cause I spent the next ten years doing just that.

Sue Schlockmann

Shark was elated when the film began breaking records. He was still resting at the beach house, but was constantly on the phone to Dad. I was happy for him, and of course for Dad too. I was just sorry their success had to come from such an odious and amoral piece of artless crud.

By Friday night Shark was actually kind of manic, feeling giddily omnipotent. "Let us remember this night, Sue," he said, "as the first major victory on the road to my conquest of Hollywood. This is my Beer Hall Putsch!"

I was startled by the Nazi reference, despite the ironic manner in which he'd made it. I'm quite sure Shark didn't realize at the time, anymore than I did, that Hitler's Beer Hall Putsch had actually failed.

I suppose there are peak sexual moments in every life, and who knows why they occur when they do. But that Friday night with Shark was certainly one of mine. I won't be pornographic. Even now I can't bring myself to cheapen that experience by describing it in detail. I will say only that I did not fall asleep until the dawn's first light, and by then I was dreamily exhausted and satisfied as I had never been before.

I woke up in the early afternoon, the bed empty beside me. I heard Shark on the phone in the other room, though I couldn't make out what he was saying. Presently he came back into the bedroom, a sun-drenched Greek god, though I could have sworn he looked ill.

"Who died?" I said as a joke.

And Shark smiled and came down the bed, taking me in his arms. I'll never forget how I felt that dazingly hot August afternoon as he kissed me so sweetly and said, at long last, the words I so wanted to hear.

"I love you, Sue. It scares me to say it because as you've undoubtedly deduced my heart has been broken severely in the past. But I can't play it safe any longer. I love you, and I want to marry you, Sue."

We left for Mexico late that afternoon.

Elliot Bernstein

Subconsciously, I don't think I ever forgave Shark for marrying Sue that weekend in what amounted to a crass and desperate act of self-preservation.

Sue Schlockmann

We were married in Ensenada by a seedy little man with extremely bad teeth and a linty blue suit. We were pretty looped on margaritas by the time the ceremony took place, both of us weaving and slurring our vows. We thought it was quite hilarious at the time. In retrospect it was strictly F. Scott and Zelda—which is to say, sad.

The motel was even sadder, though that sequence too seemed delightfully madcap at the time. We drank toasts to the cockroaches and laughed hysterically when, as we made love, the bed collapsed. Several times I voiced a desire to call my parents and break the news. But Shark would always laugh and pull me from the door back to the bed.

Minnie Schlockmann

From Saturday till Monday we heard absolutely nothing, and we were worried sick. It's hard to imagine now how terrified everyone was that weekend. That murders like that could occur right there in Beverly Hills!

Sue Schlockmann

We got back to the beach house in Santa Monica around eleven Monday morning. We hadn't seen any newspapers or heard the news on the radio—Shark made sure we didn't, I see now. When I saw Elliot's Renault and Woody's VW parked at the house I sensed that something odd was going on.

Elliot and Woody came running out to meet us as we parked, both saying they'd been afraid something might have happened to us. At first I didn't understand what was clearly a paranoid overreaction. Then Woody described what had happened Friday night at Sharon Tate's.

Elliot Bernstein

I felt gut-punched when Shark mentioned that he and Sue had got married. I was stunned because I knew in my heart I still loved her. I said very little as Woody told them about the Cielo Drive murders. Later I would remember that although Shark acted astonished, as if he was hearing about the killings for the first time, his performance was not quite convincing.

Sue Schlockmann

As Woody described the Tate murders detail by detail I began to feel as if I were peaking on bad acid. Because, you know, the parallels between what happened on Cielo Drive and the plot of *Sex Kill à Go-Go* were just too numerous to mention. The isolated house in the canyon, the beautiful young blonde woman married to the foreign director—French originally, modeled on Jean-Claude Citroen, though fearing that similarity was too close, Shark had made the director and his visiting friends, dear God, Polish instead.

And of course there were hippie killers in the movie—even some of their nicknames proved similar to the Manson family members who were arrested several month later. The degree of prescience was really quite terrifying. You couldn't avoid the thought that the movie had in some bizarre mystical way actually *caused* the murders. As crazy as that sounds now, it made perfect sense in the summer of 1969 that art, or even trash, could affect real life.

Shark got right on the phone to Dad. It didn't take long to confirm that in fact Dad had done what he had no choice but to do.

Sam Schlockmann

It broke my heart to pull the film. But it was a matter of taste and pressure from the community. It was like you'd made a movie about a fictitious U.S. president who got bumped off in Dallas and opened wide on November 20th of 1963.

I have to admit when I read about the Tate girl and her friends up there and saw the similarities, it even spooked me. I turned to Minnie and said, "You know, for the first time in my life I feel unclean." Then I picked up the phone and said, "Yank it."

Woody Hazzard

Shark told me years later that he'd heard about the Tate murders early Saturday morning, and that the only reason he married Sue was because he thought Sam might freak out and dump him. Shark said he saw right away all the similarities between the film and what had happened, and knew Sam would have to pull it, and figured Sam's great comeback success was going to turn into a "terrible, odious debacle," and his first reaction would be to blame it all on Shark.

Knowing what a piece of shit the film was, Shark had made sure his name was nowhere near it, even using a pseudonym for the shared screenplay credit. "But if Sam decided to make me the scapegoat and went public about my true role in *Sex Kill*," Shark said, "I knew it could contaminate me and destroy my career when it had just barely begun."

Shark felt that if he was married to Sue, Sam would be compelled to temper his anger.

He also knew Sam had a bad heart. "Once Sam checked out, his studio and fortune would be effectively mine, since everything would go to Minnie and Sue, and I had both of them wrapped around my finger."

Sam Schlockmann

I didn't blame Shark for what happened. Far from it. It was his instinct, I felt, his marketing genius, that had taken us as far as we'd gone.

Once the Mansons were arrested I began to see the whole matter in a much clearer light. It was, after all, just a freak coincidence. Say you make a movie that has a car crash, then somebody leaves the theater and crashes their car. Do you blame the movie? It was proved eventually that none of the Mansons had seen *Sex Kill à Go-Go*. I would bet good money they never even saw the ad.

I figured this out eventually, but the first few days after I pulled the picture I was extremely depressed. I was low when Shark and Sue came by the house and told us they'd been married in Mexico. Minnie started bawling, but I smiled cause I saw the dark clouds lifting. I had warm feelings for Shark, you see. I felt like we'd built this beautiful ship, the Titanic maybe, that had struck an iceberg on its maiden voyage. But we could build another ship. And another.

"Welcome to the family," I said, and we all drank a toast. Then I gave my new son-in-law his first studio deal.

8 / No Fat Chicks (1969–1972)

Paige Petro

I suppose the early seventies were really Kathy's time, weren't they, if we truly believe we're only young once. Kathy was surely at her best in those years, and America was thirsting for the sunny goodness she personified—especially after the dark excesses of the previous decade.

Kathy Petro

The early seventies were really my time, I guess, if as Mom likes to say you're only young once. I certainly had fun, I'll say that. No matter what happened, or what strange things I saw—for much of the world is sadly not at all like Southern California—nothing ever really seemed to spoil my mood for long.

Once in Italy, in some little village near Naples, Jean-Claude made me look at this deformed person in a cardboard box. It was just this little creature with no arms or legs and a funny-shaped head. At first I thought it was a strange doll or something. Then it moved and I said to Jean-Claude, "Oh my God, I'm going to be ill."

And Jean-Claude said, "This is what happens when your father's chemicals affect the unborn."

But I just felt like he'd deliberately polluted my mind. "Look, Jean-Claude," I said. "You can't blame *Daddy* for *that!*"

I saw Jean-Claude for almost two years, but it was very off and on, because I was having too much fun to be tied down to any one man. I considered modeling fun at the time, even though the hours could be long, and boy, did I get tired standing on my feet! But everybody was always so nice to me, I still don't know exactly why. Except in those days I tried to be nice to everyone, whether they

127

were a famous movie star or just a simple Spanish peasant. People were just people as far as I was concerned.

I knew Jean-Claude was in love with me. And I admired his creative genius, but he was just too old to take seriously. I inspired him though, he told me that in so many words, and he was just always pursuing me. I'd have sex with him every so often. But in those days I found it hard to concentrate on sex with anybody. I can't explain it, but right in the middle of sex I'd always start thinking of something else, like: Oh, I should do my nails tonight. Or I'd think of a funny scene in a movie and start to laugh. Or I'd think of some song I liked and start to hum it. I don't know, I didn't dislike sex, but I just couldn't keep my attention focused on it. Mostly my feeling was: Let's get it over with so we can go out.

I never really mentioned Shark to Jean-Claude because it was something I just didn't like to think about. Those years were blessedly Shark-free. The present was so full, the past seldom crossed my mind. And Jean-Claude never told me about humiliating Shark at UCLA because I guess it just wasn't that big a deal to him.

Jean-Claude could be really cruel if he sensed competition. I saw him savage several young men who idolized him and longed for his approval—as I learned later he'd once savaged Shark. Mostly I wouldn't understand what he was saying to them though, because it would either be in French, which I never really mastered, or even in English it would be this intellectual talk I could never make heads or tails of. But there was a rumor that one young man had gone out and jumped off a bridge right after Jean-Claude dressed him down.

Jean-Claude was always trying to start an argument with me. "Why must you be so American?" he'd say.

And I'd say, "Because, Jean-Claude, I *am* American."

Then he'd talk politics until I said, *"You're boring me!"*

Then he'd explode and start to leave. But he'd always stop as he reached the door and turn and say, "Oh Kathy! Only you can do this to me."

Then he'd come back and kiss me and we'd make love.

Then one day in Paris he attacked me for having my picture on *Time* magazine, which in a way was kind of the summit of my whole modeling career. It did make me nervous though, in a way I didn't totally understand. There was just this feeling that *Time* was for politicians and Gandhi or something. But the only reason I was on the cover was because I'd been on so many other covers in such a short period of time. Because I was "Super-Model Kathy Petro." So I was feeling a little insecure and out of my element, and Jean-Claude stormed in and went straight for my throat.

"Look at this!" he shouted, waving the magazine at me. "You've turned yourself into the ultimate product, a celebrity, you're ruined. With this you've created a psycho-visual loop which is bound to destroy you and give you cancer. You are made of paper now, a smile, a face and nothing more. Famous for being famous, the ultimate capitalist decadence."

He just went on and on until I was sobbing. Finally when he wouldn't stop I threw my hairbrush at him and cried, "Why are you doing this to me? This is how I make my living. Why are you doing this now?"

He wouldn't tell me. He just walked out the door and this time he didn't come back. Later I found out why he was so mad. He thought *he* was going to be on the cover of *Time* that week. But they'd bumped him at the last minute, deciding that it was the seventies and he was *out* and I was *in*.

Sue Schlockmann

I remember the period when Kathy Petro seemed to be on every magazine cover. I assumed that Shark saw those magazines as well, though we never discussed it. That is, he never mentioned her name, and despite my curiosity I never asked him directly about her.

Once as we lolled in bed after especially good sex I told him about a boy who'd broken my heart in junior high, thinking he might in turn tell me about his similar experience with Kathy. But when I was finished he just said, "Yeah, it's tough when shit like that happens," and got up to make some calls.

Then one afternoon he came into the den in a rage. "Why are we subscribing to this piece of shit?" he yelled, waving a copy of *Time* magazine. "These fucks are still apologizing for the war." He went on and on about *Time*'s politics, which was in itself odd since by that time Shark considered himself post-political.

Of course it was the issue with Kathy's picture on the cover.

Elliot Bernstein

Black Light disbanded in the spring of 1970 after the Dilday twins OD'ed on heroin one night in San Antonio right before a gig. Woody and I were jolted. We didn't even know they were using smack. But there they were, two blue bodies side by side on a ratty backstage sofa. I think that night Woody and I both knew beyond any doubt that the sixties were really over.

I came back to L.A. and cut my hair and thought about going to law school. But instead I went to work for Shark, and in so doing began my Hollywood career.

Sue Schlockmann

Dad gave Shark quite a generous deal. He got the biggest office at the Palms studio, except for Dad's. He had both the office and the Santa Monica beach house redone with authentic thirties rattan furniture, potted palms and ceiling fans—that tropical decor which at the time had not yet been done to death. We'd taken mescaline one night and watched a couple of von Sternberg movies in the basement screening room, *Morocco* and *Shanghai Express*, both of which gave Shark a series of "sustained mental orgasms"—I believe that's how his infatuation with the "exotic" began. Soon he was buying up old Hawaiian shirts, which he wore with baggy khakis and a short 1930s haircut a decade before Indiana Jones.

He also had a vintage soft drink machine installed in the beach house foyer, which he stocked with his beloved cream soda. He was virtually always nursing a bottle. That taste was always in his mouth. Even now when I smell or taste vanilla it triggers a sense-memory of Shark's kisses.

One weekend he procured some cocaine, which was just becoming fashionable then, and wrote the screenplay of *Tropics* in two days flat. On Monday morning he showed the script to Dad.

Sam Schlockmann

I could tell by page five there was no way we could do it. It was period for one thing, 1930s, and called for filming at a South Seas locale. Beyond that it was boring. Amelia Earhart and her navigator stranded on an island. All they do is talk. Should they or shouldn't they? Ten years pass, I'm not kidding, and they still haven't. Then finally they're about to. By now it's 1950. Just as they kiss there's a nuclear explosion. Turns out they're on an island right next to Bikini Atoll.

I told Shark, "Look, it's too expensive. It's at least two million, which is four times more than I've ever spent on a picture."

He said it would still turn a profit. So I said, "Okay, look, we'll talk about it later. Maybe if you can solve *Redneck Scum* . . ."

Elliot Bernstein

I went to work as Shark's story editor, which of course meant that I was working closely with Sue. Initially I thought I could handle it, but it soon became apparent I could not.

One night as Sue and I were working late coordinating the revisions on *Redneck Scum* I impulsively tried to kiss her.

"Don't ever do that again, Elliot," she said. "Or I'll have to tell Shark."

I should have quit then, I suppose. But she didn't tell Shark what had happened, and he promoted me to associate producer, which gave me my first hands-on filmmaking experience—a trial by fire with *Redneck Scum*.

Sue Schlockmann

Redneck Scum was one of Dad's pet projects. The script had been around for years, revised to the point of total incoherence. Every time Dad read a new version he'd shake his head and say, "I just don't understand why we can't get this thing to work. I know it's a money maker."

Shark completely rewrote the script in one night and Dad approved it the next day. That was the last script Shark ever personally wrote. Of course, he knew it was a piece of shit and wisely used a pseudonym.

Elliot Bernstein

We shot *Redneck Scum* in something like ten days on a ranch near Lancaster that was supposed to be the Mississippi delta. The lighting was so bad I don't think anyone could tell the difference. It was a *Baby Doll* rip-off, only extremely violent. Libidinous white trash girl kept prisoner in her bedroom by her cretinous father, gangraped by morons and bikers, everybody blown away at the end. It cleaned up though.

Sam was grateful but he still wouldn't do *Tropics*.

Sue Schlockmann

In late 1970 Shark bought a shelved Taiwanese film about a bunch of topless girls in a bamboo jungle prison. He had new dialogue dubbed in without bothering to get a translation, and for a while he wanted to call it *Caged Twats*.

Sam Schlockmann

Shark showed me the artwork with the title *Caged Twats* and I said, "Shark, let's go for a walk."

We walked around the lot and I told him, "Shark, we can't put a word like twat on a marquee, it's a dirty word."

He said, "But it's the seventies. All those barriers have broken down now."

I said, "I may be an old man, but twat's still a dirty word. It's dirty in the South. It's dirty here in L.A. I guarantee you, the *Times* will refuse the ad."

We went back to our offices. In a while Shark calls through the door: "Sam, take line two."

So I do and it's Charles Champlin, who in those days was the big movie critic at the *L.A. Times*. And Champlin says that Shark called him and the *Times* would have no objection to running an ad for *Caged Twats*, because twat is basically just a somewhat bawdy expression of American slang. So I say, "Thanks, Chuck." But after I hang up I call him right back. But the real Charles Champlin's voice is different and he doesn't know what the hell I'm talking about.

Elliot Bernstein

Sam finally agreed to call it *Slit Bamboo*, which was suggestive without being blatantly obscene. Shark always referred to the film as *Bamboo Slits*.

I don't know why I stayed at Regal. The situation was becoming incredibly painful. We were doing this utter shit, and the proximity to Sue was killing me. And then during the *Tract House She-Devils* period Sue began to put on weight—lots of it—and that was horrible to witness as well. She was still insisting that she and Shark were happy, but in her heart I'm sure she knew that their marriage was a lie.

And by then Shark was far from the friend I'd once known. Though I didn't want to see it he had already begun to put into practice the crazed crypto-Nietzschean philosophy he'd begun spouting in his letters from Santa Barbara. He was becoming a powerfreak, an egomaniac screamer, the epitome of everything we'd smirked at as crass and uptight a few years before.

And yet he did have a terrible charisma. He was honest, he didn't kid himself, he knew what we were doing was shit. And he still spoke with a kind of messianic idealism of someday making great films that would matter. Indeed, his commitment to that abstract goal seemed to grow in intensity the more corrupted he became. You wanted to believe he might yet do something astonishing. Perhaps a brutal jungle mentality was necessary to get the job done. Hollywood was not a tea party for poets after all. A true artist needed toughness and low cunning to survive, and Shark had plenty of both.

Sue Schlockmann

The sex stopped first, *then* I started eating—that was the chronology, I see that now. But at the time I let Shark confuse me into believing it was the other way around. As I became fat he'd say I was no longer attractive, and then in frustration I'd eat even more. He was always working late, months passed and he didn't even touch me. And I stuffed down my hurt and anger with pies and ice cream and cookies till I ballooned up to two-ten, which on my five-four frame was more than plump.

Shark's sarcasm was merciless. "Jesus, you're turning into a real sow, you know that?" he'd say when we were alone. Once he made an oinking sound as I was coming up the hall with several other people.

Then one day Shark and I and several others were walking to our cars in the studio parking lot. Shark had recently purchased a Porsche Cabriolet and when I saw the bumper sticker he'd placed on it I truly wanted to die. NO FAT CHICKS it said. The car had been there like that all day. Everyone on the lot must have seen that slogan and known it referred to me. Humiliated, I ran back to my office in tears.

Elliot Bernstein

One afternoon Sue broke down over lunch. It was just the two of us at a Mexican restaurant not far from the studio and she alone had ordered enough for two people. She'd just inhaled the enchiladas and was wolfing down a burrito when she began to sob uncontrollably. Everyone looked and I was embarrassed for her, so I paid and quickly got her outside.

In the parking lot she told me how severely Shark had been emotionally abusing her over the weight issue, and how they hadn't slept together for nearly six months. She was just abject and I'm afraid I didn't handle it very well. She finally grabbed me and said, "Oh, Elliot, why didn't I stay with you?"

You've got to understand she was just huge then, in a floral muumuu stained at the moment with burrito sauce, as was her chin. "Elliot," she pleaded cloyingly, and as much as I loved her—loved the Sue that was hiding somewhere beneath those layers of fat—I recoiled.

"Sue, please." I pried her fingers from my shirt.

She was silent as we drove back onto the lot, angered by my rejection. As I parked she got out without saying a word and vanished. A minute later I looked out the window and saw her screeching off in her Mercedes convertible.

I was worried but afraid to tell Shark what had happened. Perhaps it was nothing, she'd just gone for a drive. I tried to concentrate on the script I was reading, Neal Ridges's *Desert of the Daylight Kill*. Since Neal was a friend of Shark's from UCLA, I tried to be forgiving, but I found the script extremely irritating. Arty in the worst sense of the word. Stilted, laconic dialogue, an incredibly vacant, boring story of lovers on the run. Murders in the desert set to Verdi. In truth I was so subliminally worried about Sue I don't think I would have liked anything I read that afternoon.

Shark stepped in around three. "Where's Sue?"

"I don't know," I told him. "She left after lunch."

"She was probably still hungry," he said and laughed. Then he picked up Neal's script which he hadn't seen yet.

"It's got some serious problems," I told him. And he laughed as if he were sure it did, and took it back to his office.

An hour later he stepped back in with Neal's script in his hand. *"This,"* he said, "is our ticket out of here."

At first I thought he was joking. Then I saw that he wasn't. Then the phone rang and we found out that Sue had just tried to kill herself.

Sue Schlockmann

The dam just burst that day. For two years I'd been living on lies, telling myself that Shark really loved me, when I knew it wasn't true.

I drove back to the beach house in a black-out state. God only knows why I didn't crash on the freeway. Once inside the house I just went insane. I looked at all that rattan crap and knew he cared more about that *stuff* than he did about me. I started breaking furniture and tore his beloved *Blonde Venus* poster of Dietrich from its frame and ripped it to shreds.

I was crazy as I found myself in the garage. As fate would have it his Porsche was there that afternoon. He'd been about to leave that morning when he saw that one of the tires was flat, so he'd ridden in with me. The keys were still in the ignition. I wanted to destroy that car, but there wasn't a sledgehammer around. So in my crazy sorrow and rage I tried to destroy myself instead.

Elliot Bernstein

It wasn't Sue's time, thank God. One of the neighbors had noticed the exhaust coming out of the cracks around the garage door and called the police. By the time Shark and I arrived they were loading Sue into an ambulance, after having given her oxygen to save her.

Shark was furious. He began yelling at her. "You stupid pig. You fat, dumb twat. What the fuck were you trying to do?"

I'd had it. "Shark, shut your goddamn mouth," I said, pulling him from the ambulance. He swung and hit me, splitting my lip.

He glared at me, ready to strike again, and I had a true moment of clarity, finally admitting to myself what I'd denied for far too long. He didn't give a shit about Sue. Or me either. Or anybody. If this was Hollywood, then fuck it. Life was too short.

I stood there by the garage, still trembling with adrenaline, as the ambulance took Sue away. Shark had gone in by then, and I heard him explode anew as he discovered the damage in the house. As I turned to leave I saw for the first time the NO FAT CHICKS bumper sticker on his Porsche.

"My God, you fucking animal," I thought out loud. "You drove her to it."

Minnie Schlockmann

Sam and I were about to step into Sue's hospital room when Shark came dashing up the hall and said, "Please. Let me see her first."

Sue Schlockmann

Shark kneeled at my bedside and wept against my hand. "I'm so sorry, baby, I love you so much. That's why I got mad. I wouldn't get mad like that if I didn't love you. Oh my God, I almost lost you."

He was very convincing. Shark was nothing if not a good actor. I started crying too.

Then my parents came in. I was so embarrassed about what I'd done.

Sam Schlockmann

We were all upset. Shark drew Minnie and me aside in the hospital hallway and told us Sue had done some damage to her mind with drugs back in her Berkeley days. He said she'd taken some LSD and drugs like that, which I'd always suspected, knowing that a lot of kids did that then. Shark explained that she'd had flashbacks and episodes of depression, but they would pass if she got the right care.

Minnie and I were upset. We wanted to believe Shark when he said he'd take care of our daughter. He told us how much he loved her, and that he knew a doctor who could help her emotionally and at the same time help her deal with her weight. Shark walked us to our car and we felt reassured.

He could talk a good line.

9/ **White Desert** (1972–1973)

Sue Schlockmann

Shark sent me to see Dr. Rinker, a psychiatrist on Bedford Drive. He was about sixty and very distinguished-looking, and I'd heard nothing bad about him at the time. I just poured my heart out to him and he was very compassionate. Then he wrote a prescription, saying it would help me lose weight. It was for Desoxyn, which of course I knew was speed. But I'd never really taken much speed and thought I could handle it. How I deluded myself, repressing the crushing insights that had precipitated my suicide attempt, believing yet again that if I simply lost weight my dream marriage might somehow be saved.

Well, I lost weight all right. But I also lost my mind.

Elliot Bernstein

I left a message with Shark's service, saying I was quitting. I didn't want to talk to him ever again. Then I went in on a Sunday to clean out my desk. Apparently the guard called Shark and told him I was there, because on my way out Shark and Sue pulled up in his Porsche. I couldn't help noticing that the NO FAT CHICKS bumper sticker had been hastily removed.

Shark begged me to stay, repeating that Neal's script, which he'd renamed *White Desert*, was going to be our ticket out of exploitation-land. He'd convinced Sue of this as well. "El, don't give up right before the miracle," she said.

Well, I was dumbfounded. I see now they were both into heavy denial, trying to pretend that their personal problems were somehow the result of the kind of dispiriting crap we were churning out. And I suppose I was still naive enough to believe in the redemptive power of art. For whatever reason, I stayed.

And things were better for a while. Shark got the green light from Sam to produce *White Desert*, and there was a tremendous surge of energy and enthusiasm, especially from Sue. She began to shed the pounds, so consumed with *White Desert* that food no longer mattered. I knew she was speeding, of course. Once her prescription ran out and she went right through the ceiling, screeching into the phone to the nurse at her Beverly Hills doctor's office. "You tell that fucking asshole I need a refill and I need it now!"

Neal Ridges

I was deeply ambivalent about Shark buying my screenplay. On the one hand I was just starting out so any sale at all was a positive step. But Regal Pictures—I mean, it was just one rung above writing for TV. When Shark told me he had big plans to make it a "breakthrough film" I was heartened, but knew there'd be problems. Nobody decent would work for Regal.

Elliot Bernstein

Shark approached a number of top directors, people like Altman and I think Sam Peckinpah and Arthur Penn. Several were interested in the script, but not as a Regal production, not even after Shark's high-powered "breakthrough film" pitch.

Then he went to several big stars, but the same thing happened. So he stopped before he'd gone through everybody, and went to Sam.

Sam Schlockmann

Right from the start *White Desert* felt like a winner. It was a simple, straightforward story with a love angle and enough violence to hold your average viewer's attention through even the artiest camera work. It could be that rare breed, both an audience and critical success. So I was hurt and saddened when Shark came to me with his proposal.

Sue Schlockmann

I'll never forgive Shark for what he did to Dad then, though at the time I was callous enough to go along. I blame the speed for that. It destroys your sense of humanity.

Elliot Bernstein

Shark convinced Sam to surreptitiously finance *White Desert* through a complex series of dummy corporations and a prestigious European bank. The deal was set up so Sam would eventually get a large chunk of any profits from *White Desert*, but no one except the accountants would know. Shark told Sam they would have to manufacture a falling-out for the trades, and Shark would have to publicly trash Sam in order to gain the credibility he needed to mount *White Desert*.

Initially, I found it quite astonishing that Sam would so easily agree to such an insulting arrangement.

Sam Schlockmann

Shark said Sue's recovery depended on making *White Desert*. "She's pouring her soul into it, working twenty-hour days. If this project bites the dust I'm afraid Sue might too."

I let the bum have his way because I loved my daughter.

Hollywood Daily, April 9, 1972

"TRAGER GOES INDIE, LASHES REGAL"

Producer Shark Trager announced an abrupt departure from Regal Pictures yesterday to set up an indie company, Balboa Productions. According to Trager, who is only twenty-one, "I'm fed up with the soul-destroying crud I've been forced to churn out at Regal. Working on films like *Redneck Scum* and *Tract House She-Devils* left me demoralized and physically sick. But I'm young enough to rebound, and make the kind of serious artistic and commercially successful films that have always made our industry great."

Trager, who is married to Regal topper Sam Schlockmann's daughter Susan, plans to house Balboa Productions in the Gower Studios. First on Lido's slate, per Trager, is *White Desert*, described as a "violent love story" set in the American Southwest, but "metaphorically about our involvement in Vietnam."

Neal Ridges

I don't know where Shark got the Vietnam angle, though everybody said that sort of thing at the time. Actually the story was based on a real-life incident that occurred in Arizona in 1964. These incestuous brother and sister twins, who were clinical idiots, themselves the product of incest, killed a family in Tuscan and went on a joyride in the family's station wagon, running down a number of tourists in Monument Valley before they were both shot in the head. I did a rewrite and Shark made me lose the brother and sister angle—he didn't think people were ready to deal with incest yet—though we retained the couple's clinical idiocy because Shark felt that did make them "more sympathetic." He saw them as "innocents, mindlessly controlled by the consumerism and instant gratification depicted in ads and the media." I was disturbed by this watering down at first, afraid we might be "going Hollywood." But when Jack Hardin came on as director, I was ecstatic, all my apprehensions swept away.

Sue Schlockmann

Jack Hardin had just scored critically with *Scalp Cody and Wanda McBride*, one of the last truly great revisionist westerns—he was just the perfect choice to direct *White Desert*. He was young, handsome, extremely virile and masculine, with the lean, spare artistic sensibility the project called for. I worked quite closely with him in the pre-production phase, and it became quite obvious something extraordinary was about to happen.

Elliot Bernstein

Jack Hardin was a complete asshole in cowboy boots and Stetson—affecting the whole western thing even though he came from Ohio or someplace. I hated him on sight and he hated me. He was hot then, however, and he was talented, so I tried to think of the picture.

Then one night I walked into Sue's office and she and Hardin were having sex on the floor. She'd lost a lot of weight by then. She was back to being lithe, leggy Sue.

"Elliot," she said, "please don't tell Shark."

In deep pain I stepped out and closed the door.

Sue Schlockmann

Yes, I had an affair with Jack Hardin, and it was rather animalistic. I was a bit crazed by that time because of the speed, and I sure wasn't getting laid at home! Here I'd lost all this weight and Shark was still a cold fish.

"I'm exhausted," he'd say. "I don't even think I can get it up, honey."

Well, Jack Hardin could!

Elliot Bernstein

Principal photography began in July of 1972 in Tuscan and it was hellish from the start, the temperature rising to 115. It was Jack's idea to cast unknowns in the leads, though we could've got almost anybody, mainly because of Jack. At one point Shark was talking Ali MacGraw for the girl, and I said, "Can she play an idiot?" I don't remember what Shark said. We talked about Tim Bottoms and a few other young actors who were hot then for the guy, but Mike and Julie were really perfect, we knew that as soon as we saw them. They auditioned on different days, but when Shark saw Julie he said, "My

God, she could be a twin of that guy we saw yesterday, what was his name?" So we cast them mainly because of the eerie resemblance.

It was not until late into the production, after we'd shot the notoriously "graphic" love scenes, that we discovered that they were in fact brother and sister.

Neal Ridges

Shark had me change some details about the family that got killed, he said for legal reasons. And when I visited the location, they were shooting the murders. They had the father lying "gutted" on the floor in front of a wrestling match on TV, and the mother was dead in the kitchen covered with blood and right-wing hate tracts. I was stunned when I first saw her because she was a deadringer for Loretta Young—but the Loretta Young of the thirties. I mean, I knew it wasn't *really* Loretta Young.

Then Elliot told me, "That's Evelyn, Shark's ex-stepmother." And he said the father was Mac.

Sue Schlockmann

Arizona was crazy because we were all there. I mean, Shark was there as executive producer. And Elliot and I were co-producing. And I knew Elliot was still in love with me, but I just couldn't say no to Jack.

Then at some point I began to go psychotic from the speed. I was hearing voices, and everything people said took on a double meaning. And through all that Jack Hardin was just using me. I didn't see it at the time, I was so used to being used. But he was literally fucking me for inspiration. They'd be lighting a shot and he'd say, "Sue, the trailer." So we'd go in there, ostensibly to go over some production details, and he'd just screw me brutally, as if I were some sort of outlet for his nervous tension. He was the kind of guy who believed he had to fuck a lot to be creative.

Finally one day I just came unglued.

Elliot Bernstein

Everybody knew Jack was fucking Sue silly, including Shark. I'd glare at him every time Jack and Sue went off to the trailer, as if to say: Christ, aren't you going to do something?

Obviously he wasn't. Obviously he didn't care. The dailies were astonishing, that was all he cared about.

Then one afternoon we heard Sue yelling obscenities at Jack in the trailer. Then glass broke and Jack moaned, "Oh no. Oh no."

Well, I just assumed he'd done something to Sue. But a moment later he staggered out of the trailer, holding his bleeding stomach.

Sue Schlockmann

I don't remember breaking the beer bottle and jabbing him with it, I really don't. I was so crazy and paranoid I didn't know what I was doing.

Elliot Bernstein

For me it was Sue's suicide attempt all over again—except this time she'd turned her anger outwards. But Shark was just as clearly responsible for this. I was literally imploding with pent-up rage at him. But we had to get Jack to a hospital. Sue was completely hysterical by then, and Shark said, "Elliot, get her out of here now. Take her back to L.A."

Neal Ridges

I was on the set when Sue jabbed Jack. Shark was crazy at first. There was a lot of blood and he was afraid Jack was going to die. "Please don't do this to me," Shark actually said to him at one point. Once we got Jack to the hospital and realized his injury, while grisly, was far from terminal, Shark began to worry about the publicity. He threatened the cast and crew that if any of them talked he'd destroy them. Then he called Elliot who'd taken Sue back to L.A. and said, "I want that bitch locked up in a psycho ward until we've wrapped this film."

Elliot Bernstein

I was not about to place Sue in a mental hospital, when what she clearly needed more than medical attention was love. I stayed with her at the beach house, with the help of Thorazine and Librium carefully withdrawing her from speed.

As I did, her sanity returned. Finally one morning she slipped her arms around me and said, "Oh Elliot, I was such a fool to leave you."

Well, this time I did not recoil from her.

Sue Schlockmann

I now see my marriage to Shark Trager as the saddest, sickest episode of my life—an example of what happens when you marry strictly on the basis of fantasy and sex. Elliot is my true, destined mate in this life—supportive, loving, gentle. Shark was the emotionally maso-

chistic daydream of a lonely young woman with very low self-esteem.
That young woman—thank God—has since learned to love herself.

Neal Ridges

I went with Shark to see Jack in the hospital, and Jack raved on and
on about Sue, "That bitch is fucking insane, she nearly killed me,"
and Shark agreed with everything he said.

"Yeah, she was too much for me a long time ago, man," Shark
commented wryly. "I guess she turned out to be too much for you
too."

They ended up laughing about the whole thing—like a couple of
cowboys who'd both tried to tame the same horse and been thrown.

Then at the wrap party the shit hit the fan with Mike and Julie.

Virgil Homer

I played one of the state troopers in *White Desert*. It was no secret
to any of us that Mike was banging Julie off camera as well as on, so
I was not surprised when I came upon them in a state of undress in
the back seat of a car during the wrap party there in Monument
Valley. I was backing off when Mike pulled up his pants and said,
"It's okay, Virgil, we're all done. Stick around and have a drink."

So I did, and they told me how they were real-life twins who'd
killed their parents.

At first I thought they were pulling my leg. Then after a while I
didn't. "We're just *into* each other," Mike said, and they were still
kind of feeling each other up. They said their parents hadn't understood, and wanted to know what I thought.

"It's fine by me," I said, and stuck around till we finished the
bottle. Then I went and talked to Jack and Shark.

Neal Ridges

Shark just completely shit when Virgil repeated what Mike and Julie
had told him, and Jack turned white as a sheet. We all knew *White
Desert* was going to be a very great film, and we all saw it going
down the toilet if what Mike and Julie had said was true.

Shark sent Virgil back to get some more details so we could check
to see if it was true, but by that time Virgil was shaking. He did it
though. "Where'd you say you killed your folks? I guess you had to
change your names after that, huh? What did you say your real name
was?"

Shark checked it as soon as we got back to L.A. Their real name
was McBurney, Jon and Jan McBurney from Eloise, Indiana. They'd
crushed their parents against the side of a barn with a tractor, slam-

ming them repeatedly until they were both squashed like bugs. Then, like so many other midwestern fugitives, they'd come to Hollywood.

It was grim news. Shark was deeply depressed, and Jack was nearly suicidal—here was his masterwork and it looked like we might have to shelve it. It was as if we'd been flying as high as any plane had ever flown, and suddenly our engines had gone out.

Shark paced in his Gower Gulch office and inevitably hit upon the idea of exploiting the truth. See actual killers portraying actual killers! See twin-like idiot lovers played by real-life incestuous twins!

But Jack wouldn't go for it. "I don't want people to see the film for those reasons," he said. "If you go that route you might as well be back working for Sam."

We all fell into silent thought until Shark said suddenly, "I've got an idea. Why don't we pay somebody to shoot Mike and Julie in the head? They can die in real life as they did in the movie."

Of course, it wasn't a serious suggestion, and right after that the meeting ended. As Jack and I were walking up the corridor to his office, a production assistant came up to him and said, "You'd better brace yourself. Mike and Julie are dead."

Well, I reeled. Though I knew the feeling wasn't rational, I half-expected to hear that Mike and Julie had been shot in the head.

Sue Schlockmann

I was in bed with Elliot when we heard about the plane crash that killed Mike and Julie. I hadn't talked to Shark in weeks, not since the jabbing incident, but I knew he was back in L.A. I knew he'd be devastated, so I called him.

"It's a terrible tragedy," he said. "But they will not be forgotten, not with what we've got on film." Then he said it was a shame they died before they'd done the looping. "But then, the same thing happened with James Dean on *Giant* and that turned out okay."

Neal Ridges

Shark had trouble containing his elation. Of course, he used the Dean analogy. Their demise was the best possible luck for us, provided the truth could be contained. There were only a handful of us who knew that Mike and Julie were actually twins who'd killed their parents.

"But when the film comes out, won't somebody recognize them?" I said.

"Eloise, Indiana, is a small town, I've already checked," Shark said. "But just to play it safe, we'll lose the whole state."

"But somebody who knew them is bound to see a magazine photo, especially if the film does well," I said. "Maybe we should just 'fess up now."

At that Shark exploded. "Listen, you spineless pussy, honesty never got anyone anything in this town. You know where all the honest people are? They're all jacking off in their beer in some crummy little apartment on Yucca Avenue, wondering why they never made it. If anybody loses his nerve on this, you or Jack or Virgil or anybody, you are going to be *dead* in this town, do you understand me? You'll spend the rest of your lives playing with yourselves in a third floor walk-up in the Arbuckle Arms at Ivar and Yucca."

Sue Schlockmann

Elliot and I heard that Shark had taken a bungalow at the Chateau Marmont, where he slept between three-day work marathons with Jack and the editor, and that he'd begun using a lot of cocaine.

Neal Ridges

It was a crazy schizoid time because the film just kept getting better and better as Jack cut it. But all the while there was the sense that everything could blow up at any moment if the truth about Mike and Julie came out. There were already magazine pieces on them, because they were young and attractive and then suddenly dead, which struck everybody's fancy. I think on a largely unconscious level they became emblematic of the whole sixties thing, which was also dying. Of course, the media used their fake biographical information, which Shark had checked as well, and Mike and Julie had been fairly ingenious. That we all continued to think of them as Mike and Julie, rather than Jon and Jan, is perhaps an indication of how effectively they'd remade themselves. They had developed incredibly intricate false backgrounds: born in midwestern towns destroyed by floods and tornados respectively, so that hospital and school records had been lost, both of them drifting through a series of anonymous foster homes and obscure odd jobs after having been abandoned by relatives who had since vanished—their manufactured pasts were virtually uncheckable.

Still we held our breath. All it would take was one Indiana farm girl twanging, "My God, it's them! The McBurney twins! The ones who squashed their parents with a tractor!"

But Shark walked this tightrope over the abyss in a state of unnerving calm, cocaine having replaced the harsh amphetamine acceleration of his UCLA days. Shark thought of cocaine as his "wonder drug" in those days—in retrospect, how naive we all were about its ultimate effects. A toot or two of his snow and Shark was in perfect *control*, down to the slightest vocal inflection.

He knew just what to say to get his way with Jack, which wasn't easy because Jack had a tremendous ego. But in terms of the final editing and every other crucial post-production question Shark won every point. Not that Jack or anyone else really minded, since what'd we'd all accomplished together truly transcended ego the way a collaborative art form can but seldom does.

When I saw the answer print I wept. The film was that good.

Elliot Bernstein

Sue and I were lolling on the beach one afternoon when we looked up and saw Shark. We were both apprehensive—you could see he was coked to the gills—yet as he approached us he exuded cordiality. What then occurred was a classic example of well-Vaselined Shark Trager audacity. He said he bore neither Sue nor me any hard feelings and hoped we would all continue to be friends. Of course, he understood that she'd want a divorce, and that would be no problem, though he did want the house—which had been a wedding present from Sam and was really their only asset—for, he said, "mystical reasons." I took this as an allusion to the lingering vibrations of Selznick and Thalberg which, at least for Shark, still infused that stretch of Gold Coast beach.

He made the house, which was worth perhaps four hundred thousand in '72 dollars, sound trivial compared to the inevitable megabuck profits from *White Desert,* and he offered Sue gross points in the film as her share of the divorce settlement. He was quite convincing and Sue nearly agreed on the spot, until I intervened, saying, "Honey, you should really discuss this with your attorney."

Well, for just a moment Shark appeared ready to go for my throat. Then he laughed expansively and invited us to a screening of the film.

Sue Schlockmann

The film just blew me away. In 1973 I was still naive enough to believe that genuine art would be acknowledged in the marketplace. So I let Shark keep the house.

Elliot Bernstein

We were all bowled over by the finished film. The screening Sue and I attended was truly cathartic. Sue and Jack made up, both apologizing, Sue tearfully. It all seemed worth it—Sue's psychosis, Jack's stab wound—since the end result was a milestone in American cinema. I wept at the end, where the state troopers shoot Mike and Julie in the head, thinking: God, these two beautiful young kids—how many people who live to be ninety come anywhere near achieving the grace and purity preserved here forever in these few precious pieces of time?

I hugged Shark after the screening. "Goddamn it, you've done it," I said. "You really have."

Neal Ridges

It was a time of very great elation—until Shark screened the film for Benjamin Klieg, the president of Mastodon Pictures. Klieg had personally requested the screening, telling Shark he'd heard some "truly astonishing things" about *White Desert*. Shark assured us he had no intention of accepting Ben's offer, however generous it was, since Mastodon, known in the industry as "the dreck factory," had the least prestige of any of the majors. But a juicy offer from Mastodon would definitely provide leverage with the other studios.

Ben remained poker-faced throughout the screening, Shark said. But he was so sure Ben "had to know" how well the film was going to do that he began talking really outrageous terms as soon as the lights came up.

But Klieg stood abruptly and said, "Look—I think we're gonna pass on this."

Shark was speechless. And then he wanted to kill Klieg. "This fucking dinosaur, this tight-assed ancient fuck, is telling me this film's not commercial!"

But he held his tongue. Shark wasn't stupid. Dreck factory or not, Mastodon was a studio to be reckoned with, and Ben Klieg was one of the two or three most powerful men in town.

But Shark was shaken. He knew word of Mastodon's pass would spread quickly, and he feared that Ben Klieg was going to personally bad-mouth the film as well. "He hates me," Shark said. "I could see it in his dead fish eyes. He envies my youth, my virility, my vision. He's going to spread the word that this film is too bizarre, or too arty or too violent or too something—he's going to scare everybody else off if we don't act fast."

Shark called me at two o'clock that morning. "Do you have a passport?" he said. I told him yes and asked why. "Because we're taking this fucking movie to Cannes."

10/Cannes
(1973)

Cindi Dinkler

I was fifteen in 1973 and I thought Kathy Petro was really cool. I used to study her pictures and copy her hairstyle, and then when she started doing the Sun-Ray makeup ads I started buying Sun-Ray lipstick and eyeliner and all that, and everybody was always saying how much I looked like her. So naturally when Babcock's department store in Encino had this Kathy Petro look-alike contest I entered. I couldn't even believe it when I won!

It was just so cool, and then right there at Babcock's this guy came up and laid this line on me about being a big Hollywood producer. I thought he was kidding at first because he was so young, but he *was* cute so I gave him my number. Then he called and asked me out, and my parents were fighting so I said: Well, okay. Then he took me to a movie studio and we watched *White Desert* and when his name came on the screen I knew he wasn't lying about being a producer.

Then he said, "How'd you like to go to France?" And I said, "What about school?" He said, "Play hooky." And I said, "I'd better ask my parents."

But we left without telling them.

Elliot Bernstein

Sue and I nearly crapped when we saw Cindi. Shark had already been in Cannes several days when we arrived. We entered his suite at the Carlton without knocking—the door was ajar—and there he was on the balcony with Cindi, both of them naked. In the noisiest, sloppiest manner imaginable, Shark was going down on her.

147

Sue Schlockmann

I reeled. At first I thought she *was* Kathy Petro—the resemblance was really frightening. Then I realized she was much too young to actually be Kathy—*much* too young. It was insane. Shark was jeopardizing everything we'd worked for, for a cheap and futile exercise in sexual nostalgia.

Neal Ridges

I took a dim view of Cindi's presence since she was so obviously underage. Lest people think it was a case of exploitation, it should be said it was obvious to us all that Cindi had been around. She was a knowing, calculating Valley Lolita, a tough little nymphet who knew just what she wanted, and she had Shark wrapped around her finger—though I doubt that she had a clue as to the real meaning of his attraction to her. When she told me where she'd met Shark, I got a bad premonition, since I knew they'd conducted those Kathy Petro look-alike contests in many cities all across the country.

Ultimately though, I had little time to think about the situation. I was too busy helping Jack push the film.

Elliot Bernstein

I quickly became exasperated with Shark. He was spending all his time with Cindi, just locked into her in this cloying sexual way at the very time we needed him most. We wanted the film to be shown in competition, and we were about to succeed in that even though it required an extraordinary last-minute jury approval. But an aura was growing about *White Desert,* you could almost say a kind of frenzy. An unprecedented wave of anticipation was building. And then the worst thing possible happened.

Just as we were about to screen the film for the jury in our bid for inclusion in the prize category, we were told that one of the jury members had taken ill, necessitating a last-minute replacement. Barely had these words been translated for us than the new juror arrived breathlessly from Paris. It was Jean-Claude Citroen.

Neal Ridges

I finally found Shark on a small deserted beach where he and Cindi were going at it as if there were no tomorrow. "Maybe you'd like to know that Jean-Claude Citroen just scuttled your film," I said.

Well, Shark froze. "What are you talking about?"

I explained that Jean-Claude had persuaded the other jury members to bar the film from competition.

I thought Shark was going to have a stroke. His face turned red, his entire body seemed to turn red, he began hyperventilating. Cindi was worried too. "Shark, are you okay? Shark?"

It would have been funny had it been a film. A real case of over-acting—Charles Bronson about to go on the warpath. He started toward his rented Renault like a naked red killing machine.

Elliot Bernstein

I saw Shark on the Carlton terrace and he was just possessed. "Where is he?" he said, scanning the crowd. It was a mob scene, you know Cannes.

"I don't know," I said, though I'd just seen Citroen chatting with Godard and Bertolucci a few minutes earlier.

"Let it go," I told Shark, and explained that Jack and I were already making arrangements for the film to be shown out of competition. "Jean-Claude can't stop *White Desert*. You wait and see, Shark. We're not finished yet."

Cindi Dinkler

I don't know if I fell in love with Shark exactly or what. But France was really cool and we did a lot of coke, and that was cool too. Then suddenly after some French guy put down his movie, Shark just lost interest in me totally, and I got really bored.

Neal Ridges

The night of the screening we were all crazy. As we walked down to the Palais Shark said, "By the way, somebody should find out what happened to Cindi." He said he hadn't seen her since the night before, and her billfold and clothes were still in the room. "Everything but her bikini."

We had no time to worry about it. The Palais theater was packed and you could feel the expectation. It seemed as if every major figure in film was present—name someone and they were there. Jack was trembling, his cowboy cool disintegrating. As the lights went down I gripped Jack's arm, and Sue squeezed my hand. Down the row Shark watched the screen with a face of stone, the stark white titles reflected in his dark glasses, which he wore for the duration of the film.

Simone Gatane

I ran into Jean-Claude in Cannes soon after he had Jack Hardin's film barred from the competition, and he savaged it mercilessly. "It is pure shit. If it were allowed to compete we might as well open the doors to American TV shows as well, and place *The Conformist* against 'Bonanza,' or *Cries and Whispers* against 'My Mother the Car.' "

"But you laughed at 'My Mother the Car' in L.A., don't you remember?" I said to him.

"Yes. But it's not art."

"Are you sure you don't hate this film merely because Shark produced it?" I said.

"No, it's shit. Go see for yourself."

So I did.

Sue Schlockmann

It was the strangest screening I've ever attended. For a hundred minutes there was literally not a sound. I swear, there was not a single cough, a single movement in a seat, let alone a whispered comment or a gasp or a snort or a laugh. There was not a single walkout, and I tell you as well, there was not a single mental vibration. Usually, even if the audience is quiet you can feel how they're responding. But that audience in Cannes was absolutely blank. They had entered the film, they were *inside White Desert,* they had *become* the motion picture to such an extent that as viewers, *as perceivers,* they had ceased to exist.

Neal Ridges

It's true, there was a feeling of vacancy in the theater, a sense of silent spatiality, which was precisely what I'd striven to suggest in the script, and precisely what Jack had placed on the screen. The genius of *White Desert* is that in a very real sense the screen—*as* a "screen," and all that that implies—is simply removed.

I was fearful as the film reached its conclusion. When you go that far you're never sure how people are going to take it. They can feel used—soul-robbed or mind-raped—and hate you afterward for what you've shown them about themselves.

Elliot Bernstein

I've seen quite a few standing ovations since that night in Cannes in 1973, but never one like that. The audience applauded for twenty minutes—I timed it. Jack was flicking tears from his eyes—it was his moment of course. We all had damp eyes—Sue, Neal, Shark.

Neal Ridges

The applause went on so long I had time to reflect. Jack rightfully took the glory, but so much of the picture's genius did rest with Mike and Julie AKA Jon and Jan, those poor gifted if twisted twins. I hoped no one would ever discover the truth about them. Nothing should taint what they'd given us all here.

As I looked at Shark I felt a terrible poignance. In a rare moment of genuine self-effacement he had his arm around Jack, rubbing his shoulder, granting him all of the credit.

But I couldn't help thinking of Shark's *Pillow Fuck*, that ingenious, insane lost masterpiece, the chances he'd taken back then, chances he himself would never take again. For he had been hurt so badly then.

Then I glanced back and saw the man who had done the damage.

Simone Gatane

I had been clapping so long my palms were sore when Jean-Claude tapped my shoulder. I was on the aisle in the back and he had just come in. He appeared quite puzzled.

"What's going on?" he said. "Why aren't they showing the Chabrol film, it should have started five minutes ago."

Then suddenly he saw Shark and realized what was going on. I will never forget the look that came to his face.

Elliot Bernstein

Toward the end of the ovation I caught sight of Jean-Claude Citroen standing just inside the door. He was pale and profoundly shaken. Of course, his own career was in trouble by that time, his radical anti-narrative didacticism having passed out of vogue. *White Desert* was indisputably an art film, and yet it had a "story," which no doubt infuriated Jean-Claude on a theoretical level—though I'm sure the devastation he felt was occurring on a much less rational plane.

Later, I wished I'd pointed him out to Shark, so that Shark might have seen how thoroughly he'd won. Jean-Claude was beaten, there was no need for further revenge. Instead, I steered Shark's attention away from the door, afraid if he saw Jean-Claude something might happen that would spoil this ecstatic moment.

Simone Gatane

I went up to Shark and we embraced cathartically. As we did he said, "Have you seen Jean-Claude?" And I saw a terrible look in Shark's eye.

"No," I told Shark, "not for many years." Though, you know, I had seen him less than one minute before. Now when I looked back, thank God, he had gone.

Elliot Bernstein

As you know, *White Desert* received a special award, the Palme Noir—there was just no way they could allow Jack's genius to go unacknowledged. It was a joyful, magnificent moment when Jack's long-time idol, Pierre La Douche, warmly presented him with the award, and the next few days were spent fielding the avalanche of distribution offers. Shark held off, growing increasingly testy and temperamental. I thought the cocaine might be catching up with him. Then too there was the matter of Cindi. She had been missing for several days by then, and I was beginning to wonder if our moment of glory might yet degenerate into the scandal of an underage corpse on the beach. We had people looking everywhere for her to no avail.

But Shark seemed more interested in finding Jean-Claude Citroen. He actually grabbed Eric Rohmer by the lapels in the Majestic bar when he overheard the director relating a conversation he'd had with Citroen the previous evening. "Where is he?" Shark demanded. "Where is he staying?" It was quite embarrassing.

I managed to calm Shark, and later he told me, "It's all right. I just want to *talk* to Jean-Claude, that's all." I almost believed that— I knew he'd been carrying on an imaginary mental debate with Jean-Claude for years. But I feared Shark's temper, his short fuse even shorter than usual thanks to the cocaine. I breathed a sigh of relief when we heard that Jean-Claude had left Cannes.

Then one afternoon Shark and Jack and Neal set out for Saint-Tropez to see Derek Horus.

Neal Ridges

Jack and I had a script idea that was somewhat akin to *Performance*, about a rock star living in seclusion in L.A. Since Jagger had already done that turn, Derek Horus was the obvious next choice. In '73, remember, Down in Flames was one of the top superstar rock groups, right up there with the Stones and Led Zeppelin—though tragedy would render their time in the sun quite brief. They'd taken an indefinite break from touring that spring, and we knew that Derek was fielding film offers. Jack called him cold and it turned out that Derek was crazy about Jack's western. And the fact that he'd just won the Palme Noir didn't hurt.

Shark and Jack and I arrived at Derek's villa one sunny afternoon, and the meeting could not have gone better. Derek cut quite a figure, his blond hair running down to his lower back, shirtless as always in lowcut bellbottoms, tight with no underwear. He brought out some astonishingly good dope and soon all of us were riffing, throwing out script ideas, on this tremendous elating roll, just convinced this was going to be the best film ever made. Shark and Derek especially fell into immediate sync, their creative rapport instantaneous and ecstatic, so much so that both of them reacted with considerable irritation when Derek's girlfriend of the moment called from the next room in a grating, whiny voice: "Honey? Have you seen my stash? Hon-ey?"

Everyone turned to look as Kathy Petro stepped through the door.

Kathy Petro

I could not believe Shark was really there. I mean, here I was on the Côte d'Azur, which is a long way from Newport Beach, and who shows up but the last person in the whole world I ever want to see again. Derek tried to introduce me, and I just said, "Look, I just really do not want to deal with this."

So I didn't. I just went and found my stash, and went straight upstairs and skin-popped some heroin, which I thought I was using just recreationally that spring. Boy, was I stupid as it turned out.

Neal Ridges

It was a stunning moment when Shark saw Kathy, a Hitchcock moment—Shark's expression like James Stewart's in *Vertigo* when Kim Novak steps out of the shadows transformed.

Then track in on Kathy, wearing a micro-bikini, very tan, very fresh, very Kathy Petro: the patented California Look—except that, you couldn't help but notice, so skimpy was her bikini bottom, there were tell-tale injection bruises in the otherwise flawless flesh of either cheek.

Kathy took one look at Shark and stormed out, leaving Derek quite puzzled.

Shark was so shaken he completely spaced out, which effectively trashed the mood of the meeting. Jack didn't understand what had happened, he didn't know about Shark's past with Kathy. I was the only one who could begin to imagine what was going on in Shark's mind. I saw the way he was now looking at Derek. A few minutes before Derek had been an icon of cool, but now he was evil, the Satanic rock star working a terrible black magic on Kathy, leading her into addiction and ruination. I could almost hear Shark's thoughts as he glared at Derek: You fucking scumbag, what have you done to my Kathy, I should kill you, you evil pig.

The vibes got so bad I knew we had to get out of there before something happened. Jack felt it too. I got Shark up, and by now he looked literally psychotic. We were moving toward the door, but Derek didn't understand what had gone wrong. Maybe he just thought the dope had made Shark paranoid, because he kept cajoling Shark, trying to loosen him up again, trying to get him to laugh, and I wanted to say: Back off, man, just let us go.

Then, just as we reached the door, a Jaguar pulled up to the house. Jean-Claude Citroen got out and came around to open the passenger door for Cindi, who'd been missing for five days then. The auteur had quite a smile on his face until he saw Shark.

Kathy Petro

Granted I was nodding, just floating on this smack high which I thought was so harmless—Jeez, was I dumb!—when I looked out the window and saw Jean-Claude and this girl getting out of a car below, and thought: God, how weird! Because this girl looked *just like me*— I mean, a lot of girls did then, kind of, because they were copying my look, but she *really* looked like me, you know what I mean? And I thought: Oh my God, does this mean Jean-Claude's doing that awful *Vertigo* number? Like only beingattracted to girls he can remake in my image and everything? Because obsession is such a bore!

Then I saw Shark coming out and, well, I guess you know what happened then.

Neal Ridges

The second Jean-Claude saw Shark he got a trapped-animal look, because he knew what was going to happen. He didn't have time to get back into the car, so his feet made tracks. I've never seen anyone take off so fast, and Shark was after him like a bullet.

Shark chased Jean-Claude down along the path to the beach, it was quite a long chase, with the rest of us running along after Shark. Shark chased him out along the water's edge. Jean-Claude was lithe and on fire with adrenaline, but Shark finally caught him at the nude beach. By the time the rest of us got there Shark was just beating the living shit out of Jean-Claude.

Simone Gatane

As it happened I was there on the Saint-Tropez nude beach sunning myself with my new boyfriend. When suddenly we looked up and there was Shark kicking a fallen man in the face. The man's face was so bloody that at first I could not even tell it was Jean-Claude. People were screaming and covering themselves with towels, it was so horrible.

Neal Ridges

We finally pulled Shark away from Jean-Claude, but that was no easy task, because Shark was like a man on angel dust. It took all of us to subdue him, and then he turned on Derek, calling him a "demonic snake" and demanding that he "let Kathy go," as if it were obvious that she was with Derek against her will.

Jean-Claude was wasted. He was conscious but his jaw was broken, his face was red pulp, and he was feeling around in the blood-soaked sand for several of his teeth. When Cindi saw him she became hysterical.

Cindi Dinkler

I was on acid. I'd run into Jean-Claude on the beach at Cannes after Shark started ignoring me—I thought Jean-Claude was really cool since he reminded me of my real father. We had sex and everything and he kept calling me his Lolita, which at the time I thought was a French term of affection—years later I saw the movie on TV with Sue Lyon. Then we took all this acid and the whole Riviera turned into something like you'd see at Disneyland. Then suddenly Shark was just killing him, and there was all this blood and violence where minutes before there'd been nothing but naked French bodies. I just freaked.

Kathy Petro

By the time I got down to the beach it was all over, and I mean, Jean-Claude was just a mess. It almost made me sick even from a distance—I stayed back by the path so Shark wouldn't see me. Then suddenly this girl who looked so much like me came running back up the path, kind of keening.

Cindi Dinkler

I thought I was hallucinating at first when I ran into Kathy Petro, I just couldn't believe she was really there in France. Then I looked and looked and saw that she was real. Then I went kind of crazy, like I thought she'd stolen my identity or something, this weird acid thing. So I started to scratch her, saying, "Give me back my soul, you bitch."

Neal Ridges

It was just sheer insanity. The next thing we knew Cindi was attacking Kathy, and Derek and Jack went to intervene. Simone was there too, and had called an ambulance for Jean-Claude. Somehow I managed to get Shark back to the car.

Elliot Bernstein

Sue and I were checking out of the Carlton when Neal and Jack returned with Shark. Shark was in pretty bad shape emotionally—he hadn't slept for days and was muttering angrily under his breath. Far from satisfying his desire for revenge, the beating he'd given Jean-Claude had only whetted his appetite for blood. "I should have killed him," he kept saying. "I want to go back, the job's not done." We knew we had to get him out of the country.

There was just one loose end. We dispatched Sue to round up Cindi.

Sue Schlockmann

It was the last favor I did for my soon-to-be-ex-husband. I drove down to Saint-Tropez and found the poor girl trembling in the bushes near the nude beach as the sun was going down. I gave her some Valium and on the drive back to Cannes she became lucid again and mentioned in passing that her folks were sure going to be mad when she got home since they had no idea where she'd gone. "They probably think I got kidnapped or something," she said, clearly relishing the likelihood that they were worried sick.

I cursed Shark, certain our moment of triumph was about to give way to scandal.

Then when we got back to Cannes everybody was going crazy because Shark had disappeared.

Kathy Petro

It must have been about nine o'clock that night and things had finally quieted down. Derek and I had quarreled though and weren't speaking, so I decided to do some more junk. I went into the upstairs bathroom and was right in the process of popping myself in the rear-end—I was still telling myself I wasn't a junkie since I didn't mainline, if you can believe that!—when suddenly there was this tap on the window. I looked over my shoulder and saw Shark in the window and I just almost died! I mean, I went into this whole big flashback to the peeping-Tom movie thing in Newport Beach. Here I was in the bathroom again, and there he was at the window again! At first I was too stunned to even speak. Then he pushed open the window and started to crawl in, saying, "Kathy, I've come to rescue you, it's all right." But I just started screaming. He said, "No, no, Kathy, don't scream." But I couldn't stop, and Derek came running in and saw Shark in the window, and then went to get his gun. And for some reason, as much as I hated Shark I didn't want to see him dead, so I said, "Get out of here, you asshole. Derek's getting his gun."

Shark saw I wasn't kidding, and suddenly he looked at me in a way that both frightened me and touched something strange and unfulfilled in me too. "You're the love of my life," he said. "Do you know that?"

And I said, "Get out of here," because Derek was coming. And Shark took off.

Elliot Bernstein

We were all frantic. We'd even alerted the hospital in Nice where they'd taken Jean-Claude, afraid Shark might be on his way there to "finish the job." Then suddenly he walked in. He was dead on his feet, exhausted but oddly calm. "Let's go home," he said.

On the plane he told me he'd gone to see Kathy, but his mood was still tranquil, acceptant. "It's all right now," he said. "I know that she loves me. And she'll be by my side when the time is right. In the meantime, Elliot—" Here he squeezed my arm. "—we have much to do, much to do."

"Get some sleep, Shark," I told him. But the rest of the flight he stared out the window, though there was nothing out there but black sky, and I could see his thin, serene smile reflected in the glass.

Sue Schlockmann

Cindi sat beside me, leafing through magazines and singing Rolling
Stones songs under her breath all the way into L.A. At one point she
came upon a cheerful fashion photo of Kathy, and observed to me,
"You know, she may have a nice smile. But underneath it she's slime."

I was too tired and disgusted to respond with more than a grunt.

Neal Ridges

We were all aware of the potential for disaster with Cindi, and somehow it fell to me to drop her off at her parents' house in L.A. We'd
checked the papers upon landing, there was nothing about a missing
girl. Still, I half-expected to be surrounded by cop cars when I pulled
up to her house. It was all in my head though. Nothing happened.
Nothing ever happened.

Cindi Dinkler

My parents were assholes and drunks who didn't give a shit what I
did. When I walked in my stepdad said, "Oh, are *you* back?" So I
said, "Yeah, but I went to France, which is further than you'll ever
go, loser." My stepdad called me a liar. Then when I showed him
the stamp on my passport he slapped me hard across the face.

Later, I tried calling Shark a whole bunch of times, but every time
I did he had either just stepped out or else he was in some kind of
meeting.

11 / *The Condoist* (1973–1975)

Mac Trager

I saw that *White Desert* movie one night at the Balboa Theater. I went by myself and sat in the back and got madder and madder, gripping the arms of the seat so hard that my knuckles hurt. 'Cause everyone there was snickering at the parents—that smirking, superior kind of thing, you know?—even as the parents got cut up and killed by the young retarded couple. And it didn't take a genius to see that those parents were copied from Evelyn and me.

Evelyn Burns

A friend called from Fort Worth and said, "Evelyn, you know that former stepson of yours, the one you bragged was a Hollywood producer? Well, I just saw his movie, and all I can say is, if I were you I'd sue."

Well, I looked to see where the movie was playing, but it was already gone. I guess it didn't do very well, now did it? Not long after I finally saw it on TV a few years later I suffered my first stroke.

Elliot Bernstein

The very first day back at the Gower Studios Sue and I heard Shark explode in his office: "Goddamn it! Oh, *fuck*, no!"

We rushed in to see what was wrong, and Shark threw a sheaf of legal papers at Sue and yelled at her, "You fuck-cunt! You and your fuck-cunt father! I should've ripped the guts out of both of you!"

Well, I snapped, and decked Shark, a nice clip to the jaw. Just one blow, and he didn't return it, he was much too stunned for that. He held his jaw and looked at me, and for a moment I thought he was actually going to cry. He really thought I'd gratuitously turned on

159

him, you see. He had absolutely no concept of how long-suffering I had been.

"You are out of my life, Elliot," he said finally, his voice trembling. "I don't ever want to see you again." Then he indicated Sue without looking at her. "And take that fuck-cunt with you."

Well, it turned out he'd read the fine print in his financial agreement with Sam.

Sue Schlockmann

It was no way to say good-bye. But I have to say that when I found out what Dad had done I understood Shark's anger.

Neal Ridges

The deal was almost indecipherably complex, but what it amounted to was that if *White Desert* went even slightly over budget—and it did just that, by something like two thousand dollars—Shark would owe Sam, through the European bank and a string of dummy corporations, the entire cost of the production plus interest plus all the moneys Shark had been advanced to set up Balboa Productions. The contract provided Shark a 48-hour "window"—long since past at the point he discovered the fine print—in which he could pay Sam off before a "triple-budget clause" went into effect. Shark would then owe Sam three times the cost of the film. The film had come in at roughly two million, which meant Shark owed Sam six million, plus interest and penalties and various odds and ends which came to another four million. He owed Sam ten million dollars, and even if he could pay it Sam would *still* assume ownership of the film.*

Sam Schlockmann

You could say I had the last laugh.

---

* In the wake of this contractual debacle Shark enlisted the services of Jerry Bratman, the high-powered "attorney to the stars," who represented him in all his legal affairs until 1981. From 1983 on, Shark was represented by Steven "Little Barracuda" Ging, who took over many of Bratman's clients after the older attorney was machine-gunned in a Las Vegas casino parking lot in a still unsolved murder. The labyrinthine deals of Shark Trager might themselves form the basis of an intriguing book on the financial workings of Hollywood. Unfortunately, Shark's files "vanished" within hours of his death, an event about which Steven Ging, despite his role as executor of Shark's estate, claims to know nothing. Ging is among those who declined to be interviewed for this book.

Neal Ridges

The day after Shark attacked Sue and Elliot, Sam Schlockmann came in for the kill. The phones went dead at Balboa Productions, they came for the furniture. Shark was enraged and humiliated, and the whole thing became a legal and financial nightmare. There were lawsuits and counter suits. Simultaneously, Shark's divorce from Sue was going through, and on that count at least he got what he wanted. In the rush of elation after the initial screening of *White Desert* Sue had signed an iron-clad property settlement agreement giving Shark the Gold Coast beach house.

But it was doubtful he was going to be enjoying it for long if he didn't reach a cease-fire with Sam. Shark had to deal and deal fast to save his own skin. I could understand that.

The full-page ad in *Hollywood Today*, thanking his "mentor" Sam Schlockmann "for his keen intelligence and artistic guidance" in helping to bring *White Desert* to the screen, was a virtual retraction and public apology, as unctuous as his previous trashing of Sam had been harsh. The day the ad ran, Shark called to confirm the obvious: a deal had been reached with Sam.

It devastated me—and it literally killed Jack!—when we found out what the deal was. Mastodon Pictures was bailing Shark out as the first step of a generous multi-picture production deal. They had reached a settlement with Sam for an undisclosed sum and assumed outright ownership of *White Desert*—an act, we all felt, which was tantamount to giving K-mart exclusive rights to sell the works of Picasso.

Bill Kemmer

I was a vice-president in charge of production at Mastodon then and had seen *White Desert* at its extraordinary premier at Cannes. I'd been overwhelmed, and made our acquiring the film a personal crusade, even when I realized it meant throwing a rather expensive cut of meat to Sam Schlockmann. I put my career on the line, giving Ben Klieg no peace until he agreed. I sensed correctly that *White Desert* wouldn't make money—it was an art picture in a time when art pictures were dying—but at the very least it would bring us a shot of sorely needed prestige.

More importantly it would bring us Shark. "He's a genius," I told Ben, "another Thalberg. Whatever you may think of *White Desert*, or of Shark Trager as a personality, he is the future of this business. If we don't bail him out, somebody else will. And we'll be kicking ourselves a few years down the line when he's pouring millions into someone else's coffers."

Sonya Heinz, *French Quarterly Review,* Summer 1973

Not since last year's *Last Tango in Paris* has there been a movie that redefines an art form the way Jack Hardin's *White Desert* does. With a loose, zingy, wigged-out abandon Hardin takes both violence and eroticism to the point where they become the same thing, which is something only a young film genius—Welles was one—can do. This isn't the coy, ditsy, tuned-out sex we've come to expect in Hollywood movies, this is sex the way it really is: ugly, mean and violent. At the same time Hardin's violence has a thick, sweaty, pendulous sensuality, a sinewy wised-up cowboy wooziness. This is rapturous cathartic violence, the kind that makes you understand why some people prefer violent movies to actually having sex. Jack Hardin is a virile young Peckinpah on mescaline. He's likely to become the Sam Shepard of film if the studios don't destroy him first. That danger is real. With the businessmen taking over Hollywood again, *White Desert* may be the last true American art film we see in some time.

Neal Ridges

It *was* an art film. It should have been opened slowly and carefully with a hip, intelligent ad campaign, all of which Mastodon was incapable of comprehending. Let's face it, of any of the majors they were the crassest, junkiest studio. They only knew how to spew out mass-produced crap—greasy french fry movies for the malls. Which was just what they did with *White Desert*.

But to push it as a comedy was truly unforgivable.

Bill Kemmer

I always knew the ad campaign was a mistake. But when we sneaked it in Bakersfield, and the audience laughed, the marketing people took over and I lost control.

Neal Ridges

I'll never forget the day Jack first saw the ad. The busy cartoonish illustration and the intentional play on *Bonnie and Clyde*'s famous tag: "They were young, they were stupid, they killed a bunch of funny people." And the legend:

WHITE DESERT. A Crazy Kinda Comedy.

Jack was too destroyed to even get angry. He sat slumped in one of the few chairs left in the Gower Gulch office—it was the day Shark was moving into his new offices at Mastodon—and finally looked up at me with tears in his eyes, which was itself shocking, because Jack was a very macho guy. "You know, I can take anything except being laughed at," he said.

Bill Kemmer

It was a crazy kinda flop. Most of the audience came expecting a comedy and left angry and confused. The film actually did okay in the hipper houses where the Cannes prize carried some weight. And of course it had a long afterlife as a cult film—I think it finally broke even in 1979.

It was sad though about Jack Hardin. Because there was a man with talent.

Elliot Bernstein

For a long time I held Shark responsible for Jack's death. Even though Jack technically drank himself to death in Arizona, we all felt that he'd died of a broken heart.

Neal Ridges

My first thought when I heard the news of Jack's death was to blame Shark. In retrospect though, I think both Jack and the film were essentially victims of the seventies. Despite his tough-guy exterior Jack was emotionally frail. When people laughed at his masterpiece it simply crushed his spirit. He should've seen what was coming, the vapidity which would dominate that decade in American film. He should have gone to Europe where people understood his kind of movie. But like so many of us he had Hollywood dreams. And in the end they killed him.

Whatever else you might say of Shark, he knew how to swim with the tide.

Bill Kemmer

Ben Klieg never stopped hating *White Desert*—though he pretended to have changed his mind—but he genuinely reversed his opinion of Shark, especially when the story got out about how viciously Shark had mangled Jean-Claude Citroen.

"It was artsy assholes like him who almost destroyed this industry," Ben said of Citroen. "Thank God all that shit's over now, and we can get back to the business of making movies."

The crucial meeting between Ben and Shark occurred over lunch at Chasen's. Ben came into my office afterwards beaming, as he hadn't beamed in some time, and said, "You know, Bill, you were right. Shark Trager is—what's the expression?—a cool drink of water. I see blue skies ahead."

The expense of settling with Sam Schlockmann aside, the deal Ben gave Shark was quite lavish.

The first project Shark chose to develop was a treatment dashed off by Mrs. Benjamin Klieg, a truly wretched idea that had been lying around the story department for years. You know Jean Klieg, the quintessential L.A. socialite, the dilettante who is always coming up with a "fabulous movie idea." Well, you don't tell the boss's wife to stick to charity work. We had a foot-thick file full of worthless Jean Klieg notes.

But Shark said, "This is it, this is my next movie." It was *The Condoist*.

Neal Ridges

When Shark showed me Jean Klieg's treatment I guffawed. When he asked me to write the script I was insulted. But when he said he would pay me two hundred thousand dollars to write it—well, what would you have done?

I suppressed the bad feelings I had toward Shark about Jack Hardin's death and with what I termed resilience swallowed my bitterness over *White Desert*'s fate, and plunged into *The Condoist* with zeal—like any young whore just starting out.

Shark kept little more than the title. Immediately I saw that the new story had strong autobiographical elements. That is to say, he intended the wife who would be terrorized by voodoo zealots to strongly resemble Kathy Petro.

Then he added a Derek Horus figure. The condo where the wife and her husband were vacationing in the Bahamas would be haunted by the tortured ghost of a dead British rock star.

The condoist himself, the leisure-suited real estate tycoon–cum–"spiritual detective," initially resembled Shark, though he eventually decided that the condoist should be played by a much older man—Ernest Borgnine and Lorne Greene were both mentioned. Shark anticipated a TV series derived from the movie, and believed that middle America preferred her episodic heroes "square and stout."

Shark's ideas changed from day to day—he was doing a lot of cocaine. And the script became increasingly bizarre, an eclectic brew of contradictory occult elements—voodoo and demons, ghosts, vampires, telepathy, black magic, poltergeists, you name it. I was constantly rewriting, juggling his whims, trying to maintain some semblance of logic and plausibility.

Finally I'd had it and told Shark I quit—I'd gone far beyond the number of revisions called for in my contract.

"You can't quit now," Shark responded in his enormous office on the fourteenth floor of the Mastodon Building. He'd had the space remodeled to resemble Raymond Massey's office in *The Fountainhead*, a severe retro-Expressionist decor he sardonically termed "forties crypto-fascist."

"Shark, I'm exhausted and befuddled," I told him. "The script's not getting any better, it's getting worse."

"You're a pussy," he said without warning. "You're a pussy and a loser, and a no-talent fuckheaded schmuck."

Well, I sensed he was coked, but that was no excuse.

"Why don't you eat shit," I said, and started for the door.

I heard him coming around from behind his desk to head me off. "I should've done this five years ago," he said, "when I caught you fucking Simone in my loft in Sherman Oaks!"

He pulled me around in the doorway and swung at me, but I jumped back and he hit the heavy crypto–Frank Lloyd Wright door with his fist. It was extremely painful for him—he broke several bones in his hand.

"Good-bye, Shark," I said, and as I walked out past his stunning young secretaries I actually felt sorry for him. He was riding a tremendous elating wave of pure Hollywood power all right, but I had been the last of his true friends.

Jean Klieg

I adored Shark initially. What a charming young man he seemed! Naturally I was flattered that he'd chosen one of my humble musings as the basis of his first film for Ben.

However I must say I was disturbed when I saw Neal Ridge's screenplay. About the violence more than anything.

But Shark assured us he had in mind a tasteful, stylish thriller with major stars. And then of course he approached our dear friend Lawrence Granger, surely one of our finest directors.

Neal Ridges

I was sick with disgust and laughter when I heard Larry Granger was going to direct. Of all the tired old hacks! He hadn't had a hit since *Romanesque* in 1959. But he still played tennis with Ben Klieg.

Shark's lips were brown with dinosaur shit.

Lawrence Granger

Frankly, I never understood the sixties, and I hadn't cared for *White Desert* at all. So I went to see Shark with some apprehension, which was quickly allayed. For here was a businessman, neat, articulate, in a finely tailored British suit, good shoes. Clearly a man of taste and style who appreciated fine art and literature—I recall our shared admiration of both Whistler and Henry James.

"I'll do it," I said. "When do we start?"

"Don't you want to read the script first?" he said, and we had quite a good laugh about that. I suppose that gives you some idea how enthusiastic I initially was.

Bill Kemmer

The script was incoherent, and I personally found some of the more sensational elements distasteful. But the genre was hot, and we knew Friedkin was doing *The Exorcist* complete with piss and masturbation and the works.

The squashing scene bothered me though—you know, where the piano drops on Anthony Cray. The script said something like, "His guts go flying every which way as if the piano were a shoe that had stepped on a bug."

"Tony Cray's a ponderous old bore," Shark said. "America secretly longs to see him crushed like a bug."

"What about Laura's decapitation?" I said. By then we knew we had Laura String for the mother, but she was such a fine and distinguished actress, I mean right up there with Helen Hayes, that I felt a little crummy about it.

"She's a twat," Shark said. "A right-wing cooze who fingered her friends during the witchhunts and deserves a thorough trashing. When those steel jaws grab her head and rip it off America's gonna pee in its pants with secret glee."

Lawrence Granger

I was high on Ali MacGraw for the lead, but Shark insisted the actress must be blonde. I proposed Faye Dunaway, but he shook his head. "Not California enough," he said.

"It's a pity we can't get that Petro girl," I quipped. "She's certainly California."

Shark absolutely froze. "You fuck," he said, which I considered in very poor form. "What are you trying to do to me? How dare you try and fuck with my head?"

At the time, you see, I knew absolutely nothing of his, shall we say, *obsession avec la femme Petro* [sic]. I merely assumed that he'd heard she'd recently been cast in a film. That proved not to be the case, however. For as I mentioned the occurrence his anger soared to new heights—though I thankfully was no longer its object.

Trembling with fury he buzzed his secretary Mrs. Clive: "Find out everything you can about *Manhattan Holiday*," he said to her urgently. "Andreji Pavlavo . . . whatever that Yugoslavian idiot's name is, he's directing it in New York."

Kathy Petro

Derek and I finally had this really awful fight, and he gave me this big black eye even though he knew I had to do a *Vogue* session the very next day. So I said, "Look, I really don't think I need this," and left even though I was afraid I might be just a teensy-weensy bit strung out on smack. Boy, was I right about that!

On the plane to New York I went into withdrawal. I had chills and sweats, my teeth were chattering just like one of those sets of toy false teeth! And this really nice man, who was Andreji Pavlavojac, sat down next to me and put a blanket around me and held me all the way into Kennedy. He wasn't much to look at, I mean compared to Derek, but he just exuded this niceness which to be honest I hadn't felt from anyone in I don't know how long. I just felt safe with him for some reason, and I heard one of the other passengers say, "Oh, you know he's the Yugoslavian Woody Allen."

Bill Kemmer

Andreji Pavlavojac had come to the West from Yugoslavia in the late sixties, to France initially, where he had directed several modest comedies including *Papa Always Said So*, a substantial art-house hit in the States, which had finally brought him to America to make *Manhattan Holiday*. Shark was obsessed with seeing a script, which I couldn't provide since the picture was an indie production—there just weren't any copies of the script floating around like there are with most major Hollywood pictures.

Then Shark wanted the picture "killed."

"There must be some way to stop it," he said. "Call in some favors, Bill. Scare off the backers."

"*Why?*" I wanted to know.

"Because I'm developing a property that's just like it," Shark said.

"How do you know if you haven't seen the script?" I asked him.

"I know. I've heard enough about it to know that."

Much later I realized his real motive was jealousy. For by then it was known that not only had Kathy Petro been cast as the romantic lead opposite Andreji—like Woody Allen to whom he was so frequently compared, Andreji was directing himself—but Kathy and the Yugoslavian wunderkind were simultaneously engaged in a passionate real-life affair.

Kathy Petro

Andreji really saved my life then. He took me straight to this private clinic up in Connecticut and got me off junk, and just kept all the *Vogue* and agency people and everybody else at bay. He'd come and visit me and we'd walk around the grounds and he was so adorable in that little Mets baseball cap he always wore.

Then he showed me the script for *Manhattan Holiday*, which was just this sweet, light-hearted little romantic comedy, and when he said he wanted me to play the lead girl I thought at first he was joking.

"Andreji," I said. "I've never *acted*. I'm not an actress."

"Yes, but you have sometheeng," he said. "A special sometheeng, Kathy. How do you say? A spark."

I just giggled like a schoolgirl 'cause his accent was so charming. How could I say no to a man who made me feel so good inside?

Bill Kemmer

I finally convinced Shark there was nothing we could do to stop Pavlavojac's film. "There are only so many ideas floating around in the air. He grabbed it first, Shark. Those are the breaks."

Of course, by that time we had far more urgent matters to tend to. *The Condoist* had a start date and we still hadn't cast the female lead. Then literally at the last minute, Shark came up with Karen Quall. I'm still not sure where he found her.

Carl Stook

I was with Westwood Detective then, and Shark Trager hired us to track down all the winners of the Kathy Petro look-alike contests nationwide and compile dossiers on each of the girls. It seemed a bit eccentric, but then he was a Hollywood producer, so we assumed he was looking for a certain type for a film.

Karen Quall

I was a senior in high school in Kansas City when I won the Kathy Petro look-alike contest there, then I came to Los Angeles to go to UCLA and study theater arts.

One day I had just finished doing a scene from *Romeo and Juliet* in the UCLA theater when Shark approached me. "How would you like to be in a major motion picture?" he said.

I did a double-take and recognized him from a photo I'd seen in *Variety*. I remembered the photo because he was so good-looking and so young and yet so successful that I'd thought at the time: God, I wish a producer like *that* would pull the casting couch routine on me.

So it was like a dream come true—and I didn't even have to sleep with him to get the role.

We did have lots of sex later though, after the film started. And at first anyway it was really great!

Lawrence Granger

I found Karen quite the comely beauty, if somewhat eerily reminiscent of Kathy Petro. Her acting abilities were crude at best, but then let's be honest, *The Condoist* did not require the virtuoso skills of, say, an Audrey Hepburn or a Deborah Kerr. Karen was bright and cheery, and therefore we would care when she was brutally terrorized.

Last but not least we cast the condoist himself. I wanted Sir Laurence Olivier though Shark favored William Conrad of television's "Cannon." In the end we compromised and gave the part to Bud Squat, who had for many seasons charmed America as the mean but lovable male nursemaid in the situation comedy, "The Dinkleberry Brood." The cameras rolled in late October of 1973 on location in enchanting Jamaica.

Bill Kemmer

I flew down to Jamaica with the film company, and upon our arrival an incident occurred which really marked the beginning of my disillusionment with Shark. No sooner had we all cleared Customs than Shark relieved his secretary Mrs. Clive of a metal briefcase she'd been carrying. In his hotel room that night Shark opened the briefcase and removed a false bottom to reveal an enormous amount of cocaine.

Well, of course Mrs. Clive had no idea she'd been risking arrest, and I considered it unconscionable. Here was an infinitely decorous Englishwoman then in her early sixties, a legendary Hollywood secretary who as a young woman had worked for both Irving Thalberg and David Selznick, which was of course why Shark had lured her from retirement—as a kind of "good luck mascot," he said—only to turn her into his unwitting drug mule!

Cynthia Clive

That's absurd. Shark could never have done such a thing to me. Obviously, Bill Kemmer had his own reasons for denigrating Shark now, but I shall not allow him to involve me in his lies.

I cannot say I was wholly unaware of Shark's use of cocaine. Everyone knew why Gramps came around.* Initially, I was perhaps

* Veteran character actor Ernie "Gramps" Prichett, known for his wry chuckle and homespun manner in such classic films as *Dustbowl Dina* and *This Blessed*

guilty of romanticizing the practice somewhat. Freud had partaken of the stimulant, hadn't he? And Sherlock Holmes. It seemed a harmless vice, one that went with the territory. Perhaps every genius from time to time required an extra bit of zip.

I suppose it must be said as well that I was initially quite taken with Shark, and it was never any secret to me why. He bore quite a strong resemblance—in the first few years especially, before the drugs began to age him—to the man I still considered the love of my life, though our affair, my last, had been quite brief that glorious summer of *The Dawn Patrol*, the year before the war. How like a youthful, rakishly charming Errol Flynn Shark was that autumn of *The Condoist* in Jamaica.

Karen Quall

Everything was great at first. Lawrence Granger was just wonderful, so kind and considerate. But then he and Shark started to get into it because Shark had this vision of the film.

Then I fell in love with Mark LeManns, who was playing my husband in the movie. And that caused tension because Mark fell in love with me too, even though by then I was having all this sex with Shark.

Bill Kemmer

I flew down in January because Larry Granger was threatening to walk off the picture. "Shark said things to me which I can neither forgive nor forget," Larry said.

It seemed that Shark had exploded one evening at the dailies, calling Larry a "fatuous, insipid hack" in front of the actors and crew. "This is supposed to be a visceral, wrenching thriller, you silly old fool! Not Holly Golightly skipping down Park Avenue with Fred Astaire."

Then in a blind rage Shark had stayed up all night drawing up an intricate storyboard for the rest of the film.

"Shoot this, you dodo," Shark told Larry in the morning. "Or you'll never do another picture."

Larry had called Ben Klieg in quite a state.

Town. Allegedly one of Hollywood's most likable and reliable drug dealers until his death by dismemberment in 1981.

Jean Klieg

Shark called us from Jamaica to explain that Larry was suffering an emotional breakdown. This was sad news, but not a complete surprise, for Larry had been treated for alcoholism and emotional problems in the sixties.

"Don't worry though," Shark said. "I intend to ignore his ravings and do whatever it takes to hold this picture together."

No sooner had Shark hung up than Larry called, and indeed his grip on reason seemed tenuous at best.

Karen Quall

At first sex with Shark was really super. Then one night after we'd got it on he just looked at me a long time in this strange appraising way, as if he were suddenly dissatisfied with me. I had these freckles on my breasts, you know? And he said, "You shouldn't have these freckles. It spoils the effect."

"What effect?" I said. "What do you mean?" But he wouldn't tell me.

I didn't know then he had this thing about Kathy Petro, but I did know I was supposed to look like her in the film. I learned from makeup and wardrobe that he'd given them pictures of Kathy and said, "I want Karen to look like this."

Lawrence Granger

I found myself taking Valiums simply to get through the picture. I followed Shark's storyboard, but it was all I could do to keep a tap on my rage.

Then William Rickard, the fine black actor, who was to portray Dr. Voo, contracted a virus and had to be flown home. And Shark replaced him with Man Lafitte, a Haitian non-actor, who was already on payroll as our "voodoo adviser," though I had avoided him like the devil—which was precisely what he was. A genuinely frightening man!

Karen Quall

When I found out I was going to be ravaged by Man Lafitte I almost died. He'd been hanging around the set from day one, though the first time I saw him I thought he was some poor local derelict and told the AD he should be removed. "He's Shark's buddy," the AD said.

And it was true. He and Shark were always going off to the trailer together, ostensibly to discuss voodoo, but really I assumed to do coke or smoke dope.

Man Lafitte was just filthy, he never bathed. You could tell when he'd been around because his smell lingered. "You're not going to touch me," I'd tell Shark. "Not until you wash your hands and air out this trailer."

I pleaded with Shark to get a real actor to play Dr. Voo. But he said, "Man's perfect. His eyes are filled with a terror and insanity that no actor could ever fake."

That was true enough.

Mark LeManns

I thought I was in love with Karen, and when I heard Man Lafitte was going to play Dr. Voo, which meant he would actually kiss her and maul her bare breasts, I saw red. I marched straight to Shark's trailer, but before I could knock I saw Shark in there with that grungy Haitian varmint. Man was muttering something in dialect, then he jabbed a pin into the chest of the voodoo doll he held. I couldn't help noticing the doll was wearing a little crudely fashioned Mets baseball cap.

Kathy Petro

Andreji and I were alone in this loft in SoHo where he was editing *Manhattan Holiday*, looking at some footage on the Moviola when Derek Horus burst in. Well, Derek was drunk and crazy and he wanted me back. Andreji told him to leave, and Derek started shoving Andreji. Then he grabbed Andreji, who was much smaller, by the lapels and started slapping him around, and it was just sheer sadism. "Derek, stop it," I said. But Derek just laughed, and then he took Andreji's Mets baseball cap and put it on and started mugging and doing this vicious impression of Andreji's accent. When suddenly without warning Derek grabbed his chest and reeled back and crashed through the window, falling six stories to the street below.

Later they said he'd had a massive heart attack.

Karen Quall

We started doing the scene where Man Lafitte had to attack me, and on the first take he tore open my blouse and started mauling my bare breasts. He smelled horrible, there was dirt under his fingernails, and he was mumbling this voodoo mumbo-jumbo right in my face and he had really awful breath. When he began rutting against me, and I felt his big, hard thing rubbing through his filthy pants right up against my bare thigh, I just lost it and started screaming.

Larry yelled, "Cut!" But Shark yelled, "No! Keep rolling!"

Finally Mark intervened and spoiled the end of the take. Shark used the take right up to that point though—he had to because I wouldn't do it again.

Then, thank God, Man Lafitte disappeared.

Mark LeManns

I asked Shark where his friend had gone and he said, "Back to Haiti." Then he smiled ironically, as if he knew something I didn't. The stereo in his trailer was blasting a Down in Flames album, I remember, as a kind of requiem for Derek Horus, whom we'd heard had died of a heart attack the day before in New York.

Bill Kemmer

Several months after *The Condoist* wrapped, Shark came into my office at Mastodon looking frightened and pale. "We've got to take care of this or we could be in big trouble," he said and showed me a letter.

It was barely legible on greasy, stained paper but the gist of it was: "You send me one more check for fifty thousand dollar or you will lose your sex tool, Shark." It was signed Man Lafitte with a Haiti address, and a P.S. "I have your pube hairs, friend, so don't jerk me."

It was clearly some sort of crackpot voodoo threat, but Shark appeared genuinely shaken.

"What should we do?" I asked him.

"Either put out a contract on him or issue a check."

Well, by then we sensed that *The Condoist* was going to be a blockbuster. So I issued the check.

Lawrence Granger

Poor sweet Karen! What an ordeal that film was for her. Dear Laura String and Tony Cray—what a joy to work with both of them again, though sadly how times, and tastes, had changed. Frankly, I was thankful Shark had storyboarded the decapitation and squashing sequences. I delegated that unsavory business to the second unit director, a brash and eager young man thirty years my junior, and proclaimed for all to hear, "As far as *I'm* concerned, that's a wrap."

12 / **Boy Wonder** (1975)

Greg Spivey

Shark hired me as his story editor in early '75, while he was in post-production on *The Condoist*. I was a couple of years out of USC film school, and had been scraping by as a freelance story analyst, when it came to Shark's attention that I had been the only reader in Hollywood to give the first-draft screenplay of *Angel's Flight* a positive report. When the film was eventually made, and surpassed *Chinatown* as the top-grossing Los Angeles period film of all time, Shark tracked me down and called me in for a meeting. I'd been there maybe ten minutes, we'd made little more than jokey small talk, when he offered to make me his "right-hand man."

I couldn't believe my good fortune. How could I possibly know it was the beginning of a professional and personal relationship that would eventually cost me two marriages, my sense of humor and self-esteem, and permanently damage my physical health. Whether or not it was worth it is still a very difficult question. Shark Trager did have his upside, and in 1975 that was all I saw. His energy, his magnetism, the heady sense of being "where the action was." Shark wasn't just hot then, he was the hottest producer in town, since the advance word on *The Condoist* was that it was going to be a mega-hit, which of course is what came to pass—though I don't think even Shark was prepared for the magnitude of the success. He really had only one serious bit of competition. I don't think he ever forgave Steven [Spielberg] for making *Jaws* the same year.

Malcolm Stale, *The New Adlai Review,* June 23, 1975

The Condoist is a whacking good thriller. Beats *Jaws* by a country mile as top-notch summer entertainment. Lawrence Granger is back with a stylish vengeance. Not since *Romanesque* have we enjoyed this sort of good old-fashioned cinematic vim and verve. Bud Squat is surprisingly effective in the title role. Laura String and Anthony Cray are by turns wickedly delicious and utterly delightful. Newcomer Karen Quall steals the film with her pert desirability and fresh-scrubbed "California girl" charm. The film does have its violent moments but Granger tends to these with such incomparably good taste that only the most squeamish could possibly be offended. A five-star crackerjack movie. They just don't come any better than this.

Bill Kemmer

I suppose it's no secret the film saved the studio. We were in deep financial shit after a string of flops in the early seventies, and had a great deal more riding on *The Condoist* than most people knew at the time. But Ben knew. And he also knew that Shark had single-handedly saved the picture. Left in Larry Granger's hands it would have degenerated into unreleasable drivel, so it would be difficult to convey the true depth of Ben's gratitude.

But he still wouldn't let Shark make *Tropics*, his Amelia Earhart "fantasy romance." He was diplomatic with Shark, citing the most recent budget which was something like eighteen million. But privately he told me, "The script's so bad it defies comprehension. But every so-called genius has at least one truly terrible idea. It's part of my job to see that Shark doesn't embarrass himself. Or us."

Greg Spivey

Tropics did represent a blind spot on Shark's part. It was awful, an interminable, stickily romantic, cliché-riddled exercise in delayed gratification that was guaranteed to infuriate any audience. I was truly at a loss for words when he told he was determined to make it his next film.

Of course I see now why he was so irrationally attached to the project. The entire story was a metaphor for his thwarted longing for Kathy Petro. He projected himself into the role of Frederick Noonan, Earhart's adoring if taciturn navigator. How he ever came to associate Kathy with the famed aviatrix really confounds understanding though—have any two women ever been more dissimilar? Of course on a purely emotional level the Earhart myth does possess an intrinsic sadness, doesn't it? A yearning for the past, which when you think about it is rather poignant—that Shark at twenty-five was already steeped in a nostalgia for a love that had never really even existed, except in his mind.

Jean Klieg

We very nearly lost Shark over *Tropics*. He stormed into Ben's office, which no one ever did, not into *Ben's* office, and *demanded* that Ben greenlight *Tropics* or else. *The Condoist* had just passed the hundred million mark, so Shark no doubt believed Ben would cave in.

Well, he didn't know my husband. No one told *Ben Klieg* what to do.

Then Shark made the mistake of insulting me. "*Tropics will* make money," he yelled at Ben. "*Of course*, it's excessively romantic, but that's *a plus*. Who do you think decides which movie a couple's going to see? Ask that cow you're married to."

At that Ben rose up behind his desk on the twenty-first floor of the Mastodon Building, a towering figure of indignation against the vertiginous view of L.A. "Now you see here, you young punk! Nobody calls the woman I love a cow! You'd really better watch it, Shark. You may be riding a wave but you could sink like a stone if people ever found out certain things about you."

"What things?" Shark asked, clearly shaken.

"Everyone has a past," Ben said, cryptically. He was bluffing, of course. But he was fairly certain Shark had done something in the sixties he wasn't too proud of. In those days, you know, a lot of people Shark's age were rather frantically trying to cover their tracks.

Greg Spivey

I remember well Shark's extreme anxiety after that meeting. Without really wanting it I suppose I had already become his chief confidant and "best friend"—in effect taking Elliot Bernstein's place.

"What can Ben know about me?" Shark said.

"What have you done?" I said, jokingly.

But Shark looked at me with real fear in his eyes.

Not long after that he had the beach house swept for electronic bugs. One Saturday I was there for a story conference when he said, "Let's go for a walk."

Once we were out on the beach—away from the hidden microphones—he said, "You know, Greg, I think I may have killed a man."

I was jolted for a moment, thinking maybe he really had, a drunken hit-and-run perhaps, something he couldn't completely remember. So I was relieved when he told me about the voodoo curse which had been directed at Andreji Pavlavojac but which had by fluke, Shark believed, caused Derek Horus' death.

"But Shark, voodoo's bullshit. Derek Horus' heart attack could only have been a coincidence."

"But he was wearing Andreji's baseball cap," Shark said. "Just like Man Lafitte's doll."

"Was it your intention to give Andreji a heart attack?" I said.

"No!" he replied, almost hysterically. "I just wanted to make him impotent. But Man Lafitte stabbed the doll in the heart not the penis. I realized too late that the doll Man Lafitte used didn't even *have* a penis. Greg, I fucked up bad."

"Shark," I said. "You're overwrought. Maybe you should take a vacation. God knows, you've earned it."

What I really wanted to say was you should get off the cocaine. It was obvious Shark had an addict's personality. Once he took to anything there was never enough of it.

Cynthia Clive

As Shark's cocaine usage escalated it became increasingly difficult to regard his partaking of the drug as a romantically mischievous vice. I found myself cringing when I saw Gramps coming, no longer charmed by his folksy manner, knowing full well what a new delivery meant. And God forbid Gramps should be late! Shark's impatience had became chronic, one could barely complete a sentence without his interrupting, and by noon his voice would be hoarse from shouting into the telephone.

His temper could be frightful. We'd been trying to reach Robert Redford for days, when finally I got him on hold. "Shark, Redford on two," I called, and no sooner had they said hello than I accidentally pressed the wrong button and disconnected them. Shark stormed out to my desk. I shan't repeat the stream of obscenities he uttered.*
Suffice it to say I stood trembling and said, "Never, in all my years in Hollywood, has anyone ever spoken to me as you just have. Not Mr. Thalberg, even at his testiest. Not even Mr. Selznick, when I occasionally lost my way in his furiously dictated memoranda. I have worked for the giants, Mr. Trager. But you, sir, are a very small man."

I tendered my resignation on the spot, and departed posthaste lest he see my tears.

An enormous bouquet of red roses was waiting on my Brentwood doorstep when I arrived home less than thirty minutes later. Shark appeared at the door an hour or so after that, at sunset. The light, I

---

* According to Julie Dess, an assistant secretary, it went something like this: "You stupid English cooze. You idiotic British twitch-box. You soft-headed, kidney pie-brained old sow. You cocksucking Queen Victoria, you simpering third-rate Deborah Kerr."

shall never forget, was a soft, nostalgic orange, such as one finds in the title sequence of Mr. Selznick's masterpiece.† Never had Shark more resembled the youthful Errol Flynn than he did then bathed in that poignant glow.

"I am so sorry, Mrs. Clive," he said with a boyish, touching earnestness. "I swear upon my mother Winnie's grave, if you come back I shall never from this day forward speak to you in any but the most civilized, respectful and kindly tones."

And you know, right up until the end, he never did. (*weeping*) I'm sorry.

Greg Spivey

Almost losing Mrs. Clive gave Shark a certain pause. "I still feel like stabbing my tongue with an icepick when I think of the things I said to her," he told me. "She's really quite dear to me, you know."

But his cocaine-fueled rage at everyone else reached new heights. "Then choke on my rod, you cocksucking whore," I heard him yell over the phone to a hot young director he'd grown tired of trying to woo. Later that same afternoon he flared in a meeting and threw his telephone at one of the town's most powerful agents, yelling, "You're trying to gouge me, you fuck. I'll give you a *real* gouge." The cord stopped the phone an inch from the fellow's face, but everyone present was shaken—including Shark. The next morning he said, "Greg, you're right, I've got to get out of town, I've got to cool out. One way or another, I've got to stop this goddamn brain."

Well, I was relieved, preferring to ignore the darker implications of what he'd said. But when he simply vanished, telling no one where he was going or when he'd be back, and several days passed without his even checking in by phone, there began to be a great deal of concern.

Betty Ray

I was working at a Jack in the Box in Monterey, California, when Shark pulled up to the window in this fantastic Porsche. Right away he started coming on and I finally gave him my number because the cars behind his were honking.

He called that night and we went out and ended up spending the weekend together in this super-expensive oceanview hotel suite in Carmel. I was nineteen then and had never done anything like that before, but he was so handsome and charming I couldn't say no. And when he told me he had produced *The Condoist* I was really im-

† She can only mean *Gone With the Wind*.

pressed, since except for *Jaws* that was about the biggest movie around.

He was really sweet and a very good lover—better than I'd ever known up to then—and we walked on the beach and went to that mission where Kim Novak fell from the tower in *Vertigo*. We even climbed up to the top of the tower, though we weren't supposed to, and really caught hell from some nun.

I'd told Shark about winning this Kathy Petro look-alike contest, so when he saw that her movie *Manhattan Holiday* was playing in Carmel he said, "Let's go."

Even though the movie took place in New York City, it seemed almost like some foreign film, especially with that funny little guy in the baseball cap who played the lead opposite Kathy. He had a real thick accent. It was hard to believe that Kathy was supposed to be in love with him, since he was so dumpy and all. And Kathy just stunk. I mean her acting was so bad I really felt sorry for her. I guess Shark did too. He kept shaking his head and looking really sad.

He didn't tell me that he knew her or anything though.

Kathy Petro

The reviews really killed me, and they hurt Andreji too. They accused him of being dazzled by me, and not being able to see what a bad actress I was and that sort of thing. Andreji kept picking at me, critiquing my performance after the fact in this compulsive post mortem that seemed to go on forever. "Kathy, if you'd only listened to me when I say, 'Take it down.' " Or we'd be watching the movie for the thirty-fourth time and he'd say, "See? Here, I tell you not to be so wooden. But look how stiff you are!" Finally I just exploded and said, "I never wanted to do it in the first place." So we ended up having this big blow-out on Fifth Avenue and I ran off up the street in tears.

I just felt so rotten I didn't want to do anything. Then some photographer at a party offered me some junk, and I broke into a cold sweat. That was when I knew I had to get out of New York.

Dad had this place on Maui, a beautiful little house in Hana just up the road from where Charles Lindbergh went to live the last years of his life in solitude and sorrow. So I went there, to be alone.

I see now there must have been an item about it somewhere. You know, "Super-model Kathy Petro goes into seclusion on Maui to lick her wounds."

Betty Ray

The way it ended with Shark was really strange. We stopped at this market in Carmel to get some stuff for a picnic—it must have been Monday morning, I remember we were both raw and exhausted— and he went over to the newsstand while I went to get the food. A minute later I glanced out the window and saw him running to his Porsche. By the time I reached the door he was already pulling away. As I stood there, angry and confused, I noticed this *People* magazine on the floor by the newsstand, opened to a picture of Kathy Petro. It was just some little story about now she'd washed out as an actress and gone into seclusion somewhere.

Bill Kemmer

I was with Ben and several other executives in Ben's office, and we were all frantic about Shark, really afraid he might have gone off and OD'ed somewhere—Ben was even saying, "If I'd known *Tropics* meant *that* much to him . . ."—when Shark burst into the room.

"*Hail!* just went into turnaround, right?" he yelled with an infectious enthusiasm that instantly told us how unfounded our worry had been.

"Yes, I think it did," I said. "Didn't it, Ben?"

After topping the best-seller lists for thirty weeks, Richard Dreckley's novel *Hail!* had gone through development at half the studios in town. Despite the story's photogenic Maui location, the film remained unmade for a variety of reasons, not least of which was the concept's essential preposterousness.

Ben nodded cautiously. "Yes, I believe Universal just passed."

"Get it!" Shark yelled. "It's our next blockbuster!"

I tried to dissuade Ben. But when the marketing people ran a plot synopsis through the computer and projected domestic rentals of *at least* a hundred million my objections fell on deaf ears.

Greg Spivey

It was decided that *Hail!* would be Mastodon's big picture for Christmas, which meant that we had to move fast. Structurally, it was your basic disaster film: an all-star cast trapped at a posh island resort during a horrendous freak hail storm. The concept itself of course marked the reducto ad absurdum of an exhausted genre. Earthquakes, burning skyscrapers, tidal waves, capsized ships, bees—everything but hail had been done. And there were technical as well as esthetic reasons for this. The special effects were going to be a tough, expensive nut to crack. The script called for hail stones the size of basketballs to come crashing down through hotel skylights, to pulverize sunbathers on the beach like meteorites, and to crush people in their cars.

Shark brought Frank Gleese on to direct and whip the script into shape, and together they flew to Maui in June to scout locations.

Frank Gleese

I may be one of the few people in Hollywood who can honestly say he always got along beautifully with Shark. But then I've always believed in the collaborative nature of the filmmaking process and find prima donna egotism extremely wasteful and tedious.

Greg Spivey

Frank Gleese was a true director for the seventies, that is to say a colossally overpaid hack, a colorless, styleless, dutiful mediocrity—in short just the sort of director Shark needed if he were to stamp his own vision on *Hail!*

Frank Gleese

Shark and I quickly chose the Kalahali resort complex on Maui as the principle location for *Hail!* The resort was new then, sprawling and gleaming, precisely the sort of clean, modern look we were after. We imagined the miniatures, and the special effects shots where the tanned and screaming teens would be bludgeoned with hailstones on the picturesque beach. We studied the stupendous skylight over the lobby, picturing the mob of tourists keening hysterically under the bombardment of hail and shattered glass, and knew it would work.

The next day Shark and I planned to drive out to the Haleakala crater. I came down to the lobby in the morning only to be told he'd already taken off by himself in the Jeep.

Kathy Petro

Hana's so great cause it's so primitive. It's not all trashy and built up with tacky resorts like the rest of Maui. It's the way all the islands were fifty years ago. Just one road in and a dinky little airfield, and even the grocery store is primitive too. Staples, no gourmet deli.

Which was fine with me. I was so happy in that ramshackle house. I felt like I was relaxing for the first time in years. The air was so warm and heavy, and the house was so private, most of the time I wore little more than my clogs. The storms would come and go— God, the spectacular cascading view down to the ocean, kind of like Big Sur only better! I can barely describe the serenity I felt as I whiled away the balmy days cooking brown rice in the buff, and lolling for hours in the hammock, wearing nothing but my glasses as I savored the poetry of Rod McKuen.

I had dozed off one afternoon midway through *Listen to the Warm* when a voice called my name, jolting me awake. I looked up to see Shark peering through the front door back in the house.

"Kathy?"

In terror I grabbed my sarong, though not before he saw me in the all-together as he stepped into the house. "What are you doing here? How dare you come here?" I said, panic welling up in me. The house was so isolated, screaming wouldn't help.

"Take it easy," he said, coming closer. "I just want to talk to you." His voice was calm but he had that look in his eyes.

"Why can't you just leave me alone?" I said. "You have no right to come here."

"I have every right, Kathy," he said, and my skin crawled—even as another part of me was strangely excited. His shirt was open. He did have a good body. But I thought: Wait, this is crazy. I can't be attracted to this man, not after all he's put me through. I'm not that sick, I'm not!

So I said, "Please, just go."

He smiled and said, "Look, I don't blame you for hating me, Kathy. But let me make up for the things I've done. Let me make you a star."

"I am a star," I said. "I don't need you, or anyone, for that."

"I mean, a movie star, a *real* movie star."

Well, that touched a nerve. I didn't even want to think about movies ever again. "This is crazy," I said. "I don't even know why I'm talking to you. Get out."

But he had this script and he tried to hand it to me. "This is going to be my masterpiece," he said, and I saw it was *Tropics*. "I want you to play Amelia Earhart."

"You're crazy," I said. "Haven't you seen *Manhattan Holiday?*"

"I saw it," he said. "You were wretched. But that wasn't your fault. I know about film, Kathy. I can turn you into another Dietrich or Garbo."

I could tell from his manner that he was coked. I figured he was capable of anything so I said, "Okay, give me the script, I'll read it," just to get rid of him.

"It's about us," he said, as he handed it to me, and for some reason that remark just twisted my insides.

"What do you mean, *us?* There is no us, Shark. There never has been, except in your mind. I can't stand you, I hate you, you make me sick, you always have." Then I just went crazy and started hitting him with the script, screaming more things at him, until he finally stopped me, holding both my wrists.

Our faces were close and then, inevitably, he kissed me. But I pulled my mouth from his and spit in his face. Well, that jolted him, and I could see he was mad. So when he let go of one of my wrists to wipe off his face I broke away.

I ran out across the porch and out across this big grassy field over-looking the ocean, and he was right behind me. I was really more scared than I had ever been, not sure if he was going to rape me or kill me or both.

Suddenly I came to the edge of the cliff, and there was nothing but the crashing surf and the rocks far below. I whirled around as Shark approached me. "If you come any closer, I swear I'll jump," I said.

He stopped a few feet from me. We were both out of breath, our hearts pounding.

"I don't believe you'd do that," he said finally.

"Touch me and see what happens," I said.

"That sounds more like an invitation than a threat," he said, and smiled rakishly, which enraged me.

"I hate you so much," I said. "You're the only person in this world I've ever really hated."

"That's not what I see in your eyes," he said, and took a step towards me, opening his arms.

I stepped back. "I'm not kidding, I'll jump."

"I don't believe you," he said.

Then, just as he took another step towards me, I looked past him and saw Daddy up on the windy hill, just towering above us, the wind whipping his white slacks, and even at a hundred yards I could just feel his searing rage.

I was so startled by Daddy's presence that when I stepped back again from Shark I almost fell. Shark grabbed my arm in time. I guess he saved my life, though for a long time I refused to think of it that way, since after all he was the one who'd driven me right up to the edge of that cliff in the first place.

When Shark saw Daddy he let go of my arm as if I were suddenly no longer there. He just glared at Daddy, who was starting down the hill, glaring at Shark with the same kind of hatred, his fists clenched.

"Please, don't do anything, Shark," I said, because even though Daddy still looked strong, he'd had a bypass operation.

But Shark was already in an attack mode, no doubt flashing back on the time Daddy beat him to a pulp in Huckleberry Finn's Family Restaurant. Then before I could say another word, they were charging each other like angry rams.

It was no contest because of Daddy's condition. Shark slugged Daddy in the stomach, knocking his wind out. Then he pushed him back against a tree and kind of pinned him there, and just started smashing Dad's face in. Shark was just berserk, I knew Daddy was going to end up like Jean-Claude if I didn't stop it. So I pulled Shark away, my sarong slipping open as I did, so that my bare breasts pressed against Shark's bare muscular chest, as Daddy slumped to the ground.

"Please, go," I said to Shark. But my nipples were hard and a part of me wanted him. Crazy as it sounds, a part of me wanted him right there in front of Daddy.

And I could see he wanted me more than anyone had ever wanted me, or ever would.

Then we heard voices back in the house. My mom and several other people who had come on this surprise visit with Daddy.

Shark glanced down at Daddy and said, "You'd better get him stitched up." Then he kissed me gently on the mouth and said, "So long, funny face," and took off as my mom and the others came out.

Greg Spivey

Hail! rolled on Maui in July. Despite its complexity, the filming went fairly smoothly. An extra looked up when he shouldn't have, and lost an eye to a plastic hailstone, and one of our has-been matinee idol stars was nearly arrested for having sex with an underage Hawaiian girl. But Frank Gleese kept the film on schedule.

Then one afternoon Dean Sutter arrived and I realized something was up. I knew Dean from USC, where he'd directed a prize-winning short, then gone to Europe where he'd made an art film in Spain. I assumed he was there to discuss a future project with Shark, but both he and Shark were very furtive and secretive—neither would tell me what was going on.

Then we had a break and the three of us drove out to Hana.

We reached a remote house and Shark said, "Wait here," and walked up to the house.

As Dean and I waited in the Jeep, I said, "What are we doing here?"

"Scouting locations," he said.

"Locations for what?"

Again, the furtive air. *"Tropics,"* he said.

"What are you saying? That Klieg actually approved that?"

"Not exactly," Dean said.

Then he explained how they were going to shoot it on the sly, hiding the cost in the *Hail!* budget.

"Shark's a genius," Dean said, and tooted some cocaine. "He planned it this way from the beginning." He said that a small cast and crew for *Tropics* was due to arrive next week.

"This is insanity," I told him. "You're jeopardizing your career."

"Art means taking risks," Dean said, and offered me the vial.

I went to the house to find Shark.

The place was closed up tightly. I found Shark sitting on the porch, holding a soiled sarong and a weather-beaten book of Rod McKuen poetry, seemingly lost in thought.

Dean Sutter

I knew we could get into fairly serious trouble, but then you always can when you're really making art, and *Tropics* was a script I wanted to do. I was always aware that Shark took the story seriously, that it represented a romantic bent of his personality that he did not realize was kitsch. In this sense he was very much like Selznick, and I went along, humoring him as it were, though I always saw *Tropics* as a coolly ironic hommage—a kind of blissfully neo–von Sternbergian orgy of deadpan narcotic camp.

Greg Spivey

"You can't hope to get away with this," I told Shark.

"I don't expect to," he said. "But by the time Ben finds out about it, it'll be too late to stop it. And if he tries . . ."

Well, of course, Ben found out.

Bill Kemmer

I was aghast, we all were, when we discovered what Shark was doing. I think *Tropics* had been shooting for a week in Hana, even as *Hail!* continued filming on the other side of the island, when our spies confirmed Shark's incomprehensible audacity.

Ben was livid. But also fearful of scandal. It made us all look very bad that Shark had been able to hide the entire cost of *Tropics* in the *Hail!* budget without anyone noticing.

Ben and I flew to Maui, then spent three hours simmering in the Kalahali complex waiting for Shark to return from the *Tropics* location. The infuriating thing was that *Hail!* was still rolling smoothly and the footage we'd seen was sensational.

Ben was near the explosion point when Shark finally pulled up in his muddy Jeep. "You goddamn son of a bitch," he yelled at Shark.

"Look at it this way, Ben," Shark said, jauntily. "You're getting two films for the price of one."

"Nobody pulls this kind of crap on me," Ben said. "I don't care who you think you are, mister, I'm going to destroy you."

"No, you're not," Shark said, turning lethal. "You're going to kiss my ass, old man. You're going to kiss my ass and sing my praises— when you take home your seven-figure bonus next year after *Hail!* goes through the ceiling."

"You son of a bitch!" Ben yelled again. "I'm pulling the plug on that piece of shit you're shooting in Hana right now!"

"No, you're not," Shark said.

"And you're off *Hail!*," Ben added. "The next film you make is going to be a Super 8 production in Soledad prison."

Shark paused for effect, and then simply said, "Ben . . . the negative."

Ben didn't get it at first, then he did, and a tremor ran through him. "You son of a bitch," he said, but this time his voice was weak and shaky.

We checked and found out it was true. All the film shot so far had been shipped back to L.A. for processing, then removed by Shark's people to an unknown location.

Ben knew Shark was crazy enough to destroy the *Hail!* negative if it came to that. Ben was abject, nearly suicidal. His own career was at stake. Finally, he said to me, "I'll speak to George [*McSlot, chairman of World Leisure Petroleum, the parent company, Ed.*] and tell him I approved *Tropics* on a wild hunch. Prepare the announcements. We'll cover our tracks."

Dean Sutter

I only had one real blow-up with Shark, and that was over the length of our female star Jane Hegel's hair. I'd had it cut short, like Earhart's, and the first time Shark saw her he went through the roof. "What have done? Where's her hair?"

Jane had had long blonde hair when we'd cast her, but I said, "Shark, it's the nineteen-thirties. Do you want her to look like Kathy Petro?"

At the time I knew nothing of his past with Kathy.

He exploded, calling me every name in the book.

"Then fuck you," I said. "You don't like what I'm doing, *you* direct the picture."

This stunned him into silence. It was obvious I'd touched an old wound. He apologized profusely, blaming his irritability on cocaine, and basically left me alone after that.

Paige Petro

Shark gave Jack quite a licking on Maui, though I suppose it looked worse than it was. Jack's face was just ghastly for several weeks. I was all for pressing charges, and shutting down Shark's films. Jack certainly had enough clout in the islands to make life there quite painful for Shark.

But Jack did nothing—except glare accusingly at Kathy, as she stalked about petulantly, refusing to acknowledge him. "I can't believe I am back in this house," she would say, as if Newport Beach were a prison. "I'm twenty-five and I'm back in this goddamn house."

Of course Jack did have his mind on other things. It was the beginning of the cancer suits. Suddenly it was chic to blame chemicals for everything. Within a few years the empire Jack had built from the ground up would be besieged from all sides.

Kathy Petro

I couldn't even look at Daddy without thinking about how he'd seen me with my bare nipples pressed against Shark's chest, and without thinking how for a second I'd really been ready to have sex with Shark right there in front of my own father! God, I felt so sick.

But I had no place else to go. I'd spent all my modeling money on junk, except for the two hundred thousand I'd loaned Andreji to finish *Manhattan Holiday*. Fat chance I'd ever see any of *that* again!

And suddenly nobody wanted me anymore. The agency dropped me, saying I was overexposed. "Your time is past," they said. "This is Cheryl Tiegs's time now." And I'd see Cheryl Tiegs on a magazine cover and think: You rotten bitch, you stole my job.

I even started thinking: Gee, maybe I *should've* done *Tropics*. Then I'd think: What's wrong with me, am I crazy? Then I started having all these dreams about Shark.

C. Glibb, *Face* Magazine, September 2, 1975

FROM "SHARK TRAGER: HOLLYWOOD'S NEWEST BOY WONDER"

He's young, he's good-looking, and he's sitting on top of the world. In a town where you're only as good as your latest picture, Shark Trager is *hot*—this year's definitive Hollywood wunderkind. At twenty-five, the producer of this summer's blockbuster *The Condoist* is out to top himself with not one but two new pictures filming concurrently on Maui: *Hail!*, a "big splashy thrill-packed all-star disaster epic for the whole family," and *Tropics*, a "serious romantic fantasy for young couples everywhere."

How does it feel to be a mega-success at such a young age? "Mighty fine," quips the magnetic go-getter with a rakish grin. "I've got everything I've ever wanted, almost, and I'm ecstatic! Who says material things aren't important? I've got a spectacular beach house, the Porsche of my dreams, top-of-the-line you-name-it—and it's all a gas! People who try and trash success are just sore losers."

And in the love life department Trager's not complaining either. "Power is a major turn-on, there's no doubt about it. I need a steam shovel to keep away the babes. If I didn't pace myself I'd be doing nothing but you-know-what twenty-four hours a day."

"But movies are my life," asserts the self-confessed workaholic. "People fail you eventually, but movies never do. They're like dreams."

Do we detect a wistful tone in Trager's voice? "Oh, maybe. There are still a few things money can't buy, I suppose."

Like what, for instance?

Before Trager can answer the phone interrupts. Juggling two productions on the island paradise isn't easy.

"I love the phone," Trager says a minute later with a half dozen calls on hold. "It's like sex to me. Movies are like sex, too."

And what's sex like?

"Like going to the movies," the boy wonder retorts.

With an attitude like that, it's a good bet Shark Trager's going to be around for some time.

Bill Kemmer

Both *Hail!* and *Tropics* wrapped in September, and Shark took *Tropics* to a secret Los Angeles location for editing, afraid Ben might attempt to seize it once the *Hail!* negative was in Mastodon's hands.

I will say this. However thinly he may have been spreading himself, Shark's meticulous zeal to see that *Hail!* was ready for its scheduled Christmas release was unrelenting.

Cynthia Clive

Shark worked ceaselessly, going without sleep for days, until he was reduced to a state of hallucinatory agony, such as a handsome RAF bombardier might know toward the end of a ceaseless string of air assaults against the industrial might of Hitler's Germany.

One morning he was so exhausted I insisted he let me drive him home. He yammered all the way in my ancient Renault—in retrospect I imagine he'd been taking cocaine to stay awake but had consumed a sedative of some sort to counteract the stimulant's jangling effect in anticipation of sleep. He went on at great length about a woman he vainly loved, who was anonymous at first, then confessionally revealed to be Kathy Petro. I tried not to listen, sensing correctly that he would regret these personal revelations later, but there was no stopping him.

As we streamed down the freeway he said, "You know, Mrs. Clive, you remind me a great deal of Lorna, my aunt. You're a bit older of course, but you're physically quite similar. Oddly enough, I believe that Lorna is the single woman in this world whom I have neither loved nor hated, but simply cared for."

At that Shark rested his head in my lap as I drove and fell soundly asleep like a child.

13 / **Scars**
(1975–1976)

Bill Kemmer

As much as Ben wanted *Hail!* to succeed for the obvious business reasons, on a purely emotional level I think he was secretly praying it would fail so miserably that it would spell Shark's demise as a Hollywood power. "If this turkey doesn't fly," Ben confided to me on the eve of *Hail!*'s massive release, "Shark Trager is going to be standing under it. And I'm going to make sure everybody sees him covered with feathers and entrails and blood."

It didn't turn out quite that way, of course. By the time it was all over *Hail!* had become the top-grossing film in the history of Mastodon Pictures, despite generally negative reviews.

Barry Crown, "A.M. America," DBC-TV, December 20, 1975

Big, dull and boring. Like a tired ride at Disneyland, *Hail!* is no fun at all. Unbelievably crummy considering how much it cost. The special effects are cheesy, the acting listless, the direction nonexistent, the concept preposterous, the overall results indescribably depressing. Vacantly, blandly, dismally bad. On my one-to-ten scale, gets a *minus seven!* It stank! I hated it! If you go, and incredibly there were long lines when I saw it, don't say I didn't warn you.

Jean Klieg

The film was "review-proof," wasn't it? As Ben was always fond of pointing out, there were "a lot more average schmucks buying tickets than critics." And there was certainly no dissuading the schmucks that winter.

Privately Ben deplored Shark, even as he was compelled to publicly laud him as the maker of *Hail!* "I've got a bad feeling about Shark," he said to me once. "Not just because of the *Tropics* extortion, but just a bad feeling in general. I think someday Shark may do something truly and colossally unconscionable."

I asked Ben to elaborate, but he simply looked out the window at our Bel-Air grounds and shook his head as one might, anticipating the horrors of, say, World War III.

Bill Kemmer

Through some miracle the true story behind the making of *Tropics* never saw light. I believe Ben called in some favors with people in the trades. There was talk, of course, but we had covered ourselves, exploiting the relative novelty of "two films shooting at once." Besides, in a business as financially baroque as ours it's probably beyond the power of any single mind to ever pin down where all the money is coming from and where it's all going.

As much as Ben loathed *Tropics* he didn't try to quash it. He didn't have to. The problems were all intrinsic to the film itself.

Dean Sutter

When I showed Shark my cut he exploded. "You stupid, ignorant fuck, you've ruined it. This is shit. I'm going to see that you never direct another picture."

Well, I was exhausted and flew off the handle. I'm not a physical person, so I was astonished to find myself grappling with Shark on the floor of the screening room. The next thing I knew he was actually *biting into my forearm.* You can still see the scar.

Greg Spivey

Shark told me later he'd lost control in the fight with Dean, though the fight itself had been planned. He just wanted an excuse to get rid of Dean so that he could cut *Tropics* himself. Which he did, endlessly. He just couldn't get it right. But then nobody could have. The performances weren't the problem. It was the script, the whole concept of the film itself, that sucked. I tried to tell him this tactfully, but he wouldn't hear it.

Eventually, after months of trying to save the film in the editing room, Shark simply ran out of steam. He never admitted defeat in so many words, but the work prints were put in storage. And so his von Sternberg hommage died with a whimper, his rotten mango romance, it seemed, permanently shelved.

There followed a long stretch—actually most of 1976—during

which Shark did little more than rest on his laurels. We had a number of projects in various stages of development, but there was an unspoken sense that none of them was really *it*.

One of the oddest projects was the "Riviera romance" Shark insisted on calling *The Thrill of It All.* The story, which went through a number of permutations, was something of a pastiche of Hitchcock's *To Catch a Thief* and *Rear Window,* and the Michael Powell cult film *Peeping Tom:* a voyeuristic Saint-Tropez catburglar spying on a blonde model inadvertently photographs a murder. Shark drove the writer crazy with new plot twists and changes, before finally abandoning the idea after Universal refused to let him use the title of their 1963 Doris Day film. "There's no point to doing it if I can't use that title," Shark said, which I didn't understand at all. Of course, about that time he discovered the British art-rock group Roxy Music, which became his favorite group from that point on, and they had a song called "The Thrill of It All," which Shark played obsessively at home and in his car. It was a strange, calamitous, driven song, the lyrics speaking of hopeless romantic loss and subsequent dissipation—spiritually about as far removed from a Doris Day comedy as you could get.

There were other scripts, other deals, but nothing held Shark's interest for long. There were weeks on end where he didn't even bother to come into the studio. Of course his old high school friend was back in the picture by then.

Woody Hazzard

The early seventies had been a bad time for me. I got busted in Mexico with a hundred keys of grass, and did eighteen months in a rathole Chihuahua prison before being returned to the U.S. as part of a prisoner-exchange deal. Then I did another nine months at Chino before I got paroled. I was in real bad shape when I called Shark from a phone booth in L.A. and he invited me out to the beach house.

I ended up staying there for over a year. At first I was a little intimidated, cause he had all these heavy-weight movie star types running in and out of there day and night. But I got into the swing of it soon enough. In a lot of ways it was like a replay of our summer at my mom's place in Newport, except instead of surfer girls we had starlets. Instead of acid and grass, we had bushels of Thai sticks and huge fucking mounds of cocaine.

Talk about bitchin summers, man, I couldn't believe it. After two and a half years in the joint I was starved for snatch—to say I made up for lost time wouldn't quite describe it. I don't know what Shark's excuse was. But we had more pussy than we even knew what to do with!

Of course every girl in town was dying to fuck Shark, since he was the man of the hour. And even though he still liked the blondes the best—especially if they looked the least bit like Kathy—he had 'em coming and going in all sizes, shapes and colors. I guess in some ways Shark had put a lot of his sex drive into his work up to then—maybe that was *his* excuse—and now he was reaping the rewards.

So I wouldn't feel like a freeloader he hired me on as his assistant/bodyguard, but the whole concept of money no longer even seemed to matter. I remember seeing a check from Mastodon once, either profits from *Hail!* or *The Condoist,* for the sum of fourteen million dollars and change. It was just sitting on his desk, man!—this check for fourteen million dollars!—along with the gas and electricity bills.

He had servants—there was a great Swedish cook for a while—but they were always quitting because a lot of the times during the day Shark went around without any clothes on, and then he'd be fucking some starlet on the dining room table or something. He got off on that, being something of an exhibitionist. Then when he hired Lupe that really got out of hand.

Lupe Sepulveda

I was new in Los Angeles from Mexico when Shark hired me as his live-in maid. I had a nice room above the garage. Then right away he started making love to me, which I didn't mind because he was very handsome. But then he promised many things that turned out to be lies.

Woody Hazzard

Lupe was stunning, though she did have a tough edge. Visually, she really could have been an actress—but who knew if she could act? I think Shark fed her a line about a remake of *Ramona,* this time with a real Hispanic girl in the Loretta Young part. He promised to give her a screen test and all that and proceeded to just fuck her senseless. I mean, it was sex-object city. I'm sure a lot of the attraction was based on the fact that Lupe did greatly resemble Juanita, the young whore he'd fucked on the Blue Fox stage in Tijuana and smuggled across the border in my car trunk in '66. Shark was always a glutton for nostalgia.

One day he was giving it to Lupe dog-style on the balcony, which wasn't too cool since it was a crowded day at the beach, and anyone who happened to look back up at the house could've seen what they were doing. I was lying by the pool below when he called to me, "Hey, bro. Check it out." I looked up just as he withdrew from Lupe and fired off this huge fuckin' load in a big arc through the air.

When she and Shark weren't getting it on Lupe was still doing the housework, but I sensed she was getting sick of waiting for her screen test, and that sooner or later something bad was going to come down.

Grey Spivey

In the fall of '76 Shark became briefly obsessed with developing a "prestige literary property." He was hungry for Academy recognition. Despite the gargantuan success of *The Condoist* and *Hail!* neither film had garnered more than a few technical award nominations. I understand a recording of his side of one of our phone discussions from that period exists.

Shark Trager, Audio Cassette, October 2, 1976

Greg-O. How's it hangin', you get laid last night? Yeah, I've had her. You're more generous than I am. Talked to Ben? Yeah, that figures. I wonder how much it would cost to have a 747 crash into his office. No, I'm hot for Jean. Don't be so sure, I saw her number on the Polo Lounge men's room wall. "For the meanest blow job north of Sunset—" *(laughs)* Greg, I've got Ovitz on two, let me put you on the speaker-phone and give you my notes. *Finnegans Wake:* Pass. Irish shit always goes down the toilet. *Pale Fire:* great title, but I'm not sure who we're rooting for. *Gravity's Rainbow:* maybe, if Bill Goldman can find the spine of the tale. *Catcher in the Rye:* up the offer to one million five. *Naked Lunch:* John Milius might bring it off, but do this decade's kids know the title? It sounds like a Crown International picture. *On the Road:* yes, if we can make it contemporary. Neal Cassidy as a disco fanatic, driving cross country to a big dance contest. It needs a sure-fire *Rocky* ending. *Giles Goat-Boy:* pass. Sounds like a Disney film. *Humbolt's Gift:* yes, if we can snag Robby Benson for the lead. *Our Lady of the Flowers:* send this to Steven [Spielberg]. If his UFO yarn's the dog I hear it is, he might like a change of pace. Greg, I've got Laddie, Michael Eisner, Sidney Korchak, Swifty Lazar, Nicholson's people, and Annette Funicello on hold—gotta go, kiddo. Oh, hey—track down *The Searchers*, will you? Ciao."

Neal Ridges

I had fallen on hard times since writing *The Condoist* which despite its phenomenal success had earned me nothing—thanks to the trickery of the studio accountants. I'd had a few bullshit development deals, but was basically scrounging. So I swallowed my pride when Greg Spivey called and said Shark was eager to discuss a "remake of *The Searchers.*"

The day I arrived at the beach house the door was open and I caught a glimpse of Shark going down on his Mexican maid in the kitchen. It was a kind of real-life porno situation. She was wearing one of those short, frilly French maid costumes, and no panties.

"I'll come back another time," I said when Shark saw me.

But he just laughed, and wiped his chin, and said, "No, that's okay, Neal, this can wait. Come on in."

Well, he was in good spirits, but the girl Lupe wasn't—I picked up those vibes right away. With considerable charm Shark asked my forgiveness for his "inexcusable behavior" during *The Condoist* writing period, which he attributed to "pressure, low-grade cocaine and creative nerves." I accepted his apology, and his praise of my "unique filmic genius," and we began to discuss the new project. It soon became apparent that what he had in mind was less a remake of *The Searchers* than simply another of the "updates" of the basic *Searchers* plot that were so popular at the time. It would be an "urban version," Shark said, with the "racial aspect" of the original brought to the fore. The girl Debbie, abducted by Indians in the original, would be kidnapped by black men and taken to live in Watts.

As we talked Lupe began banging pots and pans and angrily slamming cupboard doors in the kitchen. Several times Shark shouted, "Hey, I'm in a meeting." But the noise continued, until at last she began breaking plates.

In a rage Shark stormed in the kitchen, and there were heated words, hers in Spanish. Then Shark groaned, and staggered back into the room, bleeding from the stomach. She came at him with the knife again—a serrated steak knife—which I managed to get away from her. Then Shark collapsed in a pool of blood, as Lupe, sobbing now, held his head. "Oh God, what have I done!" she wailed. "Please don't die, Shark, I'm so sorry! Oh God, why couldn't you just love me!"

Woody Hazzard

I was out surfing the day Lupe stabbed Shark, but I rushed to the hospital as soon I found out. It was an evil jagged wound but they said Shark was going to make it.

He could've had Lupe charged with attempted murder, of course, but instead he chose to cover for her. He told the cops he'd been running past her to answer the phone when she turned abruptly with the knife in her hand and accidentally poked him.

Later I asked him why he let her off.

"Because I had it coming," he said, and smiled. "I knew she was in love with me. But to me she was just an incredibly wild and hot little fuck."

Then he looked at the scar on his stomach—we were catching some rays by the pool—and smiled again and said, "It was worth it."

But he seemed changed. The partying tapered off radically after that. He didn't care if I brought girls around, but he started keeping to himself again.

Then one day he said, "I'm sick of sitting in the sun. My brain's starting to atrophy. It's time to make another movie."

Lupe Sepulveda

This guy called me from Shark's studio and said, Here's ten thousand dollars, get out of town. I said, I don't want your money, I want a screen test for *Ramona*. He said there was no *Ramona*, so I took the money and moved to Santa Barbara and began going to night school there.

It turned out to be a blessing. I earned a business degree, became a U.S. citizen, and today have my own company, Ramona Industries, manufacturing douche bags and related products. In my spare time I am a poet, a gifted painter and a serious, dedicated female body builder.

It would be many years before I saw Shark again, and it would not be as I imagined it.

Bill Kemmer

We handled the maid, and kept the incident out of the papers. It was a blessing in the long run, of course, because it had a sobering effect on Shark and brought him back to work.

We were quite troubled at first though by Neal Ridges's neo-*Searchers* script *Scar*, which Shark insisted must be his next film.

Neal Ridges

I always thought the idea sucked, but I was sick of eating macaroni. I felt it was racist for one thing, especially the scenes where "Duke White," the neo–John Wayne uncle character in the script, starts tearing up Watts in search of his niece "Nattie"—played by Natalie Wood, you may recall, in the original. The first draft was virtually a scene-for-scene transliteration of the Ford classic, and I found Shark's new version both ridiculous and extremely offensive to write. The women's jail episode, for example, where the cops show Duke several white girl prisoners who've been "shacked up" with black male criminals—in the original John Wayne encountered a group of white pioneer women whose years in Indian captivity had driven them insane. "If she's still alive, *this* is what your niece will be like," the cop tells Duke. "*Now* can you tell me you still want to find her?" At which point the white girls, their hair frizzed out in horrendous Afros, begin screeching in black ghetto dialect: "What you lookin' at, mothuhfuckuh? Fuck yo' face, you jiveass honky," as we track in on our conservative protagonist's look of unfathomable horror.

Our white-bread hero goes on to shoot out a dead drug dealer's eyes and so forth and wins his showdown with the evil pimp Scar. But when the ultimate moment of truth comes, and he chases his Negroized niece back into a Watts riot-gutted Pioneer fried chicken outlet, he's so unhinged from the infernal rhythm & blues sex-beat pulverizing his Rotarian brain than instead of rescuing the girl, in a convulsion of libidinous fury *he rapes her.*

I argued vehemently against this ending, citing the original. "Shark, if you do this the audience will kill you. You can't have them identify with Duke for ninety minutes only to have him rape his own niece in the last reel. Use your common sense. If Ethan had raped Debbie in the original it would have utterly subverted the entire meaning of the film. It was *crucial* that he said, 'Debbie, let's go home,' not 'Straddle this, you dirty little squaw.' "

"But he *wanted* to fuck her," Shark contended vehemently. "Run the film, Neal! Look at the scene!"

Well, it's one of the classic moments in American film—there's no one right way to read that scene. "Okay, Shark," I said. "You're the producer, if that's what you want, that's what you'll get. But I'm warning you."

Bill Kemmer

After I read the script I met with Shark and said, "Shark, I don't understand this. I know you're not a racist. Like most of us who came of age in the sixties you're probably a liberal or a post-political humanist or something like that, and yet this is the most virulently racist script I've ever read."

Well, he exploded, saying the script wasn't racist, the character was, and was I so stupid I couldn't tell the difference?

"*I* can tell the difference," I told him, "because I am an intelligent, educated person who understands the nature and purpose of art. But I'm not sure the average moviegoer will perceive the distinction. Face it, America is sitting on a volcano of barely suppressed racial animosity. I'm afraid there'd be white girls attacked in the ladies rooms and black men strung up against the drive-in screens in the wake of this inflammatory tract."

"It's not a tract," Shark said angrily. "It's based on my father. My father's a racist, I'm not. But it's not just my father, it's all fathers. All fathers are racists. Isn't yours?"

Well, he was. But I hardly saw what that had to do with the script. Shark was clearly irrational, the victim of volatile and unresolved subjective forces.

"Shark, there's no way we can make this movie," I said calmly.

And he stormed out, muttering, "Fucking dildo executives," under his breath.

We were all very concerned. Then the next afternoon he burst into my office and said, "Bill? Problem solved. Forget the black angle. She's kidnapped by lesbians."

At the time it struck us all as a brilliant solution. We knew from Marketing that demographically lesbians, unlike blacks, were a group we could easily afford to offend.

Neal Ridges

I was ecstatic when Shark came up with the lesbian angle. Lesbianism was a subject that had long fascinated me, though I was the first to admit that I, as a heterosexual male, could not really presume to understand what it was for two beautiful women to make sensuous love to one another. But I saw the script as suddenly giving us a chance to provide a non-judgmental, perhaps even tastefully erotic, glimpse into the exotic netherworld of sex between dreamy young women without men.

The Scar character *would* have to be a stoutly masculine mean-tempered "diesel dyke" in coveralls and flannel shirt, but I felt I could impart a kind of humanity even to her.

Greg Spivey

Everybody was crazy about the lesbian draft—except me. Not that it wasn't well-written, but I'd lived in the bay area for a while, and knew what could happen when you got a radical lesbian mad.

Woody Hazzard

The afternoon the studio rejected the black version of Shark's *Searchers* script he came home in a rage. He tossed back some Valiums with his cream soda but still didn't calm down. Finally he said, "I gotta get out of here, I'm going for a drive," and took off in his Porsche.

I know now he drove down to Newport Beach.

Kathy Petro

I found out later what happened, that apparently Shark was just driving through the neighborhood, upset about his script rejection and trying to blow off steam, when he saw Beth and me coming out of my parents' house. It was the day I was moving to Beth's, which Shark could tell, since Beth and I were putting a bunch of my clothes in her car.

When we left Shark followed us to Beth's house in Laguna Beach.

And when it got dark he sneaked up to the house and looked in the window and saw Beth and me making love.

Woody Hazzard

I remember the first day on the set in Joshua Tree—they were doing the scene where the gang of lesbians on motorcycles surround the family's Winnebago. And when I saw how they'd done up Marcia Reed I almost shit. Because, you know, they'd given her that patented Kathy Petro California Look.

"You're still weirded out about her, aren't you?" I said to Shark later in his trailer as we shared a joint.

"Who?" he said.

"You know who," I said. "Kathy, man."

"I don't want to talk about it, " he said, and looked at me kind of suspiciously. See, one night when we were drunk he'd told me about seeing her on Maui and wasting Jack Petro, and howKathy's nipples had got hard against his chest and all that—but he was so drunk I don't think he remembered for sure how much he'd really told me.

"This is kind of a low blow, though," I said, referring to the picture. "Especially if she was finally starting to have second thoughts about you.'Cause when she sees this movie she's gonna know you're trying to imply that she's a dyke."

Shark stared out the window. "She *is* a dyke," he said.

Kathy Petro

I don't know. It was a funny time for me. I don't think I was ever really a lesbian, not like Beth was, but I just got so sick of being back with my parents.

And that whole thing with Shark on Maui just really confused me. In a way I still hated him, but then I would have these dreams where he'd be making love to me in this really wonderful way—like something you've wanted for years was finally happening, that kind of sex—and then I'd wake up and be mad at myself, thinking: Why am I dreaming this?

Then sometimes I'd get mad at Shark, thinking: So if he wants me so bad, how come he didn't take me away with him after he wasted Daddy on Maui? That was his big chance, my mom couldn't have stopped him. And for that matter, why hadn't he tried harder to save me from Derek in Saint-Tropez? True, Derek had a gun, but if Shark had really been determined he could have fought Derek for the gun or something, couldn't he?

Was it possible he just liked *wanting* me but didn't really want to *have* me? Was I like some kind of fish he liked to hook and fight to reel in, only to cut the line at the last minute so he could do it all over again? Was that it, was it something like that? Or something else? I didn't know, and thinking about it just gave me a giant headache.

Then I met Beth and we just hit it off right away. She worked in a pottery shop in Laguna and seemed really artistic and bohemian and we talked for hours in her quaint little house, drinking herb tea and listening to Holly Near records. She was very frank about her lesbianism, which was no big deal to me, and she was also a feminist and made a very powerful case about how my whole life had been controlled by men. I mean, I could really see it, being a model and all, and the thing with Derek where he hit me and everything—Beth was really enraged when I told her about *that*. She even knocked my romantic affair with Andreji, saying, "You were just a fetish for him, a masturbatory icon, otherwise known in male religion as a madonna."

At first I just started staying over at her place, and we'd sleep in the same bed without touching. Then we started holding each other. Then more happened, and I can't really say it was bad or anything. But I think mostly I just wanted to get out of my parents' house.

Marcia Reed

Scar was supposed to be my big break. I always had mixed feelings about the role of Nattie, because of the lesbianism mainly, but my mother convinced me it was exactly the kind of daring debut that could turn me into a major Hollywood star overnight.

I loved Steve Riley, he was just a dream director, but I hated Shark from the very start. He wanted me to have this Kathy Petro look, but I said, "Come on, she's past it. I don't want to look like some washed-up old model." That really infuriated him, and Greg Spivey told me later in strict confidence that Shark had had some kind of thing for Kathy Petro and I should never, ever mention her name again.

But Shark kept baiting me, treating me as if I were actually the character I was playing. It was kind of disguised as a joke but you could tell he really hated me. Like he'd sing, "Hey there, lesbo girl," to the tune of "Georgie Girl." Then he'd get really crude, saying, "Hello, muff-diver." Or: "Here comes the pussy-bumper." Or: "Someone bring Marcia a toothpick. I think she's got some cunt hair stuck between her teeth."

Finally, I walked right up to him and said, "If all guys were like you, Shark, I *would* go lesbian."

He hauled off to slap me, but Steve stopped his hand.

Bill Kemmer

There was some friction on the set, which was actually a good thing. Some of the best films come out of a charged combative atmosphere, and *Scar* looked to be a case in point. I was on the set in Victorville—watching Steve Riley shoot the scene in the lesbian bar where Burt Grady, delivering an Oscar caliber performance as Duke Manmann the protagonist uncle, has disguised himself as a bull dyke and first encounters his niece being ordered about by Wanda Gerkin, doing a brilliant, hair-raising turn as the domineering Scar—when someone tapped my shoulder and said there was an urgent call from Ben.

Right up to that point Ben had been gung-ho on the picture. I knew he shared my opinion that the dailies were astonishing, so naturally I was floored by what he had to say. In a stunned daze I went to Shark and Steve, feeling especially bad for Steve since this was his directorial debut. "We're dead," I told them. "It's over. Ben has just ordered an immediate halt to production."

Nobody could quite believe it. Shark got on the phone but Ben wouldn't take his call. In a rage Stark started for his Porsche.

I tried to stop him. "Look, why don't you come back and try and calm down? Ben does have his reasons—"

Shark knocked my hand from his shoulder and jumped into his car, screaming off down the highway toward L.A.

For a while I was actually relieved. At least *I* wasn't going to have to explain Ben's reasons for canceling the film to Shark. At the very least the explanation was awkward, but I didn't know the half of it—until I discussed the matter with Greg Spivey. "Oh my God, Bill," Greg said. "There's an awful lot you don't know. We've got to warn Ben."

I tried to reach Ben, but his secretary had been given strict orders to hold all calls.

Kathy Petro

Eventually I told Beth all about Shark, though I left out the part about being turned on by him on Maui, because I knew she'd consider that sick. Well, needless to say she was completely outraged. "A man like that should be castrated," she said. "Or shot in the head the way you'd shoot a mad dog." She went on for hours and hours about how evil Shark was, how he'd violated me with his camera which was a "male instrument," how the whole history of cinema was a sexist attempt to dominate women and reduce them to visual objects. She was beside herself with fury and said if she ever saw Shark she would literally tear his testicles off with her bare hands.

Then one day she came back from a trip up to Los Angeles in a total blind rage. "This will be stopped!" she yelled and threw down a script, which I saw was *Scar*.

When I read it I became physically ill because you could tell—anyone could tell—that the lead character who was abducted by lesbians was me. She had the California Look, and even talked like me and everything. And the evil lesbian Scar was obviously based on Beth, because you know Beth had this big scar on her cheek where her ex-husband had cut her with a knife. I was completely freaked out, thinking: How did Shark know about us? Is he watching us? Is this place bugged? I mean, anything was possible. He was rich enough to hire detectives to spy on us round the clock.

Beth was ready to kill and kept saying, "This will be stopped, it will."

"How, Beth? How?" I said. "The movie is already shooting."

You see, I knew her only as Beth Womun, which was a feminist name she'd given herself cause she hated everything paternal. But finally she told me what her old name was.

Mark Klieg

It was a moment of truth for my sister. Beth knew if she "came out" to our dad he'd disinherit her, and she hated to lose those millions. She had confided in me her desire to someday channel that money into an Orange County lesbian services center, which was a kind of ultimate treason because we both knew our dad had an especially virulent animosity towards lesbians since the first woman he'd ever loved—before he met our mother—had dumped him for a WAC.

Beth called me at Stanford in a complete rage, telling me what she'd just learned about *Scar*. Even though I was thoroughly heterosexual—in desire if not yet in practice—I had long been sympathetic to her and, as she well knew, definitely had my own reasons for hating our father. She said she just couldn't let Shark Trager get away with making *Scar*, which, the personal affront aside, was essentially to lesbians what *Birth of a Nation* had been to blacks. She said *Scar* was beyond being merely "politically incorrect," it was "tantamount to artistic genocide," and she had a moral obligation to stop it at any cost.

"Be careful, Beth," I told her. "You know what happens when you tangle with Dad."

She blew up and said, "Listen here, little brother. He may have beaten the courage out of you. But he hasn't molested it out of me."

Kathy Petro

Beth and I marched into her dad's office, and he caught the drift before she even said a word. "No compromises," she'd said to me beforehand. "Can the femme act! *Cut the fluff!*" So we went in *butch*—in boots and dungarees and sloppy white tanktops showing our unshaven armpits, without the makeup or deodorant or other oppressive trappings of what Beth called "male-defined *beauty.*"

"Hi, Dad," Beth said belligerently. "As you can see I'm a dyke— that's right, dyke, D-Y-K-E, dyke! And this here is Kat, my equally dyke lover. And we've come here to tell you that if you don't stop *Scar* right now, we're going to tell the whole story of your Mafia financing, *Dad.*"

At the mention of the Mafia her father went kind of pale.

Bill Kemmer

Of course, Hollywood financing is incredibly baroque and complicated but . . . Frankly, I prefer not to get into all this.

Kathy Petro

"Kill the film, you snake," Beth said to her father, indicating the phone. "Kill it now."

Ben nodded okay, but as soon as he reached Bill Kemmer at the location he swiveled around in his chair, speaking low into the phone so we wouldn't hear, though I picked out the words "Mafia," "a couple of lezes," and heard him mention my name.

"What are you doing?" Beth yelled, pulling his chair back around. "What kind of male trick is this? I'm not kidding you, *Dad.* I've got copies of your secret files going back to 1956—provided by Leona, your loyal private secretary, who just *happened* to be the *lesbian* who brought me out!"

That pretty much knocked his breath out.

"That's not possible," he said weakly. "Leona and I—"

"That word's *rape*, Dad. You sexually harrassed her for a decade, and then *raped* her, you goddamn male rapist molester."

He got this really stunned look.

"Kill it," Beth said. "Kill *Scar.*"

For a second Ben couldn't even speak. He looked so bad I almost felt sorry for him. He was breathing kind of funny, which for some reason scared me a little. Finally, he just said, "Bill? Can't explain now. Tell Shark it's over." He banged down the phone, kind of missing the cradle.

I wanted to go then, but Beth was too wound up to stop. She just kept berating her father, attacking the whole nature of the film industry as male-dominated, making more and more demands. And Ben Klieg was so broken he kept agreeing to everything she said.

"You are going to do an epic version of Gertrude Stein's *The Making of Americans*," Beth yelled. "With an openly lesbian director and an all-lesbian crew!"

"All right, okay," Ben said, still breathing funny.

I knew Beth was stretching her luck because she didn't really have any proof of Mafia financing. It was just a guess on her part that at some point or other her father had probably had dealings with someone like that. I finally started pulling her toward the door.

"You are going to do a non-sexist, politically correct remake of *The Children's Hour* in which Audrey Hepburn and Shirley MacLaine live happily ever after as proud lesbian lovers—*after James Garner hangs himself!*" Beth was still bellowing as I backed into Shark.

Bill Kemmer

Greg Spivey and I arrived at Ben's office a few minutes behind Shark, having leased a chopper and flown into L.A., hoping to beat Shark there. We dashed in to find Shark and Beth grappling violently on the floor, Kathy Petro screaming, "Kill him, kill the son of a bitch," as she kicked Shark in the side.

Kathy Petro

It was one of those rage things, I guess. I just lost control. 'Cause, you know, I did have all this repressed anger at Shark over everything he'd done to me.

Greg Spivey

I pulled Kathy away from Shark, which wasn't easy. She was kicking and scratching and just possessed. Then Bill somehow managed to get a choke-hold on Beth. Shark was wasted, his face scratched and gouged, and in the aftermath everybody was completely winded, gasping for breath. Except Ben Klieg.

Bill Kemmer

I knew Ben was dead the second I saw him, you could just tell. Sitting there in his seat of power, mouth open, eyes staring, the lights on his phone blinking with calls he would never return.

Jean Klieg

I blamed Shark entirely for Ben's stroke. Certainly it was not Beth's finest moment, but once I understood the nature of her outrage over *Scar* I was not entirely unsympathetic.

Frankly, I never believed the story that she threatened to reveal a Mafia connection in her father's past. How utterly absurd, since no such connection existed.

Furthermore, nothing could ever convince me that my daughter's death was a "gangland execution." I still have my own theories about that.

Mark Klieg

My mother was full of denial, trying to lay the blame for everything on Shark. I didn't think much of him myself, but I also saw the larger picture. "Mom, face reality," I said to her in the limousine on the way to Dad's funeral. "Dad was a monster. He's been beating me for years, and he molested Beth when she was still in her crib. He used to get drunk and poke his pud through the slates of her playpen. It wasn't quite 'Father Knows Best,' Mom—"

My mother became hysterical and ordered the driver to stop. "Get out of the car. You will not be welcome in my house again until you take back those pathological lies."

Well, it was all true, as my mother well knew. Our rift didn't last long however. We made up a few days later—in the wake of Beth's execution-style death.

Woody Hazzard

Shark was totally demoralized after they shut down *Scar*, and when Ben Klieg checked out it threw everything into chaos.

More than anything though I think he was blown out by the way Kathy had acted when he was fighting with Beth.

"It's just like *Scar*," he'd say, sitting on the deck, looking really bad with all these scabs on his face. "Beth controls her now. She's turned Kathy into a man-hating dyke. Kathy's lost to me now, she really is."

Then—it could not have been more than a week after Ben Klieg's death—Shark got a call from Bill Kemmer saying, "Have you heard? Beth Klieg's been murdered."

Greg Spivey

I'm sure it was the Mafia, regardless of what Jean Klieg may wish to think. Shark could be ruthless, but he wouldn't have jeopardized his own future by arranging a hit.

The confrontation between Beth and her father was loud. Many of the studio secretaries overheard. Beth's Mafia allegation had quickly became prime gossip, and clearly it reached someone who took lethal offense.

Kathy Petro

I was really weirded-out after Ben Klieg's death, especially by Beth's attitude, 'cause she was saying, "Damn, we came so close. That old snake was going to give us everything! Millions of dollars for lesbian art! Now it's all lost. The studio is already being passed on to another pair of sweaty male hands."

She went on like that for days until I began to think, you know, sexual politics aside, maybe Beth was just really not a nice person.

Then one day I went to the market and as I came back I saw two big men in leisure suits leaving the house. I had a bad feeling as I watched them drive away in this baby blue Eldorado with Nevada license plates. I parked and got out and went up to the house, where a Holly Near record was playing way too loud.

"Beth?" I said. Then I stepped in and saw her lying on the carpet. They'd shot her in the back of the head. I just started screaming.

Woody Hazzard

When we learned the details of Beth's murder I said to Shark at one point, "Poor Kathy. Finding Beth like that must've really fucked with her head."

"No more than she's fucked with mine," Shark said. Then he walked to the window and looked out at the ocean and announced in this momentous voice: "From this day forward, I forbid anyone to ever again mention Kathy Petro's name in my presence. As far as I'm concerned she no longer exists."

Kathy Petro

All these cops came and everything and took pictures of Beth's body and asked me all these personal questions until I was just numb. Finally they stopped and I was sitting alone on the porch swing when I saw Daddy pull up in his Silver Cloud. He talked to the head detective for a minute, all the while glaring at me. Then he started up and I was really afraid. 'Cause he knew now I'd been a lesbian and everything and I just thought he was going to kill me. He was just trembling with all this emotion as he suddenly grabbed me under the arms and lifted me way up in the air like he was going to throw me through the window or something. I was so scared!

Then very gently he put me down and said, "Kathy . . . let's go home." And I saw there were tears in his eyes, which I'd never seen before, 'cause he was just like John Wayne that way, he never wept. But the tears came now, and I wept too, just shaking and sobbing, hugging my daddy like a frightened little girl.

14 / **Carol**
(1976)

Greg Spivey

Shark knew it was time to leave Mastodon Pictures. Although Crane Hurter, the pragmatic Harvard-trained executive who replaced Ben Klieg, was eager to retain the studio's chief asset, Shark knew that at the very least the freedom he had enjoyed under Ben would be severely curtailed in the aftermath of the *Scar* fiasco. Then, too, he was well aware that Jean Klieg, who retained considerable influence within the parent company, blamed him for Ben's death and was pressing several members of the board for Shark's "total destruction." The possibility of hostile interference from the top, which would leave Shark "impotent and castrated as a filmmaker," compelled him to reach an amicable parting of the ways with Crane Hurter.

And so for a time Shark was without a studio—and he didn't even seem to care. Not that there weren't overtures from every studio in town. In spite of *Scar* everyone wanted him. *The Condoist* and *Hail!* were still among the ten top-grossing films of all time.

But Shark seemed to have lost interest in everything.

Woody Hazzard

It was a strange time for Shark. Nothing seemed to get him off anymore. This beautiful young actress came by once, she and Shark went up to his room. Ten minutes later she comes down, and says, "He fell asleep in the middle of it."

"That's okay, honey," I told her, "I'm wide awake."

Shark would light a cigarette and look at it and say, "This tastes like shit," and punch it out.

One day I noticed a couple of grams of cocaine in the trash. "It bores me," he said.

This new Porsche he'd ordered came in—a blue Turbo, the first car I'd ever seen with a speaker phone, which of course became one of his trademarks later. That was the ultimate Shark Trager power call: that booming metallic speaker phone voice with the Porsche engine screaming in the background as he revved it and changed gears to punctuate what he was saying.

But even that bored him. He'd go for an aimless drive up the coast, Roxy Music blasting on the tape deck, and use the phone to order a pizza delivered, which would be cold by the time he got back to the house. "I've got everything money can buy," he said to me once. "And none of it means shit."

It got to be a drag to be around him. I was glad when he finally split for that Zen monastery in the mountains, and I threw a horrendous party while he was gone.

Elliot Bernstein

Shark's experience with Zen Buddhism during the time he was seeing Judy Oshima in the mid-sixties had never completely left him. Indeed, in the years after Judy's death he had more than once wondered if that brief affair, and its tragic end, had not in fact been the true turning point of his life.

"If Judy had lived," he would say from the beatific vantage point of the mid-eighties, "I think the chances are good I might have eventually come to love her in a far more genuine way than I have ever loved anyone. And I might well have left the sorry peeping-Tom episode with Kathy where it belonged—among the discarded wreckage of my troubled adolescence."

He felt as well that a serious commitment to Zen practice would have altered his life course to an incalculable degree. "I believe I would have still pursued film," he said, "but I would have made a different *kind* of film, the result of a cleaner, purer vision. With a Zen clarity I cannot imagine that I would have ever felt compelled to imitate a discursively cerebral filmmaker like Jean-Claude Citroen—I would surely have been spared the emotional disfigurement which resulted from that excessively idolatrous act."

No doubt it was this train of thought which led him to the High Sierra Zen Monastery in '76, and accounted for what happened when he arrived.

Woody Hazzard

Shark said when he pulled up to the Zen place the first thing he saw was this gray Vespa motor scooter parked by the gate. It was just like the one Judy Oshima had been riding the night she was hit by the Petro-Chem tank truck in 1966.

Even though he knew it had to be just a freaky coincidence he started breathing hard, feeling real weirded out.

Elliot Bernstein

The Zen monks were expecting Shark, he had made a reservation to attend the week-long meditation *sesshin*. But he was a few minutes late, and the other attendees had already assumed their positions in the meditation hall as a monk led Shark in.

At the far end of the hall he saw a Japanese woman sitting in a lotus position, her back to him as she faced the wall. He could see little more than the line of her cheek, but his heart began pounding.

"It was completely insane, I see that now," he told me. "Of course, Judy was dead. There could be no doubt about that. Any conceivable scenario explaining how she might have actually survived would be hopelessly gothic and preposterous. But I made no attempt to devise a baroque rationale for what I felt. I simply knew it was her."

Shark pushed past the Zen monk, going straight to the woman. "Judy," he cried, touching her shoulder.

"Even when I saw that it was clearly not Judy, I still believed it was. She would have been thirty by then—in ten years her features might have changed, grown puffy."

He still thought it "might be" Judy, even after the Zen monks, unable to tolerate the disruption, had gently shown him out. "I stood there by the gate, by her Vespa, waiting for her to remember me and come out. It began raining and still I waited, my heart pounding. Then I noticed the light flashing on my car-phone. Somehow that mundane occurrence brought me back to earth."

It was a call from Brian Straight in New York.

Greg Spivey

I'd stayed on with Shark in the wake of *Scar*, overseeing a few pointless development deals, but I'd begun exploring other career opportunities, thinking that Shark might be taking an early retirement. I was therefore heartened, indeed extremely excited, when Shark called to say he was flying back to New York to meet with Brian Straight, the president of Acropolis Pictures, and Harold Gay, chairman of the board of Sadcom, the parent company. Acropolis was really *the* happening studio then.

Woody Hazzard

Shark told me later what happened in New York, in fact he told everyone. It became one of those classic Shark Trager stories, like something from a gross screwball comedy.

He'd got a suite at the Sherry-Netherland and it was the night before his big meeting at Sadcom and he had absolutely no idea what he was going to say. Here was this guy who was supposed to be the ultimate boy wonder bursting with energy and a jillion fantastic film ideas, and he said he felt "like the macho equivalent of Anne Bancroft in *The Pumpkin Eater*" after she'd had a hysterectomy or something. Like completely blank and depressed. He didn't know what his life was about or anything, and what had happened at the Zen monastery was still weighing heavily on his mind.

So he ordered a bottle of whiskey from room service and drank most of it down way too fast. Then he stepped out on the balcony to look at the Manhattan night skyline, and without warning threw up onto Fifth Avenue below.

Then two minutes later there's this violent knock on the door and he opens it, and it's Carol Van Der Hof and she's totally livid in a full-length mink coat that's wet and matted and stinking of whiskey.

Carol Van Der Hof

You bet your breeches I was livid, and I gave Shark Trager quite a piece of my mind. "If you can't hold your drink, mister," I berated him, "I strongly suggest that you board the next plane back to California!"

At that he called me a spoiled socialite, though he was already grinning in that insidiously charming Errol Flynn manner of his.

"My dear sir," I said, "it may interest you to know that far from being a spoiled socialite, everything I own in this world is on my back. And just look what you've done to it!"

Then, furious at myself, I began to sniffle, for this indeed was the low point of my life.

His manner changed then as he noticed I suppose how truly ratty that pathetic mink was. "Say, you're not kidding. You are down on your luck." Then he attempted to remove the coat. "Come on now, that's a good girl, we'll have it dry-cleaned in a jif—"

But I swung free and proclaimed, "How dare *you* patronize *me*, sir? I'll have you know I come from one of the first ten Dutch families ever to set foot on this sliver of Indian marshland. If there were any justice in this world I should be a billionairess many times over." At that the dog-eared treatment for what eventually became *Mondo Jet Set* slipped from my mink coat pocket.

"What's this?" Shark said as he reached down and picked it up. I rather imagine it was then that he first became aware of my clubfoot.

Brian Straight

Poor Carol—it had been a rough time for her. That truly horrendous business with her father. Really one of the first big society murder scandals, wasn't it?

Carol Van Der Hof

I'd adored my father right up until that hideous Christmas morning in 1972 when he stepped into the parlor of our lovely Connecticut manor house with an antique but operative Thompson submachine gun in each of his ruggedly masculine hands and opened fire, obliterating three generations of Van Der Hofs before turning one of the weapons on himself.

Fortunate me, I'd stepped into the kitchen to replenish Uncle Bill's toddy, but I *heard* it all. How could I ever forget Dad's last words, try though I might: "I've slept with you all, and if you really want to know . . . none of you was that hot."

Then the ghastly rat-tat-tat—the soundtrack of the Paul Muni *Scarface* superimposed with a deafening ferocity upon that quaint Currier and Ives tableau.

Brian Straight

The sad thing for Carol, aside from the tragedy of losing her family, was the cruelty of her father's will. There were millions left to her in a trust, from which she was to receive only a minuscule fraction of the interest on a quarterly basis—little more than cigarette money—until she reached age sixty-five. If at that time, according to a stipulation of the will, she could undergo a medical examination which would verify that she had remained a life-long virgin, the principle would at last be disbursed to her. If she failed to "pass" the medical exam on her sixty-fifth birthday she would automatically forfeit her inheritance, and the Van Der Hof fortune would be used to establish an endowment fund for paroled murderers.

I know this because as a long-time friend Carol came to me with the will. We consulted the most powerful attorneys in New York, but the document was iron-clad, not a thing could be done.

"This is my father's revenge," Carol said. "Because unlike the others, I spurned him." Then she turned wryly philosophical. "It's a moot point anyway, Bri," she said. "I doubt I'd pass that exam even if I *were* to remain chaste for the next forty years. You see, I broke my hymen on Gogol when I was twelve." Gogol had been her horse.

"In that case, you may as well live it up, Carol," I told her.

But nothing was ever quite that simple for Carol.

Tony Borgia

Carol—God, what a character! If she were in a movie no one would believe her, and she had the same problem in life, I can tell you. Of course, she was really the ultimate film buff, and as a result she knew everyone in the New York film scene. It's hard to recall a significant screening without seeing Carol somewhere in the crowd, chain-smoking those terrible unfiltered Camels—God, her stained little fingers, the nails bitten to the quick!—chattering loudly and fiercely in that Katherine Hepburn diction some assumed she affected, but was as natural to a Van Der Hof as polo and incest. And her hair, a Dutch bob parted on the side and plastered down, like Gloria Vanderbilt I suppose, though it was really more like Ayn Rand. She had a pretty face, though she took great if unconscious pains to obscure the fact, in an obvious attempt to discourage male overtures. Although she made light of it, I'm sure her clubfoot had a profound effect on her character.

Brian Straight

She frequently made painful, feeble jokes about her deformity. "A Reuben for me, a club sandwich for my foot," that sort of thing.

As a result of her physical aberration—she wore a special shoe and walked with a slight limp—she had withdrawn at a very young age into a world of books and films. Then, too, I believe she'd known on some level what her father was up to with the other members of the family, and no doubt wished to escape from that.

Her feelings toward her father remained profoundly complex, and knowing Jack Van Der Hof, it was easy to see why. He cut quite a dashing figure. A sportsman, yachtsman, and finally an alcohol-deranged cocksman, he bore a strong resemblance to Errol Flynn.

But then so did Shark, didn't he?

Tony Borgia

Her father was a truly evil man, in that he used his looks and charm as a means of exploring the outer limits of the demonic and forbidden. I think Carol felt her clubfoot had spared her from her father's incestuous advances—and yet subconsciously she'd taken his lack of interest in her as a devastating rejection.

I adored Carol though. My God, her mind! She was quite literally a genius. Her loft in SoHo was lined and piled with books, thousands of books. She just devoured them. I didn't doubt her when she told me that she'd once "slammed through" Dostoyevsky's *The Idiot* in its entirety while waiting for a date to join her at the Russian Tea

Room—only realizing as she finished the book that she'd been stood up.

And when it came to film she had a literally photographicmemory. She could give you a detailed shot-for-shot analysis of anything she'd ever seen. No wonder her loft became a virtual non-stop salon.

But when it came to practical matters, like say putting out a cigarette or walking through a door . . . well, let me put it this way, we used to joke that Carol couldn't walk through the arch in Washington Square without managing to bang her shoulder, and she set her bed or a sofa or something on fire at least once a month.

God only knows how I ever thought she could function as a producer.

Brian Straight

I had given Carol and Tony Borgia a development deal once, for a New York action picture which Carol was to produce, though I knew she was essentially incompetent. Not that she wasn't brilliant—in fact she was too brilliant. Her body was just something that hung from her mind, that was the feeling you got. Of course the deal fell apart as I knew it would. She had no budget, no sense of what a budget was, just astonishingly brilliant ideas and pockets full of illegibly scrawled notes. She really was committable, you know.

But I'd often think: If only someone could ground her!

Carol Van Der Hof

I shall never forget that first night with Shark, for I quickly sensed it was the beginning of one of the most profound relationships of either of our lives. "My God, this is fantastic!" he cried, as he read the treatment of what eventually became *Mondo Jet Set*.

"Do you really think so? I'm rather fond of it," I said, and he exclaimed: "Yes, yes, *yes!*"

On a wave of euphoric rapport we soon found ourselves at Elaine's, neither of us able to contain our elation as our minds sparked and flashed together like the cascading fireworks behind Cary Grant and Grace Kelly as their lips met in *To Catch a Thief*.

"Yes, of course!" I cried, as he expressed his desire to someday produce a science fiction masterpiece in terms which quite accurately predicted *Blue Light*. "But it *should* allude heavily to classic fifties 'Red Scare metaphor' sci-fi, Shark! It *should* be a parodic hommage, even as it functions on a higher plane of genuine if pop religiosity!"

"My God, you're right!" he shot back. "It *could* work on both levels, couldn't it? I really *could* have my cake and eat it too!"

With what joyful abandon we laughed, Shark as taken with my filmic notions as I was with his. A nearly terminal giddiness seized us as I outlined a concept of mine called *Isabela, the Talking Anda-lusian Mare,* which I envisioned as a wickedly Buñuelian send-up of the Francis pictures with Donald O'Connor.

"Christ, I can't quit laughing," Shark cried, holding his stomach, oblivious to Capote's censoriously cocked eyebrow at the next table. "But wouldn't it be funnier still if instead of a mare it were a don-key . . . Yes, I've got it, a Mexican donkey in a sex show . . . and . . . and he loses his partner—let's call her Lupe—and becomes a detective, tracking her down."

I laughed so hard I nearly spit out a mouthful of tea. "Yes, yes, of course! My God, how utterly and deliciously outrageous, Shark! Of course, no studio will ever back such a picture." Needless to say, it was the germ of what eventually became *Looking for Lupe.*

Eventually we found ourselves back at my place in SoHo, gibber-ing like jaybirds on amphetamine till dawn—though neither of us had taken a thing, we didn't need to! He told me about his meeting that morning at Sadcom and I said, "Oh, don't worry about Bri. He puts on the tough act to compensate for everyone's unspoken knowl-edge of his homosexuality. But beneath that brutal businessman's fa-cade beats the heart of a sentimental Heidi."

"You mean, Brian Straight is gay?" Shark said.

"Good Lord, you didn't know?"

"But he's been going with Margo Fray for years."

"Really, Shark, how naive you are. Margo owes her entire career to being photographed with powerful gay boys."

Shark was clearly shaken. "And Harold Gay, is he also . . . ?"

"No. Harold Gay is straight. That is, he's straight now. Dad knew him at Harvard and said he was gay for a time back then. And Brian Straight was straight as an arrow at Yale, only discovering his true bent after he moved to L.A. So Harold Gay was gay but went straight, and Brian Straight was straight but went gay. Though there *is* a rumor that Harold Gay may have never truly gone straight, but may still be quite guardedly gay, and that he and Brian Straight may in fact be secret lovers—although Brian may actually be straight and merely acceding to Harold's homosexual desires in order to advance his career."

Shark appeared confused. "I wish you were coming to this meeting with me, Carol. In fact, why don't you?" At that he focused on me with all his smoldering charm, punctuated with a rakish grin so like Flynn's in *The Sea Hawk.* "In fact," he said, "why don't you and I become partners, Carol?"

"Good God, Shark, it's almost seven A.M.," I said, my heart burst-ing with joy. "I thought you'd never ask."

Brian Straight

Harold and I were both quite impressed with the projects Shark and Carol presented to us that morning, and their enthusiasm was indeed infectious. Privately, Harold expressed reservations about Carol, but my instincts told me to go the distance for them. "Harold, I smell success here, I foresee blockbusters and mega-bucks. Don't ask me to explain it, filmmaking isn't rational, but I sense a synergetic rapport between Shark and Carol that plunges deep into the heart of what movies are all about. Carol as the holy lunatic, Shark as the ruthless pragmatist. They need each other and we need them. If we pass on this opportunity, we'll be kicking ourselves for the rest of our lives."

"Okay, but it's your ass," Harold said. "And if you're wrong I'm going to personally carve a new hole in it, Brian."

Greg Spivey

We were all elated by the Acropolis deal. The new offices on the Inglewood lot were even more posh than the ones we'd had at Mastodon. And everyone without exception was crazy about Carol.

Cynthia Clive

She saved him, you know. Though I suppose he saved her as well from a lifetime of floundering. But what a change there was once Carol was about. Her diabolically infectious laughter, her incessant yet devastatingly brilliant talk! Shark was alive again, you could see it, living and breathing film as he was meant to. What years of joy those were!

Woody Hazzard

Yeah, Carol was great if, you know, very East Coast. But she was definitely good for Shark, and she moved into the Santa Monica beach house right away. They practically lived in the basement screening room, watching everything you could imagine. They'd invite other people over in the evening, but long after everybody else had left, Shark and Carol would still be down there—Carol with her popcorn, Shark with his cream sodas—devouring movies till dawn.

After maybe a month I moved out and went to stay with this girl I'd been seeing up in Malibu. "I don't want to cramp your style," I told Shark, assuming he and Carol were getting it on. But he set me straight about that.

Greg Spivey

It was fairly obvious, if you thought about it at all, that Carol was probably a virgin at age twenty-seven. Though you didn't think about it, that was the thing. She was just so cerebral, so asexual. Certainly I never thought for a second that Shark and Carol were involved romantically, though some people may have, since they were constantly together and soon developed the kind of shorthand you associate with lovers or, perhaps more to the point, a long-married couple. But Carol was really the antithesis of the sort of woman, the Kathy Petro sort of woman, Shark found most arousing.

In retrospect though, it's only too clear that Carol was in love with Shark from the start.

Woody Hazzard

Not long after I moved to Malibu I got this idea for a screenplay about surfing and told it to Shark. Not a stupid beach picture like *Gidget* or something, but the real story of surfing as only a real surfer could tell it, about what it was like to surf in Orange County at places like Trestles and Huntington back in the sixties before everything got fucked up.

"I think it's a fantastic idea, Shark," Carol said, and convinced Shark who was dubious at first since I wasn't really a writer. Besides by then he had decided he wanted *Mondo Jet Set* to be his next movie and was working hard with the writer on that.

But I had this idea for a structure that even Shark liked too, since he was real big on structure. I said it would be the story of these surfers who go to Redondo Beach and then struggle to make their way back home to Laguna with various adventures along the way like in *Ulysses*, which I'd just seen on TV, with Kirk Douglas.

"Shark, we must say yes, we will, yes. Woody may well be the James Joyce of the South Bay," Carol said, in reference to the famous book on which they'd based the Kirk Douglas movie *[sic]*.

So I got a deal to write it and set off one afternoon on a research surfing trip to Orange County. That was when I ran into Kathy Petro.

Kathy Petro

I was scared for a long time after Beth's death that the Mafia might try and rub me out too. Of course, it was never proven that it was in fact the Mafia, but in the mid-seventies hit men in leisure suits meant only one thing.

But after a while it kind of seemed to blow over, and I was seeing this shrink three times a week and everything, but I was getting bored so I'd go for these long drives down the coast in the 450SL Daddy had given me.

One afternoon I'd stopped at San Onofre, which was this really famous surfing spot with a nuclear reactor and everything, when who should pull up but Woody Hazzard.

At first I wasn't sure how I should feel about seeing him, because it did bring back memories of the acid days in the sixties and Jeff Stuben and the chainsaw. But then I thought: That wasn't really Woody's fault.

So we sat in my car and talked a long time. And then, as the sun went down and the lights on the nuclear reactor blinked on, Woody kissed me.

Greg Spivey

Shark completely exhausted Tim Randolph, the original writer of *Mondo Jet Set*, and then dumped him and brought in a three-man / one-woman team and exhausted them as he distilled the script to its "superficial essence."

"This film must be all visual surfaces," he said, "with flat, one-dimensional characters who are nothing more than what they seem. I want glamour and chic iconography here. The music must carry the emotion, the people should be nothing more than sexy, appealing cartoons."

Brian Straight

I read the script for *Mondo Jet Set* beside the pool in Palm Springs over the Labor Day weekend of 1976. "Harold," I said to our chairman who lay tanning beside me, "this is going to be our blockbuster for next summer."

He read it, then said, "Brian, it's all music."

"That's because it's a musical, Harold."

"All right," he said. "You're the movie mogul. But I doubt that I'm going out on a limb by telling you now, if this mindless mishmash so much as breaks even, I will personally give you the meanest blow job you've ever had."

"I'd just as soon take a cash bonus equivalent, Harold. How much would you say one of your blow jobs is worth?"

"One point five million," he said without hesitation.

"Uum. Mean, indeed. Could you put this in writing, Harold?"

He did. And we all know what happened.

15 / ***Mondo Jet Set*** (1976–1978)

Carol Van Der Hof

What can you say about Rome in the fall? What a heady adventure our first filmic enterprise was. I believed that Joe Scalli was right for *Mondo Jet Set,* a youthful director with a bold style derived from Fellini and Welles and Nick Ráy—an eye for the startling which I felt certain would assure Shark and me of the big commercial hit we so urgently needed.

I found the story quite charming, slight though it was, and thought Tom Reese most endearing as the fair-haired young Iowa Writer's Workshop novelist hurtled on a wave of sudden fame into *le monde jet set.* The spine of the tale—simplicity itself, as our young innocent moves through an increasingly bizarre and decadent Roman nightlife in pursuit of a blonde vision of equal purity. Shark insisted on the disco music—I'd been all for Nino Rota or perhaps Leonard Cohen— but he correctly foresaw that, however tedious it may have already become, the disco craze had yet to peak.

Shark convinced Joe Scalli to give Rita Flay what he called "the classic California girl look," though I argued vehemently against it, for it was all wrong, far too outdoorsy and natural. "Shark, Rita must be a rarefied ice princess, a haute couture madonna, remote and stylized, the antithesis of the tanned and vapidly grinning West Coast beach bunny."

We argued the matter quite passionately, until at last I simply surrendered, though Shark never did convince me he was right.

Greg Spivey

As co-producer, in effect line producer, of *Mondo Jet Set* I was wired for sound on adrenaline, working far too speedily to watch everything I said. Once in a meeting with Shark and Carol, I made a passing reference, which Carol didn't even catch, to Rita Flay "sure looking like K.P. now," and Shark drew me aside afterwards and told me never to allude to Kathy Petro, by using her initials or by any other means, in his presence ever again. Then he asked me—he virtually pleaded with me—never to mention his past obsession with Kathy to Carol. "Carol is the best thing that's ever happened to me," he said, with a peculiar sort of fervor I found quite puzzling since I knew they weren't romantically involved. "And I won't have our relationship contaminated with the mistakes I've made in the past."

He went on to blame his fixation on Kathy on his cocaine use, which at this time had ceased. With the "childlike joy" Carol brought him, he said, he didn't need cocaine. It was only too clear he was merely using me as an acquiescent sounding board, trying to convince himself more than me that he was over Kathy—when it was obvious to anyone who watched the dailies of *Mondo Jet Set* that he wasn't.

Carol Van Der Hof

One afternoon we'd all come up for air from the catacombs on the outskirts of Rome—where Joe was filming the extraordinary chase/dance sequence—when Shark saw a woman among a group of American tourists just beyond the trailers and absolutely froze. She was Japanese, perhaps fifty but quite youthful-looking, and she was just as startled to see him.

I followed as Shark approached her. I sensed correctly their history had been turbulent.

"Hello, Shark," she said guardedly.

"Carol, this is Miko Oshima," he said without taking his eyes off of her. "An old . . . I can't really say friend, can I ? I'm not sure what we were."

"I don't think we were anything, Shark," she said. "My mind was closed to you because of my hatred for your father." She glanced about a bit nervously. "I sense that you haven't heard."

"Heard what?" Shark said.

At precisely that moment a man stepped around the trailer—I saw him a bit before Shark did. In his late fifties, he was stocky, with a steel-gray flattop, and bore a certain resemblance to the actor Glenn Ford.

"Come on, Miko," he said to the woman, before he noticed Shark. "Everything's closed 'cause of all this movie bullshit. Might as well mosey on back to Rome."

When Shark and his father saw one another they both froze in shock.

Mac Trager

One afternoon in the fall of '75 I was leaving the Newport Beach post office when I saw Duke Wayne coming out of Gritt's Hardware store. I'd seen him around from time to time, but I hadn't spoken with the man since he quit coming into the station twenty-four years before. He was up in years by then, and something told me it might be my last chance to shake his hand and tell him how much I'd always admired him.

He was unlocking his Eldorado when I caught up to him.

"Hello, Mac," he said right off. And it kind of got to me that after all those years he still remembered my name.

We talked there for a minute, and then he said, "Say, I could use a drink. You in a hurry, Mac?"

Well, who would say no to a drink with John Wayne?

"This place all right?" he said when we came to the Yojimbo Steak House a couple doors down. It was some kind of Jap place I'd never been in. But if it was okay with the Duke, it was okay by me.

Then we stepped in the door and saw Miko Oshima. She was the hostess. "Howdy, Miko," the Duke said.

She glared at me. "I'm sorry, Mr. Wayne. But I cannot seat this man."

"Why the hell not?" the Duke said.

"I must ask this man to leave the restaurant," she said.

The Duke dug out a bill, and tried to slip it to her. "Let's just forget it, okay?"

She rebuffed him. "I don't want your money, Mr. Wayne. This is a question of moral principle."

"All right, that does it," the Duke said, losing his temper. "You don't know it yet, lady, but you just lost your job. Where's Yukio?"

The Duke started looking around for the owner, but I grabbed his arm. "Hold the phone, Duke," I said. "She's got a right to be sore."

But Miko was so sure she was going to be fired, she threw down her menus and took off back through the restaurant. I went after her.

When I caught up with her in the kitchen she was crying. "Look, I know you hate my guts," I said.

"Go to hell," she said.

Just then some waitress screamed, and a bunch of armed Japanese guys burst into the kitchen. "Hands up or you're dead," one of 'em yelled, and we all raised our hands, scared to death. Miko whispered under her breath: "Yakuza."

It was some kind of a shake-down deal, and the Duke had walked out right before they arrived. In a second two more of 'em pulled Yukio the owner into the kitchen and started forcing his face down over a pan of boiling water on the stove.

"You gonna pay? You gonna pay now?" they were yelling at Yukio, when I saw my chance and grabbed the one nearest me. I got his machine pistol away from him just as the others turned and I let 'em have it, spraying all four. They all dropped their weapons, wounded in their shoulders and arms, one guy with his trigger-finger shot off. Then another one came through the door and I threw that boiling water in his face—brother, did he howl! Then the one I'd disarmed grabbed Miko, and pressed a meat cleaver to her throat, but I shot him in the foot and he dropped it.

Luckily, the cops arrived then, since there were a half dozen more of those goddamn Yakuzas out in the dining room. When the cops stormed in they all gave up.

"Are you okay?" I said to Miko, who was shaking like a leaf, and she nodded.

"Look, I'm sorry about what happened in the past," I told her.

"I know," she said. "I'm sorry too."

We both smiled a little, and then I said, "Come on, I'll take you home."

Carol Van Der Hof

Shark and his father stared at one another, as if the film crew activities about them did not even exist, until at last Mac Trager ventured a smile. "How ya doin', son?"

Shark appeared incapable of speech, his eyes now roving to-and-fro between Miko and his father. I too found the union difficult to comprehend, given what Shark had told me of his father's right-wing prejudices and especially virulent hatred of the Japanese.

But then love and hate are very close, aren't they?

Mac Trager

Miko had had a tough life since her husband died, and as we got to talking I realized the war had cost her a lot too, what with being put in that relocation camp and all. I can't explain what happened really, except to say it was years of hatred giving way to the miracle of love.

Carol Van Der Hof

"Look, son," Mac said to Shark. "I gotta tell you, I was real sore for a long time after I saw that *White Desert*, since it was plain that you based that couple that got gutted on Evelyn and me. But . . . I guess we probably had it coming."

Mac chuckled good-naturedly. But Shark's eyes were beginning to take on a lethal glint.

"Shark, I've changed," Mac said. "It's just that simple."

"He really has," Miko said, holding onto Mac's arm. "We both have."

"Son, I love Miko the same way you once loved her daughter Judy—"

"You *fuck*," Shark spat at his father, adding to no one in particular: "I want these people off the set." With that he stormed away.

Mac sighed, appearing sadly resigned, but Miko started after Shark.

Mac tried to stop her. "Honey, it's a lost cause." But she followed Shark into his trailer.

I simply couldn't resist stepping over to the trailer window so that I might overhear their conversation.

"Mac's forgiven you, why can't you forgive him?" Miko said.

"Do you want to know why your daughter's dead?" Shark said, ignoring her question.

Miko was silent a moment, then changed the subject. "Shark, I don't think you appreciate what it means that your father and I have come to love one another—the years of bitterness and hatred, the sense at least on my part that I was destined to live the rest of my days alone and never love another man. It's not a small thing that we've found each other before it's too late."

"Oh, that's beautiful," Shark said. "I'm really fucking moved. I'll tell you what killed Judy. My fear of that evil old scumbag out there, of his pathological bigotry."

"No, Shark," Miko said softly. "It's time to forgive your father, and yourself, as I've forgiven both of you. A Petro-Chem tank truck killed Judy, nothing more, nothing less."

"Look, I think we can end this meeting now," Shark said sarcastically. "I'm really not interested in doing a remake of *Cry for Happy* or *Teahouse of the August Moon.*"

"Then how about *Sayonara?* I'm dying," Miko said. "I've got cancer, a brain tumor, I'll be dead within four months.* That's why Mac married me, that's why he cashed in his life insurance policy so we could take this trip around the world. That's the kind of man your father is now, whatever he may have been in the past."

"Here, blow your nose," Shark said, and handed her a tissue. She was sniffling.

"Well, I'm sorry that you're dying," Shark said quietly. "But if that's the case, you'd really better get cracking. If you catch the next bus back to Rome, you just might reach the Colosseum before the darkness descends."

---

* Worth mentioning here that this was a lie. Miko Oshima-Trager declined to be interviewed, but according to a close friend, Yuki Peterson: "Miko had always wanted to go around the world, but Mac was so cheap she felt that making up the brain tumor story was the only way." Mac and Miko were divorced in 1978.

Mac Trager

Miko was upset when she got back to me. "What did he say to you?" I asked her. "I want to know."

"Let's just forget it, Mac," she said. "There isn't time."

Carol Van Der Hof

That night as we viewed the previous day's rushes, which were absolutely sensational—Tom and Rita darting about the catacombs in an intricate ballet set to a Donna Summer scratch-track—Shark sat there looking utterly glum.

"You're still upset about your father, aren't you?" I whispered.

Shark looked at me and for the first time ever said, "Carol, shut up."

Woody Hazzard

After I got it on with Kathy in her car at San Onofre I got real disturbed, knowing Shark would kill me if he knew, and swore I wouldn't see her anymore.

But since Shark was in Italy making *Mondo Jet Set*, one thing led to another, I broke up with this girl I'd been staying with in Malibu, and I ended up seeing Kathy again. By that time I was back at Shark's place in Santa Monica, house-sitting for him, and the first time Kathy came over it was a little freaky.

"So this is how Shark lives," she said, wandering around the house, touching things, both of us kind of scared in a way, half expecting Shark to walk in the door, even though we knew he was in Rome.

At first we'd just get it on in my room and then she'd drive back to Newport Beach so her folks wouldn't worry. Then she started making up stories and staying over, and we started sleeping in Shark's bed since it was bigger and more comfortable than the twin bed I had. Then she started staying the whole weekend, and it seemed cool at first. Since everyone knew Shark was in Europe, no one was coming around.

Then one afternoon Kathy and I were making love on the living room floor when Neal Ridges came by and saw her through the window.

"You must be insane," he said to me. "Both of you must be insane."

"I can't help it, Neal," I told him. "I really fuckin' love her."

Carol Van Der Hof

Joe Scalli was a genius, and a fast one, which is rare. He seldom exceeded three or four takes. We wrapped a full week ahead of schedule, which was virtually unheard of. Brian Straight was elated and dying to see Joe's rough cut, which was nearly completed since Joe—what a dynamo!—had been cutting as we shot.

We made plans to meet Brian in New York—Harold Gay was dying to see it too—but Shark said, "You and Joe take the film to New York, I'm flying straight back to L.A."

"Why?" I asked Shark, who seemed obscurely troubled. "Is there anything I should know?"

"I'm not sure why," he said. "I just have a feeling I should get back."

Kathy Petro

I really loved Woody, I'm still not sure exactly why. He was really cute, I'm sure that was part of it, he had this really great surfer's body and was really gentle as a lover. I'd got so sick of guys always manhandling me, I think that's why I was so vulnerable when Beth came around, and in some ways Woody was very similar to her. So sweet and tender, just taking his time for hours, until we were almost living in this sensual daze.

It was strange being in Shark's house though, surrounded by his movie posters and everything, yet in another way it seemed so right. I don't know—I still don't understand this—but sometimes when Woody and I were making love in Shark's bed I would imagine that Shark was watching us—being forced to watch us, but bound and gagged and everything so he couldn't interfere. And I'd be thinking: See, Shark? *This* is what you've always wanted, isn't it? Only *you can't have it.* But I'm giving it to your *best friend* for free! Then I'd think: God, what a mean thought, what's happening to me?

So I finally said to Woody, "Look, I don't want to see you in this house anymore."

So about a week before Shark was due back from Europe Woody rented this little house a few miles up the coast in the surf colony at Topanga Beach, and I told my parents I was moving up to L.A. to be closer to my psychiatrist.

The afternoon Woody was moving out of Shark's we started kissing and ended up in Shark's bedroom making love when suddenly we heard Shark coming in the front door.

Woody Hazzard

I almost shit. Kathy dived for the bathroom as Shark came up the stairs, calling my name, and he saw her! I'll swear to this day he saw her—but maybe his mind just wasn't willing to believe it was her, or maybe he just saw her bare ass and back.

"Hey, man," I said, adrenaline pounding through me.

"What's going on?" Shark said coldly. But I realized then he didn't know it was Kathy.

"What do you think?" I was just standing there with my dick all sticky, though my hard-on was rapidly wilting.

"It would really be cool," he said, "if you kept this action confined to your own room."

"Oh, yeah, I know. I'm sorry, man. But she's really wild, and I just have that small single bed."

Long pause. Then he said, "She's wild, huh?" And kind of smiled.

"Yeah," I said. "She's wearing me out."

"Oh yeah?" He definitely smiled. "You need some help?"

"I don't think she'd go for that. She's actually pretty straitlaced. Though I'm changing that." I tried to chuckle.

"Yeah, and rich too," Shark said, and I almost shit 'cause I realized he was referring to Kathy's 450SL parked out front. It even had these vanity plates that read: KATHY 76. But it must have been parked at an angle so that Shark hadn't seen the plates.

"Yeah, she's some Beverly Hills princess," I said. "I picked her up at Zuma."

He glanced at the bathroom door and spoke low so she wouldn't hear. "So why don't you get back to it, man?" He indicated the balcony that connected to the next room. "Part the drapes a little so I can come around and watch."

"She might see your shadow. If she did, man, she'd freak."

"Oh, bullshit," Shark said. "She must be super hot or you wouldn't be trying to keep her to yourself. Come on, man." He whipped out his dick. "Let's make a pussy sandwich."

He was laughing like it was a joke, even as he was ready to do it. So I laughed too and kind of shoved him back from the door, saying, "No, man, really. This is not that kind of scene."

When suddenly we heard a car start up and I knew it was Kathy's Mercedes. I got to the window just in time to see her pulling away below. The 450SL had its top off that day so I could look right down into it and see that Kathy was totally bare-assed naked, man! Like she'd climbed out the bathroom window and made it down to the car wrapped in this towel that fell off in the driveway or something. A couple of beachgoers were staring at her slack-jawed as she gunned off down PCH. By the time Shark got to the window the car was too far away for him to make out either Kathy or her plates.

"She must've heard you talking," I said to Shark. "You scared her away."

Brian Straight

With *Mondo Jet Set* Shark most definitely delivered. I still believe it was the definitive disco musical, with *Saturday Night Fever* later that year a kind of cheesily home-grown imitation. Some people forget how phenomenally well we did, which I suppose is understandable, since '77 was also the summer of *Star Wars*.

Julian Christopher, *Fire Island Review*, June 14, 1977

I'm in love with Tom Reese, the heart-breaking young star of *Mondo Jet Set*. He's a perfect blond doll and quick as a whip to boot. I'd lick his penny loafers if I were into that sort of thing. Who knows, maybe I am. If I were straight I'd be in love with Rita Flay too. What the hell, I am anyway—she's the loose, ecstatic soul of what's happening today. I'm wearing out the soundtrack album. I'm not kidding, I am. The Chumps, the Dill-Does, the B.J.s, Georgine Bazoom—*Mondo Jet Set* is a Who's Who of disco. I'm dancing as I write this—I'm serious, I am. I've seen this movie five times already, and used up all my poppers, and the summer's barely begun.

Neal Ridges

Shark was riding high on the success of *Mondo Jet Set* when he gave me a deal to write and direct *Looking for Lupe*. Well, at first I was sure it was one of those ideas that would never be made, and took the deal strictly for the money, thinking: A talking sex donkey searching L.A. for his former "girlfriend"? I mean, come on. How low I had sunk since the high-art ambitions of *White Desert*.

Then as I worked on the story with Shark and Carol something extraordinary happened: I began to have fun. Of course, the concept was inane, the movie could never be more than trivial, vulgar entertainment. And yet we began laughing, holding our stomachs in convulsions of laughter, as we devised increasingly outrageous situations. "Shark, this will never be made," I'd say periodically. "We're going too far."

But it became more and more obvious, as *Mondo Jet Set* continued to rocket into the box office stratosphere with no ceiling in sight, that Acropolis was ready to do anything Shark wanted.

Carol Van Der Hof

It was a golden time for us all. Has anyone ever laughed as hard as we did that summer developing *Looking for Lupe?* How I adored Neal from the very start, for I sensed he was an artist, and in his own way needed Shark as desperately as I did if he were to survive in the Hollywood jungle.

Greg Spivey

Brian Straight was aghast when he saw the *Looking for Lupe* script. In a way, of course, it was *The Searchers* again, with Hector the Donkey in the John Wayne role. Naturally, those of us who were close to Shark knew the object of Hector's search was modeled on Lupe Sepulveda, Shark's former maid. The intrinsic raunchiness aside, Brian was concerned that Hector might be perceived as a kind of ethnic slur since he spoke with a Mexican accent. "Would you mind looking at thees peecture of my girlfriend Lupe?" he would say at the door of an Ozzie and Harriet house. "I understand she used to do thee housework for thee gringos in thees neighborhood."

Shark assured Brian we'd make it clear that Hector, whatever else he did, was a "supremely intelligent, sensitive individual, far wiser and more considerate than most human beings actually are." Needless to say, that wasn't good enough, and the script was eventually altered quite a bit.

Brian Straight

I knew we had to drop the idea that Lupe and Hector had ever actually slept together.

"But it's not just crass sex," Shark argued. "They're genuinely in love."

"Shark, that's not the point," I told him. "Hector can express his longings in the most elevated poetic terms, but that doesn't change the fact that he's still *a donkey!*"

Neal Ridges finally came up with the perfect solution: "Okay, they're *just friends*. A sentimental Flicka/Black Beauty type friendship between a winsome Mexican girl and her beloved talking pet. In the Tijuana flashback, they pretend they're *about to* stage a live sex show. But once the thrill-hungry gringos have paid their money, Hector and Lupe split—without actually delivering."

Greg Spivey

I was worried at first, fearing that Neal had fatally compromised the basic premise of the film, but it was a classic case of outsmarting the censors. Despite all the plot disclaimers to the contrary, the intimate tone Hector eventually took with Lupe left little doubt as to what was really going on between them. "Oh, *ba-by*, I just keep thinking about how *good* we were together," Hector tells her on the phone, which is not, you know, the sort of thing talking animals usually say to their platonic keepers.

Neal Ridges

I had never mentioned catching Woody and Kathy Petro together to Shark, I just felt it wasn't my place.

Then one day Shark and I were out scouting locations for *Lupe* and stopped by Wood's place at Topanga Beach unannounced.

Woody was alone but seemed rattled to see us. I saw evidence of a woman in residence and put two and two together, and managed to move Shark toward the door as Woody became increasingly nervous.

Then on a pretext Woody drew me aside and said, "Don't ever let Shark come here again without calling. Kathy's staying here, man."

I told him I'd deduced that, and agreed to keep quiet, but I felt very uncomfortable about it. Here Woody was still working on his surfer screenplay, still taking money from Shark, and actually shacked up with Kathy Petro. It was just a double murder waiting to happen.

Carol Van Der Hof

Woody finally showed us what he considered the finished screenplay and, well, to be frank, it was pretty bad. But Shark said, "I'm not sure how objective I can be since Woody is my best friend. Why don't we get Brian's opinion?"

I told him that was pointless, but he gave the script to Brian anyway. It seemed fairly inconsequential at the time. *Looking for Lupe* had begun filming, and all of our energies were focused on that.

Brian Straight

It's funny how it happened. I think I'd seen the coverage of Woody's script, which of course advised a pass, when Woody called to find out my reaction, and for some reason I took the call. Something in his voice, that boyish sun-drenched surf vernacular, set off a spark of intuition. Maybe we shouldn't blow this project off just yet, I had a hunch. And so I set up a meeting.

Once I met Woody, this youthfully tanned and blond archetypal surfer in the flesh, I was even more convinced we might in fact have something here. And so I did something I never did in my capacity as president of the studio. I agreed to work on the screenplay personally with Woody on weekends at my place in the Colony. Together, I was sure we could yet shape his material into a workable script.

Neal Ridges

When I heard that Woody was working closely with Brian Straight, I perceived yet another dimension to the disasters looming ahead—if the rumors of Brian's homosexuality were true. Woody was not the kind of guy who would graciously decline an advance of that sort. He'd probably knock Brian's teeth out or worse.

But then nobody seemed to really know the truth about Brian. It was true he was thirty-four and had never been married, but he didn't run with a gay crowd. In fact most of his "friends" were the much older A-party set, the sort of ancient farts you have to court if you want Brian's kind of power.

Brian Straight

I was a very lonely man. I'd throw the Malibu bashes with all the right people. I'd wine and dine them all and appear to be oh-so-happy. But after all the couples had gone home, there I would be, alone—the great masturbator with his porno tapes and VCR.

In fact, I may as well tell you, as long as I'm telling you everything, that at age thirty-four I'd only had sex twice in my life, and both of those times with women.

Kathy Petro

Woody started spending more and more time working on this script up at Brian Straight's place until I started getting a little jealous. 'Cause I really loved being with Woody and was really happy for the first time ever—with all these creamy sensations from Woody's lovemaking, and from this great new mood elevator my shrink was giving me.

Then one day Brian came by the Topanga beach house. It was a Saturday and he was dressed casually, driving this blue Ferrari, but I got a funny feeling about him right away. He looked at me and said to Woody, "So this is the woman you live with." The way he said it was weird and for some reason gave me a shiver.

Then Woody walked him out to his car, and I watched them through the curtains as they talked in the driveway. Right before Brian got into his Ferrari he gave Woody a quick kiss on the cheek.

Woody Hazzard

I remember the afternoon I told Kathy I was gay. We'd just made love for what I knew was going to be the last time since Brian Straight had asked me to move in with him. So I told her as gently as I could where it was at as we lay there in bed watching this bitchin sunset.

She started to cry. "It's not fair. The first time I'm really happy and everything and then you go and . . . Woody, how *can* you be gay when you just made love to me the way you did?"

"I don't know," I said. "Life's weird, I guess. I never thought I was gay—"

"Is Brian paying you?" she said.

"No. I'm still living off the screenplay deal, you know that."

"Then what is it? He's certainly not that attractive."

"I don't know what it is, Kathy," I told her. "All I know is that I like the things he does to me, and the things I do to him. I like it when he sucks my cock till I come all over the place, and I like to chow down on his fat juicy knob. I like to punch my rod up his hot little bunghole, and I even kind of like it when he sticks his finger in mine and wriggles it around, thought I haven't let him fuck me yet—"

At about that point Kathy covered her ears and started screaming.

But she calmed down eventually after she took another pill, and I said I still cared about her as a human being and everything, and we agreed we would continue to be friends.

Neal Ridges

Looking for Lupe was a fairly smooth shoot, though we did have some problems with Hector the donkey. At first he kept springing a horrendous erection, usually during the middle of a take. His trainer began to feed him saltpeter, which took care of the hard-on problem, but seemed to make him generally more obstinate and testy. Then Shark became obsessed with the head movements and the braying in the close-ups which we planned to dub with Hector's dialogue. Shark wanted "absolute lip-sync perfection," which needless to say was a futile dream, so we shot a lot of useless film.

Then one night there was a fire in the stable where we were keeping Hector. Not a serious fire really, it was quickly put out, but it panicked Hector enough that he kicked through the stall door and escaped to freedom. The next morning I noticed the red T-shirt Hector's trainer had been using to direct the donkey's attention as we filmed, and I couldn't help observing that it was soiled with hoof prints and a large quantity of dried donkey semen. The trainer explained that the T-shirt had been draped over the stall door and that Hector, panicked by the fire, had ejaculated in terror despite the saltpeter, thus drenching the T-shirt a moment before he kicked it as he broke through the stall door that was trapping him. As the trainer offered this rather odd explanation I noticed for the first time that the T-shirt in fact bore a likeness of Kathy Petro—the famous bathing suit shot from the early seventies posters. At the time it never occurred to me that her picture could have in any way "registered" in Hector's mind—though certainly what happened nearly a decade later in our nation's capital leads one inescapably to that conclusion.

Hector was even more temperamental after the fire, and soon began urinating and defecating on the set, which was funny in a way, though not to the guys who had to clean it up. There was one shot like that, of Hector defecating in the dining room of the suburban ranch house, which Shark fought to keep in the film right up to the answer print. He said it was a chance occurrence we could exploit as a gag. In the scene Hector had just read the riot act to this square gringo couple who had hired Lupe as a babysitter once, and Shark wanted to dub in a new line of Hector saying: "And another thing—" just before he took this humongous dump on the shag carpet.

I told Shark it was too much, but he wouldn't listen. Finally Brian demanded we take it out or he wouldn't release the picture.

Carol Van Der Hof

Bri was right of course. The inclusion of that moment would have tipped the balance of the film. And what a tightrope Neal walked! With what finesse he negotiated that high wire of diabolically clever wit, greased ever so lightly with a soupçon of raunch, without ever once plummeting into the netless abyss of tastelessness and simple-minded crudity. We sensed it would be a massive hit with college audiences and the Westwood sneak proved us right.

Neal Ridges

When Woody arrived at the Bruin sneak with Brian Straight my most errant speculations were confirmed. I knew Woody had moved in with Brian in the Colony, allegedly to work on that godawful script. And now here was Woody with hickies on his neck, wearing a tight LaCoste shirt and even tighter 50ls, which seemed to be a kind of gay uniform in those days.

Shark was unbelievably dense about it though. "So you guys come stag?" Despite the rumors I don't think Shark could believe a guy as tough as Brian could be gay. And Woody . . . well, it seemed inconceivable.

I caught up with Woody in the men's room. "You'd better be careful," I told him. "I don't know which is going to enrage Shark more.

Your going gay, or the fact that you were shacked up for four months with Kathy."

"The latter, I'm sure," he said with a new, fey edge to his voice.

"Is she back in Newport Beach?" I asked him.

"For the moment."

"What does that mean?"

"Haven't you heard?" We were at the urinals. He shook off and buttoned up. "Mr. Brian Straight plans to wed Miss Kathy Petro in June. Betcha can't guess who's gonna be the best man?"

16 / Tropics Redux (1978–1979)

Carol Van Der Hof

How elated we were when *Looking for Lupe*'s first weekend broke nearly every record! And what legs the film had!

Of course the teens all adored it, and it was just "hip" enough for the young adult set. And even the critics who found the premise somewhat vulgar were compelled to acknowledge Neal Ridges's virtuoso stylistic flair. With what irresistible panache he'd cribbed both Eisenstein and Bertolucci!

Cord Bucky, *Eastern Collegiate Review,* May 22, 1978

Had Vladimir Nabokov paused while writing *Lolita* to dash off a film script with the working title *Francis Goes to Suburbia,* and had Stanley Kubrick directed it on Spanish fly, the result might well have resembled *Looking for Lupe.* Visually astonishing—not since *The Conformist* have I been put away like this—the film is at once a hilariously raunchy crowd-pleaser and, to anyone who cares to notice, a subtly profound critique of Ozzie-and-Harrietism grounded in a long-take/deep focus pictorialism which operates in seamless counterpoint to a blindingly brilliant neo-*Potemkin*-like use of montage. If the film has any flaw it is the casting of Diana Chadwick as Lupe, the runaway Mexican donkey-act star. The olive makeup has a faintly green tinge, you can see her blonde roots, and her Spanish accent wavers. Then again this could be intentional, a wry comment on Hollywood's notorious history of casting WASP actors in ethnic roles, for indeed *Looking for Lupe* is chock-full of just this sort of Buñuelian prank. Maybe that's why I've already seen it five times, and I'm on my way back for more right now—if my sore stomach muscles can take it. My girlfriend is threatening to leave me. The last time I said to her, "Come on, *ba-by,*

233

let's go home," she gritted her teeth and walked away in disgust. What have you done to my love life, Neal Ridges, you diabolical genius?

Greg Spivey

That Hector's last line in the movie became *the* pop-cultural cliché of the year certainly didn't do the film any harm. It seemed that everywhere you went someone was saying, "Come on, *ba-by*, let's go home" in a bad Spanish accent. It became the pickup line of the summer, parents were saying it to their children in supermarkets, employees were repeating it mindlessly in the workplace, you heard it from kids, teens, senior citizens, cops, TV talk show guests, President Carter worked it into a major foreign policy address *—until it did become a bit grating. But then that's our media-saturated culture, isn't it? I was happy for Neal.

Neal Ridges

It was a great moment for me after years of anonymous struggle. But I held my breath, expecting murder and scandal to poison our success at any moment, once Shark found out about Brian and Kathy's wedding plans. I wasn't going to be the messenger who brought him that news.

But June came and there'd still been no announcement. Were the wedding plans off? Had Woody been lying? I had no idea why Woody would invent such a dangerous rumor, knowing as well as anybody what it would do to Shark, but the more I thought about it, the more incomprehensible it seemed. How could Kathy Petro, still so beautiful and desirable, ever agree to such an intrinsically demeaning arrangement?

Kathy Petro

I don't know, I guess I just kind of changed my mind about Brian after a while. I hated losing Woody to him and everything, and I talked to my psychiatrist about it, and he put me on a more powerful mood elevator and after that I just didn't care. I missed the sex with Woody for a while, but then I started eating all this ice cream—I just became addicted to Häagen Dazs vanilla—and I'd just get this giant sugar rush and think: Gee, you know, this is almost as good as when Woody used to make love to me, only I don't have to worry

---

* "And I say to Mr. Brezhnev, if he sincerely wants to meet with me in Geneva in an effort to halt the escalating nuclear terror which threatens both our great nations, then: 'Come on, *ba-by*, let's go home.'" President Jimmy Carter, Princeton University, June 28, 1978.

that this ice cream is going to go gay on me or anything. I mean, I know that sounds crazy, but that's what I thought.

And Woody and I were still friends. I moved back to my parents' in Newport, but it was so oppressive that I was really glad when Woody and Brian started inviting me to Malibu for dinner and everything. Brian was really nice to me, and even said nice things about my performance in *Manhattan Holiday*, which coming from him really made me think: Gee, maybe I wasn't that bad after all. He was charming and everything and one night he asked me if I'd like to go to an A-party with him, and I looked at Woody and said, "Do you mind?"

And Woody said, "No, of course not, why should I? We're all mature, sophisticated adults."

Brian Straight

I went a little crazy with Woody, I suppose. I'd repressed my sexuality so long, spent so many years as a lonely, celibate workaholic— I was the J. Edgar Hoover of the film industry!—that in the ecstatic joy of finding Woody I very nearly destroyed my career.

The Oscars in March of '78 were a typical example. Although I nominally escorted Dame Mildred Danvers, Woody was also at my side, his neck covered with my hickies, both of us reeking gay sex. It was all I could do to keep my hands off him when they lowered the lights to show the clips—in point of fact I couldn't resist giving his tuxedoed crotch a quick squeeze—and a part of me just didn't care anymore.

But word reached Harold Gay, who summoned me to New York and said, "Brian, the time has come for you to get married."

"That will never be, Harold," I told him. "For like you I am gay."

"I'm not gay," he told me. "I have been married to a woman I adore for twenty-three years and I am as straight as they come."

I was flabbergasted. "But Harold, I always thought that was merely a marriage of convenience."

"That story only started because of my association with you," he said. "As I'm sure you know, there have long been rumors, Brian, that you and I are having an affair."

"Yes, I've heard those rumors. The absurdity of it. I was a celibate masturbator until a few weeks ago. But that has all changed, Harold."

"Yes, I know. I know all about this young lad."

"I won't quit seeing him, Harold."

"I'm not asking you too, Brian. All I ask is that you be discreet. And that you take a wife."

"And live a lie?"

"Brian, we have a corporate image to protect. If you want to be a flaming queen, I suggest you go into interior design or hairdressing. But this . . ." He gestured to the Manhattan skyline. ". . . is American business."

Woody Hazzard

Brian was real freaked out after his boss told him he had to get married. "I'm going to force the world to acknowledge us," he said one night as we lay in bed after sex.

"If you do, you might lose everything," I said.

"I don't care. I could live anywhere, even in some seedy Silver Lake bungalow, as long as I'm with you."

But I thought that house in the Colony was really bitchin, so I said, "Why don't you marry Kathy? She'd probably go for it. I know she's sick of being at her parents'."

At that Brian got real worried, 'cause by then I'd told him all about Shark's thing for Kathy. He knew that sooner or later Shark was going to find out I'd had a thing with Kathy, and he was going to find out about Brian and me.

"I like Kathy," Brian said. "But I couldn't do that to Shark."

What he really meant, of course, was that he didn't want to lose Shark, since his movies were raking in millions for Acropolis.

Then something came down that changed his mind about Shark.

Brian Straight

One afternoon in the spring of '78, I met Shark for lunch at Celine's in Beverly Hills. Things were good. *Mondo Jet Set* was setting new records abroad, and we were gearing up for a wide release of *Lupe* which, our minor differences over a few scenes resolved, now smelled like a winner. As Shark and I schmoozed the subject of his early films for Sam Schlockmann came up, and we were laughing about that period of his life when I mentioned *Sex Kill à Go-Go*, the original, much-altered script of which he'd written with Tom Field.

"Really a shame about Tom," I said, "A true film genius. I knew him at Choate."

Shark laughed and said, "Tom was a pussy. Though I'll say one thing for him, he could sure suck cock. I let him blow me once, you know, though it was definitely one-way. That's why he killed himself. 'Cause I wouldn't let him cop my joint again."

Well, I virtually imploded right there in Celine's. For I had worshipped Tom Field. At Choate he had been the first, albeit secret and unrequited, love of my life. Tom was the reason I'd come to Hollywood, hoping that someday I might work with him. His suicide, while I was still an agent, had soured my heart forever.

I smiled as Shark went on to talk about all the "Malibu snatch" he was sure Woody and I were getting. But deep inside the sealed chamber of my heart I made a vow then to destroy Shark Trager.

Kathy Petro

I couldn't believe it when Brian proposed to me, I thought he was joking at first. But then he explained how it would be in-name-only and everything, how I could live anywhere and do anything I wanted. All I had to do was go to a party or a premier with him once in a while and do some charity work and things like that. Otherwise I could spend as much money as I wanted, and see other men or even another woman if I wanted to, as long as I was discreet.

It seemed kind of phony in a way, but the more I thought about it, it sounded like a lot better deal than most guys had ever offered me. Plus, I was already thinking that someday I might like to try acting again, except this time do it right and take lessons and all that. And if I did decide to do that, being married to a studio president sure couldn't hurt. So I said yes. And we talked about this big June wedding, which was just the kind I'd always dreamed of someday having.

Then suddenly, right after *Looking for Lupe* opened and became this really huge hit, Brian said, "Look, I want to postpone the wedding until next fall."

I was really angry and disappointed at first, thinking Brian just didn't want to have the big falling out with Shark our wedding was bound to cause until after *Lupe* had pulled in all those millions of dollars.

Then Woody explained to me what Brian was really up to. "For personal reasons he wants to really fuck Shark over, and a golden opportunity's come up."

Carol Van Der Hof

In the ecstatic rush of *Looking for Lupe*'s phenomenal success I persuaded Shark to do the one thing I'd long desired which he had always refused: to screen for me the work print of *Tropics*.

"I futzed around with it so long I can't tell if it's genius or shit," he said.

Of course by then the film was legendary, either as a lost masterpiece cruelly shelved by the ignorant business powers of Hollywood, or as the worst film ever made—depending on whom you talked to.

In the screening room there at our Gold Coast haven I watched all four hours of it, reserving comment until the bitter end.

"Well?" Shark said.

"It's dreadful," I told him bluntly. "It's stilted and pretentious in the worst sort of way, it's an atrocious travesty of von Sternberg and yet . . . I believe it can be made to work."

"How?" he asked.

"In a word, it needs to be brutally recut," I said. "Tightened to ninety-five minutes. Then released as an American art film, on one level self-consciously kitsch, on another exceedingly profound."

"Of course!" Shark cried. "That's precisely how it might work! My God, you are a genius, Carol! Will you do it? Will *you* recut the picture?"

"We can do it together, Shark," I said, squeezing his wonderfully masculine hand on the red velvet arm of the screening room chair.

Woody Hazzard

Brian saw *Tropics* as a chance to really humiliate the shit out of Shark. The film was so "inalterably, stupefyingly bad," Brian said, that no matter how Shark recut it, it would still be like "a bomb exploding in his hands."

"I'll give it a special press screening well in advance, inviting all the major critics," Brian said. "The reviews will be so savage no one will blame us for dumping it, and Shark's devastation will be intense."

By then Brian had told me about the Tom Field thing, which was one of the shittiest things I'd ever heard of Shark doing, so I agreed he deserved to take a tumble.

But I was worried about Carol. "I hear reviving *Tropics* was her idea," I told Brian. "How's she gonna feel?"

"I'll do what I can to warn Carol at the appropriate time," he said, "though it may already be too late. She's under his spell." He continued in the coldest voice I'd ever heard from him: "You've got to understand something, Woody. This is just the beginning. I'm going to fuck Shark Trager till he bleeds. And then I'm going to keep right on fucking. And anybody who tires to block my path is going to get fucked too, or at least splattered."

Cynthia Clive

Poor dear Carol. It was clear to us all that she was hopelessly in love with Shark, and therefore on a collision course with heartache. I was tempted to sit her down for a stern talking to, and I will always regret my lack of temerity. I might have pointed out how futile her longing was, for by then I knew well of Shark's obsession with Kathy Petro—not that he and I had ever discussed it. Far from it. No doubt the only reason I'd lasted as long as I had in his employ derived from my pretended ignorance of his personal affairs.

But the torture Carol endured!

Carol Van Der Hof

It was during the intense and intimate recutting of *Topics* that my long-sublimated feelings for Shark drove my heart to the point of no return. The long hours of close physical proximity, as we sat side by side at the flatbed installed in the basement of the Gold Coast house, eroded my most elaborate mental defenses. How I longed for him to kiss me, I could no longer deny it, at least not to myself. And I knew he did love me on a plane far more profound than he could possibly love the others. And there were others. The blondes.

I'm quite sure *bimbo* is the word. Vacuous California airheads, Marina del Rey girls, all bonded teeth and perfect breasts and high-lighted hair. An endless parade of one-night-stand Cindis and Debbis and Jodis—the "small *i* girls," I called them.

"*Hi,*" one chirped to me once, padding down to the kitchen one morning in Shark's robe. "You must be Shark's sister. He mentioned that he lived with his sister." It was all I could do not to hurl scalding coffee in that vapid beach bunny's smug Barbie doll face.

Neal Ridges

Shark and Carol invited me to a private screening of the recut version of *Tropics* at the beach in August of '78. I'd been in Europe pushing *Lupe* and hadn't seen either of them in a couple of months and Carol looked bad. I thought it was just exhaustion at first. Then she drew me aside after the screening and said, "Neal, I can't take it much longer."

"Take what?"

"I love him so," Carol said, and began to cry.

"Oh Carol," I said, and hugged her. She'd sat beside me during the screening, whispering a remark at one point about the Amelia Earhart character looking too much like Kathy Petro. Amazingly, I realized, Carol was still unaware of Shark's past with Kathy. I was finally about to blurt out everything I knew—about Shark and Kathy, and Woody and Kathy and Brian and Woody. There'd still been no public announcement of Brian and Kathy's wedding plans, but there was just a sense that the time bomb had quit ticking and was about to explode, and I knew I had to warn Carol.

But Shark stepped up to us before I could speak. "Hey, what are you doing, Neal? Trying to steal my partner?" he joked, for I was still hugging Carol.

He saw her tears. "Jesus, you're crying. I guess that's a good sign, if as many times as you've seen it the ending still gets to you."

"Yes," Carol said, avoiding his eyes. "I'm a fool for sad endings. I still weep at *Now, Voyager*, you know that, Shark."

Tropics, despite the extensive re-editing, was still wretched by the way.

Carol Van Der Hof

I suppose on some deeply buried level I always knew that, recut or not, *Tropics* remained by any objective standard something of a piece of shit. But the waves of rapture I felt toward Shark quite literally blinded me to that reality.

Still, I believe it may well have been a subconscious sense of what lay ahead which compelled me, the evening of the initial press screening, to at last show my hand.

I was dressing for the screening when Shark stepped into my bedroom. "Come on, we're running late," he said.

"Shark darling, would you be an angel and zip me up?" I said breezily.

As he complied I turned abruptly and took him in my arms. "Oh Shark," I sighed, and fool that I was, tried to kiss him.

He jumped back with a look of shock. "What on earth are you doing?" he said. "Have you lost your mind?"

"Shark, I love you," I said. "I love you and I know you love me."

"Carol," he said, recovering his composure, "I love many things about you. We've had more fun, you've brought me more joy, in these last few years than I've ever known. You mean more to me than all the women I've ever slept with combined. But I'm afraid I find you physically repulsive. Come on now, hop to it, we're late."

Well—if I'd had any pride or self-worth I would have walked out the door then and never come back. At the moment, I suppose, I was simply too devastated to take such a forthright action.

We drove in silence to the studio in his Porsche. As we mingled with the critics prior to the screening I felt disembodied. Shark was in his element, charming them all, even Sonya Heinz, who'd trashed everything he'd done since *White Desert*. Finally, as the lights came down I broke. Pushing my way to the aisle, much to Shark's irritation, I stumbled into the foyer, colliding with Brian Straight.

"Oh, Bri," I cried, and fell weeping into his arms.

"Get out, Carol," he said, after I told him what had happened. "Cut yourself free of Shark before it's too late."

"Why can't he love me, Bri?" I sobbed. "Is it my clubfoot?"

"It's not your clubfoot, Carol," he said. "It wouldn't matter if you were perfect in every possible way. Shark Trager is a man incapable of love. He worships a vision, a dream of love, a dream of blonde perfection no one could ever possibly fulfill. Not even Kathy Petro herself could live up to his masturbatory fantasy of her."

"What are you talking about?" I said, though on some unconscious level I'm sure I already suspected, for the images of Kathy proliferating through Shark's films could not all have been a simple generic similarity. I knew Shark and Kathy Petro had both grown up in Newport Beach. Once I had even asked Woody if Shark and Kathy had known one another. "You'd better ask Shark about that," he'd said, which was certainly a tip-off in itself. I suppose I hadn't wanted to know how impossible my love truly was.

Now Brian told me everything, all that Woody had shared with him, of Shark's pathological fifteen-year obsession with this mindless blonde paper doll!

"And Kathy and I are going to be married," he added.

"But Bri, I thought you were gay."

"I am—now," he said, and told me about Woody.

I was speechless.

"Get out now, Carol. Don't be at ground zero when the bomb goes off."

I don't know how long we'd been talking in the foyer. But suddenly I became aware that people were laughing in the screening room—that hideous, snide laughter of critics who've discovered an "unintentional comedy."

Then Shark burst through the doors, scarlet with rage. As he did I heard Sonya Heinz' distinctive cackle, and she'd been sitting *next* to Shark—the reaction was that out of bounds.

"Let's go," Shark said to me. "Before I kill someone."

"Slough it off, Shark," Brian said with a venomous, insinuating sarcasm. "What do the critics know?"

The affront caught Shark utterly off guard. He could not then begin to imagine why Brian should so relish his mortification, let alone arrange it. Incredulous and enraged, as another gale of laughter erupted in the theater, Shark literally yanked me out the door.

"I think I know now why you don't care for me, Shark," I said as we approached his Porsche in the studio parking lot.

And then I let him have it, telling him everything Brian had just told me. I'm sure I wanted to hurt him as badly as he'd hurt me, which was why I concluded, "So you see? Your precious Kathy prefers sex with your gay best friend, and a fraudulent marriage to your gay best friend's lover, to even *once* going to bed with *you!*"

I'll never forget the way he looked at me then. If a dog were to look at you that way you'd know you had no choice but to have it put to sleep. For an endless moment I was certain he was going to physically attack me, and I was prepared to cry out for help. Instead, he got into his Porsche and screamed out of the lot with a stunning insane ferocity.

Kathy Petro

I was staying at Brian's house, and had just taken a shower and put on my nightie when I heard the phone ring downstairs. It was one of those rare humid L.A. evenings, the air at the Colony all sultry and sensual so that we had the windows open, but you just felt all sticky and wearing much at all didn't really make sense. So I went downstairs, just wearing this sheer nightie, feeling kind of hot and crazy since I hadn't had sex in a real long time.

So there was Woody in the den watching *The Long, Hot Summer* on the big-screen TV as he talked on the phone, wearing these tight little swimtrunks Brian liked him to wear.

I could tell by the way Woody looked at me we were both getting the same idea, even though he was gay now and everything. So I stepped over to get a cigarette and my nightie kind of came open, and I was right next to where he was sitting and he slid his hand up between my legs and I started getting really excited.

I could tell after a while he was talking to Carol who was at the studio where they were screening *Tropics*. But Woody kept asking her what she was talking about, because he was getting more and more distracted, until finally he just put down the phone and buried his face in my you-know-what.

Very soon nothing else mattered except what Woody was doing to me, and I was only vaguely aware of Carol's voice still going, "Woody? Woody?" on the phone, when suddenly this whole big plate glass window just *shattered*, and at first I thought it was a bomb or an earthquake. But it was Shark.

Woody Hazzard

Shark threw this deck chair through the window, which really shocked the shit out of us. Then the next thing I knew he was in the room, pulling Kathy off of me. He made out like he was going to slap her, but I caught his arm before he could, and then we both hit the floor. We struggled there for what seemed like forever, and at one point my face was real close to his and I wanted to say: Why are we doing this? This is so fucking stupid, I know we fuckin' love each other, man. But he was really trying to kill me, it was too late to stop, and my own adrenaline was going totally apeshit.

Then suddenly the gate guard was there pulling Shark off of me, and the security patrol guy was there with his weapon drawn—it seemed Shark had rammed through the gate barricade in his Porsche. We heard sirens in the distance, and then Brian came dashing in. Kathy rushed to him and he put his arm around her, the way a husband would in a movie if he'd just rescued his wife. By that time

Shark was just panting on the floor, and he wouldn't look at any of us, almost like he was embarrassed that he'd been taken alive.

Brian Straight

The sheriff's deputies arrived and placed Shark in handcuffs in the back of their car. But I declined to press charges, and in fact did some pretty fast talking to stop the matter there, which seemed prudent at the time. I wasn't eager for a tabloid scandal to negate the entire point of my marrying Kathy.

Kathy Petro

I think Brian paid everybody off. I watched from an upstairs window as the deputies let Shark go. He went to his Porsche, which was damaged in front, and right before he got in he looked up right at me, even though I was peeking very cautiously through the blinds in this completely dark room—there was no way he could've seen me. But somehow he knew I was there. It gave me this awful chill, the way you might feel if someone you hated was reading your mind.

Then, while the deputies watched him, he got in his car and roared away.

17 / **Red Surf**
(1979–1981)

Sonya Heinz, *French Quarterly Review,*
Winter 1979

FROM: "WHY MOVIES AREN'T ANY GOOD ANYMORE"

"Why are movies so dippy these days?" a transsexual friend asked me recently, and I couldn't help recalling how I'd felt after seeing Shark Trager's deliriously woozy, low-kitsch mock–von Sternberg movie *Tropics.*

"Because in Hollywood filmmaking has become a business, and all the films there are made by businessmen now," I told him/her. "The real artists have given up, leaving the businessmen in charge of everything."

Tropics shows us what happens when businessmen make what they think of as art in a place where all the businessmen are failed, bitter artists. They end up making vacant, jittery, turn-off movies, scuzzy, deadening camp movies filled with howlers, bad-art films that make us long for even the grungiest of the sick-joke counterculture movies of a few years ago.

Tropics is an angry, rejected artist's idea of raw, thick film sensuality. If David Selznick had been a frustrated lesbian he might have produced films like this. (And the comparison is apt, for though Dean Sutter nominally directed, this is a Shark Trager film. Does anyone even remember anymore who directed *Gone With the Wind?*) Trager, who began his career as a low-trash producer (*Redneck Scum, Tract House She-Devils*), before going on to mediocre big budget crowd-pleasers (*The Condoist, Hail!*), fey, bitchy "dance" movies (*Mondo Jet Set*) and gross-out/donkey act/teen raunch comedies (*Looking for Lupe*), originally wanted to be a director.

While at UCLA film school in the late sixties, Trager made a

notorious sixteen-millimeter feature, *Pillow F**k*, which earned
him a reputation as "the next Orson Welles," though the plot-
less, experimental film probably owed a much greater debt to
Jean-Claude Citroen, Trager's idol. When Citroen savaged the
film, a tearful, petulant Trager destroyed the negative, and he's
had it in for artists ever since. "God hath no fury like a woman
scorned," the "Aviatrix" deadpans in *Tropics*. And the same is
true of artists, who can also marry for money and become re-
spectable whores. Whores don't kiss, according to custom, because they're saving their hearts for the time when they retire.
But the sad thing about a whore like Trager is that he's been
saving himself for nothing. From the sickly, gooey, spoiled fruit
evidence of *Tropics*, it's depressingly apparent where his mouth
has been.

Cynthia Clive

Shark wept when he read that essay, the only time I ever saw him
cry. Of course, you know he'd once adored Sonya Heinz, devouring
each new review with joyful delight as far back as junior high. He
credited her infectious love of film as a key inspiration, and even
mentioned once in passing how uncannily she resembled his late
mother Winnie. How desperately he longed for her nurturing approval.

Brian Straight

At the risk of appearing somewhat unsympathetic, I must admit I
snickered as I read the Sonya Heinz piece, knowing how deeply it
would wound Shark. He was still on the lot, but I anticipated an
imminent departure. Carol was staying in Laurel Canyon with her
old friend Tony Borgia, who in the wake of *Dogs of Saigon* was quite
hot. I'd long been high on Tony's passionate brand of filmmaking,
and looked toward a rewarding future with Tony and Carol—sans
Shark.

Tony Borgia

Sonya's essay was pretty rough. And I felt somewhat responsible since
I was the one who'd told Sonya about Shark's UCLA experience,
never suspecting she'd use it so viciously.

As Shark but few other people then knew, Sonya Heinz was actually my mother—though I'd been taken from her, and given to Fed-
erico and Ethel Borgia, shortly after birth. As she told it, my real
father had been a "sexually magnetic Italian drifter," with whom
she'd had an "ecstatic two-hour affair" in the grease pit of a Baton

Rouge Flying A gas station one sticky summer night in 1949. As a struggling Southern intellectual barely supporting herself as a dancing snake lady in a French Quarter freak show, my mother had seen little choice but to give me up for adoption, in the process of which she'd been told only that I was to be placed with a "lovely out-of-state Italian couple." Free of the burden of raising me she'd been able to earn a Ph.D from Tulane, write eleven books, including *From Blanche to* Boom!, the definitive study of the films of Tennessee Williams, and eventually become the nation's foremost Cajun film critic. It was not until I was twenty-six that, as obsessed as James Dean in *East of Eden*, I finally tracked her down in New Orleans, by which time, ironically—never suspecting that I was in fact her son—she had already given my first two films ecstatic reviews. Though our mother-and-son reunion was mutually cathartic, we agreed to keep our true relationship under wraps so people wouldn't say, you know, "Well, of course she likes his films. She's his mother."

But Shark knew and that was why I braced myself when he called me at home one Sunday shortly after the piece appeared. "Shark, please don't take it personally," I told him. "Mom's on the rag, that's all. You're just an easy target. Actually, she liked *White Desert*—"

"Hey, it's no big deal," Shark said. "Your mother's a critic, that's what critics do. If you can't take the heat—" He laughed good-naturedly.

"I'm sorry *I* never got a chance to see *Tropics*," I stammered.

"Hey, pal, not many people did. I think it played a couple of days in Pacoima before they ripped up the seats and threw 'em at the screen." Again, he laughed, as if to say: Win a few, lose a few, roll with the punches.

"Anyway, Tony, there *is* a reason I called."

I glanced at Carol, who'd been staying in my guest room since her fight with Shark. They hadn't spoken at all in the several weeks since that night, conducting their business affairs through third parties. But Shark knew she was staying with me.

"Carol doesn't want to talk to you, Shark," I told him bluntly.

"I know, I know," he said in a pained voice. "That's not why I called. But Tony, I do still love her. You might want to tell her that."

I wanted to ask him just what kind of love he meant, but couldn't very well with Carol standing there. "Sure, will do," I said.

"Tony," he said, abruptly shifting gears, "I've decided I want *Red Surf* to be my next picture. Has Carol shown you the script?"

I knew *Red Surf* was the most recent title of Woody Hazzard's screenplay, and I had looked at his original draft, which was so depressingly amateurish I'd only read a few pages before tossing it aside.

"Look, Shark, I'm from Michigan. I don't know shit about surfing. And frankly a beach picture modeled on the Ulysses myth strikes me as a bit—"

"Oh, no, no," he interrupted. "You must have seen an old draft. It's not like that anymore. The Ulysses plot's been completely junked. It's a crime thriller now. It's about a vicious serial killer who preys on surfers, both guys and girls."

"*Huh.*" I felt a subconscious click.

"Tony, this script was made for you. It's like *Taxi Driver* and *In Cold Blood.*"

"*In Cold Blood* was a true story," I observed.

"So is this." And then he told me all about Brad "Pus" Jenkins, his tortured boyhood friend, whose eventual rash of homicides, the so-called Surf Killer murders of 1967, had terrorized Orange County and spoiled the Summer of Love for more than a few local teens.

"My God, this is extraordinary," I said. "And there's never been a book?"

"No, it's virgin territory, Tony. A virgin crime. Let me send you the script."

Well, the messenger delivered the script an hour later, and before I was twenty pages in I was trembling with excitement.

Carol Van Der Hof

"Come on, Carol, forgive and forget," Tony said to me repeatedly, conveying Shark's wish that I join Tony and him in "the great adventure" *Red Surf* was undoubtedly going to be. By this point Shark had sent flowers, which I had returned with the accompanying apology note torn into little pieces.

But I had read *Red Surf*, and I had to admit it was pretty damn good. Brian's guidance had considerably improved Woody's writing, though the tone remained crude, primitivistic, visceral precisely the raw material of a stunning Tony Borgia film. Still, I refused Shark's calls, even as he and Tony began meeting to discuss the project.

Then one morning I stepped out to get the paper and there in Tony's driveway was a car with a vanity license plate: CAROL. It was a bright red vintage MG sportscar restored to perfection, precisely the kind always driven so recklessly by jilted, spoiled debutantes in 1950s films—as Shark and I had amusedly noted more than once through the nights of our marathon screenings. For a moment I thought it was a cruel prank—for as Shark well knew, I had never learned to drive. Then I opened the envelope attached to the steering wheel, and found a gift certificate for driving lessons. At that point I began to weep.

Through my tears I saw Shark standing sheepishly at the foot of Tony's drive. Cathartically, we rushed to one another and embraced. As they never had before his lips pressed mine. It was not as one says a "soul kiss," though I was so blindly mad with love for him in that moment it might just as well have been.

I moved back into the Gold Coast beach house that same day.

Kathy Petro

Shark sent Brian and me this really horrendous silver service as a wedding present—I mean, it must have cost thousands of dollars—with this note wishing us eternal bliss and everything. I showed Brian the note and said, "Is this a joke or what?"

"I'm not sure what it is," Brian said, and he seemed kind of nervous and scared and everything, because the wedding was only a few days away and we were all afraid Shark might still do something to spoil it.

Then suddenly Woody came in from surfing and said, "Guess what? Shark wants to do my screenplay."

Woody Hazzard

I was surfing at Sunset, which Shark knew was one of my favorite spots, when I looked up and saw him getting out of his Porsche at the side of the highway. I was just coming up out of the water and I had this big rush of fear for a second, thinking, you know, maybe he's got a gun or something. Then as I got closer I saw there were tears in his eyes. And I got this big fuckin' lump in my throat, 'cause I mean we'd been through everything and I still loved the guy. We went into this big bearhug even though I was wet and got his vintage Hawaiian shirt all wet.

"You're still my brother, man," he said, patting my back.

"I'm sorry, man," I said. "About Kathy, I mean. I don't know, it just happened. It was crazy. I didn't want to hurt you, man. It's been such a weird fuckin' time for me . . . all this fuckin' sexual ambivalence—"

"It's okay, it's okay," he said. "Life's just a play, isn't it? We all switch partners and play many different roles."

"Yeah." The way he said it made it sound real profound. Like why do people fight anyway, when we all secretly know how fuckin' much we love each other?

Then he told how he wanted to do *Red Surf*. "Aside from making an astonishing film," he said, "my fondest hope is that the process will somehow bring us all together in laughter and joy."

Brian Straight

"I don't want you to see Shark Trager," I told Woody.

"Look," he said, "I'm not your fuckin' wife, man. Don't tell me what to do. Shark's my best friend in the whole world."

"My God, have you forgotten what happened?" I shouted.

"He accepts us, Brian. Why can't you accept him?"

I refreshed his memory on the subject of Tom Field.

"I mentioned that to Shark," Woody said. "It didn't happen like that at all. He only told it that way 'cause at the time he thought you were straight. He said what actually came down with Tom and him was very beautiful. It was his only gay experience, and it was like something in a Walt Whitman poem."

"I'm not sure I believe that," I said.

But Woody kept after me, constantly nagging me to do *Red Surf*. "Brian, you helped me write it, man. Tony Borgia's a fuckin' genius. You know it'll be good."

I finally gave in against all my better judgment. The budget Shark submitted came to a little over nine million. The economics did make sense, unfortunately. And then when Tim Stroll agreed to play the lead for scale—well, he was getting two million a picture in 1979— it was a package I couldn't refuse.

Still, I made it clear I would only have dealings with Carol.

Kathy Petro

We were on our honeymoon in Tahiti when Brian told me he'd approved *Red Surf*. "I don't believe it," I said. "You're actually going to work with this man again?"

"Kathy," Woody said. He and Brian were lolling in bed together and I had just come back from shopping. "Kathy, it's going to be a great picture. It'll be my first screen credit, plus Shark wants me to surf in it too."

"Oh, I see. We're one big happy family now. Is that it, Woody? Well, you can count me out."

"Settle down, Kathy," Brian said. "This is the nature of the film business. It's a small town. If you hold grudges—"

"All right, all right, mister gay baby mogul," I said. "But just don't you ever invite Shark Trager to our house. I'll do the charity work and smile on your arm at the Oscars. But don't you ever ask me to play polite hostess to that man who has ruined my life."

Carol Van Der Hof

Once *Red Surf* received the go our imaginations shifted smoothly into fifth gear. Tony spoke messianically of "transforming the mundane," and it soon became apparent that what in mediocre hands might have been little more than a teen slasher film was to be instead an hallucinatory epic of the American suburban dream.

The extreme violence did bother me at first, especially after Tony researched the actual murders and found that Woody had really been a bit squeamish in the script. "We've got to put in everything," Tony proclaimed. "No matter how ostensibly 'disgusting' or 'deranged.' The film itself is *about* excess—the excess bred of stifling middle-class repression. The theme here is 'homeliness versus beauty.' The rage of the rejected against the vapid blonde icons of California perfection, for Pus Jenkins was the ultimate victim of an image-crazed culture that worships superficial appearance at the expense of more enduring values."

I was easily won over, for I already shared Tony's view of art as catharsis. In this light I believed that with *Red Surf* Shark might well exorcise his obsessions once and for all—for it was difficult not to notice that many of the blonde surfer girl victims were generic Kathy Petros.

Through the alchemy of art Shark might still the past at last. His fetishistic longings vanquished he might see with clear eyes the love that stood before him, a love not blonde but genuine.

Greg Spivey

You know, I'm not sure to this day why Shark drew Carol back into his life at the time of *Red Surf*. I think maybe he did really love her in a way, perhaps he even *wanted* to find her attractive, but simply could not do the necessary psychic rewiring.

He did play with her emotions though. "You know, if you lost twenty pounds I just might do something crazy," he'd joke with her in the pre-production period.

But Carol took the remark seriously, enough to become a bulimic with a serious addiction to cocaine.

Carol Van Der Hof

I had long eschewed cocaine since it tended to make me jittery. But now for some reason I reacted to it quite differently, indeed began to see what the fuss was all about.

I found it quelled my appetite so that I magically shed pounds. I felt omnipotent, breathless, as I raced down the Pacific Coast Highway in my fire-red sportscar—for with *la cocaina* learning to drive had been a snap! How like a young and carefree Grace Kelly I felt the day I veered through the amusement park set, skidding giddily to a halt a few feet before Shark!

Tony Borgia

The original amusement park in Long Beach where Brad Jenkins had worked the summer of the murders had since been torn down. But the setting was crucial as a sexual metaphor. The libidinous grunge of the moldering arcade, the seedy freak show and the urine-scented house of mirrors—the raunch of the id in opposition to the antiseptic superego of the Disneyland we would associate with Brad's vapid victims.

Brian Straight

I was jolted when I saw the revised budget which, including the amusement park set and Tony's adjusted shooting schedule, upped the cost to twenty-one million.

But I approved it with a growing intuition that Shark might well be constructing his own doom. Which would be just fine since by this time I was secretly plotting a move to Mastodon Pictures. My "sudden departure" would be announced shortly after *Red Surf* commenced principal photography. Woody would never be able to say I hadn't supported the film. If—or more pointedly *when*—the film failed miserably I would be watching the flames at Acropolis from the safe vantage point of my new presidential chair at Mastodon, plausibly blaming the failure on the nervous new regime at Acropolis.

If on the other hand it grossed a hundred mil domestic—in this business anything could happen—I would be well within my rights to claim credit for having guided the development of a major hit.

Woody Hazzard

I guess I first sensed that things might be getting weird the day we went down to Newport Beach to scout locations. It was Shark and Tony and the location manager and me, and we drove all around the old neighborhoods until we came to the house where Pus Jenkins had killed Debbi Henderson, this ultra-wholesome girl who'd got me fired from the Taco Bell the night I'd first met Shark back in '66, for saying that I'd spit in her burrito. It was just this nondescript tract house on Abalone Drive, a few blocks from where Shark's dad still lived. Understandably bummed out, the Hendersons had sold the place shortly after the murder in 1967, so some other family was living there now.

We all went up to the door and said we were making a movie and everything, and the woman let us in to see what had been Debbi's bedroom, which was where the murder had taken place. Well, you could tell the woman didn't even know there'd been a murder there— I guess it's not the kind of thing real estate people point out—and we didn't tell her about it either. Shark just said he was making a "sixties nostalgia movie," and she signed the location release form and everything in exchange for a few thousand dollars.

Then we drove over to the Jenkins house, which was right across the street from Shark's dad's place on Mackerel Drive. I noticed Shark eyeing his boyhood home as we went up to the Jenkins' front door, but it didn't look like Mac was home.

Mr. and Mrs. Jenkins were real apprehensive at first, till they recognized Shark as Pus's boyhood friend. Then they smiled as if they hadn't smiled in about twenty years, and invited us in. Shark charmed them into letting us see Pus's old bedroom, and it was totally bizarre, because they'd kept it *exactly* as it had been the day the cops took Pus away in 1967. Tony was fuckin' awed. "This is better than any set could be," he said to me on the sly.

Finally Shark told the Jenkinses he was going to make a movie about the murders, and for a second they almost freaked out. But Shark was totally coked and did some real fast talking, saying how the film was going to make people understand how a basically good boy like Brad could become so confused and everything. But the capper was when he told them Tim Stroll was going to play Pus. "Yes, he does look something like Brad," Mrs. Jenkins said, even though he didn't at all because Tim was this total pretty boy, like just the opposite of Pus.

"So you don't mind if we shoot a few days here?" Shark finally said.

"Well, you should really ask Brad about that," Mr. Jenkins said.

Shark asked what Mr. Jenkins meant, and he said, "Well, we've tried to keep it quiet, but Brad was released from Vaccaville two months ago. He's been staying at a halfway house in Whittier and doing very well. And he's coming home next week."

Brian Straight

Red Surf commenced principal photography on April 29, 1979, in the two-million-dollar amusement park set constructed on the site of the old amusement park in Long Beach.

Coincidentally, I learned that same afternoon that the Mastodon presidency was going to Bill Kemmer. My tenure at Acropolis suddenly extended, I was more than disturbed by the early reports from the set. I refer of course to the infamous first shot—though infamous is admittedly an entirely inadequate word.

Carol Van Der Hof

Tony very simply wished to top Orson Welles's opening shot in *Touch of Evil*—though perhaps build on the master's precedent might be a truer way of characterizing his intent. Welles's four-minute tracking shot is a classic, inimitable bit of virtuoso filmmaking. But Tony was determined to "sustain the same level of seamless, unbroken cinematic elation" for a good twenty minutes not simply for the sake of showing off, but because he believed the overall complexity of that single shot was integral to the meaning of *Red Surf*. In terms of its sheer technical sweep, of course, the shot rendered Welles's accomplishment rather creakily rudimentary. If only dear Orson had had a Steadicam!

Greg Spivey

The shot was insane. The camera had to track backwards through the arcade crowd, then track in on Tim Stroll and follow him into the house of mirrors where it was his job to clean the glass and mop the floors—all without the camera being reflected in any of the mirrors, of course. Then it follows Tim back out, lingering on several of his obnoxious future victims, before picking him up again in time for the snub from the first victim couple; then it follows him back to the men's room where an obviously homosexual man makes a furtive and panic-inducing overture; then it follows him out to the beach where he finds the couple making love and in spontaneous confused rage stabs them repeatedly with his Boy Scout knife; and then of course we track back for reasons of taste as he alternately simulates sex with each of the bodies. I mean, it was a monstrous shot, with literally thousands of things that could go wrong, and I think every one of them did.

The camera showing in the mirrors—that must have ruined twenty takes. Or the male arcade extra with an earring, which guys didn't wear in '67. Once we got all the way to the murder and Tim broke character when he had trouble opening the knife.

Actually, you could say that Tony was very patient. After twenty-seven days he was still saying calmly, "All right, people. One more time."

Brian Straight

"He's been shooting for a month and he's still on the first shot?" Harold Gay yelled over the phone from New York. "It's unbelievable!"

"It's a complex shot, Harold. It's supposed to run twenty minutes."

"One shot for twenty minutes? That's stupid. Boring and stupid.

Tell him to break it up or else."

"I've tried, Harold. He refuses. And Carol and Shark are on his side."

"Then pull the plug," our chairman said.

Carol Van Der Hof

We were up to take two hundred and seven and keeping our fingers crossed, when Shark rushed into my trailer and said, "We've got problems, Brian wants me at the studio."

Well, he hadn't seen Brian face-to-face since the trouble in Malibu. "I'll go with you," I said.

"No. I'll handle this. But you can do me a favor and run down to Newport Beach to pick up Pus."

"Pus? You don't mean *our* Pus?" I said.

"Oh Christ, I haven't told you, have I?" Well, he hadn't but he did now. It appeared that he and Tony and Tim Stroll had already met with Brad "Pus" Jenkins on several occasions since Brad's release from Vaccaville, as part of Tim's preparation for the role. "He's been at his parents for almost a month now and he's climbing the walls," Shark said. "Adjustment's been hard and he needs a job, so I offered him one, it's the least I could do."

"What sort of job?"

"Technical adviser. It's just a title."

It was really more than I could digest at the moment. "Shark, I can't leave now, we're about to try for another take. Surely you can send a driver—"

"Actually, Carol, he's expecting you. I've told him quite a bit about you, sort of paving the way, you might say. He's a big fan of *Looking for Lupe,* which he saw shortly after his release. When I told him the film was based on an idea of yours he flipped."

"Yes, I'll bet."

"I want you to look after him—"

"You're mad—"

"Carol, he's harmless. After fifteen years of powerful drugs and innumerable electroshock treatments and—this is privileged information—Brad was castrated in 1971."

"Good God."

"Yes, it was part of an experimental treatment program for criminal sex offenders, the theory being I suppose that without their testosterone the men's hyper-aggressive tendencies might be curtailed. And it worked apparently. Brad's a gentle, squishy lamb. You'll see."

Shark scribbled Brad's parents' address. "In any event, you're safe," he quipped as he climbed into his Porsche. "I think the gentleman preferred blondes."

"Ha-ha-ha," I called after him, and went into my trailer, expelled the enchiladas I'd recently consumed, and grabbed my car keys and a gram.

Brian Straight

The gate alerted me when Shark arrived and I had several studio guards standing by in the next room in case there was trouble. I admit I was trembling as Shark was shown into my office—not with fear but excitement—for my time to obliterate Shark Trager had come.

"Don't sit down," I said, as he swaggered in. "You won't be here that long. You've done what I've always secretly hoped you'd do. You've gone too far. I'm shutting you down, and that's not all."

"No, you're not," he said, but I barely heard him. I'd waited too long for this moment to stop now.

"I'm going to destroy you," I said. "I've got a file on you, you son of a bitch, a dossier of sleaze ten inches thick. I know every shitty thing you've ever done, you evil little scumbag. I even know that Mike and Julie were really brother and sister—that you knowingly starred a pair of incestuous twins in *White Desert*—yes, I'm even going to level your one great film. You're finished in this town, you despicable piece of crud. By the time I'm through spreading the word on you, you'll be lucky to get a job producing hygiene films in Korea."

Shark remained virtually impassive throughout my harangue—only the mention of Mike and Julie caused a slight wince. He must have always known that would return to haunt him.

When he said nothing, merely staring with glazed, coked-out eyes at my framed photograph of Kathy, I added, "If there were anything more I could do to you I'd do it. If I could get away with it I'd strangle you right now with my own bare hands for what you did to Tom Field."

At last he looked at me, then sighed wearily and turned to the door. I thought I had won. This was Shark Trager beaten. But he stopped at the cabinet by the door, and the next thing I knew he was switching on my VCR, pulling a cassette from his pocket.

"What do you think you're doing?" I said. But a panic was already welling up inside me. I had anticipated that he might counter by threatening a public mention of my homosexuality, and I was prepared to tough that out—now that I was married to Kathy. But abstract allegations were one thing, graphic proof quite another. I recalled the several occasions on which Woody and I had fooled around on a seemingly deserted Tahiti beach. Was it possible Shark had dispatched video spies?

So I was quite relieved when I saw that his tape was in fact a vintage color film—until the crimson title seared the azure Spanish sky: *El Cristo Fugitivo*—directed by Rafael Avila. I knew of the supposedly lost surrealist film, I'd heard talk of its content, but since very few people had actually seen it, you always wondered how much to believe.*

Well, it was all true, I realized soon enough, as Shark fast-forwarded to a scene of the cowgirl Mary Magdalene having sex with the outlaw Cristo in the ruins of a church. Suffice it to say, their intercourse was clearly not simulated, though in no sense could the sequence be termed pornographic. Indeed, the scene radiated an aura of almost embarrassing innocence, an utter lack of prurience, as if its maker were guilelessly unaware that there are those in this world who deem such things obscene. The glazed colors infused the activity with a dreamlike intensity. Visually, the film echoed and subtly par-

---

* *El Cristo Fugitivo* [*The Fugitive Christ*] was filmed in Spain in 1956 with an international, largely non-professional "bohemian" cast. Ostensibly the story of a western outlaw gang, the religious allegory isn't difficult to locate since "Cristo's boys" all bear the disciples' names. A rowdy fun-loving band, they ride through the surrealistic landscape, having sex with nuns, sheriffs' wives, schoolmarms, and each other, barely staying a jump ahead of a posse of enraged lawmen, husbands and priests. Along the way Cristo performs numerous surreal "miracles," including the resurrection of Mary Magdalene, a prostitute who had died of syphilis, by having sex with her apparently lifeless body. She subsequently joins the gang as a joyfully hard-riding cowgirl, but when she and Cristo pair off as lovers, the outlaw savior's chief sidekick Judas succumbs to the "true sin" of jealousy and, in league with the posse, lures Cristo into a trap.

As Edmund R. Frye stated in 1988 when *El Cristo Fugitivo* received its first belated public screening at the New York Film Institute: "The surreal crucifixion and subsequent resurrection, despite their considerable nudity, and some will say blasphemous sexual content, are among the most astonishing, authentically spiritual sequences ever placed on film. Rafael Avila, one of the original surrealist filmmakers, compelled to flee Spain after the Civil War and seek refuge in Hollywood, where, like his contemporary Buñuel, he toiled for over a decade dubbing insipid American films for export, came home in 1956 and made his masterpiece—indeed one of the greatest films of all time."

It was a film that was very nearly never seen. On the basis of a false script— a pious tale of nuns reforming roughnecks in old Arizona—the movie had been co-financed by the Catholic Film Consortium and the Spanish government; Avila found himself a fugitive in his homeland when, shortly after completion of photography, the true nature of the project became known. Although it was rumored that Avila had, at the time of his arrest, completed his editing of the film at a clandestine Barcelona facility, it was believed for many years that all the materials related to *El Cristo Fugitivo* had been confiscated and destroyed. According to legend, Generalissimo Francisco Franco was so incensed by the film's "sacrilegious obscenity"—a view still shared, incidentally, by numerous religious groups in 1988—that he ordered the surrealist's execution by "clutch-hook disembowelment," an event the Spanish dictator allegedly had filmed for subsequent home viewing.

Precisely how Shark Trager came into possession of a print of *El Cristo Fugitivo* remains unknown.

odied the glossy Hollywood western and its Biblical counterpart. And Cristo, with his flowing hair and beard, indeed evoked the classic 1950s Jesus seared into all our minds.

How finally to convey the ecstatic essence of the sequence? As the camera panned around the joined couple, it provided a passing view of the other randy outlaws, the apostles as it were, all but naked in the sun-drenched cemetery, laughing, several of them playfully fondling one another. Labels seemed beside the point. *El Cristo Fugitivo*, it was clear in even those few moments, was a rapturous ode to the polymorphous perverse, a transcendent joining of the sacred and profane, a joyous marriage of Heaven and Hell, indeed a rebirth of paradise in a landscape destroyed by stifled desire and its end product, war.

It was beyond all doubt the most astonishing film I had ever seen—the monitor seemed to open into another dimension. The amazing love in Cristo's eyes, the tenderness with which he made love to Magdalene amid the rays of sunlight, superimposed dissolves showing his coming crucifixion and Magdalene's imminent tears.

I was quite frankly so swept away I had virtually forgotten why Shark was showing me the film, until the picture dissolved to a close-up of the exquisitely soulful Magdalene—and my amazement gave way to shock.

I had no sense of how it could be, which was perhaps why I hadn't realized it sooner. But there was simply no denying that the luminously saintlike face was that, albeit twenty years younger, of our chairman's lovely wife, Arlene Gay.

Shark tossed a revised budget on my desk. "We're going to need another twenty million," he said and walked out, leaving the cassette running.

Arlene Gay

"Is it true?" Harold asked me on our penthouse terrace after speaking to Brian in L.A.

"Well . . . yes," I replied, steadying myself against the rail.

"How could you do such a thing?"

"Harold, I was only twenty, a drama student with a headful of bohemian ideas on a Spanish holiday. Rafael was then an aging but still charismatic *enfant terrible* of surrealism, and we had a mad affair. He convinced me the film would be art, and it *is* art, I suppose—"

"I know what it is, it's filth," Harold said.

"It seemed very brave at the time." I began to cry. "I lost my head, I see that now, due in part to a near-constant use of Yenge, a powerful strain of Moroccan hashish. But you've got to understand, we all lived the film as we shot it, isolated as we were on Mallorca. We were all terribly in love with one another, or thought we were. Jan Delft, the Dutch actor who portrayed Cristo, was so truly—"

"You'll stop!" Harold roared, raising his hand as if to strike me, though he did not.

"Upon my return from Spain I discovered I was pregnant," I continued in a moment, sniffling. "I became hysterical and confessed everything to Dad [*aviation hero and Sadcom founder Rusty Diver, Ed.*]. I entered a private sanitarium, convinced by then I *had* gone mad. As I recovered my sanity and decency, eventually giving birth to twins which were put up for adoption, Dad spoke without my knowledge to his old pal the generalissimo." I sobbed anew, stung with a guilt I'd secretly carried for twenty-four years. "I can't imagine how a print survived."

Harold stared across Manhattan. "There are twelve of these . . . these apostles, as memory serves. How many of them do you do it with?"

"That's not a fair question."

"Answer me."

"No. You're trying to make the whole thing sound cheap. Harold, if you could only *see* the film—"

"That will never be," he said definitively. "I've heard enough to know that this . . . this *El Cristo Fugitivo* is undoubtedly the most offensive film ever made."

"I dispute that," I said shakily, averting my eyes from his judging gaze.

"Your lack of genuine remorse appalls me, Arlene. I shouldn't even care what happens to you now, knowing that you've done these vile things. And yet I do. And because I do . . ." With a terrible wounded tenderness he touched my cheek. ". . . I'm afraid we've no choice but to give Shark Trager everything he wants."

Carol Van Der Hof

I drove to Newport Beach with considerable apprehension, but Brad proved to be precisely as Shark said. Gentle, docile, and poignantly overweight, that flabby, squishy marshmallow obesity one associates with eunuchs. He barely fit into my compact MG, his bulging thigh pressing the stickshift all the way back to the Long Beach location.

How terrible was that vacant stare, the lobotomized manner in which he spoke. Here was a being who had truly paid for his transgressions in spades.

"I really liked that *Looking for Lupe*, Carol," he said. "For a girl you sure got some sense of humor. That talking donkey was *so* funny."

For his sake I tried to steer the talk away from his criminal past, but he seemed compelled to allude to those events if only to set me at ease. "I don't really know for sure why I did those things," he said. "I guess I was jealous 'cause I have the kind of skin that doesn't tan. If you didn't have a tan in those days people said mean things."

"I've never cared for the beach myself," I told him. "Exposing myself to the sun, that is."

"Why? Because of your clubfoot?" he said, which startled me a bit. But really what refreshing childlike directness! What absurd circumlocutions most people negotiated in their efforts to avoid mentioning the obvious.

"Yes, I suppose my clubfoot is a factor. It's not very esthetically pleasing, I'm afraid."

"I've never cared much for beauty," he said. "Perfection is admirable, but it's not very lovable."

"No, I suppose it isn't, is it?"

He smiled so peacefully that I couldn't help thinking: My God, he truly has been cleansed. That a man who once committed such unspeakable crimes should be metamorphosized into such an innocent butterfly-like creature actually quite moved me. What a pity he had to lose his testicles in the bargain. If only life resembled mythic poetry more than it does a lurid tabloid collage, then Brad would surely have been reborn as a virile and muscular Byronic he-man instead of this heart-rendingly roly-poly glob.

Brad Jenkins

I started getting funny feelings as soon as I saw that amusement park set. The way Carol and I came in it looked almost real except for these big movie lights overhead. But the people that were standing around on the arcade looked just like they had that night I killed the first couple. Only everybody was real quiet, all looking off toward the beach, which was all lit up, and then I saw what they were looking at. It was the murder, and something in me just snapped.

Tony Borgia

It was take 209 and every nuance was perfect up to and including the stabbings, where exasperatingly most of our problems had occurred. There was nothing remaining but the backward tracking as Tim simulated sex with the corpses, and really there was little that could go wrong there. We were perhaps thirty crucial seconds from our first perfect take when I heard Brad scream. "No, no, no, stop!"

"Keep going! Don't look at him!" I shouted to Tim, for Brad was not in the frame yet—and we could easily dub the sound. But Brad was running out across the beach toward Tim.

"Stop that man!" I yelled.

Crew members converged on Brad as he screamed hysterically.

"No, don't do it, stop, stop, stop!" They piled on Brad, throwing him to the sand a few critical feet outside the camera range.

But when I turned back to the scene I saw that Tim had stopped and was looking. "You're *looking!*" I screamed, for the take was ruined. "You stupid idiot, I told you not to look!"

"Cut cut cut cut cut," I yelled as I charged over to Brad, really ready to kill.

Brad was sobbing plaintively as a grip helped him to his feet. "Tony, don't do this, don't make this movie," he wept. "I didn't know it would be like *this.*"

"Do you have any idea what you've just done *now*, Brad?" I said, but he was so pathetic the rage was draining out of me.

He grabbed my shirt, tears running down his fat cheeks as he whimpered, "Tony, this movie will make other people kill. That's why I killed those people—because I saw *Psycho.* I thought Tony Perkins was *so cool . . .*"

I didn't believe that for a second. For starters, there'd been a seven-year lapse between *Psycho*'s release and the murders. Beyond that it was obviously a line some bleeding-heart psychologist had fed him, a specious pseudo-humanist, anti-art argument I found fascistic and despicable. I pried Brad's fingers from my shirt. "I want this man off my set," I told Carol. "You get him out of here now."

Brad Jenkins

I cried like a baby all the way to Carol and Shark's house in Santa Monica. I just wanted to be free of the past!

Carol Van Der Hof

Poor Brad. Once home I made a place for him on the sofa, and gave him a Valium and he finally calmed down. Then, just as I was climbing the stairs toward my room, he said, almost to himself, "I know the real reason I killed all those people. Shark made me do it."

I stopped and looked back down at him. "What do you mean, Brad?"

"Shark made me read books I should never have read. Books like Camus' *The Stranger.*"

I was relieved. For a moment I'd suspected he meant something much more literal. "Perhaps you should stick to uplifting books, Brad."

I was nearly to my door when he spoke again. "Carol?"

"Yes, Brad."

"You won't tell Shark I had sex with Kathy Petro?"

I was stunned. Apparently in his confusion he believed he'd already revealed this to me. Needless to say, he had not. Until now.

"No. No, of course not, Brad," I said, concealing my utter astonishment. "I assure you, that bit of information stops here."

Greg Spivey

Shark got back from the studio as we were setting up for take 210. "Brian's approved the jack-off dream sequence," he told Tony elatedly.

Tony was flabbergasted. "I don't believe it! I don't believe it!" He broke into a gleeful dance.

I could barely believe it myself. The very aptly named "jack-off dream sequence" was just that—a fantasy occurring in Brad Jenkins' mind as he masturbated, a truly deranged fantasy Tony had written near the end of a four-day stretch without sleep. Though this new sequence ran only five pages, it would easily cost an additional five million, for it required an untold number of hallucinatorily violent special effects as well as the outright destruction of an entire block of suburban homes.

Tony Borgia

The word Shark used was "carte blanche."

"Brian feels the genius of this," he told me. "We're crossing a line, Tony, into a rarefied realm where money means absolutely nothing in the face of posterity. Hold your breath, my friend, for we have entered the sphere of pure art."

If I'd been gay I would have kissed Shark then. I felt omnipotent, both godlike and satanic—as I imagine Leni Riefenstahl must have felt when Goebbels told her, "Just make a masterpiece, *liebchen*. Don't worry your pretty little head about the bill."

The news spread quickly through the cast and crew. After a month of infuriating wheel spinning, how we needed that surge of speed in our veins! "Let's get it right this time, people," I shouted, and called "Action!" on take 210. And by God, sweet Jesus, we did! The cheers went up as Tim climbed off of Wendy's bloody corpse and I cried, "Cut! And . . . *print it!*"

Brian Straight

After Long Beach the film moved to location in Orange County for some relatively inexpensive surfing sequences, though that dragged on for days as Tony waited for the right wave.

Woody was doing the surfing and from him I learned the details of the coming "jack-off dream sequence." Woody was delighted— like everyone else he was steam-shoveling cocaine—but I was appalled.

"Harold, they're insane. This is going to be another *Heaven's Gate*," I told our chairman. The Cimino film, shooting then in Montana, was already notorious, drawing the heat away from us. But that wouldn't last forever.

"Don't expect this to stop at thirty million," I told Harold, citing my rough projection of the final budget with the "jack-off dream sequence" added.

"Who knows?" Harold said philosophically. "The film might still be a hit. Another *Dogs of Saigon*." Tony's last film had come in at roughly eighteen million, and grossed nearly five times that, despite head-on competition in the stoned-futility-of-Vietnam genre from *Apocalypse Now*.

"I'm hearing bad things, Harold," I told him. "Bad, sick things. Excessive, sick things that make *Dawn of the Dead* sound like a Disney film."

"I've got the attorneys on it," Harold said. "In the meantime we're going to have to tough it out. I won't have Arlene's name dragged through the mud, that's all there is to it, Bri."

Carol Van Der Hof

I spent several days calming Brad in Santa Monica, even as the film moved on to Laguna Beach.

"You think then that art can be cathartic?" Brad said as we strolled on the white sand beach.

"Yes, I'm sure of it. If it's art, that is, as opposed to prurient trash. And Tony Borgia is most definitely an artist."

"But what about those fatal stabbings that occurred during that gang picture?" Brad said, referring to several incidents which had abruptly squelched Hollywood's "gang-picture" cycle a year or so before.

"Brad, there've been fatal stabbings since civilization first began," I responded, "since long before cinema was even a twinkle in Lumière's eye. Besides, plenty of people have been stabbed at MGM musicals and Benji films. Why don't our self-appointed moral guardians ever mention that fact?"

"It's just that Tim Stroll is so handsome!" Brad said. "I'd hate to have anybody think if they killed a bunch of people they'd become as handsome as him."

"Tim's handsome in real life, Brad. But he hardly is in *Red Surf*. That's why he was so eager to play you, so that he might overcome his pretty-boy image. Perhaps you didn't notice but the makeup crew's done wonders, he's really quite a geek now. The sickening-looking plastered-down hair, the oozing acne—" I stopped myself. Although Brad's acne was only scars now, his hair was still quite plastered down. "If anything, I believe the film will serve as a simultaneous release *and* deterrent to anyone toying with the idea of serial murder," I said.

"If so, the movie might actually be serving a very noble purpose," Brad observed.

"Indeed, it might," I replied, thinking more of Shark's personal catharsis, which I believed more than ever once the tides of *Red Surf* had receded would bring him at last to my arms.

Brad Jenkins

One nice sunny day Carol and I drove down to Laguna Beach where they were shooting the surfing, even though Tony didn't want me around. We stood on a bluff above the camera and watched Woody Hazzard do these fancy show-off moves.

"I stalked him once," I said to Carol. "Once I saw him at the drive-in with some blonde girl. I followed them down to Crystal Cove and watched them sit in his car and smooch. And other things. Then another couple came and parked in their car. And I thought about doing all four. But I left."

I didn't even know why I'd told Carol this, except I liked her, maybe 'cause she wasn't blonde. Then she asked me about the time I had sex with Kathy Petro, and I said, I thought I told you. But she said no, so I told her then.

Kathy Petro

It happened one summer afternoon in 1966, long before Pus committed any of the murders, when we were both sixteen and he was working at the Doolittle Camera Shop. I had just completely avoided that place since Shark's peeping-Tom movie thing, but I still felt raped just walking past the shop, knowing that Mr. Doolittle had seen that film.

Then one day I was home alone just relaxing on the patio in my bikini when the door bell rang. It was Pus. "I just thought I'd drop off these photos of your father's," he said.

I took them and said, "Gee, this is nice. You didn't have to drop them off."

And he got this funny look and said, "Oh, that's okay, I don't mind. By the way, I found this old movie film. I can't quite tell whose it is—"

When he took out this little reel of eight-millimeter film my heart just started pounding. "There's some girl in it though." He held the film up to the light. "And it looks like she's—"

"Let me see that." I grabbed the film from his hand and looked at it, and it was the peeping-Tom movie Shark had made of me.

Pus said it was a copy Mr. Doolittle had made for himself before turning the original over to the police.

I started to tear up the film and Brad grabbed it away from me. "Not so fast, Kathy."

"Let me have it," I said.

"That's what I'd like to do more than anything in the world," he said with a leer.

"If I let you do that, will you give me the film?"

He said yes. So we went into the den. When it was over—and it didn't take long—he gave me the film. I waited till he was outside, then I locked the door, and screamed at him through the grilled window. "You make me sick, you ugly dork. You're so stomach-turning no one's ever going to love you," on and on, all these horrible things, in revenge for what he'd just done to me.

I never told anyone about it. Then after he was arrested for the murders I just almost died, wondering if he was going to tell about me now. Or even if I'd wounded him so badly that I was partially responsible for, you know, what he'd done.

Brad Jenkins

Carol and I were still standing on this bluff when Shark spotted us and came on up. I thought he was going to get mad but he didn't. Instead, he said, "Hey, Brad, I know you're not an actor, but how'd you like to play a small part in the film?"

Tony Borgia

I was always against it, but Shark convinced me to let Brad assay the part of Debbi Henderson's father. It was a very small part, basically a matter of visual presence, with only one line, where he opens Debbi's bedroom door and finds her dismembered body. "Oh my God, no!" he cries, and I agreed to let Brad do it. If the line reading sucked we could always loop it. The thing was, Brad *was* physically right for the part. Mr. Henderson had been quite obese himself, unlike the fellow we'd cast, so I said: All right, let's go for it.

Greg Spivey

I didn't know about it until the day they were setting up the shot. We'd been at Debbi Henderson's old house for a couple of weeks filming the murder sequence, and we were already getting some heat from the neighbors, a number of whom had been living there since the time of the crimes and still knew the Hendersons, who were now living in San Diego. A lot of the complaints were the usual ones about how we were disrupting the neighborhood. Then somebody saw

Brice, our special effects wizard, bringing in the dismembered body parts, which of necessity looked quite real. "You're sick!" one of the housewife neighbors called. "You Hollywood people are sick!"

Then Brad stepped out of one of the trailers in costume, a Petro-Chem work uniform like the one Mr. Henderson had worn. Some of the neighbors saw him. "My God, that's Pus Jenkins! That's *him!*"

The first shot of Brad had him pulling up to the house in his Petro-Chem truck, and one of the neighbors said, "My God, they've got Pus Jenkins playing George Henderson! They've got the actual killer playing the father of the girl he killed!"

And the crowd grew larger as more neighbors heard about it, until we had to call extra police to keep them at bay. Again and again, Tony filmed Brad getting out of the truck, every take disrupted by catcalls and abuse from the increasingly hostile crowd—though that wasn't what bothered Tony, he knew he could dub the sound later. But the crowd was making Brad nervous. He kept screwing up, dropping his lunchpail, or catching his shirttail in the truck door as he closed it, until Shark finally fed him so many Valium he just oozed across the lawn to the door.

Brad Jenkins

I wanted to explain to those people what this thing was about, that we had to do this so it would stop someone else from killing other people. But Shark wouldn't let me go talk to them. Then he gave me Valium, which made everything seem like a dream.

When we got to Debbi's bedroom scene it did bring back memories. There was all that pretend blood everywhere, and the real-looking arms and legs, and the broken hacksaw blade. "Which window did Tim climb in?" I asked Shark, since they'd already done that part.

"That one," he said.

"Oh, that's wrong," I told him. "I crawled in this one over here."

"Don't tell Tony that," Shark said, looking around. "Or he'll want to reshoot the whole scene."

We did the scene a couple of times where I'd open the door and find Debbi's body. And on the third time something happened and I started to cry.

"What is it, what's wrong?" Tony said after he stopped the camera.

"I guess I'm just seeing this through Debbi's dad's eyes," I said. "And understanding for the first time what the sight must have done to him."

I was crying really hard and Carol put her arm around me. Then Tony called a lunch break, and as we went to the tables some guy in the crowd threw a rock at me.

Mac Trager

The first I knew they were making a movie was when I came home one night and saw the trailers and what-not parked a few blocks up on Abalone Drive. The next day I found out that it was Shark's film based on the Pus Jenkins story. I figured Shark was over there, but I hadn't seen him since the deal in Rome and my attitude was: To hell with him.

Then the location guy came around one morning and said: We want to use your house. I said: You know where you can stick it, and he said: Look, we'll pay you money for it.

"How much?" I said.

And he said: "Two hundred thousand."

I said: "Man, you must be crazy. It's only worth one-fifty. What the hell do you want to do, blow up the place?"

And he said: "That's right. You must have been talking to your neighbors." Most of them had already signed.

I thought about it for a few minutes, then caught up with him at the Gruntleys' house. "All right," I said, "but you'd better make that a cashier's check."

Paige Petro

Of course you know Jack had refused to attend Kathy's wedding, and had prevented my attending as well. I hadn't been too keen on the marriage myself—one had heard, shall we say, certain unappetizing rumors about Brian Straight—but I was willing to attend for Kathy's sake. Jack's chief objection was Woody Hazzard's presence as best man, and he and Kathy did have words about that.

"Have you forgotten that man's role in Jeff Stuben's tragic death?" Jack said to her.

Of course, at the time we had no idea Kathy had in fact been *living* with Woody up north. How dreadful this entire affair is!

When we first learned that *Red Surf* was planning to film in the bad part of town, Jack's initial attitude was one of benign disgust. At that point I believe we both thought it was some sort of nostalgia beach party film.

When we learned it was in fact the Brad Jenkins murder story Jack became incensed. "They're actually going to film poor little Debbi Henderson's murder in the very room where it occurred, if you can imagine *that*."

Jack made some inquiries with the city to see if all the permits were in order. Unfortunately, they were.

But the casting of Brad Jenkins himself as Debbi's father was the last straw.

"This is a moral atrocity," Jack said. "I think it's time I had a word with my son-in-law."

Kathy Petro

I was sunning topless by the pool at Malibu when Consuela came out and said, "Your father, *Señora*." Before I could even pull on my top Daddy was there, and he was just fuming.

"I want to have a word with your husband," he said.

"He's upstairs," I said, rattled and everything, trying to pull on my top without him seeing my nipples.

So he started for the stairs, and then I said, "No, wait. Let me get him." But it was too late, he was already going up the stairs.

I finally got my top on and started up after him. Then I heard this terrible slap and Daddy yelled, "You goddamn queer!"

Woody Hazzard

I was buttfucking the bejesus out of Brian when the bedroom door flew open and I almost shit, 'cause there was Jack Petro, towering above us like a red-faced Sunday school god in white Dacron slacks. Before I could even react he knocked me away from Brian, and started pummeling Brian with his fists, calling him a queer and stuff like that.

Then Kathy was there, pulling her dad off Brian, and as the two of them struggled Kathy's breasts slipped out of her top. This flustered her dad, and then I jumped him, and then Consuela the maid stepped into the room and stopped everything 'cause she had this shotgun trained on Jack Petro.

Paige Petro

Jack returned from Malibu in a blind red fury. When he told me what he'd seen I dashed to the bathroom where I was physically ill.

"Our dear Kathy," I said upon my return.

"Kathy is dead," he said. "This is the limit. As of today, I have no daughter."

"Jack, you can't mean that. You're exhausted, that's all. You'll see it differently in the morning. We'll find a way to rescue our daughter."

"Not this time," he said, and poured himself a large bourbon. "I don't know, Paige. I just don't know anymore. I've tried to live a decent life. I started out as a paperboy and built a goddamn empire. There was a time where that meant something, but not anymore. Now the bleeding-heart environmentalists control everything, the fruits and the whale-lovers and the left-wing attorneys. Ever since the sixties . . . God, how I despise that decade."

"They're a pack of envious jackals," I said, referring to his proliferating enemies. "False accusers, the lot of them. There's always been cancer, Jack. Long before Petro-Chem was even a twinkle in your eye."

"Bless you, my darling love," he said. Which . . . I'm sorry . . . proved to be his final words.

He retired to his study, taking the bourbon bottle with him, as he frequently did when he wished to be alone with his thoughts. I went to bed, though sleep was impossible. A little before eleven I heard a single, obliterating shot.

Greg Spivey

We wrapped at the Henderson house and then it was time for Mackerel Drive. Shark had secured the entire block for use in the "jack-off dream sequence." But first we had to shoot what was surely the most grisly of any of the murders where it had actually taken place—in the Jenkins' garage.

We had Mackerel Drive cordoned off, which kept the crowd of hostile neighbors some distance away down on Eel Road, but some of the people in that block of houses which we had in effect "bought" were still moving out, and the crowd on Eel Road was taunting them, as if they were union scabs: "Don't let 'em do it! Don't let 'em use your house!"

Of course, the people on Mackerel Drive could hardly refuse. This was essentially a middle- if not lower-middle-class neighborhood, remember, and the checks from Acropolis were more money in the hand than any of these people had ever thought they'd see.

Carol Van Der Hof

I observed a touching moment between Brad and his parents as they were loading their personal possessions into a U-Haul trailer. Shark had insisted, and paid them handsomely, to leave their furniture and "set dressings" behind in the house, though naturally it was quite all right for them to take personal items such as clothing and old photographs, anything that couldn't be observed with the camera's eye.

They were almost ready to leave when Mrs. Jenkins noticed that in the process of laying camera tracks the crew had savagely trampled her tenderly nurtured flowerbed, and she began weeping. Brad, who was back at the garage acting out for Tony the double-murder he'd committed there, noticed his mother and rushed to her, hugging her as best he could considering his girth. "There, there, Mom," he said.

"It's for the best. Once this house goes up in a big cathartic explosion, the past that took place in it will be gone too."

"I know," Mrs. Jenkins said. "Your father and I can buy a whole new life with three hundred thousand dollars. But I still hate to see people trample my pansy garden!"

On their way out, I understand, after fifteen years of compassionate acceptance, their Newport neighbors threw stones at the Jenkins, shattering the windows of their car.

Mac Trager

As soon as I got that cashier's check I moved out lock, stock and barrel, leasing a beach-front Laguna Beach condo at four thousand dollars a month. I was out a good five days before that movie crew moved over to Mackerel Drive. Then while I was unpacking I realized with cold shock that one precious thing was missing.

So I went back to Mackerel Drive, hoping they hadn't blown up the house yet, and they hadn't. They were all across the street at the Jenkins' place as I ducked up the driveway into the garage and found my old wire recordings of Joe McCarthy right where I knew they'd be, stuck behind the workbench in a green fishing tackle box.

I was coming back up the driveway when I saw this girl all covered with blood being chased across the Jenkins' lawn by the actor who was playing Pus Jenkins. She started to scream but he covered her mouth and started dragging her toward the Jenkins' garage when all of a sudden the Borgia guy yelled, "Cut!" 'cause I had walked into the camera range.

Everything stopped and Borgia started over, cussing me out, when suddenly Shark stepped up and said, "Ease up, Tony. He's my dad."

Shark came over and said, "How you doin'?"

"I'm okay," I said.

"Your hair's white now," he said.

"Well, I'm sixty-one," I said.

"I heard you and Miko split up," he said.

"Yeah. I got pretty sore when I found out she wasn't really dying," I told him. "Took her all around the world for nothing."

"I guess I judged both of you kind of harshly in Rome," he said.

"Yeah, well—" I didn't like thinking about that.

"Are you all right?" he said. "You got a place to stay?"

I told him about the Laguna Beach condo.

He was wearing dark glasses but he took them off, and his eyes were crazy-looking and filled with tears.

"Dad," he said, and then he tried to hug me.

I jumped back, by instinct, and said, "All right now, none of that Hollywood queer shit."

Just then that old fishing tackle box snapped open, all those wire spools of Joe McCarthy's speeches spilling out everywhere. I remember seeing a funny look on Shark's face right before I went after one spool that was rolling back into the garage. As I bent down to pick it up Shark jumped me from behind. He was like a madman. The next thing I knew he had me pressed back across that old freezer, the same one we'd found Winnie in, and he was choking me, cutting off my wind. A couple of the movie guys finally pulled him off.

Greg Spivey

"Shark, what happened?" I asked him in his trailer after we'd calmed him down.

"I'm not sure," he said, pouring himself a large whiskey. "When I tried to hug him, he rebuffed me—though I should have expected that. Then, when I saw those wire spools . . ." Shark winced and cupped his crotch, as if making some sort of subconscious sense-memory connection.* "I don't know . . . I just wanted to kill him."

Later that evening we heard about Jack Petro's suicide. At the time we knew nothing of the altercation in Malibu, pitting Brian and Woody and Kathy against her father; Petro's suicide seemed a distant, almost obscure event.

"That figures," Shark said when he heard Petro had done the shotgun-in-the-mouth routine. "He was definitely a Hemingway kind of guy. Tough on the outside, but underneath a pussy through and through."

Woody Hazzard

I was having sex with Kathy at Malibu the day after Jack Petro paid his surprise visit—by this time I'd kind of decided I was pretty much bi for all practical purposes—we were making love slow-like to some Marvin Gaye song when the phone rang by the bed and Kathy reached for it, real irritated.

"Hello?" she said. Then: "Mom, please don't start—" Then she just listened for a minute and hung up without saying anything.

"What is it?" I said, as we started moving again.

And she said, "I'll tell you later. Don't stop."

So we kept going, but pretty soon she started crying, like crying really hard, and I started to pull out, but she held me to her, saying, "No, don't stop."

But it was too weird, so I rolled back beside her, and by then she was really sobbing and said, "Daddy's dead."

I just held her for a long time after that, rocking her gently while she cried.

* See childhood snagged penis incident circa 1954, page 8.

Brad Jenkins

That scene in my garage made me feel real funny, 'cause by the time I finished showing Tony how the murders came down and they got ready to film it, it was almost like it was happening again. They had the guy who was playing Eddie tied up to the work bench, just like he'd been when I'd made him watch. And they had that actress Kit who was playing Becky Childers stripped right down to her panties, which were the exact shade of pink they'd been in real life. Then Tim would lift her up as she wriggled helplessly and start moving her wriggling body across the bench toward the power saw, the same saw I'd used in '67 to bisect Becky Childers right up the middle. And it all looked so real I began to get excited, even though I knew I shouldn't.

Then when that actress Kit lost her big toe I guess I kind of lost control.

Tony Borgia

It was just one of those terrible accidents that sometimes occur no matter how careful you are. The power saw blade, I felt strongly, should be real. The audience can tell when something like that is fake—it's the first thing they look for. We had the shot carefully blocked out and rehearsed. There should not have been a problem.

Actually, Brad became excited first, that was why Tim moved slightly off his mark. The saw began humming, and Kit was writhing, mouth and wrists taped, breasts undulating sensuously as Tim moved her toward the blade—well, the scene *was* supposed to be horrifically arousing.

Greg Spivey

Tim was moving Kit's feet toward the saw blade, which was to move up between her legs almost but not quite to her crotch—when suddenly out of nowhere Brad appeared, stepping right into the scene, his pants already down around his knees as he masturbated furiously. Well, it was a truly surrealistic moment: this crazed figure so grotesquely obese he could barely reach himself below his bulging abdomen—and no balls to boot!

Tim was so rattled by the sight he stepped back slightly, and in a bright splash of blood the blade took off Kit's big toe. A second later Brad spermlessly ejaculated in a paroxysm of pathological ecstasy.

For the first time I really began to wonder why I was involved with this film.

Carol Van Der Hof

Poor Brad was in absolute torment afterwards. "I don't know what happened, Carol. I thought those feelings were all behind me."

He began banging his head against his parents' kitchen wall until Shark intervened. Then he fell whimpering into my arms, as I stroked his amply padded shoulders.

"Take him over to my house," Shark said. "Give him a Placidyl and put him to bed in my old bedroom."

I did as Shark said, as well as I could, for Shark's boyhood house on Mackerel Drive was all but empty, his father having taken all the furniture. In what appeared to have been Shark's old bedroom however there was a beaten twin mattress surely thirty years old. On this I held poor Brad, his head in my lap. Rocking him I sang "Hush, Little Baby," and a slew of similar lullabies, until at last the sedative took effect.

Tony Borgia

Kit was rushed to the hospital where they were able to sew her toe back on. But I had to let her go. Obviously, the scene wouldn't play with her foot bandaged. Then Jerry Spark, who'd been playing her boyfriend in the scene, physically attacked me, saying Kit's injury had been all my fault. So we had to let him go too.

"Don't worry," Shark said. "So much of art involves exploiting chance. I think I know just the pair to replace Kit and Jerry in this scene."

Carol Van Der Hof

I was binging on Häagen Dazs in my trailer when Shark stepped in and said, "Call your friend Brian. Tell him I want Woody and Kathy on the set at six sharp tomorrow morning."

"You've gone mad," I said, realizing that he meant them to replace Kit and Jerry. And I wondered: Was it possible that he'd planned this all along? Could Shark have incited Brad to masturbation on the set at precisely that crucial moment, anticipating that it might cause a disruption and injury to Kit that would necessitate her replacement? My mind was racing crazily, for in the escalating dementia *Red Surf* was rapidly becoming, very little remained unthinkable.

"Shark, you can't be serious," I said, in response to this absurd casting whim. "Woody and Kathy are far too old. There's nothing as dispiriting as thirty-year-olds portraying teenagers."

"They're young at heart. We'll light them carefully. Make the call."

"Kathy will never do it," I said.

"Brian will convince her to," Shark said. And when I asked him why he thought so he told me for the first time of the print he'd found of *El Cristo Fugitivo*, featuring a graphically sexual Mrs. Harold Gay. Of course, I knew of Rafael Avila's suppressed surrealist masterpiece, rumored to have been perhaps the single greatest, albeit to some most offensive, film ever made. But the notion of Arlene Gay née Diver, unctuous star of the cloying Ginger film series,* portraying an incandescently obscene Mary Magdalene a scant two years before her brief time in the wholesome Hollywood sun, was not easily assimilated, though Shark assured me it was so.

"I see, then it's blackmail," I said, in my astonishment perhaps needlessly spelling out the obvious. "That's the reason Tony has carte blanche. It has nothing to do with art at all."

At that Shark fixed me with a look of weary contempt which I sensed had far less to do with what I'd just said than with his feelings, or lack of them, about me in general. For it was precisely the absence of any passionate emotion which made his gaze so devastating. Hatred, anger, even intense irritation, would have been preferable to that look of terminally bored disdain.

"You know, Carol, you really are a very stupid, silly woman," the man I adored said to me. "Once we finish this film I'm going to pack you and your ugly clubfoot right back to New York where you belong."

Well—I felt as if he'd killed me then, as if my life were over. I picked up the phone and wanted to throw it at him, but felt utterly drained of all strength. I dropped the phone on the floor. "Call Brian yourself," I said, and limped out into the night.

Woody Hazzard

Around eight that night Kathy and I were watching TV in the Malibu den while Brian took a call in the other room. Kathy was still real grief-stricken about her dad's death, feeling like it was her fault, and I was saying, "Kathy, come on. It's an ego trip to think you're responsible for somebody else's suicide. Your dad was depressed about a lot of stuff."

"I know," she said. "But why wouldn't Mom let me go to the funeral? Why, why, why!" She began to cry again.

I was comforting her when Brian came back into the room, looking

---

* *Ginger and the Clergyman* (1958), *Ginger Goes to Guam* (1959), *Ginger Goes Cuban* (1960). Acropolis Pictures' attempt to copy the successful Tammy formula, the first two films were hits, but the third entry bombed, a victim of changing attitudes towards Castro's Cuba, and ended the series. Arlene Diver made one more movie, *Isn't He a Dream?* (1961), before marrying Harold Gay and retiring from films.

real drawn. He took a deep breath and said, "How would you kids like to do a bit in Shark's movie?"

Kathy looked at him like he was crazy, and then went through about nineteen changes, all of them bad, as Brian tried to calmly explain what the roles entailed. There were just a few lines of dialogue, and the partial nudity would be tasteful, but when he got to the part about the power saw that had cut off Kit's big toe, Kathy exploded.

"Brian, the answer is no! Do you not know that I would rather die first?"

"I don't think you understand," Brian said, and told us about the surrealistic movie Shark had that showed this grinning cowboy Jesus cleaning out Arlene Gay's box.

"We've *got* to give Shark what he wants," Brian said to Kathy, "if only to finish *Red Surf* before it bankrupts the studio."

"And you want me to be in a Shark Trager film with a real power saw moving up between my legs? Well, *you are crazy!*"

"I'm telling you you're going to do it!" Brian yelled. "I've come too far to watch my entire career go down in flames becauseyou—"

But suddenly Kathy was shaking violently. It was almost like that scene in *Alien*, where that thing burst out of the guy's stomach. She fell back on the sofa, her tongue lopping out, her eyes rolling back showing the whites—like this total balls-out fit.

"Oh my God, she's having a grand mal seizure," Brian said, and he and I tried to help her. "Christ, put something in her mouth before she bites off her tongue."

I grabbed the first thing I saw on the coffee table—this raunchy old leather cock ring. She nearly bit it in two, but it saved her tongue.

Carol Van Der Hof

I returned alone to the Santa Monica beach house that night, more profoundly depressed than I had ever been. I was planning to pack my things and leave the City of Angels and the motion picture industry and Shark Trager forever. But I paused to binge on several Sara Lee cakes—those sticky sweet metaphors for all the erotic pleasures I had not, would never, share with Shark. I had barely finished throwing it all up when the phone jingled harshly. It was Brian.

"Kathy had a seizure," he said. "She was rushed to Saint John's. The doctors aren't sure yet but they think she might have lupus as well."

"You're telling the wrong person," I said.

He asked what I meant.

But suddenly I had a brainstorm, and quickly covered my tracks. "I mean, I'm mad at you, Bri. Why didn't you mention that Shark was blackmailing Harold Gay? No one tells me anything. It's sheer sexism."

I let Brian respond flusteredly to that, then steered the conversation back to the matter of Kathy's inability to appear in the film. "Don't worry, Bri. Not even Shark could blame an actress with lupus for missing a six A.M. call. Besides, I've got an excellent replacement in mind." Off the top of my head I named a young actress.

"Bless you, Carol," Brian said, adding, "Woody will be there though."

"Shark will be happy to hear that, I'm sure," I said. "And don't worry about *El Cristo Fugitivo*. I'll see that Shark comes to his senses on that score. Ciao, Bri."

Greg Spivey

It was close to two A.M. and Shark and Tony and I were still going over the next day's schedule in Shark's trailer when Kathy called. At least I thought it was Kathy as I took the call. It just didn't occur to me at the time that it might be Carol doing the impression she'd occasionally employed for comic effect during the pre-production period, though never in Shark's presence. Kathy's voice isn't difficult to do, I suppose—it's more or less that classic Southern California beach girl speech pattern, which New Yorkers especially seemed to have just discovered in those days as an endless source of snide amusement—though Carol's mimicry had always contained a rather transparently envious and bitter edge.

Tony Borgia

"It's for you," Greg Spivey said, offering Shark the receiver.

"Take a message, damn it," Shark snapped. By this time our nerves were shredded.

"It's Kathy Petro," Greg said.

Well, track in on Shark—it was that kind of moment. Shark took the phone from Greg. "Hello, Kathy," he said with the utmost tenderness as he irritably waved Greg and me out of the trailer so that he could speak to her in privacy.

Carol told me later what transpired.

"Hi, Shark," Carol said, imitating Kathy's voice. "I know it's late and everything. But I just wanted to talk to you, I guess. Can you talk now? Am I calling at a bad time?"

"No," Shark said gently. "No, no, not at all."

"Shark, listen," Carol said. "I know this is going to sound really crazy. But I'm just really looking forward to being in *Red Surf* and everything, even if I only get to play a murder victim. Because, I don't know, this is going to sound really weird, but I can't get you out of my mind."

Shark was silent for a moment, and Carol was afraid he'd detected the ruse. But he hadn't. "Do you know that you are my life?" he said, his voice trembling with emotion.

"Oh Shark," Carol replied with a provocative sigh. "This is so crazy, but I really think that maybe we're meant to be together or something."

Shark could barely speak. "I have been waiting all my life to hear you say that," he finally said.

"Oh Shark," Carol sighed again. "I wish I were with you right now. I just wish you had your arms around me and everything. I don't know, it's just really what I want. I think . . . this is so weird . . . but I think I really love you or something. You know?"

Again, Carol was afraid she might be laying it on too thick. But Shark fell for it hook, line and sinker. "Are you in Malibu?" he said.

"Yes. Shark, I wish my naked tan body were against yours right this second. Really, that's what I wish."

"Come to me, my angel," Shark said. "Come to me now. The freeways are empty. We're only an hour apart."

"Oh Shark, oh yes," Carol sighed, pressing her luck. "Oh. I'm already *wet*, oh I really am."

Even before making the call, Carol said, she had found an old bottle of Clairol left behind by one of Shark's house guests and dyed her hair blonde.

Carol Van Der Hof

I roared down the freeway, utterly blitzed on cocaine, my freshly blonde hair drying in the wind. I reached Mackerel Drive shortly after four in the morning and parked around the corner so Shark wouldn't see my car. A guard was posted, who recognized me, though he did a double-take, because of my hair no doubt. Then too as I passed him my trenchcoat flapped open in a sudden gust, revealing the scanty bikini I wore underneath—a bimbo souvenir that had long adorned Shark's bedpost.

Mackerel Drive was silent, most of the trailers dark, though a light was most definitely burning in Shark's.

I was trembling as I called his name in a stage whisper, fearful someone else might hear.

Shark appeared in the trailer door. "Kathy?"

I darted back toward the Jenkins' garage, through the maze of cables and lights awaiting the morning's shoot, knowing he would see me.

He came toward the driveway. "Kathy—"

I turned before the open garage, knowing the overhang would

shield my features from the moonlight, and suggestively removed my coat. I was so thin by then Shark was easily deceived, seeing in the shadows what he wanted to see.

As he approached I waited until the last possible moment, then began lowering the garage door, blocking my face from his view. He stopped the door halfway down, crawled under it, and lowered it the rest of the way.

Then in the near-total darkness of that garage all of my rapturous dreams of love with Shark Trager came true, in a manner of speaking.

Woody Hazzard

I reached Mackerel Drive around five-thirty that morning and went to Shark's trailer but he wasn't there. A lot of the crew people were already out, and Greg Spivey came over and said, "Did Kathy come with you?"

And I told him, "No, are you kidding? Don't you know what happened?"

So I told him and he said, "She can't be in intensive care. She called Shark at two in the morning."

So we're still trying to figure this out, and meanwhile other people are arriving, including the DP and the special effects guys and Tim Stroll, and I'm saying, "Shit, man. You mean you don't have a replacement for Kathy? Then how are we gonna do the scene?"

Then Tony Borgia comes out of his trailer and says, "What's the matter?"

And then I see Brad Jenkins coming out of Shark's old house, rubbing his eyes.

Then we hear this scream coming from Jenkins' garage, and everybody looks, but nobody can fuckin' believe it, because the garage door's open and the power saw's running, except it's been knocked over on its side. And Shark and Carol are standing there, Shark totally naked except for his socks, and Carol's naked except for this bikini top hanging from her shoulder and she's got her hair dyed this really phony-looking blonde. But the worst part is she's like totally cut off her foot.

Tony Borgia

It was bad. There's something about real violence . . . I don't know . . . It kind of made me sick.

Apparently, a few of the crew guys had come up to the garage without Shark and Carol hearing them and abruptly raised the garage door. Well, in the sudden dawn light Shark saw instantly that he was having sex with Carol, rather than Kathy Petro, and his mind just stripped its gears.

He pushed Carol away so hard she fell back and knocked over the power saw, and the switch was hit as it fell on its side.

Shark stared at Carol, just completely destroyed. For something like two hours, after all, he'd thought that his ultimate dream had come true.

Carol was crazy by that time too, and she told me she could literally, viscerally, *feel* Shark's hatred as he glared at the body he'd been worshiping with his mouth only moments before in the dark. With a special disgust he glared at her clubfoot, Carol said.

"What is it, Shark?" she said to him. "Wasn't it good? As good as you ever thought *Kathy* would be? What is it that keeps you from loving me? Is it *this*? Is it my *foot*? Well, *that's* no problem, Shark."

At that Carol ran her ankle up against the spinning blade. It was over so quickly, a grip later said, there was barely time to wince, let alone intervene.

Greg Spivey

It was madness. Carol, once the pain hit, screaming ceaselessly, her leg spewing blood. A script girl was throwing up, one of the caterers was hysterical, even the grips looked peaked and they were pretty tough guys. And then Brad Jenkins ran up to the garage, just completely crazed and driven, and started masturbating in a pathetic frenzy at the sight of all the blood, until I and several of the prop men grabbed him, pounding him to the ground.

Woody Hazzard

The ambulance came. As they loaded Carol in she started laughing hysterically in pain and shock, and yelled at Shark, "Everyone's had Kathy, it's no big deal. Everyone but you! *Even Pus!*"

I'll never forget the look on Shark's face. He was just totally fuckin' devastated, man. Just completely wrecked.

He looked at Pus, who was laying on the lawn after Greg and a few other guys had creamed him. And Pus kind of gave Shark this sheepish smile, confirming what Carol had just said.

Then the ambulance was screaming away and Shark turned to me and his eyes were just totally insane.

The next thing I knew he was grabbing me, trying to pull me into the garage, screaming, "Get in there!" Then, to the crew: "Tie his arms and gag him. Let's shoot the scene."

He was so out of it I just knocked him away. Then he grabbed the Roto-Rooter snake, which had been the murder weapon used on the guy I was supposed to play, then he pushed me again. "Bend over the work bench. Pull down your pants. Move that fucking camera up here. Let's shoot the fucking scene!"

He was just cracking up, and Carol's blood was still everywhere, and everybody was like totally bummed. Tony finally came over and said, "Shark, that's enough."

Shark looked around and saw how everyone was staring at him and finally seemed to realize how bad he'd flipped out. He was breathing hard and sweating, just totally crazed. Then he dropped the Roto-Rooter snake and reeled off toward his trailer.

That was it for me, man. I split.

Tony Borgia

I was shaken. I don't know . . . when real violence actually happens to someone you know, someone you care about, it's hard not to feel something, I guess.

But filmmaking is like war. There comes a time when you have to be ruthless, when you have to leave your wounded behind.

And so I hired two new actors, and Brice brought in the cow intestines and the split-woman dummy, which *was* rather extraordinary. And we shot the scene.

Carol Van Der Hof

Luckily, the power saw cut was quite clean. As a result they were able to sew my foot back on. I'm quite glad they did now. What an act of madness on my part!

And yet it did serve a kind of purpose, for it made me see the light. Convalescing in the hospital, simultaneously detoxing from cocaine, I knew that I was over Shark, that my life with him had been a self-induced form of torture I would never subject myself to again.

I even felt a twinge of pity for Shark, knowing he was stilldown there in Newport Beach, in his own way as abjectly selfdestructive as I had been, hurtling toward the crazed *Götterdämmerrung* of what would undoubtedly be his last film.

Greg Spivey

Shark was absent from the set while Tony finished the Henderson garage scene—he was sleeping in Santa Monica, I guess.

Then as we began to set up for the "jack-off dream sequence," the production really reached a new pitch of madness. Tony was insane by then, coked out of his mind. It was harrowingly apparent that he'd crossed a line from irresponsible genius into sheer disembodied delusion. He began talking about junking the rest of the film, the "story" as it were, and just having a four-hour dream sequence of perpetual, unmotivated violence. *"This* is reality," he said as we began setting up for the slaughter. "The 'plot' is the dream."

By then we were keeping the TV crews at bay as well, because the story of Brad playing the part of Debbi's father had broken. There were headlines: KILLER PLAYS FATHER OF VICTIM IN FILM, that sort of thing. There was general outrage in all quarters, and quite a concerted effort to make the city shut down the film—but on that count I have reason to believe that some major money changed hands. Brad had been sent back to his parents, smuggled past the crowds on Eel Road in a catering van.

We were nearly ready to go on the dream sequence when Shark returned to the set.

Tony Borgia

I know people want me to say I was crazy then, that I was on cocaine, that I went too far. But I will never say those things. I regret nothing. I expect to be hated the rest of my life. But I will die happily knowing that a thousand years from now when money no longer exists people will be astonished and swept away by *Red Surf*.

Greg Spivey

The sequence was covered as no sequence had been covered since *Triumph of the Will*, with fifteen separate Steadicams. Tony wanted it to have a swirling hallucinatory feeling, or as Shark said, "Like an endless William Burroughs fantasy."

"Yes!" Tony would say. "Except with both girls and boys. We should have a boy hanging here in the Andersons' backyard, as a conscious Burroughs hommage. But I want fifteen Girl Scouts strung up here on the McPhersons' porch, their breasts lopped off in unison, so nobody think's I'm gay."

Essentially the scene called for Tim Stroll to work his way up the street, torturing and slaughtering the families in each house along the way. It was all shot at night, the lights tinged red. For at least two miles as you came up the coast highway you could see the hellish glow of that nightmare suburban inferno.

Tim Stroll

Yes, I saw Hell then. For five solid months I lived in a preview of Hell. Satan controlled my mind and body with drugs, that is all I wish to say about it now. Today I live in the light of Jesus Christ, my Lord and Savior, whose infinite love has cleansed my soul of my Satan-ruled Hollywood past.

Greg Spivey

Poor Tim. Hadn't he been raised as a Pentecostal or something? It was all too much for him. He was coking heavily and became, perhaps inevitably, unhinged.

Who wouldn't have? Who didn't? Brice's special effects were gruelingly real. The body parts flying, the gutters of Mackerel Drive literally clogged and overflowing with Karo syrup blood. The "Girl Scouts"—God, how many did we go through? The hysteria, the screaming stage mothers. Minds were being destroyed but nothing would stop Tony and Shark.

Then one night I came upon Tony looking at rushes on the Steenbeck set up in what had been Shark's boyhood house. He was alone, or so I thought at first. Then I saw the blonde woman's head between his legs. That was all—just her head, one of the very realistic dummy heads used in the decapitation sequence.

I stepped out to Mackerel Drive and threw up by a pile of latex surfer torsos. Then I walked off the set and did not come back.

Tony Borgia

Charitably, I would say Greg imagined that. Perhaps he was thinking the sequence in the film where *Tim* has sex with the severed head. Admittedly, it was a time for all of us when the line between art and reality became smudged.

Brian Straight

I was utterly sickened by what was going on and pleaded with Harold to let me stop it. The flak we were catching over Brad Jenkins playing his murder victim's father was unbelievable. What kind of studio would make a film like this?

Harold wouldn't budge. "Let's tough it out," he said from New York. "It can't go on much longer."

"Oh yes it can, Harold. This so-called dream sequence isn't even scripted. Tony and Shark are making it up as they go. They're both completely demented. Left on their own, they'll *never* stop!"

Harold sighed. "The board is meeting tomorrow. Perhaps . . ."

He never finished the sentence. A moment later Arlene came on the line. "Brian, would you please hang up so I can call the paramedics? I believe Harold's having a stroke."

Tony Borgia

We were set up to shoot the final scene of the film when Brian Straight screamed past the barricades in his Ferrari, jumped out and ordered a halt to the production.

"You're finished," he yelled at Shark and me as he approached our command position on the top of the hill. "You are not exposing one more foot of film!" As he reached us he glared at Shark and said, "Harold's dead. And so are you."

I looked at Shark with a sense of terrible desperation. I had been literally seconds from calling Action when Brian arrived. Every detail of the scene was ready, the houses wired with explosives, all of the cameras ready to roll. It was, to use a sexual metaphor, like being on the verge of an excruciating orgasm and being told to stop.

By the look in his eyes I saw that Shark felt the same way.

"Shoot the scene, Tony," he said.

"Tony—" Brian whirled around to me.

"This is a take," I said into my walkie-talkie.

As the horn sounded Brian tried to grab the walkie-talkie from me, and Shark grabbed him. Each camera and soundman checked in as Shark and Brian struggled. Then, just as I called, "Action!" Brian saw something behind me and cried, "Oh my God, no!"

I looked just in time to see the man coming at Shark, a fellow about fifty in a Petro-Chem work uniform, whom I recognized in the glare of the first explosion as Debbi Henderson's father. He had a large knife. "Goddamn you to hell for what you've done to my little girl's memory," he screamed and drove the knife into Shark's stomach.

Shark reeled back, clutching his stomach, as Brian and I and a couple of grips subdued George Henderson, who was sobbing hysterically by then.

When I turned my attention back to Shark I saw that he was staggering down Mackerel Drive as, one after another, the houses began exploding around him.

There was no way to go after him, debris was flying everywhere. It was horrible to watch. He just staggered and staggered, trailing blood as he moved down the center of the street. At the time I was certain he was ruining the sequence, though we did save it later, cutting around him.

At last he reeled up his driveway and disappeared behind his old house. Then, in an especially large explosion, his old house blew up.

Brian Straight

We were certain Shark was dead. The entire block had been leveled. In the aftermath there was just complete chaos and Tony was nearly arrested—the local police and fire department had been deliberately kept in the dark as to the intended magnitude of the destruction. The debris had been scattered for blocks, in one case killing somebody's dog.

It was after midnight when the firemen finally found Shark. I ran to the spot as soon as I heard, ducking past the smoldering ruins of his boyhood home, back to where the firemen were gathered in the rubble of what had once been the garage. They were lifting Shark's blood-soaked body from an old freezer he'd climbed into, which was all that had saved him from being killed in the blast.

18/ Buying It
(1981)

Brian Straight

While Shark was in the hospital I surreptitiously borrowed Carol's keys—she was on the floor below his in the same hospital—and searched the Santa Monica beach house. I found a stack of rusty film cans containing a 35-millimeter print of *El Cristo Fugitivo* hidden in the wine cellar. Among Shark's extensive video tape collection I found a cassette labeled *The Eddy Duchin Story*—an unlikely movie for him to have saved—which proved to be another copy of the surrealist film. Fearing there might be still more cassette copies, similarly mislabeled, I took and destroyed his entire cassette collection—though I couldn't bring myself to destroy what I hoped was the last existing print of that scurrilous but astonishing film. I locked it away in my home vault, telling no one, least of all Arlene, when I reached her that night in Palm Beach, where she'd gone into seclusion following Harold's private funeral.

"I suppose there's a chance Shark ran off more cassette copies," I told her. "And yet I somehow doubt it. Shark's a tough negotiator on the major points of a deal. But he bores quickly once he feel he's won, and tends to leave his ass in the air on the back end."

"I don't care if he does have another copy," Arlene said, her belated bravery inspired at least in part by the sedative which was also slurring her speech. "I should never have allowed Harold to give in to this blackmail in the first place. I should never have given in to my own shame. This film *is* art, after all. It's not as though I appeared in some sort of tawdry loop—"

"It's art, all right," I said. "But that won't stop millions of people from being enraged by it, Arlene."

"But in the proper setting, in the Museum of Modern Art, say, might it not be perceived in its true avant-garde light—"

"It's a moot point now."

I felt for her on one level, but on another I'd just about had it with her. Preserving her precious reputation had got us into this mess. The truth was I wanted Shark's blood so badly by that point I didn't much care if he'd already shipped cassettes of *El Cristo Fugitivo* to the *National Enquirer*, the Legion of Decency, "Sixty Minutes," and *Christian Life* magazine.

By then I knew Kathy had left me, you see. She'd disappeared from St. John's Hospital, where, I'd discovered, she hadn't had lupus at all. For days I'd heard nothing, had no idea where she was, or what she planned to do or say. I was frantic, so was Woody.

As for my career—sweet God. The way the press was ranting at Acropolis you'd have thought we'd bankrolled an epic kiddie-porn snuff film. The outraged response to the "unauthorized" Newport Beach detonations seemed to have no end, the lawsuits were already flying. The TV news kept showing the family who'd lost their collie in the blast, the kids crying over "Tippi"—again and again those crying kids. It was as if we'd deliberately disembowelled Lassie.

George Henderson, confined for observation to the psych unit of the Orange County Jail, was already being perceived as an all-American martyr, a decent dad driven over the edge by the soulless exploiters of Hollywood. Clearly, that was going to be his defense. God only knew how deeply his attorneys might dig in their attempt to shift the blame.

I flew back to New York for an emergency meeting with Clarke Tower, the new Sadcom chairman, and only then learned the *real* reason the board had allowed the madness of *Red Surf* to go on to the end.

"Harold told me privately about the *El Cristo Fugitivo* blackmail," Clarke explained in his office on the ninety-third floor of the Sadcom Building. "But I was certain the board would never acquiesce simply to preserve Arlene's reputation. And so . . . Harold and I told the board Shark had the goods on Sadcom's Nazi dealings."

"Nazi dealings?"

"Oil shipments via Spain during the war," Clarke said vaguely.

I was stunned. "Sadcom sold oil to Germany during World War II?"

"No, no, of course not. The shipments stopped with Pearl Harbor. But we had to tell the board something. Understand this, Brian. I would have gone to any length to spare Arlene," he said fervently of the woman he would marry six months later. "I've adored her from afar for over twenty years, since the moment I first beheld her fresh-scrubbed angel sweetness in *Ginger Goes to Guam* in 1959. I revered her then, and I revere her now—one lurid Spanish summer be damned."

I was touched. A secret love was something I could always relate to.

Clarke outlined our strategy. "We're going to blame the whole thing on Harold. We'll say he was charmed and tricked by Trager, the board in turn charmed and hoodwinked by Harold. If that doesn't play, we'll say Shark had proof of Harold's cannibalism."

"His *what?*"

"An incident in Arabia back in the thirties, not worth going into now." Clarke walked me to the door. "We're going to try and spare you, Brian. You've been our brightest light. God knows, this debacle was not your fault." He sighed. "Is any of it worth saving?"

"We should know soon enough," I said, expecting to view the damage upon my return to L.A.

Before I'd left I'd dispatched armed guards to seize the negative of *Red Surf*—though in fact it would take us another week to discover where Shark, on the phone from his hospital bed, had ordered it hidden.

Tony Borgia

Somebody at the lab tipped me off that Brian was seizing the negative, but by the time I got there it was too late. I drove straight to the studio and entered Brian's office, more than prepared to beg.

"Brian, please, for God sake, let me have my film back."

"You're finished," he said.

"I swear I didn't know about *El Cristo Fugitivo*," I told him. "I was stunned when I found out. I thought you believed in me, in my art—"

"You fucking megalomaniac prick!" Brian yelled at me. "Do you know how much this piece of shit has cost so far?" He closed the door so the secretaries wouldn't hear. "Fifty-seven million dollars."

I was sobered but said, "All that means is that we've come too far to stop now. I'm the only one who can put the pieces together. Please, another ten million, that's all I ask."

He began yelling again, and I swallowed what was left of my pride and fell to my knees before his desk. "Please don't do this to me, Brian, I beg you, in the name of God and Mary, mother of Jesus. Don't nail me to the cross like Erich von Stroheim." An allusion, of course, to the silent film genius's martyrdom over his masterpiece *Greed*.

"The spikes are already driven through your hands," Brian said. "Get the fuck out. I don't want your blood on my carpet."

Cynthia Clive

Rather like a war bride I had remained at Acropolis throughout the *Red Surf* production period, keeping the home fires burning. Naturally, tales of the battle atrocities did reach my ears, but that was war, wasn't it? Or in this case art. I refrained from passing judgment on the basis of Shark's enemies' propaganda and—tellingly, I see now—I refrained as well from viewing the rushes which might have led me to independently conclude that Shark and Tony Borgia had indeed lost their minds in that heart of darkness where one can only lament as Conrad had: "The horror, the horror."

How much of what I knew I suppressed in the name of compassion, playing nursemaid to Shark upon his release from the hospital. He convalesced from his stab wound in the Santa Monica house, I moving into the garage apartment to be close by as he conducted his affairs from home. His wound was severe, the stitches quite ghastly. He took Percodan for the pain initially, and then despite my firmest admonitions, resumed use of cocaine. The stimulant as always made him cross—though he was considerably more than cross the day he learned Acropolis had seized his film.

Tony Borgia

From my confrontation with Brian I went straight to Shark, roaring down the freeway in a blinding apocalyptic rage, my future vanishing before me. To be this close to my ultimate artistic achievement only to have it ripped away me was more than unbearable. Certainly, I had growing doubts about Shark's character—what had happened with Carol had given me great pause—but nothing could be allowed to stand in my way now, not friendship nor sentiment nor human decency, so-called. We were in the suburbs of Moscow, the spires of the Kremlin in sight.

Shark had known for several hours that Acropolis had seized the film. By the time I arrived his initial fury was spent. "I'm afraid we've lost our leverage, Tony," he said, with a strange sort of pre-occupied calm. He was convalescing by the pool, that horrendous scar exposed. In comparison, an older scar, the result of a steak knife poke from a hot-tempered maid, seemed little more than an ancient love scratch.

"Someone came into the house and found my 35-millimeter print of *El Cristo Fugitivo*," Shark explained, "as well as the single tape copy I'd made. In fact, they made off with all of my tapes, including my exhaustive film noir collection, a gratuitous act of cruelty that points a finger at Brian himself."

"Then it's hopeless," I said. "They've won and we've lost."

"It's not hopeless at all," Shark said and smiled. "I've always known it could come to this. There was always a chance they would tough out *El Cristo Fugitivo*. If they had, my friend, I was prepared to do then what I'm going to do now."

"What do you mean?"

"I'm going to buy the film."

"Dear God." I mentioned Brian's fifty-seven million dollar figure and cited what we both knew was a somewhat low postproduction figure.

"I'm worth that," Shark said mildly. "Tony, sit down. Have some blow or a drink. I'm expecting a call from the bank."

Well, the call came. And easily, too easily, Shark got what he wanted, though he had to put up literally everything he had.

I broke down and wept.

"Don't cry," Shark said. "Only high-strung little ballerinas cry. Get up, Tony, and go to work. This is going to have to be the best goddamn movie ever made or we're both going down the toilet."

Brian Straight

I actually experienced a kind of physical seizure of glee when I learned Shark wanted to buy *Red Surf*. It was only too perfect. "What do you think? Should we let him have it?" I asked Clarke Tower.

You could have hung up the phone and still heard him laughing in New York.

The timing couldn't have been better. The transaction was barely complete, our separation from that deranged cinematic monstrosity had just been officially announced, when the whole matter surged into the headlines again in the wake of George Henderson's freakish death.

Greg Spivey

Somehow, he was electrocuted while watching "The 700 Club" on an Orange County Jail TV. They'd just scrubbed the floor or something, it was still wet, and the TV was bolted into a metal frame, which he touched. Tragically, his release on bail was imminent, a George Henderson Defense Fund having been established with that as its first objective.

Of course, the media and the public blamed Shark and Tony, their exploitation of Debbi's murder having driven her father so far over the edge that his death seemed somehow tragically inevitable. No one seemed to blame George for having tried to kill Shark. On the contrary, nearly everyone asked in a random street sampling said they would have done the same thing.

Brian Straight

The guy's death was sad, there's no getting around it. But it did spare us all a big messy "Hollywood made me do it" sort of trial.

Woody Hazzard

Brian made it a condition of the sale of *Red Surf* that Shark use a pseudonym for my screenplay credit.

"But what if the film turns out to be a hit?" I said.

"That's not going to happen," Brian said. Then he showed me a tape dub of some of the footage from the so-called dream sequence and all I could say was, "I see what you mean."

I was driving by Shark's place one day when I saw a lot of activity out front, guys moving in Steenbecks and stuff like that. And I wondered, you know, if maybe I was wrong, if Brian was wrong. I mean, what could you tell from raw footage? Maybe Shark would pull it off yet, weirder things had happened.

Just then I caught a glimpse of Shark and some babe he was with. But there was no way I was gonna stop and talk to him or anything. I still really hated his guts for what he'd done to everyone in the name of art or whatever the fuck it was.

I was on my way to visit Kathy that day actually. She'd filed for divorce through her attorneys and everything, and made me promise not to tell Brian where she was.

Kathy Petro

Gray was the doctor on duty in the St. John's emergency room that night I was brought there after my seizure. He was so handsome and kindly and said, "Look, you don't have any history of epilepsy, I strongly suspect this attack was psychosomatic in origin. Are you under any pressure? Why don't you tell me about it, Mrs. Straight?"

Well, the dam just burst, I began sobbing and told him everything. About Brian wanting me to be in this film with the power saw, and about Brian being gay and my marriage being a sham. I just sobbed and sobbed and Gray held my hand—but it wasn't sexual or anything, just comforting.

"I don't want to go back there," I said.

"You don't have to," he said.

I guess in a way I fell in love with him right there in that hospital that very first night. He was so young and sandy-haired and innocent and everything. He was smart, the ways doctors are, and yet so gentle and kind. I just looked into his blue eyes and felt really safe for the first time in years.

Tony Borgia

The post-production on *Red Surf* was difficult because of all the assholes we had to work with. Initially, we hired one of the top editors in town, a woman whose work I'd long admired. So you can imagine how I felt when she turned to me at the Steenbeck one day and said out of the blue: "This film is sexist garbage, and you're a very sick man."

I was hurt for a second before I said, "Then take a hike, ball-buster, before I edit your nipples with this splicer."

A lot of people quit, mostly because of Shark. I controlled my temper for the most part, but he didn't. I don't think I'm being paranoid when I say a lot of people wanted me to fail. That was certainly the feeling in the industry at large, and it extended to the people who were supposedly on our team. There were many instances of unconscious sabotage disguised as incompetence or "mistakes brought on by fatigue." But my worse enemy of all proved to be Shark.

Ray Boil

I was the fourth editor to work on *Red Surf*, and I have to say I only did it for the money, the film really kind of made me sick. Not the violence so much as the waste. You could've made twenty good films for what they'd spent. I steeled myself and gave them what they wanted, though looking back I don't think what I made was worth the grief.

It was a real bad environment, everybody coked out of their skulls, which I don't object to per se. But Shark and Tony were way beyond being jacked up—they were both fried right out of their minds, constantly screeching at each other like monkeys in a cage. It got physical too, but they always made up more or less. Shark was obligated to give Tony his director's cut, but if the preview didn't go well Shark could dump Tony and recut the picture himself, and Tony thought Shark was deliberately trying to fuck him up so that would happen.

"I'm gonna kill him," Tony told me once when we'd stepped out for some air. "I'm really gonna fucking kill him. I'm gonna shove his face into the flatbed screen and grind off his head on the broken glass."

The only sane one around there was Shark's secretary, the English gal. And I'm not so sure about her.

Cynthia Clive

I did try to be a rock of stability for Shark, for of course, however I might feel toward him in my secret heart of hearts, I had long realized that he regarded me as a surrogate Lorna figure, after his beloved aunt by that name, whom he had spoken of on any number of occasions as the only "good woman" in his life.

And I suppose however tinged with a latent romanticism my emotions may have been, they were also heavily laced with an auntly, nay maternal, concern. For the talk about Shark was exceedingly cruel. People did so want him to fail—out of envy, I never doubted. He had been a winner for *too* long, you see. The boy-wonder was thirty, a boy no more. There were schools of vicious younger sharks circling and watching for the first drop of blood so that they might attack and devour him and assume his place.

It was a nightmarish ordeal for him whenever he ventured out to one of the "in" spots, a never-ending gauntlet of malevolent glares and snide grins. The cocaine and lack of sleep made him even more sensitive to it, I suppose. Needless to say, the worst example of that sort of thing was the incident at Breton's.

Tony Borgia

Breton's was a trendy new restaurant in Beverly Hills that year, *the* place to be seen for lunch. Shark and I were at a table with a distribution honcho and a couple of his underlings, and the lunch had not gone well, so Shark was already testy when he saw Jean-Claude Citroen come in. Jean-Claude was with a group of people, including Philippe Villon, who was being pushed as the new Gerard Départdieu in Europe that year, and was that kind of guy, very macho and tough.

Shark smirked cockily as he watched Jean-Claude cross the room, as if clinging in this moment of colossal insecurity to the threadbare ego-thrill of recalling how thoroughly he'd wastedthe French auteur on a Riviera beach eight years before.

He waited for Jean-Claude to spot him, and he wasn't disappointed. Even though they were a number of tables away, Jean-Claude involuntarily flinched when he finally noticed Shark, and fearfully averted his eyes from Shark's stare.

"Cower, you fucking frog," Shark said under his breath. "That's right, cringe." Then he laughed in a very sick and bitter way that disturbed the distribution honcho and his underlings, and bothered me too.

Presently, we got up to leave and Shark glared at Jean-Claude once again. Jean-Claude was ignoring him now, but Philippe Villon was glaring hatefully at Shark, though I don't think Shark noticed.

In the foyer Shark said something rude and dismissive to the distribution honcho, and he and his underlings left in a huff.

"I've got to use the men's room," I said, wanting to do a couple of lines as a way of bracing myself for Shark's inevitable tirade in the car on the way back. As I ducked up the hall Shark stepped out to have the valet bring around his Porsche.

When I came out a minute later, I expected to find Shark waiting in the car. Instead, I found Philippe Villon holding Shark's arms

behind his back in the parking lot as Jean-Claude slugged him repeatedly in the stomach and the face.

"Stop it," I yelled, and pulled Jean-Claude away.

Philippe released Shark and gave me a few shoves, as Shark sort of
rolled along the hood of a white Rolls Royce, his face bleeding severely. Finally, Shark crumpled to the pavement, and by then more
people were coming out, a number of very big-name Hollywood people, and they just stepped around Shark, a few of them swallowing
laughs, a few snickering quite openly.

Shark was disoriented, trying to get up but unable to. It reminded
me of a James Dean scene, like the title sequence in *Rebel*, I guess.
Or perhaps more pointedly, Jett Rink's reeling last scene in *Giant*.

I finally managed to get Shark to the car. I drove, and he bled all
the way home in his Porsche.

Carol Van Der Hof

I received a formal invitation to the Westwood preview—if you can
imagine that! By then I was beyond either laughter or tears when it
came to Shark Trager, though the vindictive side of me did relish the
notion of witnessing what could only be his penultimate humiliation.
But I let go of all that, preferring to spend a quiet evening at home
with Joel, a sensitive young UCLA film student I'd met at a campus
screening of Cocteau's *The Blood of a Poet*. Sweet Joel, who loved
me for being just who I was, clubfoot and all!

Greg Spivey

Shark invited a number of people from the production, as if he were
really unaware that most of us considered *Red Surf* the worst experience of our lives. In the same heedless spirit, the preview audience
was packed with openly hostile industry people, executives, other
producers, agents, actors—all of the most influential people in town,
not to mention the key critics. Either Shark had a profound death
wish, an unconscious desire for catastrophic public humiliation or—
what is probably closer to the truth—he was so deluded by that time
that he really thought *Red Surf* was going to blow everyone away.

I attended even though I hadn't spoken to Shark since I'd walked
off the set. But it was just one of those nights that for better or worse
you couldn't miss.

I approached Shark in the Bruin lobby, where people were milling
around him, gleaming with phony smiles, but secretly drooling for
the kill. I could hear bits of conversation in the crowd, "It runs four
hours? I'm leaving." "It destroyed Tim Stroll. *Imagine*, that handsome young man smashing his head through a mirrored-glass window!" "I understand it's even more incoherent and lumbering than

Heaven's Gate." On and on, just trashing the shit out of the film before they'd even seen it. There was no way Shark could win that night.

He looked bad. He was thin and pale and wearing dark glasses, his face still bruised from the beating he'd received from Jean-Claude at Breton's, which of course everyone had heard about.

But when he saw me he opened his arms and we hugged. He was coked, of course, and hugged me so intensely I half-expected a Michael Corleone-style kiss and a "Greg, you broke my heart." But it was precisely as he was hugging me that he saw something outside and broke away, dashing out the door.

I stepped out after him to see what was going on. It was summer and still light out, and there were Kathy Petro and Gray Skinner, the young doctor she eventually married, cutting across the street.

Kathy Petro

I remember that evening well. Gray and I had walked down to a little Italian restaurant for dinner and were strolling through Westwood Village, where in those days it was really nice to stroll. I hadn't a care in the world until I saw the klieg lights and limos and all that up ahead at the Bruin. Then I saw *Red Surf* on the marquee and said, "Gray, I think I'm going to have an anxiety attack."

"There, there, love," he said. "We'll cross the street. None of that has anything to do with you now."

So we crossed the street, but I felt an icky, creepy feeling all the rest of the way home.

Greg Spivey

Shark told me later he followed Gray and Kathy through the crowded Westwood Village streets until they reached their apartment in the adjacent residential neighborhood. He watched as a light went on— it was dusk by this time and back at the Bruin *Red Surf* had started without him—then he sneaked up through the bushes and looked in the window.

He saw Gray and Kathy kissing in the living room, and then Gray began unbuttoning Kathy's blouse. He said Gray had his back to the window at first, and he hadn't really got a good look at him yet, but finally he did and he was shocked. Because Gray bore a very strong resemblance to Shark—a few years younger, but it's not stretching it much to say that given slight adjustments they could have almost passed for twins.

As a result, Shark was galvanized. He said it was like watching himself with Kathy in a pornographic movie, for that was what happened: Gray and Kathy made love right there on the living room floor.

Shark said he watched for quite a long time, until Gray came and then tenderly held Kathy. At that point, Shark said, he suddenly felt "dirty," because it was no longer like pornography; he could tell they were really in love. So he crept away from the window, feeling very strange and guilty. Just as he reached the sidewalk the porch light snapped on and he was afraid they had heard him in the bushes, so he took off running. He ran all the way back to the Bruin.

Tony Borgia

It was unbearable. People hissed the titles, and the boos began within the first minute of the opening tracking shot, increasing as that infinitely delicate visual dance moved inexorably toward the first murders. When the murders did take place, there were cries of disapproval and perhaps three dozen walkouts. Then the comments started, the talking to the screen. We'd laid in a voice-over in postproduction—Tim talking to himself—and people began answering that. "I don't know why I do these things," Tim would say. "Neither do we," somebody would shout and the audience would guffaw. When the second murder came there were more walkouts. "This is sick, Tony Borgia is sick!" yelled a fellow director I had long revered. Then more gales of laughter. I felt ill and ran to the john.

Greg Spivey

Shark said the Bruin lobby was empty when he returned from Kathy and Gray's, but he heard the audience laughing and knew it was all over. To brace himself he went upstairs to the john to do some cocaine. As he approached the men's room door he heard retching, and entered to find Tony clutching the sink where he'd been sick, as Sonya Heinz tried to comfort him. Well, at the time Shark knew the critic was really Tony's mother, as few other people did.

"Tony," she was saying, "what do these Hollywood people know? An artist has to have the right to fail."

"*Fail?*" Tony said spacily, by this point in a kind of stupor.

Then Sonya saw Shark. As you know, there was no love lost between them.

"I'd better go back," Sonya said to Tony. "It wouldn't look good if I were seen comforting you."

"Like a *mother*, huh?" Shark said, letting her know that he knew her true relation to Tony. And she was jolted, for Tony had supposedly told no one.

Shark followed Sonya out of the men's room, stopping her at the top of the stairs. "You *are* going to give your son's movie a good review—"

Well, Sonya was nearly sixty by then, but still one tough little Cajun crocodile. "I'm going to say what I think really happened," she said to Shark. "That Tony Borgia is one of the few authentic cinematic geniuses of the 1980s, and this might have been his greatest film. But you ruined it. You distorted the true story into a lurid, wigged-out personal psychodrama, which is always the failed, frustrated artist's woozy notion of what art is. Because that is what you are, a florid, tawdry hack and a crummy, mediocre whore, a bitter, rejected artist turned Hollywood businessman, who in his impotent rage and envy has deliberately destroyed the truly gifted artist he himself could never be, much as Salieri destroyed Mozart in *Amadeus*, which probably won't make a very good Milos Forman film, if his stumpy, wrongheaded *Ragtime* is any indication, but which does provide a useful analogy here."

"You twat," Shark said. "You dirty old twat."

Shark admitted he was "very aware" that Sonya was standing at the top of a steep flight of stairs, and was fighting back the impulse to "give her a shove," when Tony stepped from the men's room, having overheard Shark's crude remark to his mother. In a wordless rage Tony grabbed Shark by the lapels, "his face as red as a blood clot, his eyes like a poisoned rat's"—when suddenly a new group of walkouts burst into the lobby below, their vicious comments distracting Tony to the extent that Shark was able to pull free of his grasp. Shark smoothed down his jacket, snorted at Tony and Sonya with cocky contempt, and went back down the stairs.

Tony Borgia

It was just after Shark insulted my mother that the shit really hit the fan. He had just reached the bottom of the stairs when people began *pouring* into the lobby, and I could tell by the soundtrack that the dream sequence had begun. People were groaning with disgust, which seemed odd, because nothing truly horrific had even happened yet. "I don't believe it," I heard a Paramount executive say. "This is really the limit."

"I'm not going to stay and watch that man jerk off," I heard a top female agent say, and I assumed she was talking about Tim's simulated masturbation in the film . . . or, figuratively speaking, about me as an artist. I had no idea at that point that she actually meant Brad Jenkins.

Greg Spivey

It wasn't surprising that Brad got an invitation too—in a way it was perfect. He had come in after the lights had gone down—later I recalled seeing an obese man taking a seat on the side down in front. But nobody recognized him until he stood up as the dream sequence started and began masturbating furiously, his penis momentarily brushing the blonde hair of an actress in the seat before his. She let out a little cry of revulsion when she saw what had touched her, and her burly date stood, about to punch Brad out, I think, but decided it wasn't worth it. Everyone's attention was on Brad by then, and word spread quickly as to who he was, and it was just too much for nearly everyone.

I was leaving myself when Shark pushed in past me, confused at first until he saw Brad, who was still masturbating away. In a rage Shark went for his boyhood friend.

Tony Borgia

People screamed as Shark pulled Brad out into the lobby. Brad's pants were still down around his ankles as Shark pulled him through the crowd and shoved him out the door onto the Westwood sidewalk.

It was then that *I* lost control.

Greg Spivey

No sooner had Shark booted Brad into the street—where the usual well-heeled date-night couples were gasping at the sight of the pathetic, exposed castrate lying in the gutter—than Tony pulled a knife from behind the concession counter. I still don't know what that knife was doing there, an enormous, shiny kitchen knife—maybe they used it to split open those big sacks of pre-popped popcorn or something. Whatever, it was there, and before anyone could stop him Tony raised the gleaming knife in a blinding flash of murderous rage. *"You don't call my mother a twat!"* he roared at Shark.

Of course, we know where the blade came down.

Tony Borgia

I blame Shark for my mother's death. I was trying to kill *him*, that was obvious to everyone who saw what happened. Shark had driven me to that diminished state of temporary insanity, and then my mother simply stumbled into the space between us. When that knife sank into her back right up to the handle I swear to you I died as well.

Greg Spivey

It was a stunning, terrible tragedy. Sonya died instantly, which is something, I suppose. At least she didn't suffer, though you couldn't say the same for Tony.

Inevitably, there were those who suggested he subconsciously *wanted* to stab his mother out of some sort of Oedipal, or even Hitchcockian, bent of mind. I always felt that was rubbish, dimestore psychology, drive-through Freud.

Less easily dismissed was the sense of karmic retribution pervading the incident. Tony had celebrated a painless, estheticized violence for so long it seemed almost horrifyingly logical that he should have to spend the rest of his life bearing the guilt of having killed in reality the only person he'd ever truly loved without reservation.

The last time I visited him at Porterville State Hospital, he was fine, quite cordial and witty, until I inadvertently touched upon the subject of Sonya's death. Then he began to sob uncontrollably, even though it had been well over six years since that awful night.

Kathy Petro

Gray and I were watching the TV news in bed that night when the story came on about Tony killing Sonya Heinz at the preview. They showed the theater and Sonya's body under a sheet, and there was blood all over the concession stand and—I'll never forget—this one close-up of all the popcorn just soaked in blood.

"Oh God, I can't look at this," I said.

So Gray changed the channel.

Brian Straight

It was a sad thing. I'd never been a big fan of Sonya's, but still.

It was a pity in several ways. I can't help but believe that when it came right down to it, Sonya might have given *Red Surf* its only forgiving review. In the wake of her death the reviews were uniformly obliterating—"vile," "despicable," and "insane" seemed to be the favored adjectives—though I imagine they would have been nearly as lacerating even without such a literal assault on an esteemed member of the critical community. When the mother/son relationship was eventually revealed it did add a poignant dimension to the matter though.

Somehow as a result of that final cruel occurrence my desire for revenge on Shark Trager was spent. It was with no great relish that I noted his subsequent professional demise. Shark was a dead horse— or to use the more obvious metaphor, a once sleek and vicious Great White now gutted and stinking on the beach.

Greg Spivey

Shark had been on the verge of closing what was, all things considered, a reasonably fair distribution deal with Tramcorp. But after the preview they backed out, and the few other offers Shark received were so bad you couldn't really blame him for refusing them.

In the end he lost the film, of course, just as he lost everything else. When the dust finally settled, the film had gone to Sword Communications, whose standard fare was crap like *Panty Beach Massacre* and *This Film No Star BRUCE LEE*, and they didn't even bother with a theatrical release. *Red Surf,* all sixty-six million dollars of it, went directly to videocassette.

Cynthia Clive

Shark was ruined financially, so it came as no surprise when he summoned me into the house one afternoon to inform me he had no choice but to let me go. I could tell he'd been drinking in addition to his usual quota of cocaine—what little cash he had hidden away all seemed to be going for that. They'd found poor Gramps dismembered in the brushy hills of Calabasas, so a new drug man had been coming around, a horrid reptilian fellow with long stringy blond hair, though I confess my occasional attempts to confuse him away were perfunctory at best. How could I censure Shark's desire for escape now, knowing what emotional agony he endured? To have risen so high, to have had so much, only to be dropped into the abyss.

He presented me with my severance pay in cash plus a bonus which, knowing his circumstances, caused me to weep. Then he hugged me, as he never had before, for he had always respected my reserve and was not, as one usually thinks of the term, a demonstrative man. I sensed something odd in the air just before he said, "You know, Mrs. Clive, I believe you're the only woman who's passed through my Hollywood life whom I've never fucked. Why don't we rectify that now?"

At that he began to maul me, not forcefully as if he meant to overpower me, but rather as if he were sure I would readily give in. But it was pathetic, you know. All of the starlets who'd been so willing when he'd been on top had abandoned ship like rats. There was no one left to validate him, and I was not about to. Which was why I raised my knee quite abruptly between his legs.

As he buckled to the floor, I said, "Do you realize what you've just done? I was the last person in this world who still cared about you. And now you've alienated even me. You've got no one now."

He said nothing, merely groaning as he rocked on the floor, holding himself between the legs. That would prove to be my last image of Shark Trager.

Woody Hazzard

One day I was driving up PCH through Santa Monica and noticed a For Sale sign on Shark's house. I stopped, just out of some weird sense of nostalgia, I guess, since I could tell the house was empty. I peered in the windows at the rooms where Shark and I had once had some pretty bitchin times. My hatred for him was cooling out, I guess, and even though I still thought he was a pig who'd got what he deserved, I knew a part of me would always remember the good days too.

As I was leaving I saw this cream soda bottle by the chair on the patio, the same kind of cream soda Kathy always drank. The bottle had a bunch of cigarette butts in it, and I imagined Shark sitting there alone his last night at the house, drinking the soda, then smoking all those cigarettes one after another as he listened to the waves crash and stared at the stars.

19/ **Maya**
(1981–1982)

Todd Jarrett

I met Shark Trager in the spring of 1981 at the Ray-Mar Theater the night our projectionist became rabid. I was still at UCLA film school then, working nights at the concession counter. The Ray-Mar is gone now, demolished a few years ago, which was really a crime—it should have been restored. It was Art Deco like you wouldn't believe, opulent and cavernous, musty and decadent, with scuffed red velvet seats and the poignant reek of fifty years of spilled buttered popcorn and Coca-Cola and tears. There's a Ross Dress-For-Less discount clothing store there now.

Even in '81 we knew our days were numbered. The Ray-Mar was a revival house and the so-called video revolution was already eating into our business. It was sad and infuriating really. You could rent some piece of shit starring Chuck Norris for a buck a night at Music Plus, but soon there'd be no place left to show a crisp 35-millimeter print of *Shanghai Express*—which was playing, billed with *Blonde Venus,* the night Shark struck up a conversation at intermission.

It was raining that night, there were only maybe a dozen patrons, so there was plenty of time to talk. Shark had a thick blond beard at that point and was rather seedily dressed; I certainly didn't recognize him as the notorious producer of *Red Surf.* We were lamenting the state of things and he had just got around to mentioning his own UCLA film school background, when Ernie the projectionist reeled down the curving staircase in the midst of a fit. I thought it was a joke at first—he did things like that—until he fell on the Art Deco carpet actually foaming at the mouth. Fred the manager came running and I remembered that Ernie had recently been bitten by a dog. "Christ, it's rabies," I said and we called an ambulance. While we waited for it to arrive Shark took off his belt and struck it in Ernie's

300

mouth so he wouldn't bite off his tongue, and then restrained Ernie's thrashing arms despite considerable danger to himself.

As the paramedics took Ernie out Fred shook his head and said, "That's it for tonight. We can give them half their money back."

And Shark said, "Look, I can do it."

Fred was leery, we'd had some projectionists' union problems a while back. When he mentioned this, Shark dug out a projectionists' union card. Fred and I were both jolted when we saw Shark's name on the card.

"I got this a while back so I could operate my own projector," Shark explained, seeing by our reaction that we knew who he was. "It cost me a lot of money to get it, but it's completely legitimate."

Some people were already complaining about the delay, so Fred said all right. And Shark went up and ran *Blonde Venus* without a hitch.

Fred Thal

It was hard for me to reconcile my image of Shark Trager the producer with the man I met that night at the Ray-Mar. In my mind Shark Trager stood for everything I loathed about Hollywood—that greedy materialistic powerfreak schlockmeister attitude that was really destroying movies. He *had* produced *White Desert*, he had that to his credit. But everything since . . .

Yet here was a man who was paying for his transgressions, you could see that at a glance. Not just in the material sense, though for a man who was used to having everything that must have been humiliating enough. He was staying in some flophouse on Sawtelle—you know, where the illegal aliens stand on the corners to be hired for shit work—and he didn't even have a car. This guy who'd paid sixty thousand cash for his last car was now taking the bus. Do you know what that can do to a man's self-esteem in L.A. ?

But the real pain was in his eyes. It was a psychic or even spiritual pain he just carried with him every minute he was awake, though you could see he was fighting hard not to give in to it. To do so, I suppose, would have meant committing suicide.

He came back the second night since Ernie was still in the hospital and Shark definitely needed the money. We talked quite a bit and I began to have compassion for him. I began to see why his life had gone the way it had. We drank some wine in the lobby after the last show and he told me about his days at UCLA, and the rejection from Jean-Claude Citroen that must have been so devastating, though he tried to make light of it. I just couldn't help but feel for him.

Finally I got up to leave, and he did too, mentioning that he was concerned about returning to the Sawtelle flophouse, since he owed a week's back rent. "Look, why don't you sleep in the loft tonight?" I said, and he did.

Not long after that Ernie told me he was going back to Arizona as soon as he was well enough to travel, so Shark became our permanent projectionist and moved into the loft, though he didn't have much to move.

Todd Jarrett

The loft was a room that adjoined the projection booth. It was something like a press box, with a huge picture window that provided a view of the screen. The glass was a one-way mirror on the auditorium side, so you could look out at the screen but the audience below couldn't see in. The story was that Norman Mar, the guy who'd built the theater in the thirties, had these hideously deformed twin daughters, and built the room so they could watch the movies without disturbing the experience of the other patrons. That may be apocryphal, but the fact remained it was a very strange room. It had a Murphy bed and a kitchenette and its own bathroom with a shower and a bidet; it was like a little apartment with a celluloid view. Shark would stretch out on the bed and watch the movies, enjoying all the comforts and privacy of home video with the esthetic superiority of a true silver screen.

I became quite good friends with Shark and I have to say that despite what you might expect I think he was happy for quite a while. We talked about films from an esthetic or critical perspective for the most part, though of course he would sometimes refer to his own practical experience. But he didn't seem angry or bitter about what had happened to him. On the contrary, he seemed serene, as if it was finally a relief not to have to fight in that jungle anymore.

If he'd done a lot of cocaine before, he certainly wasn't now. He couldn't afford it. Alcohol was his drug of choice, cheap California wine, not rotgut exactly, but whatever was on special at Boy's Market in the gallon jugs.

I think he drank himself to sleep most every night, but earlier in the evening while he was working he would pace himself. There were never any problems with his competence on the job until the night of the Fritz Lang double-bill—a night that sabotaged his serenity and opened a series of doors that no doubt should have remained shut and locked forever.

Maya Dietrichson

I had come to the Ray-Mar with Billy Freeze, our new drummer in Spione, the group I was singing with then, so Billy could see the Fritz Lang film *Spione*, from which I had taken our name. It means spies in German. At first I had wanted us to call ourselves Spies in the House of Love from the book by Anaïs Nin, but we knew that was too long for the club marquees, so then I thought of the Fritz Lang film.

It was a silent film and this made Billy angry since I hadn't told him in advance. There was music, you know, but he was getting jumpy and I was getting angry with him. "Can't you just watch the pictures and read the occasional title? What's wrong with you? Can't you get along without mindless chatter?" I said and he became quite miffed. I was not then aware that he couldn't read.

Then the reel changed and the picture was badly out of focus and stayed that way even though people started calling out. So I became furious and went out to complain.

Todd Jarrett

Maya was just extraordinarily, stunningly beautiful in this ethereal, dreamlike way. In my mind's eye I always see Maya in black and white, a luminous close-up on nitrate film. I swear she always looked like that, as if Lee Garmes [*von Sternberg's cinematographer, Ed.*] were following her around, lighting her every move. I saw her in a Seven-Eleven once and even there she looked like that—like Marlene Dietrich paying for a microwave hamburger. A lot of it was cultivated, of course, the result of her makeup and attire, that New Wave Neo-Expressionist thing she was into. Then too there was the German accent, a sultry, insinuating Lola Lola impression, which by the time I met her had become a constant pathological affectation. For as everyone knew she'd been born and raised in Granada Hills in the San Fernando Valley.

Maya Dietrichson

I complained to Todd Jarrett and together he and I went up to the projection room to see what the hell was going on. There we found Shark passed out on the Murphy bed in that little room with the view of the screen. I shook him awake, seeing that he was drunk, and he staggered to the projector. He tried to focus the picture but was too drunk to see when it was right, so I said, "Here, let me do it. You're pathetic, you're a mess."

Todd was embarrassed and said, "I'll make him some coffee." But he fumbled with that so I said, "Look, I'll do it." So I put on the coffee and Todd left, and once he did I gave Shark some cocaine. I didn't know who he was then, he had a terrible beard. But we talked and I said, "You know, I'll bet under that beard you're quite a good-looking fellow. Why don't you let me shave it?"

So I did, using a scissors, then several Bic razors. He *was* very handsome and I became excited, and he became excited too.

"What about this?" I said, brushing his chest hair. "Shall I shave this too?"

He pulled my hand away and his strength further excited me.

"What about *this?*" I said, and put my hand on his crotch, where he was already hard. "Why don't I shave this?"

At that he threw me on the Murphy bed and we made violent love.

Billy Freeze

It was a big sex thing at first, I think. Maya and I were just friends, on account of working together and everything. Plus I'd heard too many stories about guys she'd fucked over, or who got obsessed with her or something and ended up killing themselves, which was something you could tell she would get off on. She wanted guys to worship her and die at her feet and that sort of thing.

Fred Thal

It was total sex, Last Tango at the Ray-Mar. Shark told me later it was something like two weeks before he even realized Maya wasn't really German. And she didn't know who he was for a long time either, and Shark was really elated about that. "She's hot for *me*, man," he said. "Just for me and my hot bod. Not because she wants something from me."

That made sense, I suppose, since most of the women Shark had known in his Hollywood days had been actresses on the make and that sort of thing, though it was difficult to imagine Maya, or anyone, being so deluded as to think Shark could help them now.

I had no prior knowledge of Maya since I wasn't into the local music scene like Todd was. When he began telling me about her reputation as a maneater I was tempted to say something to Shark, but I didn't, deciding to mind my own business.

Maya Dietrichson

I knew that people said I was cruel because I would let no man possess me. It's not easy to be beautiful, for people always want you and when you don't let them have you their rage and frustration know no bounds. But with Shark I initially believed I had at last found my equal in beauty. I didn't care who he was—when I found out it didn't matter. Our pasts were unimportant. I only cared about the immediate physical presence of his body.

I see now it was the high point of my erotic life, those exquisite days and nights through which we fed upon one another. Though inevitably, I suppose, when you have gorged yourself on simple fare, you begin to develop an appetite for the truly forbidden fruit.

Todd Jarrett

Maya introduced Shark to opium, which was her drug of choice. She received money from a trust fund, I think, not a lot but enough to pay for that apartment on Windward Avenue in Venice and sustain her opium habit. I smelled the sweet aroma of it wafting down from the projection room one night and went up to tell them to cool it. There they were, virtually naked on the Murphy bed, the room lit with a single amber bulb, lolling sinuously in their opium den with a view. *Morocco* was on the screen. It was all Shark could do to float to the projector in time to change the reel. I glanced back on my way to the stairs and caught a glimpse of Maya woozily going down on Shark in the flickering projector light.

Fred Thal

It was obvious things had taken a dark turn when Shark began wearing the dog collar.

Maya Dietrichson

He worshipped me, that's all, and I sensed his inner needs.

One night we were in the loft, a sentimental movie on the screen— *Somewhere in Time,* as I recall—and I began to yawn even as his fingers made me wet.

"Tell me about yourself," Shark said. "The truth about yourself."

"Why?" I said. "So we can bore one other like a normal couple?"

"Tell me about Granada Hills," he said, and I became furious.

"I don't know anything about it," I said. "I didn't grow up there, some other girl did. A bland and boring girl who dreamed dull dreams of one day owning a bikini boutique. A vacuous creature who squealed with unctuous glee when she won a Kathy Petro look-alike contest at age fifteen. Do you want to hear more?"

"No," he said. And for some reason unknown to me then he got a shell-shocked look, like a handsome sweaty-faced soldier in a war. This excited me.

"Go down on me," I ordered him with aristocratic contempt. "You talk too much and I'm tired of it. Do something worthwhile with your mouth."

He became quite excited and obeyed my command with great zeal.

"That's right," I said. "Yes. Eat me. Eat me like a dog."

Todd Jarrett

Shark never mentioned Kathy Petro to me. I knew nothing about his obsession with her. But it's funny, I do remember once noticing that Maya did bear a certain basic resemblance to Kathy Petro, and idly thinking that if Maya had remained sane and true to her Valley beginnings she would probably have become just another vacuously wholesome Kathy Petro California blonde.

Nobody ever accused Maya of being wholesome, but when she started leading Shark around on that leash I felt things were going too far. Granted, it did seem like something of a joke at first, a deliberately outrageous put-on, but still.

Maya Dietrichson

I said, "You're a dog and you love to lick me, don't you?"

And he nodded obediently yes.

So I put on the dog collar, I put it on tight, till his tongue lapped out like a dog's, which excited me. Then I loosened it a bit so he wouldn't choke. "You're my sex slave now," I said, and put the chain through the collar. "You're Maya's sex slave, that's all you're going to be."

We were in my apartment on Windward in Venice and he was naked and aroused and panting at my feet. I wanted to take him for a walk like that out along the boardwalk, but I knew if I did we'd be arrested. So instead I made him eat me while I imagined that we were on the boardwalk and everyone was watching as I made this handsome man do my bidding.

Billy Freeze

Maya lived next door to me at the Charleton Arms, this raunchy old apartment building a block up from the boardwalk at Windward and Speedway. Windward is the street with the arches where they'd shot that Orson Welles movie *Touch of Evil*, though I guess there were a lot more arches back then. The street was pretty grungy in '81, all these closed-up rollerskate shops and sun-burnt winos staggering around. Maya's third story window overlooked Windward and you could hear the weird shit she was into with Shark going on up there. Like you'd hear a slap, then a cry of pain or maybe pleasure. For a long time I thought it was just her dominating him.

Then one night we had a gig and I went to get Maya and Shark opened the door. The room reeked of opium and Shark was naked and his poor overworked crank was red as a beet. "Okay," he said, "but I want her back here by two at the latest." And there was Maya in this black corset, gagged and tied spread-eagled to the posts of the brass bed.

Maya Dietrichson

We began switching off because I got tired of doing all the work. I said, "All right, you can dominate me if you think you're man enough to do it. But I warn you, I'm going to fight you every inch of the way."

So we had our battles. But he enjoyed the idea of having to rape me. Several times I really scratched him, so he had to tie me down. I'd had him sniveling for so long, he really relished getting even.

Neal Ridges

Shark had vanished so completely from the Hollywood scene a number of people really thought he was dead. As much of a disaster as *Red Surf* had been, he could have continued on some level if he'd wanted to. I mean, look at Mike Cimino; even after *Heaven's Gate* he got deals and came back. Granted, Shark's situation was far worse, it wasn't just the failure of the film, it was everything that had surrounded it. The insanity on the location, the capper of Sonya Heinz's death. Still, Shark could have got some sort of deal somewhere. His exile was definitely self-imposed.

Then—well over a year after *Red Surf*—I ran into Sue Schlockmann on the Mastodon lot and she said, "You'll never guess who I saw last night."

Sue Schlockmann

Elliot and I had a production deal at Mastodon for a teen drama with music—the one-line concept that got us the deal was "MTV Gidget goes to South Africa"—and one night I went with a girl friend to check out Spione at Blue Angel, a music club on Olympic in West L.A. I liked their single, a New Wave remake of "River Deep/Mountain High," and thought the German girl singer had a look that was right for a Pretoria club sequence in the film.

The place was packed, and Shelia and I had tried to dress punk, but we still felt out of place, and were kind of hunkering in the back when Spione came on.

Well, the girl was everything I'd expected: cool, blonde and Teutonic. She had a long chain looped over her wrist, rather like a dog leash, though I didn't give it much thought at first since she and the guys in the group were all kind of into that leathery, chainy, punk S&M look. She sang this astonishingly affectless rendition of "Gloria" as if she were a statue, moving nothing but her lips, even as everyone else in the club was gyrating maniacally. Then they began another song, but she stopped it, distracted by something off stage.

"Hold it, hold it. This really pisses me off, you know. I bring my pet along with me and he makes a mess backstage."

So she pulled the leash, reeling this shirtless skin-headed punk out to her, the other end of the leash attached to the dog collar around his neck. I nearly dropped my drink when I realized it was Shark.

You could tell he was ripped on something, he had this glassy-eyed, fixated look. She ordered him down on his knees and rolled up a newspaper. "Bad boy," she scolded. "Bad boy." And began swatting his black Levi'ed behind with the paper.

I thought it was an act at first, which in a way I guess it was. I told myself it was okay, he was doing it because he wanted to, and a lot of people were laughing. But I didn't think it was funny.

She began ordering him to do dog tricks, like stand on his haunches, which he did, panting happily. Then she made him roll over. Then fetch—she took a bite from an apple, nonchalantly tossed it across the dirty floor, and ordered him to retrieve it. He did, picking up the dirty apple with his teeth. I'd seen enough at that point and so had Shelia. We were trying to push through the crowd when Maya Dietrichson ordered him to beg, and he did, and then—in a way you could tell wasn't planned—abruptly buried his face in her crotch. She lifted her short skirt—you could see that the gasps of genuine shock excited her—and she was wearing crotchless panties. Shark began going down on her in an extremely exhibitionistic, pornographic way. The audience was going crazy, yowling and cheering wildly, but the guys in Spione were unplugging their guitars and leaving the stage in disgust.

I supposed he eventually humped her on the stage, but Shelia and I didn't stick around to find out. I'd already seen him do that.

Maya Dietrichson

Shark wanted to take his thing out, but I wouldn't let him. Finally, I shot him in the face with a seltzer bottle, getting his handsome face all wet.

Billy Freeze

That was almost the end of Spione that night. We were all furious, though I can't say I was totally surprised. I knew Maya got very turned on on stage and had a strong exhibitionistic streak, and I guess Shark did too.

Maya Dietrichson

He told me all his fantasies, and I told him all of mine. Then we lived them. Every one. Until there was only one fantasy left.

Todd Jarrett

Shark told me later how it all came about. He said he and Maya had collapsed exhausted on the bed at her place one night after a two-day session involving bondage and discipline and copious quantities of opium and intravenous cocaine, and Maya said, "If you could die in a sexual manner how would you do it?"

And Shark said, "I would like to come and explode at the same time. What about you?"

"I would like to die violently in the midst of an orgasm in a speeding out-of-control car."

Shark said this wasn't a surprise to him since J.G. Ballard was Maya's favorite writer, and she became very aroused reading aloud grisly passages from the Ballard novel *Crash*. So they devised a way in which they could join their fantasies into one.

Maya Dietrichson

I had a Volkswagen beetle, but that wouldn't do. Shark however had been saving up his money toward purchasing a car, so I chipped in and we bought a powerful 1970 Chrysler 300 for eight hundred dollars. It was huge and made a terrible roar and began to shimmy at fifty miles an hour. The tires were bald, but that was okay. We weren't going far.

For two hundred dollars Mouse, an old friend of mine, built a powerful car bomb. He was a retired Hell's Angel who knew of such things. I told him I wished to blow up an old rival in love, and he showed me how to attach the bomb so it would go off when the car reached eighty miles an hour—using the Chrysler, he thought, merely for demonstration purposes.

"Are you sure this bitch will *go* eighty?" Mouse asked, in reference to my fictitious rival.

"Yes, she's a speeder," I told him.

"But what if she's on the freeway, trying to pass a busload of innocent children?" he said. "Why not set it to go off when she fires the ignition?"

"Because I want her to die with the wind in her stupid hair," I told him. "Don't worry, she only speeds down empty, moonlit roads."

Fred Thal

I watched Shark and Maya pull into the Ray-Mar parking lot in that Chrysler one evening and I sensed that something bad was about to happen. It was not a car anyone in their right mind would buy. Just a total piece of shit, belching exhaust, muffler dragging, a joke. Shark and Maya floated out of the car, utterly blitzed, and she went on upstairs—it was nearly showtime—as I drew Shark aside.

"Are you all right?" I said, knowing he wasn't, that he hadn't been for months.

He was so high he could barely talk. "This dream is almost over," he finally replied in a tortured Christopher Walken whisper.

"You're blowing it," I said, because lately his drug use had begun to affect his job performance. Several times he'd mixed up the order of the reels. A few nights before he'd stuck a reel of *Mean Streets* into *Taxi Driver*, though sadly only one person had complained.

"Nothing can hurt me anymore," he said spacily. "I feel good now, I feel at peace, knowing I won't have to die alone."

"What are you talking about?"

"It's almost seven," he said, focusing with some difficulty on the clock. "I want to really enjoy these movies tonight. I want to really enjoy them."

I watched him float up the stairs. Then I went to Todd and said, "I think we may have a problem tonight."

Maya Dietrichson

The bill that night was two Ava Gardner films, *The Barefoot Contessa* and *Pandora and the Flying Dutchman*, both old wide-screen prints which had really turned to shit. We smoked opium on the bed during *Pandora*, which I found really stupid and boring, so I shot some cocaine into one of Shark's magnificent veins, then hit myself up.

"I'm climbing the walls," I said around nine o'clock. "Both of these movies are so tedious and stultifying, I don't want them to be the last films I ever see. Maybe we should wait until something good is playing and choose that night to die."

Shark saw my point and said, "Yes, maybe we should wait till Saturday when we're showing two of my favorite films."

That was only two days away and the films were already there, I saw, as he tapped the cans which were labeled *The Magnificent Ambersons* and *Touch of Evil*.

"I don't know if the car will last that long," I said. "Why not show one of them right now? What can they do to you? Fire you? So what? Which of the two is your favorite?"

Kathy Petro

I was kind of out of it that night because my shoulder was acting up again and I'd been taking these codeine tablets that Gray had prescribed for me. Gray had been working really hard but had the night off, so when he said, "Why don't we go to a movie?" I said okay, even though I didn't really feel like it.

None of the current movies in Westwood sounded that exciting, so when he finally said, "Here are two old Ava Gardner movies in Mar Vista," and the titles sounded romantic, I said: Sure, that's fine.

So we went to the Ray-Mar, this grungy old theater which smelled really bad and had awful broken seats. We sat down and the movie started, but I was just kept wishing we'd rented a cassette or something so I could be home in bed cuddled up with Gray. And then suddenly without warning the picture changed. I mean, one minute Ava Gardner was talking to James Mason in this faded pink color, then suddenly it was black and white and I saw the title *Touch of Evil*, and I got this funny feeling because I'd always heard it was one of Shark's favorite films.

People started getting angry and shouting up at the projector, and then the sound got painfully loud, and I started to feel sick. "I have to get out of here," I said to Gray. "I'm having an anxiety attack."

So we went into the lobby, where the manager was trying to reassure people that the problem was being taken care of. But I still felt anxious and just wanted to go. Then suddenly I felt faint from the codeine or something and had to sit down on this old couch in the lobby while Gray went to get me a cup of water.

Todd Jarrett

I raced up the stairs to find out what the fuck was going on, and the projection booth door was locked. I pounded on it, really steamed, and Shark finally opened it.

"Are you crazy?" I said.

"What's the problem?" he said affectlessly, opium smoke wafting out the door, Maya lolling on the bed back in the loft.

"The problem is people paid to see two fucking Ava Gardner films, not *Touch of Evil*."

"Maybe," he said. "But *Touch of Evil* is by far a better film."

"It's overrated," I said, then blew up, angry at myself for even dignifying his argument. "Goddamn it, Shark, put the other film back on!"

At that point Maya drifted up to the door, her breasts exposed, which didn't especially embarrass me—but I heard someone else coming up the stairs. "For Christ sake," I said to Maya, who didn't seem to care. I looked back, expecting to see an angry patron coming up to complain.

It was Kathy Petro—heading for the ladies room directly opposite the top of the stairs. She seemed disoriented or even sick, and didn't bother to look at us.

But Shark most definitely saw her. He appeared stunned.

Fred Thal

I was about to go up to Shark myself when I saw through the open doors that *Pandora* was back on the screen. "See, folks? It's all straightened out," I said, as cheerfully as I could, and people did start going back in.

At that point I went up to the booth, passing Kathy Petro on her way down the stairs.

Kathy Petro

When I came down from using the ladies room Gray said the movie was back on the screen and everything. I didn't really want to go back in, but he said, "Oh, come on, Kat, they've got it straightened out now. Hurry, before we miss something." So we went back in.

Fred Thal

"This is too much," I told Shark. "I really can't tolerate this. This is your last night. I'm letting you go."

"That's cool, Fred. That's all right," he said.

Maya was eying me disdainfully as she tucked in her blouse. I noticed a syringe on the floor by the bed.

"I hope you know you're destroying yourself," I said to Shark.

"Why don't you leave him alone?" Maya said. "What do you know about anything? It's mediocre people like you who've driven artists like Shark to the point of seeing what a dull joke life is."

"I take it back," I said to Shark. "You're letting this psycho Valley girl destroy you."

Shark wouldn't look at me. He was looking down at the screen as if he hadn't even heard me. Or perhaps he was trying to locate Kathy Petro in the audience.

Maya Dietrichson

"Fuck all of this, Shark," I said. "Let's just go. Everything's ready. The bomb is in place. All I need to do is attach one more wire."

But he ignored me, and began rummaging through all the junk piled up in the loft.

"What are you doing?" I said. "What are you looking for? Didn't you hear me?"

Finally he pulled out a rusty old film can. Sixteen millimeter. He took out the reel and began threading it through the sixteen-millimeter projector.

"What is this film? What is it?" I said, but he wouldn't answer me.

Kathy Petro

The Ava Gardner movie was almost over, the music was coming up and everything, when suddenly the picture changed again, getting a lot smaller.

"Oh, no, not again," Gray said.

And then it came into focus and I couldn't believe it. For a long time I couldn't even move. I just couldn't accept what I was seeing.

It was a film of Jeff Stuben and me lying on the sun porch at my parents' house in Newport Beach. I saw, as Jeff began to kiss me, that it was the afternoon we'd made love there back in 1967! And I realized that *Shark* must have shot the film with a high-power lens from Woody's house down the block. Which meant that somehow *Shark*, right now, was . . . My mind couldn't handle it.

"What's this?" Gray was saying. "My God, is that *you?*"

Suddenly a voice boomed out over the speakers, which I recognized instantly as Shark's voice. "Kathy," he said in this deep, creepy voice. "This is all I've ever had of you. Just these few moments of vicarious bliss. How many times I've masturbated to this movie, Kathy, projecting myself into this scene, imagining it was me you were loving like this. Oh, Kathy, this is truly the end."

"What's going on, what's going on?" Gray said, and he was really panicked, too.

Shark just kept saying all these weird creepy things. And then on the screen Jeff climbed on top of me, and I covered my ears and started screaming, "Stop it, stop it, stop it, stop it!"

Maya Dietrichson

"What are you doing?" I said to Shark as he spoke into the microphone. "Who are you talking to? Who is *Kathy?* What is this film?"

Then I realized that the girl in the film was a very young Kathy Petro getting it on with a bulky jock. But I still didn't understand.

Todd Jarrett

It was crazy. People were going nuts again, and then Kathy Petro started screaming, and the next thing I knew her boyfriend was pulling her into the lobby. And she kind of hurtled into me, still screaming, as he charged up the stairs to the projection booth.

Fred Thal

I ran up right behind Kathy Petro's boyfriend, reaching the projection booth a second after he did. It was empty, the film running out into a pile on the floor.

"Where is he?" her boyfriend said. "Where is Shark Trager?"

I saw that the fire door was open. We reached it in time to see Shark and Maya pulling out of the parking lot below in that lumbering death machine.

Kathy Petro was still screaming hysterically down in the lobby as her boyfriend tore the film of her from the projector and ripped it to shreds.

Maya Dietrichson

We stopped at Sav-On to pick up a new syringe on the prescription I had, and then hit each other up with cocaine and Dilaudid as we sat in the car with the engine running. Then I got out and popped the hood and placed the final wire on the bomb which was taped to the manifold.

"We're ready," I said, and unzipped Shark's pants as we got on the San Diego Freeway.

"The Sepulveda Pass," I said. "We can gain great speed there, going down the grade into the Valley."

So we roared up the freeway, a Spione cassette on the deck, so I could die listening to my own coldly beautiful voice.

As we hurtled past Sunset I straddled Shark, my back against the steering wheel.

"Move the seat back," I said. "The wheel is gouging my kidneys."

He tried but the seat was stuck.

The Sepulveda Pass was coming up fast. "It's time," I said. "Enter me."

But his tool wasn't hard.

"Oh Christ, not now," I said. "What a time you've picked to be impotent."

"I can't help it," he said. "I feel rotten."

"I don't believe this," I said. "We are blistering right into the penultimate moment of existential will and you are going to start whimpering like some kind of pantywaist. I don't want to hear it."

"I don't know why I did what I did back there," he said, ignoring my anger. "I only succeeded in injuring Kathy yet again. Why, why do I always injure her, when all I've ever really wanted to do was love her?"

"Who cares?" I said. "Goddamn you anyway, you'd better start fucking me and you'd better start soon. Look, we're already pushing seventy."

But he still couldn't get it up. I tried yanking him, that sometimes worked, but not this time. We were soaring down the Sepulveda grade, the wheels shimmying violently, which excited me terribly.

"Why do people hurt each other?" Shark said. "What is love, anyway? Is all romantic love really just obsession? Is there another kind of love that's more genuine, but which by its very nature precludes sex? Is there a love that's genuine that *includes* sex and yet is not obsessional? If so, it's a kind of love I've never known."

"Look, you get that cock up right now or I'm going to scratch your face off," I said. Glancing over my shoulder I saw that the speedometer was at seventy-nine!

"I can't do this," he said.

"You asshole!" I yelled. "You coward, you yellow-bellied killjoy, you've ruined it now. We're going to die and we're not even fucking!"

But I could feel that we were slowing and heard the squeak of the brakes.

"You make me sick," I said, and climbed off of him and lit a cigarette.

"I'm sorry, Maya," he said. "Maybe I had to come this close to death to see how much more there is still to know and do and feel in this life."

"Oh, shut up," I said. "Just shut up and take me home."

Billy Freeze

I was talking with some friends in front of the Charleton Arms when Shark and Maya pulled up in the Chrysler. It was a warm summer night and there were lots of people out and everybody turned to look as that noisy piece of shit lumbered up Windward Avenue. Shark pulled over but kept the engine running and Maya got out. Then Shark jumped out and went after her, grabbing her arm as she tried to cross the street. She started yelling, "Fuck you, go to hell." And he said, "Maya, goddamn it, disarm the fucking bomb." And she said, "Do it yourself. You're so smart, you can figure it out."

He tried to pull her back to the car, but she scratched his face and broke free. Then he chased her into the Charleton Arms.

I went in after them and saw them fighting, just scratching and whacking the shit out of each other on the stairs, when suddenly there was this horrendous blast out in the street.

They stopped fighting, and we all went to see what it was. The Chrysler was engulfed in flames and you could see the burning silhouette of a man at the wheel.

Maya Dietrichson

Some asshole tried to steal the car and the bomb short-circuited. It took the cops a while to find out who he was, his wallet was burned beyond recognition. At one point they thought he might be a young husband whose wife had gone into labor in the next block. His car was in the shop and he'd run out, desperately in search of a car with which to rush his wife to the hospital. Or so the woman believed. In reality he had simply chosen that moment to desert her.

The dead man was finally identified as a sociopathic criminal who had been raping old ladies in the Venice area for months. Shark convinced the police the bomb must have already been in the car when we bought it that afternoon, and the used car dealer caught hell before the investigation eventually petered out.

I saw Shark in the flesh for the last time as we stepped from the police station that morning at dawn. By then I had cooled off, and wished to resume our relationship, but he left me standing there in the rain-slick parking lot.

Perhaps a week later I spoke to him on the phone. "You're playing difficult," I said. "Giving me a dose of my own medicine. You want me to beg for it, don't you?"

"I don't want you to do anything, Maya," he told me. "It's over."

"I've heard that before," I replied. "You're a Sunday school boy now, but that won't last. The next time that big tool of yours gets good and hard, you'll think about Maya. Face it, you're addicted to me. You'll be coming back for more. It's just a matter of time."

He hung up on me.

Many months would pass before I quit thinking whenever the phone rang that it might be him.

Fred Thal

Shark apologized for what had happened in a very sober, genuine way, explaining in an almost jaunty manner what it was all about. "This gal I've got a thing for," was how he described his sad fixation on Kathy Petro.

Though I felt for him I just couldn't trust him anymore. I had no choice but to send him on his way.

Todd Jarrett

"I guess you can do what you want with my stuff," Shark said, indicating the junk in the loft. "I don't have any place to put it."

"You don't have a place to stay yet?" I said, feeling a little guilty for not offering to let him sleep on my sofa. But my girlfriend had just moved in. And I was still quite disturbed by what he'd done.

"No, but it's summer," he said. "And this is Southern California. There are a lot worse things than sleeping on the beach."

20/ **Beached**
(1983)

**Letter from Shark Trager to
Kathy Petro, June 23, 1983**

Dear Kathy:

I hope it doesn't frighten you that I've memorized your address. Don't worry, I won't bother you—not now or ever again. This letter will be the last you ever hear of me, and I just want you to know finally and clearly how truly sorry I am for everything.

I have no excuse for what I did at the Ray-Mar except that I was truly insane that night, my mind utterly distorted with opium and cocaine. I was involved in a sick relationship then, which I knew in my heart was sick, and I think what I did was a cry for help, an attempt to reach out to the goodness I have always associated with you, Kathy, though I see now that my method was wrong and could only have caused you great pain.

I am glad Gray destroyed that old film—I should have done it myself years ago. Needless to say, I should never have filmed you with Jeff Stuben like that in the first place. Of course, you know how in love with you I was then, I suppose I just couldn't help myself.

But love is the wrong word, I see that now. I was obsessed with you, Kathy. You were always on my mind. I was like a jealous lover who had never even been your lover. God, how many times I've wished I'd never kissed you.

I'm just sorry for everything. I see now how unforgivably selfish I was. How I never really thought of your feelings, what you wanted or didn't want. I was in love with my dream of you, with my fantasies of what we might have been like together, all of which had nothing to do with the real you. I'm so sorry for the trouble I've caused. If I could go back to 1965 I would cut off my own hands for what I did to you with that camera then.

Films are like dreams, it's been said. And I've always thought

318

that dreams are a place for us to live out the things we can't, or dare not, do in real life. In that light I ask your forgiveness for all the instances in my films in which I have vented my frustrated longings for you. Remember *Tropics* if you remember any of my films at all—and if you choose not to, I will understand. *Tropics* was my dream of what might have been.

It's so easy for me to recall that movie now, it's easy for me to get in that mood. I'm on the beach, Kathy, your and my beloved beach, under a faded lifeguard station with a jug of Bali Hai. Sweet tropical wine, sweet tropical sunset. As always when I stare far out to sea I imagine the sputter of Earhart's Electra and see that silver plane going down against the sun.

I know there is an island where there is sweet music, where lovers eat guavas by the light of the moon. For three ninety-five plus tax I can go there, my love, and drown in my dream of your kisses for the rest of my life.

My dream. Perhaps this is what I've always really wanted. To live and die in my dream of you.

But you are a creature of reality. Gray seems like a super guy. Are you happy at last? I hope so, I really do. You deserve it, kid.

The sun's below the water now, it's time for me to go. Bless you, my darling love. Go on ahead with your everyday life, and forget this craven dreamer who once tried to love you but didn't quite know how. Be free and cheerful for the world is not necessarily a bad place. Love Gray, as I know you do, for he is one lucky fella to have landed a gal like you.

Respectfully yours,
Shark

Kathy Petro

I knew the letter was from Shark before I even opened it. My name and address were scrawled on this dirty envelope with no return address but it had a Venice postmark. I got very upset when I read it because I was just starting to get over what had happened at the Ray-Mar, and the letter just brought it all back.

Then I heard Gray coming in the door and hid the letter before he saw it. He'd been so mad at Shark he couldn't see straight, and I just didn't want to get him going again. Gray hugged me and I thought: Yes, it's true, I am happy now, and the past is finally behind me.

But I couldn't get to sleep that night, not even after Gray and I had made slow, beautiful love for hours. I got up and took a few more pain killers for my shoulder, which always seemed to act up whenever I thought about Shark. The codeine wasn't strong enough so I had borrowed one of Gray's triplicate prescription pads, which— not wanting to bother him about every ache and pain—I simply filled out with his name and got myself the somewhat stronger analgesics,

Dilaulid and Percodan. I tossed back two of each with a glass of Wild Turkey, and smoked a cigarette in the dark living room, staring out the window at the full moon, wondering how Shark had discovered my address.

"Wet Brain"

Shark liked that Bali Hai, but the dye in it made me sick. I stuck to short dogs. At first he had money and he loaned me some. He had some gal's bank card and knew her code. We'd go to Wells Fargo and get a hundred dollars. Then one night the machine took the card.

We slept in the Venice pavilion till the night Scooter got stabbed. Then we moved up the beach to Rose Avenue where it was safer.

He said he used to make movies and I said yeah, I was Ava Gardner's boyfriend once in Puerto Vallarta, which was true. I spent the night with her, then I became a hippie, but the peyote split my mind into forty thousand separate worlds. I had to keep my thumb and finger taped together all the time, so the universe wouldn't fly apart.

Woody Hazzard

I liked to surf Venice sometimes, and one Sunday morning I was going down to the water with my board when I almost stepped on this wino who was sleeping by the sewage drain wall. I hadn't even seen him at first underneath this cruddy blanket, and when I realized it was Shark I almost shit. He had a long dirty blond beard and was sunburnt the way the derelicts in Venice always are, and he had scabs or wine sores on his hands. He was snoring and right by his head was his empty half-gallon jug of Bali Hai.

I thought about waking him up but I didn't know what I'd say. I wasn't pissed off at him anymore but I guess seeing him like that just kind of freaked me out. So I started to split. Then I felt guilty so I went back and stuck two twenties in his pocket, and then I drove on up to Sunset and surfed there.

Lupe Sepulveda

One Sunday afternoon I was roller-skating with my husband along the bike trail in Venice when I almost collided with Shark. I didn't recognize him at first, thinking only that a derelict had staggered into my path. But I stopped and looked back and could hardly believe it.

The sight of him really touched me. I'd been so angry when *Looking for Lupe* came out since the lead character was so clearly modeled on me, though needless to say I had never slept with a donkey.

But seeing Shark now in this awful state I felt no more anger. I couldn't feel anything but pity—even when he lookedat me without recognizing me, and blaming me for the nearcollision, mumbled: "*Whore.*"

Victor, my husband, skated back around. "*What* did he say to you?"

"Nothing," I said. "He's just a drunken bum, forget it."

So we went on. If Victor had known it was the man who had used me as a sex toy and then made *Looking for Lupe* I don't think he would have shared my compassion.

Todd Jarrett

Shark became something of a fixture on the boardwalk, hanging out at the gazebo near Horizon where all the derelicts liked to gather. He seemed to have one buddy, the aptly named "Wet Brain," a lumbering schizophrenic who was even grungier than Shark. They seemed to fight a lot—that is, have verbal arguments. And Shark would respond to Wet Brain's delusional gibberish—"You are wrong, Karen Valentine is the *sister* not the *mother* of God!"—to the extent that I feared for his mind as well.

I gave him a few bucks once in a while, knowing full well that it would go for more wine, not the food he said he wanted it for. He would try to prolong the encounter, but it was really painful to see him like that, so I'd try and slip off as quickly as I could.

Then one afternoon I was coming out of an office on that chic first block of Market Street where I'd just had a screenplay ripped to shreds by an independent producer, when Shark called to me from the doorway where he was urinating on Speedway. I was in a foul, dejected mood, wondering if I wasn't wasting my time playing these stupid Hollywood games, and against my better judgement I told Shark what had just happened.

When I mentioned the producer's name, Shark said, "He's a turd. Let me read it. I'll tell you if it's any good or not."

And before I could stop him he took the script from my hand. He was obviously too drunk to read it at the moment. "Give me the weekend," he said. "We can have lunch and discuss it on Monday."

"Wet Brain"

One night Shark read a typewritten message from God. He started bawling like a baby.

Todd Jarrett

I approached Shark out by the sewage drain wall that Monday with some sandwiches for lunch—he was too grungy to take into any restaurant—but what I really wanted was just to get my screenplay back. I'd realized later it was my only clean copy, so my heart sank when I saw it beside him, torn and dog-eared and stained with Bali Hai. It was ten in the morning and he was already ripped.

"It was mag-nificent!" he said, and there were tears in his eyes. "Man, do you know this reminds me so much of the first film I ever made! Back when I was twelve years old! Before sex! *Innocent!* My very first movie with an old Bell & Howell."

"That's great," I said.

"Your story *moved* me, man!" he said, a sob in his throat. "It really fuckin' *got* to me."

Obviously it had, but in the wrong way. The script was essentially a dark and biting satire, a vicious parody of so-called heart-warming films, a merciless explication of the unctuous rot behind the sickly sweet facade of sentimental manipulators like Capra and Spielberg. All of which was lost on Shark.

"That sweet little girl," he said of the deliberately cloying little cretin known as Debbi in the script. "Not since Dorothy in *The Wizard of Oz . . .*" A tear rolled down his cheek.

He was right about the reference though. That was definitely one of the stale fantasies I meant to trash.

"Shark, can I have the script back now?" I said.

He began thumbing through the pages. "Saucers!" he cried. "Real honest-to-God flying saucers! None of that lighting fixture shit like *Close Encounters.*"

I tried to take the script from him, but he obviously held on to it. "And my God, the ending! All the missiles launched. The Reds and us both shitting! Then, at the very last moment, *Jesus* stops 'em mid-air! My God, my God!"

"It's a nice moment, isn't it?" I said. It was meant to be absurd, crypto-religious kitsch. "Can I please have the script?"

"I want to option it," he said.

I wanted to laugh but couldn't. It was too sad.

"It's being considered elsewhere," I said, which wasn't true. It *had* been everywhere, but in Hollywood true originality invariably terrifies people.

"Here." Shark dug out a quarter and put it in my hand. "This is all I've got right now, man. But I'll let you have it for a six-month option against a purchase price of two hundred thousand. We gotta shake on it now. I don't want you trying to fuck me later if we land Sean Penn for the lead."

"It's tempting," I said. I'd given options for less. "But I think I should talk to my agent first." At the time I didn't even have an agent.

"Okay, I can dig that," he said. "But Todd, I have a feeling about this. I saw the saucers in my dreams last night, more clearly than I've seen anything in years. I *know* that this movie can save both our lives."

"I'm sure you're right." I finally got the script away from him. "Keep me posted," I said, and started back across the sand. But I was really thinking: I'm going to have to make sure I don't run into him again.

Sue Schlockmann

One afternoon in the fall of 1983, Elliot and I met Neal Ridges and Carol Van Der Hof for lunch at 9 Ocean Front, a rather expensive but good new restaurant on the boardwalk in Venice. It was in one of the old arched buildings used so famously in *Touch of Evil*, though it had been extensively renovated, very clean and spare inside, the space between the arches filled in with treated plate glass. From the dining room you had an unobstructed view of the colorful boardwalk and the beach and sea beyond. But on the boardwalk side the glass was blue and opaque, shielding the chic and frequently famous diners from the stray invasive eye.

We were there to discuss a script Carol had written which Neal wanted to direct, a semi-autobiographical story of a club-footed New York socialite who marries a charming but abusive cad who leads her into drug addiction before she finally breaks free of him and discovers genuine love with a sensitive younger man. I was quite high on the concept, and we were all sparking to one another, so carried away we hadn't even ordered yet, when Carol glanced out the window and said, "I feel ill."

Neal Ridges

It was Shark, arguing with another drunk on the boardwalk directly opposite the window. Of course, he couldn't see us because of the treated glass, and we couldn't really hear him. But it was definitely Shark and he looked really bad—deeply tanned, but emaciated in a creepy checked sportcoat and filthy cords.

"Just ignore him," Sue said. "He's where he wants to be."

Elliot Bernstein

We tried to continue talking, but it was impossible to forget that Shark was there. He wasn't moving either. He and this other guy were really getting into it, a protracted, animated argument. Sue would say to Carol, "Elliot and I were both extremely impressed by your mastery of dialogue. Weren't we, Elliot?"

"Right, great dialogue," I'd say. But I was spacing out. In spite of everything Shark had done, I couldn't help thinking: That guy out there was once my best friend.

Carol Van Der Hof

I somehow thought that I'd forgiven Shark until that afternoon. Pity is so much easier at a distance. Actually seeing him in the flesh I felt rage, disgust and panic. "Let's go!" I wanted to say. "It was a mistake to come here. Why did we choose this restaurant, knowing full well this is his stomping ground now?"

Neal Ridges

Carol was getting jumpy, her eyes darting to Shark. Then she closed her eyes and said, "Oh Christ, he's coming over."

Well, sure enough he was reeling right up to the window.

"Carol, it's all right. He can't see in. The glass is treated," I said.

It was hard to believe that though, since to us it was just like window glass. And then Shark unzipped his fly.

Elliot Bernstein

I really don't think he knew there were people inside watching him. It was just a sheet of mirrored glass back in an alcove to him.

People gasped as he fished out his tool and proceeded to take a leisurely piss against the glass right next to our table. He was closest to Sue, who glanced at his member and feigned nonchalance. "I wasn't impressed then," she said, "I'm not impressed now."

Carol however was livid and jumped up, calling for someone to make Shark stop. The French maître d' pounded on the glass, which only caused Shark to scowl in puzzlement. The maître d' made a helpless gesture to Carol. "I'm sorry. These bums, they think this alcove is a pissoir."

Neal was covering his brow and trying not to laugh. I thought it was wrenchingly sad.

Neal Ridges

I thought it was both funny and sad at the same time. But I was glad when Shark finally shook off, stuffed his dick back in his pants and moved on. We were trying to calm Carol down when she said, "Here he comes again."

Carol Van Der Hof

He'd begun talking with a group of black men he appeared to know. A very rough-looking bunch, one of whom had what I believe is called a boom box. Suddenly, Shark began adjusting the knobs and we heard a loud throbbing burst of Roxy Music's "The Thrill of It All."

Elliot Bernstein

Shark took the boom box from the black guy and began dancing around with it, this awful drunken staggering dance to Roxy Music's "The Thrill of It All." He was in a kind of mesmerized trance, and refused to return the boom box. So the black guys started pushing him around, and finally got the radio back. Then he must have said something inflammatory, because the next thing we knew the black guys were attacking him, just beating him mercilessly as he stumbled back into the alcove by our table.

Neal Ridges

These guys were just pounding the shit out of Shark, and Elliot and I jumped up at the same time.

"Elliot!" Sue said, but he ignored her.

Elliot and I raced out to the boardwalk.

Elliot Bernstein

"That's enough," I yelled as Neal and I reached the scene. It could have been very bad for us, there were maybe six or seven of these black guys, but they were pretty much finished with Shark, their anger spent by the time we got there. There was some grumbling and then they moved on.

Neal lifted Shark's head from the pavement where he'd fallen in his own urine.

Neal Ridges

His face was a mess. He could only open one eye but he recognized me. "Neal?" he said. "Is that really you, man?"

"It's all right, Shark. It's all right now," I said, and felt tears in my eyes. "We'll take care of you now."

I looked up at Elliot and there were tears in his eyes too.

Elliot Bernstein

We helped Shark into the back seat of Sue's Mercedes and she bitched that he was going to get his blood and smell on the leather upholstery. He did smell pretty awful. Carol limped off in a huff because we were helping Shark, and she tore out of the lot in that red fifties' MG he had given her.

21 / **Flash Flood**
(1983)

Bill Kemmer

In the fall of 1983, at the age of thirty-two, I ascended to the presidency of Mastodon Pictures, thereby becoming one of the three or four most powerful executives in Hollywood. In the years following Ben Klieg's death the struggle for control of the company had been fierce, but through sheer tenacity and will I had at last emerged victorious.

But at what a cost. For my brutal workaholism had been fueled by increasingly horrendous amounts of cocaine, and now that I had achieved the ultimate success . . . I was coming apart. Fearfully—and not being able to distinguish real from false fear was a crucial problem—I took a three-week medical leave, supposedly to undergo a hemorrhoid operation. In fact I admitted myself to the Kolon Clinic in Palm Springs.

Neal Ridges

The Kolon Clinic was considered *the* substance abuse treatment center of choice at the time. This was several years before the beating death scandal which forced its closure, and to those inthe know Ernst Kolon was most definitely *the* recovery guru ofthe hour. Of course, the Betty Ford Center was still gettingall the publicity, which was part of what made the Kolon Clinic so attractive to the ultra-rich and ultra-famous and ultra-strung-out. If you really wanted to kick in total privacy the Kolon Clinic was the only place to go.

From the Venice boardwalk, we took Shark to UCLA Emergency where his superficial lacerations were treated. By then he was on the verge of DTs, and when the doctors told us the UCLA detox unit was full, the Kolon Clinic immediately came to mind. At five thousand a day it wasn't cheap, but Elliot and I both felt we owed it to Shark.

327

We split the expense, which we could easily afford—thanks to the breaks Shark had once given us.

He was choppered from UCLA to Burbank airport and flown to the desert. I don't think he understood where he was going, though we tried to explain. He was strapped to a stretcher and babbling incoherently as we saw him off on the UCLA roof.

Bill Kemmer

I was in the lodge chatting with Narges Pahlavi-Bardahl when the chopper set down. We watched through the plate glass windows as they unloaded the patient, an astonishingly grungy, sunburnt wino type—a complete aberration at the Kolon Clinic. Though most of us you could say were "dying inside," on the face of it we still looked pretty good. I watched in disgust as they brought the man up on the stretcher, telling myself he had to be *somebody* or he wouldn't be here, mindful of what a mess Howard Hughes had become.

"My God, I don't believe it," I said to Narges when I finally recognized Shark. "I thought I heard he was dead."

Ernst Kolon

Shark was a sickening mess at first. I put him in the detox unit for several days so he could go through the worst of the physical withdrawal. I knew who he was of course, and from his movies I knew what a sick guy he was—though I did like *Hail!*, which was good entertainment. It so happened they had been showing that movie on the plane when I flew in from Zurich in 1975 on my mission to save the élite of America from their own weakness of mind.

Bill Kemmer

Ernst was this gruff, no-bullshit "tough love" kind of guy, about sixty then but built like a goddamn Panzer tank—an accurate allusion since he'd been a medic with the Africa Korps. He claimed not to have been a Nazi per se, just a "male Wehrmacht nurse," and of course Rommel and the whole North African thing were sort of the "pure" part of World War II, weren't they? Ernst had albino-white hair, a deep leathery tan, and wore khaki shorts and shirt that only lacked the eagle-and-swastika insignia.

But the guy knew how to deal with addictive personalities. There was just no way you could con him; he knew every game. He'd been there himself, having been a benzedrine addict in North Africa, an alcoholic in post-war Munich and a heroin addict in West Berlin.

And he had no respect for money or fame or inflated star egos. No matter who you thought you were, he treated you like shit.

Ernst Kolon

The first night in detox Shark tried to get pills, a Valium or something to ease his withdrawal. "Shut up, you stupid piece of garbage!" I shouted in his face. "Suffer, you goddamn weakling! I have no sympathy for you, you make me sick. Suffer and pay for all the cowardly escaping you've bought with the bottle. And just maybe if you're lucky you will hurt for the last time."

So he was cussing me out as the boys strapped him down to the bed. He was naked and I could see he was in bad shape. Thin from not eating, and his muscles atrophied. He would be oozing the poisons for days, but he'd ooze them much quicker if he began working out. So I sent in Drake.

Drake Brewster

I couldn't fuckin' believe it when I saw Shark's name on the chart. Christ, it had been fifteen years. I told Ernst that Shark and I had a history and told him what it was—Ernst knew all about my past—and he said, "Good. He can work out his repressed hatred for you."

So I went into Shark's room and said, "All right, get that skinny wino ass in gear. I'm gonna make a man out of you yet."

And Shark almost shit when he recognized me. "Drake? Is that really you? Jesus Christ."

I thought he might still be mad, but he wasn't at all. He broke into a grin and then we hugged with me squeezing the shit out of him. "Christ, you're as thin as a delicate little girl," I said. "We gotta put some meat on you."

He couldn't get over seeing me again. "I thought you'd be in prison by now," he said, "considering all the raping you used to do."

"I did six years in Soledad," I told him, "from '69 to '75. But it wasn't till after I got out that I paid the ultimate price. See, while I was in the joint I ran an ad and started up a pen-pal relationship with a girl named Judy who lived in Tennessee. She helped me work through my anger at women—which went back to my mother who'd been alternately abusive and smothering—and predictably enough as Judy and I wrote back and forth over the years we fell deeply in love. When I got my release date she agreed to come and get me. I'd never seen her in the flesh but for five long years I'd jacked off to her beautiful photo. Then the big day came and she was nowhere to be seen. Then suddenly this stumpy broad came up and tried to hug me and I almost crapped. It was Judy all right—see, I'd received a number of replies from different lonely women and somehow mixed up the photos. I was so upset, and she was too, that on the highway back to L.A. she crashed the car. She died in my arms, and I've been kicking myself ever since. So what if she was stumpy—inside she was the girl I loved."

As always I fought back tears at that point.

"That's a sad story, Drake," Shark said. "But that was eight years ago. Why do I sense that you're still single?"

"Because I am," I told him. "I turned to weights with a vengeance after that, and now it's too late." I explained how the steroids had atrophied my nuts and dick. "It's probably for the best," I told him. "Sex was a hassle anyway. Now all my energy is self-contained right here in the world's bitchinest bod." I pounded on one of my chrome-hard pecs. I had a body by then that made Schwartzenegger look like a slob.

We talked some more and then Shark said, "Drake, listen, I feel like shit. How about rustling me up a drink, for old times' sake?"

I slapped him hard across the face—the approved Kolon response to that kind of shit. "Get up, you sniveling pussy!" I yelled. "You don't know it yet, but you've had your last goddamn drink ever. Put on your jock and your workout shorts. We're going on a grueling desert hike."

Bill Kemmer

I was in the lodge, with Narges again, and a number of other patients—actors, singers, a jet set princess and a literary lion or two, who for obvious reasons I don't feel I should name—when we saw Drake Brewster leading Shark in a jog across the desert. Shark was sweating profusely—it was maybe a hundred degrees that day, though we were protected by the air-conditioning. And Narges was already beginning to shift her attention to Shark, which was a great relief to me. As soon as she'd learned I was president of Mastodon she'd been unshakable. A distant relative of the Shah who'd escaped Iran in '79 to be near her ninety million in American assets, she was indeed beautiful, with long black hair, almond eyes, olive skin and a svelte little body that just didn't quit. Under different circumstances I might have enjoyed a casual sexual relationship with her, but she had been admitted to the Kolon Clinic against her will and clearly had no desire to achieve a state of permanent freedom from drugs. On the contrary, she was defiant and only biding her time. "I can't wait to base again," she said repeatedly. "Bill, you must come to my palace in Rancho Mirage once we are free of this concentration camp. We can have a big sex and drug blow-out to celebrate."

Well, my life and career were at stake, so when she expressed curiosity about Shark I deliberately colored the truth just to get her off my back. She was impressed by his credits, especially *Mondo Jet Set*. "He made that movie? How I adored that! I associate that film with the last great days in Teheran!"

To explain Shark's derelict state upon admission I used the Howard Hughes model. "He's eccentric."

"Yes," she said. "I can sympathize with that. A man who cares nothing for outward appearances, who sees the stupidity of fashion-plate *Gentleman's Quarterly* clothes. I too have come to see the emptiness of mere material wealth."

She was especially impressed watching Shark jog across the desert, for by then he had received a haircut and had shaved off his ratty beard. "My God, he is handsome," Narges said. "I sensed that he would be." Then she confessed, "How I would like to sit upon that handsome face and free-base at the same time."

Our attention was suddenly drawn to a British film star who was making a scene with Ernst across the room. "I've changed my mind," he was booming. "My father died at Tobruk. If I'd had any idea you fought with Rommel . . . Open the door. I demand that you let me leave."

"I don't care if your mother was fried in a tank at El Alamein!" Ernst yelled in the actor's face. "It would only be a pretext. Your addiction is like a demon that wants you to chicken out. That's why you're not going anywhere." He slapped the British star hard across the face. "Sit down and shut up, you whimpering limey sniveler!"

No one could leave, that was part of the admission policy. Once you came in you were there for three weeks unless you simply died.

I was comforting the British actor, who was extremely chagrined, when I glanced out the window and saw a new patient being led through the courtyard back toward the detox unit. I recognized the woman with a jolt.

Kathy Petro

Finally one day this pharmacist called Gray and said, "There's a woman in here trying to get three hundred Percodan with an obviously forged prescription." And I was still waiting when Gray came into the drug store and I just broke down and started sobbing. "It's all right, Kathy," he said. "It's not your fault. You're not a bad person. You're just an addict, that's all." So he sent me to the Kolon Clinic, which was expensive, but by then I had my settlement from Brian and we'd moved into this big house on Stone Canyon and everything.

I was having cold sweats by the time Gray dropped me off, and the attendants were leading me to the detox unit when I saw these two men jogging toward me. One was real muscle-bound like Arnold Schwartzenegger or somebody and the other one was skinny and drenched with sweat. I went into a kind of shock I guess when I realized the skinny man was Shark.

He was winded and everything but managed to say, "Hello, Kathy."

This horrible panic just welled up inside me and I ran for the gate. I got there but it was locked. I could still see Gray's new BMW going off up the desert road, and I called, but he was too far away to see or hear me. I started screaming and shaking the gate, and Ernst Kolon came out.

Ernst Kolon

She was hysterical. "Let me out, let me out, I can't do this, I can't be here with that man." Then she told me she had a history with Shark that stretched back twenty years. I didn't catch all the details but it was clear she was angry.

"You have resentments towards him then?" I said.

"Resentments? *Resentments?*" she yelled. "Do you know what he's done to me? *Shark Trager has ruined my life!*"

"Then good," I told her. "You are lucky that he's here. You have a golden opportunity to break up a major chunk of rage."

She began pounding on my chest with her fists, so I slapped her across the face, then put her into detox.

Drake Brewster

It was clear that seeing Kathy Petro had shocked the shit out of Shark. "What is it?" I said as I watched him take his shower. "She one of your ex-fucks?"

"You watch your goddamn mouth, Drake," he said, and I grinned. It was the first real spunk he'd showed.

"Oh, I see, it was serious then," I said.

Then he looked real sad. "It was never really anything. Except in my mind." Then a minute later he said, "Why does she have to be here now? Is it possible that after all the crap and madness . . . it really is meant to be?"

Kathy Petro

Ernst came to see me in detox. They had me on some kind of mellowing drug 'cause if I'd just stopped everything cold turkey I would have gone into convulsions. So I had this real calm feeling, like a cow in a sunny field or something, and Ernst was really gentle this time and held my hand and everything.

"How would you like to be free forever of the need to hide your feelings with drugs?" he said.

I said that sounded okay.

"How would you like to get even with Shark Trager once and for all?"

I said that sounded good too, but I didn't want to go to prison for murder. He said that wouldn't be necessary, and gave me a copy of his *43 Steps of Recovery*, and said I could do anything I wanted to Shark, starting first thing tomorrow.

Bill Kemmer

Ernst had developed his own forty-three-step recovery program, which he characterized as an "improved version" of A.A.'s twelve steps, though in fact there was little more than a structural resemblance. Ernst was extremely eclectic, borrowing from a variety of New Age therapies, both au courant and passé, as well as from old-line German philosophy—the key word in his program was "will" in the Nietzschean sense. "The forty-third step marks the *triumph* of the will," he would say, unaware I think of the allusion to the Leni Riefenstahl film.

The first fourteen steps, and the first week of the program, were devoted to getting in touch with and giving vent to our rage.

Ernst Kolon

The addict is an angry person but too cowardly to show these feelings. So we have them make a list of everyone they've ever hated, beginning with their parents, then we put them with the dolls.

Bill Kemmer

The dolls were life-size and made of spongy rubber. They were predominantly flesh-colored, though he kept black ones in stock for the occasional black singer or comedian, and they could be dressed up a variety of ways as an aid to the imagination. The rage therapy took place in a large empty room with a padded floor, rather like a gymnastics rooms, with ropes hanging down so that if the patients desired it the dolls could be suspended from the ceiling. There was a choice of weapons for use on the dolls—clubs, knives, even a sledgehammer, though the machetes tended to be the most popular.

The rage therapy sessions were private, but one afternoon I arrived for my session as Shark was still in the midst of his. Ernst was facilitating as Shark clobbered a doll in a gas station uniform with the sledgehammer.

"Tell him!" Ernst was yelling. "Tell him what he did!"

"You killed my mother, you son of a bitch!" Shark screamed, as the sledgehammer broke the rubber head apart.

Ernst Kolon

First I had Shark take it out on his parents: his father, a confused, lonely anal type with a homosexual panic complex, and his mother, a classic weakling who dressed him as a girl, then abandoned him. He destroyed both those dolls, which was good, you know. He really got it out of his system. The next time I brought in a new doll in a bikini and blonde wig and said, "You know who this is, don't you?"

At first he wouldn't act. "That wound is healed," he said. "I wrote Kathy a letter."

"Bullshit," I yelled at him. "What you are you, a saint now?"

"Hardly," he said. "But I did all the damage to her. She has every right to be angry at me, but I have no right to be mad at her."

"*Rights?*" I shouted in his face. "The human psyche doesn't know about *rights*. You're furious with her, it's all too apparent. Look at you. You're trembling like a cowardly little scaredy-cat. She teased you, didn't she? She promised you everything, the way women do, but didn't put out. Isn't that the truth of it?"

He tried to hide in confusion. So I pushed the doll at him, aping Kathy's voice: "Come on, Shark, don't you want it? Don't you want my blonde pussy? Well, *you can't have it.* I'm too good for you, Shark—"

At that he exploded and picked up the machete. If I hadn't jumped back quickly he might have hacked off my hand.

Kathy Petro

I see now that Ernst deliberately kept Shark and me separated the first week. He put us in different discussion groups and made sure we were never in the lodge or the dining room at the same time, which was really smart, I guess. I still knew Shark was around though—in fact I thought of little else. I saw him a few times going out across the desert with Drake, and I just got madder and madder. Part of it was the withdrawal—my nerves were just raw. And what a convenient focus for all my irritability he was!

Still, I almost laughed when Ernst showed me this rubber doll wearing the exact same kind of workout shorts Shark was always wearing. "Normally, we start with the parents," Ernst said. "But in this case I think your hatred of Shark is by far more immediate and compelling."

I almost couldn't do it at first, it seemed so stupid and everything. So I just picked up this billy club.

"What is the first bad thing he ever did to you?" Ernst said.

"He took advantage of me when I was on antihistamines at the drive-in," I said.

"Then pretend you are there now and respond to that," Ernst said.

So I said, "Don't do that, keep your hand out of there," and hit the doll on the arm with the club, but the club just bounced off.

"Oh Christ, he didn't even feel it!" Ernst yelled. "Come on, don't be such a nice girl! He's going to fingerbang you, then tell all the guys about it. He's going to spoil your reputation. Stop him!"

So I hit the doll really hard, and Ernst yelled, "Right!" So I did it again, and felt this big rush of adrenaline, and it felt really good.

"What's the next thing he did?" Ernst yelled.

"He made a peeping-Tom movie of me," I said, and just snapped. I just went crazy and the club wasn't good enough, so I grabbed the machete.

Ernst Kolon

The boiling fury inside the girl! She literally hacked the Shark doll into small rubber pieces, one of the most thorough ventings I have ever facilitated. In the end she was spent and wrung out . . . and free. She had exorcised Shark Trager from her emotions forever. As is always the case once the mind is emptied of the anger, the actual person seems reduced and insignificant if encountered in the flesh.

To make sure this was the case, I deliberately placed Kathy and Shark together.

Narges Pahlavi-Bardahl

We had all gone through our rage therapy, which I had enjoyed, repeatedly stabbing my brother for sending me to this place, and hacking up my late husband, Steve Bardahl the race car driver, who had died in a fiery crash, for taking his hot body from me.

At dinner I had begun sitting with Shark, for I had decided I wanted him. I knew by then he didn't have any money left, but that didn't matter, I had enough for both of us. I had a crush on him and really wanted him to fuck me, and didn't think that I could wait until we got out. Then one night we were locked in conversation at the table when Kathy Petro came in, and right away from the looks they exchanged I sensed competition.

Bill Kemmer

I remember well the night Kathy first encountered Shark in the dining room. I saw a flicker of fear in her eyes, a instant when she wanted to take flight, but she held his gaze and nodded tentatively before taking her tray to another table.

Shark was with Narges, who by that point was glued to him, and she was clearly put out when Shark excused himself and approached Kathy's table.

Kathy Petro

Shark came over and said, "Do you mind if I join you for a moment?"

I was unloading my tray and said, "I guess not. If it's just for a moment."

He sat down opposite me. His whole manner had this strangely peaceful and gentle quality to it, unlike anything I'd ever experienced from him before. It's hard to explain, but I really got the feeling that, as hard as it was to believe, he really didn't want anything from me anymore. Which is not to say I wasn't still guarded.

"You got my letter?" he said.

"Yeah, I got it."

"I was very drunk when I wrote it—"

"Yeah, I could tell."

"So some of what I said was pretty fucked-up. About living in a Bali Hai dream and all that—"

"So what's your point?" I said.

"Look, I don't want to lay anything on you—"

"Then don't."

"I just want you to know that I meant the apology part of the letter. That still goes. I'm sorry for everything, I really am. That's all."

And at that he got up and went back to Narges, whom I'd heard was a distant relative of the Shah of Iran or something.

Drake Brewster

I whipped Shark into shape, got him back on the free weights till he was sweatin' like a pig. One day afterwards he was sore as hell, so I said, "Shower off, then stretch out in here. I give rubdowns now too."

I was giving him one of my powerhouse massages, breaking up the tense knots in his back, when I said, "Boy, I see you still got lots of hair on your butt. Had all mine taken off a few years back. Electrolysis. Too much of a bitch, trying to shave your own butt."

"Yeah?" Shark said. "Well, do me a favor, Drake, and just keep your eyes off mine."

When he said that it brought back what had happened that day in Santa Barbara when I'd tried to nail that hippie gal he married eventually, then almost cornholed him. Thinking about it made me feel bad.

"Look, Shark," I said. "I know we've avoided talking about this, and I don't want to open old wounds. But I am sorry for what happened back in '68."

"I know, Drake," he said, and sat up. "You couldn't help how you were back then, I see that now. I guess I wasn't the best roommate in the world. And for that I'm sorry too."

We hugged, even though he was naked, but there was nothing funny about it.

Forgiveness was the happening thing then, I guess, since that was the big theme of Week Two.

Bill Kemmer

It was one of the apparent inconsistencies of Ernst's program that Week Two was devoted to forgiving the very people we had vented our rage on in Week One. As a result, I found myself apologizing to Shark—whose surrogate rubber doll I had bludgeoned mercilessly—though I must say I was never entirely convinced I had done anything to him that required a plea of forgiveness.

Narges Pahlavi-Bardahl

I was sunning by the pool with Shark when Bill Kemmer came up and said, "You know, Shark, I'm really sorry about the way I handled *Scar*. I hope there are no hard feelings."

Shark got up and the two of them hugged and Shark said, "No, *I'm* sorry, Bill. I was out of control then. I'm sorry I put you through that difficult time."

After Bill left I said, "This is good, Shark. Now maybe he will make our film."

Todd Jarrett

Shark called me at the Ray-Mar Theater one night and asked if my script was still available. It was—I'd gotten nowhere with it—but I said, "Well, Spielberg's reading it this weekend," which to me was an obvious joke.

"I'll pay you cash for it," Shark said. "Two hundred thousand. Is it a deal?"

I had a funny feeling. I hadn't seen him since the pathetic option discussion on the beach several months before, and had no reason to believe anything had changed. But he didn't sound drunk. "Where are you?" I said.

And he told me he was at the Kolon Clinic in Palm Springs, putting together a deal with Bill Kemmer.

Bill Kemmer

We were supposed to be incommnicado but somehow Shark got the script smuggled in. He slipped it to me one night when the attendants weren't looking, after having given me a riveting pitch.

Reading the script in bed I saw immediately how grossly he'd misinterpreted it. Far from being a "cathartic tale of spiritual rebirth," it was a vicious, cynical, sacrilegious parody that no one in their right mind would produce.

Narges had apparently missed the satire too—perhaps due to the language problem—for she shared Shark's enthusiastic belief in its potential as another *E.T.*

Narges Pahlavi-Bardahl

Blue Light really swept my heart up. It had everything: flying saucers, children, a nuclear war, even Jesus Christ! How could it not be a very huge blockbuster! It was so beautiful, like a vision you would see while basing. You know, when a drug high becomes almost religious? It was like that.

I knew also it was a metaphor for our sudden love. I knew I was in love with Shark the first night we had sex in his cabin and it came to pass that I did sit upon his face and it was almost as good as basing. And I knew the love was mutual because he told me so.

Bill Kemmer

I tried to let Shark and Narges down easy. I knew they'd begun a discreet affair, and suspected their enthusiasm for the script was woven heavily into the fabric of their new feelings for one another, as well as their recovery in general—and I certainly didn't want to unravel *that*.

"The script needs work," I told Shark.

"You won't take a chance on me, will you?" Shark said. "That's the truth of it, isn't it, Bill?"

"It might be tough," I confessed. "Jean Klieg still carries weight with the board. I may have forgiven you, Shark. But she hasn't."

"Then let's end the conversation here," Shark said. "I don't want to take advantage of you, Bill. I shouldn't have even mentioned it, I see that now. Not in this setting."

"That's all right, Shark. I'm glad to see that you're thinking about doing something again." I nervously cleared my throat.

"I took quite a fall," he said. "I suppose I'm going to have to prove myself again. Win back people's trust."

"That's not going to be easy, Shark. Once bitten—"

He smiled, and squeezed my arm, though he wasn't looking at me. I followed his line of vision to the swimming pool in the distance where Kathy Petro was executing a dive.

Kathy Petro

After Shark apologized in the dining room he really did just leave me alone. We were in different discussion groups and everything and whenever I did see him he was always with Narges and just completely ignored me. I mean completely. Like I'd glance at him on the sly to see if he was glancing at me on the sly, you know what I mean? You can tell if someone's pretending to ignore you. But he wasn't pretending, he really was.

And the weird thing was, in spite of everything I found myself resenting it. Thinking, you know, what's wrong with me? Have I changed, have I gotten old? I was only thirty-three and my body looked twenty-six, though I did have these laugh lines. Was that it? Was I too old?

It kind of pissed me off in a way, if that was it. Like he's all obsessed with me for twenty years, then suddenly I'm too old? He was not exactly some twenty-year-old blond surfer himself.

I don't know, it just really began to get to me, this number he was doing with Narges. Lovey-dovey by the pool and all that. She was pretty for an Arab, but it was bullshit, she wasn't his type. *I* was his type. I decided he was deliberately trying to play with my mind and thought, you know: Two can play that game.

So I thought, maybe I'll come onto *Bill,* that will really frost him. We'll see if I start rubbing my bare legs up against Bill's by the pool if Shark can ignore *that*—when suddenly I thought: What am I thinking, am I crazy? I love *Gray!* Gray is the only man who's every treated me like a real human being. Am I ready to throw that away just to play some weird mind game with Shark?

Ernst Kolon

Kathy came to me and said she was still having some problems in her own mind about Shark. I found it hard to believe she was still angry at him, but she said it wasn't anger exactly.

"Love and hate are very close," I told her.

And she said, "Look, I don't want to hear that."

"Why don't you start going for long walks by yourself in the desert?" I said. "In the evening when it's cool. You can walk off this residue of negative emotion."

Narges Pahlavi-Bardahl

One evening Shark and I were leaving a Thirty-third-Step discussion group meeting in the lodge when we paused to hug and watch the orange sunset and discuss the coming film.

"I don't think you should assume all the risk," Shark said to me. "We'll set up a limited partnership—"

"No, really, why bother?" I told him. "I want to be your patron. Twenty million to me, Shark—it's not that big a deal."

"It could be more like thirty, Narges."

"Then kiss me," I said.

He did but I saw that his eyes were looking off beyond me. So I turned and saw Kathy Petro walking down into the dry gulch that ran like a path through the desert toward the distant purple mountains. A breeze blew her blonde hair.

"I used to think she was really something back when she was young," I told Shark. "I was in the French *Vogue* once, and you know what they said of me? They said I was the Kathy Petro of Iran."

"There's really no resemblance," Shark said with a sudden coldness that startled me. And then, as if heavily distracted, he simply walked away.

Bill Kemmer

We had a "free period" that night after dinner, and Shark and Narges appeared to be having a tiff, so Shark and I played a game a chess in the lodge. Around eight it began to rain, one of those sudden and ferocious desert storms. I got up once to get another Perrier and heard a flash flood bulletin on the TV in the next room. I mentioned it to Shark as I sat down again. "I hope we're safe here."

"Yeah, I think we are," he said. "It's just the dry riverbeds and gulches where the shit really hits the fan."

A minute later Ernst came into the room and asked if anyone had seen Kathy. She wasn't in her room and had missed a therapy session at six.

"We saw her around five, didn't we, Shark?" Narges said, leaning in the door.

Shark looked very pale. Without saying a word he dashed out into the rain.

Drake Brewster

Shark told me later he almost shit when he reached the gulch because it was like a fucking rapids. He was really afraid Kathy had been caught in the flash flood and washed away and drowned. But he ran on down the edge of the gulch anyway, the rain thundering down as he called her name.

He went on and on for a mile or more, getting more and more freaked out, like certain she was done for, but still calling her name. He said he was so drenched he couldn't even tell if he was crying. And it was like totally dark everywhere, just this rain coming down, there was nothing but desert and then suddenly he saw this shape up ahead, a big square in the sky, which he realized a second later was a drive-in movie screen. It was this old shut-down drive-in, completely dark and abandoned, and it really bummed him out for some reason, and he cried out at the top of his lungs like a wounded animal, "Kathy!" like totally certain she was dead.

Then he heard her through the rain, calling back, "Over here!"

So he slogged up through the sand to the drive-in where the whole parking lot was like this sea from all the rain. But right in the middle of it, there was this one old wreck of a car, an old Chevy, and that was where Kathy had taken shelter from the storm.

Kathy Petro

I was sopping wet by the time I reached this old car and the rain was coming down so hard I couldn't even tell which way the clinic was. So I just climbed in the car, even though the upholstery was all torn up and everything and for all I knew there were rattlesnakes inside. But there was no place else to take cover from the rain.

My blouse was soaked so I took it off and wrung it out. My bra was all wet so I took that off too. When I heard the voice call my name I didn't realize at first it was Shark. I just thought it was a rescue party so I responded. I tried to pull on my blouse but it got caught on the door handle and ripped. I was going: "Oh darn," when I saw Shark bounding through this huge puddle toward the car.

I thought about locking the car door before he reached it, but it would have been pointless since the window was broken. He climbed in on the driver's side.

He was winded and soaked, water running down his face as he looked at me, and I could see how worried about me he'd been. I just saw everything in his eyes, that he'd been looking for me and thought I might be dead, I just saw it all—he didn't have to say a thing. And he didn't.

I was holding my torn, wet blouse in front of my breasts, and I sensed what was going to happen. And I wanted it to happen. I couldn't, didn't want to, take my eyes off of his.

For a second I thought he was going to do something really crude, like yank my blouse away. But he didn't do that, he didn't do that at all. He reached out, his hand trembling, and very gently touched my cheek. Then, very slowly, he leaned over to me and kissed me more tenderly than anyone ever has. Then he pulled back a little and I saw there were tears in his eyes. I touched his hand and he kissed me again. Then we kissed long and deep and I couldn't believe all the sweetness I felt. It was crazy, but suddenly I just knew how much he'd always loved me, that all the weird things he'd done were just expressions of stifled love. All he'd ever really wanted was to love me like this. And crazier still, I realized that as much as I'd hated him I'd always really loved him too, even though it wasn't what I thought love was supposed to be. Ernst was right. Love and hate are very close. You don't spend twenty years hating someone you're indifferent to.

His mouth moved to my breasts, and then one thing led to another. It was one of those big type of Chevrolets with a roomy front seat and we made love there with my head on the armrest. Once he was inside me it felt so right I thought: Why didn't we do this back when we were young? Not that thirty-three was that old, but we had wasted a lot of time. It was just so clear that our bodies were right for each other. Maybe *that* was what it was all about. Our bodies had just instantly wanted each other even though there were all these mental reasons why we shouldn't be together. I saw that was what had happened the very first time we had kissed at the Flying Wing Drive-In. I had wanted him then, but my mind said he wasn't appropriate. I had wanted him on Maui, but Daddy got in the way that time. So here we finally were, almost twenty years after that very first kiss, picking up where we'd left off because our bodies just wouldn't take no for an answer.

We made love all night, just lost in each other. We stopped a few times and smoked cigarettes, but were just drawn back into each other. In a way time stopped, I wasn't even aware of the passing of the hours until I noticed that it was getting light.

At first it was just this cold gray light. Then suddenly the sun cracked through the gray clouds, and like you'd turn off a tap the rain just stopped. We watched the hot yellow sun coming up over the clean rain-fresh mountains.

Shark lit our final cigarette, which we shared. Suddenly I was frightened, not sure what this really meant.

"We'd better get back," he said, the first words he'd spoken in hours. "They're probably going to be out looking for us."

"They probably think we went off to get loaded or drunk," I said, a little giddy from the lack of sleep and from what we'd been doing.

"Yeah," Shark said. But he seemed distant, as if there were still some loneliness in his soul that even this night had not touched.

"You know, this was really—" I began in what I guess was a romantic tone of voice, and he stopped me.

"Let's not reduce it with words," he said, which reassured me in a way. At least he felt there was something to reduce.

He opened that rusty old car door, and we both laughed a little as it squeaked. He really did have a nice smile.

"We'd better go back separately," he said. "So people don't think things."

Suddenly the real world came back in a rush. I thought about Gray, whom I really, really did love, and for a second I felt really awful. But guilt was stupid, I told myself quickly. Besides, what we'd just done had no effect on my love for Gray. This was something else, on some other kind of level.

The sun was burning brightly, hurting my eyes as I climbed out of the car and squinted back at Shark. Already, the night was beginning to seem like an unreal dream.

"You're in love with Narges, aren't you?" I said impulsively, both hoping he would say yes and afraid he was going to.

"It's not love, it's business," he said. He was trying to act tough and wouldn't look at me. He reached for a cigarette, forgetting he was out.

Again, I wanted to say something endearing but he'd blocked that path. So I just said, "Well, see you around," even though it seemed like a dumb thing to say after what had just happened.

Narges Pahlavi-Bardahl

Shark returned that morning maybe an hour after Kathy with a hickie on his neck. So I knew what had happened and called him on it.

"This is not a subject we will ever discuss," he said to me in a calm tone of voice but with a look in his eyes that frightened and silenced me.

Still, I was steamed for several days and wouldn't go to his cabin. But I observed that he was staying away from Kathy just as he had before. So naturally I assumed that their sex had not worked out.

Bill Kemmer

I was sure, as we all were despite their stories, that Shark and Kathy had spent the night together. In the days that followed Shark appeared strangely subdued and preoccupied. I tried my best to be supportive in a general sense, but didn't feel it was my place to pry into what had happened.

Drake Brewster

"You finally fucked her, didn't you?" I said to Shark in the weight room, and he set down his dumbbells and pinned me back to the wall.

"You fucking moron. I should rip your brain right out of your skull," he said.

"Ease up, Jack," I told him. "Sorry I mentioned it."

He cooled off later and apologized. Then he said: "Drake, how'd you like to come to work for me? As a combination bodyguard/trainer?"

I said, "You're full of shit, man. I know for a fact you don't have a dime."

He said that had been the case, but he now had a ninety-million-dollar line of credit.

Narges Pahlavi-Bardahl

Shark and I made up in the final week of the program, where the theme was "taking responsibility." We both saw that was precisely what we were doing with *Blue Light*, which we were going to push on with despite every obstacle. We began talking excitedly about it all the time, and having wild sex every night. I kept my mouth shut about Kathy Petro, since that was so clearly over.

Then two days before the program was to end I did something which today I regret. I had an appointment with Ernst, and as I waited for him in his office I noticed Shark's rage therapy folder on his desk, and I could not resist taking a peek. I only managed to read a single item—quite a juicy one—before I heard Ernst coming and quickly put the folder down.

Kathy Petro

I was really confused that final week. Shark was just ignoring me, which seemed prudent in one way, but it also kind of hurt me. He was still lovey-dovey with Narges all the time and I knew I had no right to be jealous, since I was still committed to Gray. I didn't want to leave Gray or anything but . . . I didn't know, I just felt really confused.

Bill Kemmer

The program ended on a Saturday with a group singing of "Kum Ba Yah" in the lodge. I couldn't help noticing the looks Shark and Kathy were giving one another as we all joined arms and sang and swayed in unison. When the song was finished there was an orgy of hugging, and people growing tearful with Ernst—this bastard we'd hated for three weeks but who had turned our lives around. I noticed that Kathy ducked out of the room before it got to be her turn to hug Shark.

Around noon the cars began arriving. I was watching for my girl-friend's Jaguar from the foyer when I heard Shark and Kathy in the adjoining room. I knew I was being a snoop, but I couldn't resist stepping closer so I could hear what they were saying and discreetly observe them through the crack of the door.

"I just want you to know I'm never going to forget what happened," Shark said to Kathy.

"I never will either," she replied, avoiding his eyes in an effort to suppress her emotions.

"I've always loved you, Kathy. And I always will."

"I know," she said softly.

"But you're happy with Gray, aren't you?"

She looked at him forthrightly. "Yes, I am. I love him very much."

At just that point I saw an anthracite BMW pulling up—with the license plate: GRAY. A good-looking, if somewhat haggard, young man got out—a man who bore, it was hard not to notice, a rather eerie resemblance to Shark.

"Then go about your happy life with him," Shark said to Kathy, neither of them aware of Gray's arrival. "I set you free, my darling love."

Very gently, Shark kissed Kathy . . . just as Gray stepped into the foyer.

I felt obliged to warn them, so I called Shark's name.

Kathy Petro

Shark was kissing me good-bye when suddenly Bill Kemmer called his name from the foyer, and then a second later Gray stepped through the door. He just missed seeing us kissing, but he still caught the vibes, I guess. My eyes were misty.

He recognized Shark and went through about nineteen changes in three seconds flat.

"Gray, it's all right. We've forgiven each other. It was part of the therapy."

Gray was trembling with anger, and shot a dagger look at me. "Let's go."

Shark didn't say anything, thank God. If he'd tried to be friendly I'm sure Gray would have punched him out. So we just left, but I looked back at Shark one last time. He had this sweet, tender smile like you'd see on a wounded saint, even though he wasn't looking at me, or at anything in particular.

22 / *Blue Light*
(1983–1984)

Todd Jarrett

Shark invited me up to that place in Bel-Air a week or so after he got out of the Kolon Clinic. It was a huge Italianate mansion with an electric gate and all that, one of Narges' many homes around the world. He'd mentioned that she was his "co-producer," and that she was a distant relative of the Shah or something, but I didn't really get the gist of the relationship till I met her. She was hanging all over him like some sort of femme fatale in a sex stupor. Shark had her completely . . . What's the opposite of pussy-whipped? Prick-whipped, I guess.

Narges Pahlavi-Bardahl

With Shark I lost all my desire to free-base, which is saying quite a lot, for it was a powerful addiction. Very psychological, you know? But he fucked it out of me. Quite literally.

Or so it seemed in those first fevered weeks.

Todd Jarett

Shark and Narges raved about my script, Shark calling it "Capra-esque," Narges hailing it as "truly Spielbergian in the best possible sense," both of them still completely missing the point. Shark was especially wild about the title, which he found "evocatively spiritual without giving too much away," not even catching the sledgehammer Nazi reference.*

But I kept my mouth shut and signed the contracts. And Shark

---

* He no doubt means *Das Blaue Licht*, Leni Riefenstahl's mytho-fascist 1932 German "mountain film."

handed me a cashier's check for two hundred thousand dollars. Of course, I felt like a whore and swore I'd get even with them both someday.

"It *is* going to need some revision," Shark said. "And I don't know if you're up to it, Todd. It might be too painful. I think I know what this script means to you."

It meant a lot to me actually, but not in the way he thought. I knew it was the best, the most bitterly brilliant writing I'd ever done. And now in his cloying, sickeningly sweet, born-again cokehead pseudo-humanism, Shark was going to hack off its balls. I didn't even want to hear what he had to say. But he steered me out to the veranda, his arm over my shoulder, the carpet of city lights twinkling insipidly behind him, as he raptly described his desert vision.

Greg Spivey

Shark told me about his Palm Springs "vision" during our intoxicated conversation on Christmas Eve in Beirut. He spoke of what had immediately preceded the hallucination: his night with Kathy in the abandoned Chevrolet. He said it was by far the best sex he'd ever had, though of course it was impossible to speak of it merely as sex since it involved so much more. Indeed, it was the culmination of a twenty-year desire which he realized finally was as much spiritual as sexual. It was so good, he said, that he sensed nothing else could ever come close to that night. He felt as if, through the act of making love to Kathy, he had achieved a kind of ultimate life goal. As a result he was frightened afterward, with a terrible sense that he'd just passed through the peak moment of his existence, and really wondered if there were any point in "toughing out another thirty or forty years of tedium, tepid thrills and low-level pain."

He said a brute, compulsive part of him still wanted Kathy, wanted to possess her in a very literal sense—that is, make her his sex slave, keep her chained to a bed in a room somewhere, and continue having sex with her "until one or the other of us died." He said he knew that was where it would lead, because she would be like a drug to him, there would never be enough, he would never be "satisfied." And so, with all the effort he had, he released her. Because he said he knew, a higher part of him had glimpsed, that Kathy was finally only a symbol of a great spiritual longing that, if the Hindus were right, might well have endured through many lifetimes. And he knew as well that she was a person, "a divine manifestation of the timeless Atman, or universal soul, in her own right," on her own spiritual path, and he could not simply use her as a means to his own ends.

He said he watched her heading back to the clinic that morning and knew he had reached the outer limits of what sex was. He waited a few minutes, then started back across the desert himself. The day was already hot, the sun pounding down, and he soon realized he had lost his way. There was nothing in any direction but desert, so he picked a direction and plodded on, sweating by that time, light-headed from lack of sleep and the night's dissipation.

Suddenly a flash of reflected light in the sky caught his attention. At first he thought it was a plane, a silver plane. Then he saw what it was, and for a moment he thought he was actually going to crap.

It was a spacecraft, not a saucer exactly, but a silver craft that greatly resembled a 1955 Porsche Spyder without wheels. It was humming, hovering. And then it descended before him.

At first, he said, Jesus Christ was at the wheel. The classic Jesus we all know: shoulder-length brown hair and beard, white robes, compassionate brown eyes. He said Christ placed a finger to his lips and adjusted the craft-radio, which was playing "How Much Is That Doggie in the Window?"

Then, before Shark's astonished eyes, Christ "transmuted"—something as a werewolf might in a film, only in reverse. His beard drew back into his face, his hair grew short and light, his eyes changed to blue as his features remolded themselves, and his robes reformed into a white T-shirt and red windbreaker jacket. As Patti Page gave way to Bo Diddley on the radio, so Jesus Christ had become James Dean.

But only for a moment. For as Shark watched, on the verge of peeing now, Dean turned into an alien from outer space. A Dean-oid alien however, a stylized "silver-skinned" version of the flesh-and-blood Dean, the face and hair now hard and metallic, but still identifiable as the iconographic Dean.

In this final metamorphosis, the music changed to a post-New Wave futurist sound, and the Spyder craft ascended. It paused momentarily as the Dean-oid alien—or as he would be called in *Blue Light*, "Deem"—beckoned to Shark, indicating the way back to the clinic. Then, in a blinding flash of blue light, the craft simply vanished as if it had slipped through an invisible crack in the sky into another dimension.

Todd Jarrett

I wanted to laugh as Shark told me about his "vision." I wanted him to laugh, but he didn't. Then I just wanted to get out of there. I was sure he was crazy.

Greg Spivey

Shark said he continued having sex with Narges, even though his heart wasn't really in it, only because she was able and willing to finance *Blue Light*, which he now saw as a "delivered vision" which must be shared with the world at any cost.

But finally he reached a point where the sex with Narges became so "painful," he just couldn't do it anymore. "I sensed that the only true road for me was celibacy," he told me months later in Beirut. "I suppose I'd known that in my heart ever since the night with Kathy, and I could simply no longer use my body as a female prostitute might use hers. If Narges couldn't find a way to love me on a spiritual plane, then . . . maybe it wasn't really love."

Narges Pahlavi-Bardahl

He spoke of Yogic principles, the need to conserve his energies and channel them into the film. I did not take it well.

"If I had blonde hair and a toothy smile I'll bet you would feel differently," I said, alluding to Kathy Petro.

He became quite steamed. "I told you, that is a subject we will never discuss."

I stalked off through the house, slamming many doors. I was still furious later that evening when we went to the Bernsteins for dinner.

Elliot Bernstein

Sue was not at all keen on the idea of having Shark to dinner, remaining quite cynical about his alleged transformation. She was curt and brittle when Shark and Narges arrived. Neal arrived moments later, and he and Shark stepped into the solarium for a private discussion, during which Neal passed on directing *Blue Light*.

Neal Ridges

Shark had sent me a heavily revised screenplay, which I had read over the weekend. The new writer on the script was Drake Brewster, Shark's bodyguard/trainer, who had remained behind the night of the Bernsteins' dinner—understandably, since he had once tried to rape Sue. Clearly, although Drake may have written in the changes, the ideas were all Shark's.

On one level the story was about an abused teenage girl in an Orange County suburb who fantasizes a romantic affair with an extraterrestrial who resembles James Dean. In Todd Jarrett's original draft—you could still detect—those opening scenes had been unrelievedly harsh: the sadistic redneck father savagely spanking his panties-clad teenage daughter Patti—a parody of the prurient have-it-both-ways TV-movie approach, both titillating and moralizing at the same time. Shark had toned that down—the father was now merely "overly strict" and given to "occasional caustic remarks," the cretinous alcoholic mother now newly sober and "struggling to become a wise and loving mother at last." "There are no real villains in this piece," Shark had told me. "Only hurting, misguided people."

The affair between Patti and Deem, the alien, struck me as highly insipid. He may have resembled James Dean but he talked more like Robby Benson. He and Patti cruise over the suburbs in his Porsche-like spacecraft and eventually make love, but when she gets pregnant things veer into vintage Sandra Dee. She wants to marry Deem and have his baby, society and her parents be damned. But when Patti's father discovers she's pregnant—"knocked up by a nerd," he believes—and repeatedly slaps her, Deem comes to her rescue, and the two of them take off. This part wasn't bad—going back to *White Desert*, I'd always liked lovers on the run. And when the Porsche-craft breaks down over Beirut, and the couple is pursued through the labyrinthine streets by heavily armed Shiites, you had all the makings of a neat little action film.

Drake Brewster

My favorite part was where that Air Force guy goes ahead and nukes Beirut. I got off on that, when all those A-rab bastards got vaporized. I liked writing that part, Shark telling me what to put down. "All right!" I yowled. "Let's get down in it! It's about time America started fucking again!"

Neal Ridges

Of course Patti's escape from Beirut was completely implausible. But you could see the visual possibilities as the warhead spins down through the sky directly at Deem and explodes.

The ending was too much though—and not to say expensive. The Moscow stuff as the Russians, believing the U.S. has started World War III with the strike on Beirut, launch a full-scale counterattack. The Oval Office scenes, as we respond. The thousands of missiles midair . . . when, only seconds from oblivion, Deem "rematerializes" from the ashes of Beirut and projects a "beam of love" from his heart that blankets the globe and melts every warhead before it can explode. Saved from the brink of obliteration the entire world convulses in a paroxysm of cathartic enlightenment. But the Soviet premier sobbing, "Thank you, Jesus," on his knees in the Kremlin . . . I mean, come on!

"Not Jesus," his general tells him. "Deem!" And the cry goes up all around the world, from Calcutta to Capetown, from Beijing to Boston: "Deem! Deem! Deem!" as Deem and Patti flash away through a space-and-time warp to dwell for eternity in the distant and infinite blue light.

"It's kitsch," I told Shark. "It'll be laughed off the screen." I hated being so blunt, but I felt an obligation to save him from his own . . . what? Neo-naiveté?

"I'm sorry you feel that way, Neal," he said, seeming more sad than angry. "I suppose when you've been knocking around this town as long as you have it's hard not to be cynical."

That angered me. But I sensed that Shark was someone who really needed handling with kid gloves now.

"You may be right, Shark," I said. "I'll probably kick myself later." At that we joined the others.

Narges Pahlavi-Bardahl

I was furious at Shark all through the dinner. The Bernstein woman kept glaring at me. She drank too much wine and turned nasty.

Elliot Bernstein

I knew there was going to be trouble. Shark was expounding on his new philosophy of art, the need for a "core of compassion" within all his film characters, the moral obligation of the artist to show "the redemptive power of love." And Sue kept muttering, "Bullshit, no sale."

"I believe that people are basically good," Shark said over dessert. "People basically want to love one another—"

And Sue blurted out, "Oh sure. You made that point real well with *Red Surf.*"

"I intend to make amends to the world for that, Sue," Shark said evenly. "That's what *Blue Light* is all about."

"Right," Sue shot back. "You're going to make this piece of kitsch dreck with your Iranian scumbag money—"

At that Narges threw down her spoon. "How dare you insult me! You should speak of dreck. I know what kind of shit films your father used to make—"

"At least my father didn't build an empire on torture and bleed a whole country dry like the goddamn Shah—"

Narges lunged across the table, trying to jab Sue with a butter knife. "How *dare* you speak ill of my late relative the Shah, you Zionist bitch—"

Neal Ridges

Shark and I restrained Narges as Elliot calmed Sue. But that was it for the evening. Nobody finished their desserts.

Greg Spivey

I had just finished line-producing a depressing teen computer comedy when Shark approached me about *Blue Light*. I still don't know why I took the job exactly. I didn't think much of the script I read, the one he'd revised with Drake Brewster. But I did believe that Shark had genuinely changed. He apologized at great length for the "weirdness" he'd put me through with *Red Surf*. "I've been through the fire, Greg," he said. "And I know I am not the only one who got burned. Join me in this great adventure, my friend, so that we may all be healed in a sea of genuine love and compassion."

Well, what could I say?

Several directors had already passed on the project—understandably given the script, given Shark's last film. "I wish there were someone young and gifted," Shark said. "A virginal genius who hasn't been battered and scarred yet."

I suppose I must accept the responsibility for suggesting Gary Schnell.

Gary Schnell

I was still asleep in this little Bel-Air cottage my parents had got for me when Shark showed up one morning with the script. He said he'd seen my student film which he thought was astonishing, and he wanted me to direct *Blue Light*.

I read the script that morning and I was weeping by the end. I called him with tears still in my eyes and said, "This is going to be my *E.T.*"

I mentioned that of course I'd have to talk to the high-powered agent I'd just signed with, and Shark got nervous for a second. Then he said, "Okay, but be sure and mention that we're prepared to pay you a fee of two million dollars."

Greg Spivey

I had seen Gary's short at a USC screening. It was a twenty-minute science-fiction story about a shy, chubby teenage boy—no doubt an alter-ego for Gary—who, faced with sexual rejection from a coarse high school girl, regresses back through a time-warp into a sexless Disney-ized Mark Twain world. It was extremely vapid but extremely well-made, with a number of stunning, and expensive, visual effects. It was obvious he'd out-spent the other students by a wide margin. Gary's father was Earl Schnell of Schnell Petroleum in Houston.

Drake Brewster

Gary was a fat-ass so I started whipping him into shape. He and Shark worked on that script long and hard. Shark tried to include Narges but she wasn't interested. She was still pissed off because Shark wouldn't fuck her any more.

Narges Pahlavi-Bardahl

It made me so angry I even thought about stopping the film. I could do it just like that with one phone call to the bank. ButI knew if I did Shark truly would never have sex with me again. I kept telling myself: this can't last forever. He's a virile man. Sooner or later he's going to be in a sexy mood again. So I waited. But I grew restless. So I began to base again.

Gary Schnell

I kept getting more and more excited as Shark and I worked on the pre-production. My agent had been negative at first because of Shark's past, but I convinced him that Shark had really changed. He did insist that I get my entire fee up front though, minus his two hundred thousand dollar commission.

We dropped the pregnancy angle from the script. "It makes it cheap and dirty if they actually have sex," I told Shark. "They should just kiss and be in love. It's more touching that way."

Shark saw my point and went along. "Yes, the era of frivolous premarital sex appears to be drawing to a close," he said. "As a film-maker I'm beginning to feel a strong moral imperative not to glorify promiscuity anymore."

Greg Spivey

Gary was twenty-four and, I'm sure, still a virgin. He was not bad-looking, but one of these kids who'd spent his adolescence holed up in a movie theater, who had, for whatever complex of reasons, been terrified of sex long before there was anything to especially fear.

We had an open call for the part of Patti, during which I made a joking remark to Gary about all the hordes of "young Hollywood snatch" we were seeing. Gary turned red as a beet and said, "Greg, please don't talk about women like that. I don't want anything to vulgarize the atmosphere of this film."

Drake Brewster

About a week before we left for Beirut Shark and Gary went to lunch at Breton's. I went along since that was where Jean-Claude Citroen and his frog actor buddy had wasted Shark. Even though the chances of running into them again were remote, there were still a whole lot of people around who hated Shark.

Narges came too, but she kept going to the bathroom. We knew she was coking again but Shark felt helpless. "I've tried to talk to her, but she denies it hysterically," he'd told me. By then they were sleeping in different wings of the house.

People were discreetly checking Shark out, but everything was fine till Bill Kemmer and Carol Van Der Hof came in.

Bill Kemmer

I saw Carol tense, and felt her anger, as Shark approached our table. "Give him a break, Carol," I said, anticipating what Shark was going to say.

"Carol, I don't blame you for hating me," Shark began.

"Good," she said, refusing to meet his eyes.

"I never wanted to hurt you, Carol. I think you know how much you meant to me. I was crazy, that's all, quite literally out of my mind."

Completely ignoring Shark, Carol said to me, "I smell something *dead* in here, don't you, Bill?"

"I just want you to know that I'm sorry," Shark said gently. "I can't compel, or even expect, you to forgive me."

"I know what I smell," Carol said loudly. "A dead fish! A dead rotting fish all doused with a sickly sweet cologne. But it still has that rotting fish stench!"

Everyone was looking by then and Shark was embarrassed. He maintained his saintly expression, but under his breath he said to Carol, "You cunt."

Just then all hell broke loose in the ladies room.

Narges Pahlavi-Bardahl

I was trying to base when some fake blonde bitch made a scene, saying I shouldn't do it there. "Why not?" I said, "I could buy this stupid restaurant." At that she nearly set my hair on fire, so I began to pull on hers, and soon we fell into the dining room.

Drake Brewster

Narges was rolling on the floor with some TV actress, and when I
pulled her up she bit my hand, and spilled coke on the carpet. It was
a real bad scene.

Gary Schnell

I felt bad for Shark. He was trying so hard to be a truly decent man.
You could tell that the other industry people in the restaurant were
only too eager to think cynical thoughts.

Bill Kemmer

Narges was still spitting like a viper as Drake, his hand bleeding,
shoved her into the Rolls in the parking lot.

Carol and I were climbing into my Ferrari when Shark came
bounding over. "Carol, look," he said. "I'm sorry I called you a cunt."

"Oh, go drown," Carol said, rolling up her window.

Gary Schnell

Shark was driving as we pulled up to the gate of the Bel-Air house
and saw a grungy old man yelling into the intercom.

"A friend of yours?" I said to Shark as a joke, certain the old guy
was a bum, one of the sad homeless people you saw in increasing
numbers during those years.

"He's not a friend," Shark said, as he stopped the car. "He's my
father."

Mac Trager

It ripped me up inside to come to him but I had no place else to go.
"I'm in bad shape, son," I told him there by the gate. "I went to
Vegas and lost every dime. One of those showgirls got me drunk and
kept me gambling. I hadn't slept with a woman in over five years,
not since Miko cleared out, and I just lost control."

"What about the condo in Laguna Beach?" he said.

"That's gone too," I said, the tears stinging my eyes.

"Look, son, I've changed," I told him. "It's the eighties now, and
I've left *all* my bigotry behind. It's a process that started with Miko,
who raised my consciousness about the plight of Asian-Americans.
But now I extend that same tolerance to everyone, of whatever religion or race or minority life-style. Different strokes, son. If you're a
member of the gay and lesbian community, it's fine with me, as long
as it makes you happy and you're being true to yourself."

"I'm not gay, Dad," Shark said, and then he hugged me. I wanted to jump back but I forced myself not to.

"It's all right," he said real gentle-like. "This is a time of healing. Father, come inside."

Greg Spivey

I was against Shark bringing his father along to Beirut. Mac Trager was a hard drinker with a big mouth and things were touchy enough as it was—Beirut being Beirut. I wanted to use Tel Aviv or Athens but Shark insisted on authenticity.

It was frightening. The first day we were setting up a chase scene on a rubble-filled street in East Beirut when a fire fight broke out less than two blocks away in the Western sector.

Gary was furious. "Somebody go over there and tell them to cool it. We're trying to make a movie here and they're ruining our sound."

"Gary," I said, "why don't you go tell them yourself? It might mean more if they hear it directly from you."

He started over but Shark stopped him.

Gary Schnell

I'll never forget Beirut. Until you've seen a real war you just don't know what it's like.

"I thought I told you to keep these bodies in the background," I said to a prop man one day before a set-up that involved some dummy corpses. He lifted the dummy I was referring to, but it wasn't a dummy at all, and real intestines covered with maggots slipped out. I threw up and then became more convinced than ever that *Blue Light* might be the film that stopped the madness of human violence once and for all.

Joey Joel

Playing Deem was a very physically demanding role. Once Luis had glued that silver latex Deem head in place over my own, it was on for the day, and my only nourishment came from sipping drinks through a straw inserted in my nostril. Snort, then swallow—not a fun way to drink a milkshake, believe me.

Beirut was really terrifying—especially after a group of midwestern lady Sunday school teachers who'd been staying at our hotel "disappeared." That was very freaky. They went out on a sight-seeing tour and then their bus was found, shot-up and abandoned. The rumor was they'd been kidnapped, though it was being kept out of the news because of allegedly "delicate negotiations." Whatever, it certainly didn't contribute to an atmosphere of security.

There was always so much gunfire going on in the background, not to mention the rocket attacks and bombardments, that we just gave up on the sound. Then on the last day of filming Luis came up to me after a take and said, "What's this? How did you do this?" There was a bullet hole through the top of my latex Deem head. It had missed my skull by a millimeter.

I was so shaken I went straight to Sharon's dressing room where, without even trying to remove my head, the two of us had sex. In the heat of the moment we neglected to close the blinds.

Greg Spivey

It was obvious that Gary had a crush on Sharon—that was why he'd cast her as Patti. But he idealized her, you know, confusing her with the role. So when he walked by Sharon's trailer on the last day of the Beirut shoot and saw her having sex with Joey he was very disturbed.

Gary Schnell

It did bother me, I guess. Because Sharon was really the picture of everything Patti was about: sweet and pure, a kind of fresh-scrubbed angel really. But when I saw her with Joey—they were doing it "dog-style"—I realized she was just another Hollywood slut like my dad had always warned me about.

Drake Brewster

Gary came to me that night in the Beirut hotel and said he was upset 'cause he'd seen Joey giving it to Sharon.

"It's a natural thing," I told him. "A real man has urges. I used to myself till the steroids shrunk up my nuts and dick."

Then I started to tell him about my rapist days of yore, but he stopped me and said, "I don't think I want to hear this, Drake. I don't want to stop being fond of you."

Then he went upstairs and caught Narges with Mac.

Mac Trager

From the point where Shark and I hugged by the gate in Bel-Air it was all downhill. We tried talking once but had nothing to say, so we watched a Raiders game, but Shark kept talking on the phone. Then he said, "Come on to Beirut, Dad."

So I went, thinking things might pick up there, but they didn't. I stayed at the hotel drinking in my room, bored as hell, nothing but A-rabs and dubbed Elke Sommer movies on the TV.

Then one night Narges invited me into her room. She wasn't bad for an A-rab. Real high-fashion type, none of that veil shit.

"You know, you're very attractive for a somewhat older man," she said, sidling up beside me on the sofa. The Israelis were bombing some ridge in the distance.

"You're okay too," I told her, knocking back a glass of Jack D. "But aren't you fuckin' my son?"

"No," she said. "For some time now, Shark has been opting for celibacy."

"Opting for it, huh?" I grinned at the notion. "Well, no wonder you're smokin'."

I ran my hand up her skirt, and she spread her legs and moaned. We were going at it like gangbusters right there on the sofa when Gary walked in.

Greg Spivey

Shark and I were going over the L.A. shooting schedule when Gary stuck his head in the door. "I thought you might like to know that I just came upon your father and Narges having sexual intercourse."

Shark looked stunned for a moment, then said, "Thank you for telling me, Gary. It takes a great deal of courage and moral authority to be the bearer of such news."

Narges Pahlavi-Bardahl

Gary was due in my room for a meeting, that was why I had sex with Mac. I knew Gary was a prude and would report it immediately. I only did it to make Shark jealous.

Mac Trager

Narges and I had just wrapped it up, and she was in the bathroom, when Shark barged in. I pulled up my pants and grinned at him. "Not bad," I said. "You oughta try her sometime."

"Where is she?" he said, then opened the bathroom door.

She was smoking cocaine with a torch deal and he knocked it out of her hands. "You're a mess and I'm sick of it," he said. "You haven't done shit since we got here except base your stupid brains out. I want you to go back to L.A."

"All right, Shark," she said, picking up her bra. "But let's see how you finish this film without my money, huh?"

He grabbed her arm. For the first time since I'd come around he looked really mad. "If you try and fuck me, Narges—"

"I've been trying to do that for weeks," she said. "Obviously, your father is much better equipped to do that job than you. I'll bet if *he* had made love to Kathy Petro she would still be with *him*—"

Narges Pahlavi-Bardahl

Shark got a funny, squinty-eyed look at the mention of Kathy Petro. Had I not been so high I would have realized the danger I was putting myself in.

"How dare you mention her name in that context?" Shark said. "How dare you conjure up that sort of mental image?"

"Oh, there's a lot I could conjure up, Shark," I said with foolish abandon. "I could even conjure up what happened to you in the Orange County Jail when you were fourteen years old."

Mac Trager

I got a sick feeling. It was a door that should've stayed shut.

Narges Pahlavi-Bardahl

Shark appeared shaken, which pleased me. I went in for the kill. "I saw your rage therapy folder in Ernst Kolon's office, Shark. I know all about the time you got *buttfucked by Negroes!*"

Mac Trager

Shark flipped his lid and tried to strangle Narges. I felt it my duty to come to her aid, and was doing so when Drake came in with a gun.

Drake Brewster

I'd been packing a .357 since we arrived—everybody was armed in Beirut. I aimed it at Mac, and he backed off from Shark, then Shark let go of Narges and said, "Give me the gun." So I did, seeing a second too late that he was crazy.

"I'm gonna blow your Iranian pig brains all over this wall," he said, trying to jam the gun into Narges' mouth as she screamed.

"Don't do it, Shark, not here!" I said, thinking of his future. But I was turned on. I mean, this scene was *hot*.

Narges Pahlavi-Bardahl

Shark was insane. When I saw *Blue Velvet* a few years later it was like a terrifying flashback. Because Dennis Hopper had the same look in his eyes as Shark in Beirut!

Drake Brewster

Mac tried to say something and Shark turned on him with an un-hinged fury, whacking him back and forth across the face. "You shut your fucking hole, you goddamn fuck! I should have squashed you like a bug years ago for what you did to me!"

I was getting *real* turned on! Shark was like a fuckin' animal, man, flipped out on the natch. I could see in his eyes that his mind was running to wild, crazy places way beyond right and wrong and all that phony fuckin' Sunday school shit. Man, I was *aroused!*

"I just don't know what to do with this pair," Shark said, in a low, scary Clint Eastwood voice. "You got any ideas, Drake?"

"You bet I do," I said, feeling my dick jerk. "Let's fuck 'em both, then kill 'em."

He grinned and said, "You know? That sounds like a plan."

Mac Trager

I was starting to get unnerved. Shark and Drake took us down the express elevator to the Mercedes in the hotel garage, Shark saying he'd blow our brains out on the spot if we tried anything. He was beyond reason, and Drake was egging him on. I could believe they were gonna fuck Narges, but not me, you know? But as we drove up an alley past a bullet-riddled sign that warned we were entering West Beirut I began to get a real bad feeling that anything was possible.

Narges Pahlavi-Bardahl

By the time Drake pulled to a stop on an empty rubble-strewn street in West Beirut, he and Shark were like a couple of psychopathic killers—like the pair in *In Cold Blood* perhaps, only far sicker. They had entered that realm where reason and morality no longer exist as we know them.

"Do you want to fuck your father?" Drake said to Shark. "Or should I?"

Shark considered the matter, then said, "You do it," and laughed like a fiend. "You do it and I'll watch. I'll watch while you buttfuck my dear old Dad, just like he let those black prisoners buttfuck the innocence out of a terrified teenage boy. I'll watch and relish his agony, and force Narges to watch. And blow off her head at the exact moment you come."

Mac Trager

I started hyperventilating in the back seat of the car.

Drake Brewster

Shark ordered Narges and Mac to get out of the car. By then he was talking in a Southern redneck voice, why I don't know, telling Mac again and again how I was gonna make him *"squeal* like a pig!"

I didn't much want to assfuck Mac—in fact I wasn't sure if I was up to fuckin' at all. To be blunt my dick had shrunk up almost to nothing, man. I'd been kind of hoping Shark would do all the fuckin', and I could just watch and then blow 'em away.

Narges Pahlavi-Bardahl

Shark ordered Mac to lower his trousers and lean over the hood of the Mercedes and told Drake to make Mac "squeal like a pig."

But Mac refused to do it, so Shark placed the gun to my temple, and I said, "For God sake, Mac, do as he says."

Mac Trager

I asked myself, "What would John Wayne do in a mess like this?" And I knew the answer: He'd slug his way out of it. So I came at Drake with a right hook to the jaw. I see now it was the wrong thing to do. The blow barely phased him, but it did set him off, and the next thing I knew he threw me over the hood and yanked down my pants. I saw his pecker, but it wasn't like no pecker I'd ever seen before.

Then just as the worst was about to happen, Shark said in a strangely calm tone of voice, "All right, Drake. That's enough."

And I looked back at Shark and he had the gun trained on Drake.

"What's the problem?" Drake said.

"No problem," Shark said. "This is wrong, that's all. It's wrong and it's sick, and it's really no fun. It's not joyous and loving, and that's what I'm trying to be now. Thank God I've come to my senses in time."

"Aw shit, man," Drake said. "Are you gonna puss out now? This takes the cake."

Narges was trembling, as confused as I was.

"Put your penis away, Drake," Shark said. "Dad, it's okay, pull up your pants. No one's going to harm you."

So I pulled my pants up quick and then I heard a pop and saw blood on Drake's thigh. For a second I thought Shark had shot him, but a magnum don't make a pop, you know? Then we seen a bunch of A-rabs with automatic rifles coming up the street.

Narges Pahlavi-Bardahl

Suddenly there was shooting and Drake was struck in the thigh and nearly fell. Shark pulled him into an alley, firing at the Lebanese who were armed with automatic weapons.

Mac and I ducked into the alley also. "Come quickly," I said to Mac, and we ran on ahead of Shark who was helping Drake.

"Get help!" Shark called after us.

Mac Trager

Narges and I cut between two buildings as we heard more shooting. Then we heard the A-rabs coming up the alley after us.

"In here," she said, when she found an open door. And we ducked right into a room full of Shiites who were armed to the teeth.

Drake Brewster

Shark pulled me back into a bombed-out building as the Arabs ran past us. Luckily it was so dark they didn't see my trail of blood.

"You'd better leave me, man," I told Shark. "Save yourself."

He hesitated, then said, "No, I can't do that, Drake. I realize now that you're an evil influence on me. You represent an old part of me I have to let go of. Beyond that, however, you are still a human being. So you sit tight. I'll be back with help, possibly the Marines."

Narges Pahlavi-Bardahl

As Mac and I stumbled into the room all the Shiites grabbed their weapons. I knew they were the most extreme splinter group of Shiites because of the framed portrait of Khomeini on the wall, and because all of them were ugly with evil, dirty grins and rotting teeth.

"So . . . an American," one of them said, his face an inch from Mac's.

Stupidly, I was carrying my passport. When they saw the name Pahlavi they virtually convulsed with glee, several of the more disgusting ones literally drooling.

"Put them with the others," the apparent leader ordered.

And they pulled back a long sliding door to reveal the twelve kidnapped American lady Sunday School teachers cowering fearfully in a filthy room where flies buzzed.

Mac Trager

I saw red when I saw all those Sunday School teachers. Good, decent
Kansas women, both wives and spinsters, young and fresh, and old
and sweet like dear old grandmothers. It just tore my heart out to
see 'em in that state, slop holes in the floor, bowls of that couscous
or whatever that A-rab shit is. Yet you could see the brave dignity in
those broads' eyes.

Drake Brewster

Shark told me later that right after he left me the Arabs almost caught
him. They were all over the place and he ducked into another gutted
building. As he watched them pass, he said, he smelled something
foul in the room and saw it was a corpse that had been there for days
and was rotting real bad. Fighting back nausea, he looked closer at
the body and saw it was that of a boy no older than six, though he
was wearing combat boots, his stiff fingers gripping an AK-47. It was
then, Shark said, that he truly understood for the first time the
graphic futility of war.

But knowing he was in a jungle—not of his making, but one in
which it was his duty to many others to survive—he picked up the
AK-47, checked the clip, which was full, and moved on. Then as he
ducked between a couple of buildings he heard a bunch of American
women singing "Onward Christian Soldiers."

Mac Trager

Those broads had balls, I'll say that. In what was clearly a pre-
planned act of defiance, they started singing "Onward Christian Soldiers" in unison, knowing it would drive those A-rabs nuts, and it
did. They kept screaming like animals at the women to shut up, then
started poking 'em with their rifles, which made me think: Okay,
ladies, you've made your point, don't press your luck. But those
broads were real wound up.

Narges Pahlavi-Bardahl

It was an act of sheerest stupidity. In the Islamic world the woman
does as the man tells her. The song itself was bad enough, but when
they wouldn't stop as they were told the Shiite men really blew their
tops. I believe they were only one second away from slaughtering the
whole choir when Shark burst through the door with the AK-47.

Mac Trager

It was my son's finest moment, bar none. If it had been me, I'd have blown the shit clean out of that whole A-rab crew. But Shark sensed—correctly I see now—that once the shooting started they'd have nailed him and me and Narges and all those broads too.

So he bluffed 'em. "I don't just have this rifle," he yelled. "I'm wired with twenty pounds of plastic explosives. If anybody fires the whole block's going up."

The thing was, he was wearing a T-shirt and khaki pants. The pants were baggy, but what the hell did they think? That he had the explosives taped to his ankles? It was nothing but pure . . . what's that Jewish word? Chutzpah. That's what it was. And those dumb A-rabs bought it hook, line and sinker.

Narges Pahlavi-Bardahl

It was an astonishing display of bravery on Shark's part, there is no denying it. What élan! He reminded me of the young Errol Flynn in that moment, and in spite of the terribleness of some minutes before, I fell in love with him all over again.

What a magnetically bold figure he cut, ordering those Shiites to drop their weapons, which they did in a heap on the floor. With that accomplished Rambo would have annihilated them, don't you think? But Shark was not like that—he had far too much grace and panache under pressure to ever play the macho buffoon.

As Shark covered the Shiites Mac and I steered the Sunday school teachers out the door, several of them whimpering by then, their eyes filled with tears of gratitude, more than one as she passed Shark saying a heartfelt, "God bless you."

Mac Trager

Shark ordered the A-rabs into the room where the broads had been and told me to pull the door shut and lock it. But I said to him on the sly, "Come on, the broads are out of here. Why don't you grease 'em now?"

And he looked at me like *I* was sick or something. "That's really what you'd do, isn't it, Dad? You think violence is the answer to everything—you and your generation who glorified slaughter in World War II, who got us into Vietnam in the name of your rancid Duke Wayne heroics, and last but not least invented the bomb."

"Lookie here, bud," I said. "A half hour ago you were fixin' to let that muscle-bound Rambo poke his steroid-shriveled pole up my wrinkled old bunghole till I squealed like a pig. So don't come on now like Mahatma Gandhi."

Shark got a pained look like some kind of saint, which I thought was fake till I saw the tears welling up in his eyes. "Father, forgive me," he said real gentle-like. "I knew not what I was about to do."

"Let's just forget it, okay?" I said, and locked those A-rabs up in that room so we could get the hell out of there.

Greg Spivey

The jubilation when Shark returned to the hotel with the Sunday school teachers was brief. Soon the place was swarming with embassy officials and/or CIA men, the women were sequestered, and Shark was told in no uncertain terms not to speak to anyone about what had happened. "The women are safe, that's the important thing," the ambassador told Shark when he arrived. The political situation was "just too precarious," he explained, "to rock the boat with something like this now."

Shark was confused, demoralized even, and Narges was angry. "But Shark was a hero," she said. "It's not right that he shouldn't get credit for his bravery."

Mac felt the same way, we all did.

Shark finally went to bed around dawn—by then we knew Drake was safe. The following evening, which was Christmas Eve, the call came from President Reagan.

Shark took the call in the bar, where Mac was drinking heavily. I don't really know precisely what the president said. "Yes, sir, I understand, sir," Shark said into the phone, with a final, rather sad, "You're more than welcome, Mr. President. Merry Christmas to you and Nancy too."

Shark said nothing for a moment after he hung up. Then he ordered a double bourbon. I knew it was his first drink since the Kolon Clinic and should have objected. But I joined him instead. So began our Christmas Eve soul-baring. By then it was just Shark and me—and Mac a few stools away, passed out with his head on the bar.

Drake Brewster

A bunch of Marines came and got me just like Shark said they would. On the way to the hospital one of them said, "What the hell were you doing in West Beirut?"

"Aw hell," I said. "We just went for a joyride. You know how that is."

Gary Schnell

Some of us exchanged gifts in my suite on Christmas Day. My mom had sent a tree with ornaments and tinsel and presents from Neiman-Marcus for me to give everyone. Shark seemed out of it that morning, as if he hadn't slept much, and he didn't have a present for me, but that was all right, I understood. I really thought he'd done a courageous thing and I was so glad he hadn't killed anyone. "I don't think I could live with myself if I ever killed another human being," I said to him. "Could you?" He said he couldn't.

I gave Shark an original framed gel of Bambi, which had cost quite a bit but it was worth it to see the smile of joy that came to his face. With some difficulty I had collected the complete films of Rossano Brazzi on thirty-seven leather-bound videocassettes for Narges, since I knew she had a deep affection for the actor. But she didn't come to the gift-opening party. When I asked Shark where she was he drew me aside.

"Gary, I'm concerned about the future of our film," he said very soberly.

I was shaken. "Why? What do you mean?"

"Something happened with Narges the night of the rescue—"

"What?"

"I don't want to go into it. It's too sick. And you see, that's the thing. You're part of my new, decent life, Gary. Narges, I'm afraid, is part of the old. Her cocaine usage—" Shark shook his head.

"Yes, I know. I've suspected that she uses it." I'd tried coke, but hadn't liked it. "It's sad."

"It's worse than sad, Gary. Narges is a very sick woman, if not genuinely evil. She's a selfish, promiscuous slut and I simply will not play her game anymore. I won't use drugs with her or be her sexual toy. As a result, I believe that as soon as we get back to L.A. she's going to pull the plug on the film."

In a way I wasn't surprised. With a woman as unstable as Narges it had crossed my mind before that something like this could happen. So I was not unprepared. "We don't need her, Shark," I said. "I talked to my dad in Houston just a little while ago. He'd heard some bad things about you, you know, and was never too keen on my making this film with you. But today—the State Department blackout be damned—when I told him what you'd done, he said: 'You tell Shark Trager he is my kind of American.' "

Narges Pahlavi-Bardahl

A production assistant—acting on Shark's orders, I discovered later— had given me a powerful Lebanese sleeping tablet as I went to bed on Christmas Eve. I did not awaken till the following evening. When

I did Shark was sitting on the edge of the bed. "Merry Christmas," he said, and for the first time in months kissed me full on the lips. Then he showed me Gary's gift and I clapped my hands. "But I adore Rossano Brazzi! How did he know?"

"Listen, kiddo," he said, "I want you to know how rotten I feel about sticking that gun in your mouth—"

"Let's not talk about it now, Shark, it's Christmas," I said, and placed *South Pacific* in the VCR.

As the tape began Shark caressed my shoulder, and continued: "But when you mentioned that Orange County Jail episode—"

"I was mad from basing, and from stifled desire for you. Still, there is no excuse. I had no right to examine your rage therapy file."

Shark stared blankly at the TV. "The thing is," he said, "I lied to Ernst. That's not even what happened. What actually happened was far worse. I wasn't raped by black men—"

"Oh, look at the South Seas photography, isn't it stunning?" I said, trying to change the subject. But there was no stopping his confession.

"There was *another* boy in the county jail that day," he said, as if staring into his memory. "Eighteen, I guess, though he looked much younger. Fair, blond, you'd even have to say beautiful—a kind of Orange County suburban Billy Budd." Shark continued with difficulty as the memory became painful. "It quickly became apparent that a number of older prisoners, hardened criminals most of whom happened to be dark-skinned, were going to have their way with this young blond Christ figure. And I had to decide. Do you understand what I'm saying?"

"No," I told him.

"I had to choose. Two large black prisoners held his pale body spread-eagle against the iron bars as their fellows repeatedly impaled him. My choice was to join his crucifiers . . . or to join him on the cross. I picked the former, and proved myself according to their brute animal law."

"It was a long time ago, Shark," I said to him. "It sounds to me like you really had no choice."

"He died that night," Shark said, staring out the window at the cobalt sky. "He and I shared a cell. He'd been injured internally but bore it in silence. 'I'm sorry,' I whispered to him, as he lay on the bunk above mine. 'Please . . . can you forgive me?' He said nothing. And in the empty silence I realized I couldn't hear his breath."

Shark caressed me mechanically, lost in his own pain.

"It sounds like *Sophie's Choice*," I told him. "Perhaps the stakes were not quite as grueling but the principle remains the same. Whichever way you had gone, it was still going to be very bad."

"Yes." He stared absently at the TV as Rossano began to sing "Some Enchanted Evening."

In a moment he said, "Are you in love with my father?"

The question startled me. "No, no. I was only trying to make you jealous, that's all it was."

"Then you prefer me." He slid his hand between my legs.

"You know I do. There's no comparison."

Soon we made love. "Oh Shark, I've missed this so," I cried as he moved into me.

That night he loved me more tenderly yet thoroughly than he ever had before. For a while I really felt that after all the weeks of strain and tension, capped by a momentary lapse into madness, we were at last back together where we should be once again.

Of course, I see now he was only giving me something to remember him by.

23/**Redeemed**
(1984–1985)

Drake Brewster

Shark and Greg came to get me at the Beirut hospital for the flight home. But Shark seemed funny, distant and all, and wouldn't be alone with me, which pissed me off, 'cause I felt we needed to talk.

On the plane I caught him by the toilets and said, "Hey, look, man. Don't try and lay the whole thing off on me. You were ready to fuck and kill 'em too."

And he said, "We'll talk about it later, Drake," and went and sat back down beside that simp Gary.

Then I saw him talking to Mac, and when he finished he and Mac shook hands, but Mac looked pale.

Mac Trager

Shark sat down beside me and said, "Look, Dad, I'm still sorry about what happened with Drake and me. It was an aberration, there's no doubt about it, a kind of flashback to my old psychotic behavior. But the fact remains that you are dogshit disguised as a human being, and I never want to see you again. So here's the deal. I'll give you fifty thousand a year for the rest of your life to keep your mouth shut about what happened. All right?"

Narges Pahlavi-Bardahl

Shark began acting strange on the flight home. I still felt so delicious from our lovemaking that I wanted to cuddle. But when I touched him he cringed.

Then as we set down in Los Angeles he said, "Narges, Gary's father is going to buy you out of the picture. You are dog vomit disguised as a human being, and I never want to see you again. As you may know, Earl Schnell is an extremely wealthy and powerful man with heavy Washington connections. I know what your immigration status is, dear heart. If you try and make waves I will see that you are deported back to Teheran."

I was too stunned to speak.

Drake Brewster

I was trying to find Shark after I went through Customs when Greg Spivey came up and handed me an envelope. "Shark wants you to have this," he said.

It was a thousand bucks in cash along with a note. "You are out of my life, you sick fuck," the note said. "And lest you think for a minute that you can fuck with me in any way, Drake, you should know that I have the number of a secret international feminist revenge organization. One phone call, in which I explain to them how many rapes you actually committed and how lightly you got off, and these women will stop at nothing until you are castrated and dead. Nuf said?"

I was angry and hurt. I went over to Mac and Narges and said, "Hey look, I admit I got a little rowdy but—" And they both cut me dead and went out to a limo that was waiting and drove off. I had to take the fuckin' bus, then walk up into Bel-Air. When I reached the house all my shit was piled by the gate.

Gary Schnell

"It's for the best," I told Shark when he told me he'd bid adieu to Narges and Drake and his father. "It's too bad about your dad though. There's nothing sadder than watching the love go out of a family."

"My father abused me," Shark said out of the blue, as we watched *Fantasia* at my place in Bel-Air that night. "He used to whip my bare ass in the garage . . . right by the freezer where my mother died."

"It's okay, Shark," I said and we hugged. "We'll be your family now."

Then we got in our twin beds and watched the rest of *Fantasia*, and lay there talking about the special effects for hours in the dark.

Kathy Petro

I remember when *Blue Light* was filming in Fountain Valley because they did this segment on "Hollywood Tonight" about how it was Shark's first film since *Red Surf* and everything. I was kind of half-watching the TV and half-trying to come up with a title for my book.

Gray had encouraged me to write about my battle with drugs since

I'd been a role model for so many American women and everything, but it was scary at first because I wasn't really a writer. I thought about working with someone but then I decided: No, I should tell what happened in my own words. So I sat down at the typewriter and it just poured out, all of it: my grass and acid days including Jeff Stuben's tragic death, which certainly was a warning to the teenagers of today. Then my abusive heroin-fogged relationship with Derek Horus—I could use his name since he was dead. I told about the cocaine and mood medications I'd used when I was married to Brian—though I had to tread softly there since Brian was still very powerful. I ended on a note of hope and new beginnings, my pain killers left behind forever, thanks to Ernst Kolon and the infinite love and patience of Gray, the world's most handsome, understanding man.

I was jotting down titles: *Smiling on the Outside, Dying on the Inside; First You Smile; I'm Smiling as Hard as I Can;* finally just settling on *Behind the Smile*, though I didn't really like it that much, when the TV showed Sharon Shay being interviewed on the set in Fountain Valley. And I mean I couldn't help noticing that she did kind of look like me at sixteen. And I was kind of thinking: Well, Shark's up to his old tricks again, but at least this time it's flattering, he'd not trying to "get" me or something. And just then Gray came in, looking very pale and even thinner than usual, though he'd lost a lot of weight lately—from working so hard, he said.

"Kathy, I've got cancer," he said just like that. "I just got the test results. It's inoperable. I'm going to die."

I thought he was joking at first. When I realized he wasn't I just came unglued.

Joey Joel

After Beirut the filming in Orange County was fairly uneventful. But the crisis atmosphere of the Lebanese adventure had actually served to bring us all together. Something magical happened on *Blue Light* once we were back in the States. We just appreciated America and each other in a whole new way, and we really became a kind of family. We were always hugging—everybody, the cast, the crew, even the Teamsters. The entire production was bathed in a warm glow—Gary's jealousy over Sharon and me just completely vanished. Of course, what had begun as brute tension-relieving sex had became something else entirely as Sharon and I fell deeply and genuinely in love. "I'm just glad you kids are happy," Gary said, like a benevolent father.

If Gary was our father, then Shark had come to exist for us on an even higher level. Of course, we all knew about his heroism in Beirut, though it hadn't been revealed in the media yet. I don't know how to put it—he just exuded this wondrous joy and love. I'm reluctant to use religious terminology because Shark would be the first to insist he was "just another guy from the neighborhood." But in our hearts, I think, he became something like our fondest hopes of what God might be. Knowing all that he'd been through especially, there was just no way you couldn't love the man.

Sharon Shay

I don't think there was a dry eye at the wrap party. By then we all knew from the dailies how good the film was going to be. If it failed we were all prepared to turn our backs on Hollywood forever.

Greg Spivey

There was a kind of rapturous aura about those final weeks of filming. Though I pride myself on being a bit cynical, I have to say that *Blue Light* remains the ecstatic high point of my career. On occasion I would reflect on Shark's seething dementia during the final days of *Red Surf*. But that seemed a lifetime away, the madness of another man. Shark Trager truly had been reborn.

I will never forget the afternoon Gary and Shark and I drove down to Costa Mesa. It was a few days before the end of filming and Shark wanted to have the wrap party in the drive-in where he had been born. But when we got there, just as the sun was setting, we found that the drive-in was gone.

Gary Schnell

It was an indescribably poignant moment. Shark had rhapsodized about the Flying Wing Drive-In all the way down—the neon, the fading mural, an early romantic experience he'd had there during a Doris Day film, his charming contention that he recalled *Gun Crazy* on the screen the night he was born. But when we reached the site there was nothing but a plowed-up field and a sign announcing the imminent construction of the Caligari Mall.

"Video," Shark said. "In a few years there won't be any theaters left anywhere, except small ones in museums. Everything will be rented on cassette, watched on a small, stupid box. We're a dying breed, gentlemen. The makers of the last true mythic iconography. Soon everything will be reduced to the level of a 'Hazel' rerun."

Saddened, we drove back to Fountain Valley, where we held the wrap party at a drive-in church.

Greg Spivey

The post-production period was long because of all the special effects, and Shark worked closely with Gary and the editors. Gary really is a gifted, intuitive filmmaker, but at that point anyway he was still insecure and always deferred to Shark's judgment. "He's like my big brother," Gary would say. They were always hugging and going around with their arms over each other's shoulders, the way a couple of kids might. There was absolutely nothing gay about it—it was a totally pure kind of Mark Twain buddy thing—though it was clear that Gary really idolized Shark.

We had a rough cut by May of '85 and it was just the best thing that any of us had ever seen. So Shark showed it to Bill Kemmer.

Bill Kemmer

Well, I was blown away. That screening was beyond all doubt the most affecting moment of my Hollywood life. I was really not prepared. I don't know what I expected . . . but when Deem rose from the ashes of Beirut and melted the missiles midair . . . Well, it touched something deep inside me, some primal wish which I guess we all have, which goes back to childhood, the wish of: Please, God, make it all right.

I hugged Shark afterwards. "I love you," I said, which to be frank I hadn't said to anyone for quite some time, including, sadly, my wife. But I was saying it a lot, and meaning it, after *Blue Light*. That's the kind of movie it is.

Greg Spivey

Bill was so swept away by the film it almost seemed crass to discuss money at all. It was just understood the film was going to be huge and Shark made a very good distribution deal.

Gary Schnell

My parents flew out to see the film and my mom just sobbed at the ending. Even my dad was misty-eyed and said, "Son, I'm proud of you."

Then he shook my hand real hard, but I said, "Oh heck, Dad, let's hug." And we did, even though my dad was a real tough guy, kind of a cross between Lyndon Johnson and Robert Duvall.

Then he and Shark hugged. "You steered my boy right," Dad said to him.

My mom was just wild about Shark. She had invented the first polyester pantsuit back in 1964, which had brought in a fortune, though the pantsuit business had waned in recent years. Shark kept telling her, "They'll come back, Sue Bee. Everything comes back."

"Well, you certainly know about movies," Mom would say. "Maybe you know about fashion too."

Mom hadn't been to L.A. for years so we all went out sight-seeing. We went to Disneyland, and to the Chinese Theater, and then one day we drove up the coast because Mom wanted to see Malibu. I was driving the Corniche convertible past the Colony when suddenly Shark said, "Hold it, pull over." And he got out and went up to a blond-haired surfer who was gassing up his Corvette at the Mobil station.

Woody Hazzard

I crapped for a second when I saw it was Shark. I almost didn't recognize him at first, and it wasn't because he'd changed that much physically. He looked good, healthier than during *Red Surf* by a long shot, but more than that he'd changed in his eyes, in his vibes, in his soul. That was really what I felt as he opened his arms like he wanted to hug me. It wasn't like the time at Sunset beach where he'd just been manipulating me. I sensed it was real now—he didn't want anything.

We hugged a long time. "Woody," he said. "I'm so sorry, man. I'm so fuckin' sorry. I still love you so much, man. I really fuckin' do."

"I know you do," I said. "And I love you too. Shit, you were my best fuckin' friend for years."

We talked for a while and he invited me to the premier of *Blue Light*. Then he asked about Brian, if Brian still hated his guts, and I said I was pretty sure he did, and we both laughed about that. Then he asked about Kathy, mentioning that he'd kind of resolved things with her at the Kolon Clinic, and I said, "Yeah, that's what I heard."

"Then you're still in touch her?"

"Oh yeah."

"How's she doing?"

"As well as can be expected, I guess," I told him.

"What do you mean?" he asked.

And I said, "Oh, Jeez, I guess you don't know. Gray died."

Kathy Petro

I remember the day that Shark's card arrived by messenger. I was walking aimlessly around that suddenly enormous and empty Stone Canyon house in a numb stupor as I had been for weeks. The answering machine was clogged with messages from my New York publisher about how well the book was doing, and how they knew it was a difficult time for me and everything, but couldn't I try and pull myself together enough to do Merv this Thursday night?

Well, no. There was no way I could do Merv this Thursday or any Thursday ever. How could I laugh effusively at Merv's stupid jokes when the only man I'd ever truly loved was dead?

"Dear Kathy," the card read. "I just found out. I won't devalue the profundity of your grief by facilely trying to cheer you up. Know simply that you are now and forever, with no strings attached, in my heart. You are sunshine itself, Kathy. I know that warm days will come once again to your life." It was signed: "Your friend, Shark," with a P.S.: "If there's anything ever I can do, no matter how trivial, please don't hesitate to call." And then there was a number, which I recognized as a Bel-Air exchange.

I though it was sweet, but for some reason I didn't understand I tore up the card.

Greg Spivey

The premiere of course is history now. At the Village in Westwood, klieg lights, the works—Mastodon pulled out the stops. The Village, of course, is right across from the Bruin, the site of Shark's *Götterdämmerung*. But the only reference I heard him make to that debacle was a jaunty remark to Gary: "Just don't stab any critics in the lobby, Gary. That's how Tony Borgia lost his mother and his one good review."

"I'd never stab my mother, Shark," Gary said. "I love her. In fact, I don't intend to marry until I find a gal at least half as good as her."

As it turned out Shark didn't need to worry. The critical praise was virtually unanimous. *Blue Light* was one of those rare cinematic experiences that literally pleased everybody. It was above all a *film* film, accessible and emotionally involving to the average man or woman in the street, yet so well made, so chock-full or *purposeful* filmic allusions, such an astonishing tour de force of cinematic high art, that even the most erudite and élitist of the critics were completely overwhelmed. The single bad review, as I recall, was the unconscionable hatchet job by Edmund Himmler in the *New York Review of Reviews*. But then he's always been the quintessentially vicious critic—a sour, repressed and loveless male spinster with a bitter ax to grind.

Edmund Himmler, *New York Review of Reviews,* July 16, 1985

FROM "BLUE KITSCH"

If the mothership in *Close Encounters* resembles a lighting fixture in a Las Vegas casino, if E.T. resembles a repulsive bug anyone in his right mind would squash with his shoe, then surely "Deem," the cloying alien protagonist in Shark Trager's latest cinematic production *Blue Light*, resembles nothing so much as a chrome-plated stool sample with a fruitily pouting mouth and a pair of simpering girl's blue eyes.

Are American audiences so starved for reassurance in the face of imminent nuclear catastrophe that they will embrace this nauseating swirl of demented treacle? Yes, apparently. For the film has become this year's cheap catharsis, a tearjerking resolution of the East/West conflict for scared, stupid people everywhere.

Gary Schnell

Shark shook his head and sighed when he finished reading the Edmund Himmler review. "This was written by a very sick man. You can feel the pain between the lines. I have nothing but pity and genuine compassion for him."

But Shark wouldn't let me read it. "Gary, it would be like letting you pet a mad, snarling dog."

Of course, by then one bad review didn't mean much anyway. What had started at the premiere just continued on and on: the audiences crying and applauding afterwards, carrying the sense of joy and hope out of the theater and into their lives, just as I'd always prayed they would.

In a strange way the figures just didn't seem to matter. I mean, *of course* it was breaking every house record. *Of course* it had the top grossing opening weekend in the history of film. *Of course* it was going to pass *E.T.* as the top grossing film of all time. But *so what?* To use the obvious religious analogy, you might as well try and put a monetary value on the second coming of Jesus.

Bill Kemmer

I knew it was going to be a monster hit, but not even I was prepared for what happened. And the merchandising—Jesus God! How many Deem dolls were sold the first month? They couldn't keep them in stock.

It was just a phenomenon, and I must say my heart was full for Shark. To say it was a comeback wouldn't quite describe it. As much as people had despised him after *Red Surf*, the entire industry worshiped him now. Thank God we'd closed a first-look production deal with Shark on the basis of the screening, a very generous deal, because once the picture passed the hundred million mark in a record twenty-one days he could have written his own ticket at any studio in town. Of course, the media was clamoring for interviews with Shark and Gary, all of which they refused—Gary out of shyness, I think. As for Shark, well, I can't say why.

Greg Spivey

It all got to be too much for Shark. He was happy, of course, though he would always insist it was Gary's picture. "I'm just a businessman. Gary's the artist." Which was both true and not true, because *Blue Light* in its look and texture and overall production design was as much a Shark Trager film as *White Desert*, or for that matter *Red Surf*.

I think Shark found the sheer velocity of the success disorienting. He'd had his blockbusters in the seventies, God knows, but what was happening with *Blue Light* was really on a whole other level. "I don't want to lose my balance," he said. "I can't let that happen this time."

So he checked into a Zen monastery up near Big Sur for a week of brutal, no-frills meditation. It was while he was there, incommunicado, that the inevitable happened. Despite all the government attempts to suppress it, the story of Shark's Beirut rescue finally exploded through the media.

At just the point where *Blue Light* was beginning to taper off ever so slightly, Shark Trager became a national hero.

24 / **American Hero**
(1985)

Kathy Petro

I was in bed one morning watching the *Today Show*, and Juanita was bringing me my breakfast, when the story came on about how Shark had rescued those Sunday school teachers in Beirut. And it was so thrilling I found myself saying to Juanita, "I know him. He's an old friend."

I guess that was when I knew Shark had really and truly changed. The old Shark would just never have done anything that heroic—he would have been too concerned with saving his own skin. So it really made me think: Was I being selfish myself by grieving over Gray so long? Whatever happened to my vows to help others and everything? Wasn't that why I'd written the book in the first place, so that maybe I could save at least just one other person from having to go through what I'd gone through? Maybe I should be out on the lecture circuit or something instead of just moping around all the time.

Yet I still found myself in a deep, numb depression every time I thought about Gray. So that afternoon I walked into Westwood, mainly just to get out of the house, and ended up seeing *Blue Light*.

Well, the film just did something to me. It was exciting and suspenseful—especially when they fired off all the nuclear missiles and you were thinking: My God, what can save us now? But there was also just so much love in it. It was just filled up with human compassion for everyone, even the Russians, who like everyone else were just longing for love.

But the ending especially really broke my heart. When Deem and Patti go out through space and vanish into the endless blue light it just reminded me of heaven. I don't know if Shark and Gary meant it that way, but that's how I took it. And it seemed to be saying: Yes, there is a place where people go when they die, where lovers can be together forever. I know it sounds corny, but it really made me see

378

that yes, I would see Gray again, that once you've loved someone that love will always be, since life really has no beginning or end.

I stepped into the Westwood sunshine feeling calm and healed.

Greg Spivey

As the story began breaking the White House called, and they were referred to the Zen monastery, which refused to summon Shark to the phone. When Shark found out several days later that the president had been trying to reach him, and he hadn't been informed, he became quite upset.

Roshi Guy Yokomoto

"Why didn't you tell me Ronald Reagan was calling?" Shark said to me.

"Because it was merely another distraction," I told him. "Why add one more to your monkey mind?"

"But it was the president," he said.

"That's neither here nor there," I told him. "If it wasn't the president it would be something else, which you would judge either good or bad. You are trapped in duality. Go back and sit!"

But he left. He was in love with his delusions.

Greg Spivey

Shark told me later the Zen roshi tried to "put a hex" on him. I said, "Come on, Shark, Zen Buddhists don't do things like that," but he insisted it was true.

"He told me there was no such thing as success and failure, but that since I obviously thought there was, I was doomed."

"He said that? Doomed?"

"Words to that effect."

"It's envy," I told Shark. "He's probably got an unsold screenplay in a drawer somewhere."

"You know," Shark said, "in his case I don't think so."

He went on to tell me about his meditation experience: "The oddest thing, Greg, was that as my mind began to empty, one of the last things to go was that ancient image of Kathy as she looked in the car the night we kissed at the Flying Wing Drive-In in 1964."

I was reacting to this with appropriate solemnity when the phone rang. As we expected, it was President Reagan.

Bill Kemmer

Shark told me later it was a classic bit of Reagan backtracking. The president contended that his previous request that Shark understand the need "not to rock the boat" in Lebanon had been based on a "bad briefing from George [Schultz]." With a clearer understanding of the full situation, the president said, he would be honored to present Shark with a Davy Crockett Medal of Bravery in a special Oval Office ceremony. Naturally everyone who'd been involved would be invited to attend: the Sunday school teachers . . . and Narges and Drake and Mac.

Mac Trager

I was in my new condo in Marina Del Rey when Shark's secretary called about going to Washington. She was that gal who later wrote *Teamster Secretary* before she was killed,* and I'll tell you she did sound tough on the phone. She said if I "behaved" there was a bonus in it for me. And if I didn't I might find my legs crushed by a truck.

Drake Brewster

I was mopping floors at a downtown gym when his secretary called me. She said I'd get a thousand bucks if I stayed in line at the White House. But I'd been thinking about Shark's threat to have me offed by some feminist hit squad and realized it was bullshit. So I said, "Yeah, I'll be there, no problem." But I was thinking, what with Shark making millions off *Blue Light,* and me not even getting a shared screenplay credit for all the work I'd done, the time had definitely come to put on the squeeze.

Narges Pahlavi-Bardahl

I was basing with a famous actor when Shark's secretary called me. She threatened me with deportation if I didn't "smile and act like a lady" as I met President Reagan.

---

* Stacy Joy Decker, who stepped into an empty elevator shaft after a 1986 "Nightline" appearance in which she defended her best-selling account of Teamster violence and corruption, including the sensational allegation that her one-time boss, labor leader Jimmy Hoffa, had "bragged during sex" of having arranged the "mob execution" of John F. Kennedy. Shark Trager, for whom Decker worked for less than a month, perhaps best characterized the visually kittenish but hard secretary-turned-author as "a cross between Joey Heatherton and Lee J. Cobb."

I said, "We'll see about that," and she asked me how I would like to hobble off the plane in Teheran with both of my legs in casts.

I hung up on her and thought to myself: What a scene it would be if right in the middle of the ceremony, in front of the cameras and the president and everyone, I blurted out: "Shark Trager is a madman. He was going to blow my head off, and his henchman Drake Brewster was going to sodomize Shark's father—I'll tell you what really happened." I amused myself with this scenario as I went back to basing with the famous actor.

Gary Schnell

Shark told me he read Kathy Petro's book *Behind the Smile* on the plane to Washington. He said he was deeply moved by her candid recital of her struggle with various drugs, and at the same time profoundly grateful for her discretion. Reading between the lines, he said, he knew that when she spoke of a "long-time admirer," or "a man from my teenage years who still had a crush on me," that of course she was alluding to him.

At one point she wrote of "a man who did something really awful to me once which filled me with resentment for decades to come. But I see now that I *chose* to be resentful. He was only trying to love me, but like so many of us, did not know how to show love." I asked Shark if that was about him too, and he said it was, but he wouldn't tell me what it was he'd done to her.

Narges Pahlavi-Bardahl

I began drinking heavily at the hotel bar in Washington because I hadn't slept for several days and my nerves were shot. Then the Secret Service came to get me and the sidewalk was wet and I slipped and skinned both of my knees.

Mac Trager

I met Shark in the waiting room outside the Oval Office. He was polite but distant, you know. Then the hens he'd saved started showing up, gushing all over him. And he was smiling away like some kind of goodie-two-shoes, which kind of made me sick. Then Drake arrived in a cheap-looking suit, and Shark barely said hello to him. Then the White House staffers started telling us how the thing was going to go, and then we heard some commotion and there came Narges, drunk as a skunk and all riled up.

Drake Brewster

Narges was real fucked up. These Secret Service guys were trying to calm her down as they led her in. But she was saying, "Get your hands off of me. What are you trying to do, cop a feel?" So Shark went over to her and said something, and she piped right down.

Narges Pahlavi-Bardahl

Shark was deliberately playing with my mind, I see that now. He said, "You know, Narges, I've been thinking a lot lately of how great it was when you sat on my face in Palm Springs. I was thinking how it might be fun to try that again back at your hotel after this ceremony. Of course, if you're in a foul mood . . ."

So I pulled myself together, for he was turning me on. The way he was looking into my eyes, it was just like the old days.

Mac Trager

The door finally opened and there was Ronald Reagan. Shark shook hands with the president and the two of them talked while the staffers showed everybody where to stand. Then Drake went up and interrupted Shark and the president.

Drake Brewster

I went up and squeezed the back of Shark's neck, like we were buddies, except I did it real hard. I could tell Shark was in pain but he kept smiling at Reagan. "He's a good man, sir," I said to the president. "You should send him in commando-style to take care of Khadafi once and for all. Send us both in, sir." I grinned at Shark. "We could do to Khadafi what we were fixin' to do that night in Beirut before those Shiites came along." I laughed and winked at Shark, knowing he'd get it, but the Gipper wouldn't.

"Well, I'm certainly open to any suggestions you fellas might have," the Gipper said, and kind of chuckled.

"Drake's a sociopath, Mr. President," Shark said, and slid his hand down my back. "I'm afraid you'd find his suggestions demented at best." Then, without Reagan being able to see it, Shark jammed his hand down the back of my pants and for a second I thought he was gonna dig his finger right up my butthole. So I quit squeezing his neck real fast.

"Well, I've got nothing against a sociopath per se," the Gipper said, "as long he's on our team."

Suddenly we heard something rip and Narges let out a yelp.

Mac Trager

I thought it was funny myself. The staffers were trying to move Narges back by the Sunday school teachers, but she kind of stumbled and caught her dress on the wing of an eagle statuette on the president's desk. Then she whirled around real fast and her skirt tore clean off. She wasn't wearing any panties.

Drake Brewster

There were already a bunch of photographers there, but some staff guy rushed up, waving his arms, saying, "No pictures. Come on, fellas. Give us a break on this one."

Narges was freaked out, trying to pick up her skirt. But one of the Sunday school teachers was standing on it, and when Narges picked it up, it ripped again. Finally she got it and the Secret Service guys hustled her out.

Shark was saying something to Reagan about what a pathetic case Narges was, I guess. 'Cause Reagan was shaking his head with this look of understanding pity.

Narges Pahlavi-Bardahl

I was so humiliated I had to go and base. They gave me a maid's dress to put on and I went straight to the nearest bathroom, and dug out my torch and stash.

Within moments I took what I truly believe was my very last hit of cocaine. For no sooner had I done so than I noticed a *small human mouth* growing in the palm of my hand! A mouth I recognized at once as that of my adored Rossano Brazzi. "Narges," the little mouth instructed me gently but firmly in the only voice I was still capable of hearing. "Narges, flush that cocaine down the toilet."

So I did.

Drake Brewster

After Narges split, everything went okay. The Gipper said a few words about Shark being an example of what made this country great. Then he handed Shark that bronze medal with a picture of Duke Wayne in a coonskin cap at the Alamo on it, and the cameras clicked away. Shark had to stand there for a long time posing with the president. But at a certain point he started staring out the window real hard. There was something else going on outside, a bunch of broads on the White House lawn.

Mac Trager

I saw what Shark was looking at. There were a bunch of gals out there with Nancy Reagan. And one of 'em was Kathy Petro.

Kathy Petro

It was a gathering of women from all over the world who shared the First Lady's concern with the problem of drug abuse. I'd been really honored by the invitation, and by the kind things Mrs. Reagan had to say about my book. I had heard that Shark was going to receive the Davy Crockett medal, but I didn't really know it would be the exact day and hour that I was there on the grounds. The speechmaking part of the gathering was going on a lot longer than I'd expected, so I finally slipped away to go find a phone since I had a bookstore appearance scheduled for later that day and could tell I was going to be late. As I crossed the portico I head the president of Mexico's wife saying into the microphone that she had brought "a gift from the people of Mexico," which might "come in handy" on the Reagans' Santa Barbara ranch, but I didn't really pay much attention because suddenly right there ahead of me was Shark.

I was so stunned I just stopped in my tracks. He was looking at me and I couldn't take my eyes off of his.

In the background I kind of heard Mrs. Reagan saying, "Well, I'm sure Ronnie and I can find something for him to do."

And the First Lady of Mexico said, "Well, you know, he used to be a movie star too, Mrs. Reagan."

And Nancy said, "Oh my. I'd better not tell Ronnie that. He's still trying to live down *Bedtime for Bonzo.*"

Then there was polite laughter, but it was like the sound in a distant dream, for the only reality was the man who stood before me.

The air was crisp and I didn't have a wrap. Maybe that's why my nipples were getting hard, I don't know. Or maybe it was the way Shark was looking at me as he stepped toward me. He looked so handsome that afternoon. So youthful and just . . . really so good. And his eyes were clear and filled with a kind of pure hunger.

I was trembling as he reached me, and he didn't say a word. I thought he was just going to kiss me, but instead he took my hand. Waves of raw euphoria washed through me as his fingertips touched mine.

He lead me into the White House, along an empty corridor, my heart buzzing like a hummingbird's wings. Then he thrust open a door and we entered a room with a huge old bed and an ancient portrait of Abraham Lincoln.

There he kissed me and I kissed him. And soon we couldn't get enough of each other.

Elliot Bernstein

Shark told me that as he made love with Kathy in the Lincoln bedroom he had a *"Vertigo* experience." He said they were both so fevered with desire they did not bother to remove their clothes. Rather, he held Kathy from behind against the high bed as she hiked her skirt, and he pulled his erect member from his fly. Though the scene might have appeared raunchily pornographic from a "cinematic" point of view, subjectively it was anything but, Shark emphasized. As he and Kathy connected there, he felt a swirling sensation, he said. And although they remained fixed in place against the bed, moving only in a rhythmic, locomotive manner, the walls began to move around them as if they were in a diorama composed of rear-projection screens, the room giving way, Shark said, to other times and other places. As Kathy turned her head so he could kiss her, they would be back in the car at the Flying Wing Drive-In in 1964. Then, as he thrust still deeper inside her, he would see the windswept grassy hill on Maui where her bare breasts had pressed his chest and he'd longed to take her ten years before. Then, as she gasped, they were there in her bathroom in Newport Beach—his teenage fantasy of climbing in the window and making love to her there made real at last. Then that bathroom gave way to the one in Derek Horus's house on the French Riviera as it was the night he'd come to "rescue" her in 1973. Then they were other places: in the James Dean A-frame in Sherman Oaks, in the Gold Coast bedroom, in the loft of the Ray-Mar Theater—places Kathy had never been, but where Shark had poignantly, fervently masturbated to his mental image of her. All of these seemingly futile lost moments were now redeemed.

Kathy Petro

Something really beautiful and extraordinary happened as Shark and I made love there in that quaint old bedroom. But I still feel a little crazy even talking about it. All I know is that I got so far out that I guess I began to hallucinate, the whole Lincoln bedroom and everything just dissolving away. Suddenly we'd be in that car at the drive-in when we were fourteen years old! Then we'd be on this hill on Maui doing all the things we might have done if Daddy hadn't been there. Then we'd be in my bathroom in Newport Beach the night he made the peeping-Tom movie of me. We'd be making ravenous love and I'd look over his shoulder and see his Bell and Howell movie camera all glistening and masculine on the pink tile, and I'd feel this terrible welling-up of ancient terror and excitement and a million other emotions all at once.

Then we'd be in some weird A-frame kind of place I'd never seen before, and suddenly for some reason he would look like James Dean.

And, I don't know, it just began to occur to me that Shark *was* every man I'd every really wanted. He was James Dean and Errol Flynn and Harvey Keitel and everybody else you could ever think of all rolled into one virile ball. And he was blowing those emotional floodgates—which I'd kept so tightly shut when Gray was still alive—right off their hinges! There was no reason why we shouldn't be together now just like this forever! Shark knew it and I knew it—that's why we were devouring each other.

Then suddenly we heard this braying sound—you know, this donkey going: *Hee-haw!* And for some reason my heart just stopped.

Drake Brewster

I'd watched Shark turn from the Oval Office window and ask the Gipper where the men's room was. The Gipper'd pointed to a door and when Shark ducked out I'd followed, thinking it might be my only chance to get him alone.

But instead of going to the men's room Shark cut out across the White House lawn and I soon saw why. Up there on the walkway he intercepted Kathy Petro. I hung back and watched as he took her hand and led her inside. Even at thirty paces you could feel the sex vibes, so I knew what they were up to. I was about to go in after them when the thing with the broads on the lawn broke up. I hid behind a pillar as they all trooped back into the White House, the Gipper's wife among 'em.

When the coast was finally **clear** I went in to look for Shark. It was eerie in a way, this long empty hallway. You could hear the broads yakking in some distant room somewhere, but there was no one in the immediate area, no Secret Service or nothing. I started up the hall and then I heard Shark and Kathy getting it on. You know, gasps from her and that slippedy-sloppedy sound. Why the broads hadn't heard 'em as they passed that room I don't know—I guess 'cause they were yakking so much.

So I went up and opened the door real quiet-like and there they were, doing it dog-style against this big old bed. It was pretty hot and I was getting turned on—they hadn't seen me yet—but I was just about to say something when I heard this fuckin' donkey bray! I looked back and saw this donkey—which I found out later was a gift to the Reagans from the president of Mexico's wife—just standing there in the door, like he was looking around for something. Some guy was running up from the lawn, yelling, "Come here, you stupid donkey."

Then I swear that donkey's head jerked as he looked past me and saw Kathy Petro. At just that moment she was looking back at me over her shoulder so that donkey got a real good look at her face.

Kathy Petro

I looked back when I heard the braying and saw Drake Brewster standing in the door. Before I could even react to his presence I saw the donkey behind him, and the next thing I knew the donkey was charging just the way a bull might.

Drake Brewster

It was crazy. That donkey just made a bee-line straight for Kathy Petro. I barely stepped out of the way. Shark saw it coming too, and pulled away from Kathy just as that donkey barreled into the Lincoln bedroom. For a second or two Kathy was still there braced against the bed with her butt exposed and I thought sure as shit that donkey was gonna nail her. 'Cause you couldn't help but notice it had a hard-on about two feet long. It brayed again. And Kathy screamed.

Kathy Petro

Right at the very last second Shark pushed me up across the bed. It was the only thing he could do. That donkey was coming too fast to stop it. I screamed as the donkey put his front feet on the bed, almost stepping on my hands, like he was trying to mount me. I shivered with revulsion as I felt his bulbous you-know-what touch my calf.

Shark lunged across the bed as best he could with his pants still down, so he could pull me to safety. And Drake, bless his heart, grabbed that beast by the tail.

Drake Brewster

It was just instinct, I guess. I knew that thing would kill her. But grabbing the tail was a mistake. The son of a bitch kicked me back into the bureau, where I cracked the mirror with the back of my skull.

Then he turned on me, and for a second I thought he was gonna try and mount *me* or some weird deal like that. But he brayed again—and it was worse than any sound in a horror movie. And then he started kicking that big old bed apart.

Kathy Petro

Shark was still pulling me across the bed as the donkey began kicking the frame. I screamed as the mattress and box springs fell to the floor. For a second I was trapped there in this big hollow as the donkey kicked the frame again. But at last Shark pulled me to safety and we ducked through a door that led to the next room.

Shark leaned against the door, both our hearts pounding, and said, "Go get help. I'm going back for Drake."

"No," I pleaded. "Don't go in there again, not by yourself. I'll be right back."

Suddenly the kicking in the Lincoln bedroom stopped, which was somehow more unnerving than anything. What was that donkey doing to Drake?

"Run," Shark said. "Hurry!"

So I ducked out to the hall, smoothing down my skirt, trying to collect myself. I couldn't understand why someone hadn't heard the racket and already come, but that part of the White House just seemed completely deserted.

I hurried up the hallway and went around a corner and saw all the women I'd been with having lunch in this large sunny room at the end of the hall. As I entered the room everyone stopped eating and stared, since I was quite a mess, I guess, all freaked out and everything plus probably reeking of sex. Mrs. Reagan approached me and said, "Kathy, what on earth—"

But before I could say a word I heard another *hee-haw* and looked back and saw that donkey charging into the room.

Drake Brewster

I was picking myself up, my head bleeding from the mirror, when Shark burst back into the Lincoln bedroom.

"Where's Hector?" he said. By then I guess he'd put it together that it was Hector the donkey they'd used in *Looking for Lupe*, which he explained later had been negatively conditioned to Kathy's picture on a T-shirt the donkey had been looking at during a fire in a stable.

"I guess he split," I told Shark. "Must've gone out that way into the hall."

"Oh shit," Shark said, and he and I ducked out to the hall.

Then we heard the broads scream and tore off around the corner. We reached this ballroom where all the broads were just in time to see Hector kick a Secret Service man back across the floor. Then Hector charged Kathy, the Gipper's wife jumping back with a horrified look.

Kathy tripped on the carpet as Hector closed in. But when the Secret Service man fell his gun had slipped out and clattered across the floor. So Shark picked up the gun while all these broads were going apeshit and drew a bead on Hector as he said to the broads through gritted teeth: *"Get down."*

As the broads ducked down behind the tables Shark squeezed the trigger, plugging poor old Hector in the head. The donkey lurched just short of Kathy Petro, then kind of reeled like he was stunned, blood shooting out of his head like it was coming from a hose, throwing arcs all over the white tablecloths.

Then Hector staggered over toward this grand piano, blood still going everywhere, and then he shot off. I mean that big old dick of his just fired off about a quart of donkey jiz, big old long streaks of it going every which way. The broads kind of keened. The Gipper's wife jumped back, but she still got a big old streak of donkey jiz on her orange dress.

Then Hector lurched into the piano, knocking the support out, so that the top banged down on his head. Then he croaked, just going limp, kind of hanging there, with his head caught in the grand piano.

Kathy Petro

Shark helped me up from the floor and held me, and I just wanted him to hold me forever. Most of the women were whimpering by that time from the horror of it all. Then the Secret Service just arrived en masse, and we were told that we would be adjourning to another room for coffee. But I just wanted to leave.

I was numb in a way, but I felt safe with Shark. He left me for a minute to speak privately with the Secret Service men, and when he came back he put his arms around me and said everything was going to be all right, and I said, "Please just don't ever let me go."

I kept holding onto him, just wishing I could literally hide under his jacket, as we waited for the limousine to come around. At that point Mrs. Reagan came out in a fresh dress. She told Shark that what he'd done was very brave, but she seemed troubled, and Shark read her mind.

"Mrs. Reagan, I just want you to know that as far as I'm concerned this tasteless and horrifying episode never occurred. I did what I felt I had to, but it is not something I will ever speak of to anyone. When I recall this date in my memoirs it will be only to say that you were a consummately gracious hostess as I made an impromptu stop at your utterly decorous luncheon to briefly say hello."

At that Mrs. Reagan gave Shark a hug and said, "God bless you." She smiled at me. "Both of you." Then she added, with a twinkle in her eye: "I sense a great love in the making here."

"You sense correctly," Shark told her. "Odd as this may sound to Kathy, I feel as if we've only just begun."

I felt myself blushing as Mrs. Reagan said, "I just know you're going to be very happy. Kathy, with a man like Shark you can't go wrong."

As insane as it may seem now, on that crisp afternoon, which had been both so rapturous and so revolting, I had no doubt that she was right.

Drake Brewster

The Secret Service guys took me to a hospital there in Washington to get my head stitched, and all the time the doctor was working they kept trying to get me to promise not to talk about what happened. But I kept saying, "Well, I might keep my mouth shut if there's something in it for me." And they were getting real steamed when Shark came in.

As soon as we were alone Shark said, "Drake, you surprised me this afternoon. Grabbing Hector's tail was a very courageous act and no doubt prevented an occurrence too grisly to contemplate. I am therefore going to give you one point in *Blue Light* as a token of my appreciation."

Then he went on to say he still thought I was dogshit and that as part of the deal I would have to sign a paper saying that if I ever talked to anyone about what had happened at the White House or about any of my associations with Shark in the past I would forfeit my profit participation and, he hinted, there were forces in the government that might punish me much more severely than that.

Well, I had some idea how much a point of *Blue Light* was worth, so for the last time I shook Shark Trager's hand.

Mac Trager

Narges and I got back together again there in D.C. She became abject at the White House after the Secret Service found her muttering to herself in the john. "*You* take her back to the hotel," they told me, and she sobbed in the back seat of the limousine.

"I feel so terrible," she said. "I can't go on like this."

"There, there, it's okay," I said, and put my arm around her. "Old Mac'll take care of you, you sweet Iranian thing, you. We'll get you off that cocaine one way or another."

As it turned out we were on the same flight back to L.A. as Shark and Kathy. They sat up ahead of us all lovey-dovey, but no more so than Narges and me. We got us a couple of blankets, and I finger-banged her crazy little Persian box from sea to shining sea. "Don't stop, Mac," she said over Kansas. "When you make me feel this good I have no desire for drugs."

Kathy Petro

I felt so dreamy flying home with Shark. It just seemed so right to be with him at last. We whispered sweet nothings and spoke of the future. He said he was going to buy the old VistaVision Ranch.

"I don't care where I am," I told him. "A hovel in La Puente, a tract house in Torrance, it wouldn't matter how grungy it was. As long as it had a bedroom where we could pull down the shades and stay in bed all day making love, love, love."

Then he kissed me and we melted into one another as we descended through the smog into the endless brown expanses of L.A.

25 / **VistaVision**
(1985–1986)

Greg Spivey

Amazingly, the White House donkey incident did not make the news, although there were several female reporters present at the luncheon. Out of respect for the First Lady, I suppose, and probably because there was really no way to tastefully describe what had happened, there was a kind of tacit consensus among the Washington press corps that the incident should simply be quietly forgotten.

Out of curiosity however Shark did trace the route Hector had taken from *Looking for Lupe* to the president of Mexico, and every owner told the same tale of initial elation—Hector having become more or less the "Francis" of the seventies—followed by disgust as Hector's penchant for untimely defecation and general rowdiness became apparent. It was therefore obvious that the gift to the Reagans was in fact a malicious prank, but Shark never passed this information on. Nor did he tell Kathy Petro why Hector had specifically attacked her since to do so, he told me, would only evoke the "negative obsessional energies of the past." So as far as Kathy knew, the donkey had simply gone mad.

It was obvious however that Shark's "obsessional energies" were not all in the past. As soon as they got back to L.A. Shark and Kathy moved into an unctuously picturesque Bel-Air cottage—a temporary home while the VistaVision Ranch was being renovated—and spent the last four months of 1985 doing little more than fucking their brains out.

Kathy Petro

We called it our Enchanted Cottage because that's what it was. It was just this adorable little house like something in a fairy tale with all this Hansel and Gretel Bavarian gingerbread everywhere. And the flowers! The whole lot, the whole house, was just covered with flowers, it seemed like every kind of flower you could think of. And a florist came in several times a week and put cut flowers in every room, so the whole place was just laced with natural fragrances. Flowers and sunshine and bees and hummingbirds—that's my main memory of that wondrous autumn. The flowers and the sunshine and the sweetness of Shark's love.

The dreamy days melted into one another as we made love day and night, only pausing it sometimes seemed to eat and sleep. I don't know what it was, it was sex yet somehow beyond sex at the same time. It was as if we'd been held apart all our lives by fear and complications and now that we were finally together we just wanted to merge and become one, and since we had bodies we used our bodies to do that.

Bill Kemmer

I understood how much Kathy meant to Shark—and thought I understood why he had opted for seclusion with her at a time when the media interest in his Beirut heroism was most ravenous*—but I began to grow irritated nonetheless. He had projects in development but nothing all that promising and for weeks on end he seemed to have forgotten entirely that he was in a position to make virtually any film he wished. So I was relieved when after the first of the year he began driving up to the VistaVision Ranch to check on the progress, though I understand he and Kathy made something of a lewd spectacle of themselves on several visits.

Greg Spivey

The VistaVision Ranch was essentially a gift to Shark from Jake Skyler, the chairman of Montanacom International, which had acquired Mastodon Pictures in late 1984. Jake was a tough old western tycoon, a kind of real-life John Wayne character, who took an instant liking to Shark and, significantly, an instant disliking to Gary Schnell, whom Jake referred to behind Gary's back as "No Nuts," which described only too well Gary's cloyingly "nice" and sexless personality. As a result Jake gave Shark the ranch and told him to "bill Mastodon" for the renovation expenses, which came to millions. And Gary got the Pangborn Building, a cramped Streamline Moderne one-story structure on the Mastodon lot, which was extremely rundown and pervaded with a subtle but disgusting smell—the result of decaying rats in the walls, it was said.

* Shark deflected all interview requests, and book and commercial endorsement offers, in the wake of the Beirut rescue story with a high-toned prepared statement in which he spoke of "a moral obligation not to exploit myself for doing nothing more (or less) than any other patriotic American would have done under similar circumstances."

Gary was miffed and began obsessively comparing his seedy facilities to Spielberg's headquarters at Universal. "Steven's got a game room, a projection room. All I've got is this rusty Art Deco water cooler, and even that was plugged up with something that looked like Xavier Cugat's toupée."

"*Blue Light* was only your first film, Gary," I'd tell him. "Give it a little time."

But of course it was a question of ego. And Gary was green with envy the first time he saw the VistaVision Ranch, which Shark was developing into a major base of operations, a kind of Skywalker Ranch South, set in the dry Malibu brush of Kelp Canyon.

Gary Schnell

It did bother me the first time I saw that place, because it had everything I wanted. There was a huge swimming pool and stables and posh state-of-the-art editing suites and guesthouses for dozens of people. There was a special effects facility and a helicopter pad and tennis and racquet ball courts and an astonishing view of the ocean several miles below. And the ranch house itself had been redone in this 1930s Will Rogers lodge style with deep leather sofas and antlers and all that and it had every amenity you could think of. The screening room had been expensively upgraded so that it could show anything, including old nitrate prints, and it could accommodate almost two hundred people in luxurious deep oxblood leather overstuffed chairs. There was even an abandoned church by the front gate which Shark said he was going to turn into an office for me since he knew how much I hated the Pangborn Building. But I told him I didn't think it would be right to do that to a church. In reality though, I was so stirred up inside with different conflicting emotions I didn't know if I could ever work with Shark again.

Besides, he was so busy having compulsive sex with Kathy Petro it remained to be seen if he'd ever even make another movie. It was clear to me that she was sapping his energy and pulling him down into a kind of erotic insanity. The day he showed me around the ranch I went to use the bathroom and when I came back I caught them doing something unbelievably crude.

Greg Spivey

Shark told me Gary caught a glimpse of Kathy going down on him in the ranch house den. Embarrassed, Gary quickly ducked away before Kathy saw him. But Shark saw Gary and confessed that for some reason he found the idea of Gary watching a turn-on—his old exhibitionistic streak, I guess. Of course, Shark was aware that he'd been neglecting his friendship with Gary since Kathy entered the picture, and knew Gary was feeling hurt and a little jealous, though not in any gay sense. Shark reflected on the entire matter and realized that the only way to provide Gary with a true perspective on the difference between platonic friendship and erotic love was to see that Gary finally got laid.

Tina Veer

I guess you could say I had been one of Shark's one-night-stands in the late 1970s. We got it on in that beach house in Santa Monica. It was the usual horseshit, him saying I was just right for some part and how much I reminded him of Gloria Grahame because of the way my mouth was—I'd heard that before, I guess we did have similar mouths, which along with a buck would buy me a cup of coffee. I knew he was full of shit but I fucked him anyway, 'cause in a town like Hollywood you never know. But the next film he made was *Red Surf*. That happened a lot. For some strange mystical reason I always seemed to fuck the wrong guy.

By '86 I was twenty-eight and bitter, having done a bunch of episodic TV shit and flashed my tits in a couple of raunchy teen pics. So when Shark called me out to the VistaVision Ranch—he was still in the process of moving in—and asked me how I'd like to pop Gary Schnell's cherry I laughed and said, "Well, that just all depends. What's in it for me?"

He said there might be a part in a movie and I guffawed, thinking: Yeah, sure, *riiight*.

Then he said, "Look, Tina, try and be sweet. You still *look* sweet for some reason, that's why I thought of you. Just try and pretend you're not a hard little barracuda and you just might land a hell of a real-life part too."

So what the fuck, I thought. Gary Schnell *was* a very hot director and not *that* bad to look at, his millions of dollars creating, shall we say, a certain charisma. "All right, how's this?" I said, and pursed my lips like some prim and prissy little virgin. "Is this what he wants? Is it this?"

Kathy Petro

Shark and I moved to the VistaVision Ranch in early 1986, and I really hated to see the Enchanted Cottage go. Those months had been like a timeless idyll in paradise—and I still believe that sunny autumn is destined to remain one of the peak experiences of my life. But nothing lasts forever. We both knew it was time for us to return to the world of everyday reality, Shark to make movies, me to promote my book which had just come out in paperback and to use my fame to speak out in the fight against drug abuse.

And so our period of isolation ended. For though we could still be alone in the ranch house and make glorious love for hours on end, we could frequently hear the voices of the many others on the grounds. We began inviting people in for huge breakfasts and barbecues and the sounds of joyful laughter echoed through those scrubby hills. Yet Shark seemed restless. He spent his time pouring over technical details as they completed the work on what was almost a self-contained mini-studio. But now that he had everything any moviemaker could ever want, it was like he didn't know what to do with it.

Greg Spivey

At first I thought it was just the $8^{1}/_{2}$ syndrome. How could Shark top himself after *Blue Light?* We had some scripts in development that weren't all that bad, but it was clear none of them really excited Shark.

Then one afternoon I was talking with Shark on the ranch house porch when it came time for Kathy to leave for the airport. She was going back east for a week of public appearances. Shark put her luggage in that specially built aquamarine Ferrari Clarapetacci he'd recently given her, and then they passionately and protractedly kissed good-bye. I couldn't help noticing however that Kathy was by far the more passionate of the two of them. You could just see, and feel, how crazy she was about him. And it wasn't just sexual, though it obviously included that. But you could see that she really loved *him*, if you know what I mean. Which made what followed all the more heart-rending.

For as Shark stepped back to me he appeared profoundly, indeed numbingly depressed. As we watched Kathy rumble throatily down the driveway toward the gate Shark said, "You know, Greg, it's a scary thing when you really get everything you've ever wanted."

"Yes, I know," I said, trying to sound sardonic. "The terrible cost of success."

But Shark didn't smile. "Take Kathy, for example," he said. And as I had so many times before, I sensed that he was about to tell me things that were none of my business, but which I suppose he had to tell someone.

"For over twenty years I longed for that woman with every fiber of my being. And now that I've got her, do you know what, Greg? You're going to love this."

"What, Shark?"

"She bores the shit out of me."

I was momentarily at a loss for words. For I saw that Shark was simply telling the truth. And it struck me as somehow so terribly, so desolately sad.

"I suppose we can dream of someone so long that when we're finally with them they inevitably fall short of our dreams," I said.

"She's a dim bulb," Shark said. "She's got the IQ of a stuffed toy. If she says more than two words I start to yawn."

"She's got a good heart, Shark."

"She has an unerring instinct for the trite observation and the vapid remark."

"She's an extraordinarily beautiful woman, you can't deny that."

"Yes, and she's good sex too. But do you know something, Greg? I never thought I'd say this, but I'm even bored with that."

"Perhaps you should try some new things in bed—"

"Greg." The emptiness in his eyes made me look away. "We've done it all."

"I don't know what to tell you, Shark."

"I'm scared, Greg," he said with an intensity that startled me. "I don't want to feel this way about Kathy, but I do. I knew the sex wouldn't last forever. We were burning too brightly, but . . . I must find a way to rekindle my feeling for her, or . . ." He didn't finish.

"It's too bad she can't act," I said, perhaps a bit tactlessly. By the way he stared at me I thought sure he'd taken offense.

"What makes you think she can't act?" Shark said.

"Well, *Manhattan Holiday.* I hate to even mention it, but . . ."

"But that film was a piece of shit," Shark said. "The problem was Andreji's nauseating script and inept direction. Even Meryl Streep would have stunk in that."

I didn't agree but held my tongue. It was clear that Shark's wheels were already turning, so I suppose I must take credit for planting the seed that grew into *Home to the Heart.*

Elliot Bernstein

I always felt that *Home to the Heart* was a fairly calculated attempt to woo the Academy after what happened in 1986.

Bill Kemmer

We were all disappointed but not really surprised when *Blue Light* was only nominated for technical awards, for as is so frequently the case when a film does that well, a rather severe backlash had set in. It was a terribly cruel phenomenon to witness though, a number of the critics in effect reversing their opinions, confessing they'd been "taken in" by the film's "manipulative sentimentality," many of them, I suppose, shamed and sobered by Edmund Himmler's merciless review. By the time the Academy balloting took place I think the members were skittish of voting for a "flashy special effects cartoon movie," a big slick "cheaply cathartic, crypto-religious" fantasy blockbuster, especially in a year that was heavy with small, "relevant" human dramas featuring a number of virtuoso Oscar-fodder acting turns. Of course, James Dustin's semi-autobiographical *A Farm to Come Back To* went on to sweep the awards, stealing the recognition that Shark no doubt felt should have been his.

As it happened, I was with Gary Schnell when the nominations were announced, and he became extremely dejected. I tried to call Shark at the ranch, only to be be told he was "incommunicado."

Later we learned that he was actually writing—or to be specific, dictating—the script of what I still believe will go down in history as his most shatteringly poignant film.

Woody Hazzard

I had seen Shark a few times since we made up but we were not in any sense hanging out together. Part of the reason for that was Brian, since he still hated Shark's guts, and I still cared a lot about Brian, so I hadn't even mentioned the one time I'd gone up to the Vista-Vision Ranch. I'd been real impressed by the place and Shark had said something about how I should try writing another screenplay some day, but I just kind of winced and said, "No, I think *Red Surf* was it for me."

Then one afternoon he called and said, "Woody, this is it. You've got to come up here immediately. Something astounding is happening inside me and only you can help me bring it out."

I didn't know what he was talking about and it sounded weird— *he* sounded weird—but I drove up anyway, partly out of curiosity, I guess. Besides, Kelp Canyon wasn't that far from the Colony. It was spooky driving up there though. Kelp Canyon was basically this one-lane road with lots of blind turns running through the middle of nowhere, just empty chaparral hills, and that winter was super-dry, there hadn't been a drop of rain yet, and there was a bad Santa Ana blowing, which always made everybody real jumpy.

It was a Sunday and when I got there the place seemed deserted. Shark buzzed me through the gate and I drove up to the ranch house and Shark was waiting there, shirtless and sweaty, with this funny look in his eyes, and I just knew instantly he was on something.

Then I stepped into the house and there on the table were these two mounds of powder—one was white and clearly cocaine, but the other one was brown. And I said, "Oh shit, is this what I think it is?"

"Don't lay a guilt trip on me, okay?" Shark said. "I need it for inspiration. To break through the mental blocks. I'm using it very scientifically."

"This is smack, isn't it, you dodo?" I said. "You're snorting speed-balls. Didn't you learn anything from Belushi's death?"

"Don't lecture me," Shark said. "There isn't time. I've got a movie in my head, I can see the entire thing, and you've got to write it down."

"You're nuts, man," I said. "Is this what you asked me up here for? I'm not going to be a party to this. Fuck this."

I started for the door, but he blocked my path.

"Woody, please, I'm not kidding, I need you."

"Why don't you write it yourself, Shark, if it's such a great idea?" By then I was totally pissed because of the drugs. I just saw all the weird shit from the past starting up all over again.

"I can't write it," Shark said. "I just can't do that."

"Yeah, I know," I said. "And you know why you can't? 'Cause you're chickenshit. You want somebody else to take the heat in case it goes down the tubes like *Red Surf*. That's the story of your life, you know that, Shark? You could have been a great director if you hadn't pussed out. You could've been another Orson Welles—"

"Yes, exactly, in every sense, you moron!" he yelled at me. "I would've ended up beaten and broken. What do you know about anything, you asshole? Sit down and shut up and turn on that computer."

"Fuck you," I said and went out the door. I was crossing the porch when I heard a gun click. I couldn't believe it at first, it was like something in a movie. But I looked back and he had this big fucking Colt .45 in his hand, one of those Old West models with a foot-long barrel.

"Come back in here, Woody," he said.

"You're nuts, man," I said, but I went back in.

"Sit down at the word processor," he said.

"I don't know how to use one of these things," I told him.

"It's easy," he said, and switched it on, still keeping me covered. "It's ready now. You just type the way you would on a typewriter."

So I started to sit down and he said, "Wait. Take off your clothes."

"What?"

"I want to make sure you don't try and make a run for it."

"Where am I gonna go?" I said. "The whole fucking property's fenced and the gate's a quarter mile away."

"Peel off your duds, Woody. Just do it," he said almost gently.

"This is too weird, man," I said, but I took off my clothes.

Kathy Petro

I had sensed for a while that something wasn't quite right with Shark, but I thought it was just that he hadn't decided what movie to make next. I didn't see, or didn't want to see, that he was already growing tired of me. I was just not prepared to accept that, not at a time when I had finally come to love and appreciate him in a way that really scared me at times, since my heart was right out there on the line. I had always known the early sexual intensity wouldn't last forever, I knew enough about relationships to know that. I therefore sensed that we were passing through a critical period where, if we were to last and my heart was not to be broken, we would really have to come up with something to hold us together besides sex.

This train of thought was reinforced by a conversation I had with a noted psychologist backstage before the "Donahue" Show. "Don't tell *me* these things," she said. "You should be expressing these feelings directly to Shark." She also suggested that Shark and I make separate lists of our likes and dislikes and then compare them. "You're bound to locate areas of mutual interest that way, as well as discovering the things you should never do together."

I thought about that a long time and it seemed like such a good idea I decided to cut my trip short by two days and started making my own list on the flight back to L.A. Then as we came into LAX I noticed all this black smoke up the coast in the Malibu area.

Woody Hazzard

I smelled the smoke around three that afternoon. By then I was up to about page eighty of the screenplay. Shark wasn't kidding, it was all in his head, he hardly changed a line and kept going as fast as I could type, only pausing to lean over the table and snort more smack and cocaine.

I didn't pay much attention to what I was typing at the time, I was too blown out to really visualize it as I went. All I could see in my mind was Shark sitting behind me with that gun. But I was kind of aware it was at least partly autobiographical, since his mom and dad were the main characters. Mac and Winnie. Except they weren't like any Mac and Winnie I'd ever known or heard of. His mom had checked out before Shark and I were ever friends, you know, but I'd heard she was pathologically withdrawn and probably crazy. But the Winnie in the script I was being forced to write was like some character Sally Field would play, you know? This real stand-up-and-be-counted dynamo type.

"You know, I think there's a fire over there in Tuna Canyon," I said to Shark, when I saw all these clouds of smoke to the west.

"Damn it, you made me lose it," he said, and I looked back and saw how hard he was concentrating. The gun was resting on the arm of the chair and I considered making a lunge for it. In a way I couldn't really believe he would shoot me. But on the other hand the dope was clearly affecting his mind. A lot of the story seemed ultra-sentimental as well as basically a lie, like some real boorish junkie getting all nostalgic about how great his parents were or something, you know?

"Okay, I've got it," he said, and looked up before I could go for the gun. "Interior, J. Edgar Hoover's Office, FBI Building, Day. Hoover stands before a portrait of President Eisenhower as Winnie storms in. She shakes her finger in Hoover's startled face, tears welling in her eyes. Winnie: 'Now you listen to me, Mr. Director. My husband Mac is a loyal American . . .' " It went on like that.

But the smoke kept getting worse until it turned the sun this weird cherry-red color and so much ash was drifting through the window I had to keep blowing it off the computer keys.

"Shark, I'm worried about this fire," I said. "It looks like it's just on the other side of that ridge."

"Don't be a pussy," he said. "Just keep trying. Interior, Hospital Room, Day. Winnie appears nauseated from the cobalt treatment . . ."

Then I looked out the window and saw these huge fucking flames coming down our side of the ridge.

Kathy Petro

I tried calling Shark from the airport, but the service said he'd left word not to be disturbed. "Look, this is me, Kathy," I said, and they said, "Sorry, Miss Petro, but he gave specific orders."

So I was irked, but I also had a funny feeling that Shark might be in grave danger because of the fire. I hurried out to my Ferrari and drove toward Malibu as fast as I could. When I reached PCH I saw how bad the fire really was, these huge clouds of smoke billowing out over the sea. Fire trucks were screaming past me and when I reached the Kelp Canyon turn-off it was closed off with a barricade. There was nobody there though, so I got out and moved the barricade and drove on up. By the time the ranch came into view the smoke was so bad my eyes were smarting. I opened the gate and drove up to the house where I saw that sure enough Shark's Porsche was still there. And Woody's Corvette was parked beside it. Then I saw that the fire was burning right behind the house, right up to the line where they'd cleared the brush! I dashed into the house, yelling, "Shark!" and found him wrestling with Woody, who was nude, on the floor.

Woody Hazzard

I'd finally stood up and said, "Go ahead and shoot me, man. 'Cause if we stay here we're gonna burn."

And Shark looked at me and said, "I can't shoot you, man. This old gun isn't even loaded."

But instead of being relieved I flipped. "You son of a bitch," I said and laid into him.

The next thing I knew we were grappling on the floor. It was weird, but for some reason I started to get turned on. At one point our faces were real close and I knew that on some level what I really wanted to do was kiss him, you know, just ferociously start making out. But to Shark it was just a fight and nothing more and he was determined to win, so I fought back and eventually got him in a scissor hold, you know, with my dick squashed up right in his face. And it was at that point that Kathy came in.

Kathy Petro

I reeled when I saw them like that, not really sure what was going on. At first it looked like a fight, but then I thought: Why is Woody nude? What in fact is going on here? Is this really a fight, or some sort of homosexual wrestling match? And then I saw the cocaine and heroin on the table and I just freaked.

I ran out to the Ferrari, but I was so upset I drove off the driveway and got stuck in the dirt. The wheels just spun and the car wouldn't budge, so I got out and ran down to the gate.

Woody Hazzard

Seeing Kathy jolted Shark more than it did me. He quit fighting and said, "Let me up, man. Let me up."

So I did and Shark and I were both winded, and he seemed suddenly sobered. He was holding his head like he was finally seeing how badly he'd flipped out, and saying, "Oh my God, what have I done? What am I doing? What must she think?"

Then he ran out to the porch and called, "Kathy?" But she didn't answer and the smoke was so bad you couldn't even see down to the gate. I was pulling on my pants as he dashed back in. "My God, she's taken off on foot," he said. "Come on, we've got to find her. It looks like the fire's about to burn across the road."

"Fuck you," I said. "You're crazy, man. I knew I should never have come up here."

"You're right, I've been a bad boy, you can spank me later if you want," he said. "But right now all that matters is finding Kathy. I know you still love her on some level, just as you love me, and I love you and Kathy."

"You're nuts," I said, and grabbed my shoes and ran out to my car.

He ran out after me, calling Kathy's name again. The fire was burning right up behind the house, a couple of the umbrellas around the pool igniting. I got in my Corvette and started the engine. "You better get the fuck out of here," I yelled at him, but he seemed dazed, looking off through the smoke for some sign of Kathy. "Did you hear me, Shark?" I said, and he didn't respond. So I said: "Fuck him" to myself and peeled out.

I caught up with Kathy a quarter mile down the road. "Come on, get in," I yelled as I pulled up beside her.

"Homo," she said.

"Kathy, that's not nice. Come on, get the fuck in. The fire's coming close."

"Is Shark gay now too?"

"No, no, no. It's not what you think. He was literally holding a gun to my head. Kathy, for fuck's sake, get in."

The fire was ripping right down to the road, so she finally got in. Just as I pulled out we heard this massive explosion and I saw a fireball back up the road in my rearview mirror. Then it was out of sight as we went around a bend, but it came back into view again and Kathy was looking back and said, "Oh my God, it's the Porsche! He's burning up in his Porsche! Go back, go back!"

"I can't," I said. And I couldn't, the fire had cut us off. We had to get out of there fast to save our own butts.

"Oh my God," Kathy kept saying, "Oh my God." By the time we reached PCH she was hysterical.

Brian Straight

We gave Kathy a sedative at the Colony house. I had not seen her since the divorce. "Well," I said eventually, "I suppose it's the end of an era."

"Yes, and you're glad, aren't you, Brian?" she said. "You're glad Shark's dead."

"Don't be silly, Kathy," I replied. "Shark Trager did more for the Hollywood film industry this year than any other single man."

"You're being sardonic as always," she said. "And it's not appropriate, Brian. There's a time for everything and the time for that is not now."

"At least he died trying to save you, Kathy," Woody said, with his arm around her on the couch.

"He did?" Kathy said, and Woody nodded. And she began sobbing against his chest.

Woody Hazzard

It was a very weird night. I kept making calls, trying to find out what the fuck was going on, and finally talked to Greg Spivey around midnight and learned that the VistaVision Ranch had been spared.

"I guess the brush clearing paid off," I said to Kathy, who was watching the fire reports on the TV in a numb, sedated stupor.

Then she got up and said, "I'm going for a walk on the beach."

"Are you all right?" I said, scenes from different movies where people walked in the Malibu surf flashing through my mind.

"Yes," she said. "I just want some air."

Kathy Petro

I walked along the shoreline and smoked my last cigarette. I did think about suicide. I mean, who wouldn't under the circumstances? Mostly, I was just numb though. Numb and oddly grateful that at least Shark and I had had a few wondrous months. For that was what I saw, how truly precious that time in the Enchanted Cottage had been. That ultimate pinnacle of romance and sex, instead of just one or the other. How many people in this world ever really have a time like that?

The waves crashed, the icy water getting into my shoes. The pungent smell of the fire still laced the night air, and I wiped my cheeks where soot was stuck to my tears. What a crazy roller coaster ride it had been! How could I even imagine my life without Shark Trager? As irritant, pest, pathological obsessive and finally mind-shattering lover. Sweet God, what a time we had had!

And then, you know, I saw him. As I turned back to the house I saw him coming out across the sand. His bare torso, still so hard and muscular at thirty-seven, was smeared with soot. So was his face, that boyishly handsome face, resembling in the moonlight that of a battle-weary Errol Flynn with a touch of Kevin Costner. As he came closer I saw that his dirty blond hair was singed in several places. And then I could barely see anything at all, I was crying so heavily. Then he held me and I held him.

Woody Hazzard

I'd answered the door and needless to say it shocked the shit out of me to see Shark standing there. "Fuck, man. You're *alive*."

"Yeah, I jumped out of the Porsche just as the flames began to engulf it," he said, looking past me. "Did you get Kathy?"

I told him she was on the beach, and he went right out to her. I watched them hug and kiss. Then as they came back toward the house Shark broke away from her and came up to me.

"You can tell me to fuck off, I won't blame you," he said. "But I really am sorry, Woody. It was the drugs, and it's not going to happen again. Lesson learned, I swear."

So I went ahead and hugged him, glad he was alive and everything. But to tell you the truth it was never the same, not after the other weird shit that had come down that day.

26 / **Home to the Heart** (1986–1987)

Gary Schnell

I was in bed with a woman I thought I loved when Shark called me to say he wanted me to read a new script Woody Hazzard had written. "You're too late, Shark," I told him. "Brian Straight just gave me a green light on my Houston project at Acropolis."

"You've got to be kidding," Shark said. "You can't work for him. You know how I feel about Brian."

"That's your problem, Shark," I said, as Tina kissed her way down my stomach. "You may have old enemies in this town but I don't."

"But Gary, no one else can possibly make this picture. It's a warm, tender elegy to a bygone era, but one that's coming back as people see that there were many virtues intrinsic to the 1950s that are well worth reclaiming. And it's extremely autobiographical."

"Then why don't you direct it yourself, Shark?" I said.

There was a pause and I sensed he was suppressing his anger.

"At least read it, Gary."

"Shark, I'm busy at the moment—"

"I'm coming by," he said and hung up.

"Damn it," I said, not wanting to get out of bed, not that day or ever. What a world of physical delight I had denied myself out of shyness! And the way it happened with Tina was so spontaneous and therefore so right.

Tina Veer

It was a pretty simple ploy. I just parked my old Pinto on Sunset, then walked up to Gary's gate in Bel-Air and buzzed. "Look, my car broke down and a couple of sinister guys offered me a lift. I told them to leave me alone and now they're out cruising around looking

405

for me. Please help." It was almost midnight and I was dressed square like Marie Osmond on her way home from a church function.

He buzzed me in. In the living room I grew faint and he offered me a glass of mineral water. Belatedly, I pretended to recognize him. I gushed over *Blue Light*. He said, "You're an actress, aren't you?" He actually remembered me from a bit I'd done on "Quincy" years ago.

And then a strange thing happened. Even though it was part of the plan that I was gonna break down and cry about how badly my career was going, I began to cry for real. I mean, I really got into it, and it wasn't an act.

And he became very tender, treating me like no guy had in I don't know how long. And when we made love, I don't know . . . I don't even want to talk about it. It would make it cheap if I talked about it. He touched something inside me that hadn't been touched in years. And if you think that's funny or dirty, fuck you.

Gary Schnell

Tina was in the kitchen when Shark arrived, and in retrospect I see there was something funny going on as I introduced them. Tina seemed frightened, even though she was acting like she and Shark had never met before.

Shark and I went out to the patio and he gave me the script of *Home to The Heart*, insisting that I read it right then. I did, while he went in the house to use the phone. And even though I was prepared to dislike it, I had to admit it was pretty good. The last twenty pages where Winnie was dying of cancer really got to me. It was even more wrenching than the last half hour of *Terms of Endearment*. I didn't actually cry, but I knew I would if I saw it on film, and I knew audiences would.

"Well?" Shark said, as I put the script down.

"You were right," I said. "It's warm and sweet and tender. And it's a human story about real, ordinary people, a story of heroism in everyday life, uplifting and yet heartbreaking without being a downer in any way. I've only met Woody briefly, I had no idea he was this sensitive. This script is as delicately structured as a Mozart concerto."

"Then let's make a movie," Shark said.

But I told him about my Houston project, an epic *Giant* for the eighties, telling the story of my parents and their parents before them, a sprawling saga of the oil and petroleum by-products industry, with a subplot exploring the tempestuous courtship of our close family friends, former Governor John Connally and his vivacious wife Nellie. But as I outlined the story Shark yawned.

"Texas," he said. "People are sick of all that rich Texan shit, it's been done to death. Besides, just in terms of entertainment value, your parents are basically a drag, Gary. Who gives a shit who invented the pantsuit?"

"I do," I said. "And you'd better watch what you say about my mom."

"Gary, I love your mother, you know that," he said. "She's a sensational woman in real life. But *this*—" he tapped his script "—is art, and that's a different bird. Sleep on it, Gary. Without being preachy, this film will make an important statement about traditional American values that needs to be made. And it's a small, intimate character piece with zero special effects. You need this film as much as I do, Gary, if you're to be a truly class director and not just a kid cranking out expensive cartoons. I think you already sense there's an Oscar in this for you, lots of Oscars, enough for everyone involved."

With that he left. I met him the next afternoon in Bill Kemmer's office at Mastodon. At the end of the meeting, Bill said to us. "You're on."

Woody Hazzard

Against my better judgment I helped Shark finish the screenplay of *Home to the Heart*. Part of the reason, to be honest, was the two hundred thousand dollar fee. I knew that my days with Brian were numbered. I still cared about him but wouldn't sleep with him anymore, since I'd found out that he'd had sex with a couple of other guys and I was real scared of getting AIDS. With the screenwriting fee I planned to move to the South Bay, open a surfboard shop, and hopefully meet a young gay surfer who had never actually had sex with a man before.

Shark was real pleasant as we finished the script, making a big point of letting me know the ranch hand who'd scored the cocaine and heroin for him had been fired. "If alcoholism and drug addiction are a disease," he said, "then what I had was a minor relapse, and I'm not going to beat myself up about it now. The important thing is I'm back to my true decent and loving self." And as far as you could tell that seemed to be the case.

One morning I went with him to a dealership in the Valley to pick up this new Porsche he'd ordered. It was spooky in a way—or at least it seems so now—but as we drove down Ventura Boulevard he told me the dealership was the same one James Dean hadgone to to pick up his silver Spyder the day he died. It was called Competition Motors then, but it had a different name now. Shark got into this whole trip about it as we pulled up to the dealership garage. "That's where James Dean had 'em paint 'Little Bastard' on his car, right there. He stood *right there* thirty-one years ago."

And then we saw Shark's Porsche, and it's no exaggeration to say it was the ultimate Porsche, beyond any doubt the bitchinest Porsche ever made. It was one of a kind, specially built for Shark: the Porsche 997, with a five-hundred-horsepower twin-turbo engine and a top speed of two hundred-twenty miles-per-hour. I think it set him back almost three hundred grand, but if you cared anything at all about cars it was worth every cent. When you fired that ignition, man, it made your nuts start to rumble and it was all you could do not to come all over the dash.

Kathy Petro

The first time Shark took me out in that silver monster it scared me to death. He did this big Grand Prix number on the Kelp Canyon road while I clutched the dash. "Don't worry, this fucker can stop on a dime!" he yelled. And then he proved it and I nearly peed!

Then he tore out again so fast that the gravity socked me back into the seat. I was terrified yet excited when he finally pulled to a halt at the very crest of Kelp Mountain, the ocean and Catalina stretched out far below.

"I want you to star in *Home to the Heart*," he said. "I want you to portray my mother Winnie."

"What?" I said. "Are you talking to me?" I was completely incredulous.

"I know you can do it, Kathy. You're mature now. Forget about *Manhattan Holiday* and that Yugoslavian drip—that never happened."

"But Shark," I said. "I'm not an actress. I'm an aging model with laugh lines."

"That's what I mean. You're no longer vapidly pretty."

"I'm not?" I said, feeling vaguely insulted.

"You're still pretty, but not vapidly pretty. In fact, pretty isn't the right word. You're beautiful, Kathy, you will always be beautiful. But you have a kind of inner beauty now that you didn't used to have. You've been around the block a few times and it shows, but in a positive way. You're developing a kind of earthy, wise sensuality, the sort of aura one associates with certain soulful French actresses."

"Gee, really?" I said, feeling kind of flattered, and strangely comforted. Because getting old did worry me. Especially in California you're just really aware of how much everybody worships youth and everything.

"It would be nice if I could become a serious actress," I said. "It has occurred to me that I can't go on talking about drug abuse forever. I really do need something else to do with my time."

Greg Spivey

Home to the Heart was really a fantasy, wasn't it? Shark took real characters but completely revised reality, though I guess the affair between Mac and Gladys was based roughly on actual events. The politics were so incredibly odd though—I still don't have an exact fix on that. In one sense it was a kind of liberal-humanist tract—I mean, the subplot about the black family being driven out of the white Orange County suburb. But the business of Mac's defense contractor boss being a Communist spy was nothing less than vintage McCarthyite paranoia, and a deliberate pandering to the neo-patriotic jingoism of the mid-1980s.

The roles of Mac and Winnie were essentially reversed, for as I'd always understood it in real life Winnie was the pathological weakling. Her "lifting disease" and all that. And of course she'd committed suicide, climbing into the freezer, rather than waging the valiant battle against cancer depicted in the film. The cinematic Winnie was clearly the mother Shark wished he had had, a powerhouse who forced her ninny husband to stand up for America. "I can't tell the FBI about my boss," Mac protests in the movie. "If he's arrested for selling secrets to the Russians, the company will go under, I'll lose my job and we'll lose this house."

"Come to your senses, Mac," Winnie reprimands him. "If the Reds take over this country we're going to lose a lot more than our house. You've got to do what's right!"

The real Gladys I understand was just a wayward fifties tramp with a Gloria Grahame mouth who for a time shacked up with Mac on Mackerel Drive, even as Winnie withdrew to her bedroom, becoming more and more disassociated from reality. Gladys's status as FBI undercover agent in the film did make her more "sympathetic," which of course was part of Shark's overall "humanity-affirming" slant that there were "no truly evil people"—not even the boss, who was only committing treason to finance an orphanage in Italy where, during the war, he'd accidently machine-gunned a pregnant woman. And in the film Mac and Gladys' furtive and guilt-ridden if "understandable" affair took place in a seedy motel far from the wholesome goodness and warmth of the home.

I once asked Shark why he'd excluded himself from the story, giving his cinematic parents a pair of twins instead, the five-year-olds Gene and Jan, described in the script as "perfect, angelic mirror reflections of one other, in every way except their clothes." Shark waved the question away with a smile. "Let's leave that one to my biographer, Greg."

I knew when I read the scene where the twins drown in the swimming pool that whoever played Winnie would win an Academy

Award. It was just one of those scenes. Winnie alone in the house, deserted by her cad of a husband, and by that time confined to a wheelchair with cancer of the spine. She's knitting matching sweaters when she happens to glance up through the plate glass window in time to see the twins thrashing in the pool as they begin to drown. She wheels to the patio and cries out for help as the twins gurgle under—but the next-door neighbors, seen in a cutaway, are watching Lawrence Welk on TV and don't hear. Frantically, Winnie wheels to the phone in the hall. Just as her hand touches the receiver her wheels lock up suddenly in a snarl of yarn, the abrupt stop throwing her out across the floor. As she falls, still holding the phone, the cord is torn from the wall, and . . . well, you could tell the scene was going to play for at least three minutes: as she pulls the heavy weight of her body inch by inch across the carpet toward the sliding glass door, excruciatingly, helplessly watching the twins drown . . . It just had Best Actress stamped all over it.

When Shark said Kathy was going to play the part I nearly laughed.

Gary Schnell

I did laugh. I was sure he was kidding, then I saw that he wasn't. By that time we had cast Tina as Gladys and I saw what Shark was up to all right.

"Did you even really *show* the script to Meryl Streep?" I said.

"Yeah, I told you, she's booked up until 1990."

"I don't believe you. I'm going to call her."

Shark stopped my hand on the phone. "Look, forget that it's Kathy. Just let her read, that's all I ask, Gary. If after that you don't think she's right for the part I'll never mention it again. Forget that I love her. Pretend that she means nothing at all to either of us."

So I let Kathy read. And the strange thing was, even if she hadn't been Shark's girlfriend, even if Shark Trager had not existed, I would have cast her to play Winnie after the first few minutes of that reading. She was that good.

Kathy Petro

Shark had me prepare for the reading with a method acting teacher, and luckily for me I was a quick study. I had this really big break-through the very first session and saw how phony I'd been during *Manhattan Holiday.* I'd been pretending to be an "actress" back then, doing what I thought actresses did or something. But Maurice kept yelling at me: "Don't act!" And once when I did something really fake he actually slapped my face! I ran off in tears but came back and delivered a scene from *Who's Afraid of Virginia Woolf* that terrified everyone in the class.

Greg Spivey

Home to the Heart rolled in Torrance, California, in late August 1986, as we grabbed the Mac and Gladys tryst scenes and the black family scenes first. Torrance, a South Bay suburb, had a lot of fifties motel and coffee shop architecture that hadn't been filmed before, and whatever else might be said of the film, Ernesto Fonseca's delicately gold-tinged cinematography imbued each shot with a preternatural poignance.

Kathy's scenes began when we moved to the Palos Verdes location, a glass-walled Richard Neutra-designed residence considerably more stylish than Shark's boyhood home in Newport Beach, where perhaps eighty percent of the film took place. And from the very first day Kathy was astonishing. Somehow, I'm still not sure how, she had tapped into something inside her, some depth of being, that I for one never suspected was there.

As usual, Shark was constantly on the set. While he seemed at first to be leaving all the essential directorial decisions to Gary, offering even fewer suggestions than usual, it eventually became apparent that between takes Shark was privately coaching Kathy on her performances. This began to irritate Gary quite a bit.

Gary Schnell

To be honest I never really liked Kathy that much as a person. I tried to keep my moral views to myself because in the beginning especially she was delivering quite a good performance. But in the back of my mind I could never forget that she'd once been a pig. Of course most women her age had been, because of the so-called sexual revolution. On that score I was glad to have found Tina, who at the time I believed had only slept with one other man before me. Believing that, it seemed ironic that Tina was playing such a loose character while Kathy Petro, one of the world's biggest retired sluts, was portraying this pure and noble American mom.

That's why what Shark began doing infuriated me so. Because I would spend all this time getting a quiet, restrained performance from Kathy and then Shark would whisper something in her ear and she'd come back and start playing it big and raw and sometimes downright crude—to be frank, almost as if she were in heat. Well, the idea of trying to imply that there was some sort of sexual undercurrent in Winnie's maternal character just offended me to the very core of my being.

Greg Spivey

With only a few key pages left to shoot in Palos Verdes we were rained-out for a week in late September, and so returned to Mastodon's fabled soundstage one to pick the Washington interiors. That was where Gary finally lost it, when Kathy tried to play the scene with J. Edgar Hoover without a bra.

"Cut!" he yelled. "What the hell is going on? We can see your nipples, Miss Petro. Who told you to take off your bra?"

Kathy looked at Shark.

Gary went over to Shark, trembling with anger. "It's 1957. No decent woman would walk into FBI headquarters in a tight semi-diaphanous blouse without a bra."

"I want a sexual subtext to the scene," Shark said. "I think Hoover should notice her nipples and appear flustered."

"That's not what the scene is about!" Gary screamed. "And I am directing this goddamn picture!"

"You are because I asked you to, Gary," Shark said evenly. "You exist because I gave you a break, you spoiled-rotten little prig. And I can replace you so fast it'll make your head spin."

Gary was livid. "We'll see about that, Shark."

Gary Schnell

I was enraged. I came close to walking off the picture that morning. But we had less than two weeks left to shoot, including the crucial swimming pool sequence, and I knew that despite Shark's interference I had the coverage I needed to make my best film. So I decided to fight back and called Dad.

Kathy Petro

The night before we were to shoot the swimming pool scene Shark got a call from Bill Kemmer and found out that Earl Schnell was trying to buy Mastodon Pictures. Shark got right on the phone to Jake Skyler, who assured him that Montanacom would never let that happen, but the idea that Gary would go to such lengths to gain total control of the film just infuriated Shark.

"That evil little prima donna," Shark said. "When this is over I'm going to destroy him."

"Shark, let's just finish the picture. We've only got a few days left. I don't want anything bad to happen now."

"We'll finish the picture all right," he said. "But as soon as we wrap, that double-crossing schmuck is dead."

Well, I barely slept at all that night. I was already keyed-up anyway anticipating my most difficult scene—I just didn't need all the extra tension. The next morning the vibes on the Palos Verdes set were just awful.

Greg Spivey

"You've fucked up bad, pal," I told Gary that morning. "Shark knows your dad's trying to take over the studio."

"If you're smart you'll side with me, Greg," Gary said. "Because it's going to happen."

Tina Veer

I was on the set even though my scenes were finished. But if I'd known what was coming I would have gone far away. Shark and Gary weren't speaking. And from the very first take, Gary treated Kathy viciously.

Kathy Petro

I was really trying hard to forget about the tension and get into the scene. But every time I fell out of the wheelchair Gary would call, "Cut!" and say mean things. "No, no, no! That's horrible, you're pathetic. Your twins are drowning, for Christ sake! You're acting like you just smelled the roast burning."

Again and again we'd start the scene, and he'd stop it. Finally, he said, "Boy, you stink, you know that? You just plain stink!" And I started to cry and Shark, who'd been simmering, started toward Gary with violence in his eyes.

I stopped him. "No, please, Shark. Let me try it one more time."

So I did, and Gary stopped it again and said, "Phony, phony, phony!" And I ran to my dressing room in tears.

Shark came in after me and held me and said, "Look, I've got an idea."

Greg Spivey

Without Gary being aware of it, Shark had Kathy fitted with a wireless earphone so that he could speak to her during the take, in effect directing her through it. He also instructed the camera and sound men to keep rolling no matter what Gary said, and since by that time nearly everybody thought Gary was an asshole, they went along.

Kathy Petro

It was always supposed to be this really long take of my crawling across the floor, basically this close-up of my face as I went through all these emotions, and Shark just said he would "cue" me. I was never really sure exactly what he meant, but by that time I just wanted to get the scene over with. My hip was all bruised from falling out of the wheelchair so many times.

So finally we were ready and Gary called, "Action!" As soon as I fell from the wheelchair, Shark started talking to me through the earphone. "Oh my God, *Jeff Stuben!*" he said. "He loved you but you gave him acid and he cut off his head! He picked up that chainsaw and went *bzzzzzzz!* Right before your eyes!"

I started crying and screaming, "No, no!"

"Derek Horus died too. A heart attack! He fell back through a window—there he goes now!"

And I saw it and just came unglued.

"And what about *Beth!* In a pool of blood on the floor! Is *that* what happens to everyone who loves you!"

"No, no, no!" I sobbed, as the Panaflex camera swooped in on my face. I think I kind of heard Gary call, "Cut," but I was too wrecked by then to stop.

"And your dear old dad. *You killed him!*" Shark yelled in my ear. "He blew his brains out because you knowingly married a homo. You drove him to suicide!"

By then I was crawling across the carpet, tears coursing down my cheeks. "No, no, somebody stop it!" I cried.

"And Gray," Shark said in my ear. "Let's talk about your dear, precious Gray."

"Oh no, *please*," I pleaded.

"How did you feel when you knew Gray had cancer? When you watched the sweetest love of your life die! He's dead! Gray's dead! He's gone!"

I just became totally hysterical, pounding the floor. I kind of blacked out, I guess. I don't even remember tearing off the earphone, but I understand I did.

Greg Spivey

By the time Kathy tore off the earphone Gary was beside himself. He'd called cut about thirty seconds into the take, and now it was up to nearly three minutes. For a long time he was too wiped to react with more than incredulity. "What's going on? Why are you still running?" he said to the camera and sound men. "Is everybody crazy?" Kathy was miked in such a way that Gary's comments didn't spoil the sound.

Gary Schnell

I was stunned. I've never heard of anything like that happening on a movie set before or since, a crew openly defying a director's authority. I finally just stood back and watched Kathy's breakdown—because that's what it was. In my book that wasn't acting. And I realized what was going on the second I saw that earphone.

Greg Spivey

Gary picked up the earphone and heard Shark talking through it. "Where is he?" Gary yelled and tore out to the trailers.

Gary Schnell

I found Shark in his trailer still talking into the mike, unaware that the scene was finally over. "Gray is wasting away now, taking his last breath. His death rattle, Kathy . . ."

"You monster," I said, as I grabbed him. We grappled out onto the pavement where a couple of the grips pulled us apart.

"How did it play?" Shark said, out of breath, as the grips finally let him go. As he spoke we saw Kathy being helped to her trailer in a state of abject hysteria. And Shark looked pleased. Pleased!

"You're beneath contempt, you evil bastard," I said to Shark. "I hope you realize you've just destroyed what was left of that aging slut's mind."

Tina Veer

"Ohhhh, Gary," Shark said lethally, glancing at me. "You should watch what you say about the woman I love. You're in no position to talk, my ignorant little friend."

"Shark, no," I said, sensing what was coming. "Please don't do this."

"Tina's a whore," he said. "I paid her a thousand bucks to pop your cherry. She's the biggest pig in tinsel town, pal. She's literally fucked every guy in the industry."

"Gary?" I touched his arm. I wanted so much for him to say he loved me anyway, and to explain that however it had started I genuinely loved him.

"Is it true?" Gary said to me.

"Well, not literally every guy."

"Then it's true," he said coldly, and walked away from me.

I walked up to Shark Trager and spit in his face. A year would pass before I had to look at that face again, the night I picked up my Best Supporting Actress award.

27/ **The Last Time** (1987–1988)

Greg Spivey

Kathy was admitted to Saint John's Hospital for nervous exhaustion, and from there she left Shark. He was furious and tried to locate her, but she'd covered her tracks. Or to be more precise, a number of us knew where she was but were not about to tell Shark. When it was understood what he'd done to her on the set everyone was on Kathy's side, and as the story of the incident spread through the industry Shark's reputation began sinking to a new low. How quickly people were ready to cite Shark's cruelty to Kathy as evidence that despite *Blue Light*, despite what some were even calling his "Beirut grandstanding," he hadn't *really* changed.

The awful thing was, the scene worked. Shark had a rough cut by July, and in context you believed totally that Kathy was watching her twins drown and the scene was just lacerating. But Shark kept fiddling with the film, pushing back the release date, and a lot of the reason was that he'd begun coking heavily again.

Elliot Bernstein

"I hear he's coking again," I told Kathy in late summer. After spending a few days with Woody, who was living in the South Bay after his breakup with Brian, Kathy had come to stay with Sue and me in Bel-Air.

"Maybe I should go back to him," Kathy said. "He's like John Lennon now, the time Yoko left him. Without me, he's lost."

"Don't be a sap," Sue said. "He doesn't love you, Kathy. For Christ sake, don't you understand that even yet? It was always just his fantasy of you he loved, not the real you."

"What's the real me?" Kathy said, with a terrible lost look.

Greg Spivey

"You know where Kathy is, don't you, Greg?" Shark said to me one night at the VistaVision Ranch as we watched a new cut of one of the Mac and Gladys infidelity scenes.

"No, I don't know where she is. I'm on your side, Shark. Though sometimes I wonder why."

"I'll tell you why," Shark said, as he dabbed cocaine up his nose. "Because I'm a fucking genius, and your time with me has been the most exciting time of your life."

"Your egotism is not one of your more endearing traits, Shark."

"I'm not egotistical," he said. "I just happen to be the next best thing to God, that's all. Look at this movie! Look at the stupid twat up there." He indicated Tina. "And that washed-up oaf." He meant Ben Killard as Mac, of course. "I've given those fucks new careers. And where are they now? They're off bad-mouthing me somewhere, just like everybody else in this town."

"Not everybody, Shark. It's basically just your director. It's a shame you and Gary can't patch things up before this comes out."

And I really meant that, because in spite of all the bullshit, the film was really good.

Gary Schnell

I was furious and so was Dad. It was humiliating to be kicked off the picture, even though most people knew that I hadn't done anything wrong, that it was basically because Shark was crazy. There were times where I thought: I'll just kill it. Dad could have his lawyers tie the film up for years. By then we knew his buying Mastodon Pictures was out, for some baroque financial reasons—and that pissed me off too.

Then Bill Kemmer, who was sympathetic to me, got ahold of a cassette of Shark's rough cut. Security was tight at the VistaVision Ranch, but the studio had a spy there. When I saw the rough cut I flipped. "This isn't my picture, Bill. Almost without exception Shark has chosen the very worst takes. And Kathy's swimming pool scene! It's camp now! It's *Mommie Dearest*, it'll be guffawed off the screen."

Bill Kemmer

"You're right, it's not your vision," I told Gary. "But the fact is it's a very good film. And it's the one we're going to release."

"Then I want my name taken off of it."

"I'm not sure that's possible, Gary. You did direct it."

"I don't care. I hate it now. I hate the film, I hate Shark, I hate Tina, and most of all I hate what this town has done to me. I never knew hatred before I came here. This town has taught me how to hate."

"I hear the new Robert Benton film is a dog," I told Gary. "The Pollack picture's been pushed back to '88. As for Francis, well . . . I'm glad it's not our money . . ."

"What are you saying?" Gary said.

"The same thing I've been saying all along. How old are you now, Gary?"

"Twenty-seven."

"Then you'll be the youngest winner in the history of the Academy. A certified boy wonder."

"Yeah?" Gary laughed nastily and flashed a disturbingly carnivorous grin as he warmed to the notion. "*Yeah,* maybe so. Unless some old fuck who's about to croak comes out with some stupid little masterpiece that steals all my thunder."

Brian Straight

We revived Gary's Houston project shortly after he was fired from *Home to the Heart,* but he was not the same Gary I had worked with before. To be blunt, I think the breakup with Tina Veer shattered him. He became hard and animalistic and began to drink and coke heavily. It was not a pretty transition to witness, but I didn't feel it was my place to intervene. I was going through a difficult period myself since Woody's departure, kicking myself for having been unfaithful when I'd known how strongly Woody felt that monogamy was essential in the terrifying sexual atmosphere of the mid-1980s.

Gary began running with a succession of mean, brutal women, and there were several embarrassing scenes in restaurants about town. A fistfight in Breton's, and an obscenity-shouting and vomiting incident that got him eighty-sixed, I think, from Spago. The odd thing was that no matter how belligerent and obnoxious Gary became, people seemed to have an endless supply of compassion and pity for him. I suppose because of his youth and talent and terrible naiveté Gary represented to many their own lost innocence. And as Gary viciously put down his former producer everywhere he went it was unsettling how readily people began to question the legitimacy of Shark's "new" post–Kolon Clinic persona. Of course, the story was out that Shark was coking again and rapidly reverting to his old paranoid behavior.

Greg Spivey

Shark was getting paranoid and not without reason. He knew that Gary was trashing him mercilessly all over town, and he was fearful that especially after the colossal success of *Blue Light,* his mean-spirited industry peers would be only too eager to see him fail disastrously with *Home to the Heart*. So he kept tinkering with the film, obsessively adjusting it as the months passed, even though it was perfectly fine. I'd tell him that and he'd say, "No, it's not there yet. Do you want me to embarrass myself?"

Sometimes I felt like saying, "Fear of embarrassment has never stopped you in the past, Shark."

But he was far past the point of being able to take good-natured sarcasm. By the fall of '87 we'd been through a number of editors and Shark announced one night, "I've lost my way. I can't finish this picture unless Kathy comes back. Will you tell her that, Greg?"

"I have no idea how to get in touch with her, Shark."

"You're a fucking liar, Greg. You've been talking to her for months. She's at the Bernsteins, I know that."

Kathy Petro

I guess I did put Greg Spivey in a difficult situation, because I knew he was Shark's main confidant and everything. But I really liked Greg, and in spite of what had happened I had never quit caring about Shark, and so I would check with Greg every so often to find out how he was doing. I got more and more upset, just certain Shark was spinning our of control again because I'd left him.

Sue kept bad-mouthing Shark all the time, until I finally asked her to stop. "You're just bitter, Sue," I said. "Because you loved Shark at a time when he was hopelessly obsessed with me."

"You really are stupid," she said and I became upset.

Elliot came to me later and apologized on Sue's behalf, but said I should maybe start thinking of finding another place to stay.

Then when Greg called and said Shark couldn't finish the film without me I became very confused.

"What do *you* think I should do, Greg?" I said.

"I don't know, Kathy. What Shark did to you was an unconscionable act of blatant cruelty in the name of art. But the fact is he misses you terribly, and if you don't come back I believe he'll eventually destroy himself."

"Greg, tell me one thing," I said. "Do you think Shark really loves me? I mean, *me* as opposed to his fantasy of me?"

Greg paused for a moment. "That's a tough one, Kathy," he said finally. "But if you want to know what I think, I think Shark loves you more than he himself knows. But then what do I know about love? I've never stayed with any single woman longer than a year."

"Greg, where is he now?"

"He's with the editors. He hasn't slept in two days."

"Greg," I said, "I'm leaving right now."

Greg Spivey

I didn't tell Shark Kathy was coming. But I will never forget the look on his face when he saw her there in the editing room door. He was so exhausted he nearly collapsed in her arms. And he wept. It was the only time I ever saw Shark cry. I think if I'd ever had any doubt that he really loved Kathy it was erased then. He could play intellectual games with himself forever about what love was or wasn't, what was genuine love as opposed to obsession or fantasy, and all that sort of thing. Who wouldn't become confused trying to figure all that out? But he did love her. And I know she loved him.

And he finished the film.

Bill Kemmer

I wept when I saw the finished film. *Home to the Heart* did not of course elicit the kind of joyfully tearful catharsis you experienced with *Blue Light*. On the contrary it was an ending of genuine and poignant sorrow. As devastating as Kathy's swimming pool scene was, it was her deathbed scene which literally tore out my heart. I was still teary as I got Gary Schnell on the phone. "You mustn't be an asshole about this," I told him. "It's a masterpiece and it's going to gross a hundred mil easy. We're pulling out the stops so we can have it in theaters in time to qualify for the Awards."

Gary Schnell

I finally saw the finished film at Mastodon about a week before the New York premiere, and it kind of made me sick. This little coked-out airhead I took—I can't even remember her name now—cried during the deathbed scene, and I said, "Come on, get serious. It's fucked! Shark ruined it!" Then we got into a fight in the parking lot afterwards and I said, "Walk, twat," and dumped her. I just wanted to disappear. I was sure the critics were going to murder me for a crime I hadn't even committed.

Kathy Petro

Things were beautiful for quite a while after I came back to Shark. He apologized so profusely for what he'd done to me that I was embarrassed. "I don't expect you to believe this," he said, "but I took that heinous shortcut for you. You were shutting down more and more as the scene progressed—understandably, given Gary's assaultive behavior. I saw that if I didn't do something radical, amoral even, your big screen moment was going to be blown."

"I know, baby. I know," I said, just so glad to be back in his arms.

He stopped the cocaine at my insistence, saying, "I don't need it as long as you're with me. You're all I've ever really needed."

And we made love in the big western bedroom and it was far sweeter than it had ever been, even sweeter than the time in the Enchanted Cottage, for that lovemaking, if the truth be told, did have a certain frantic edge to it. We had been making up for so much lost time. But now in those golden months of late 1987 we were somehow like an old married couple who had remained fervently in love despite the passage of years. Really, that's what it was, I see now. We had our old age compressed into a few months.

Greg Spivey

Filmmaking is an odd thing. No matter what sort of ugly crap happens during production, once a movie comes out, if it's good and a hit, everything is forgotten. At least that's usually the case. And it was certainly my sense of what was happening with *Home to the Heart* as Mastodon geared up for a wide Christmas release.

You could feel the excitement in the air. People were smiling again at the VistaVision Ranch, including Shark. There was a press screening in L.A. and as the first rave reviews began appearing our elation grew. It fell to me to try to convince Gary to attend the gala New York premiere, but he was nowhere to be found. The story was that foaring disaster he'd pulled a male version of Geraldine Page's stunt in *Sweet Bird of Youth*, roaring off across America in a restored '58 Cadillac convertible with a pound of cocaine, a case of Jack Daniels and a mean little porno actress with mainstream dreams running her hand up his leg.

Bill Kemmer

I suppose that while the applause lasted the New York premiere was one of the peak moments of Shark's life. Who could have predicted that on the very heels of that vindication an interrelated series of wrenching events would occur which would irrevocably mark the beginning of Shark Trager's end.

Kathy Petro

I sat there in this awful dress I was wearing just going out of my skin as the lights went down, wanting a Valium so bad I could taste it. Even though the early reviews had lavishly praised my performance I just didn't believe it. This was the real moment of truth, a tough New York audience, and I just couldn't take it. While the titles were still on I bolted to the lobby, Shark following me.

"Kathy, it's all right. Come on back in."

"No, I can't. I can't watch myself, it's too weird."

And so I didn't go back in. You know, I've never seen the whole film, just little bits and pieces. Once they showed a clip of the swimming pool scene on TV, but I couldn't even watch it. So Shark just held me in the empty lobby, rocking me in his arms. The picture had been playing for maybe twenty minutes when Edmund Himmler, the powerful New York film critic, arrived with his aged wheelchair-ridden mother.

Greg Spivey

Shark told me later that he felt his blood boil when he saw Edmund Himmler wheeling his mother into the lobby, recalling the critic's vicious review of *Blue Light*. He said Himmler saw him and grinned and whispered something to his mother, an ancient woman with silvery-blonde Teutonic braids, who reminded Shark of Claude Rains's evil Nazi mother in *Notorious*. She grinned too, Shark said, and his first impulse was to stomp them both.

But for Kathy's sake he quelled his anger. "This man is spiritually sick," he observed in tones only Kathy could hear. "He's a very sad man, who has probably never had sex with another human being, not even her."

But Shark said his heart was still pounding with adrenaline as he watched Himmler wheel his mother into the theater, knowing all too well that a critic of Himmler's temperament was incapable of giving *Home to the Heart* anything but a ferociously negative review.

Kathy Petro

Shark was still rocking me in the lobby when we heard the applause. "You see?" he said. "You see?" And he tried to pull me back into the theater just as the doors opened and people flooded out like some kind of ecstatic throng or something, and the next thing I knew they were all over us! People hugging me with tears on their cheeks, saying I was better than Meryl Streep and Sally Field and Debra Winger and everybody! And they were hugging Shark too, and he had tears in *his* eyes! It was like the ending of a Rocky movie or something: people were practically lifting Shark up on their shoulders. I half-expected an American flag to drop down from the ceiling and drape over him at any moment.

Woody Hazzard

Shark paid my way to New York to attend the premiere, which was the first time I saw the movie. I have to say, I think Gary saved the picture. The shit about the Communists especially—that could've been real bad, but Gary had this knack for having everybody play low-key. A lot of the lines were really pretty bad, but somehow it all came out believable.

The scene in the lobby afterwards was like total jubilation—you really expected everybody to break into some big song or something like the end of a fifties musical—and all kinds of people were coming on to me, other producers and executives and so forth, when they learned I was the writer. Let's do lunch, that kind of thing. You should direct your next script. I didn't know what to say.

I kept trying to get over to Shark, but people were crowded in around him like sardines. Then, in one of those fluke shifts, the crowd parted right in front of him so that he had a clear view of Carol Van Der Hof as she limped from the theater into the lobby.

She was with that rock video director guy Joel she'd had an on-again/off-again thing with for years. *He* got the premiere invitation, but Shark must have known the chances were good he'd bring Carol if he came. She totally froze when she saw Shark, and they just stared at each other for a long time without saying a word. Then Shark opened his arms like he wanted to hug her, and you could see all the love and longing for reconciliation in his eyes.

And Carol just cut him totally dead, like he didn't even exist. She limped past him and went up to Kathy and said, "My dear, I just want to tell you how much I enjoyed your performance." And Kathy smiled and said thank you, looking kind of dazed by then from all the compliments. And then Carol added in a voice loud enough for Shark to hear, "You know, Kathy, I portrayed *you* once. Did Shark ever tell you about *that?*"

Kathy looked confused, picking up this weird lethal vibe from Carol. And Shark pushed up to Carol, saying, "You shut your cunt mouth," and people gasped.

"I portrayed you in a pitch-black garage," Carol continued to Kathy. "And Shark made love to me as I seriously doubt he ever has to the actual you—"

"You fuck-twat," Shark said, and smacked Carol across the face hard enough to knock off her glasses. It was gasp city, man.

Joel laid into Shark, and they grappled a little, Joel clipping Shark's nose pretty good, till several guys, myself included, pulled them apart. Shark's nose was bleeding, getting blood all over his suit.

Kathy Petro

I was aghast. I had no idea at the time what Carol was referring to. I had been spared a full recitation of the events leading up to Carol's well-known power saw accident during *Red Surf*. All I knew was that this evil New York woman, who had obviously once had a crush on Shark, was marring what was otherwise a flawless night of jubilation.

I watched as Woody gave Shark a handkerchief to staunch his bleeding nose and helped him toward the basement men's room. And when I saw Edmund Himmler bringing his mother up the basement stairs in her wheelchair I just sensed that something even more horrible was about to happen.

Woody Hazzard

Himmler was pulling his mom up the stairs backwards, one step at a time, as Shark and I started down on the way to the men's room. When Himmler saw the blood on Shark's face he grinned and said in that snide George Sanders voice he had, "Well, Shark, I see you're already bleeding. But let me tell you, you're going to have to tie a tourniquet around your *neck* once you've read my scathing review of that nauseating piece of kitsch treacle."

At that Shark made a move *toward* Himmler, but I swear he never touched him. Himmler flinched though, and threw up his arms to cover his face. And his mom's wheelchair just started rolling down the stairs.

"Eddie! Eddie! Ahhhh!" the old lady cried, but there was no way to stop her plunge. The wheelchair just bounced down step after step, until it reached the bottom and she went sprawling out across the marble floor.

"Mother!" Himmler cried. And as he started down after her he tripped on his own feet and plunged down the stairs. I will swear on my own mom's grave that Shark never touched him, in spite of what people said later.

Bill Kemmer

I was sick when I saw Edmund Himmler and his mother at the bottom of the stairs, sensing even before I received an explanation that it was going to cast a negative pall over the film. The evening ended horribly with ambulances arriving—at that point Edmund Himmler was unconscious and his mother was too dazed to speak. The police questioned Woody and Shark and, lacking any testimony to the contrary, tentatively accepted their *accident* version of what had happened and let them leave. We learned soon enough that Himmler's mother had sustained little more than bruises. But the critic had struck his head hard against the marble floor and remained in a coma as Shark and Kathy returned to L.A.

Kathy Petro

Shark was extremely upset about what had happened. As much as he disliked Edmund Himmler he said he didn't wish for him to be in a coma, though inevitably at one point he did quip, "At least we don't have to worry about his review."

Almost all the other reviews were glowing, except for a few that were clearly written in the days after the Himmler incident, since they fired a few shots at Shark personally even as they praised my performance and Gary's direction of the film.

By then we knew the story was going around that Shark had pushed both the Himmlers down those steps. But Shark and I both figured those kinds of shots were just an inevitable by-product of success, especially after *Home to the Heart* had the biggest opening weekend in the history of motion pictures, breaking Shark's own previous record with *Blue Light*.

Bill Kemmer

It was a stunning victory for everyone involved. The audiences were transported from coast to coast, and the critics, with a few late exceptions, were rhapsodic in their praise. But those late exceptions bothered me, as did the persistent rumors that Shark had deliberately pushed both Himmlers down the stairs. The critic remained in a coma. Working in Shark's favor was the fact that Himmler, far more so than any other film critic, was almost universally despised. His name worked against him for one thing, with its unavoidable Nazi connotation. And since the last film he'd praised unqualifiedly had been *The Night Porter*, there were many who felt Shark had finally given him what he deserved. If only his crippled mother hadn't gone down those stairs as well.

Kathy Petro

Shark and I flew to Maui a few days before the Oscar nominations were due to be announced. I don't think either of us had ever been higher without taking a thing. We were just riding this super-big wave of self-perpetuating success, which I guess is what America at its best is all about. The film just kept going and going, and I was just inundated with scripts and offers. The Meryl Streep comparisons really pleased me the most though, because she had always been my idea of a really serious actress. I remember telling Shark on the flight over to Hana, "I want to do something with an unusual accent next time."

We had a rustic little house just up the road from the Lindbergh place, not far from the house Daddy had owned back in '75. But we never went by that house. We had no need for nostalgia. The present was plenty for us.

We had both brought along scripts to read but we ended up just baking in the sun all day and making love way into the night. We unplugged the phones, and went around nude, and just couldn't keep our hands off each other. I see now that those days were truly our last good time.

Monday night Shark switched on the TV news while I was in the shower, and when I stepped out he said I'd just missed the Awards nominations story, so I asked him how many we got.

"Eleven in all," he said. "Including Best Picture, Best Director, Best Screenplay, which will certainly get a laugh and a smirk out of Woody! Best Actor for Ben, Best Supporting Actress for Miss Veer. And the music and cinematography and a few other things."

"Is that all?" I said.

"Yes, I think so. Oh, wait. Kathy what's-her-name . . . Oh Christ, I can't think of it now. You know who I mean. Used to be a model. Made a real turkey about thirteen years ago. She got a Best Actress nomination, if you can figure that . . ."

"Oh, Shark!" I squealed with joy as he lifted me up off my feet and kind of swung me around. In a way I still think that moment was our peak. I just didn't see how things could get any better.

Bill Kemmer

Of course we were elated by the nominations. But we had one small problem: We couldn't find Gary. He'd been "missing" for weeks by that point, and his parents were extremely distraught. He had established a reputation for shyness during *Blue Light*, which we used to keep the press at bay for a while. But the stories of his unruly behavior had begun appearing in the tabloids, along with photos of Gary and some of his more unsavory companions, and we began to fear that something horrible might have happened to him.

As if to confirm our most dire projections, his American Express bill came in in late February, the charges tracing a chaotic trail across the continent, terminating in New Orleans where a number of horrendous bills had been run up at sleazy French Quarter dives, the last stubs clearly forged. I spoke to Earl Schnell and he dispatched private detectives.

Then a Beverly Hills bank called Gary's business manager about a two hundred thousand dollar check made out to the Carl Grubb Ministries in Shreveport.

Gary Schnell

I had sunk so low. I remember little of New Orleans, save one horrific flash image of Jan, my partner in Hell, injecting cocaine into a vein in my penis. I vaguely recall a seedy room with a stained mattress on the floor and an old black and white TV, on which a fuzzy picture of Carl Grubb appeared, and through which I felt the healing power of Jesus.

Bill Kemmer

"My boy's been born again," Earl Schnell told me over the phone from Houston, "and he will be attending the Awards."

I was relieved, yet in some way I couldn't quite put my finger on, apprehensive. I passed the word on to Shark, who was quite amused. It was the fateful Sunday eight days before the Academy Awards.

Kathy Petro

Shark shook his head when he heard that Gary had gone sexually and narcotically berserk and then ended up in the clutches of Carl Grubb, this really awful redneck evangelist. "It's only too predictable," he said in the living room at the VistaVision Ranch. "You take a guy like Gary who's basically a sheltered pussy—if you'll pardon the randy expression, my love—and of course he goes too far once he discovers pleasure, and inevitably feels guilty, and turns back to being a self-righteous prude."

"Well, at least he's not dead," I said. "Maybe someday he'll get tired of being a fundamentalist Christian and find some kind of balance between denial and excess."

"Perhaps," Shark said.

Later that evening we were cuddled up on the sofa getting ready to watch "Sunday Evening," which Shark liked better than "Sixty Minutes," which he thought had "gone soft." As Shark nuzzled me he mused, "You know, tomorrow is the balloting deadline. I'll bet any number of Academy members are sweating out their final decisions right now."

"I'm thinking positive thoughts," I said.

"You've got a very good chance, my love," Shark said. "Your only serious competition is Irene Greerson for her feisty grandmother shtick in *Sunset Lake*, since the word is out that she's got terminal cancer."

"It's ironic, isn't it?" I said to Shark. "That I might win for playing a cancer victim, but Irene might win for actually having it."

"I suppose it's too late to spread any rumors," Shark said, and kissed my forehead as the "Sunday Evening" intro came on.

Well, needless to say, he almost died when he saw they were doing a story on him called: SHARK TRAGER: HERO OR "SCUMBAG"?

Bill Kemmer

It was a hatchet job, plain and simple. Hank Dye was the most vicious of any of the "Sunday Evening" reporters for starters, and his lead was a blatantly inflammatory reference to Trudl Himmler's persistent allegations that Shark had actually attacked Edmund and her at the New York premiere. "What kind of man would allegedly push an eighty-year-old wheelchair-ridden woman down a flight of stairs? Is this something an 'American hero' would do? But *is* Shark Trager an American hero? We asked a few people who should know."

Kathy Petro

Shark moaned when, after recapping the Sunday School teacher rescue in Beirut, the picture cut to a closeup of Narges.

"Shark got me severely addicted to free-basing, encouraging me to resume it even after the Kolon Clinic treatments," she said. "When I finally refused to take any more drugs with him, he and his bodyguard Drake Brewster, a convicted rapist, took Mac Trager and me into West Beirut, where they were about to have sex with both of us, then kill us, when the Shiites disrupted their sick plan at the very last second. Yes, I'm telling you, it's true. Shark was about to [bleep] and kill me and [bleep] and kill his own father. That's the kind of man they gave the Davy Crockett Medal to."

Shark covered his brow and shook his head.

Mac Trager

I tried to talk Narges out of going on TV, but she wouldn't listen. By the time Hank Dye and his crew came up to the Bel-Air house she knew that Shark and Gary had had a falling out, so she figured Shark couldn't press Earl Schnell anymore to use his Washington connections to get her deported. I went for a walk around the grounds that day though. I didn't want to tell Hank Dye nothing. I didn't know for sure what *she'd* told him till I saw it myself on TV.

"Hell, that's not what happened, Narges," I said, as we watched her tell her version of Beirut. "Shark had a change of heart."

"I don't care," she said. "He played with my mind once too often. This is my revenge. And you'd better just accept it, Mac, if you want to go on humping me."

Kathy Petro

"Is that true?" I asked Shark about what Narges had said.

"No, no, of course not. The woman's insane with jealousy. She knew I wanted only you."

I squeezed Shark's hand. But he winced and I groaned as the TV picture cut to a clip of Hector the Donkey in *Looking for Lupe*.

Greg Spivey

I was watching "Sunday Evening" at my girlfriend's house. Since Shark had described to me in convincing detail what had happened at the White House after the Oval Office ceremony, I was aghast at the distorted version Hank Dye presented.

"Yet, according to informed sources," Dye said in a shocked, incredulous voice, "Trager chased the terrified animal through the *Lincoln bedroom*, virtually destroying this national shrine! Like something in a debased Marx Brothers comedy? Maybe. But what happened next was like an outtake from Trager's own dementedly violent *Red Surf*. For as a number of visiting dignitaries—including, we are told, the First Lady herself!—watched in horror, Trager 'borrowed' a Secret Service revolver and gratuitously *shot* the beloved animal point-blank in the head."

Kathy Petro

It just went on and on. They were just out to murder him. The only good thing was that at least they didn't say anything about Shark and me having sex in the White House. Drake was conspicuously absent. Thank God Shark had made a deal with him.

They interviewed Carol Van Der Hof, who said Shark had destroyed everyone who'd ever loved him and blamed him for her own drug addiction and even said it was Shark's fault that Tony Borgia had flipped out and accidentally stabbed his mother. "Shark drove Tony to it by creating the atmosphere of pornographic violence that permeated *Red Surf*, which also led to my own 'accident.' The man quite frankly is a monster. I for one never bought his 'new' Shark Trager act for a moment. He may be handsome and successful, and imbued with a certain rancid charm, but in my book Shark Trager is, was, and always will be an evil, sleazy scumbag, debasing what remains of the American dream."

Greg Spivey

I felt Hank Dye's final remarks were pandering in the extreme. "One fortunate postscript: Gary Schnell, the talented young director of *Blue Light* and Trager's current mega-hit *Home to the Heart*, seems to have narrowly avoided the grueling fate of so many others who naively trusted this man. After a near-terminal bout of drug abuse and sexual frenzy, Schnell is now on the road to full recovery thanks to the loving support of his family and a new but profound faith in Jesus Christ."

Kathy Petro

By then the lights were flashing on the telephone, but Shark was too wiped out to answer.

Bill Kemmer

It was just a nightmare. Monday we heard that the Academy was being besieged by members requesting new ballots, so they could change their votes before the five P.M. deadline. As the week progressed the reaction grew increasingly severe. The editorials demanding that Shark be stripped of the Davy Crockett Medal of Bravery. The statement of censure from the SPCA and the enraged demands of animal rights groups that Shark be prosecuted for "murdering" Hector. Of course, the White House was stonewalling that matter with a vengeance. It was deemed to be "under investigation," but the "Sunday Evening" report had obviously broken the tacit agreement of silence among the White House press corps. It was just a matter of time until the true story came out, which—as I understood it from Greg—would reveal that Kathy's salacious behavior with Shark in the Lincoln bedroom had precipitated the sex-maddened donkey's destruction of that room.

Kathy Petro

It was strange in a way. Shark didn't get angry or anything, he just withdrew. He became very quiet and just went into the den where he started working on the screenplay for the sequel to *Blue Light*. It was kind of telling, I see now, since the sequel was all set way out in space in the sphere of blue light, which I had always thought was supposed to be heaven.

He wouldn't take any calls or watch TV or anything. But I did, until I couldn't stand what they were doing to him anymore.

"I'm going to hold a press conference," I said one night when he finally came to bed.

"Like hell you are."

"I am. I'm going to tell what really happened at the White House—I can do that much at least. You *had* to shoot that donkey. It was an act of consummate bravery."

He took my hand on the sheet. We hadn't made love since the report aired. "You'll do nothing of the kind," he said. "So far, you've been spared. I won't have your name dragged through the dirt . . ."

"I don't care," I said. "I'm not ashamed of what we did."

"You will be," Shark said. "When you see how it's depicted in the media."

I felt a rush of anxiety. "You think it *will* come out?"

He squeezed my hand. "You might give some thought to cutting yourself free of me, Kathy." His voice was flat and tired. I guess I already knew he was coking again, but I didn't want to deal with it.

"Don't be absurd," I told him. "I love you. Shark, your whole life has been one long series of ups and downs. This too shall pass."

"I have loved you, Kathy," he said. "If it weren't for you I would have gone belly-up a long time ago." He leaned over and kissed me.

And then we made love for what turned out to be the last time.

28 / Hollywood Ending
(1988)

Kathy Petro

Bill Kemmer called Friday and said, "You'd better brace yourself," and explained that he understood the Saturday edition of "Hollywood Tonight" was going to do a story about what had happened at the White House.

"Let them," I said. "To quote Edith Piaf, 'I regret nothing.' "

"I don't think you understand," Bill said. "It may not be an entirely accurate version of what happened. If it were," he added cryptically, "I seriously doubt that you would still be alive to take this call."

Well, I found out what he meant soon enough. That Saturday proved to be the second most emotionally lacerating night of my life—the first being still to come.

Greg Spivey

I was with Kathy in the ranch house living room when the report came on and she quickly became hysterical. Shark was in the den with the door closed, working determinedly on the sequel to *Blue Light* as he had been all week, as if it was only through that effort that he held onto his sanity.

Kathy was sobbing. "No! No! No! It's not true!" And even though the den was well within earshot Shark did not come out. Finally, I left Kathy in the care of several of the secretaries and bolted into the den.

Shark had his back to me as I entered and did not look up from the word processor He was wearing a Walkman and hadn't heard me enter, any more than he had heard Kathy's sobs in the next room. I could hear the faint murmur of a Roxy Music song as I pulled the headphones from his ears.

"You just might like to know that they're saying that Kathy actually and willingly had sex with Hector in the Lincoln bedroom."

He looked stunned for a moment, as if he were having trouble coming out his imaginary world. There was a mound of cocaine on the desk next to the keyboard. *"What?"* he said finally, completely incredulous, and heard Kathy sobbing in the other room.

Belatedly, he went to her.

Kathy Petro

I just couldn't believe it. The "Hollywood Tonight" reporter had spoken to Drake, even though he'd signed this paper promising he'd never talk about Shark. Well, maybe that was the loophole, because he didn't talk about Shark—he just talked about *me!*

Drake Brewster

For one thing I wasn't getting my one percent of *Blue Light* like Shark had promised. It turned out it was a net point, not a gross point, and Mastodon kept giving me the runaround. So I was still broke and living in this crummy apartment near Gold's Gym in Venice, and didn't really have much to lose.

I was angry at Shark, and knew the best way to get him was to dump on Kathy—though now I wish I hadn't said what I said.

Bill Kemmer

Of course, the story was preposterous. And it was the height of journalistic irresponsibility to repeat Drake's clearly insane allegations at all. But once the image of Kathy having sex with the donkey in the Lincoln bedroom was planted in the American mind, it stuck. Factual refutation, even physiological common sense, were beside the point. It was the classic dilemma of the smeared. BEST ACTRESS NOMINEE DENIES HAVING SEX WITH DONKEY, the headlines might well scream—but the denial itself would only elicit yet another replay of the lurid images already seething in the shock-hungry popular mind.

I felt for Kathy, certain the scandal spelled the end of her career as a serious Hollywood actress. But wouldn't it be a poignant capstone to the whole ghastly affair, I couldn't help thinking, if come Monday night she nevertheless walked off with an Academy Award?

Greg Spivey

Kathy remained in seclusion all day Sunday, resting in a numb stupor in the master bedroom. Shark stayed with her for a while, comforting her, I noticed, in an oddly affectless way. Rather disconcertingly, he had yet to show any signs of anger, even when he replayed the tape of the "Hollywood Tonight" report. All he'd said as he'd watched it was, "This is silly. Hector had a gargantuan dick, at least two feet long." He indicated the female reporter who was doing the piece. "I wonder if *she'd* still be smiling if she'd straddled that."

Late Sunday afternoon I heard him mention something about his tuxedo to one of the secretaries. "Good God, Shark, you're not still going to the Awards," I said.

"Of course, I'm going," he replied in a dry, exhausted voice that frightened me. "For Kathy's sake. She's going to win, you know."

Kathy Petro

Shark never came to bed Sunday night. I woke up Monday morning and then went right back to sleep again, I just didn't even want to get out of bed, ever. I just wanted to leave Hollywood and never come back. Or maybe just regress—I even thought about that. Maybe just go insane and become a little girl again so I wouldn't have to deal with anything ever again.

Then sometime in the early afternoon Shark came in and said, "Come on, Kathy, it's time to start getting ready for the Awards."

I couldn't even speak at first. The thought of all those people made me start to hyperventilate. Finally, I managed to say, "I can't."

"Come on, kitten," Shark said, kissing my shoulder. "I know you're a fighter. This is one of those times when you've got to show the world what you're made of. I'll be beside you all the way."

"I can't, Shark," I said. "Don't make me go. I can't face all those people, knowing that when they look at me they'll be thinking just one thing."

"We can't be quitters, Kathy," he said. "Not when we're this close to victory. I'm going to go. Rambo couldn't stop me. But to be frank, I'm nervous too. I could sure use the gal I love by my side."

Suddenly, I realized how selfish I'd been. Of course, he needed me, more now than he ever had before. We needed each other. "All right, you win," I said, and sat up. "Where's that stupid gown?"

Greg Spivey

The limo pulled up to the ranch house a little after five, and Shark and Kathy emerged looking as sensational in a way as either had ever looked, Shark in a sharply cut black tuxedo, Kathy in a sensuously slinky black gown with a plunging neckline she seemed a bit self-conscious about. Both of them wore shades.

They were almost to the limo, where the chauffeur waited by the open door, when Shark said impulsively, "Let's take the Porsche."

With that apparent whim, I've always felt, Shark Trager connected with his fate.

Kathy Petro

I will never forget that drive into town. It was sunset, one of those painfully beautiful sunsets when the sky seems to stay orange forever, and you feel that you somehow understand what California is all about. We drove in silence and for once I was not afraid of the horrendous power of that car. Even when I noticed he was pushing it past ninety I still felt safe. I realized then that whatever did or didn't happen, none of it mattered as long as I was with Shark. Even if we went broke somehow and ended up in some grungy little tract house in Azusa, so what?

As we reached downtown Los Angeles, the sky turning azure blue before us, he switched on the tape player, saying, "You know, this has always been my favorite song."

It was that old Roxy Music song, "The Thrill of It All," which I'd never much cared for because it sounded like several songs playing all at once. But I realized the title was the same as the Doris Day movie that had been playing at the Flying Wing Drive-In the night Shark and I first kissed so many years before. As we got off the freeway—how Shark did love the Los Angeles freeways—the song came to an end.

And so, as the Music Center loomed up ahead and Shark pulled over, parking arrogantly in a red zone, I kissed the man who was responsible for both the best and the worst moments of my life for the last time.

"Whatever happens tonight, know that you have been my life," he said as we drew apart.

"Don't be so final-sounding," I said, and tried to smile. "We'll get through this. You know that."

And he smiled too, a thin, sad smile I will never forget. Then we got out of the Porsche.

The Music Center was up at the end of the next block. You could see the limos pulling and the bleachers where the fans were. We were just about to cross the street when Shark said, "Wait here, I forgot something," and went back to the car.

I had a good idea what he was going to do, so I went back after him, and caught him bending down to the glove compartment, tooting up a really huge amount of cocaine. He stopped when he saw me. "I thought I told you to wait," he said softly.

"Give me the straw," I said. "I need some of that too."

"No," he said. "You've been clean since the Kolon Clinic. I won't let you . . ."

"I can handle it," I said. "Give me the straw. You're not the only one who needs some artificial courage tonight."

Reluctantly, he handed me the straw. As I sniffed several thick lines he was already feeling the effects of the drug, and not liking it at all. "This stuff is shit," he said with a scowl. "I used up my own supply and scored this from the pool man just before we left. It's been heavily cut with speed."

He was right. I could feel the harsh amphetamine high as we started up the sidewalk again. My heart was pounding furiously as Goldie Hawn came into view, stepping from her limo to the applause of the fans. I felt breathless and vaguely paranoid as the klieg lights momentarily blinded me.

"Oh Christ," Shark said under his breath. "Oh Christ."

He was grinding his teeth, his hands forming red fists, as if he were going into a state of violent rage. He'd told me that he couldn't handle speed, that it did bad things to him, as it had in his teens when a doctor had prescribed it for weight control. He'd even admitted that in his early obsessive feelings toward me the drug had been a major factor, that he would never have made that peeping-Tom movie of me if he'd hadn't been high on speed.

"Goddamn it," he kept saying under his breath, as we approached the red carpet. And by that time his face was turning red too.

"Shark, please don't cause any trouble," I said. "I just want to get through this. Whatever happens tonight, won't you at least try and be gracious?"

Elliot Bernstein

Sue and I were up near the door, where we'd paused to exchange gushy inanities with a few people, when we saw Shark and Kathy arrive. I had to give them both credit for having the guts to show up. But that feeling quickly gave way to apprehension when I caught the aura of anger emanating from Shark.

Sue Schlockmann

You couldn't help but feel badly for Kathy. Exuberantly idolatrous toward Goldie Hawn a moment before, the fans fell deadeningly silent as Kathy passed. Shark led her quickly along that gauntlet of accusing stares. It was so very sad. You know the sort of overzealous, possessive fans who crowd those bleachers every year for a glimpse of their favorite stars. Well, only days before they had cherished Kathy. But now it was if she had committed an act of personal betrayal against each of them. They looked upon her with a scorn they might have shown their real-life mother, where she to be accused of a similar act of depravity and raunch.

Elliot Bernstein

I sensed trouble when I saw Shark drawing Kathy toward the TV reporters—Doug and Cindi from Channel 8—who were grabbing the arriving stars for a few quick words. The trouble was that after a word and a smile from Goldie Hawn, both Doug and Cindi were turning their attention to Bette Midler, whose limo was just pulling up, looking beyond Kathy and Shark if they were not even there.

Kathy Petro

It was so terrible. Cindi got this look of shock when she saw us coming and said something to Doug, and then they just ignored us. It was like we were invisible, but Shark was pulling me over, and I said, "No, let's skip it. Let's just go in."

And Doug was looking beyond us, saying, "Well, here comes Bette Midler . . ." And Shark was steering me up to Doug and Cindi, saying, "Goddamn it, they are going to acknowledge you."

Elliot Bernstein

Ignoring Sue's admonition that I not get involved, I started over to Shark as he spoke to Doug. "Hi, Doug," he said, knowing they were on the air. "Don't you think Kathy looks lovely tonight?"

Doug stared right though Shark, saying into his mike, "And I see Steven Spielberg pulling up now too . . ."

And Shark grabbed Doug by the lapels, saying, "I asked you a question, fuckface."

And Doug said, "Oh my God," knowing the obscenity had gone out live, since the pre-Awards broadcast was live, to millions of people.

"I want an answer, you smiling puke, or I'm going to cram that microphone down your throat," Shark said, as I reached him.

"She looks lovely tonight," Doug said, extremely rattled. "She looks lovely, doesn't she, Cindi?"

"Someone stop this," Cindi said through her smile, as several TV crew guys started toward Shark.

I took his arm. "Shark, for God sake—"

"Agree with Doug," Shark said to Cindi, covering her microphone with his hand—which didn't stop millions of viewers from hearing him spit: "Agree with him, you cocksucking Barbie doll."

"Yes, Kathy Petro has never looked lovelier," Cindi cried, and dropped the microphone, as several of the TV crew guys pulled Shark away.

Kathy Petro

I was humiliated. Thank God for Elliot. And then Neal Ridges came to the rescue too.

Neal Ridges

I was inside when I saw the commotion and dashed out to help. It was essentially over by then, Elliot and a couple of the TV crew guys restraining Shark out of camera range as Doug and Cindi tried to regain their composure. Kathy looked like she just wanted to disappear. The TV director was furious and had called the security guards. I did some fast talking to assure everybody that it was all okay now, and hustled Shark and Kathy inside.

Shark was still angry as we moved through the crowded lobby, and every eye was on him. "What are *you* looking at, you simple shit?" he said to one of the Best Director nominees.

"Shark, get a grip on yourself," I said.

Kathy Petro

I felt panicky and claustrophobic in the lobby, my heart pounding frantically after what had happened outside. I still expected someone to come up at any moment and ask Shark to leave. As far as I was concerned the evening was already ruined, even though it had barely begun.

Everybody was staring at us, *everybody*. Neal and Elliot were trying to calm Shark, and then Sue, the last person I expected to do such a thing, offered me the support of a friend.

Sue Schlockmann

I saw that Kathy was jacked up on something, literally trembling like a terrified bird, and appeared on the verge of tears. I couldn't help feeling for her. "Come on, hon'," I said. "Let's go to the ladies room."

Shark glared at me as I began to lead Kathy away.

"Where do you think *you're* going?" he said to her.

Elliot calmed him. "Simmer down, Shark, it's all right."

Elliot Bernstein

Shark was just flipped out, there's no other way to describe it. Completely stuck in this pugnacious, paranoid, cocky mind-set—like an extremely depressing parody of a James Cagney gangster. He stood there, sort of bouncing on his heels, punching his fist in his palm, confronting as many staring eyes as he could.

"You're a twat," he said to a three-time Oscar winning actress. "You've always made me sick, you know that?"

"Shark, cut it out," I said.

"Up your asshole," he said to a young actor, giving him the finger. The fellow started over, but his girlfriend restrained him.

Neal Ridges

I realized that Shark was looking around for someone and I feared it was Gary Schnell. Since I knew Gary and his parents had already gone to their seats, if we could keep Shark in the lobby until the show started I thought we might be all right.

So I was actually relieved when Shark said he had to use the men's room.

Elliot Bernstein

I accompanied Shark to the men's room, and I was quite angry with him by then, though I tried not to show it. But I was thinking: This man is a mental case, he should be in Camarillo [State Hospital] not the Dorothy Chandler Pavilion, because I am not a goddamn psychiatric nurse.

"Do you want to hold it for me?" Shark said with a smirk as he stepped to the urinal.

"I don't know why I even care what happens to you, Shark," I said as I turned to the mirror to check my hair while he took a leak.

I was stunned a second later to see in the mirror that Shark had actually grabbed, and appeared to be trying to yank off, the dick of the man at the urinal next to his.

Sue Schlockmann

Kathy began sniffling in the ladies room as I dug a couple of Valiums from my purse. "Here, take these. And blot your eyes before the mascara runs."

"Sue, I don't know how to thank you," Kathy said.

As Kathy tossed back the Valiums I heard a loud, familiar voice: "Don't you *smell* something, Jane? *I* certainly do. An extremely rank and raunchy *barnyard* smell?"

Kathy whirled around with a frightened, wounded look and saw Carol Van Der Hof gloating at her in the mirror.

Neal Ridges

I was waiting for Elliot and Shark to return when I felt a soft hand on mine. "Neal," Simone Gatane sighed, and kissed me on the cheek. "It's been years."

We hugged and she asked, "What happened? I understand there was some trouble with Shark."

"Everything's okay now, I think," I told her. "He's in the men's room with Elliot."

Simone gasped. "But Neal! I am back with Jean-Claude. And he has gone to use the men's room, too."

Elliot Bernstein

"I'm going to rip this thing off and flush it down the toilet, you fucking frog," Shark yelled as he pulled Jean-Claude Citroen's penis. *"I worshiped you! And you destroyed my life!"*

Jean-Claude keened in agony, helplessly waving his arms in the air, as I and two other men grabbed Shark and finally forced him to let go. Jean-Claude crumpled to the floor, cupping his penis as he tried to catch his breath.

Sue Schlockmann

"Frankly, I'm surprised she's still standing," Carol said of Kathy to the actress next to her at the mirror, who seemed terribly embarrassed. "Though she does walk a bit strangely, doesn't she? Precisely as if she'd once squatted upon a truly gargantuan—"

At that, Kathy pulled Carol around. "If you have something to say, Carol, why don't you say it to my face."

I couldn't help but admire Kathy's courage, a forthright bravery that in fact echoed several of her finer moments in *Home to the Heart*.

"I find *that* prospect exceedingly revolting," Carol said to Kathy. "For really now, who knows where *that face* has been."

Kathy slapped Carol, and I didn't blame her a bit.

"Why, you've knocked out my contacts, you pea-brained blonde pig!" Carol yelled.

And before any of us there could stop it, the two women were on one another, pulling each other's hair.

Neal Ridges

Simone and I heard the commotion in the men's room and dashed in to find Elliot and several other men restraining Shark. Simone ducked down to Jean-Claude, who was rocking on the floor, teeth chattering, as he cupped his genitals.

"My God, are you all right?" Simone said to Jean-Claude. Then she glared up at Shark. "You're a madman!"

"French whore," Shark said, and tried to kick Simone in the face.

Elliot and I pulled Shark back out to the lobby, guiding him back into a more or less private alcove. "Shark, you get it together right now or we will have security remove you," I told him.

"You know something, Neal? You owe me everything," he said. "There are thousands of guys with more talent than you in their little fingers who will never do shit. But you had the luck to know me. It's just too bad I never made you suck my cock."

"You're sick," I said. "You're pathetic." I let go of him, feeling more contempt for him at that moment than I'd ever felt for anyone. "He's all yours," I said to Elliot, and went to find my girlfriend.

Inside, the orchestra had begun to play.

Sue Schlockmann

A number of us managed to separate Carol and Kathy, but not before Carol tore one of the thin straps of Kathy's gown, and ravaged her hair. I pulled Kathy to the ladies room foyer, where I tied the strap back in place even though it looked like hell, and did what I could to smooth down her hair. Carol was still carrying on loudly back in the ladies room, and Kathy was still quite worked up, so I said, "Come on, let's go in, I hear the music starting."

Kathy Petro

I could barely believe I had lost it so badly since I am really not a violent person. But I was just not ready to take what Carol said.

As we found Shark and Elliot in the lobby, Shark said, "What's wrong? What happened to your dress?"

"It's nothing," I said. "Let's just go in."

Elliot Bernstein

Nearly everyone was seated by the time we entered, the orchestra playing a medley of movie themes, and Shark and Kathy's seats were in the middle of the row about half way down. I saw a little flare-up as they moved down the row, Shark apparently stepping on a woman's feet. He said something to her, and her husband stood up threateningly. But Kathy pulled Shark on to their seats. Sue and I were mercifully on the far side of the aisle.

Woody Hazzard

Brian and I took our seats late too, since we had been in this men's room stall all during the thing between Shark and Jean-Claude Citroen, and we had to wait till everybody left before we could come out.

I'd come with this girl Margo who lived next door to me in Hermosa Beach, and Brian was there with some eccentric actress friend of his.

When we saw each other in the lobby something just happened. We just started looking in each others' eyes, and it was like nobody else was even there. I knew we still really loved each other, and he knew it too. "You know what I'd like?" he said in this totally intimate voice, and I really wanted to fuckin' kiss him right there. "What I'd really like is for you to give it to me right now."

And it was crazy—I mean, at the Academy Awards, man! But my dick started doing its number.

Brian glanced toward the men's room. But I said, "Wait, I don't know, man. I'm real freaked out about this AIDS thing."

And he said, "Woody, the few others guys I saw—we only had safe sex, I swear. Do you think I'm stupid?"

"I don't know."

"Woody, if you come back to me, I promise you I'll never step out again. It's not worth it. I love you too much." There were tears in his eyes.

"Oh man." I choked up.

"Look, I've got a rubber in my wallet," he said.

So the next thing I knew we were in this stall, like completely into this passionate if Trojanized scene, when suddenly we heard the commotion with Shark and Jean-Claude and like totally froze. We didn't move or make a sound till everybody'd gone. Disengaging and pulling ourselves together real fast. I guess we weren't too careful.

I noticed people looking at me funny as I made my way to my seat. But I had no idea till later that I had this used rubber stuck to my right shoulder. Margo didn't see it either since she was seated on my left.

Brian Straight

I nearly died when, taking my seat, I saw Woody several rows below with the condom on his shoulder. But there was no way to alert him, save passing a note. Surely, I thought, someone else would bring it to his attention, but the minutes crept along and no one did.

At least as disturbing however was the presence of Shark four rows below me. And three rows below him sat Gary Schnell with his parents. You could actually feel the moment when Shark spotted Gary.

And Gary felt it too, touching the back of his head as if Shark's stare were a death ray.

Gary Schnell

I did feel Shark's presence, but I did not turn around. There was nothing to be gained by making eye contact with Satan, for by then I had little doubt about which force of the universe Shark was serving. And so I closed my eyes and prayed that Jesus might protect me and that He might through a miracle enter Shark Trager's heart.

Greg Spivey

I watched the Awards on TV at my girlfriend's. Hecton Preck, the master of ceremonies, seemed nervous from the start, flubbing his lines as he introduced the guy from Price-Waterhouse and all that.

Hecton Preck

We had a crisis meeting moments before we went on the air, and I was all for having Shark Trager arrested. The sort of language he's used in the pre-show interview was completely unconscionable, though mercifully that had been a local telecast. But now we were going out to two hundred million people all around the globe. The man was a foul-mouthed sociopath. And if by chance *Home to the Heart* won . . .

But the word was he'd taken his seat, and the next thing we knew it was thirty seconds to airtime. If we removed him now, the first thing those millions of viewers would see . . . Well, there seemed little choice but to tough it out and hope the worst was over. How I regret that decision now.

Bill Kemmer

I arrived late with Tina Veer. I'd rushed to UCLA Emergency after her roommate had called to inform me that Tina had dressed for the Awards and then, still despondent over Gary's rejection, slit her wrists. By the time I reached the hospital her wrists had been bandaged and she was pumped full of Thorazine and eager to continue on to the Music Center.

"Tina, are you sure you're up to it?" I said.

"Yes, I see now how foolish I was," she said in a numb affectless voice. "Besides, these bandages match my dress."

In fact, she was wearing a rather gauzy white gown.

We found our seats as Twain Roberts won the Best Supporting Actor award for his portrayal of "Catfish" Rivers, the poor but patriotic black janitor in *Home to the Heart*. And in more ways than one it was an indication of how the evening was going to go.

Sue Schlockmann

What Shark did during Twain's acceptance speech was unforgivable, conclusive evidence if it were needed that Shark had gone completely out of his mind. Twain was surely one of the finest and most distinguished black actors in America, and it seemed doubly ironic that Shark chose to echo the contention of one or two critics that the part he himself had created for Twain was a regressive racial stereotype.

Kathy Petro

When Shark started singing "Zip-A-Dee-Doo-Dah" in a darkie voice I just wanted to die. It was just so stupid and unfunny, it was almost beyond belief. Poor Twain!

Brian Straight

I cringed. Sad to say, a number of people, while offended by the interruption, seemed almost equally baffled, failing to comprehend why comparing Twain to the beloved Uncle Remus should even *be* an insult.

A lot of us got it though. Several of the people closest to Shark were furious, and words were exchanged.

Kathy Petro

A distinguished old producer sitting directly in front of Shark turned around and said, "*You*, sir, are an idiot." And Shark mashed the man's face back, saying, "Siddown, fuckface."

Several other men stood up, and I grabbed Shark's arm. "Please, for God sake," I said.

Then everybody started applauding Twain Roberts, practically a standing ovation to show their admiration for his dignity in the face of Shark's insult. And the other men sat down again, but the producer and his wife left. So Shark put his feet up over the empty seat.

"Actually, I like Twain," Shark said. "I've got nothing against black people, as long as they don't go around raping teenage boys in prison."

Elliot Bernstein

Shark fell quiet for some time after the Twain Roberts incident, scrunched down in his seat, legs over the chair in front of him, occasionally rubbing his crotch. As the Best Costume Design winner— for *Star Cop IV*—thanked the Academy at length, Shark began to loudly snore.

Bill Kemmer

By the time the Best Supporting Actress Award came up, the fellow next to me had filled me in on what had occurred earlier during the pre-Awards broadcast. After what had happened with Twain Roberts I feared an even greater embarrassment—if Tina won.

Tina Veer

It was both the best and the worst night of my life. It didn't even register at first. But suddenly Bill was nudging me, saying, "You won."

Sue Schlockmann

I sensed that something was terribly wrong when I saw the strangely mechanical way Tina was moving to the stage. I noticed what appeared to be bandages on both of her wrists. Though they might have been part of her costume for the evening—they did match her gown, which was eccentric—I sensed they were not.

She seemed to stand there forever clutching her Oscar before she finally said, "This is a miracle. You know, I . . . I tried to kill myself tonight."

There was no one in the Dorothy Chandler Pavilion who didn't gasp—except possibly Shark.

After a lengthy, wavering pause, Tina concluded with a fervent: "I love you, Gary."

And a split second before the tumultuous applause, Shark very distinctly made an *oinking* sound, and Gary Schnell shot up from his seat like a ramrod.

Gary Schnell

For a moment I did want to kill him. For I had come to realize how harshly I'd judged Tina. I had prayed that she would win and that I might have a chance to speak to her that night, for I knew then, having passed through the fire myself, that Jesus Christ could wash away any amount of sin. When I saw how she had mortified her own flesh I longed to embrace her in Christ's forgiveness. And when Shark made that sound I was ready to rip out his heart with my bare hands. But my father restrained me. "Gary," he said, "don't spoil the best night of your life. It's not worth it. Shark Trager is finished in this town."

Kathy Petro

When Shark saw Gary stand up and glare at him, he began to unzip his fly as if he were going to pull out his you-know-what and wave it at Gary. I stopped his hand. "Oh please," I said. "Please, just stop."

"He's a punk," Shark said. "Look at him. He's a pussy. He doesn't have the balls to come back here."

Thank God Gary sat back down.

I just kept thinking: God, I wish I could climb into a time machine and zip ahead an hour to when this will all be over. Needless to say, if I'd known what was going to be happening in an hour, I might have wished to go back in time to some nice, safe place, like 1955, instead.

Woody Hazzard

I never really thought I had much chance of winning the Best Screenplay award. I was up against some real heavyweights, especially that English guy who wrote *Schweitzer*. He was sitting down the aisle with his wife, and it seemed like they were both glaring at me. I really expected him to win, so it took me a second to realize they'd actually said my name.

Margo squealed in my ear, and the next thing I knew I was floating down to the stage. It was like totally unreal.

Greg Spivey

"What's that on his shoulder?" my girlfriend said as the camera followed Woody to the stage.

"I don't know," I said. "If I didn't know better, I'd say it was a used rubber."

Brian Straight

I couldn't look.

Greg Spivey

"My God. It *is* a used rubber," I said as they cut to a close shot of Woody accepting his Oscar.

Woody Hazzard

"This is really weird," I said at the microphone, and there was this strange rumble going on in the audience, like they knew something I didn't, which was definitely the case. I almost felt like looking down to see if my fly was open or something. "I really feel like I don't deserve this," I said, and several people clapped.

"I wouldn't even be here," I continued, "if Shark Trager hadn't held a gun to my head."

Neal Ridges

There were a few scattered boos when Woody mentioned Shark's name. There was something on Woody's shoulder, but from where I was sitting you couldn't tell what it was. The people in the first rows could though, and the word quickly spread on a wave of astonished disgust.

Kathy Petro

"What's that on his shoulder?" I said to Shark. And then we heard somebody say, "A condom? Oh my God, I don't believe it. What's happening tonight?"

And Woody was kind of rattling on nervously, saying, "Yeah, this is really only my second screenplay. I guess you know what the first one was." When suddenly Shark called out, "Hey, Woody. You've got a rubber on your shoulder."

Woody Hazzard

I looked and saw it and almost fuckin' shit.

Neal Ridges

I have to say, I think Woody handled the situation with considerable élan. He simply peeled the condom from his tuxedo shoulder as if it were a wet leaf, nonchalantly looking around for someplace to dispose of it. Hecton Preck, clearly livid, ducked out and gingerly took it from him.

"Thanks," Wood said sheepishly, and then picked up his Oscar, saying into the mike, "Thanks for this too."

Hecton Preck

The incident was a low point in bad taste. That's really all I care to say about it.

Bill Kemmer

After Woody's award Debbie Swann sang the final nominated Best Song, Paul Vichy's poignantly nostalgic "Home to the Heart," and it appeared for a time as if the music had soothed the savage Shark. He fell quiet, making a waving motion in the air with his hand. But it was a stealthy, menacing sentimentality, and for some reason it suddenly occurred to me: My God, he's Jett Rink in the last scenes of *Giant*.

Elliot Bernstein

When "Home to the Heart" won as Best Song, Shark jumped to his feet, clapping violently and yowling as one might at an especially rowdy rock concert. As Paul Vichy, an extremely gifted and sensitive man, accepted the award, you could see he was shaken by what had happened so far.

As Paul said, "And most of all I want to thank my loving and infinitely patient wife Fran . . ." Shark yowled raunchily, casting a horrendously inappropriate sexual pall over the remark. Pressing the point he yelled: *"Ow! Get down in it!"*

Hurt and angry, Paul quickly concluded his remarks.

Simone Gatane

I remained with Jean-Claude in the lobby where he rested, still shaken from Shark's physical assault, though he claimed the pain in his genitals had begun to subside.

"I wonder," Jean-Claude said as I lit his cigarette, "if there is anything to what Shark said about my ruining his life."

"Your criticism was merciless," I replied. "Even though it has been twenty years I can still see that terrible scene as if it were only last night."

"The truth is," Jean-Claude said in an admission of frailty less rare than it once was, for with his advancing age he had mellowed. "The truth is—I was jealous of Shark Trager. I was envious—and frightened of his genius. For with his very first film, his maiden student effort, he had taken all of my ideas as far as they could go. This intuitive boy wonder had, in effect, already made the ultimate Jean-

Claude Citroen film—thus rendering my life's work meaningless. I had no choice but to attack him with all the force I had."

"Yes, I know," I said, unable to hold Jean-Claude's gaze. "I know what you're saying is true. I've always known."

Jean-Claude sighed. "He might have been the Rimbaud of the cinema, the greatest director of all time. He had that kind of passion and fire and audacity. But with a few cruel words I broke him. If there were a God, He would punish me for what I have done, Simone."

There was nothing more to say. I knew these things were so.

From inside we heard polite applause as they announced the Cinematography award.

Kathy Petro

Shark had been glum through several song and dance numbers and awards—for Best Editing and a few other things that went to other pictures. When Ernesto Fonseca won Best Cinematography for *Home to the Heart*, Shark shrugged. "The camera work was pedestrian," he said, as if the award only showed how dimwitted the voters were.

Then, as they started to read the Best Actor nominations, Shark pulled out the bag of speed and started dabbing more of it up his nose.

"My God, are you crazy?" I said, as the couple on the other side of him got up to leave.

"I'm getting bored," he said. "If they have one more lame production number I'm going to personally go down there and take a giant *shit* on the *stage!*"

At that I saw another couple seated behind us getting up to leave.

Then Shark was just flabbergasted when Ben Killard didn't win as Best Actor.

Bill Kemmer

When they announced that Reginald Wheaton had won for *Schweitzer*, Shark sat up and did this big antic shocked shtick, like a coach on the sidelines reacting to a bad call. "That wasn't *acting*," Shark said, in reference to Wheaton's quietly powerful portrayal of the great humanitarian. "That was *makeup*."

Kathy Petro

Shark kept making these scoffing sounds all during Reginald's acceptance speech. I knew what was coming next so I finally said, "Shark, if you love me at all, please just stop."

And then, strangely, he did. As they applauded Reginald I felt a sudden wave of love coming from Shark, a warm glow of intense affection I'd thought I'd never feel again. As Hecton Preck introduced the Best Actresses presenters, Shark took my hand. Astonishingly, after all that had just happened, he was gentle again, and it was almost as if we were alone. In fact, there was space all around us because of all the people who had left.

He kept holding my hand as Mary Trish Beth, the previous year's winner, read the nominations. It occurred to me as she read my name that the TV cameras were showing a picture of me in a little square on the screen, that eight hundred million people all over the world were examining me with a microscope. But I kept my attention focused on Shark. What a painful tenderness I felt as we looked at one another, and at ourselves, reflected in one another's dark glasses.

"I love you," Shark said, as Mary Trish opened the envelope.

Greg Spivey

Mary Trish should have won an Oscar herself for her performance when she saw the name of the winner. At least twenty seconds passed as she ran the gamut of facial reactions from giddy shock to bleak disgust before finally saying, "I suppose I may as well tell you . . . the winner is Kathy Petro."

Sue Schlockmann

Well, there were the gasps, then that terrible rumble of incredulous murmuring, and finally worst of all that feeble smattering of applause. My heart just went out to Kathy, though I must confess I was too stunned to applaud myself.

Bill Kemmer

I was not that surprised, since I'd always felt it would be either Kathy or Irene Greerson. Once the donkey story broke I had actually prayed that Kathy would lose, if only so she wouldn't have to face that condemning crowd. I must say she did prove what she was made of that night.

Kathy Petro

How can I possibly describe the mix of emotions I felt as Mary Trish read my name? The utter terror and elation. The joy that my peers had once wished to so honor me, stained with the knowledge that if they could recast their votes now I would surely be stripped of the award and ostracized forever.

Shark held my hand fiercely, a tear shooting down his cheek from beneath his dark glasses. "Shark, I've got to go down there," I said, and he finally released my hand.

Neal Ridges

Kathy was still wearing her dark glasses as Mary Trish, snide Vassar bitch that she is, handed Kathy the statuette with an air of haughty distaste.

I'll never forget the way people gasped as Kathy stepped to the microphone and, with impeccable dramatic timing, tore off her shades. For the look in her eyes was absolutely stunning. Brilliant, hard, defiant. You could tell she was about to kick ass. And she did.

Bill Kemmer

Her gaze was withering, and so was her voice. "I know what some of you are thinking tonight," she said. "You're wishing there were some way to take this away from me."

There was scattered applause, but Kathy cut into it like a knife: "Well, let me tell you something! I worked hard for this! I put everything I had into this role . . ."

Then she added, in what I think was a really stunningly brave tactic: "I don't believe in doing *anything*—anything at all—half-assed!"

Neal Ridges

That remark showed real courage and style. It would have been so easy for Kathy to use her time to deny the donkey story, to try and appear victimized by the media, to beg her peers, and the world, to believe she was innocent. Instead, she was saying in effect: Even if it *were* true, it wouldn't change the fact that I damn well earned this award!

Sue Schlockmann

"There are many people I could thank for this," Kathy said, and I braced myself. "But there are only two I will thank. It's a shame they're at odds tonight. Because I know deep down they love each other as much as two men can without actually being gay."

Gary Schnell

That remark disturbed me. Though Kathy's voice was trembling with seemingly heartfelt emotion, I sensed demonic forces lurking about her. I wished she'd just sit down and shut up.

Sue Schlockmann

"I want to thank Gary Schnell," Kathy said. There was a burst of applause, and then I really braced myself. "But first and foremost I want to thank the man without whom *Home to the Heart* would have never been made, the man I love, the man I know that deep in your secret hearts many of you love too. I want to thank Shark Trager."

Predictably enough there were boos. I saw that Shark had his fingers pressed together at his lips, as if he meant to seal them with prayer.

Bill Kemmer

The boos angered Kathy. "Shark Trager is exactly what you've made him, nothing more and nothing less," she cried defiantly.

And in the silence following that remark someone let loose with a piercing imitation of Hector the donkey's rowdy bray.

Well, everyone gasped in shock. And I saw that it was Carol Van Der Hof, her hands cupped to her mouth as she brayed again with an astonishing force and malevolence.

Kathy glared at her heckler. "*That* says much more about you than it does me, Carol. You're an extremely bitter woman, and I think we all know why . . ."

At that point someone cued the orchestra, which began playing "Home to the Heart." Then Hecton Preck stepped up, leading the applause to get Kathy off the stage.

"I'm not finished," Kathy said.

The mike picked up Hecton saying, "Oh yes you are, my dear."

Hecton took her by the elbow to steer her away, and as she twisted free of him the strap of her gown came undone, revealing her bare breast to the millions.

Greg Spivey

"My God, I don't believe this," my girlfriend said as the TV picture cut from a flash of Kathy's breast to a wide shot of the audience. You could see Shark making his way toward the aisle as Elliot Bernstein ducked down to intervene.

Elliot Bernstein

I grabbed Shark just as he reached the aisle. I had truly had it with him by then. "Shark, you sit down and shut up or I am going to personally knock out your lights," I said.

Shark was incensed, glaring at Carol, who looked back at him and smirked. But I'd stopped him long enough for Kathy, who was hastily retying her broken gown strap, to make her way back up the aisle. As she reached us, Shark helped her retie the strap and then, still shooting murderous looks at Carol, guided Kathy back to her seat. I took the empty seat beside Shark to keep watch.

Kathy Petro

At the time I was too angry to care that millions of strangers had just seen my breast. That really seemed the least of it.

Woody Hazzard

The next award was for Best Director, and when the guy said, "And the winner is . . . Gary Schnell for *Home to the Heart,*" the whole place just went wild. Practically everybody was on their feet. I stood up too, mainly so I could see how Shark was taking it.

He had sunk back down in his seat, his legs up over the empty seat in front of him, and he was yawning like he was bored. Beside him Kathy was sulking, her shades back on, as if the awfulness of how people had treated her was belatedly hitting her real hard.

Bill Kemmer

The applause for Gary seemed to go on forever. You could see tears glistening in his eyes by the time people sat back down.

"To me," he said, holding up his statuette, "this award is about love. And the miracle of love that can come shining through even the darkest night. You can't stop love, no one can!"

Woody Hazzard

A lot of people started to cry during Gary's love speech.

Greg Spivey

I found Gary's remarks extremely unctuous and manipulative, but my girlfriend began to sniffle.

Neal Ridges

"Love," Gary cried. "That's what this movie is all about. Some of us seem to have forgotten that! The love of a husband and wife for one another, the love of parents for their children, and children for their moms and dads. The love of a white family for a less fortunate black family!"

Elliot Bernstein

At that point Shark said, as an aside to me, "The love of Mac for Gladys's hot little snatch." He sniggered nastily.

Bill Kemmer

"There was so much love packed into this film that nothing or no one could dim its glow!" Gary said. "Even if Satan himself had been given final cut I believe that the pure light of love in this film would still have come shining through!"

There was applause.

"I did not make this movie by myself," he said, and went on to list a number of cast and crew members—with the notable exception of Kathy. "But more than anyone," he concluded, "I want to thank one man without whom this film would never have been possible."

There was a rumble of apprehension.

"A man who has suffered and given more than any of the rest of us can ever possibly comprehend."

Kathy Petro

I was touched by Gary's apparent generosity. But Shark said, "He's gonna shit on me, wait and see. He'll kill me with the capper."

Bill Kemmer

"A man so far ahead of his time that the rest of us forced him to pay the ultimate price," Gary said. "A man who is finally not a man at all, though he bore his lonely agony like a man!"

Elliot Bernstein

"My God, he loves me," Shark said.

Bill Kemmer

"I want to thank Jesus Christ, my Lord and Savior," Gary cried. "Good bless you all and good night."

Elliot Bernstein

As the applause erupted again Shark appeared stunned—he'd really thought Gary was talking about him. "What? Jesus Christ?" he said sarcastically. "There was nobody with that name on the picture. I've seen the payroll."

"Settle down, Shark," I said. But in fact he wasn't angry. On the contrary, his mood had turned cocky and arrogant. There was only one award left, the big one. And despite the flurry of activity in the last twenty-four hours before the balloting closed, Shark clearly believed, on the basis of what had happened so far, that *Home to the Heart* was going to win.

The lights came down as they showed clips from the nominated films, and I noticed several security men watching Shark from either aisle, ready to move in if he made any more trouble.

Shark looked bored during the first three clips. When they showed Kathy's swimming pool scene from *Home to the Heart*, he yowled and clapped wildly, though the response from the audience was noticeably ambivalent, indeed confused. On the one hand they wanted to acknowledge Gary's direction again. On the other, they knew who was going to pick up the award if the picture won.

Bill Kemmer

The clips concluded with the epidemic scene from *Schweitzer*, and at precisely the most affecting moment Shark loudly snored. In fact, at three and a half hours the film was extremely lumbering and tedious. But it was just the sort of uplifting prestige picture that so frequently wins the top award.

How can I describe the tension, the visceral excitement and dread, that permeated the Dorothy Chandler Pavilion as the lights came back up? What was going to happen? What exactly did the last-minute change of votes mean? Had there been a rush to vote for *Home to the Heart* because of Gary? Or against it because of Shark? I think we all literally held our breath. The tension proved too much for Harold Hawkor, whose job it was to present the award.

Neal Ridges

Hawkor was eighty-nine, and he clearly didn't have much time left. Really one of the last great Hollywood directors, the sole remaining member of the club which had once included Hitchcock and Ford. Well, he'd been trembly, like Kate Hepburn, for years, so that was nothing new. But I had a bad premonition as he fumbled with the envelope.

Elliot Bernstein

It was excruciating. "And the winner is . . ." Then he dropped the envelope and couldn't bend over to get it. So Hecton Preck rushed out and picked it up for him.

"And the winner is . . ." But his hands were shaking so severely he couldn't break the seal. So Hecton Preck came out and did that too.

"The winner is . . ." But he couldn't read it. So he fumbled for at least half a minute, pulling his glasses from their case, nearly dropping them, putting them on, adjusting them. "For best picture, the winner is . . ." Then he dropped the envelope again.

Woody Hazzard

That guy was driving everybody crazy.

Elliot Bernstein

"Come on, goddamn it!" Shark said through gritted teeth, as Hecton Preck picked up the envelope for Harold Hawkor a second time, and stood by to make sure he read it.

"And the best picture is . . ." Hawkor gasped. And the rest is history, I suppose.

Greg Spivey

Hawkor dropped the envelope again, clutched his heart, and collapsed in Hecton Preck's arms. The way his eyes rolled back in his head you just knew it was a case of sudden massive coronary thrombosis. People were running out to the podium, the audience gasping with horrified incredulity, as Hecton Preck cried into the microphone, "The winner is *Simple Folks.*"

Bill Kemmer

I was stunned. *Simple Folks* was the ultimate dark horse of any of the nominated films, a truly dim little Southwestern character story about a tight-lipped widower and a plain, laconic waitress.

Fortuitously, the producers of *Simple Folks* were the only ones of any of the nominated films not in attendance that night. Therefore, Hecton Preck was able to say, "On behalf of Rex and Betty Rogers, the Academy accepts the award," as Harold Hawkor's lifeless body was removed from the stage.

Kathy Petro

I couldn't believe it. I started crying. I guess a lot of other people did too. But Shark was angry. "*Simple Folks?* This is ridiculous! That film is dogshit! *Schweitzer*—I could see losing to *Schweitzer!* The movie was a yawn, but at least Schweitzer the guy was okay. But *Simple Folks?* That film was a zero, ninety minutes of dobro music and people saying, 'Pass the ketchup.' A boring film about boring people. A stultifying little naturalistic fart in the desert breeze!"

"For God sake, Shark," I said. "Harold Hawkor just dropped dead. Doesn't that mean anything to you at all?"

"He was eighty-nine," Shark said. "What do you want me to do, sob? He made more films than I ever will."

Elliot Bernstein

Hecton Preck said, "Good night," to the cameras and that was it. People got up to leave, most in a state of numb shock, though quite a number of the women were still crying.

Shark remained slouched in his seat as people moved up the aisles. "This is fucked up," he said to me. "Something stinks about this whole thing. I can't believe that stupid film won."

"Go home, Shark," I said.

"I'm not going anywhere," he said, "until I get what's mine."

I got a sinking feeling when I saw that he was looking at Gary Schnell.

Kathy Petro

"Shark, let's just go," I said. "I can't take anymore, I really can't."

Then I saw that he was staring at Gary Schnell, who was moving up the aisle with his parents. The security men were still watching Shark, but by then the crowd was too thick for them to intervene.

Gary Schnell

I saw Shark coming up the row to intercept me and I began to pray. He had a bad look in his eyes. "I want that, I earned it," he said, indicating my Oscar. "Give it here."

"You're crazy," I said, and he came at me.

Woody Hazzard

It looked like Shark tried to grab Gary's Oscar, but Earl Schnell and a couple other guys stopped him from doing it. Then Shark pulled free of them and lunged for Gary again, and Gary pushed his way frantically through the crowd trying to get away from Shark.

Brian Straight

I was in the hallway that led to the press room when Gary pushed past me, and I looked back and saw Shark slamming through the crowd after him.

Tina Veer

I was in the press room when Gary burst through the door, Shark right behind him. Shark tackled Gary and they fell amid the TV cameras as the astonished reporters jumped back.

"This is mine!" Shark yelled as he got the Oscar away from Gary.

Everyone was horrified as Shark got to his feet, clutching the Oscar like some kind of crazed fiend. Gary was angry by then too—at least as angry as he was scared—and got up ready for a fight. Reporters jammed the doorway, photographers clicking away, as Shark and Gary stood each other off.

"You're a very troubled man, Shark," Gary said. "That is not yours, you did not win it. Give it to me."

"I earned it," Shark said, his insane eyes flitting over the crowd, surely realizing on some level that it was all over. "It *should* be mine," he said, his voice cracking painfully. "It was my movie. Winnie was *my mother!*"

Elliot Bernstein

It was a sad, terrible moment, everyone staring at Shark, at the tortured pathetic spectacle he'd become. "Give Gary his Oscar," I said to him evenly.

Kathy held out her Oscar and said, "Shark, we have this one."

"Let me have it," Gary said, his voice trembling.

"All right," Shark said finally with a weary, defeated sigh. "I'll let you have it, Gary."

And then, before anyone could stop him, Shark jumped on Gary, threw him face down on the floor and tore down Gary's tuxedo trousers. "I'll let you have it just the way you've always wanted it!"

Some of the women present screamed.

Woody Hazzard

Basically I guess Shark tried to shove the Oscar up Gary's ass, though he didn't actually do it, people stopped him before he could. But I'll never forget the glimpse I got through the crowd—it was like a one-second shot in a movie—of Shark digging that statuette into the crack of Gary's hairy little butt while Gary went: "Oh. Oh. Jesus, oh no."

Neal Ridges

It was just insanity. It took maybe five or six of us to restrain Shark. Hecton Preck was there by then, a towering paragon of Biblical rage: "Sir, you are a disgrace to the motion picture industry!"

Gary was shaken, needless to say, and when Earl Schnell arrived and heard what Shark had done, he had to be physically restrained as well. The security men hustled Shark to an adjoining room.

Bill Kemmer

God knows I wish now I had not intervened in Shark's behalf, but I did, convincing the security chief not to turn Shark over to the police. "Just go," I said to Shark, and by then he was relieved that he wasn't going to be arrested.

"Okay, okay, no problem," he said cockily, looking around for Kathy.

He spotted her in the adjoining corridor, where Sue was offering her support.

"Kathy!" he called sharply. "Let's go!"

Sue Schlockmann

"You don't have to go with him," I whispered to Kathy.

"Yes, I do," she said quietly.

And I see now that she meant that their fates were joined.

Kathy Petro

"Oh my God," I said more than once as we walked to the car. "What have you done tonight? What have you done?"

"Oh, shut up," Shark said. "You won your fucking Oscar. What are you moaning about?"

"How could you do that to Gary?"

"It was easy. I only wish I'd had some Vaseline. Maybe next year."

"There isn't going to be any next year, Shark. Not for either of us after this."

"Oh, you never know, my love. They said I was finished after *Red Surf.*"

When we got into the Porsche he opened the glove compartment and took out another baggie of speed.

"For God sake, Shark, no more," I said. "That was half your problem tonight."

"And what was the other half, my darling love?" he said sarcastically.

So he snorted up some more of it and said, in this rowdy rock-and-roll manner, "Oh yeah! Okay! It's all right now!"

As he started the engine I said, "You make me sick."

"Well, the feeling is quite mutual, I'm sure." He peeled out so brutally the force threw me back against the seat. "You know, Kathy, you haven't turned out to be quite what I used to dream about."

"That's right, destroy me too," I said. "You've destroyed everything else tonight."

"That can be arranged, my sugary sweet," he said, veering dangerously around a sharp corner.

"Slow down, for Christ sake," I said. "*You* obviously have a death wish, but I don't."

"Shut your hole," he said, and switched on the tape deck. That Roxy Music song came on loud.

The downtown streets were virtually empty, all these big, silent buildings everywhere, as he roared over a bridge toward the freeway entrance. He must have been doing sixty or seventy. I clutched the dash and pressed my foot to the floorboard. "You really are an asshole, you know that?" I said.

Then I saw her. I had no idea what a woman with a baby carriage was doing on that empty downtown street at that time of night—but there she was in the crosswalk right in front of the freeway entrance!

"Oh my God, look out!" I yelled as we hit her.

I screamed as the baby hit the windshield and bounced off. There was a *clump-clump* sensation under the wheels as we dragged the mother. I looked back as Shark floored it and we shot onto the freeway, finally releasing the woman's body at the end of a long red smear.

"Oh my God, oh my God!" I screamed.

"Shut up!" Shark yelled. "Shut your goddamn hole!"

"Oh God! Go back! Go back!"

"We're on the freeway, baby! There *is* no going back!"

He turned the tape deck up past the threshold of pain, snapping his fingers to the beat like a fiend.

I became hysterical. "You're insane! Stop the car! Let me out! Let me out!"

"Can't stop, baby! *We're on the freeway!*" he yelled above the music, the speedometer passing a hundred. "But if you want out, then get out!" He reached across me and opened my door.

"So long," he said, and pushed me out of the Porsche.

29/ Movies Till Dawn (1988)

Greg Spivey

I think it's safe to say that Shark Trager's last twelve hours must have been the most tortured and lonely of his life.

I arrived at the VistaVision Ranch shortly after eight Tuesday morning and entered the ranch house. The coffee in the mug beside Shark's bed was still warm. I couldn't have missed him by more than a few minutes.

The bedroom TV was showing snow and you could see how he'd spent the night by the cassettes scattered on the floor before the VCR. *Touch of Evil, Rebel Without a Cause, Vertigo, The Searchers,* his own *White Desert,* and absurdly, poignantly, as a kind of frothy dessert, *The Thrill of It All.* Indeed, I remember thinking: Yes, these are the remnants of Shark Trager's last cinematic meal.

I cleaned up the cocaine residue just moments before the sheriff's deputies arrived—even then protecting him by rote, as I see now I had done far too frequently before.

Woody Hazzard

I'll always think that Shark died believing he'd killed Kathy. What else could he think? It was nothing short of a miracle that she survived. He might have heard about it on the Porsche radio, I guess. But my hunch is that Shark was too far gone by then to be listening to the news.

He had to believe he'd run down an innocent mother and her baby, too, since it wasn't till the next day that the truth about that began to come out: that the woman he hit was actually a fugitive homeless psychotic lady wanted by the cops for letting her pit bull terrier severely maul a couple of Salvadoran refugee kids in a park in down-town L.A. The woman was totally flipped out, just wandering around the downtown streets with this baby carriage. Kathy was certain Shark shared her impression that an actual baby had bounced off the windshield. It all happened so fast they had no way of knowing it was really the woman's pit bull wrapped up in a dirty blue baby blanket, and that the dog was already stiff as a bat, having starved to death at least a week before.

Ellen Weir

I'd seen the story on the morning news where they said that Shark Trager had mowed down a woman with a dead pit bull in a baby carriage and then pushed Kathy Petro from the car. They said the car was a silver Porsche, and I understood that our house on Mackerel Drive was built on the spot where Shark Trager's boyhood house had been before he blew it up in that movie. So when I saw a silver Porsche with blood on the hood cruising slow past our house I put two and two together and called the police.

Woody Hazzard

I think Shark took a sentimental journey, like he did a lot when things in Hollywood got too strange. I think he probably just drove all around the old neighborhood, thinking about how things used to be. Maybe he was thinking of killing himself, or of trying to get away, and was trying to make up his mind which to do.

I don't know why he pushed Kathy out of that car. I know he loved her. I guess he just went crazy after he ran down that woman he thought was an innocent mother with her baby. In fact, it was the crazy woman's fault. According to Kathy, she was crossing even though the sign said: Don't Walk.

I think when Shark fully realized what he'd done to Kathy it must have really killed him. Even though she irritated the shit out of him at times, she was his fuckin' life, man. Everybody knows that.

Gus Cord

Yeah, I remember that day all right. It was hot, hot for March, one of them Santa Anas blowing. I was the clerk there at U-Lock-It Stor-age, which was right alongside the Newport Freeway, and I did a double take when Shark pulled up in that big silver Porsche. I didn't know who he was or about nothing that had happened, since I hadn't watched the Awards show the night before. But you could see some-thing real bad had happened to the Porsche.

"Yeah, I hit a dog," he said when I asked him where the blood came from. "He was a mean dog too. Tried to bite my nose off."

I sensed something bad about him, but let it go at that. He signed in for unit fifty-four and drove on down to it.

He was still down there maybe ten, fifteen minutes later when a sheriff's car coming down the highway spotted his car and made a hard U-turn and lunged into the lot with his siren yelping.

Elliot Bernstein

The storage unit had apparently been rented during *Red Surf*, so that Shark could store the things from the Mackerel Drive house he didn't wanted destroyed in the film, namely, his bedroom furniture and a number of mementos—including his original Bell and Howell eight-millimeter movie camera, which I understand Kathy now has.

Kathy Petro

I went down to that storage place with Mac about six months after Shark died. It was difficult physically—I was still in a lot of pain then—*and* emotionally. Mac and I stood there and looked at Shark's things. When I saw the camera I felt a chill but said, "Do you mind if I keep this, Mac? It has a certain sentimental value."

Mac said, no, he didn't mind, but he wouldn't look at me.

When I saw that old, fire-blackened freezer I asked Mac why Shark had kept something like that. But Mac wouldn't tell me.

Gus Cord

Shark jumped back in his Porsche when he heard the cops coming and tore out of there like you wouldn't believe. I mean, that car was fast!

Orange Country Sheriff's Deputy Glenn Smegg

We pursued the suspect up the Ramona Highway, which runs parallel to, then under, the Newport Freeway into Costa Mesa. At the intersection of Ramona and Don Diego Road, three more Sheriff's units joined the pursuit. Four Costa Mesa Police Department units converged on the suspect's vehicle from a northerly and southerly direction on Loretta Drive as he crossed that thoroughfare at a speed of approximately ninety miles an hour. The suspect's vehicle then jumped a curb and careened through the parking lot surrounding the Caligari Mall.

Woody Hazzard

There was some restaurant under construction alongside the main mall building, some franchise place—the Norman Rockwell Pancake House or something like that. But it was basically just a framework then and Shark plowed right through it. In the back, where it was flush against the mall building, there was just a bunch of plywood. And on the other side of the plywood was the Caligari Cineplex, one of those places with eighteen separate movie screens.

Neal Ridges

We figured out later that the Caligari Cineplex was actually built on the exact spot where the Flying Wing Drive-In had once stood. And so Shark died where he had first kissed Kathy Petro and where he had actually been born—taking fourteen innocent children with him.

George Harl

Home to the Heart was playing in theater five, our largest, with a capacity of three hundred, and the first show that day was packed. The little retarded children from a nearby special school had arrived just as the movie was beginning, so they were occupying the less-desirable remaining seats down in front. There had been some disturbance from them during the movie, gibbering and so forth—the protracted swimming pool drowning scene seemed to especially agitate the children. So as manager I was standing in the back as the film entered its final few minutes, planning to guide the retarded children and their teachers toward one of the lower exit doors.

Kathy Petro was dying on the screen and a number of patrons were crying. By then, I believe, most everyone had heard that she'd been pushed out on the freeway after the Awards the night before and was in critical condition and not expected to live. And I think everyone who had judged her on the basis of that donkey business was feeling more than a little contrite. Her personal life aside, it really was a heart-rending screen performance. She was in her death bed, saying good-bye to her friends and family—and you couldn't help thinking: My God, life is imitating art, the poor woman is dying for real in the hospital right now, though not even able to say good-bye. And as many times as I'd seen the film I too was beginning to weep when I heard a crash and a screaming engine as Shark Trager's silver Porsche came through Kathy Petro's face on the screen.

Kippi Morgan

It was my idea to take the kids to see *Home to the Heart*, which at least was a decent, all-American film. If I'd only known! That car came right through the screen and didn't stop till it plowed through the first three rows! Those kids never had a chance!

Orange County Sheriff's Deputy Glenn Smegg

As we entered on foot through the large opening the vehicle had made in the movie screen, the suspect was climbing out of his Porsche. I suppose when we saw the maimed children all about, some of us in a sense lost control. As the suspect staggered towards us with a shiny metallic object in his raised hand a number of the law enforcement personnel on the scene opened fire.

Woody Hazzard

They obliterated him. It was never proved, but I'm pretty sure at least some of those kids died from stray police bullets. 'Cause I saw Shark's body at the morgue and it was just ripped to shit.

Alfredo Barabbas Dillinger

It was something else. We were sitting halfway back, but my girl-friend still caught a round in the shoulder, though we didn't know till later since she didn't feel nothing and the blood matched her dress. Man, those cops kicked out the jams, I'm talking *serious* rock-and-roll! *Bam! Bam! Bam! Bam! Bam!* Blood flying everywhere, big fuckin' squirts of it arcing through the air like wet scarlet flares, big splashes going every which way like bursting red roses, while Trager jerked and shook in a mean hucklebuck like a man having ten thousand orgasms at once. He *yowled* like Warren Oates at the tail end of *The Wild Bunch* as his body blew apart and the girls and women keened, and those heavy-duty cop guns kept on belching rounds like nickel-plated hard-ons packed with cherry bombs: *Bam! Bam! Bam! Bam!*

Sister Mary Madelyn

"Please, in the name of Jesus, *stop*," I prayed through my tears, clutching my rosary beside Sister Teresa perhaps ten rows back from the screen on the side.

And then, for a moment, they did stop. And in that moment there was a kind of silence, even the whimpering of the injured seemed to taper off, there was only the dim whir of the projector.

Shark Trager turned, his face in the beam of bright movie light. It seemed to blind him and he dropped a small object and held up his hands, both of which were pierced through with bullet holes.

I will never forget the look in his eyes then, as the beam projected Kathy Petro's tear-streaked face onto his. Or perhaps the tears were his, I don't know. He reached up to the light and spoke her name, "Kathy," as if he believed she were already up there somewhere beyond the light and he was now to join her.

Sister Teresa and I crossed ourselves as the police opened fire again.

George Harl

The police response was perhaps excessive, though at the time I didn't think so. I was so shocked and enraged by what had happened I wished I'd had a gun myself.

I have to say, however, contrary to the police version, that while Trager did have something in his hand initially, his hand was not raised in a threatening gesture, and it would have been very difficult to mistake what he was holding for any sort of weapon.

Greg Spivey

To my mind, what happened at the Caligari Mall was nothing more, or less, than a tragic accident. I believe Shark meant to escape the country, and when the cops pursued him he simply lost control of that horrendous car. The fact that he died on virtually the exact spot where he'd been born creates precisely the sort of vacuous symmetry Shark himself had such an unfortunate weakness for in his films. It's just the sort of fluke irony that lends itself to facile overinterpretation, and there's certainly been no lack of that.

Neal Ridges

It was obviously his fate. And his karma that he would die in an orgy of wanton self-destruction complete with the taking of the most innocent lives. Though Shark Trager had at times brought joy to millions it was intrinsic to his megalomania that he would eventually bring agony as well.

Elliot Bernstein

The question of just how innocent Shark's victims really were presented itself, to my mind, as soon as it was learned that their supposed retardation was in fact a cynical hoax employed by their teachers to save a few dollars on a group handicapped admission—a hoax which of course required the children to convincingly "act like a bunch of spastics," as one of the survivors put it. By then it was apparent that they weren't, technically speaking, *children* at all, but rather in their early teens, and a disturbingly nasty, mean-spirited adolescent crew at that.

I sensed there was going to be more to the story. But I don't think anyone was prepared for the bombshell revelation that the teenagers' so-called private school was in fact a heavily guarded neo-Nazi training facility.

Those of us who initially condemned Shark have been compelled to reconsider our judgment in recent weeks as we've watched the TV investigation reports showing the hateful parents and defiant, un-abashedly right-wing extremist "school" officials, as we've seen the displays, following the FBI raid, of the weapons caches and textbooks espousing racism and bigotry of the most demented sort, all of it paid for with hundreds of thousands of dollars of fraudulently obtained state and federal aid. Far from being "innocent," the smirking little California Reich *Jungen* killed at the Caligari Mall were as close to an embodiment of pure evil as we in America are ever likely to know. It's entirely conceivable that Shark, in one of the stunning paradoxes that punctuated his life, may have in the seemingly wanton slaughter of his death scene actually saved the world from a grassroots Amer-ican Hitler.

Sue Schlockmann

That's crap, and Elliot knows it. There is absolutely no way to prove such a flagrantly outlandish contention. The crucial point is that Shark didn't *know* those kids were neo-Nazis when he mowed them down. Anyway, they were still human beings, for God sake, and I for one don't believe that anyone is unsavable. Had they lived, any number of them might have eventually escaped their parents' influ-ence and come to see the light. In fact, several of them were actually gifted—geniuses really. Who's to say one of them might not have gone on to discover a cure for cancer or AIDS or a means of elimi-nating nuclear weapons, or at the very least become an accom-plished, life-affirming painter or musician or poet?

Shark was an egomaniacal, life-denying, narcissistic pig who never gave a damn about anybody but himself, that's the truth of it. Any-one who got in his way, whether it was a talented director or a chairman of a parent company or a pitiful schizophrenic woman with a dead pet in a baby carriage—they met the same fate. Not even his most passionate apologists can begin to excuse what he did to Kathy—the woman he supposedly *loved?* He didn't know the meaning of the word. To the various strained attempts to resurrect Shark Trager I say: Pass. *No sale.*

Elliot Bernstein

Certainly, there's no excuse for what Shark did to Kathy, other than to say he was clearly out of his mind. I believe he had come to genuinely love Kathy though, despite the early years of mental obsession, despite his final lapse into madness, and I think Sue knows that as well. It isn't difficult to understand why so many of the women who passed through Shark's life remain so irredeemably bitter.

Carol Van Der Hof

"Arrivederci, scumbag," I sing.

Narges Pahlavi-Bardahl

I think of him now as merely the worst side effect of my cocaine addiction.

Maya Dietrichson

He had a great body, that's the main thing I choose to remember. So did I in those days.

I'm not bitter though. We had our fun.

Greg Spivey

"I'd like that to be my epitaph," Shark said to me once at the end of *Touch of Evil.* Of course, he was referring to Marlene Dietrich's pronouncement following Orson Welles's collapse into the garbage-clogged Venice canal: "He was some kind of man." To which she adds poignantly: "What does it matter what you say about people?"

Woody Hazzard

There was no funeral service. Everybody hated Shark's guts at that point because they still thought he'd killed a bunch of innocent retarded kids instead of a bunch of evil neo-Nazis.

According to Shark's will his body was supposed to be dumped into the ocean at a certain spot off Catalina in a burial at sea. Greg Spivey made the arrangements, but he said he wasn't up to going out on the boat.

I went down to the boat in San Pedro, and I kind of figured somebody else would show up, maybe Elliot or Neal, somebody who still had some good memories of Shark. But there was nobody. I was the only one.

Then, just as they were about to raise the gangplank, Simone Gatane pulled up.

Simone Gatane

It was an astonishingly beautiful day, so clear and cloudless, the sky such a brilliant blue—the kind of day Shark would have loved. As the ship coursed toward its destination Woody and I shared a chilled bottle of wine, and despite the nightmarish events of less than one week before, we found ourselves reminiscing about the good early times we had both known with Shark so long ago.

"I can still recall the first time we met," I told Woody, "how Shark spilled hot chocolate down the front of my blouse as I watched *The Nutty Professor* on the flatbed at UCLA. How incensed I was. How sweetly we made love that night in the James Dean house in Sherman Oaks."

"I remember the night Shark and I got busted in Newport Beach," Woody said, "and Shark swallowed the evidence—ten thousand micrograms of acid. And I held him in the drunk tank as he shook and quaked like there were bombs going off inside him. I held him like that all night."

I saw a tear in Woody's eye.

Woody Hazzard

It was sadder than shit, especially when they finally dumped his body. It was just wrapped in this old canvas sack, and you could see where the blood was kind of starting to soak through, which I guess was the whole idea. I don't think it was even legal, but Shark had paid a lot of money up front to make sure they did it the way he wanted.

They tossed him overboard, and the sack wasn't even weighted, but it was at this real specific spot off Catalina, so I guess Shark knew what was going to happen.

The sack disappeared under the water. There was a lot of glare on the surface, but I saw the dark shape of a fin. Then suddenly it was like thrash city, man, with fins and tails flying, and the water was red with Shark's blood.

Simone Gatane

I couldn't watch. I knew it was what he had wanted, but it was too horrible. I poured myself another glass of wine as the thrashing continued. But it didn't last long.

Woody Hazzard

A seagull came screaming across the sky, and then it was over. The blood dispersed, and the sea was blue and sparkling again, the waves rolling on just like they had for thousands of years.

Elliot Bernstein

The police eventually revealed that the object in Shark's hand when he died was a small reel of eight-millimeter film—that was what he had gone to the storage facility to retrieve. As I understand it, the film is now in Kathy Petro's possession.

Kathy Petro

The police said it was an old film of me, that's all they told Mac before he gave it to me. I ignored it for a long time. The little reel was rusty and then I saw that some of the rust was actually dried blood. But finally one day I drew out the film and held it up to the light. I was fearing the worst, thinking that it might be a copy of the peeping-Tom movie, but I saw soon enough that it wasn't. So I found an old eight-millimeter projector and ran the reel, and there I was at age fourteen sitting on the beach with several girl friends. Shark must have been a short ways up the beach, I had certainly not been aware of him, and could not remember the day, it was so like so many other days. I was snapping my fingers to a song on the radio, and as he zoomed in on my face, I could read my own lips. I was singing "Hold Me Tight," that early Beatles song. I laughed at something one of my girl friends said, and then a man with big tan shoulders passed through the frame. Probably Jeff Stuben because I was blushing. Shark's camera held my face as my expression turned sad, as if I were a girl who thought she'd never find real love. I had a crush on Jeff then, I guess, and probably thought he didn't know I existed. The way Shark's camera held my face—there was this terrible kind of tenderness to it. It was as if he was *really* holding my face, gently, in his hands. I don't know . . . The film ran out.

As I switched off the projector I thought for a moment that I might cry. Then I looked down at the scars on my legs and I didn't.